Avalon Dreams

Alexa Whitewolf

Avalon Dreams
by Alexa Whitewolf

Copyright ©2016 Alexa Whitewolf
ISBN 978-1-9994499-6-4

Cover design by **Y. Nikolova at Ammonia Book Covers**
Interior design by **Ascendant Formats**

Sixth Edition

To the two pillars of my existence,
Mom & Steven,
For giving me strength, courage and
much needed encouragement

ACKNOWLEDGEMENTS

Behind every great author, there is a supportive team.

I am profoundly grateful to the love of my life, Steven, for the encouragement and support you've shown every minute of every day, even when at times I wanted to give up.

I want to thank my mom, for all the trust you put in me, and encouraging my dream of writing as of when I was a little kid, and helping me publish my first book at 14.

To everyone who helped with readings, edits – you know who you are! - thanks for taking the time out of your lives to help me out with this.

And lastly, this book would not have been finished without a good dose of relaxing – provided by Zeus and Achilles, furry masters of mischievousness in the household.

CHAPTER 1

The wind rushed through her hair, the strength of the horse's back between her legs, the breeze in the air lifting her spirits.

King Adrien's daughter enjoyed freedom a little too much on the sunny day. Riding astride on her faithful steed, Shadow, satin gown billowing in the wind, she was acutely aware her behavior was entirely un-princess like.

Still, she joyously opened her arms, welcoming the wind, while the stallion neighed and kept galloping.

"Lady Vivienne!"

Shouts came from behind, and she glimpsed a group of guards following from far away, evidently trying to catch up. The closest one pushed his horse on, heading for the monarch.

Vivienne chuckled at his disheveled appearance, and threw a mischievous smile his way, emerald green eyes glinting. Shaking her midnight-colored hair loose, she bent over the horse, clutching onto its mane, and laughingly commanded, "Run like lightning, Shadow!"

His sturdy muscles bunched under her legs, picking up speed and leaving the knights in the dust. The royal gleefully giggled along, eyes closed in delight.

* * *

Vivienne was in a half awake fantasy state, fragments of the dream and horse's neigh still around her. The faint glow of a lamp illuminated the bedroom, always on. A sound had woken her up, but she could not pinpoint it immediately.

She blinked, slowly waking up. The faint breeze flowing through immediately shook her – the windows were always, without a fault, locked tight at night.

As quietly as possible, Vivienne tried to reach under the pillow for the dagger hidden there, but touched only the smooth satin pillowcase. She froze at a sound, mindful there was someone else in the room.

"Looking for this?" The disembodied voice came from the corner next to the closet.

Vivienne could make out the intruder's shape, and tried to hush the beating of her heart, hiding the fear and racing pulse.

She sat up in bed, keeping the covers wrapped tight around her, and turned towards the voice. A glint of metal shone in the dim moonlight, the same one she had religiously kept around her nightstand for ages as a precaution. How ironic that it would be the same weapon endangering her now!

Vivienne distinguished the contours of a male shape, but no discerning marks.

"If it's money you're after, I don't have any," she confessed truthfully, proud to keep her voice firm and unshaken. *I wish Alistair was here right now.*

A crude laugh echoed, brittle and harsh as nails scraping on a chalkboard.

"Well, isn't that too bad? I'm sure we can find another, *better* arrangement."

As he spoke, the shape stepped right, and the young woman had the confirmation she had been waiting for. Judging by his build and outline of the body, the intruder was undoubtedly male.

Despite squinting harder, she still could not make out the features of his face, as if it was blurred to her eyes. At his scrappy, sickening voice, her stomach curled in disgust. No exit was possible, due to his nearness to the only door.

Vivienne's senses tingled, fully alert, muscles tensing as she slid towards the opposite edge of the bed, preparing an escape.

"What do you want?" she questioned, in a vain effort to gain time.

For all response, the man advanced to the bed. His intent to hurt was apparent, but in a split moment, Vivienne's problems doubled – quite literally. Her vision became a confusing fog, and two shapes faced her instead of one.

As it had come many times before, the signs were the same: the bile in the throat, the flare in the stomach, the spinning of the room.

"You've got to be shitting me!" Vivienne muttered out loud, and the man paused for a fraction of a second.

The young woman knew that if she passed out, the

situation would get out of control. She tried to push the sensation away, but only resulted in making it stronger, whilst the intruder continued his approach.

Vivienne grasped at straws of reality in a last effort.

Close to the bed now, the man went to grab the covers. Vivienne jumped to her feet, already losing grip on the clamoring reality.

The intruder managed to grab her wrist, tugging on it. He breathed on her neck, emanating a foul odor, and she spun around. With a force Vivienne did not recognize possessing, let alone a move she had never learnt, she struck.

When her closed fist connected with his jaw, Vivienne fell, the floor and darkness beckoning.

The last thing she noted before giving in to the blackout, was a luminous bolt shooting towards the intruder . . . but emerging from her hands.

* * *

Vivienne Du Lac, Viv for all her friends, considered herself a wild twenty-five-year old, with a mean streak for speaking her mind, and a gift with animals. Though not Snow White by any designation – the jet black hair and rosy lips had often times gotten her the comparison – the small creatures had always connected with her.

Unfortunately, it was a gift the young woman learned to keep under wraps, realizing it set her apart from everyone else.

Another thing differentiating her from fellow humans was what Vivienne called a unique gift – or curse, depending on the day – déjà-vus.

Dictionaries define a déjà-vu as a sensation of having experienced a situation already, though it is only happening for the first time. In Vivienne's case, a tornado of flashbacks would hit, sometimes more than once during a day, and she would lose all notion of time and space.

This rather odd ability began manifesting in childhood, when at seven-years-old, her parents bought a gorgeous white Andalusian foal. The vineyard Vivienne grew up on, in Nice, France, was nothing if not fairytale, as were her parents.

When she had met the foal, she had jumped for joy. During that first ride, something happened – the nice breeze brought echoes of a different ride, flashes of unfamiliar landscapes, and another horse.

Vivienne could recall, to this day, waking up from the vision on the ground, her parents terrified the horse had thrown her off, and forbidding her to ride again. It did not work out, as the young girl snuck around and formed a bond with the animal. Eventually, they gave in, and returned the riding privileges.

From that first day on, Vivienne's nights were populated by weird visions, half-dream and half-imagination, where she was a pampered monarch in a faraway kingdom. In the morning, she would recount these nightly adventures to her parents, and at first they found it endearing.

As she got older, it became apparent something more was going on, and they decided a shrink would be a good idea. Following the experience, Vivienne promptly realized her uniqueness, and learned to hide the déjà-vus.

To the present day, aside from her best friend, Jennifer, and the faithful Alistair, no one knew what happened whenever she zoned out. Even at work, whenever she was required to meet in person with clients, no one guessed the truth. They had no idea that her precarious departures had nothing to do with the migraines she lied about, but rather with foreseeing the incoming déjà-vu and preferring to avoid passing out in front of strangers.

Luckily, her profession as a historical researcher – and the more than sizeable bank account her parents had set up – gave Vivienne the freedom to never worry about the secret getting out. Whenever she was on assignment researching papers or books for the people contracting her, she was careful.

Her parents still lived in Nice, while Vivienne herself had chosen to navigate away towards Venice, then London, and had finally settled in the ancient city of the popes, Avignon. She had rented a small town home in one of the quieter corners, away from tourists – her own little haven of peace to return to from trips abroad.

Rather unfortunately, the déjà-vus followed everywhere, and no amount of therapy could get rid of them – not that Vivienne needed them gone anymore. They were a part of her life, despite being rather hazardous at times.

* * *

A kink in the neck woke Vivienne up – a startling pain, followed by the coolness of the hardwood underneath. She peeled herself slowly off the floor, blinking at the morning's sunrise filtering through the window. The previous night's episode flashed in her psyche, and she jumped up, urgently scanning her bedroom.

She was alone, and the bed was untouched.

Vivienne ran to the bathroom, taking off the nightgown hurriedly and checking her body in the large vanity mirror. She had no bruises, no scratches. In fact, there were no marks whatsoever on her body to indicate any kind of struggling.

Confusion was setting in, a nagging doubt now rising. Could she have imagined the entire situation? Yet it had been much too real – the hair at the back of her neck rising, the panic, wishing Alistair had been there . . .

"You can't have dreamt it!" Vivienne argued with her reflection in the mirror, green eyes sparkling with anger and fear. Once again, she inspected her back for any visible bruises, with no luck.

Had it been all imagined, a trick of the mind? Sometimes, reality and fantasy became so intertwined with her trances to the point of creating false memories.

Vivienne gave up on the bodily inspection, now sure nothing had happened, and went to shower. Minutes later, exiting the bathroom, she noticed the window of her bedroom open – same as from the so-called dream.

Vivienne tip-toed to the bed, lifted her pillow, and frowned in confusion upon noticing the blade missing. She inspected the area around the bed and finally found it near the bedside table, on the floor.

It was still sheathed in leather, but could not have fallen there on its own. To top it off, the dagger was precariously close to where the intruder had been the last time she had seen him.

All the pieces combined in her mind, pointing to the only possible explanation – the intruder was not only real, but had disappeared after last night.

Vivienne's first thought was to call the police. The second, quickly following, was, *Who would even believe me?*

Aside from the weird situation, she lived in a rental town home off a private lot, and the neighbors kept to themselves. They generally did not interact, so the chances of them remarking anything odd the previous night were slim. As well, the fences around her own backyard pool kept anyone from getting too close.

The ring of a cell phone snapped Vivienne from her musings.

She rushed to retrieve it from the kitchen, picking up on the last ring breathlessly. "Hello?"

"I don't know what game you think you're playing, you little witch, but that was some trick you pulled last night!" The angry voice was unmistakably familiar, and Vivienne froze, rooted to the spot, the hairs at the back of her neck rising yet again.

"I don't understand what you're talking about," she tried, but got interrupted.

"We'll see about that."

The line went dead, leaving her even more confused. The call had come from an unknown number.

Almost in a daze, she set the phone down and started to get dressed. She had barely finished tying her long, inky hair in a ponytail, when the doorbell rang.

Vivienne felt his presence – and annoyance – before even opening the door.

A hundred plus pound of dog jumped up in greeting, large paws reaching for the young woman's shoulders, grey and black hair flying everywhere. Vivienne laughingly embraced him as he licked anywhere he could attain.

"Honestly, I can't fathom how you handle him!" Jennifer, her best friend's voice, echoed from far behind.

Vivienne adjusted Alistair's weight in her arms, and glanced around him. A petite blonde woman stood further back in jeans and a low-cut top, high heels, straining with the leash.

Jennifer's blue eyes flashed in annoyance, but the rosy cheeks and blonde hair were still as flawless as the last time they were together. They had been friends for over five years, since Vivienne had first run into her in a café by the house, as though by fate. Even after all this time, there was an unspoken connection between them.

"He's honestly not that bad," Vivienne chuckled, collecting the leash from Jennifer. "Maybe a bit overexcited."

"My childhood cat was overexcited when he ate, Viv. Your dog is a demon."

Alistair, wisely sitting down by his mistress' feet, tilted his head and growled menacingly, causing Vivienne to frown at him. Big enough to pass her hips, the massive Caucasian Shepherd's body was strung up with anger.

The breed of dog was particularly designed for protection, and they viewed their human as the absolute charge, and anyone else as their enemy. Vivienne had chosen him from a litter of pups based on one stare – as though they were long lost friends.

Although the display of attitude was a daily occurrence between Alistair and Jennifer, she presumed the occasional sleepovers helped smooth out their relationship. After all, her friend had volunteered to care for him whenever Vivienne was out of town doing research for a new contract.

"He's not that bad," the young woman muttered again, moving past the entryway to let them in.

Once Alistair's leash was removed, he bounced around, before settling on his favorite couch to observe them both. Caucasian Shepherds were distinguished for their loyalty and vigilance, and her dog was no exception.

Half shrugging again at his behavior, Vivienne concentrated on Jennifer.

"So, what did I miss?"

"Nuh uh, girl," the young woman giggled, "you first. How was Rome?"

Vivienne grimaced, the recollection of last night still bugging.

"Uh oh," Jennifer's voice interrupted her thoughts. "That bad?"

"No, no, it was alright," Vivienne shook her head, giving an evasive answer. "How about we go get a coffee?"

Despite the casual tone, after one glimpse at her friend, it was apparent Jennifer was not fooled. Perceiving her uneasiness and deciding not to pursue it further, she simply nodded. "Whatever you feel like."

"Great! Alistair can get his walk too!"

Vivienne chuckled at Jennifer's groan, and picked up a small navy messenger bag and Alistair's leash as they exited the house.

***

A short stroll from Vivienne's house later, they ended up by a café down the street. The owner knew them and had no objections to giving them a street table, even procuring a bowl of water and a croissant for Alistair.

Jennifer accurately interpreted Vivienne's silence as not in the mood to expand on the trip to Rome. Instead, she order espressos and pastries and filled her in on the latest drama in her family's soap-opera life – including the part about a cousin running away with some construction worker, and the parents' indignation.

Vivienne, still fixated on last night's events, was having a hard time focusing. As she glanced about, observing the street, Alistair perked up. She craned her neck in the direction of his stare, immediately drawn to *him*.

The man could not have been more than six feet tall, strolling around in a dark leather jacket and jeans. There was nothing overtly gorgeous about him, rather an implacability which commanded attention. This was someone not ruled by emotions.

He could have passed by, never looked her way, and they would have been none the wiser. But Alistair, quiet up until that moment, stood up and barked his loudest thunder-bark.

Jennifer, unperturbed by the characteristic behavior, rolled her eyes and prattled on. "In the end, it doesn't astonish me. Much. She's been stubborn since the first day I met her."

Having calmed Alistair with a tug on the leash, Vivienne risked a peek in the stranger's direction, and heat instantly flamed her cheeks – he was still there. Furthermore, he was staring back with the most peculiar, shocked expression.

Something about his features was familiar, but the heat in his eyes was an entrancing echo of things past. There was a stirring deep within Vivienne, and a sensation akin to curiosity

– or was it a warning? – prickled her skin.

Had his stare not enthralled her, the leather jacket, bruised knuckles, and scar on the side of his jaw would have raised bells of alarm. The onyx eyes, however, were a trap Vivienne could not disengage from.

In a single glance, the man's dismay was apparent, as was her shock at being ogled so openly. When his gaze continued to warm in recognition, images flowed at the back of Vivienne's head – a swift snippet of a champion bending over a lady's hand, a flash of metal, a chaotic overflow with no heads or tails.

The torrent threatened to consume, when the man stepped in the street, towards her. In that one second beat, an insistent honk – and a car rushing by, narrowly missing him – broke their connection. As swiftly as he had emerged in her field of vision, he broke eye contact, and retreated.

With him gone, the images evaporated as well. Alistair attempted to get up, but Vivienne yanked on the leash hard enough to instill the command to sit. With a resigned glare, the dog settled back down, grunting heavily in displeasure.

Vivienne zoned back into the conversation, in time for the end of Jennifer's tirade about the relative, carefully hiding her uneasiness under a blank mask of neutrality. The day had escalated to full-blown weirdness, as of precisely three minutes earlier.

"Yeah," Vivienne shrugged in response to Jennifer's rant, while massaging the sides of her temples to dull the incoming headache.

"What's wrong? Is it another one of those flashbacks?" Jennifer pounced on her friend's vulnerability.

Vivienne was about to deny, pass it off as a normal occurrence – as unlikely as those were – but something stopped her. A nagging voice in the back of her head asked, *Why have a friend when you won't even trust her?*

At that exact moment, she peeked at Jennifer, with the uncanny sensation the thought had come from the young woman.

"Not really," Vivienne began, despite an odd reluctance within her. "More of a connection. It was a man this time."

"Cute?" Jennifer enquired, but despite the gossipy smugness, her attention was focused.

Vivienne could not help a small smile recalling the eyes, the lips, the strong jaw and Roman nose, all definitive ruggedly handsome good looks. "Yeah, of course. But, there's something about him . . ."

Jennifer arched a thin eyebrow – gift of nature – questioningly.

"He brought up stuff," Vivienne continued.

When Jennifer's expression remained blank, Vivienne continued, "Things I've never done – walks in the moonlight, knights, swords . . ." She stopped with a derisive shake of her head. "I'm not sure, Jen, it was weird."

"Coming from you, it must be serious," her friend stated matter of factly, before taking a sip of the espresso. She was avoiding Vivienne's look, now fidgeting with the cup.

Vivienne frowned, both at the words and actions, and murmured, "I guess so . . ."

"Is there anything else?" Jennifer pointedly enquired, not fooled by the monosyllabic answers. "Anything to suggest he recognized you?"

Again, Vivienne hesitated, before haltingly disclosing, "He stopped, and for the longest time stared at me. I thought he was going to come here, but he changed his mind."

She had to wonder at the disappointed tone in her own voice. What was wrong with her – on top of everything else, she now craved a stranger's attention, too?

"Wait," Jennifer interrupted Vivienne's mental tirade. "You're saying he noticed you?"

"Yeah. I was listening to you, when I looked towards him and saw him pass by. Alistair barked, and he looked straight at me."

Jennifer dropped the usual sarcastic attitude and fidgeting, an assessing gleam replacing the vagueness in her eyes. "Anything else?"

"Umm . . ." Vivienne stopped with a cup halfway to her mouth and pondered honestly, tilting her head to the side. "Only that I have a hunch I know him – *really* know him. Stronger than others."

There was a flash of almost fear in Jennifer's eyes as she recoiled, causing Vivienne to wonder at its reason. The tension in her head – which had previously eased off – returned with a vengeance, causing her to almost drop the coffee cup at the pang of discomfort.

Though her vision blurred, Vivienne noted Jennifer's peering, and distinctly heard her voice asking, *Can it be him already?*

"What did you say?" Vivienne murmured, confused. Her friend's lips had not moved, but the question had been as clear as if spoken out loud.

Jennifer froze at Vivienne's words, before forcing a tight-lipped smile. "I forgot, but I have to go." With a nonchalant shake of the head, she got up from the table in a hurry, and spilled the cup. "Damn. I, um," she trailed off, wiping the mess quickly with a napkin, before adding, "I promised Jacques I'd meet him at noon. And it's almost time."

Vivienne raised her eyebrows, beyond surprised at the boyfriend's name. *Didn't she break up with that guy a few nights ago? Or did I dream that, too?*

When she voiced the thought out loud, Jennifer shrugged and explained, "Well, yeah! But I have to get my things from his apartment. I'll call you about tonight. Ciao!"

In a whirlwind, she was gone, and the atmosphere dropped a few degrees. Vivienne shivered, and the dull ache in her head also eased off. Alistair whined low, pleading for attention.

"That was weird," she agreed while petting the pup, having long ago gotten past the bizarreness of speaking to her dog in public.

* * *

As soon as she was out of the café, Jennifer pulled out a cell phone and dialed the pre-programmed number.

When a male voice picked up, she hurriedly conveyed, "Advise him he's here, saw her, and she's remembering things. I'll stand by for instructions."

Jennifer then strode over to her own place, frowning at the unexpected turn of events.

* * *

The man hung up the cell, and entered back into the church. Situated on the edge of a cemetery, at one point, the religious establishment had been great, a tourist attraction even. Now, only an abandoned building remained.

On the outside, the walls were falling apart, overgrown weeds eating into the stone, covering past great architecture. Parts of the building had collapsed, but the main structure still stood the test of time. A few windows had been broken by the elements, and pieces of glass streaked the ground, along with broken bottles and beer cans from teenage rebels.

As the man advanced past the faded brown door hanging on its last hinge, he could barely suppress a disgusted sneer. Inside the building, the remaining oak benches were either painted with graffiti, in pieces, or flat out faded and unusable.

There was only one thing untouched – an altar, with a red tablecloth thrown over it, a few chandeliers, and a large brass cross adorning the opposing wall. A few tiny candles stood in a circle around it, waiting to be lighted in prayer.

"Who was it, Braydon?"

The speaker stood in front of the altar, only his back visible to the one called Braydon. He wore a faded brown cape, with a large hood.

Braydon put away the cellphone – there was no love for such contraptions with his master – and said, "Jennifer, master. She said he's back. And Vivienne's reminiscing has begun."

The man threw his head back in an almost relieved sigh, lifting both arms up to the ceiling in a V shape.

"Hallelujah!" he sniggered mockingly, before lowering them. "Then it can begin."

He drifted around the altar, picking up some remaining pots, throwing them with such emphasis they shattered, and the oil tainted the tablecloth. With a single hand wave, a blazing candle dropped on the material, inflaming it. He stood behind the blaze, a cruel sneer playing on his lips, as the last remnants of faith in the building evaporated.

* * *

Having finished the coffee, Vivienne got up and paid the bill, grabbed her jacket and bag – as well as Alistair – and left the little coffee shop to get some air. The dog followed docilely. She only kept the leash on to avoid alarming people due to his large size, but with or without, his obedience was never in question.

As they walked, she breathed in deeply the autumn air. There had always been something appealing about the multicolored leaves and crisp air, although why, Vivienne could not place it.

Strolling down the street towards her favorite spot in the city, a fountain in the Place des Corps Saints, the stress eased off her shoulders, as if removed by an invisible hand. Her gait became more relaxed, and Alistair trotted silently, enjoying his walk on the cobblestone paths.

Vivienne anticipated a few minutes of peace when they arrived at their destination, as the water always aided reflection. However, as she got to the little roundabout where the fountain was located, her usual spot by the ancient tree was already occupied.

The young woman stopped dead in her tracks, jaw

dropping as she recognized the man from earlier. As though alerted by an inaudible alarm, he snapped out of his deep thinking and turned her way, eyes widening in surprise.

Almost lazily, he straightened from the trunk he was leaning against, and moved forward, eyes locking across the distance. Vivienne advanced before making a conscious decision to do so. She could not break the stare, enthralled.

Before she could step again, he was gone, in two long strides getting into a silver car parked in one of the adjacent alleyways. In a rush – almost a panic attack – she ran towards it, but the car sped away.

As soon as it disappeared, Vivienne became heedful of the weird sensation in her chest, almost as if a hand was squeezing the center. Alistair's bark made her jump, though he was frozen to the ground, also staring after the car.

"What the hell is wrong with me?" she wondered out loud angrily. It was impossible they had met before, of that she was certain. Yet his hold on her was undisputable.

Frowning, Vivienne stepped towards the fountain, sitting down on the ragged edge, still mulling over the unfamiliar man. Alistair settled on the ground, patiently waiting.

His mistress peeked down, exhaling heavily. "If at least I knew his name, maybe I could understand what the hell is going on with me . . . and him."

The moment the words left her mouth, a breeze picked up, blowing against her flushed cheeks. As it always did around an oncoming flashback, her skin prickled in warning. Alistair whined – a telltale sign the déjà-vu was coming. Vivienne braced for it, but only the wind responded, with a gentle caress as soft as a feather.

Then, so hushed she almost missed it, a name.

"Sébastien."

Startled, Vivienne jumped off the stone, eyes darting around her surroundings to identify where the name had come from. *Am I beginning to actually lose it?*

The déjà-vu hit before she could prepare, and all that was left to do was submit to its insistent pull.

* * *

Vivienne was in a garden – a vast, filled with ever flower, type of garden. The cold air of the night surrounded, and the full moon was high in the sky. The sand underneath indicated she was somewhere in the desert, yet the encompassing palace was luscious, and not a mirage.

As far as the eye could see were a multitude of flowers and trees. Her gown, of the finest silk, wrapped across her body whimsically, a lover's caress to a heated skin.

He came out of nowhere – leather armor on, weapon in hand. The love of her life. He had always been there, always solid.

The guardian strode towards Vivienne, and the welcoming smile on her lips died at the grieving in his eyes – something was not right. He stepped into the moonlight, and she frowned at the regret in his expression, heart lurching agonizingly.

"I've failed," he rasped.

"Sébastien . . ." the name was uttered softly, lovingly. As he got in close proximity, Vivienne detected the sheen of sweat on his face, and the blood oozing from a gut wound.

"No!" she screamed – but it was too late. He crashed at her feet, murmuring words of love, as Vivienne bent over his body, sobbing uncontrollably.

Later, when Sébastien's body had become cold and lifeless, she cried to the moonlight, and begged to be allowed to join him in the afterlife.

* * *

Something wet licked her hand, and Vivienne's eyes fluttered open. Alistair was bent over her, his warm doggie breath in her face. Her head rested on the cold ground, apparently having fallen against the fountain during the recollection – which also explained the irritating soreness around her neck.

It was not a surprising occurrence, considering the weird nature of the flashes assailing her, which more often than not resembled time travel.

Normally, a déjà-vu is only a familiar sensation, fading smell or taste. Vivienne's, on the other hand, were a cross between a déjà-vu, a memory, and getting whacked over the head by something incredibly solid. Whenever they happened, she was literally transported somewhere else, reminiscing, losing complete connection with the current reality. It made the return much more aggravating, and her life even more confusing.

Oddly enough, this particular flash was one of its kind. Previous ones had mostly been centered in a medieval time, but this one was ancient in its environment, as though from a different lifetime. And there was something incredibly familiar about the champion who had died at her feet . . .

Using the dog's sturdy frame to manoeuver herself up, Vivienne managed to get to a standing position, well-versed now in the art of recovering. Alistair peered at her questioningly.

"I'm fine," she grimaced weakly. "Let's go home, maybe a nap will help."

They took their time getting back to the house, on account of Vivienne still being dizzy. As soon as they cleared the backdoor, she went straight to bed and passed out. Alistair inspected the house quickly, and then joined his dormant mistress, head over his paws, an alert gaze fixated protectively on her.

Vivienne, through restless sleep, was soon dragged into another vision, with Alistair helpless to stop it. This time, she was not in the desert, but in a different recollection, similar to the ones from medieval times.

* * *

"You summoned me, father," Vivienne curtsied in front of the old king, then straightened up and grinned at him.

King Adrien could not help returning it, despite the hour spent attempting to calm down the head of the palace guard, and the guards themselves. They had been beyond furious after Vivienne had, once again, run off with her stubborn horse, and had to give up the chase across the vast plains of the realm Elsior.

Vivienne was his only daughter, and after Vevila's death, Adrien's beloved wife, he had raised her freely – perhaps a bit too much. The young princess was so full of life and laughter, he simply could not restrain her, cringing at the thought of imposing limits. And yet, the challenges awaiting her, especially once he would no longer be of this world, would be worse for wear without protection.

Thus, much as the king hated to, he had listened to the reports, and finally given in. Adrien landed a severe stare on the princess to impress the gravity of the situation.

"Yes, dear daughter," he finally acknowledged out loud. "You are driving your guards quite mad, so I have taken the liberty of hiring a new one. He is knighted, and comes highly recommended from various courts across our land, where he has secured his charges to the satisfaction of his employers. Please, meet Sébastien Dubois."

Vivienne tilted her head in the direction king Adrien was pointing to, but the haughty reply died on her lips when their eyes met. Green met midnight, and the instant connection was impossible to miss. The grand throne hall disappeared, the only thing existing was his unflinching stare.

The new guardian was taller than the royal, with broad shoulders that were intimidating, if not enticing at first. The look was completed with hair as somber as Vivienne's, and eyes of pure onyx, still fixed on her.

Sébastien broke eye contact first, and inched forward. He kept a respectful distance, less than an arm's width, before kneeling at her feet on one knee. "My lady," he began in a deep, hoarse voice, a delicious caress of the senses.

His hand gripped Vivienne's gently, rough pads grazing the skin. When his lips pressed to it in greeting, the princess' knees wobbled. What was it about this man that stirred her to the core, when none had ever managed to before? He had spoken no more than two words, yet she was left without speech.

"Rise," Vivienne rasped, and cleared her throat at the breathless tone, keeping her features as impassable as possible.

Sébastien did as he was bid, and towered over the monarch momentarily, before retreating a few steps. Vivienne tried to ignore the scrumptious new guard, instead glancing back to the king.

"Father, is this truly necessary?"

"Yes, my dear. I appreciate your independence and I do not wish to limit anything from it, but he will be travelling with you during your lessons with your mentor, and anywhere else you wish to go."

"How is it I am supposed to get some time to myself?" Vivienne argued, eyes narrowing.

"You still will . . . But he has to come everywhere. Please do not push this issue any further, Vivienne."

The princess was about to protest, but the king's tired tone hit her. For the first time discerning it, she frowned at the pallor of his skin, and replied softly. "Father, as you wish," and curtsied again.

She was about to depart, when a shadow emerged from the corner of the throne room and came to her. Everyone present gasped at the size of the animal, and Sébastien's hand automatically went to his weapon. When he realized neither the king nor Vivienne were fazed, he remained immobile, observing silently.

The dog, if he could be called such, nuzzled Vivienne's hand, until the royal peered down at him. His head passed her waist, the rest of the body as large as a young bear. The black fur which had permitted him a seamless blend with the shadows, now stood in contrast with the whiteness of the floors.

The dog's eyes travelled to the new guard, whose hand still gripped the sheathed blade. With a dismissive snort, he strode to the king, walking up the stairs to the throne, and set his huge head in the old man's lap. As if preparing to yawn, the massive jaws opened, and a breath came out in puffs of white smoke, which Adrien inhaled.

The king's cheeks regained some color, eyes now glowing with resolution. Vivienne retained a relieved sigh. Alistair, her familiar, had done it again, invigorating Adrien with life essence, when his was failing.

She could not help but glance towards Sébastien, curious what his opinion was of all this. Sensing eyes on him, he turned to her. Before even deciding to, the princess stepped forward, back in his vicinity, drawn to the new knight against all odds.

Alistair retreated from the king, and came to his mistress' side. "Thank you," Vivienne murmured to him, before turning to Adrien. "You should have told me your health was getting worse," she chastised, half reproachful.

"My dear," he extended a hand out, which Vivienne hastened to grip. "You are aware I will not be long for this world. Old age cannot be avoided, which is why I need you safe, at all costs."

She bit back the tears threatening to escape, before nodding. "If it will bring you happiness and ease your burden, then I shall accept this new guard."

Sébastien knew not what happened – whether the monarch's words, kindness or beauty did it – but his next actions stunned even himself.

He unsheathed his sword, and progressed towards Vivienne, as if incited by an invisible hand. Alistair sharpened his gaze on him, but foreseeing the intent, did not intervene. The princess' confused stare settled on him instead.

Clutching the blade, Sébastien knelt at her feet once more. He uplifted it, on the flat of the palms, and the words escaped his lips with a rushed intensity. "Lady Vivienne, I swear to you on this day my arm and body to protect you. I will let no harm come to you, and will be there to prevent any perils coming your way. Please accept my oath and bless my sword."

"Interesting," Alistair rumbled in his mistress' head.

Comfortable with his telepathic messages, she did not react visibly. However, Vivienne could not agree more with the assessment. Sébastien had taken a basic oath of allegiance, and transformed it into the promise of a lifetime of defending.

As she extended a hand to graze the metal, some magic seeped into it, without her actively willing. It gleamed, before being absorbed, making the metal shine brighter for a few moments. "I bless it," she declared, "and accept your oath, Sébastien."

Their eyes met again, and this time the guard's stare did not waver. Something passed among them, and Vivienne became aware of a yearning deep within, as if it had woken up after years of lying dormant. She was the one to break contact, curtsey to the king, and saunter away, Alistair following close behind.

"She is stubborn, but will get attuned to you," king Adrien maintained, noticing the guard's rapt expression.

Sébastien absently agreed, still endeavoring to clear his head. He had come to the castle for duty, but upon contemplating his charge, already control over his emotions was slipping.

The oath was not one the knight had ever given, and it weighed upon his soul now that Vivienne was gone. A sweet citrus perfume assailed his senses, lingering in the air. If he was not careful, the so-called assignment of watching over her would become more complex than intended.

CHAPTER 2

Vivienne woke up with her mind in a haze. She had only intended to nap, but it was now evening, the darkened sky visible through the window. Holding the side of her head, she groaned, trying to stand up.

Alistair's head sprung off the bed, tilting in query.

She tried to beam confidently, but it came out as a grimace. "I'm alright, pup, just weird nightly hallucinations . . ."

Even as she said it, Vivienne wondered if the words were true, or denial. Had it been a dream, and only coincidence that both names were hers and the man's from the fountain? That his features were fully recognizable in the champion she dreamt of? Or was there more to the story?

The young woman examined the phone on the nightstand, and noticed five missed calls from Jennifer. She listened to the voicemails, none too surprised to find out her friend would be picking her up in less than an hour for another girl's birthday bash.

Stifling another pained moan, Vivienne thrust herself out of bed and into the shower. As the jet of water cascaded down her back, the dream nagged still, and the odd impression of belonging within it. When waking up, it felt wrong, as if the fantasy was where she needed to be, not the reality she was currently living.

As she got out and grabbed a towel, something fell far away. Vivienne momentarily froze, before quickly wrapping the towel around her body, and picking up a pair of scissors off the vanity. She opened the door and waited uneasily, listening for anything out of the ordinary.

"Alistair?"

Nothing happened for a moment, then the Caucasian Shepherd appeared around the corner and sauntered forward with his tail wagging. Vivienne exhaled loudly, her entire body relaxing. "You silly doggie! Did you knock something over?"

He sat down sheepishly, which spoke volumes. Sure enough, when she went in the kitchen, one of the plastic bowls – which had previously been filled with snacks – was now on the floor, empty.

Vivienne rolled her eyes at Alistair. "Well, at least you fed yourself!"

He nudged her hand, staring inquiringly at the scissors, causing his mistress to admit, "I figure I'm being too paranoid, but better be prepared than not, right?"

She put the scissors away, thoughts already turning to

finding something suitable to wear.

* * *

Vivienne was sipping a drink, aware of someone watching her. It had been going on the entire night, and she could not pinpoint where it was coming from. There was only a vague notion of recognition, a tingling above her neck.

After the events of the afternoon and the previous evening, her body was quick to react, becoming tense and restless. It was quickly becoming apparent home was a better spot to be than the bar.

These days off work were supposed to help Vivienne relax, not end up with an anxiety attack. The lack of information about the intruder, and the call following the next morning, was a warning on its own. If there was something to worry about, it was better to figure it out sooner, rather than later.

Vivienne squinted to the right, vaguely in the direction Jennifer had left.

Her companion was off somewhere with a group of friends, and although Vivienne enjoyed the solitude, it was high time she left the bar. A stroll by the river with Alistair sounded much more appealing than being in the middle of a party.

As she stood up to leave, the image of the handsome stranger from the fountain floated in her mind, and he nearly spilled her drink on the bar. A hand grabbed Vivienne's in time to avoid it – a warm, hardened hand, with a firm grip that reached deep within.

In a flash, the dream flitted in her head, and the sensation of the princess' hand in the guard's own. The fantasy blurred with the reality, yet the man's grip was still firm, an anchor in a turbulent sea.

How did I not see him, standing so close by?

Vivienne raised shocked green eyes to be met with onyx ones. Her lips parted in disbelief as she recognized, even in the dimness of the bar, the man from earlier at the café.

"You!" The word was almost an accusation.

His eyes widened, an undeniable glimmer of recognition flickering within their depths, stunning her into silence.

"Vivienne," he said, eyes searching hers, as if he had not gazed upon her in ages.

Vivienne experienced recognition and longing all at once, filling every fiber of her body. The contrast served to annihilate the confusion seeping within the reality.

"Sébastien," she voiced aloud, placing the name from the fountain. Green eyes dropped to his lips, then back up.

Completely absorbed, his heated gaze bore into hers, and the air around crackled with newfound electricity. Vivienne's body leaned towards his, responding to an invitation as old as time itself.

It was as if the world around them stopped. Clichés had never been her thing, but never had a phrase described a situation better than that. All Vivienne was conscious of was the closeness, the heat coming off the stranger in waves, the impression of his hand in hers. They stared in each other's eyes, wordlessly communicating.

As his lips descended on hers, the embrace was soft, yet persistent; reckless, yet tender. Conflicting thoughts affected both their judgment, and norms were no longer important. For instance, Vivienne was well aware the normal thing to do was to shove him away and demand an explanation – a normal girl would do exactly that.

After all, one could not go around making out with strangers, or letting them do the kissing, in bars. But she could not – did not wish to – push him away, as her lips melted against his. The embrace was natural, as if it was not the first time. When the déjà-vu hit again, images flashed behind her closed lids with irritating resolution.

* * *

There was a knock at the bedroom door. Vivienne jumped off the bed, opened it, and threw herself in his arms. "I was afraid you were harmed."

Tears of relief escaped from behind closed lashes. Sébastien's arms went around her waist, gathering his beloved close to him, whispering comforting words and promises of a future to come.

Still within the circle of his arms, he maneuvered Vivienne back in the room and locked the door behind. In the darkness, their mouths found each other, hands roamed through clothing, anxious, seeking more.

"We don't have much time," Sébastien withdrew and murmured, darting a swift glance towards the entrance, but Vivienne yanked his mouth back down.

Bodies pressed together, desperate for contact. A touch of skin, breaths quickened, until finally, they landed on the bed.

"Vivienne!"

The royal opened her eyes, startled from a slumber in the middle of the day. She sat up on the bed to find Alistair nearby, head tilted questioningly. Interpreting her aura, his mouth opened wide, in his version of a doggy grin. "I see your new guardian left a lasting impression."

Vivienne blushed crimson, before throwing the closest pillow at her protector. He ducked it, barking out a laugh.

* * *

Sébastien was the one who disengaged, leaving her dazzled, confused, and still in the aftermath of the trance. Oddly enough, Vivienne had managed to remain standing this time, and the entire scene had lasted only a few seconds behind her closed eyes.

Focusing on him, the young woman saw the midnight visitor from the vision, the reckless lover, and not a complete stranger. Her entire being recognized him, trusted him.

"Vivienne," he said again, the name so easily slipping off his tongue. Then his expression changed, filling with worry. "Oh hell, you have to get out of here, please!"

She blinked, the words finally penetrating, though incomprehensible. His urgency should have been alarming, yet within her was a perception of familiarity and belonging as Vivienne had never felt before. Leaving his side was the last thing she wanted to do.

Sébastien's midnight eyes were a sea of confusion, as unnerved by their connection as she was.

Slowly but surely, he regained control, and tugged on Vivienne's hand. "Please listen to me. Get away from here. Go to the fountain, to the Place des Corps Saints." His French was flawless, yet no accent remained in English. "I'll meet you there in an hour. I swear to you, I won't fail. Not this time. Not again."

"What are you talking about?" Vivienne wondered, shaking her head, frowning as the reality of the situation finally sank in. "Who *are* you?"

He froze in his urgent tug, eyes narrowing onto hers, mumbling, "You don't remember . . ..?"

Sébastien searched her expression, growing more astonished by the moment at the answers found in there. He compelled forth a reassuring smile, murmuring as he caressed her cheek softly, "One hour, please," and was gone.

Vivienne was left staring at his retreating back, but soon lost track of him in the crowd. It was as if the bubble she had been in burst open, and the noise and ambiance came crashing down, amplifying the chaos.

"Viv?" Jennifer's voice penetrated the surrounding haze of confusion.

Vivienne whirled to see her friend rushing by her side, eyebrows raised curiously, slightly out of breath. "Who *was* that?"

"Jennifer," she bit her lip, still staring at where Sébastien had been, utterly disoriented now. "A total stranger kissed me, and I didn't stop him because–"

"You actually had a reason?" Jennifer smirked, implying she should have kept going.

Vivienne paused before continuing, though an intuition deep within her suggested she keep silent.

"Oh my god, was it him? Viv, was it the guy from the

café?" Although she sounded earnest, something in Jennifer's eyes set Vivienne off, and her response was an automatic shake of the head.

"No, he came on to me and –"

"Viv, that's awesome!" Jennifer simpered, interrupting yet again, and seemingly sincere. "Go for it! Who cares if you just met him, heck he was yummy enough for me to go after him."

The young woman formed a noncommittal reply, and the night went on. She waited for the opportunity to run away and meet Sébastien impatiently, hoping despite everything to get some answers.

* * *

The stranger, Sébastien, disappeared before Vivienne could figure out where he was headed, and blended with the shadows. Earlier, when he had seen her at the café, he could not believe it. And now, to have been so close . . . What a fool he was!

After all this time, lifetimes later, and Vivienne had to come back when he was not master of his own fate. Keeping a distance was the best option, as it was evident there was something wrong and she did not remember anything from the past – *their* past.

So why did she react to the kiss as if she knew me?

Words and images from a different existence assaulted his senses. Long ago, they had known each other, had been more than friends to one another. Sébastien had been her guard, Vivienne his charge, and they had fallen in love. That was the past, and he could not bear to ruminate over all that had been lost, or the reasons why.

He closed his eyes in an effort to hang on to a semblance of sanity. To be so close, yet so far away, was beyond tormenting.

Sébastien's entire being craved to be with Vivienne, the promise to meet her lingering, a hope for something – anything. Yet she would require explanations, and he did not have the slightest idea of where to begin.

How could he reveal the truth, that they were pawns in destiny's clutches?

"Sébastien!" The male voice broke past his fuming ruminations. It was not a soft inquiry, but rather a command.

At a loss, Sébastien did the only thing he could. He wrenched his longing stare from Vivienne, and went to his jailer.

* * *

An hour later, close to midnight, Vivienne crossed the roundabout and arrived by the fountain. Sébastien was there, standing up from its edge when they were in close proximity. He extended a hand, almost as if to reach for her, but appeared to think better of it and dropped it.

"You came," he murmured, almost as if not trusting she would have. Without the noise of the crowd, the full effect of his voice permeated, and the young woman shivered at the husky tone tugging on her senses.

Vivienne melted the closer she got to him. She had never reacted such to a man, an impression of completeness as though he was a missing piece, and the world was set right just by being in his vicinity.

It was freaking her out, and she tried not to anticipate what her parents would say about meeting an unfamiliar man in a secluded place, in the middle of the night.

All these musings crossed Vivienne's head, yet they were still staring at each other. The night was silent, with no one else around. Even the alleyways from the roundabout were deserted.

Their eyes collided, and that instant connection hit them both. Vivienne heard Sébastien's intake of breath, and her own lips parted in response.

"Is this crazy?" she wondered passed the dry throat, clogged with emotion. She bit her bottom lip, shifting on her feet, and something softened in his countenance.

There was so much in that one gaze, but all Sébastien did was reach for Vivienne's wrist, and gather her close. She tipped her head back to meet his eyes, and noticed the clenched jaw, as though he was aiming for restraint.

When her eyes lowered to his lips, Sébastien gave a small groan, bent her head back over his arm and kissed her, tenderly at first, allowing Vivienne plenty of time to shove him away.

"If this is crazy, or an illusion, I'd rather never wake up," Sébastien confessed against her lips. Then he pressed her tighter, the graze of his mouth against hers changing in intensity. Vivienne clung to him as though he was her rock in the midst of a tornado.

The urgency from her flashback was there, barely held back, in the tightness of his body. She longed to ask him about it, dispute it, but all she could do was give in. He was the breath of life she did not realize was missing.

When Sébastien paused, minutes later, Vivienne moaned in displeasure. He pulled away, leaving barely a width of space between their lips. "Tell me if I should stop."

She shook her head in denial, voicing the only question that mattered, "Do you want to?"

"Never. I've waited too long for this."

And she needed nothing more – tonight would be enough. Wrapping her arms around his neck, she gave in to the sinking sensations. They embraced under the stars, and it went on, and on . . .

* * *

Vivienne strode the little path to her house in a daze. Sébastien had just dropped her off in his silver Jaguar and she was grateful for it, considering her legs were jelly from being around him for so long.

It was near sunrise, but nothing could have stopped Alistair's enthusiastic jumps. The minute she opened the door, he was there to greet her, extremely vocal about her prolonged absence. Abruptly, his exuberance settled, and he started a thorough sniffing.

"You're so nosy, Alistair!" Vivienne giggled, prodding him away. "Yes, I met a guy, and no, we didn't do anything, only made out . . . Yeesh!"

He sat down, yapping a powerful thunder bark. She knelt down in front of him, burying her head in his fur. "It's so surreal, Al. First the other night, this place gets broken into –"

The dog disengaged from her grip, and Vivienne deciphered real alarm in his eyes. Her canine friend had always been intelligent, but certain displays almost gave him a human air.

"I'm fine, I promise."

He nudged her hand, sniffing again, and slowly licked it, making her shake with laughter at his antics. "I had one of my flashbacks when the intruder was here, then woke up and he was gone. I'm not sure what to conclude, but I'd rather not involve the police yet."

Alistair whined in potent disapproval, but settled as she continued.

"Anyway . . . Remember the guy at the fountain?" He tilted his head, asking for a scratching behind the ear as his mistress went on, "I ran into him tonight, and he's the one I spent the last couple of hours with. It feels so right, Al, I can't even explain it. Does it sound crazy?"

Alistair butted her shoulder, then followed it with a lick on the cheek, which Vivienne interpreted as denial. *I have to wonder at the reasoning behind that, considering I'm the one talking with my dog about my romantic life . . . Clearly not a good judge of the crazy scale.*

Shaking her head, Vivienne got off the floor and went to shower, before getting into bed. It was only as she lay down, musing over the last hours spent with Sébastien, that she discovered she was still lacking his last name. His kisses had been so compelling – topped with the comfort of his arms – that Vivienne had simply forgotten.

She smiled to herself at her own air-headedness. After all, she was entitled to it, and having never felt this way for another man, it was long past due. In the end, Vivienne finally surrendered to sleep, and the déjà-vu that ultimately arrived with it.

* * *

Sébastien had been at the castle for two weeks, and it had been an education, to say the least.

First and foremost, he learnt the mentor Vivienne visited most mornings was none other than Merlin, the renowned mage. He had accepted Vivienne as a pupil, and so most mornings, she would wake up and, accompanied by Sébastien and the fair Lancelot, would go to Merlin's to practice magic.

Cue the not so large surprise – Lady Vivienne was no ordinary princess interested in knitting and dancing. Her mother, Vevila, a common born, was a descendant of the Celts, daughter of an influential priestess, Kyna. When Kyna's husband, Vivienne's grandfather, died young, she sent Vevila to live with a distant relative who happened to be working at the castle of King Mihail, in the realm of Elsior.

A happy king, Mihail had one son, Adrien, a frail young man since birth. Vevila, a kind young woman, came into his life like a tornado, and filled him with a newfound vigor. With her, Adrien grew into a robust man, made his father proud, and inspired the people.

It was only natural that when his father got too old, he withdrew from power and Adrien became king, choosing Vevila as his queen. Unfortunately, the young queen died while Vivienne was still young. But from her mother, Vivienne received her skills, which she was learning to use and dominate to safeguard her land from various threats and to perhaps create a proper alliance with the Pendragons line, and its current leader – Arthur.

And lastly, Sébastien was none too bewildered to find out Vivienne's pet was a demon dog, appeared out of nowhere. No one knew his story, only that he became the princess' companion as a child. According to the stories, one day the young Vivienne had gone out – and come back accompanied by the demon dog. He had never left her side since.

All in all, Sébastien was intrigued, but conducted himself as a proper guardian to the lady, knowing full well there could never be anything between them – despite the obvious attraction and deeper sentiments he felt.

What also killed him, however, was Vivienne's overt fondness for Lancelot, out of all the other knights. A player and carefree man, younger by a few years than Sébastien, he was interested in anything with a skirt.

Sébastien had kept quiet on the matter, and from what he had detected, there was no intimacy there. But considering the knight was about Vivienne's own age, the new guard could see the appeal. Although half-afraid sooner or later he would have to act to secure her heart, in the meantime, he had no choice but to observe and serve.

* * *

Vivienne snuck to the stables before one of the lessons with Merlin, smiling at Shadow as she let him out of the stall. "Let's go for a ride, you and me."

She had barely mounted when Sébastien strode out of the

shadows with his own mare, Illyria. "May I join you on your ride, my lady?"

"No, you may not," Vivienne scowled. "I am in the mood for some alone time."

"I apologize, but I cannot allow that."

"Allow?" She leveled a smug look on him. "I can get rid of you with a wave of my hand."

"So why don't you?" Sébastien counteracted.

Vivienne was left speechless. Clearly, the reason she could not was because her magic was only used for good. The small victorious gleam in the new guardian's eyes implied he knew it, yet the monarch was not prepared to give in.

With a small shrug, she kicked Shadow's shins, and the horse ran forward. Sébastien got out of the way in time, and she was gone.

Vivienne enjoyed her ride for a few moments, before sensing a presence behind. She swirled around to find Sébastien following at a close pace on Illyria, evidently not having lost him.

"Go away!" Vivienne yelled.

"Can't do that, my lady."

His tight smirk infuriated the princess even more than the fact she could not escape him. Did the man never lose his cool?

Sensing fury boiling under the surface, Vivienne bent over the horse and clutched onto his mane. "Run like lightning, Shadow!" she commanded in his ear.

Despite the lengthening in his stride, and the rapidity of the landscape passing by, she still could not shake the stubborn guard. His mare was smaller than Shadow, thus her stride matched him easily.

They raced across the plains at increasing speed, until they arrived by a stream. Vivienne ordered Shadow to a halt, mindful of his thirst.

In the short moment Shadow came to a full stop, Sébastien was already there to help her dismount. He extended a hand out, and she ignored it, instead sliding down on her own. Vivienne learned the mistake too late, as when she turned, the knight was pinning her at the front, with Shadow at the back.

The young woman glared at the guard, incensed, but he was just as furious. His nostrils flared wildly, eyes smoldering, jaw taut with the force clenching it.

"Your disregard for your own safety is quite astounding, my lady," Sébastien gritted out. "But you will not shake me, no matter how hard you endeavor to. I have played all these games before, and I am good at them. So we can continue this way, or you can accept the fact you cannot shake me."

When he backed away, it left her taking in deep breaths to calm a racing pulse, his nearness affecting Vivienne more than she preferred to let on. Still furious, she stalked off to the stream, Shadow following close behind.

In the moments passing by, as he drank his full, Vivienne thought back to her father's tired expression, and the whole reason behind needing protection. With a muffled cry of annoyance, she headed back to where Sébastien stood. Her horse continued to drink until finally satisfied, then trailed behind his mistress.

Sébastien was patting Illyria down, whispering soothing words, yet the tautness of the back muscles spoke of his mood.

"Very well," Vivienne kept a level voice as she conceded. "You win."

His back remained frozen for a few long moments, before he whirled around, features still stormy. Vivienne forced the rest of the words out.

"I do not wish for my father to worry more than he already does, thus . . . You win."

Sébastien inclined his head, graciously accepting her defeat. "Thank you, my lady."

He offered a hand to mount, as a sign of peace. Vivienne gripped it, and gasped at the shock running right through both of them. She glanced at Sébastien, noticing the same astonishment reflected in his gaze.

For a moment, the briefest of instants, he stared at her as a man to a woman. But it was soon gone, as he helped her onto Shadow's back, and went to mount Illyria.

* * *

Vivienne woke up with a gasp, eyes flying open, and sat upright. It was raining outside, a big thunderstorm, and at first she thought it was the cause of her waking up. Alistair snoozed on the bed, a normally calming presence, but her pulse thumped wildly.

The dream came back to her in a flash.

"Oh hell," Vivienne clamped a hand over her mouth to keep from screaming. "I'm losing my sanity."

Tears filled her eyes, the stress of it all becoming too much. She brought both hands up to her face, muffling the sobs as much as possible. Within moments, the mattress shifted, and Alistair crawled closer, prodding a muzzle against her shoulder.

"I'm losing my sanity, Al," Vivienne repeated louder. "What my parents were afraid of, it's finally coming true."

He nudged more insistently, and she wiped at her eyes, finally meeting the dog's scrutiny. There was something in there, a calming, soothing glint, and slowly Vivienne's heartbeat rebound back to normal and the chaotic thoughts eased away.

"Yes, I'm a bit better," she admitted aloud, at the silent question in Alistair's eyes. "It was another nightly vision, similar to the one from yesterday. Except it was no dream, but seemed like a . . .a memory."

Vivienne curled back under the covers, missing the speculative look in his eyes. The sound of the rain outside lulled the young woman back to sleep, but the dog remained standing, watching as he always did.

* * *

Braydon leaned against a wall, biding his time. His eyes were trained on Vivienne's house, and the shadows drifting within. He could, on some level, understand his master's fixation on her.

"Hey, handsome!"

His musings were interrupted when Jennifer sashayed around the corner, body deliciously clad in low hip jeans and a V-neck top.

"You're trying too hard, darling," Braydon smirked, snickering as she pouted in response.

Once she was by his side, she inspected their surroundings. "What are we doing here?"

"Not taking any chances. Carleigh demanded I send some of his minions to scout the connection between Vivienne and Sébastien."

Jennifer grimaced, throwing a glare full of hate towards the house. "If only she'd hurry up and die!" Before the sorcerer could react, she stomped up to the door, hissing under her breath, "You don't even know the power you dominate, you stupid bitch, do you?"

"Now, now, my dear." Braydon scolded, in an instant close by and cupping her chin menacingly. "No crazy actions. We agreed to follow the master's plan here."

Jennifer scowled, and nodded tightly in response. As Braydon removed his hand, she added, "What about her dog?"

"What about him?"

"In the past, he was influential, a thorn in Carleigh's side."

"We're not even sure it's the same dog," the sorcerer declared with a shrug.

"Well, he sure hates *me*," Jennifer grumbled, as if that alone was proof.

Braydon stayed pensive, tilting his head with an evil glint. "Alright, let's not run any risks. I'll send the same guy to eliminate him. Did she mention the intruder?"

Jennifer shook her head slowly, trying to case the meaning of the question. "No . . . Why, should she have?"

"I would imagine so. He was damn freaked when she went all supernatural on him."

"She's incompetent, and doesn't even remember

anything!" Jennifer cried, and Braydon drew an index up to his lips, motioning for her to hush, and to edge further away.

"No . . . I don't imagine she does," he murmured in response once Jennifer joined him back in the alleyway. "It must have been some defense mechanism."

The warlock was quiet for a few moments, staring intently at the house, before speaking again.

"Carleigh will send his minions to test them," he informed Jennifer, scanning the house again. "You, my dear, have to do as I bid you."

At the eager glint in her eyes, so similar to a puppy, he continued, "Use your body to interfere with them. In no way can we let them be together again. Understood?"

Jennifer nodded, pressing closer to him. "In the meantime, it's been so long . . ."

"Not now!" the sorcerer exclaimed curtly, pushing her away. "Maybe another time. Now get out of here before anyone notices us."

He waited until she retreated around the corner, and followed suit the other way. If Jennifer was right, and the dog was supernatural, it was too risky to use otherworldly skills so close by them. It was much better to be cautious in the meantime.

* * *

Alistair was snoozing with one eye open, when footsteps under the window awoke him. His head snapped up, and he slowly slid off the bed, making sure not to wake his mistress up.

The dog stepped to the window and glanced outside, but

there was no sign of an intruder. He turned his gaze to the pool, then the back doors, with the same results.

Alistair was about to go back to bed, when voices drifted upwards. He trotted down the stairs, paws silent as a wolf, until he was in the living room. A different waft came from the entrance door, causing him to lift the head, sniffing the air, a low growl building in his throat.

He gravitated slowly to the entrance, and noticed someone right outside, their shadows visible under the door. There were murmurs, more than one person, and he was about to alert Vivienne, when they left abruptly. With one last glance, Alistair went back upstairs and settled by the bed.

The odor coming from underneath the door could not have been real, as he had only smelled it long ago. It must have been young kids from the neighborhood – or so he tried to convince himself. Regardless, he would defend Vivienne with his life, if need be.

* * *

Sébastien parked the car in the garage of the rented home, and slowly made his way inside. When Tony had demanded his presence on a trip to get in touch with a certain branch of the "family" this far off, the young man had not deliberated much.

Now, he was beginning to distinguish complications arising, with the way certain business transactions were going. The end result would involve Sébastien remaining in the city for a little while longer.

He never would have expected to find his soul mate here, of all places. Sliding in bed, analyzing tonight, he knew it had all been a risk – seeing Vivienne, touching her. It was the truth, yet he would not have done anything differently.

Sébastien peered up at the moon, wondering if his beloved was home in bed, and wishing to be her guardian, friend, lover, as once before.

But he could not afford to bring Vivienne into his world, not into the mess he had created. Despite his deepest desires, when the time came to depart, he would have to follow Tony. Allegiance was owed to the man, and he always collected – that was Sébastien's life now.

* * *

Vivienne returned to the café the next afternoon, ordered the usual espresso and sat down in a shaded spot with Alistair by her side, and a book in hand. She soon got lost in the story.

It had been a few hours, perhaps two, but the moment he strode by, Vivienne had an uncanny urge to look up. He was only a few meters distance, facing away from her, but she knew instantly it was him.

"Sébastien."

She had only whispered, but he swirled around immediately, eyes locking across the distance. The way he stared at her, and how his body leaned towards her, all Vivienne could think of was the Sébastien from her dream.

She snapped out of the reverie to note his internal conflict – one step in her direction, body turned away – as if hesitant to approach. The young woman wondered if it had anything to do with his entourage – a group of men dressed in business casual, busy piling in a few limousines further off – yet he did not appear to be the type to care for such frivolities.

Vivienne smiled tentatively and, like a moth to a flame, Sébastien drifted towards her table.

"Hi," she greeted once he neared.

"Hi," Sébastien replied back. He drank her in, eyes roaming over her body and features as if it was not only last night she had been in his arms, lost to the sensations of his mouth on hers.

Vivienne's cheeks heated, a telltale sign of a blush, even as Sébastien smirked, guessing her thoughts.

It was only a fraction of a second later when he peered down at Alistair, and froze. Vivienne could almost hear his tendons lock into place.

"He doesn't bite," she offered helpfully, thinking the reaction was due to an innate fear of dogs.

Sébastien did not reply, staring at Alistair in shock. *That's her demon dog, yet she's suffering from some amnesia, and he strikes me as a normal dog. Something is incredibly wrong here.* For the first time, his ruminations went to the asshole responsible for their predicament, swearing vengeance for everything lost.

As if listening to his private thoughts, the dog squinted at Sébastien. There was a glint of recognition in the canine expression, followed by frustration. He half expected the dog's booming voice in his head, but no such thing happened, and he groaned. *What the hell is going on?*

"Sébastien?"

Vivienne's soft voice penetrated and he conveyed his attention elsewhere, to another problem. Namely, the people in the luxury cars, whose attention he silently prayed not to attract.

"How are you?" he enquired instead, locking eyes with Vivienne's.

She hesitated for a tiny second, barely perceptible, before responding, "I'm alright . . . You?"

"Good." An idea hit him. "Are you going back to the bar tonight?"

"I—No, I wasn't planning to. Why?"

"Good." He breathed a sigh of relief, ran a hand through his hair distractedly, and glanced behind again to ensure his entourage was still busy getting into the cars.

"Why?" Vivienne persisted, drawing his attention.

Sébastien shifted on his feet, gaze falling on Alistair again. How could he explain the hazardous reality of his life, without revealing what he did now for a living?

He tried to find a way without sounding like a control freak, and finally settled on, "There have been some incidents there, and it's not the most secure place. I'd prefer for you to be out of harm's way . . ..When you're not with me, I mean."

Vivienne beamed at the words, her body relaxing. "Am I, then? With you?"

"I wish you would be."

Shit.

It was not the response he had intended to give. Sébastien longed to advise her to run away, far away from him and everything in the vicinity. Trouble was in the air, coming for Vivienne – some intuition alerted him there was more going on here than either of them understood.

Sébastien also yearned to leave with her, and regain what had been lost – something which, deep down, was impossible. He had formed a promise, long ago, one which had to be kept.

The most he could do was spend time with Vivienne, ensure she was unharmed, as long as his entourage did not notice him missing.

It's the least I can do to make up for lost time, he mused.

Vivienne had been his charge long ago, and perhaps he could care, this once, without all hell breaking loose. And maybe, along the way, help her recall the truth, and what happened. If the reason behind the amnesia was found, then he could punish those responsible.

If she ever remembers.

Unaware of Sébastien's internal battle, Vivienne grinned wider at his words, and Alistair peeked from the man to her, and back to him. There was an insistent gleam in his eyes, which could not be ignored.

"Are you free tonight, then?"

Vivienne tilted her head back in an innocent way that drove him crazy, recalling times past. Her long, raven locks fell out of the ponytail, framing her heart-shaped face, lips parted in a sensuous smile.

"Is that a proposition?" she breathed, unaware of the raw invitation exuded with those few words.

Sébastien wondered at the logic of the situation, and finally smiled. "Yes . . . I'd like to take you somewhere."

He regretted the suggestion the minute it was voiced. Not because being alone with Vivienne was a bad thing – rather because it would be too addictive, and something he would want more of.

"You can bring your dog if you prefer," Sébastien added to save face. *Please bring him.* "I have to finish some work related business, but afterwards . . . Could you meet me at the fountain for six?"

Vivienne nodded, unaware of the mental battle he was enduring.

Aware of being constantly under watch, Sébastien tried to communicate with his eyes what he could not otherwise. "Tonight," he reiterated with one last look, then spun on his heels and returned to his own personal hell.

* * *

The drive in the night was smooth, but Vivienne's nerves were frayed. Sébastien's Jaguar slid noiselessly amid the streets, and he was a great driver, so the problem was not there.

She had not brought along Alistair as had been suggested, rather preferring to be alone. The drive had started out fine, but it was not long before tension took hold of Sébastien's body, easily discernable.

With each passing second, he drove as if the hounds of hell were on their heels – leading her to second guess the decision to come without Alistair.

"Is everything alright?" Vivienne tried to probe after long moments of silence.

Sébastien peeked her way, measured her expression, and slowed down a bit. His shoulders relaxed infinitesimally. "I apologize, truly. It was not my intention to drive like a maniac and scare you."

"That's okay, I don't mind fast," she smiled. "Bad day at work?"

"I guess . . ." His expression turned sheepish and he focused back on the road – not before glancing in the rear-view mirror rapidly. "But mostly, I wanted to get us out of the city."

"Oh." There were too many things to enquire about, so Vivienne went with the easiest. "What is it you do, anyway?"

Sébastien hesitated for a barely perceptible second. "I'm in real estate."

Had it not been for that barest of pauses, she would have believed him. But there was something in his voice, a note Vivienne could not put her finger on. She decided to let it go, instead enjoying the drive.

However, thoughts would not stop churning in a chaotic mess in the young woman's mind, so she voiced another one. "You know, I never asked your last name. Silly, right?"

He half-smiled at that, "It's Dubois. Sébastien Dubois."

"Mine's Du Lac."

"Of the lake," he murmured, translating the French last name to English. There was an almost reverent odd tone to the way he said it, but again, she could not place it.

After a moment, Vivienne shrugged it off and pressed, "So, where are you taking me?"

Sébastien relaxed for good, with a grin that hit her all the way to the core. "That, babe, is a surprise!" He reached over and clasped a hand over hers.

Vivienne beamed back, squeezing his hand in response. She was stunned at how natural it felt, as if they had always belonged together.

Somewhere during the drive, she must have dozed off, because when she woke up, the sun was setting, the air was fresh, and there was water all around them.

Vivienne inspected the surroundings, glimpsing Sébastien

out of the car, on the shore of a gorgeous body of water. He must have driven them out of Avignon, because she was not aware of such a place nearby.

Almost as if sensing her awake, he came to open the door.

"I'm sorry I conked out, not sure what came over me," Vivienne apologized, dazedly getting out of the car, holding on to the door for support.

"Restless nights, perhaps?" Sébastien's eyes were intent on her, as if attempting to decipher her soul.

"That's one way of putting it," she grumbled.

"Do you want to talk about it?"

Vivienne was unsure how much to divulge. When she glanced up at Sébastien, and noted the concern, it all came out. "I've been getting these odd dreams. They seem more real than fantasy, and I'm weary of not being able to rest properly."

"What type of dreams?"

"Silly ones," Vivienne shrugged. "Me being a monarch, meeting a knight, ruling a kingdom . . ." The chuckle came out strained. "Like I said, silly."

Sébastien's lack of response was confusing, and Vivienne glanced at him. He was smiling, not laughing at her, but almost a tender smile, though the expression in his eyes was undecipherable.

"Nothing about you is silly," he declared. "Now, come." He extended a hand, and she slipped hers in his, stepping away from the car.

Sébastien dragged Vivienne up to the edge of the lake, and as she gaped in wonder, he circled behind and easily wrapped both arms around her. A click formed in her brain, and a notion of familiar comfort settled over.

More at ease than she preferred to admit, Vivienne tried to joke. "So, how many girls do you bring here on a first date?"

At Sébastien's unresponsiveness, her stomach churned in anxiety for a few moments. Finally, his chin settled on her shoulder, and he murmured, "None. You may not believe this, but I don't have time for frivolities."

Vivienne barely stifled the relieved sigh threatening to escape her. For some reason, the idea of him with any other woman set her teeth on edge. "Because of your job?" she enquired innocently.

Again, that hesitation. "Among others, yes."

Sébastien was quiet for a moment, before informing her, "This is one of the closest bodies of water I could find. I figured with the sun setting, it'd be a nice place to bring you. I always come here to reflect, and I wanted to share it with you."

After a pause, he continued, voice softening, "I'm even happier I decided to, since you shared your sleeping issues. There's something about this place that has the ability to soothe. That's my take on it, anyway."

Vivienne took in the lake's glinting surface, breathing in the crisp evening air, enjoying the breeze. "I can feel it, it's so —"

The words died on her lips, as her eyes widened. The world around spun, and the young woman clasped Sébastien's forearm for support, to no use.

"Crap!" Vivienne had time to mutter, right before she went limp in his arms, surrendering to the shadows.

CHAPTER 3

All Sébastien knew was, he had positioned Vivienne towards the lake, hoping the sight of it – and the resemblance to the past – would be enough to summon up some memories.

Her admission of the dreams had given him hope. If they were indeed recollections, her subconscious bringing them to the surface implied it would all eventually come back. All he had to do was wait for the right time to explain it all.

When Vivienne's eyes had fallen on the water, Sébastien had waited with baited breath for a reaction – and he'd gotten one.

Her body had tensed, and for a moment, he had hoped it was due to her memory returning. But when she mumbled something and went limp in his arms, panic arose.

"Vivienne!"

Sébastien grabbed his beloved by the waist right before

she hit the ground, and slowly lowered her.

"Vivienne, answer me!"

He was silently cursing himself for bringing her out here so soon. Of course she would pass out, if there was some damned curse blocking all her memories. *What kind of an idiot am I?*

And yet to anticipate the lake would have an adverse effect on her, who could have foreseen it? The irony did not escape Sébastien, considering it had been, in the past, Vivienne's place of power.

* * *

The lessons had been going fairly well, or so Sébastien concluded. Merlin had brought Vivienne in the midst of a meadow for the day, to teach her the art of illusion by way of water.

The princess knelt next to a pond, hands extended towards it, and practiced the mage's exercises. Merlin sat on a boulder next to her, while Sébastien stood a few feet behind, monitoring the area and ensuring their safety.

The knight had been unable to keep his eyes from returning to Vivienne every few moments, drawn by an invisible force, unable to stay away. It was due to the close observation he noticed her demeanor changed, radiating tension.

Sébastien cast an eyeful at the wizard, and noted Merlin's peculiar scrutiny as well, before inching a few steps closer. The old man barely spared him a glimpse, disclosing nothing as he concentrated on the royal.

"Vivienne, that is enough for today," Merlin advised out loud.

She ignored him, fixated on making the incantation work.

"My dear, it is fine. We will pick it up tomorrow."

With a grunt of frustration, Vivienne dropped her hands from the liquid, and stood. She gasped upon noticing Sébastien so close, and a slow blush spread across her cheeks.

He bowed, then extended an arm gallantly, glad beyond words Lancelot was not around today. The joy of strolling by her side would be his alone.

"Ready when you are, my lady."

With one last glance to Merlin, they parted ways. Vivienne clutched the guardian's arm as they walked the short way back to the castle.

Sébastien was prompt to notice her frown. "Forgive me for my boldness, but is there something bothering you?"

Vivienne shrugged, and for a moment he dared not presume an answer. Eventually, it came in a whisper, like the most secret of wishes.

"You would imagine that as the precious daughter of a king, I would be happy. Yet there are nagging doubts tugging at me. It is not easy being different, and I am afraid that some things which are coming, I am not prepared to tackle."

Sébastien frowned, wondering if any of it had to do with Lancelot. "I am sure you will figure it out, my lady. You have a bright head and compassion, and those two things are enough to ensure you decide the right thing at all times."

Vivienne swirled around, smiling for the first time that day as their eyes met. The breath caught in his throat at her radiance as she replied a sincere, "Thank you."

Sébastien's heart constricted and the longing within was almost agonizing. He craved nothing more than to kiss her, wipe away the shadows and make the princess happy. However, he knew her affection was with another, and she was out of his league.

Lancelot was of noble blood, and if Vivienne so desired, she could have him. But Sébastien, though knighted, was of common blood, not suited for a princess.

He bowed his head, fighting against the rising sentiments, and murmured, "My pleasure."

They continued the rest of the way in silence, until Vivienne was securely back at the castle.

* * *

The next day, Vivienne spent it in a meadow, playing with magic. Surrounded by quiet, the monarch was carefree as she let the charm flow through, while listening to Alistair's tales of his own world. Though usually fairly hushed on his past, today he was in a talkative mood, and she was happy for the distraction.

Letting spirit flow through her, Vivienne imbued the ground and the flowers with her essence, helping them bloom.

At the sound of a twig snapping, she whirled around. Narrowed green eyes scoured the forest, and she breathed a sigh of relief when Sébastien advanced between the trees.

"My lady," he bowed in greeting. Words got stuck in her throat, even whilst her pulse started beating in frenzy at the sight of him.

At Alistair's abnormal silence, Vivienne glanced down,

frowning at his fixed stare on the knight. Sébastien met and held it for a few moments, unaware the demon dog was using his otherworldly powers. Through different eyes that saw their auras, he observed in silence their interaction – what he was looking for, not even he knew.

"That is truly odd," Vivienne said out loud.

"My lady?" It came as a question.

She answered distracted, still intent on her protector. "Alistair has never been so subdued around a man before. It is unusual."

At Sébastien's silence, Vivienne looked up with an almost evaluating glint, before shaking her head and enquiring politely, "Was there something I could help you with?"

"Not particularly. I intended to keep my distance and not disturb you. As you recall, I have to be with you at all times."

Vivienne sighed, pushing aside the disappointment. Of course he was there out of duty, and nothing else.

"I am almost done," she assured him, releasing the earth from her magic's hold.

"Please, my lady." Sébastien stepped forward, hand extended, but stopped at the wariness in her countenance. "You were so carefree, I would rather not be the reason you stop. I can go back to the shadows, until you are prepared to retreat to the castle."

He bit down the words threatening to escape, of the love blooming, and his inability to get her out of his head.

And yet Sébastien could not help but wonder, was that another blush spreading across her cheeks? Before he could probe, Vivienne turned away, but her rushed words floated on the breeze.

"It shan't be necessary, Sébastien. There is nothing more

to do at this point. If I could figure out why I block the spells, sometimes subconsciously, I would have a better idea of how to work them."

She tucked a strand of long, raven hair behind a delicate ear, her gaze lost on the water nearby. "Not many people grasp the occult, and being one among few, I have learned it is not always easy. I am either feared or revered, from one extreme to the other."

"I cannot imagine the complications of your life, princess. But your strength and purity will prevail, no matter what."

At the rough timbre of his voice, heavy with unspoken sentiments, Vivienne focused on the knight with a sad little grimace. "It must be ironic to think I do not have everything I desire, is it not? To be a defender of my realm, I constantly use enchantments, yet I cannot enjoy... Such basic pleasures..." She trailed off, the corners of her lips trembling. "Forgive my ranting. You may retreat, Sébastien."

The words stuck in his throat, thus he simply bowed his head and went to the woods, watching her in silence. Only her back was visible as she conversed with Alistair.

The demon dog, who had been observing the exchange the entire time, disregarded Sébastien. Done with his examination of their auras, he turned to his mistress.

"His energy is different than the others, princess," his loud voice boomed telepathically.

Vivienne inclined her head towards him, noticing the flicker of red in his eyes. "Yes, it is," she exhaled wistfully. "But I cannot afford distractions, Alistair. You understand better than anyone. It was you who warned me I would have to confront obstacles befitting my station – and power – on my own."

"Perhaps I was hasty in my predictions, majesty."
Alistair approached, nudging one hand until she began petting
him automatically. "There is something between you two, and
I have witnessed it rarely in my existence. Do not close your
heart to the man just yet."

Vivienne bit her lip as the words sank in, and finally
joined Sébastien. Alistair on their heels, they headed back to
the castle in silence.

Before dropping his charge off at the main entrance,
Sébastien grazed her arm, and she glanced up. "My lady,
please feel free to talk to me. I may be only a knight, but I
promise to keep your confidence and make an effort to ease
your burden."

Vivienne smiled at the words, and stood on her toes to
kiss his cheek. "Thank you," she murmured in his ear.

The trace of the princess' citrus perfume lingered in the
air long after she was gone. Sébastien was left bereft, wishing
for more – always more.

* * *

Vivienne opened her eyes, noticing the inky sky, and a heat
behind. She tried to get up too hastily, and a settling hand
came into focus.

"Easy, take it easy."

"What happened?" Vivienne groaned, clutching her head,
at the same time sagging against Sébastien's chest. She was
sitting between his legs, his arms wrapped around her and
facing the lake.

"You passed out," was the gentle answer.

Vivienne stopped moving at the words, afraid to even comment. Silence surrounded them, whilst she attempted to figure out if she should confess to him that this was a daily occurrence, nothing to worry about, or rather explain what truly happened.

On top of that, the déjà-vu the young woman had woken up from was very much present in her head, and she was having a distressing time separating the Sébastien holding her from the one in the flashback.

As if sensing her internal conflict, Sébastien shifted Vivienne in his arms so she was in his lap, facing him. She could not help gawking like an idiot, recalling the look in his eyes, from so long ago.

Sébastien had been busy with a quick examination to ensure his beloved was awake and unharmed, but peering closer, he detected a peculiarity behind her regard – the shadows of the past dancing within. He tried to hush the excitement threatening to overflow, but when he stroked Vivienne's shoulder, an electric current zapped his fingertips.

They both froze, staring at each other. The young woman's eyes darkened with desire, and every fiber in his body responded. With a groan, Sébastien pulled her close, dragging her mouth to his.

When their lips grazed, it was a detonation to her senses, and before long, Vivienne pressed against him, deepening the embrace. It was what she craved and more, the world tilting right on its axis, no longer torn between reality and fiction. The only truth existing was Sébastien's lips, moving against hers, melting, coaxing, plundering, giving and taking, over and over.

It was moments before Sébastien forced himself to

withdraw, ignoring his body's groan of agony. "I know this is crazy, but I never want to let you go," he murmured.

Vivienne bit her lip, confusion warring within. His words were a promise, much like long ago. Meanwhile, she was still attempting to understand what was happening, desperately perceiving only pieces of the puzzle that had now become her life. And yet he was so strong, so sure of himself, she let herself be swept by the surety exhibited.

Sébastien's eyes raked over his beloved's features, noticing the now normal gleam of her eyes, and he forced a reassuring smile. The moment was gone, uncertainty looming, and his excitement had to be quieted. "Would you like to watch the rising moon together?"

Vivienne's gratitude shone in her eyes. "Nothing would please me more."

She settled in Sébastien's embrace, and enjoyed the first truly normal hours of the last couple of days.

* * *

The couple was returning to the Jaguar, when Sébastien froze, surveying the surroundings. His pose, the way he scoured the area, immediately reminded Vivienne of Alistair – or any guard dog, for that matter.

"What's wrong?" she wondered aloud.

Sébastien's hand tightened on hers, maneuvering Vivienne behind, his own body becoming a shield.

"Reveal yourselves."

Vivienne shivered at the ire in his voice. It was unfamiliar, as she had not been aware of it even in her visions.

There was a snap of a twig, and a shadow detached itself from the trees, followed by another, and another.

It was the first Vivienne saw of them – long black cloaks billowing in the wind, blank expressions, as though not masters of their own bodies. They were all men of various ages, under a dozen.

Sébastien let go of her, this time effectively placing the rest of his body to shield her. "Who the *hell* are you!?"

Vivienne could only glimpse the back of his head, but the crackling fury emerging, surrounding them, was stifling and violent. How the men could not perceive it was beyond her.

"We come for her."

The young woman froze at the man's words, peeking from around Sébastien to view the stranger effectively pointing her way. *Me and my damn luck! This just keeps getting better.*

"Like hell you do."

Before Vivienne could dispute Sébastien's words, he was covering ground, advancing and engaging them in a fight. He did it so admirably, somehow getting himself in their midst, yet keeping the strangers far away from her.

He acted swiftly, with a feral grace reminiscent of a panther attacking. Imminent danger surrounded them, but all Vivienne could fixate on was Sébastien, eyes drawn to his fluid form, to the vigor he exhibited.

He thrust one opponent in a tree, ducked another's punches and slammed a shoulder into one's stomach. The remaining men hesitated, evidently not having expected the fight. One of them observed Vivienne with blank and unfocused eyes.

What the hell kind of drug are they on? She shivered

despite herself. His unblinking stare raised goose bumps on her arms.

Then like a force of nature, Sébastien was there, dragging Vivienne to the car. He pushed her in, closed the passenger door, hopped into the driver's side and shifted into gear. They were gone before the attackers were any wiser.

Once they had put some distance between them, Sébastien slowed down a bit, and clasped her hand. "By all hells and heavens, you have a will of steel, babe. You're not even shaking."

"No . . . I just haven't yet processed the fact this truly happened."

"Vivienne," he squeezed her hand, "this isn't one of your dreams. Are you alright?"

She nodded, but realizing he could not see it in the dimness, replied with a faint, "Yes." Biting her lip, the young woman squinted behind them, but no obvious shapes caught her eye. "Who the hell were those guys?"

"Not friends of yours, I take it?" Sébastien's query sounded more like a grunt.

Vivienne shook her head in denial, ever as her throat closed up, tears filling her eyes. "What the hell is going on?" she choked out, right before bursting into tears.

Realizing the shock must have hit home, Sébastien swore, and pulled over on the side of the road. It was risky, since they had not put enough distance between their stalkers, but Vivienne's sobs were wrenching at his soul.

He scrutinized the obscurity behind them and around for figures hiding in the shadows. Not sensing anything, he gave up and concentrated on his beloved.

Sébastien unbuckled the seatbelt, dragging her in his lap. Both hands went to Vivienne's cheeks and he caught her haunted gaze with his.

"I'm not sure what's going on here, but all I can say is, I want to care for you. So whatever's happening, I'm going to be by your side, not letting you go." He rested his forehead against hers, praying his words helped. "You have to trust me, and I'm begging you to let me bring you to my place tonight. Whoever those guys were, they might have an idea of where you live. Is that alright?"

Vivienne nodded her head in silent assent. "Brave girl," he praised, with a rapid peck on the lips meant as a reward. Sébastien then moved to capture her waist to manoeuver her off him, and they both froze as the electricity hit again.

The conflict was apparent on Sébastien's features, the sudden lock of his jaw, the tightening of his hand on her hip. His reasoning was simple – Vivienne was too vulnerable, and he preferred not to act impulsively at such a time.

They stood frozen for a beat of a second, before Vivienne's body tilted betrayingly towards his. It was all the encouragement Sébastien needed, as he dragged her mouth down to his with a free hand, and they were making out again, in a way different from before. It was insistent, arduous, as all Vivienne yearned for was to experience something, anything.

When he plundered her mouth, taking over like a conquistador, Vivienne surrendered with a moan, her softer body glued to his chiseled muscle. She pressed closer, wanting to become one, and her hands reached under his shirt . . .

Sébastien broke it off again, panting. His eyes roamed her features, searching, and she muttered, "Guess you felt it too, huh?"

His laugh was a calming wave, washing over Vivienne, taking the angst and desire with it. When Sébastien shifted her back into the passenger seat, she gave into its warmth, settling peacefully as they took off.

* * *

Braydon cringed as he entered the church where his master lay in wait. He had apprehended it was a huge bet – but damn! The druids had been utterly useless, real puppets with no strings.

The only thing resulting from it was the certitude Vivienne did not have supernatural skills and Sébastien still wanted to secure her safety.

No revelation there. I'd protect that body too.

Braydon progressed past the shambled door, his eyes narrowing on his master, sitting cross legged in front of the alter ashes. The man was in his early thirties, with a mop of black hair reaching his shoulder in straight strands, slightly oily in the light. His build was neither muscular nor frail, but somewhere in between, as though he had never finished growing.

What currently kept Braydon's stare was the deathly ashen sheen of the warlock's skin. Eyes closed, palms on his knees, he was a real yogi in the making.

At least, if one was to ignore the murky creatures at his feet, surrounding him in a pool of darkness, and feasting on the ashes of the sacred altar. They were manifestations of the darkness clinging to the sorcerer, taking the shape of snakes, spiders, insects in general, forever in his proximity.

Braydon stopped dead in his tracks when Carleigh opened pale gray eyes, and stared at him expectantly.

"You've heard," he stated, a hint of fear in his voice.

A cruel sneer distorted the master's already angular features. "That my acolytes were disposed of by bare human strength? Of course. Which is why I am ensuring the new ones will be properly equipped. Though I do not expect much from my minions, I do have to ensure they truly waste Vivienne's time – and resources. Watch and learn."

The necromancer muttered an incantation, calling forth the most disturbing energies. The snakes and spiders at his feet writhed in anticipation, jumping up like eager puppies to their master. Braydon had goose bumps being this close to them.

The air crackled with malevolent energy, even as the temperature dropped a few degrees. Carleigh grunted in pain, then his back arched in an unnatural pose.

As though in a trance, his mouth opened and out came a smoke, thick and compact, the color of night. It floated to the ground, encompassing the creatures, and whirled in a circle, like a tornado, faster each moment, until it stopped. An eerie silence floated.

The smoke settled on the ground, where the altar had been, imbuing the stone with corruption. When it was absorbed, the surface became smooth and shiny, a newly created black mirror. A moment later, the its surface bubbled with an ugly gurgling sound, and shapes exited.

Carleigh stood up with a victorious smirk.

"Now we can begin our attack. These new druids will have some juice. Either way, they are intended as a means to an end. I will ensure to stay off the grid to better manipulate them." He met Braydon's astonished gaze. "I have not spent lifetimes in waiting to be countermanded at the last moment . . . No. The plan will succeed, mark my words."

* * *

Sébastien's house was not far off Vivienne's, a fact she pointed out when he parked in his secluded driveway.

"The coincidences keep on coming . . ." he muttered, shaking his head and turning off the engine. "But I don't actually live here, it's only a rental for a short time."

He got out of the car and opened the door, unaware of Vivienne's stricken expression. When they entered the house, Sébastien directed her to the couch, and poured her a shot of cognac. "Drink."

Vivienne gulped it down, relishing its fiery path to her stomach. It was a welcome distraction from other thoughts. "So if you're renting, where do you live?" She tried to keep an even voice, but it was harder to maintain her composure at Sébastien's answer.

"Here, there, everywhere," he shrugged, serving himself a glass as well. "My job brings me different places."

When Vivienne did not respond, he glanced to see her tearing up again. "What's wrong?" He frowned, sitting down and pulling her in his arms.

"For some stupid reason, I assumed you lived here . . . I . . ." She shook her head, tried to get up, but his iron grip kept her. "Please let me go. I should go home."

"Vivienne, babe, talk to me." Sébastien urged her chin up with his index, anxiously searching the young woman's features for a clue that would explain the sudden change. "What happened?" He stifled the panic at the thought of her leaving, especially after witnessing the danger courting her.

Vivienne breathed in, as if preparing to plunge somewhere deep, and returned the stare. "You cannot be making promises of protection if you're here temporarily. I think this was a big mistake. We both get the attraction is there, but I don't do short term affairs. And considering my life has attained a new high on the complication index in the last couple of hours . . . It's best I leave."

Sébastien frowned, and his hold loosened enough for Vivienne to get up and head to the door. Before she could move further, he was up following, tugging the wrist closest to him, and forcing Vivienne to face him.

"Wait."

He watched her silently, noticing she was fighting back tears, biting her lip. Sébastien knew the behavior well enough, and the stubborn will behind it. The tightness in his chest became more pronounced. How could he reveal this was an old enemy, when she was not even aware of the different past they shared?

"You're right," Sébastien started, trying to find the words to console without lying. "We both feel the attraction. But I don't lie when I promise to look after you. Though my assignment here is only temporary, I'd like to get to know you, spend time with you, and protect you after what we saw tonight. I'm not asking we jump into anything. Just . . . Please, stay for tonight. I cannot explain it myself . . ."

He trailed off, unsure of how much more to divulge. At the mention of the night's events, Vivienne bowed her head.

"I'm so sorry."

"What for?"

"For tonight. And what happened."

"It's not your fault," Sébastien immediately noticed the emptiness of the words, and tried to cover it by adding, "But I would like any information you have on those guys, if only to better shelter you."

"I honestly don't know, but . . ."

The young woman peered at him, green eyes earnest and wondering if she could trust him. Sébastien tried to keep an open expression, showcasing his concern and intent. Once her body posture relaxed, he moved close enough to hug her.

"This is going to sound insane," Vivienne began in his chest, and Sébastien noted she was warring with the idea. "But you and me, I'm under the impression it's already happened. In the past." She paused, glancing up – there was no surprise in his eyes.

"In another life," she finished off, but Sébastien's facial expression still did not change. "Either you think I'm crazy, or you actually give credence to this, and I can't figure out which to fear more."

At that, he winked. "You're not crazy." Relief spread through him, at being able to admit at least a portion of the truth, and his arm around Vivienne tightened. "I've sensed something between us from the moment I first laid eyes on you. That's what I was having such a hard time explaining to you. I can't guess what it is, but I would like to find out more. I'm not the type to give up easily, or to make promises I won't keep. Right now, I promised you safety. And I would like, in the meantime, to be with you, learn more about you."

He kissed the side of her temple, moving them backwards to rest on the couch once more. Once Vivienne was settled against him, he added, "So for the time being, I suggest to go with it, and see what happens. I'm willing if you are."

For all response, Vivienne snuggled into him, resting her head on his chest. Exhausted from the day's events, she passed out in a matter of moments.

Sébastien listened to her breathing, vowing that before he left Avignon, her life would be safe once more, with all menaces eliminated.

* * *

Sébastien was dreaming of old times past, when the environment changed, and he was in a dimmed room with a mirror. He did not wish to approach it, but a disembodied voice ordered him to.

As the guardian followed the command, his own reflection sneered back. He had blood on his hands, a cruel glint in the eyes, and a blank expression.

"This is who you are," the voice accused. "You are damaged. You do not deserve Light, and should stand by your promise."

Like a movie, his last life flashed before him, and the promise made when Vivienne died – to stay away.

Sébastien's eyes snapped open. Vivienne was warm in his arms, still asleep, trusting him wholly. Though he was no longer quite the man she had known, he could still be worthy of that trust. He longed to reveal everything, but it was much too soon – or so he convinced himself.

In reality, he was afraid of the questions his beloved would have. The fear of losing what they had now, small as it was, crippled him. Yet still he was aware they could not regain what they had been gifted with in the past. That was a path he could not follow, no matter how much he yearned to.

As Sébastien struggled with using his better judgment, Vivienne snuggled deeper, and mumbled, "Love you."

It was such an unexpected declaration, probably brought forth by whatever memory she was lost in, that he froze. Then his gaze softened, and he kissed the top of her head. His arms tightened around her, his decision made in a snap – he had to stay. At least until she was safe.

* * *

"Did you sleep at all? You look like you didn't get much rest," Vivienne said, caressing his cheek.

She had woken up on the couch, snuggled against Sébastien, to find him watching her.

"I generally don't," he chuckled. With his mussed hair and sleepy eyes, she could not help but conclude he was adorable.

Sébastien pressed his lips to hers slowly, languorously, enjoying the embrace and teasing them both. As Vivienne's body reciprocated in desire, a phone rang, and he froze.

"Aren't you going to get it?" she wondered on the fifth ring.

He groaned, gently moved her off him, and flipped his cell open. "Tony expects you. Now." The caller hung up without further explanation.

"Sébastien? Are you alright?"

Vivienne's concerned tone broke past the raging haze, and Sébastien realized what caused her reaction. His body had become stiff, heedful of where it had to go. He attempted to shrug carelessly, schooling his features in a mask of annoyance.

"Work, an emergency that can't be avoided. Rain check on the breakfast?"

"That's okay," Vivienne shook her head, "I'll go home."

"No, let me drop you off."

"It's fine," she smiled. "I doubt those creeps would try anything in daytime and, whatever the emergency with work is, I can tell it's got you worked up. I'd rather not keep you."

Sébastien hesitated, thankful for the understanding, but unwilling to let her go. The decision was made for him when Vivienne got off the couch, and he sighed, "Thanks, babe."

As she passed by, he enticed her for one last kiss, and let go only when Vivienne's pupils dilated with desire. It was hard to leave her wish unanswered, but the unpleasantness of what awaited him was definitely a mood killer.

"Are you free tonight?" Sébastien asked on a whim.

"Ye—um, actually, no. Jennifer, one of my friends, begged me to go with her somewhere."

"Text me the address when you have it, and I can meet you there tonight."

Vivienne nodded then waved one last time, and left. It was only after she was gone that Sébastien let his scowl take over. He had a feeling her "friend" would be yet another complication, one he was well familiar with.

* * *

Later that day, Vivienne was minding her own business at the bar, when Jennifer, beyond tipsy, trotted up with a man on her arm. She already regretted coming, but her friend had insisted, and she always did have a tough time saying no.

Vivienne had texted, as promised, Sébastien the address, but he had not shown yet. She could not help but think back to the morning, and the normalcy of the scene. For two people who had promised to take it slow, it sure had not felt that way – not that she was complaining.

When Jennifer bumped into her, Vivienne whirled around, already annoyed at the man's insistent gaze fixed on her.

"Keep him entertained, I'm going to visit the washroom," she slurred.

The minute she left, the man crept in her personal bubble. "*Vivienne*, huh? Is that French?"

She curled her lip in disgust. He was as drunk as Jennifer, eyes raking over her like a piece of meat, breath stinking of booze. No friend rule mentioned she had to suffer the lewd conduct.

"Not quite," Vivienne responded curtly.

"I bet you're a real good kisser," he delivered the corny line, and immediately attempted to get in her space.

"Back *off!*" She managed to shove him away, but he came back again.

"Come on—"

"Hey babe."

Vivienne half-turned, but a hand wrapped around her

waist, and next thing she knew, hauled her in a sound embrace. Familiar lips cut off any air supply, and she was lost.

That night, Sébastien was different. The way his lips shifted around hers was pure seduction, skillful and alluring, and she gave in. Her body melted against his, surrendering the reins to his mastery.

They broke off at a muttered curse behind. Vivienne was about to confront Jennifer's date, but Sébastien's arm tightened, maneuvering her into his side. His hand splayed across her lower back in a possessive gesture.

He leveled a dark glare on the man. "Got something to say?"

It was a roar more than an interrogation, his voice tight with warning. Vivienne shivered in response to this strange side she was not familiar with – the timbre of the voice similar to how he had greeted their cloaked attackers. Her knees quivered at the danger he exuded, and the man blanched, retreating.

"You okay?"

Vivienne peeked up at Sébastien, and smiled shyly, "Yeah." He was looking sexy without even trying, in navy jeans and a fitted white shirt. The arm around her was strong, causing an enhanced sense of security – more than she had felt all day in the house.

"Who was the guy? Another one of your friends?" he scowled, glowering at the man's retreating back.

"Not quite, no. Only some loser my friend dumped on me."

Vivienne stopped talking, flabbergasted at the ice in her voice. She had never gotten mad at Jennifer before, regardless of whatever stupid behavior she was guilty of. But something about this particular night was extremely bothersome. With a start, she recognized the anger stirring underneath the surface at her friend.

Sébastien arched an eyebrow in response to his beloved's tone, and he glanced over her head, then back down. "Is that your friend heading here now?" he enquired, in an all but welcoming tone.

When Vivienne looked over her shoulder, she glimpsed Jennifer arriving by their side. Her friend eyed Vivienne in Sébastien's arms, not shying away from ogling the man himself. There was something in her eyes that did not quite fit with the drunken behavior, an almost calculating glint.

Still, she broke off the gawking, and sneered at Vivienne. "Well, where's my date gone to?"

"Not here, obviously."

Jennifer's expression showed her shock at being greeted so icily.

"He hit on me, Jen. Quite aggressively. So, nice freaking going."

"Oh Viv, I'm so sorry—"

Vivienne shook her head, lifting her palm in Jennifer's face. "Save it. I'm *so* not interested. This was never my scene, hence why I'm leaving. Enjoy your night."

Without another word, Vivienne snatched Sébastien's hand and sauntered away, inhaling a large gulp of air once outside.

Sébastien's eyes narrowed on the tightening of her muscles, and the faint lightning in her eyes. He longed to divulge the truth now more than ever, having caught on he was not the only one masquerading in her life. *More than one peril courts her . . .but how much unsaid is left there?*

And yet, part of the truth would not do, that much was clear – it would have to be all of it. Sébastien did not wish to put Vivienne through the pain, having hurt her in the past. The reality was, he was not prepared yet, as it would involve letting go.

With a loud exhalation, he mused instead on how to neutralize this one threat for her. Vivienne's pacing soon distracted him, especially the shimmering dress clinging to her curves. In the dimness of the bar, he had missed his chance to observe, but now . . .

"What?"

Sébastien raised his eyes to notice Vivienne now staring at him, staring at *her*, and chuckled guiltily, "You're gorgeous, babe, that's all."

She blinked, disconcerted, and beamed as the words registered. The blaze was now all but gone from her countenance.

"Feeling better?" Sébastien asked, spreading his arms welcomingly for a hug.

Vivienne shrugged, approaching slowly, but stopped as something dawned on her.

"You weren't—you didn't—" she stopped, shaking it off. He fought back a grin at her confusion.

Vivienne breathed in, and tried again. "What I meant was . . . Jennifer, you weren't affected by her."

"*Affected?*" By that point, Sébastien was flat out laughing. "Is she a virus of some sort? Your words sure point that way."

"She is," Vivienne complained, then clamped a hand on

her mouth. "What the—I'm so sorry, I'm not usually this catty. Must be the lack of sleep, or stress . . . Or something."

Sébastien could not help an outright laugh. Vivienne clearly did not realize her personality was in metamorphosis, with the past and present selves merging, and it was hilarious to behold. "I assure you, I'm quite enjoying myself. But what do you mean by affected?"

Vivienne shrugged, tucking a strand of hair behind her ear. "I'm not sure how to explain it, but guys are always weird around Jennifer. They, for lack of a better expression, fall at her feet."

Sébastien gave a tight-lipped smile, an odd crackling in the air again. "Do they, now?" It was murmured almost to himself, and for a moment he was somewhere else, thinking of another siren in their past.

After a beat, he snapped out of it, eyes locking with Vivienne's, honesty apparent within their depths. "I'm not most guys, babe. And trust me when I say, my interests lie only with you."

His words spread a now familiar warmth deep within, and she beamed. Sébastien reached for her hand, tugging her close, stealing another kiss. When they pulled apart, Vivienne buried her nose in his neck, inhaling the crisp scent of his skin.

"How did your emergency go, at work?"

"It got handled."

Vivienne was dismayed when Sébastien froze, his entire body going rigid. *How can a real estate job be so stressing?* Despite her inner thoughts, she refused to ruin the moment by probing for more answers. *Later.*

Instead, she pressed her lips to Sébastien's neck in a light peck, and confessed, "Can we go get something to eat? I'm a bit tipsy, and food would be great."

His body shook with a silent chuckle, and the tension seeped out of him. Vivienne beamed, proud for the little victory, even as Sébastien replied, "As you wish, my lady."

At the words, she disengaged abruptly, flashes hitting her like an avalanche, similar to the time at the café. No vision came, but there was an odd sensation in the pit of her stomach, halfway between a need to cry and a craving to kiss him.

"What did you just say?" Vivienne breathed, searching his features.

Sébastien met her confused stare.

"Anything you wish?" he repeated, frowning.

"No, the last part."

"My lady?"

She nodded, biting on her bottom lip.

"What's wrong?" Sébastien's brow furrowed, still searching for a clue.

"Nothing, it's . . ."

Vivienne hesitated, but realization dawned on him before she could finish.

"Is this part of those dreams of yours?"

Sébastien deciphered the admission in her eyes, despite the lack of response. With a shake of the head, he huddled closer, one hand going up to caress her cheek. "Well, maybe there's some truth in there, after all."

Vivienne nodded, but the moment was interrupted when her stomach roared. She ducked her head, sheepishly wondering, "Too late for the food?"

"Nah babe, anytime."

* * *

Sébastien accompanied Vivienne to get some food at one of the little joints open late, and relaxed and enjoyed something basic and uncomplicated. He warily kept an eye out for any other interruptions, but whoever the cloaked figures from the previous night had been, they seemed to have given up for the time being.

When he dropped her off, Vivienne invited him in, and he could not deny the yearning within.

Alistair was there, joyously accepting his mistress back home, for all intents and purposes acting like a dog. But Sébastien was not blind to the assessing glint in his eyes whenever their gazes met.

After a movie, Vivienne dozed off against him. She did not stir when he shifted, picked her up, and carried her to bed, tucking her in. He took a minute to glance around her bedroom, but a sound behind caught his attention.

Alistair had followed them, and his dark eyes settled on Sébastien with their odd human intelligence shining within.

"If only you'd remember . . . We could figure it out together." He ran a hand over his face, groaning. "Maybe it's best you don't."

Alistair's low whine distracted him from tumultuous ruminations, and he peered at the dog. "I miss your counsel, old pal."

They both froze as someone knocked on the door.

Alistair growled, moving stealthily in its direction, his massive body prepared to attack. Sébastien followed behind, getting a strong impression the night was about to head towards the worst.

He opened the door to find Jennifer standing there. Her shocked regard met his, and Sébastien crossed his arms, blocking the only way in.

"You look sober." He kept a low voice for Vivienne's benefit, but the sarcasm was apparent. "But then again, you were never drunk, right? Nice to see you again, *Guinevere.*"

CHAPTER 4

Guinevere scowled at him, her pretty features twisted in annoyance.

"It had to be you! And you remember everything. How unsurprising . . . Always the knight in shining armor, huh?"

Sébastien did not respond, instead evaluating the menace. Her presence suggested nothing good, and he wondered if it had anything to do with Vivienne's amnesia.

"What the hell are you doing back here?" Guinevere demanded.

"The better question is, what are *you* doing masquerading as Vivienne's BFF? There was bad blood between you."

"That's in the past."

"Bullshit," Sébastien snorted.

Alistair grunted in approval.

Guinevere glowered at both of them, before shrugging

dismissively. "Whatever, I don't have to explain myself to you. Let me see Vivienne."

"She's unavailable," Sébastien stated, gritting his teeth.

"Seriously!?"

"Yeah."

Sébastien's tone left no room for debate. It registered in Guinevere's eyes, as she took in his tense stance and folded arms. "You're not the same you were. Why would she be?"

"Either way, it's none of your business."

"I'll reveal everything."

"No, you won't. Whatever twisted game you're playing requires Vivienne to remain ignorant of the past, and you prefer her unaware. So, scram. You're done playing."

"Who the *hell* do you think you are!?"

Sébastien uncurled his arms and advanced in one motion, his countenance overshadowed with barely restrained fury. Guinevere backed away, and real fear registered in her face.

"You *have* changed."

"Get out. Now."

Guinevere whirled to depart, but glanced over her shoulder one more time. "You can't have Vivienne, and you know it. Not to worry though, you'll be gone soon enough. Enjoy it while you can."

Sébastien waited until she disappeared down the road, and retreated back in, Alistair shadowing his footsteps. He went to the couch, and Alistair came to sit in front of him.

He stared at the beast for a long beat, wondering if it was worth it, and decided to give it a shot anyway.

"I'm crazy for talking to a dog," Sébastien inhaled deeply, and blew out his repressed fury, keeping a cool voice. "But

I'm hoping you're in there, old pal. I can't figure out if you don't recall either, but this isn't the first life we've lived. You, me, Vivienne, Jennifer also known as Guinevere . . . The last time we were all together was in King Arthur's time. Crap happened, and you were gone."

He paused, running trembling hands through his hair in frustration, before continuing, "I lost Vivienne, and I had to do some not so good stuff to bring her back. But here's the thing – she doesn't remember anything of her old life, doesn't register she's in danger, and that someone's after her. I'm afraid it might be the guy that got her in the last life, Carleigh . . . And I need your help to keep her safe. So for now, whatever you do, please stay around her if I'm not here, and keep Guinevere away. Please."

Alistair had been listening attentively during the entire speech. Once it was done, he approached to nuzzle his hand.

"Paw me if you get it, old pal." Sébastien did not even attempt to keep the pleading out of his voice.

The dog squinted at him for a frozen moment, then his left paw came up, tapping Sébastien's hand.

"Thank the fates for little miracles," Sébastien murmured. He positioned himself to have a better angle on the door, and lay down on the couch.

Time to become what he had always been meant to be – Vivienne's guardian, once more.

* * *

The night was silent as Sébastien was on his rounds. Though the grounds were hushed, he perceived a presence following and drew his sword out, shifting to confront the unknown menace. He was met with the midnight eyes of Vivienne's demon dog.

Sébastien hesitated. He could not well attack the monarch's familiar, could he?

"Lower you weapon, knight," a deep voice rumbled in his head.

The tip dipped to the ground, as did Sébastien's jaw. He caught himself and, unsure of what to add, sheathed the sword, surreptitiously glancing at the dog – he really was massive.

"Forgive me, but I am unsure how to address you," Sébastien spoke out loud, feeling ridiculous as the words echoed in the night.

"Alistair will do," the voice in his head came again.

Sébastien nodded, but a horrible presentiment hit him, envisaging the dog might have a reason for being present. "Is Vi—Is my lady alright?"

"Yes, she is resting. I came to join you on your rounds tonight."

When Sébastien did not answer, Alistair advanced to his side. Together, they stepped back out onto the grounds, the dog trotting next to the man, silent at first.

After a few moments, the voice came again in his head, "I am not an evil demon, knight. If I was, I would not be finding nicknames for you, and engaging in conversation. You can stop fearing I will eat – or otherwise harm – you."

Sébastien gaped down at him, bewildered once more. "You can read my mind?"

"Not easily, but when the thoughts are as loud as yours

are, it is fairly simple to tune in."

Sébastien walked in silence for a few moments, then wondered, "If you are not evil, then what exactly are you? You are most certainly not a dog."

Alistair formed a sound like a cough, and the guardian realized it was laughter. "No, I am not truly from the canine family," he finally admitted. "I simply chose this body for its usefulness. Eons ago, I used to be a divinity."

"You were a god?" Sébastien tried to mask his astonishment, and failed.

"Yes. There existed different realms, governed by different gods, some more influential than others. I was amongst the middle ones. Unfortunately, some gods grew greedy, and commenced playing politics. The resulting wars were worse than you ever experienced in your few human years. I fell amongst them, and instead of doing good, as I was mandated, I became cunning. After the wars, when some gods established their rule over the others, they punished those who had disobeyed."

Alistair paused for a few moments, surveying the inky sky, and shook his colossal head. "I was one of them. They cast me out of the skies, and sent me to the underworld, where I became a demon lord, forever intended to influence for evil, never interfere. For eons, I did this, but I grew tired. The more I interacted with humans, the more I assessed them as pawns, too easy to manipulate."

They rounded a corner and wordlessly agreed to head on the outskirts of the castle grounds, to ensure the sentries were standing guard.

"It was during these incursions," Alistair continued his

story, "that two things occurred. First, I came across a wizard going by the name of Merlin. He was young at the time, but still formidable. I tried to influence his decisions towards evil, as I was supposed to, but found I did not have the soul for it. He noticed my presence, and over time, we spoke."

"You did not attempt to kill him?"

"No, for I found him entertaining." At the guardian's surprised look, the old god laughed again. "Yes, the young version of the wise man you now see was truly something else. Regardless, I also eventually realized that Merlin would play a big role in the future of humanity."

At Sébastien's silence, the dog went on, "There is a prophecy of a young boy who will lead humanity out of the dark ages. His name is Arthur, and he is intended to be a leader the likes of which man has never experienced."

"I know of him," Sébastien said, "whispers in the countryside I always presumed were rumors or old wives' tales."

"Yes, everyone is under the same impression. But he is very much real, living in Camelot, and already on his way to becoming a great ruler. Merlin will be the one to lead him to his glory."

Sébastien pondered the words for a moment, and wondered, "What about the other one? In your incursions, the second thing that happened."

"I met Vivienne. Her pure spirit drew me in like a moth to a flame."

"I can relate," Sébastien sighed, barely keeping the longing out of his voice.

The demon dog ignored him, continuing, "And I have

been her guardian and protector as of when she was a little girl. Until you came along."

"I sense a threat coming," Sébastien muttered.

Alistair stopped dead in his tracks, peering with a menacing flame in his eyes. "No, knight. A promise. Just as you swore an oath to Vivienne, I have one for you. If you ever hurt the princess, you will pay with your life."

Sébastien inclined his head in assent, declaring, "I will never hurt her. On the contrary, I fear I might be falling in love with her, and it is not something I planned to let happen."

Alistair did his odd cough-laugh again, sauntering away.

"What's so funny?" Sébastien scowled, hurrying to keep up.

"You humans are. Love cannot be limited, nor planned. I have learned that much in my eons of existence. It was, still is, and always will be, the only thing which fights evil, over and over again."

Sébastien was silent and the dog left him to his musings. That night, they roamed the grounds for hours in companionable silence.

Over time, it became a habit, and a bond of friendship forged between them. For the most part, the rounds were spent chatting about security, and the past.

One night, everything changed. They were in the midst of a discussion, when Alistair paused. He looked around, his nose up in the air, then a low growl started deep within his chest. Without a warning, he took off on a run.

Sébastien sprinted after him, and ended up in the prison tower. Alistair was pacing from one end to the other like a caged lion, snarling like the hells of fury.

The knight watched in growing amazement as the dog sniffed the ground, his entire body arched in tension. The enormous jaws opened, and he blew out a mist, staring with obvious intent as it spread over the ground. It was an icy blue, thin-like fog, and the temperature in the tower dropped by a few degrees following its apparition.

Alistair waited as it covered the ground, lighting each bit of sorcery left behind, until the entire area seemed carpeted by blue fireflies. He sniffed again, this time tasting the malevolence in the specks. Having gathered enough, he shook his head, and the mist dissipated, along with the fireflies.

"Blood magic was used here for nefarious purposes," Alistair mumbled at Sébastien's approach, an uneasy glint in his opaque eyes. "Go stand guard by Vivienne's side tonight, until I join you."

After the knight turned his back, the demon dog squinted at the moon and thundered, "Damn full moon!"

Sébastien was already racing across the grounds to his mistress' quarters, body tightly wired for a fight. Noticing the door to her chambers open, he burst in, just in time to glimpse the shadow bolting out the window.

He unsheathed his sword and ran after it, but by the time he looked out the window, it was gone.

Vivienne jumped up in bed, startled out of sleep, and dragged the bedclothes to her chin. "Sébastien! What's the matter?" The second after her outraged cry, she noticed the blade in his hand, followed by the fury on his features.

Sébastien tried to survey one more time the grounds, but it was useless. Despite the full moon, there was an unnatural gloom enveloping the castle. His human eyes were no match for it.

He stepped to Vivienne, attempting to calm his breathing – and ignore the sight of the princess in bed, hair a tumbling mess, a vulnerable look in her eyes. He craved nothing more than to bring her comfort in ways other than as a knight.

Sébastien met her confused stare, and began explaining the night's events. It was both an effort to both distract his errant thoughts, and wipe her anxious look.

Alistair showed halfway through the explanation, looking rougher for wear. He placed his head on the bed by the royal's feet, and waited.

When Sébastien was done, Alistair tilted his head, and his voice echoed in both their minds. "You must have learnt by now that whenever used, the occult drops traces of magic behind. In the tower, the black art throbbed still. I am not sure whom it was, or what they intended, but I will be keeping an eye out. Meanwhile, Vivienne, you should use defensive barriers around your bedroom each evening. It is useless to pretend this was not an attack aimed towards you."

Though pale, Vivienne had reined in her original reaction, and was now much more in control, agreeing to the protector's suggestion without flinching. Noticing this, Sébastien realized his presence was no longer required.

He was about to depart, leaving the royal in capable paws. Her voice stopped him, emerald eyes trapping his.

"Thank you, Sébastien," Vivienne spoke softly.

"My pleasure, my lady," he mumbled hoarsely, keeping silent the rest of his emotions – at an extreme price.

"You did well," Alistair's voice mentioned for his ears only. "We will catch him, whoever this menace is."

* * *

Sébastien woke up from the recollection with a start. He had not allowed himself to remember the past for a reason, but it was odd he had subconsciously summoned up that particular time.

Perhaps it's all starting as it did back then, with midnight visits and stalking, he could not help but muse.

Uneasy, Sébastien got up from the couch and went over to his beloved's bedroom. He opened the door, noticing Alistair snoozing on the bed. Reassured by the sound of Vivienne's peaceful breathing, he returned downstairs.

Much like in the past, he did a tour of the house, both outside and inside, checking for anything peculiar. The night was hushed, the grounds peaceful. With a sigh, Sébastien retreated back inside, locking everything behind.

If it truly was starting as before – which all signs pointed to – what Vivienne faced was infinitely more hazardous to her life whilst she remained ignorant of the past. She would never discern the incoming enemy, nor register danger. And there was the matter of magic – without it, she would be lost.

Sébastien knew he had no choice but to stick around. Sensing the tug of fatigue, he settled back on the couch, and fell dormant into restless dreams.

* * *

Guinevere headed up the stairs to the house, getting her keys out. A heel caught on one cement tile and she wobbled, the keys dropping from her hand.

She bent over to pick them up, and straightened only to find herself a hair's breath away from Braydon.

"What were you thinking!?" he growled.

Guinevere's eyes widened at his furious tone. "I—"

Braydon shoved her up against the door, hand gripping her throat tightly and pressing down. Guinevere tried to gasp for air, but to no avail.

"Why did you confront Sébastien, you stupid bitch?" he snarled.

She tried to scan right and left for help from neighbors, but no one was out at the late hour. Air was missing, and Guinevere still attempted to breathe in anything past the vice around her throat. Eyes closing, wheezing, she was about to pass out, when Braydon's hand shifted infinitesimally to allow a bit of room to breathe.

"I didn't think it would be such a big problem," she whispered, tearing up. *Is vengeance upon Vivienne really worth it?*

This was no fairytale Guinevere was involved in, yet to have been in close proximity to death was making her question the side she had chosen.

"No, you clearly didn't!" Braydon retorted, backing away and removing his hand, still scowling at her. "You better have had a good reason."

Massaging her rapidly bruising neck, Guinevere muttered, "I hoped to throw him off his game."

"Did it work?"

She looked away, recalling Sébastien's defensive stance and the dog by his side. "No."

Braydon got nearer, and Guinevere cowered in fear. "Stay

away from him until further notice from me," he ordered in a deadly calm voice. "I will handle it. If Carleigh's plan is to work, Sébastien should fixate more on the intruder than you."

As the sorcerer walked away, Guinevere stepped into the house, locking the door behind her with trembling hands. Only then did she slide to the ground, sobs shaking her petite frame.

The crisis lasted mere moments, before she picked herself up, a cold glint replacing the fear in her eyes. Yes, vengeance was sweet, and it was too late to back out anyway. If she was to suffer – or die – then she would drag Vivienne down with her.

* * *

Vivienne woke up in a cold bed. She glanced around, finding Alistair by her feet, snoring peacefully. Something was wrong, and immediately she thought back to the break-in, scanning the room – but there was no one there.

The young woman recalled Sébastien had been there the previous night. Since it was still pitch black outside, she got up and headed into the living room. The man of her dreams was still there, getting snoring softly on the couch.

Tiptoeing over, Vivienne planned to snuggle next to him, but stopped when reaching him. There was a meager sheen of sweat on Sébastien's face, and he was moving his head from side to side with jerky movements.

He's dreaming.

The feeling in her chest grew stronger, oddly unsettling. Vivienne sat down next to him and, driven by instinct, stroked his arm. There was an electric shock, travelling from her fingertips up, and then she was no longer in the living room – rather, she was in Sébastien's head.

They were in a dim room, with a large mirror right in the middle.

Sébastien stood in front of it, frozen in the perusal of his reflection. It was a bloody caricature of the man she knew, with a taut jaw, clenched fists, and a shifty image unfamiliar to Vivienne's eyes.

She approached him, but a disembodied voice warned, "You promised. And you will pay for breaking your oath. The new version of you does not deserve Light."

Vivienne frowned, both at the words and the slightly familiar voice, but shook it off, and continued to Sébastien. She grasped his shoulder, and he whirled around, shock in his eyes. A soft glow enveloped them in the nightmare, and they both woke up.

Vivienne got off his chest, and her stunned gaze clashed with his.

"What the hell?" Sébastien grumbled, rubbing the sleep off his face vigorously.

"What just happened?"

They gaped at each other, mirror images of confusion, until the ring of Sébastien's cell startled Vivienne. He hesitated, before removing it out of the pocket and answering. Eyes still fixated on her, he clipped an annoyed, "Alright, I'll be there in ten."

Vivienne glanced away, but he grabbed her chin, rushing on. "I can't even begin to fathom what happened any more than you do, but we have to talk about this. My place, your place, I don't care, so long as it's after I handle this for work."

"I'm not sure that's a good idea, Sébastien."

She tried to avoid his eyes, but his grip was firm, the gaze intense. "Don't do this. Don't withdraw because of how confusing and weird this is. Give us a chance. Breakfast today."

Vivienne bit her lip, finally meeting his eyes. "I'm scared."

His tense expression eased and he said, "I get it. Breakfast, *please*." There was desperation in Sébastien's voice, and she gave in.

"Alright, breakfast."

Sébastien let go, and got up. Before leaving, he embraced her softly, a promise of more to come. It was oddly comforting, though shorter than Vivienne would have liked.

It was only after his departure that it hit her – what real estate job wakes one up at four in the morning?

* * *

True to his word, Sébastien showed up on Vivienne's doorstep at noon. Earlier, she'd had a stroll with Alistair, bathed, and changed into a pair of jeans and a forest green tank top. When the knock came, she rushed to open it.

Sébastien stood there, hair still dripping wet from a shower, in a pair of navy jeans, shirt and a leather jacket. *Yum,* Vivienne's mind voiced, before she advised it to kindly shut up – the talk planned for that day was serious, no distractions needed.

She did not notice the way Sébastien's eyes raked over her casual outfit, taking in the way the jeans rode low on her hips. The green top that brought out the color of her eyes, whilst displaying her narrow waist and the swell of her chest.

Sébastien swallowed past the lump in his throat at the young woman's loveliness, fighting primal desires stirring underneath the surface. He had sworn away distractions until they spoke of the morning's events, and intended to keep the promise to himself.

With that in mind, he forced an easygoing grin and caught her hand. "Shall we?" he enquired with a mock bow.

Vivienne chuckled and followed him out the door, clutching onto his arm. As they walked the short way to his place, Sébastien was aware of her closeness and soft fragrance, but his will remained strong. It was only as they arrived at the house that his restraint slipped.

He was unlocking the door, when Vivienne peered up at him. The vulnerable, trusting glint in her eyes undid him, and he hauled her close for a comforting kiss. The minute their lips grazed, though, it was not enough.

Sébastien maneuvered her against the door, pressing his body against hers. Overtaken by the sensations, Vivienne wrapped her arms around his neck and inched closer, kissing him back.

His hands roamed down her back, causing shivers of delight. Sébastien broke the embrace, instead moving his lips down her neck, on the side of her jaw, and back again to her mouth. It was a fever under their skin, and he craved to –

"No."

Sébastien drew back while it was still possible, taking in Vivienne's shocked expression, heedful his features must betray his own surprise – the word had come from him. He could not – *would* not – be intimate with her unless she was fully aware of the history between them, of his history since, and still chose to be together.

Sébastien inhaled deeply, and followed it by a sheepish chuckle. "I'm sorry, I'm acting like a teenager. I didn't intend to be a total cad. I've honestly brought you here for breakfast, and to talk."

Vivienne laughed, smoothed down her hair and opened the door. He followed her, in time to notice her enchanted smile at the breakfast table. There was an assortment of fresh bagels and different breakfast foods set up, with two mugs of fresh coffee, orange juice, eggs and bacon.

The young woman's eyes danced when she faced him. "You shouldn't have done all this, but I appreciate it."

Sébastien acquiesced distractedly, avoiding Vivienne's eyes. *I'm not going to be able to stay away from her,* he complained internally, already missing the way her body felt against his. A cold shower was definitely a must.

In desperation to cool down, he said, "I forgot dessert. I'll run to the bakery at the corner, be back quick." The words were barely out of his mouth, that he ran out as if the hounds of hell were after him.

Vivienne was no fool, realizing the prompt departure was more related to their chemistry rather than dessert. Whenever they were close, the electricity passing between them was impossible to ignore, getting worse as they spent more time together.

Yet, she had spent all morning reflecting, realizing there were obviously things about Sébastien she had been ignoring. Despite it all, Vivienne still trusted him, a notion she could not give up on. But she yearned to at least get a glimpse of the man inside, without the confusion of flashbacks.

Sébastien's place did not reveal much, considering it was rented. It had the bare amount of furniture, no pictures, and was extra clean. As Vivienne examined the surroundings, she noticed a little box on one of the book shelves in the living room. Though not intending to snoop, curiosity got the better of her, stronger than any morals. After a tiny hesitation, she opened it . . .and stared at the gun nestled on a bed of velvet.

"What the *hell*?" Her eyes narrowed, but before she could think it through, the door opened once more.

Behind her, Sébastien dropped the dessert on the table. He arranged the pastries by the rest of the food, unaware his beloved's hunger had evaporated with the sight of the weapon.

"Vivienne, come on over. We have to talk."

She gripped the box and entered into the dining room. "Yeah, we do."

Sébastien looked up at the tightness in her voice, and froze noticing the box.

"Why do you have a gun?" Vivienne demanded.

Sébastien's gaze locked with hers, noticing the hurt. She had concluded, with good reason, that he had lied. With a frustrated sound, the guardian sat down on the couch, and ran a hand through his hair.

This was a problem, for a variety of reasons. If he revealed the truth, Vivienne would run off scared, and protection would be impossible. Furthermore, this particular information would probably increase the list of bad people after her, so that was no good, either.

Sébastien hated lying to his beloved, but it was a necessity.

"A while back, I had a break-in at one of the other places I rented at the time. It was related to some violence going on in the area, also at that bar I warned you to stay away from. I got a gun for safety, and I bring it everywhere I rent now."

Sébastien could tell the explanation made sense to Vivienne, but still she pressed, "And the odd calls?"

"I own a real estate company, flipping houses." He shrugged, forcing himself to appear nonchalant. "Emergency situations happen morning and night, babe."

Satisfied, Vivienne set the weapon aside and approached him, settling in the comfort of his open arms. "I'm sorry for the inquisition, it's just been a weird couple of days."

"Tell me about it."

They were silent for a bit, until Sébastien exhaled. *Might as well.*

"About this morning, the nightmare . . ."

Vivienne peered up at him, reading his tension. "I have no idea what that was, Sébastien, I swear to you. I did nothing except touch you, and all of a sudden, I was in there with you. Try as I might, there's no reasonable explanation for it." She hesitated, then whispered, "My parents, when I was small, put me with psychiatrists to "fix" my problems, but it never worked. I'm only warning you of this, so you know what you're getting into."

Sébastien stared at her, his heart tugging in sympathy. How could she imagine, for a single second, that she was less than perfect in his eyes?

He gently caressed Vivienne's cheek, trying to communicate, in some way, the extent of his affection without alarming her. "Babe, I don't care. I'll be the first to admit what happened scared me too, but if we're going to be honest, the truth is we had a connection from the instant we ran into each other. I imagine it's partly to blame for this morning."

"What are you implying?"

Sébastien could see Vivienne was struggling with the idea of reality not being quite what she thought it was. Still, accepting its flexibility was the first step towards the truth.

"Alright, well, these dreams you've been mentioning, maybe they're happening for a reason. There are people whose minds are more sensitive to external stimuli."

She frowned, trying to understand his meaning. "Such as?"

"I'm not an expert, but there are lots of cases where kids have recollections from past lives, stuff science can't explain. Maybe it's something similar to what's happening to you."

Vivienne pondered the words for a moment, before asking, "So what am I supposed to do?"

"Go with it," he shrugged again. "See where these flashes take you."

"What if it's somewhere I don't want to go?" The young woman's voice dropped an octave, but Sébastien caught the words.

"You're not even a bit curious to find out how this story you keep dreaming of ends?"

Sébastien could almost hear the wheels in her mind turning, praying silently she did. A complete disinterest would not bode well, making him look crazy. And what Vivienne needed at the moment was someone stable, not crazy.

"A bit, yes."

Thank the fates.

"There's your response," Sébastien hid the relief flowing through him with a neutral mask. "Once you get to its inevitable conclusion, maybe it will clarify things."

"But do you think it's actually possible? A past life . . ." Vivienne trailed off, but the unspoken query hung in the air.

"Anything is possible, babe. Only you can decide that."

Sébastien wished nothing more than to reveal everything, to help her remember quicker, and accept the past. But he was afraid of doing more harm than good, and also of what Vivienne would find when she looked back.

"So, all I can do is wait and see . . .. That's your bright idea?"

"Yup."

Vivienne sagged back, resting her head on his chest, deep in thought.

What Sébastien mentioned made sense. For once in her life, someone truly understood, and the fact he was still there after what she had revealed warmed Vivienne in a way even his lips could not.

And he was right about her nightly troubles. She should not be stressing about it without first comprehending its true nature. The best course of action really was to go with the flow.

In the last couple of days, more déjà-vus had assailed Vivienne than in an entire lifetime, but also, the pieces were falling into place. If she could find out the truth of the story, a nagging feeling suggested that one way or another, it would set her free.

Another idea hit her. "Sébastien?"

"Mm?"

He sounded sleepy, and she hated to bring it up, but it was a nagging thought that would not go away. "Those guys back at the lake . . . Do you suppose it's also related to this?"

"What do you mean?"

"Could they be after me, because of something I'm not remembering, or . . .who the hell even knows . . .?"

Sébastien was unresponsive for so long, she presumed he dozed off. His words were unexpected.

"I guess they could be. It's weird them having found you the way they did. No one knew where we were going, except for me. I strongly think that for the time being, the best course of action is to have either me or Alistair with you at all times."

The young woman inclined her head in agreement.

"You hungry now?"

"Yep!" Vivienne admitted, and they got up to eat.

* * *

After feasting on the rather large breakfast, the couple spent the day relaxing. In the late afternoon, Sébastien suggested a stroll. Vivienne figured it was a good idea to burn off the morning's calories.

"There's a pathway by the river, off the Parc du Dome. I'm pretty familiar with it, and it's nice and quiet this time of day," he mentioned, and she grinned in assent.

They drove the Jag to the park, left it behind, and strolled down the cobblestone paths. One way took them by a small manmade stream, with a beautiful statue of Venus in the middle, and a few more down.

They were in no hurry, and closeness to the water

invigorated Vivienne, as it always had. The park was normally busy during the day with families and children, but so close to the sunset, only a few people were out and about, further off.

They had been walking for a bit, when they hit a dead end, with another fountain in the middle. "Fountain again, huh?" Vivienne beamed up at Sébastien.

"Right," he chuckled. "That's where I saw you for the second time."

"Which reminds me, what were you doing there?"

"Whenever I'm in Avignon, I sometimes go there to reflect. That particular day, I had to sit down after seeing you. I felt like I got hit by a train."

"You and me both . . ." Scouring the space again, Vivienne murmured, "This could be a nice dancing spot."

Sébastien let go of her hand, and did a mock little bow, "Humor me, my lady. Shall we?"

She laughed out loud at the sheer romantic side of him, and the silliness of the situation. But nevertheless, it was too good an opportunity to pass on. So Vivienne mimicked the bow, and accepted the extended hand.

The wind was their music, the fountain a crescendo. Sébastien's hands were on her waist, leading into a waltz, circling around, lips to her temple – a truly fairytale moment.

During a twirl, Vivienne lost her footing. Rather than fall towards the ground, it was another vision that called out to her.

* * *

The music filled the ballroom of the castle, and Vivienne grew tired of switching partners. She strode out in the gardens for a breath of fresh air the first chance she got, making sure she was not followed. Within a few minutes, Sébastien joined her.

"Are you alright, my lady?"

Vivienne spun to face him at the odd note in his voice, almost tormented. When their eyes met, there was restraint, regret and frustration in his gaze.

"Perhaps I should be asking you this," Vivienne said softly.

The harsh glint in the guardian's eyes softened visibly. "I apologize. It was not my intention to frighten you."

"What is troubling you, Sébastien?"

"Nothing, my lady," he responded immediately. At her insistent look, he forcefully unclenched his teeth.

"These dancing balls have me on edge. Aside from the security risks, the men are apt at behaving like imbeciles, and one hears things."

"Such as?"

"Nothing suited for the ears of a lady."

"Tell me," Vivienne commanded, guessing where he was going with it.

"Comments about your beauty, my lady . . ." Sébastien answered, avoiding her eyes. " . . . and celibacy."

"I see." Vivienne let the words hang in the air for a moment, before sharing, "I appreciate you making an effort to shelter me from it. But I have heard it all before. They deem me unnatural for not letting a man rule me, and yet they all want to bed me."

Sébastien's jaw tightened again at her statement.

The princess could not help from inching closer, and

running a finger alongside it. The muscle jumped under her fingertips, drawing her rapt attention. "Relax, Sébastien," she whispered close to him, and rose on her tiptoes to kiss his cheek.

Then she walked past him, adding, "They cannot harm me with their words. I am simply weary of the night and wishing it to end. Enjoying dancing is impossible with all the muttering about."

Sébastien swallowed past the lump in his throat, shifting to face her once more. "Perhaps I can help with that, at least ... If I may." As Vivienne frowned in confusion, he added, "A dance with no strings attached."

Her gaze was unflinching on his features, even as he held his breath. For all intents and purposes, Sébastien expected a rejection. The opposite stunned him.

"I'm not stopping you," she declared.

It was all the encouragement the guard needed. Straightening to his full height, Sébastien stepped up to her, and slid an arm around her waist. With the music filtering from the ball, he led them in a waltz.

Vivienne gave in to the comfort, relaxed enough to feel the music and enjoy it. Sébastien's strength renewed her vigor, and his muscle was the stone she needed to rely on.

When the singer inside stopped with her enthralling voice, Sébastien reluctantly dropped his hand. Vivienne looked up at him, her gaze unreadable in the dimness, then retreated back inside. He was left staring after, wishing things were different.

* * *

Vivienne came back to in Sébastien's arms, moaning in pain. This time, the déjà-vu had been stronger, and it left a bad headache behind.

She was lying down on something cold, with a dripping sound close by. It was coming from the fountain edge Sébastien had laid her on. She was half in his arms, half on the marbled edge.

At the sound of her awakening, Sébastien's arms tightened, and she whispered, "I'm alright, just a bit dizzy. Might need a painkiller . . .or five."

When silence answered, Vivienne urged her eyes to open. Sébastien was hovering over her, but staring at something insistently, his entire body strung up.

The young woman craned her neck in the direction of his fixation. An unfamiliar male stood half hidden in shadows, with a gun pointed in their direction.

"You've got to be shitting me."

"Babe, lay low."

Vivienne did not even have time to properly gauge the situation. In the next breath, Sébastien got up and moved towards the gun, palms up.

"Put the gun down," he snarled, quite convincingly to her ears.

There was a moment of silence, then the man answered, "I don't think so. Not until you give her to me."

Vivienne shivered, not because of the threat, but the voice. It was the same intruder from nights ago!

"Over my dead body." Steel coated Sébastien's voice, and he advanced unhurriedly towards the man, his gait confident that the situation was handled.

"That can be arranged," was the cold-blooded reply.

There was a click as the man took the safety off the gun, and Sébastien shifted, at the same time as a gunshot rang out. A bullet whizzed by and Vivienne slid off the fountain, ducking to the ground.

She squinted in their direction, witnessing Sébastien fight for control of the gun. He had the upper hand, but was also doing double duty, trying to manoeuver the intruder away from her area. It put him in a vulnerable position.

Once the stranger was pushed away, Sébastien landed a punch that put him down into the ground, on his knees. He then swiftly took the gun away, but rather than throw it, he pointed it back at the man's head.

"Sébastien, let's get out of here," Vivienne whispered, afraid of the direction he was heading to.

He glanced towards her and, for a moment, the attacker did too, before sneering. There was a glint of silver and he tried to stab Sébastien, who jumped out of the way in time. The man got up, punched him, seized the gun and clocked him over the head with it, then ran off.

Vivienne sprinted to Sébastien's side, where he was kneeling and clutching his head.

"Are you alright!?" she panicked.

"I'm fine. I'll have a bad bump and headache, but it'll be fine." He got up slowly, more annoyed at letting the man get away and incurring an injury in the process.

"You?" Sébastien concentrated all his attention on Vivienne, hands roaming over her anxiously. "Did the bullet hit you?"

"No, no, I'm alright."

"Then let's get out of here." His body shielding hers, they walked back fast, and got to the car with no further incidents. The return drive was silent, but rapid.

The entire time, Vivienne was debating on informing Sébastien that it was the same intruder who had broken into her home earlier in the week. Logically, it was important information he needed to know. But there was the other side of him, the somber side, revealed whenever she was in peril, which caused Vivienne to fear for the life of whoever endangered her.

The last thing she wished for was Sébastien getting into trouble on her behalf. She was too absorbed by the internal debate, not immediately recognizing his own tension.

After he assured himself his beloved was unscathed, all Sébastien was conscious of was Vivienne's living body nearby. He craved a touch, to reassure himself of her safety, and check each inch of her body. Only the drive home distracted him in the small enclosure of the car.

The minute they entered the house, Vivienne was about to enquire about something, and grazed his shoulder to draw attention. With that timid touch, Sébastien's restraint flew out the window.

He maneuvered her body between him and the wall, mouth descending on Vivienne's with a newfound determination, as if the world was coming to an end. Placing both hands on either side of her head, Sébastien ensured she was well and truly trapped. His lips were pure seduction, causing sensations that made her head spin, and knees wobble.

When they stopped, breathing heavily, the incident was far away for Vivienne, as was the decision to apprise him about the intruder.

"Stay here tonight," Sébastien pleaded. "Please. I need you safe."

Vivienne nodded wordlessly, trying to read through his reaction – though the stiff jaw, rigid muscles, and his restraint spoke volumes. She was about to mention something, but Sébastien effectively cut her off with another burning kiss.

CHAPTER 5

Vivienne woke up in Sébastien's bed, warm in the t-shirt borrowed last night, and pinned down by his arm around her waist.

Surprisingly, their rather hot make out session had ended with a movie, rather than a tumble in bed. She did not even remember drifting off, let alone Sébastien carrying her to bed.

The arm holding her hostage tightened, and a voice rough with sleep grumbled, "Are you awake?"

"Yeah," Vivienne smiled into the pillow.

Sébastien's hand moved off her waist, instead digging into her hip. He maneuvered Vivienne on her back and rolled over, hovering above.

"You were talking while sleeping."

Uh oh, was Vivienne's first thought. The second, rapidly following, was that Sébastien seemed wide awake, and not in a good mood.

"Umm . . ." She trailed off, racking her brain to figure out what exactly she would have been dreaming of, to get him so annoyed.

"Something about an intruder?" Sébastien growled.

Vivienne bit her lip, aware there was no other option but to tell him now. Despite the sticky situation, she could not help but find his concern endearing.

"About that . . . I was going to mention it last night, but it didn't seem like the right time to . . .."

She stopped off at Sébastien's pissed off glare.

"Vivienne, if I'm going to protect you, I have to know everything. No exceptions."

Shifting under him, the young woman tried to get away, but found his weight an impossible boulder to move. "Could we maybe have this conversation outside of bed?"

"No," his tone was unflinching. "Tell me, *now*." To illustrate the point, Sébastien pressed his body downwards, effectively pinning her to the bed.

With a heavy sigh, Vivienne recounted the whole thing – more to keep her imagination away from each impenetrable muscle of his against each one of hers. Not to mention the fact she was more turned on than she ever had been.

Sébastien tried to keep calm as the story unraveled, but his body tensed with each passing moment. *This danger is worse than I could have ever realized!*

When Vivienne got to the end of her narrative, he bit off, "And you didn't call the police because . . .?"

"I couldn't figure out if it had been real or not. At least not until the call came after. Plus, I was afraid they were going to think me crazy."

Sébastien's eyes softened, all the anger evaporating like thunderclouds once the sun came out. "Babe, they wouldn't. But considering the cops are no longer an option, I'm going to handle this my way."

"Meaning?"

"Until we figure out what these nightly visions of yours are alluding to, and what these people are after, I'm going to be around you, permanently."

"That's no hard feat," Vivienne chuckled, and Sébastien's chest constricted again. *How much longer do I have?* The agonizing question was a torture eating at his sanity each day.

"We'll see about that," he replied instead, smoothing out the panic from his voice. He bent over and kissed Vivienne swiftly, not trusting himself around her – in bed – much longer. He jumped up the second after, and tugged her up as well.

After she used the bathroom to shower and get changed, and he followed suit, they ended up cooking breakfast together.

The scene was cozy – too cozy for less than a week of dating – but Vivienne allowed it, easily falling into a normal pace. As they sat down and ate bacon and eggs, she recalled his nightmare.

A question escaped past her lips after a short internal debate. "When I stumbled into your nightmare . . . What was that about?"

"Not sure," Sébastien shrugged. "It's been recurring for the past week or so."

The young woman froze with the fork halfway to her mouth. "Since you met me?"

They locked gazes, and Sébastien put his own utensil away, as though he had been hit by a brick.

"Since we ran into each other, yes," he admitted slowly, following the statement up with a chuckle. "I'm fairly sure we established it's definitely not the first time we met."

"And at the bar? That time when you kissed me . . . Do you feel it too?"

"You mean the feeling of everything falling into place? Yeah. Every time I'm around you." He echoed her musings so matter-of-factly, as though it was a daily occurrence, and dug into his breakfast.

Vivienne frowned, insisting, "It's not normal."

"Nope," he spoke around a mouthful of bacon.

"And it doesn't bother you?"

"Nope." Again, that sexy grin, and her pulse accelerated.

Vivienne insistently stared at her eggs, with an inkling of missing something, as per usual. The ring of a cell was startling, and Sébastien pushed it towards her.

Jennifer's name was on the caller ID, and Vivienne acknowledged it with a stifled sigh. "Yeah, hey Jen."

Sébastien continued eating, but remained focused on the conversation. Vivienne could understand why his first impression of Jennifer was unfavorable, and could not blame him.

"Viv, hey," the young woman was saying. "Listen, I'm sorry about that night . . . Can you please not stay mad at me?"

"I'm not mad, Jennifer."

"You're not?" Confusion tinged her voice.

"No. It's just not my scene, so you'll have to excuse me if next time I don't come with you."

"Okay, that's fine, no problem." Jennifer was too hasty to agree, and Vivienne's eyes narrowed. "How about coffee today?"

"Coffee today?" She repeated, glancing at Sébastien, silently questioning if they had any plans. When he shrugged, she said, "Yeah, it's fine. Meet you in an hour at our spot."

Vivienne hung up, but had barely breathed, when the phone rang again. This time, it was a private number. A shiver crept up her spine, an instinctive reaction to what was coming.

"What is it?" Already attuned to her, Sébastien reacted to the change in demeanor.

"Private number," Vivienne declared, showing him the phone's screen.

"Go ahead, pick up." He stood and moved behind her, placing a calming hand on her shoulder in support. "I'm here."

Vivienne hit the answer button before better judgment suggested otherwise. She tapped the speaker button for Sébastien to listen in to the conversation.

"One of these days, your defender won't be around, and I will get you. My master is getting quite impatient."

"Your master?"

Sébastien grasped the phone out of her hand. "You can advise your master I want to have a word, if he's so inclined to hurt Vivienne. He should find it easy to reach me. My name is Sébastien Dubois."

When the voice on the other end sputtered a reply, he hung up.

Vivienne was the first to break the silence. "Now what?"

"Now, we finish breakfast, you go meet your friend, and I go to work. By tonight, if he contacts me, I'll set this straight, once and for all."

"Please be careful."

Sébastien bent over, grazing his lips against hers for a kiss. "Always."

* * *

Jennifer was waiting for Vivienne when she got to the café, Alistair's leash in hand. She was not in a mood to confront her friend without at least some support, and the pup required a stroll anyway.

Upon noticing the sour expression on her friend's face, Vivienne was glad to have brought Alistair along.

"Were you with him?" Jennifer's first words confirmed her doubts.

Vivienne's grin immediately died off, and Alistair responded with bared teeth. The young woman stopped in her motion to sit, instead deciding to stand. It appeared the conversation would be shorter than anticipated, as her figurative defensive walls immediately came up.

"Who?" she probed frostily.

"The guy from the bar. Sébastien."

"Not that it's any of your business, but yes." Vivienne threw her friend a warning glare, silently warning to let it go.

"Vivienne, there's something wrong with him—"

"Seriously, Jennifer?" Vivienne's temper flashed, hand tightening on the leash, as she fought an urge to slap some sense into her. "I come here for a truce, and this is what I get?"

"I'm trying to help," Jennifer insisted, standing up to be at the same level.

Alistair growled, and she stopped halfway before approaching Vivienne. Her blue eyes glanced uneasily at the massive dog.

"No, you're not," Vivienne said, features schooled blankly. "You're selfish and only care about yourself. I'm only shocked it took me this long to figure it out."

The softness went out of Jennifer's baby blue eyes, and in came a cruel glint. "Did *he* tell you that?"

"I have no idea what you're talking about," Vivienne's eyes narrowed. "Why are you being so nosy?"

"I'm not, Viv, just trying to be a good friend!"

"Well, do me a favor and *don't*!"

Without a backwards glance, Vivienne stalked off, dragging Alistair behind.

* * *

Although the neighborhood was not the best to be in, Vivienne figured with Alistair around, she could not get into much trouble. Plus, it was simpler than taking a taxi, and a walk to cool off would serve her well.

After the showdown with Jennifer, they had been striding around downtown, until Vivienne got tired. By the time twilight came around, she figured it was time to get back home, and took a shortcut.

She had used the alleyways that led to the back roads many times, without hesitation. Yet as she stepped into the first of many that day, a nagging feeling of doubt crept up her spine.

A whine by her side had Vivienne slow down, peering

down at Alistair. He sat on his hind, refusing to go any further, and she paused as well. "I get it, Al, it's not the smartest decision, but Jen was being unreasonable, and I didn't want to deal with it. Plus, we're almost home."

His head tilted to one side, almost as if listening, and she shrugged. "Come on, let's go."

Instead of budging, he kept still – too still. It was the hair rising on his spine, and her neck, that was the first clue, before the words came from the misty shadows.

"If only I had anticipated it would be this easy, your majesty, I wouldn't have bothered setting up such a flawless trap."

Vivienne gasped at the voice, the same as a few nights earlier. Alistair got up too, advancing in front of her. She gripped his leash tighter, even as his entire body strained, prepared to attack.

"Al, no!" the young woman urged, not yet able to identify more than a faint outline in the ill lighted area by the garbage bins. It was oddly murky, as though that particular corner was eclipsed on purpose.

To her utter stupefaction, Alistair turned his head, making eye contact, and pointedly looked behind her. Vivienne glanced in the same direction – to the street lamps, and cars passing by. The bump in her legs was Alistair nudging her away.

"Aw, ain't that cute, a doggie," the same voice snickered.

Alistair stared at Vivienne one more time, insistently, almost demanding, until the young woman took a step in the direction. "You're trying to tell me to get away," she realized, eyes widening in shock.

He bent his head, acknowledging it. The following instant, gleaming canines snapped at the leash, cutting it in half. In the same breath, he lunged towards the shadows.

"Alistair!" Vivienne yelled.

A scream answered, followed by a gunshot from the shadows, and she could make out struggles. Alistair's ferocious roar filled the night, as did another gunshot. Vivienne shouted for help, at the same time running towards them, intent on one thing only. *I can't let another protector die.*

The young woman could not figure out where the thought had come from, only a faint feeling that something similar happened in the past, an event she never wanted repeated.

The eerie silence gave her pause, a few feet away from approaching the bins. Two masses were in the shadows, and as Vivienne got nearer, one of them advanced out. It was Alistair, dragging his back leg.

"Alistair!" she yelled again, and he wobbled closer.

Vivienne knelt down as he arrived by her side. Panting, jaws filled with blood, he lowered his body to the ground.

"Are you ok!?" She frantically patted Alistair down, checking for injuries. From what she could tell, only his hind leg bled from a gunshot wound on the thigh.

"You poor dog, don't worry, I'll get you some help." Vivienne did not even realize tears were streaming down her cheeks until he licked them. His tail thumped unsteadily, but the heartbeat under her hands was strong.

Another gunshot rang out, startling them both. Alistair stilled, and Vivienne screamed as if in anguish herself. His eyes closed for a moment, and with an enormous effort he got up slowly. Once more he turned to defend, despite the second wound apparent in his ribs.

"No, Alistair!" Vivienne cried, and extended an arm to hold him back.

It closed around air, as he lunged again, aggressively growling. There was human swearing, an animal snarl, and both shadows dropped down once more. This time, the young woman did not hesitate, and ran towards them.

Alistair lay down, heavily breathing. The pitiful whines escaping from his unmoving form wrenched at Vivienne's soul. A few feet away, a man attempted to drag himself away, bleeding heavily. He was crawling across the pavement and leaving a trail of blood behind. She marched to him, rage making the blood pound in her ears.

At her approach, the man rolled on his back. She did not recognize his features, only the voice. He could have been anyone on the street with longish brown hair and riddled features.

"Your highness," the man croaked with a lopsided leer.

"Who the *hell* are you?" Vivienne screamed, towering over him.

He ignored her, instead glancing past to Alistair. "That stupid demon lord of yours was never far away. Well, at least I leave you with no defenses. What will you do now, princess?"

"You're a madman," Vivienne spat, desperation tinting each word. "What the hell are you rambling on about?"

The intruder stared at her for a long moment, and paled some more when he realized she was serious. The victorious glint died in his eyes, replaced by a stupefied one. "You don't know?"

"Know what?" Vivienne frowned in annoyance.

"How the hell don't you know?"

"Know *what*?" This time, she grabbed onto his shirt, pulling the man up, adamant to get some answers.

"The stupid irony," he croaked, and went limp in her hands, eyes rolling in the back of his head.

Vivienne let go at once, disgusted. To her utter amazement, the minute his corpse made contact with the ground, it blurred. At first she thought maybe another vision was upon her, but then the body split into tiny pieces, transforming into grey, sooty dust.

It was as though he was cremating under her eyes – without a fire. As she blinked, the ashes were swept away by the wind.

A whine behind recalled her attention to more important things than the ravings of a lunatic.

"Alistair!"

Vivienne rushed to the dog's side. She was able to see him better this time, as the eerie gloom had evaporated along with their assailant. Alistair, unfortunately, did not emerge in good shape from the fight.

She pulled out her cell and planned to call Sébastien, but her finger did not even get to the buttons before it hit again – the headache, the dizziness. Vivienne gripped onto Alistair's fur as anchor, but it was to no avail as the déjà-vu came.

* * *

"You will recall me explaining enchantments have to come from deep within you. They cannot be used for evil, only for good, and selfless reasons."

Vivienne was tempted to roll her eyes, but knew Merlin would have things to say about such unladylike conduct.

"Yes, master," she agreed instead.

Merlin shook his head at the monarch's antics, the crinkles around his sea blue eyes deepening. "Perfect. Now, it is time. This dove yearns to fly again."

Vivienne fixated on the bird in his hand, its wing bandaged. As she had done many times before, she reached deep down for a well of power, and gripped a tiny drop of it. Her entire being centered, as though a chain linked her to the earth, and it to her.

The incantation spread its warmth from the deepest corners within her, to the fingertips. Vivienne closed her eyes, at the same time circling a hand above the dove. She wished it could fly again today, imagining the freedom under its wings, the clouds above, just as the bird itself would.

The wave surged within Vivienne, more than intended, but nonetheless it unfurled gently.

"Look."

Merlin's voice caused her eyes to open, and watch as tiny gold wisps escaped her palm, enveloping the bird's wing in a halo. It shone brighter for a moment, then dimmed, until the light was completely gone, absorbed within.

The dove tried to flap the wing, and upon realizing it worked, flew away. Vivienne smiled as it circled them twice, and then flew into the distance.

"Well done, Vivienne," Merlin praised, approval evident in his voice.

The princess beamed gratefully, but became distracted by the sound of a horse nearby. She whirled around, her pulse beating wildly as Sébastien approached.

"My lady, your father asked for a word," the knight informed his mistress once he was within hearing distance.

Vivienne inclined her head in acknowledgement, then peered over a shoulder at Merlin. "I have to go."

The speculative glint in the mage's eyes was not lost on her, as he observed the dynamic between her and Sébastien. However, instead of commenting on whatever he perceived, Merlin beamed paternally and waved Vivienne away.

"Tomorrow, then?"

Vivienne nodded, already retreating. Sébastien extended a hand, and she mounted behind him, wrapping both arms around his waist. It was then she remembered, and glanced behind once more. "Oh, and Merlin?"

The old man blinked, appearing to disengage from a trance.

"Tomorrow, I would like to meet this Guinevere you keep mentioning to me."

His laugh echoed behind as they left.

* * *

Vivienne's eyes flew open at Alistair's low whine. *Thank the fates the flashback was not long this time.* She patted him down, conscious of the blood flowing out of his wounds.

"Please don't leave me," she cried out, eyes filling with tears even as she clutched his fur in a futile effort to keep him.

There was an insistent gleam in the dog's eyes, and she recalled how he had tried to get her away from the alley. Something inside Vivienne rattled. Perhaps it was the realization that reality and fiction were not so far apart, after all. Sébastien's words echoed in her mind, as did his advice to let the story play out to its end.

"Tell me what to do," she sobbed. "How can I help you? This flashback, is it real? Was I able to use spells at some point?" It sounded insane when said out loud, and Vivienne held her breath.

Alistair's eyes were closed, unresponsive for a few moments. Then, as if it was taking his entire strength, he blinked. Staring intently at the young woman, his massive head nodded once.

Vivienne knew it was impossible, but asking her dog for advice – and listening – could not be crazier than the whirlwind romance she had been having with Sébastien.

Having been different all her life, she now realized there was a reason for it, one which society would not accept or deem real. The notion was comforting, in a way – scary, but nonetheless comforting.

You have nothing to lose, Vivienne told herself.

She closed her eyes and reached within, as in the déjà-vu. There was nothing there to tap, nothing which responded, causing a frustrated scream. Alistair nuzzled her hand, stretching as far as his condition allowed.

Flashes hit Vivienne – a massive black dog, sauntering by her side, fighting, defending, a companion and a friend. The similarity to the Alistair she knew was undeniable in the way he gravitated and shielded her, always vigilant. Only instead of the warm dark chocolate eyes she was used to, flames flickered in his opaque eyes.

Blinking back to the reality in front of her, Vivienne took

a deep breath. *I have to try again.*

This time, when she searched deep inside, there was something under the surface. Vivienne insisted further, yearning for nothing more than to heal Alistair, and a tiny wisp stirred at her call. It was tough to concentrate as she had in her recent recollection, with so many thoughts distracting her.

Then Alistair lifted his paw over her hand, and everything quieted around her. His fur was warm, but she could feel the wetness of his blood against her skin.

She might have had no idea of what she was doing, but the magic definitely did. It flowed from within, into both hands, and out her fingertips. There was a soft vibration at the top of her fingers and Vivienne opened her eyes. She gaped, fascinated, as the golden incantation traveled over Alistair's body in wisps, bundling together on the gunshot wounds.

At first, the bullets were extracted out by the magic, and the glow stopped the bleeding. The wounds closed, until the dog's body was fully healed, and the light faded, absorbed into his fur.

"You're alright!"

Ah, finally . . .I am, a voice rumbled in her head, and Vivienne gasped.

"You—"

She watched in amazement as the previously bullet-ridden dog got up, shook his enormous body as though he had been bathing, and glanced at her. Alistair's eyes had always been intelligent, but now they shone ferociously – she even noticed a tiny flame in their depths.

My dear princess, Alistair began again, bowing his head.

All this time I have been wanting to speak to you, but my abilities were linked to yours, and this instance was required for them both to be unlocked.

"What are you implying?" Vivienne questioned, feeling like her eyes were bulging out of her head. "I must be going crazy. Psychotic breakdown, or something!"

No, you are not, and it is time to recognize who you were. You have lived other lifetimes in the past, and are being hunted now by an old enemy.

The young woman tried to shift away, rubbing her throbbing temples. "I must be losing my sanity . . ."

No. Alistair shoved a muzzle towards her, grazing the side of one cheek. Vivienne could sense something entering her mind, searching to unlock it, and a headache spread. The agonizing probe was tortuous, growing worse by the second, and she screamed out loud.

The dog backtracked, shock displayed in his eyes.

No! This is not supposed to be happening! The discomfort eased away as he withdrew the spirit from Vivienne's mind, though she was left panting for breath.

"What the hell was that?"

My apologies. I presumed I could help you remember, by entering your thoughts, but it does not seem so.

"Remember *what?*"

Your past life – lives, rather. This is not your first human existence, highness. You lived in the past, around the same time as King Arthur.

"Arthur? But he's a myth!"

In this world, yes, but not ours. And if you believe that is strange, you have not even begun to remember your previous lives before that.

"Lives? What... So... What, I'm a reincarnation?" Vivienne was attempting to wrap her mind around the new information, but it simply made no sense next to what she had been taught.

Your soul, yes, it lives on, and reincarnates in the next era.

"But Arthur's story was ages ago... Shouldn't I have lived—?"

Since then? Indeed. The dark eyes grew speculative. Which is a mystery for me to solve. Furthermore, what happened to your memories is not normal.

Vivienne stopped rubbing her temple enough to frown. "What do you mean?"

There are usually two reasons for a person to reincarnate. If you have unfinished business from your previous existence, or if you are a large player in the battle of good versus evil.

Ignoring Vivienne's widening eyes and jaw dropping, he continued, *When the soul reincarnates, it normally commences a fresh slate. But remnants of the past stay behind... Most of the time, they are triggered by a soul mate or other such phenomena.*

The young woman clutched her head, as it throbbed again.

"Unfinished business? Battle of good versus evil? What are you going on about?"

Majesty... You have lived unaware in this life. From the beginning of time, good and evil have fought for balance, each choosing a champion for their side. You were that champion!

Vivienne shook her head, cringing as it pained her even

more. "I don't believe you."

You must! Alistair pressed closer, locking eyes with hers. *This is no game. It is the truth, and you are* not *losing your mind.* When she was about to deny it again, he pressed on, *Remember when you were with Jennifer, and you heard her say something she had not voiced out loud?*

Vivienne stopped mid-shake, mouth opened in surprise. "You know about that?"

Yes. I have been able to observe, but not act. That was an instance of your abilities.

She gestured to his body, thinking of the gunshot wounds. "What about the . . .whatever I did? To heal you?"

Magic.

"Right," Vivienne snorted.

The dog inched nearer. *You were powerful in the past and your abilities are simply dormant. If you trust in yourself, they will be unleashed.*

"Powerful? Me?" Vivienne scoffed. "Next you're going to reveal Merlin really was my mentor?"

Alistair stared at his mistress, patience evidently tried, before replying, *Yes, highness. And under his tutelage, you became the Lady of the Lake, and protected your realm and Camelot. You have been reborn because this world needs you, much as the past one did. I understand how incredulous this must seem, but the magic – your gift – is still with you, except it needs to be released.*

Vivienne shook her head, disbelief across her features. "I'd rather not. I wouldn't have any idea of what to do with it. I'm more interested in these recollections you speak of. Are they the dreams I've been having?"

Dreams? Such as the one of you being a monarch you spoke to me about?

"Yeah . . . And the ones in the desert. Back in another palace, too."

Speaking out loud in an alleyway to her dog was no longer daunting to Vivienne. She was getting more answers than she ever had been – though, granted, they confirmed she was insane. Even more incredulous was the fact Alistair had been able to understand everything, through all the talks they had shared.

Yes, they are.

"So why can't I remember it all?"

I am not sure, Alistair admitted with a tilt of the head. The life before Lady of the Lake, it is quite normal. You have lived and loved, and the experiences fade with time. The time to recollect those years was during your previous life in Arthur's era. As for your most current ones, you might be blocking them, requiring more time . . . Or it could simply be, I am not the person who can help with them.

"Then who is?"

Your knight – Sébastien.

"That's . . . How . . . You've met Sébastien?"

I have. Him and you, majesty, are two sides of the same coin. You have always lived together, loved each other . . .

"And lost each other."

The silence between them lengthened, as Vivienne pondered the instinctive words. They had come from deep down, though she knew they were true. The visions had communicated one point across – the threats her and Sébastien had tackled, and the strength of their love. But it was yet unclear how their last life together had ended.

Speaking of your champion . . . I would very much like to talk to him.

Vivienne's gaze snapped back to Alistair, startled as she was out of her musings. "I'm not sure that's such a good idea . . . This was a big enough shock to me. I can't imagine how he would react."

Trust me, princess, Sébastien *and I are old friends. And he owes me some explanations.* Alistair raked a long look over his mistress, taking in her tiredness. *But first, it is time to get you home.*

Blankly, the young woman got up, and followed him back to the house. Still in a daze over the recent revelations, she passed out as soon as her head hit the pillow, falling into another memory.

Alistair waited until Vivienne was fully dormant, only then exiting the house. He faced it and blew a breath of magic towards the building, watching with glowing demon eyes as it blanketed over the house, then around the windows and doors, like a translucent mist.

It would stop anyone from entering while he was away, with a zap of electricity similar to an electric fence. Modern human television had its perks, as it had given the dog multiple options to protect his mistress. Now, with some powers back, he could imagine those same options he had thought about, being put into place.

When Alistair was satisfied with the result, he set out to track Sébastien's scent.

* * *

Accompanied by two of her defenders, the loyal Lancelot and the new Sébastien, Vivienne walked over to Merlin's lair. She tried to ignore the guardian's eyes on her, and fixate on the enchantment lessons ahead. When they entered the circle though, Merlin was not alone.

Next to him was a beautiful, young blonde woman with blue eyes. As she faced Vivienne, the two men behind froze at her beauty. The princess, as well, was astonished – but more by Merlin's cool aura.

There was nothing in his demeanour that was remotely welcoming of Arthur's beloved. On the contrary, even his body was averted from her.

A closer look at Guinevere soon revealed the glimmer of calculation in her eyes, and Vivienne held back a shudder.

"So pleased to meet you, Guinevere," Vivienne bowed her head in acknowledgement.

The young woman returned the smile, and curtsied low. "Lady Vivienne, the pleasure is all mine."

Vivienne's features tightened, barely controlling her reaction to the beautiful maiden – and jealousy it was not. With otherworldly vibes, she could detect something around Guinevere, a web ready to ensnare. When peering at her aura, Vivienne noticed it was of a murky color, like a weed wilting in the sun.

The royal surveyed her two companions. Lancelot could not take his eyes off Guinevere. She was afraid to witness the same thing with Sébastien, but still could not help glancing out of the corner of her eye.

The guardian met her gaze steadily, and Vivienne registered with a jolt he never wavered, seemingly immune to

Guinevere's beauty – or so she concluded too swiftly. His eyes flickered betrayingly towards the other woman, and Vivienne looked away in anger.

She missed Sébastien's frown, as it was not with longing, but cold investigation that he observed Guinevere. He was perplexed not only at Lancelot's reaction, but his princess' own uneasiness.

Soon, Guinevere departed for the castle, accompanied by Lancelot. Sébastien waited by the horses for Vivienne to be done with Merlin. Eyes glued to her pacing form, he noticed the tautness of her shoulders as she spoke with the mage, unaware her stressful demeanor was because of him.

With an annoyed cry, Vivienne stopped pacing and focused on Merlin. His eyes had never wavered from her countenance during the – rather long – soliloquy.

Except, she noticed now, he was busy staring at Sébastien. "I understand they are both enthralled with Guinevere, but–"

"Both, my dear?"

Vivienne narrowed her eyes, wondering what the old man was getting at. Silently, she waited for an explanation.

"I only observed one's eyes on her, Vivienne. And the other's were on you. My dear, Sébastien is quite infatuated with you."

Vivienne's frown deepened, even as she urged her quickening heartbeat to settle. "Lancelot, however, is smitten with Guinevere. We have to be careful, Merlin. She's–"

"I, too, have apprized the situation," he admitted. "She is a trap, yes. But Arthur has fallen in love already. I will shelter him as much I can, and perhaps my presence there will deter *betrayal of another sort."*

Vivienne inclined her head in assent.

"How about those lessons now?"

* * *

Hours later, Sébastien accompanied an exhausted Vivienne back to the castle. He dropped her off at the main entrance, and intended to follow within, when she stopped him.

"Thank you. I will be fine from here."

She departed without a backwards glance, and Sébastien could not help following at a distance, despite being dismissed. He convinced himself it was to ensure the princess was not suffering.

The truth was, the guardian had noticed the way she peeked at Lancelot, while the youth gazed at Guinevere, and guessed at her sentiments. He was not surprised when Vivienne used a shortcut to end up at the stables, sneaking in by way of the back door.

Sébastien kept to the shadows, close enough to witness Vivienne walk to where Lancelot brushed his horse.

"Lancelot, we have to talk."

"Lady Vivienne," he bowed with a gallant and confident grin.

The princess wasted no time in getting to the point. "Meeting Guinevere today, I gather you fell to her charms, but she is betrothed."

Sébastien could not help but admire Vivienne's bluntness, as everything else about her person. Lancelot's response, however, shocked him.

"I am aware of that," the man admitted, with barely an ounce of regret in his voice.

"Are you really?"

Sébastien peeked around the corner in time to see Vivienne touching his arm. "Please Lance, be careful."

Once she departed his presence, Sébastien did not follow.

The pain in his chest was blinding as he walked the opposite way. Illyria waited by the main entrance, and without considering anything else, the knight jumped on the horse and rode far, far away.

Not even the distance between himself and Vivienne was enough to wipe her desolate expression from his imagination. Of one thing, Sébastien was absolutely sure – he was in love with a woman out of his league, whose heart belonged to another.

And the only thing the knight could do was watch – and suffer – in silence, as the other man destroyed it.

CHAPTER 6

Sébastien arrived in the Jag in front of an old townhouse. He craved nothing more than to call Vivienne, find out how she was doing, anything to take his mind off the job at hand. But there was no escaping Tony's orders.

Parking in front of the house, he hesitated, then got out of the car and marched past the beat-up garden to the door. He knocked three times, and a forty-something man opened it, paling the minute he recognized Sébastien.

"I don't have it."

"Do I care?" Sébastien drawled. "Tony expects me to collect."

The fear in his eyes was palpable. "I'm serious, I don't have any cash around. Please, give me a few more days, I can—"

Sébastien's fist in his nose stopped the rush of words.

Tony wanted to deliver a message, and he would. The hit was followed by another punch to the head, and another to the gut. The man slumped to his knees, coughing out blood.

Sébastien was about to deliver one more blow, when a voice stopped him.

"Daddy?"

He glanced over a shoulder to notice a kid, no older than six, staring at them both. The judgment in his eyes brought back the stupid nightmare all over again, and he lowered his fists.

"You have two days," he said to the kneeling man. "Otherwise, Tony will send someone way worse than me."

Avoiding the child's look of horror, Sébastien got out of there as promptly as possible, sickened by the situation. He hit the gas and pushed his Jag as fast as it would go, trying to outrun his own demons.

For hours, he drove around the city. Tony called and he delivered his report, after which he drove around some more. He was slowly coming to realize doing this job was not something he could maintain.

Vivienne was innocent and immaculate, and one way or another, his private life would cause her problems. The best course of action was to talk to her as soon as possible, end things so she could find true happiness. And while she struggled to recall her past, he could keep her safe from the shadows.

It was not ideal, but in the long run, the hurt caused now would be better than any future devastation.

Sébastien recognized – incited by a rapidly darkening mood – that despite the chemistry between them, nothing more could ever exist. In truth, once he had a taste of Vivienne, it would be impossible to stay away, and not a choice that was truly his to make.

No, the best thing for Vivienne, was Sébastien being a shadow – his original duty. It was with a heavy heart he drove back to the rented house he called home.

* * *

Hours later, as Sébastien paced in the living room, he still had not called Vivienne. Conflict tore him apart – the need to be with her, yet knowing he had to stay away.

Halfway through his ruminations, a sound echoed outside his door, and he rushed to open it. A bundle of fur and muscle jumped on him, and they both tumbled to the ground.

Sébastien recognized it as Vivienne's guard, Alistair. And, sure enough, the beast's growl suggested he had done something wrong.

You have no idea just how bad you screwed up, do you?

The familiar thunderous voice tore in his mind, and he winced. "Alistair! You're back, too?"

The dog eased off, and sat on his hinds as Sébastien scrambled to his knees. *Vivienne had a taste of the supernatural tonight, trying to heal me after I saved her from—*

His heartbeat raced, and he made a move towards the door. "Is she alright? I have to see—"

Alistair's growl settled Sébastien back down. *You will not be with her again until we talk and you fill in some blanks here.*

"Whatever you require, demon dog," Sébastien agreed,

resigned. He had postponed the decision for too long, and now it had been brought to him.

I am not a demon now, but a dog with limited abilities. They were linked to Vivienne's, hence why years passed by before I regained the ability to speak. Had I been aware you were in town, I would have tracked you down ages ago.

Sébastien sighed, shaking his head. "Why didn't you signal this, when I was at Vivienne's?"

Alistair tilted his head to the side, and his dark eyes burned amber. Do you have any idea how complex it is to think as a dog? I would no sooner have an intelligent thought, that it would be driven away by hunger, or a crave to play. With Vivienne's magic blocked, it meant my own normal capacities were . . . flawed. Anytime I tried to do something to attract your attention, I would forget instantly, like a damned curse – though it could not have been one.

"Are you sure?" Sébastien frowned. "What about Vivienne's amnesia, isn't that a spell? It would explain why you, as her protector, would be affected, due to the strong link between you."

It was not the reason. Vivienne's dilemma has nothing to do with a curse, but something else. Which is my reason for coming here – after I am finished with you, and I have the full details I need, you will go to her.

Sébastien opened his mouth to disagree, but the dog beat him to it. *To put it simply for your human intellect, I am more dog than demon here. When I died in the past, due to all the interventions I did on your behalf, I lost more of my status – and abilities. I have informed you before about the cardinal rules of my old deity pantheon. They do not forgive insubordination easily.*

"You're not the only one who suffered a demotion," Sébastien grumbled under his breath.

Alistair shook his head, gave a little grunt, and continued, *Regardless . . . Where have you been?*

"I've only recently come into town." At the dog's insistence, Sébastien shrugged, "I travel a lot. But enough about that, let's get back to what you were saying. Why do you need me? And what happened tonight?"

One thing at a time. First, Vivienne had a showdown with Guinevere, after which we got attacked by some man with a ghastly stench of evil on our way home. Vivienne appeared to recognize him – it was probably the same guy who broke into her house a few days back, as the smell matched. Either way, I ended him, but got hurt in the process. Vivienne unlocked an enchantment to heal me, and thus freed me, too.

Sébastien was quiet for a moment, then whispered, "When I was with her a few nights ago, we were attacked by a group of druids by a body of water."

Druids? How is that even possible? They are peaceful . . .and almost extinct in this modern world.

Sébastien ran a hand through his hair in frustration, muttering, "They were not peaceful, I can tell you that much. In the past, Carleigh was able to transform a few of them into warlocks, with no regard for nature's power. I have my suspicions, of course, but for him to be alive again . . ." He trailed off, biting his tongue before the bottled rage escaped.

Alistair's short silence was indicative of his own pensive mood. *It cannot be anyone else but Carleigh. He has unfinished business from the past, and he has always been a champion of evil. If he made a deal with the occult in order to be reborn, it is not surprising. Which is why it is even more imperative to get rid of Vivienne's amnesia.*

"And how do you propose we do that? She has visions when she's with me, not recollections."

Alistair stared at him for a beat, unconvinced. Vivienne was having those flashes for years. They have been more frequent since you found her. The pattern is changing, and it is our best chance to get her to remember everything – about you, your history, Carleigh, Merlin . . . The whole bit.

"You realize if she recalls everything . . ." Sébastien shuffled his feet, before re-focusing an uncertain gaze on the dog. "Vivienne will also remember the truth about her father. I'm afraid of what will happen once she finds out."

It is a risk we must live with, and an agony you must help her withstand.

"You have me confused, Alistair. I'm not the man I once was."

Another growl. Then why are you around Vivienne? If you are not her knight in shining armor, why be near her at all?

"I wasn't aware of her presence here!" Sébastien admitted, breaking eye contact. "You have to believe me. It's only thanks to your bark I saw her in the coffee shop, and I haven't been able to stay away."

So what is it exactly you have been doing?

"Nothing. I was hoping she would remember me – us – but it's only been these flashes so far, and . . ." He trailed off, unwilling to disclose everything.

And what? Why have you not insisted for more?

"Because of what I mentioned – her past contains horrible events in it. This time around, I was afraid it might change

Vivienne, hurt her. I only long for her to be happy. And I knew by revealing a little of what I know, the rest would soon surface."

She cannot be happy living with all this unknown.

The dog's words echoed Sébastien's own conclusions, and he bowed his head in shame. "There's something else I have to explain."

Clearly. Considering she died under your protection, am I to assume our attempt to rewrite your fate did not succeed?

"Not quite, no. Despite us being soul mates, the end was the same. Merlin said Carleigh's sorcery overtopped the balance between good and evil, and that's why he won. Regardless, he killed Vivienne, but not before cursing her."

Alistair bared his teeth, *The son of a—*

"He cursed *me* through her," Sébastien interrupted, intent on getting the confession out of the way. "He wanted to keep us apart, and he's managed to do so."

What is it you are implying? Alistair tilted his head to the side, cueing in on Sébastien's hunched shoulders, and his avoidance of all eye contact. A closer look at his aura showed the guardian's shame, and regret – but over what?

What the hell happened to you?

Sébastien's sigh was full of unspoken burdens, even as his shoulders curled inwards. "I've lived two other lifetimes, without her. This is my third. I can't fully recollect the previous lives, only that they weren't pleasant. This particular time around, I became an orphan shortly after being born, and grew up in an orphanage. Life wasn't easy, and it toughened me up."

The dog watched as Sébastien's face got a faraway look,

as though reliving the story, and contorted in a self-pitying grimace. "As I grew up, I got a reputation for being able to get results. A man came to me . . . Tony Lombardia. He's the head of the biggest Mafia around this side of Europe. He offered me an easy life, and in exchange I was to work for him. I accepted and the rest, as they say, is history." A shrug, and he said, "I've been in his debt ever since, unable to decide my own destiny. Not that it would matter, at this point . . . It's too late for me."

Alistair hung his head, in deep meditation. *If only he knew the other half of the story,* Sébastien mused. He had not yet informed the dog of the details of the curse, and exactly why he had to stay away from Vivienne.

If the full truth was revealed, Alistair would try to keep him away from Vivienne. And while that had been exactly what Sébastien intended earlier in the night, he craved a few more days of being with his beloved. Despite his bravado, letting her go was not an option.

What will you do now?

Sébastien snapped out of his thoughts and shrugged. "All I can. I know I can't have what we once did, and it's but an illusion I'm contenting myself with now. But I'll be damned if I don't make Vivienne safe again before Tony goes back on the move. And the only way to do this is to eliminate Carleigh and his corrupted druids."

Alistair nodded, but the dark eyes spoke volumes. You cannot do it on your own, and as I mentioned, my powers are limited this time around. If I intervene by attempting to change things again, I will cease to exist as a demon.

"But she needs you, Alistair. You can't surrender."

The dog snorted, and coughed out a laugh. And it is not my intention. I can keep Vivienne safe to some extent in this form, but I cannot be the one to provide her answers. The reason I am telling you this – and at the risk of repeating – is because it is clear we have no choice but to summon back her memories. Put aside your personal wishes. With Carleigh around, and Vivienne's magic . . .. She has to remember everything, and you have to help.

Sébastien sighed, sitting on the couch and rubbing his neck pensively. He had guessed this day would come, and now it had. His next actions were pre-written, and as unavoidable as the incoming storm.

"Is there no other way?" he pleaded, hoping for a miraculous different solution.

Alistair shook his massive head. *Regardless of the outcome, those memories are key. Vivienne's mind is vulnerable now, and whatever blocks them will be easier to destroy. Tonight is the time to push.* He stood and pushed closer to Sébastien's knee, nudging him. *You have to go to her. This menace, whatever it is, is real, and Vivienne has to recover access to her magic.*

"And where are you going?"

To have a chat with an old friend.

Sébastien nodded and dragged himself to his feet, following the dog out the door.

* * *

The next day during training, Vivienne decided to observe the knights, convincing herself it was to keep an eye on Lancelot.

In truth, it was to stare at Sébastien.

The royal supervised their sparring from afar, and could not help herself from stepping in their direction. She was drawn to the new knight's vigorous movements as he lunged and parried the other man's blows.

Lancelot, with his childish jabs, was a boy next to him. The way Sébastien covered the ground, with a feral grace, caused the young woman to wonder if he would be the same way in bed.

Vivienne blushed at the thought, and almost as if to spite her, Sébastien's gaze captured hers in that exact moment. It was blazing, whether from the heat of the training or their connection, she could not guess.

At the same moment, Lancelot lunged, and with panic she saw the sharp metal of his sword graze skin. In instants, a thin line of blood emerged from Sébastien's shoulder to his abdomen.

"Sébastien!" Vivienne yelled, but he was already moving towards his rival, his strikes much more ferocious.

By the time she was near, Sébastien was breathing hard, and Lancelot was on the ground. His body was covered in dust, mouth open in shock at having been defeated so soundly.

"Sébastien," Vivienne murmured, and the knight whirled around.

Ignoring as best as she could the scrumptiousness of his physique, the princess instead gestured for him to join her.

He strode closer, stopping at the fence separating them. Sébastien did not trust himself around her, thus he avoided eye contact as much as possible. He had not intended to come so close to injuring Lancelot, but noticing Vivienne there, admiring the empty-headed knight, had caused the tight rein on his emotions to snap.

"Would you care to join me on a brief stroll by the stream?" Vivienne's soft question was music to his ears, and a cooling wave to his blazing passion.

When Sébastien met her gaze, there was something there she could not quite grasp. Before she had a chance to probe, it was masked with an incline of the head. "Of course, my lady."

Dropping the sword still in his hand to the ground, Sébastien put his shirt back on, and the blood immediately soaked it. He smoothly hopped over the fence, and they strode side by the side, arriving by the stream in a matter of moments.

When Vivienne faced him, Sébastien feared admonishment due to her frown. Instead, she whispered, "Does it hurt?"

He peered down at the bloody garment and shrugged. "It is only a scratch, my lady. I will be fine."

Shaking her head in denial, Vivienne stepped towards him. "Please, let me heal you."

"Why?" His gaze scorched as it plunged into hers, causing butterflies to flutter in the pit of her stomach. Vivienne had the impression he was trying to figure out her very soul, and thus carefully chose a response.

"It was my fault you got hurt. I distracted you and . . . I do not wish you to be in any discomfort."

Sébastien stared for a beat longer, bowed his head in assent, and she reached for the shirt. He bent over to remove it, watching as Vivienne knelt by the stream to wet it with cold water.

When she got back up to clean the blood and sweat off his

chest, the gentleness of her touch surprised him. As did the patience in her countenance. Sébastien could not recall the last time any of his charges had shown much compassion – but Vivienne was special, and that was the crux of the problem.

At the first contact of the cool material, Sébastien gasped, but then he settled – though his muscles jumped under the princess' touch.

"I am sorry if the water is cold," she spoke softly.

"It will do," Sébastien murmured, but his voice sounded strained.

Once she had the wound clean, Vivienne peeked at him. A soft gasp escaped her when she realized how close their bodies were.

"I –" Vivienne's hand stilled, mesmerized by the blaze in his eyes again.

Sébastien felt the magnetism, tilting towards Vivienne, pushed by a primal need as old as time itself to taste her lips for a single moment – one touch of heaven. He stopped a hair's breath away from her lovely face, and forced some self-control. Leaning backwards, he successfully added some distance.

Vivienne willed herself to do the same, but her voice came out raspy, through a parched throat. "I was going to ask if it is alright to use an incantation?"

"Yes," Sébastien briskly agreed. Anything to be done with it, and get distance from her before he burst.

Vivienne bowed her head over him, placing both hands on his chest – a very naked, stony and chiseled chest. Stop it, she told herself. Healing is the priority, not jumping his bones.

She moistened her lips, then continued without looking at

him, "I only ask because although magic heals the wound faster, not everyone is comfortable with me using it around them."

At the silence that greeted her words, Vivienne peered up once more. The knight was gazing through half-closed eyes, but the intensity was unmistakably there.

Sébastien bit down the words of comfort he wanted to speak as a lover. He heard the rumours around the palace, and in the village – not everyone liked having a gifted sovereign.

With great effort, he swallowed past the lump in his throat, and instead said what a guardian could. "I am not one of those people, highness. No matter what, I am and always will be on your side."

Vivienne's lips trembled, and she bit down hard to stop it, staring back at the wound to hide the rising emotion. Never had she felt so connected to someone, as she did in that moment with Sébastien.

Focusing back on healing, one palm became ablaze, as did the other. The enchantress held onto the golden glow, rather than letting it escape in wisps. She kept it in her palms as they drifted across Sébastien's bicep, slowly to the side and down the front, following the gash over his chest.

Through it all, she surveyed the tough guard from under her lids, wondering at his closed eyes, and why he was biting his bottom lip. His neck tendons strained as though tormented, and he inhaled sharply.

"Am I hurting you, Sébastien?" Vivienne asked, though her hands kept moving. Already, the glow had closed half of his gash.

"Not in the way you think, my lady," he groaned through gritted teeth.

She could not fathom how to respond.

When the wound was closed, fully mended, Vivienne silently thanked the magic, and extinguished her palms. She backed away, immediately regretting the heat of his body.

"It is done."

Sébastien opened his eyes and admired her handiwork – there was no trace of the blade's cut. "Thank you, my lady," he bowed. "Is there anything else you desire?"

Quite a few things, Vivienne mused. Out loud, she said, "No, that will be all. I can find my own way back."

* * *

The instant her eyes opened, Vivienne jumped out of bed and threw herself at the presence in the room. They crashed into the dresser and landed on the floor. Their brief tumble ended with her straddling the adversary on his back, in a shoulder lock.

"Vivienne!"

She froze, and her name on Sébastien's lips was her undoing.

How the hell did I do that? Her body had followed a pattern never learnt from before. She was not a fighter – at least not physically. Last time an intruder had entered her bedroom, Vivienne had been searching for a weapon. Now, her body was it.

She let go of Sébastien and shifted off him, but remained in a kneeling position. He rolled to his back, coughed twice, and proceeded to breathe evenly.

"Well. At least I taught you well."

"What are you doing here in the middle of the night?" Once his words registered, Vivienne frowned. "And what do you mean, *taught* me?"

Sébastien half sat up, eyes never wavering from her face. There was an apology in his voice when he spoke. "I was there with you, Vivienne – in the past. Everything you've been dreaming, we lived it together. Alistair came to my place tonight, and sent me here. He told me you used magic to heal him, and to come to you, and help you with remembering."

She gaped for all of two seconds, and Sébastien took advantage of her surprise to kneel in front of her. After a few stunned seconds, Vivienne recovered enough to ask, "So it's real? You remember now, too?"

Though Vivienne could not read Sébastien's eyes in the dimness, his hoarse voice confessed, "I always did, my love."

Sébastien backed a few inches, still kneeling. His hand moved and she saw the action before it happened. With a quick flick of her hand, she deflected his wrist, pinning it to the ground – unaware he had only intended to caress her cheek.

Almost immediately, Vivienne let go, shocked at the rapidity of her movements.

I wish I knew why she cannot fully recall everything. Her body instinctively reacts, yet –

"Stop it!" Vivienne realized the loudness of the words only when Sébastien's eyes widened, his eyebrows shooting way up.

"You have your full abilities back? And you can hear me as you did before?"

The young woman shook her head, in full denial.

"Sébastien, I'm losing my sanity here. I had an out loud conversation with my *dog*. I healed his *wounds*. With *magic*. Something apparently I've had all along, as did he, but he couldn't access it considering I didn't know I had any. Now that I have it back, apparently I'm supposed to be able to do quite a few of things, except for one problem – I have no idea how!"

Sébastien's voice was soft. "You evidently intuit more than you recognize. The way you tackled me proves it."

Vivienne stood up, moving to turn on the light, and Sébastien followed suit.

"Please. I need to understand this," she pleaded.

"What would you like me to explain?" he asked warily. "I'm afraid my answers will be pretty limited."

Vivienne threw her hands up in the air. "What's been happening, the last couple of days, for starters. Alistair told me who I was, but . . . You know more than you've revealed, and right now I'm too confused to be mad at you. I have to put together all the missing pieces."

"That, I think I can help you with."

"How?"

Vivienne peered into his eyes for an answer, unprepared for his lips meeting hers. The moment they grazed, warmth spread within her and she gave in – what was the point of fighting against a rising tide?

As their lips meshed in unison, flashes of things stirred within Vivienne's mind, as though they would split it open. Too many memories were pushing past her walls, eager for the young woman to experience them all at once.

Groaning, she drew away from the embrace, longing for

the pain to stop.

"Vivienne?" Sébastien's voice broke past her haze of discomfort.

She reached out to him, almost unconsciously, snuggling in the comforting cradle of his arms.

"Shh," he whispered, pressing a light kiss to her forehead and tightening his hold. As if that simple gesture could remove any distress.

"What *was* that?" Vivienne gasped, head still throbbing. The vibrations of her voice only added to the pain.

"I hoped to help you unlock certain things. In the past, you've always had these memories surfacing when we were kissing, or together. Alistair's theory is your mental barrier is more vulnerable tonight. And since that's what's causing your amnesia, I was hoping a kiss might bring everything back."

"It did, I think. In a way."

"What exactly did you see?" Sébastien frowned, wondering how much he had unwillingly revealed.

"Too many things at once. I can't process them all, which is probably why it hurt so much."

He tucked a strand of her hair behind her ear. "It makes sense, in a way."

Vivienne's eyes were pools of confusion, and she bit her lip. "Can you fill in the gaps?"

"Some, yes. I'm sure Alistair revealed this isn't the first life you've lived, Viv." When she nodded, he continued, "Your déjà-vus are basically memories of your past experiences. But one thing common to each of your lives was that each time we met, each time we fell in love, and each time, I lost you."

The truth of Sébastien's words resounded in the young woman's body, heart, in her very soul.

"You knew about this . . . This entire time, after we ran into each other?" Vivienne beseeched him, struggling still to get rid of the pain at the back of her head. She moved away from him, unable to think in such close proximity.

"Yes." The pain in his voice tugged at her heart strings, but she forced herself to listen to his words. "I've been waiting for you for a long, long time, my love. When I saw you at the coffee shop, I thought I was hallucinating. Later, as we got together, I couldn't decide whether to tell you, or let things play out. I was afraid of this, of hurting you, and you thinking I was crazy."

"You tried to shield me, as you've always done," Vivienne realized.

"Yes." Her lack of anger was a relief to Sébastien, and he found himself relaxing infinitesimally.

For Vivienne, everything was finally falling into place. Why she had never disputed his words, but trusted him unequivocally despite the short time they had spent together. Subconsciously, she *did* know him, and already trusted him from past experiences. To some extent, the crazy explanation of spells and past lives was rational enough.

Her gaze fell on Sébastien, trying to guess at his thoughts. Now that everything was out in the open, the little bubble they had been in no longer existed. "So, what do we do now?"

"Well, your memories are in your head. It's only a matter of you processing them. You'll have to go at your own pace, of course. My bet is, the visions will probably continue, as will the dreams. Eventually, it will all come back."

Vivienne rubbed the side of her head. The throbbing was very much still present. "And until then?"

"Well, I'm hoping your magic works like your fighting reflexes. Maybe you don't have to actually remember how to use it, and it comes naturally. You'll need it to fight those who are after you."

"Are they the same as in the past?" Vivienne frowned, grasping at some elusive tidbit of information. "I can vaguely recall a menace . . ."

"Yes," Sébastien grumbled. "Carleigh was an apprentice of Merlin, and he was cast away when the old wizard chose to train you. He's been after you ever since. And he had the upper hand in the past, leading to your death."

Sébastien ran a nervous hand through his hair, continuing, "Carleigh had a few too many people at his command. Those guys we ran into, at the lake? They seemed to be druids . . . Their evil twin version, anyway." At Vivienne's confused look, he added, "Warlocks, cloaked in sorcery. And they must have come back some way, with him. My fear is he has dabbled into more than dark arts at this point – necromancy, to be more precise."

A flicker of fear passed in Vivienne's expression, and Sébastien stopped talking, pulling her back into his arms.

"I can't stand keeping a distance between us," he murmured against her head. "Not after all this time." Deep down, he could not reveal his intention to depart – not yet.

Vivienne shook her head in his chest, then wrapped both her arms around his waist. "This is crazy."

"That has always been our life, beloved."

She drew back a bit, whispering, "Our. I love the sound of that."

Sébastien's eyes softened, and when they kissed, it was tender and sweet. As always, forces out of their control dragged them into a myriad of sensations, rapidly spiraling out of control.

Hands acting out unspoken wishes, Sébastien ended up with Vivienne in his lap, wrapped around him in an enticing way. He managed to gently break her hold around his neck, barely keeping a lid on his own raging desires.

When he peered down at her swollen lips, flushed skin and eyes alight with desire, he knew he was in deep. And much like before, he would never be able to leave her side.

"My love," Sébastien began, voice rough with emotion, "much as I would enjoy continuing this, it's your magic we have to work on."

"How, exactly?" Vivienne smiled sheepishly.

Sébastien cupped her cheeks in his hands. ""First, the pain, just now. Have you ever felt it when we kissed?"

"No," Vivienne shook her head. "This was unbearable, like my head wanted to split open with these flashes. It hurt so bad, I was close to passing out."

"Has it ever happened after your flashbacks?"

Vivienne thought about it for a second. "Not really. I've had headaches most times, but nothing this bad."

"And the psychiatrists you mentioned your present parents brought you to, did they ever do anything to you? Try to access your mind? Hypnotism?"

"No," Vivienne shook her head again, "only normal therapy sessions."

Sébastien let go of her, muttering to himself. "I can't figure out what it could be, aside from what you mentioned.

Unless you're blocking—" He stopped, clamping his mouth shut, gaze frozen on the enchantress' features.

Vivienne noticed something working behind his eyes, yet she could not tune in to the thoughts as before. *Great. The one ability that could be useful, is an on and off thing,* she grumbled silently.

Out loud, she asked, "You had some type of revelation?"

Sébastien had, but he hesitated to explain she was probably subconsciously blocking everything because of the deaths she had been witness to in the past, including her father's.

No, he decided, *being there for her once she finds out is one thing, but I won't be the one to deliver the blow.*

"Close your eyes," he said instead as another idea struck.

Vivienne stared at Sébastien for a beat, uncomprehending. At his determined yet silent pleading, she followed his instructions and waited. His hands were warm on her skin at first, then their temperature cooled off. Sébastien whispered something, and the wretched agony was back in her head.

Something surged inside the young woman, a warm vibration aspiring to explode. Vivienne tried to hold it back, but it was impossible to focus past the pain – and she lost control of it.

Vivienne opened her eyes, gaping as Sébastien flew in the air, hitting the wall of her bedroom. She got up to her feet, shouting his name, but brightness in the room distracted her.

She looked down at her body – only to realize it was coming from her. A glow within her skin, turning it translucent.

"Vivienne," Sébastien called out.

She gazed at him, sprawled on the floor, expecting him to be irritated, at best. After all, he had only been trying to help. Instead, it was a reverent grin on his face, one she identified only too well.

Sébastien read the worry in her eyes, and said, "It's unimportant. My well-being is nothing compared to yours."

Vivienne was about to dispute the words, but he continued, "I never had any supernatural abilities, but this was something taught to both of us by Merlin – to access the soul mate bond linking us. In so doing, I trust I freed a portion of your abilities. The rest, only you can do."

He got up, approached Vivienne, and knelt down in a position similar to one from a long time ago. Raising his right hand to his chest, Sébastien then bowed his head in allegiance. "I am at your service, my lady, as I always have been. I pledge my life to you, to do with as you wish."

A memory filled Vivienne as she gazed down, of when Sébastien had first vowed to protect her, and she swallowed past the lump in her throat.

"I accept your pledge. Please, rise and kiss me, Sébastien."

He did as she bid, and when they separated, rested his forehead against hers. "You did it – accessed your raw power. Now it's only a matter of time before everything else comes back."

Vivienne wanted to agree, but something prevented her from doing so. Namely, the room spinning – rather dangerously.

"Are you alright?"

Sébastien's concerned voice came from far, far away, and

she collapsed when the blackout hit.

* * *

Realizing she had overspent energy, Sébastien carried his beloved to bed so she could rest in comfort. The exertion was bound to catch up at some point, considering she had been accessing areas of her powers she had not for ages.

He could not help worrying, hoping certain aspects of the past would stay at bay for a little longer. He did not wish the burden of remembering the worst of her past onto his beloved.

Sébastien should have been happy Vivienne remembered him, and knew the so-called hallucinations were real, and they could discuss them. Yet no matter how deep he searched within himself, all that responded was an instinct of dread.

As if to prove his point, his cell vibrated. He checked the caller ID, noted it was Tony, and hit *decline*.

There was only one way this could work out, and it was if Sébastien left his employer. He had more than enough money set aside in the past lifetimes and the current one to keep him comfortable, so unemployment was not a concern.

It would not be a clean slate, seeing as his soul was much too damaged for that. But perhaps it would be enough to get a second chance to be Vivienne's friend.

He contemplated the enchantress' dormant form longingly – if only.

When the cell vibrated again, Sébastien shut it off. He took his boots off, and got into bed, on top of the covers. Vivienne snuggled closer, and he wrapped an arm tightly around her.

Sébastien knew the nightmare awaited him, but hoped

against everything that it would not come.

At least for this night, let me rest in peace, he pleaded silently.

CHAPTER 7

Braydon entered the church apprehensively.

"What happened?"

He jumped as his master Carleigh emerged out of the shadows, silent as a ghost.

"She regained her magic, and I believe the mutt his."

"Has he, now?" Carleigh's eyes narrowed pensively.

"Yes, I believe so," Braydon answered with an odd stare. "Last I saw of him, the dog was headed to the knight – without Vivienne."

"Perhaps it's time I go have some fun with him." The sorcerer picked up one of the spiders from under his sleeve, and pointed it towards the servant. "Show me your hand. You will guard the portal in my absence."

When he hesitated, Carleigh seized his hand forcefully, and slapped the spider in it. Braydon gritted his teeth as the beast dug under the skin, becoming one with him.

His master muttered an incantation, and Braydon was immediately drawn backwards, mere inches away from the malevolent mirror. He was frozen, a true statue of silence, while the portal bubbled at his feet, eagerly waiting.

Carleigh glanced down at it, then at the acolyte. "The portal will waver if I do not feed it with the opposite energy. Now that I've commenced this sequence of events, I have to ensure it remains alive."

He paced for a few moments, tapping an index to his chin thoughtfully. "There is only one place in this city where the mutt would go if he truly regained his abilities. If he went to Sébastien, his next order of business will be to speak to Merlin. And coincidentally, he will be heading to the same place I have to go. Gathering good spirits for sacrificing to the portal is no easy task."

"Master," Braydon croaked through immobile lips, "what if they find out what you plan?"

"That *is* the point!" Carleigh snickered. "Vivienne, being as smart as she is, will figure out what I plan. I need her to! They can prepare for it to no avail – consequently the reality will be so much worse than they can ever foresee!"

He cackled evilly, backing away, and let darkness feed on his most loyal servant. From afar, the new batch of cloaked druids watched, unblinking.

Sticking to the shadows, Carleigh crossed to the middle of the city, where a fountain stood. Being so attuned to darkness, he was nearly blinded by the light radiating off the fountain, from centuries of spiritual faith fueling it.

Yet the sorcerer drifted closer, and dug a hand in the

fountain. There was a zap, and a charge of electricity aimed to throw him off. The fountain itself perceived the corruption animating the sorcerer.

Carleigh stood his ground, digging deeper. It was only liquid he stroked at this point, still within the real world, when what the necromancer desired was the power within it. He closed his eyes in concentration, needing to see by means of the supernatural and not human eyes.

With a snarl of annoyance, he dug the other hand in, preparing for the worst. When the electricity zapped again, burning through the darkness emanating from the skin in an effort to purify him, he gripped it in his mind.

There was a blinding flash in Carleigh's head, and a door opened, as though he had projected his spirit within, in another dimension. He propelled the energy past the small opening, finally coming upon the magic now at his fingertips.

The electricity increased, and his teeth gritted against it. Carleigh extended the hand closest to the circle of spirit, capturing a handful, and disengaged. Regaining the real world, the sorcerer squinted in the fountain, where his hands were still submerged. In his right palm was an orb, the size of a tennis ball. It shimmered of a golden light, feathery soft to the touch.

With a satisfied grin, Carleigh withdrew it, and tucked it underneath his cloak. He backed away from the fountain, swaying.

"Damn," he muttered, the electricity having done its job and purified some of the maliciousness from him. A much needed session of recharging would wait back at the church, but for now, it was time to put on a good face.

The necromancer turned slightly to the side, sensing a presence nearing. "Ah . . . Finally, the fun is about to begin."

Carleigh faced the fountain once more, placing his back to the mutt that was coming close. His legs were weak, weakness flowing through the human body still hosting his spirit – not for much longer. He would have to ensure the dog got the right information, but nothing stopped him from having a little fun.

With a muttered incantation, he cloaked the scent of the little sphere, as well as his own pain.

* * *

After he dropped Sébastien off at Vivienne's, Alistair headed to the Place des Saints Corps fountain. It was dusky enough now that no tourists would be out around the area.

He required a source of water in a spiritually-charged spot to communicate with Merlin. The fountain had been there long enough to be impregnated by the city's power. Avignon had always been a spiritual city, with the popes choosing it as their own over centuries – truly a perfect place for the reincarnation of the Lady of the Lake.

With a shake of the head, the demon dog focused his energy onwards. He rounded a corner, ready for some explanations.

As he came within sighting distance of the fountain, Alistair noticed a figure standing there. At first, the dog presumed it was another tourist, before noticing the outdated cloak, and the nebulous aura surrounding the man. Then the breeze changed direction, and the murky odor hit his nostrils.

A snarl erupted from his throat. *Carleigh!*

As if hearing him, the shadowed figure whirled away from the fountain, and Alistair got confirmation. The warlock had not changed – same grey skin and beady eyes, same lanky build and awkward movements. However, there was a new rotten flavor to the shadows following him around, trailing his footsteps and turning the night darker.

Peering closer, Alistair realized Carleigh's shadow moved of its own accord, and the truth dawned on him. He had spent enough time as lord of the underworld to connect the dots. When the scale had tipped in the past, Carleigh must have ensured his survival by making a pact with darkness. Probably within that pact, was a deal to bring his previous servants into the new world.

Alistair had never missed his old abilities as much as in that moment. He would have preferred his older, stronger and quite larger body, but the present one would have to do – even if the powers he possessed now, compared to the past, would be close to useless.

Despite the obvious fact, Alistair knew he had to find out as much as possible to help Vivienne. And if matching his strength could not be done, at the very least, he could outwit Carleigh to play his hand.

What are you doing here? Alistair thundered, facing the sorcerer.

"I've come to finish what I started long ago, since her highness is back." The voice was that of an old man, so unnatural in someone younger.

The price of necromancy is high, Alistair mused thoughtfully, once more struck by the changes in Carleigh.

You will do well to stay away from Vivienne, he warned the warlock, locking stares and baring teeth.

"I am afraid I cannot do that." Carleigh sniggered, privy to his own joke. "Rather conveniently for me, she has to finish tipping the scales in my favor."

What the hell are you on about? As he spoke, Alistair paced around the fountain. He never lost sight of the warlock, but was attempting to find a good angle of attack.

"The princess has access to pure magic, the types of which can win the war against good and evil." Carleigh stopped, staring away from the dog as though listening to music only he could hear.

It was as he paced from one end to the other of the fountain that it dawned on Alistair – either the sorcerer was cocky to be so exposed, or he had something else planned. There was no rhyme or reason to exposing the plan, or himself, in this way.

As though deciphering his thoughts, Carleigh continued, "My plan is to corrupt her, effectively ruining the balance, and assume her magic for my own."

And why would you divulge this?

"Because, demon dog, you won't live long enough to warn anyone."

Merlin was right about you, foolish one. You always were too greedy for your own good!

"Don't bring him into this!" Carleigh's visage twisted in pure rage. "That man is no mentor of mine. He cast me away like garbage the minute he had the chance!"

Alistair shifted to the side, to find an opening, while keeping him talking. *The way I heard it, you were dabbling into forbidden arts and Merlin tried to put a stop to it, before you got any stronger.*

"Well, I guess he failed in that."

Indeed.

"If he was here now, I wouldn't object to giving him a piece of my mind."

Alistair cocked his head, disconcerted at the words. *What if I can bring him?*

It was Carleigh's turn to project incredulity, and his guard dropped for a moment. It was enough for Alistair to catch a longing in his eyes, similar to a child's for a parent.

Interesting . . . Despite the bravado, his attachment to Merlin still remains, Alistair mused to himself.

Then the masked slipped back on, and Carleigh yelled, "You're lying!"

I am not. Speaking with him is the reason for my presence here. I can bring him forth, long enough for you to get some closure.

"And why would I trust you?" Carleigh snarled, more rabid dog than human being.

Because despite your words, you long to see him again, to prove you have grown into the man he'd never expect of you.

While talking, Alistair attempted to pierce Carleigh's fortified shield, but promptly realized he had no chance. The senses that helped him usually discern an aura, could only distinguish a thick, immovable fog around the sorcerer, invisible to the naked eye.

Carleigh's silence snapped Alistair out of his thoughts, in time to notice darkness seep, and jump out of the way. The curse's shadow slithered as a snake in the sorcerer's hand, gathering in a sphere of midnight fire.

The warlock kept it steady, sneering like a lunatic.

"Who's the fool now, mutt? To think it was so easy to play a part, poor me needing Merlin's approval!" He snorted, preparing to throw once more.

Alistair tried to feint, but the minute it was launched, the orb made hit him full force, and he flew into the wall of the building. He struck the cold brick, grunting, and slid to the ground, his small body fighting the electric charges.

I have to warn them, was all he could think, angry at having fallen for the sorcerer's tricks.

Carleigh inched by, the air crackling around him. The dog could barely tilt his head, giving a low whine.

"Sorry, mutt, time to say good night."

With a last effort, Alistair pushed off the ground and lunged at him, seizing onto a leg and clamping his substantial jaws down. Despite Carleigh's scream, he kept at it insistently, until the bone gave way with a sickening crunch.

A bolt hit Alistair again, and this time he rolled off, leaving Carleigh to moan in agony on the ground. In spite of the futility of his action, the demon dog got up, straining in a crouch. He growled, snapping his jaws towards the warlock. Their eyes locked for a split of a second, before he pounced.

At the same time, Carleigh uttered an incantation, and the darkness surrounded him, shielding him in a black mass. When Alistair landed, he was gone, but his odor was more potent than ever.

Heavily panting and exhausted by the fight, Alistair dragged his body back to Vivienne's home.

* * *

Carleigh groaned in pain, reappearing on the outside of the church. He used the wall of the building to hoist himself up, leaning heavily on it as he walked in.

Braydon's eyes followed the master's walk to the pool. With one sweep of the hand, Carleigh released the servant from the darkness' clutches.

Braydon immediately stepped away, still trembling from the torture darkness had caused him. For the entire time Carleigh was gone, his mind had been a prisoner, the negative forces feeding on all his doubts, insecurities, anger, pushing for a breaking point. It had suggested death, havoc, chaos.

He shook his head in an effort to clear it, then glanced back to his master. Carleigh was now kneeling, the spiders and other creatures crawling over his form, their tiny bodies glowing black as energy pulsated through his skin.

Braydon did not ask what happened, as the master had a satisfied smirk on his face, despite the pain. Without speaking, he reached in the cloak and pulled out the orb of spirit, showcasing it to his servant. Then he hid it again, and sank into the now liquid pool.

Hours later, once darkness had recharged him and healed the wounds the fountain and Alistair had inflicted, Carleigh would re-emerge stronger than before.

* * *

Sébastien was sparring with a young devil, conscious of Vivienne observing him, always attuned to her presence these days. He did not understand whether she was around only for Lancelot, but either way, their eyes always met.

Since she had healed him, the guardian yearned for nothing more than to hold her and erase the other man from her mind. Yet all he could do was watch over the princess, while trying to ignore the tightening in his chest each time her eyes went to Lancelot – and failing.

The sound of metal clashing and an abundance of noise broke his tumultuous ruminations. Sébastien turned around, immediately remarking two younger pages sparring close to where Vivienne had been standing.

Before he could react, she marched to the two youngsters, yelling at them to stop. This despite the fact one of them had a very real weapon in his hand.

When the page whirled at the sound of her voice, he swung the sharpened sword clumsily around. Sébastien's own blade came to block the blow, only inches from Vivienne's cheek.

The youth's hand shook, and the sword clattered to the ground. He fell to his knees, his face a mask of shock and angst. "Lady Vivienne! My heartfelt apologies!"

"What do you two imagine you're doing?" Sébastien snarled between clenched teeth, unmoved by their youthful appearance. The anger – and fear – that hit him at the idea of Vivienne being injured was staggering.

Even the young woman cringed at the fury coming off him in waves. She clasped his shoulder, ignoring the way heat permeated her own skin and travelled through. Sébastien inhaled deeply at the soft touch, inclining his head to her.

"I am unharmed, Sébastien. It was my fault, I should not

have gotten so close."

The battle was still clear in his eyes, as he had not yet calmed down. Vivienne disregarded him, kneeling instead by the younger youth who was bleeding.

"May I heal your wound?" She kept her expression open and warm, so he would realize he was not in trouble.

The youth nodded, awestruck by her beauty and kindness. Sébastien knew only too well how he felt. He could draw Vivienne's features with his eyes closed – countless sleepless nights thinking of her would do that.

Blissfully unaware, Vivienne healed the young boy in mere moments. She then turned to the still-kneeling boy. He also had a cut, but was curled unto himself and barely breathing, as if hoping his presence would be forgotten.

"What is your name?" she asked.

"W-W-William," he stuttered.

"You will not be punished, William. But I would like to understand what happened here. May I heal you in the meantime?"

Enthralled by Vivienne – and with a nervous peek at Sébastien – the child recounted a silly story about a stupid fight over a girl. He concluded with a contrite, "I'm terribly sorry, my lady."

"It is quite alright," she smiled. "Off you go."

Sébastien advanced to intervene, but she glared his way. "Follow me, Dubois."

Once they reached a secluded corner, Vivienne whirled around accusingly. "You scared that poor boy to death!"

"Poor boy, my lady?" Sébastien gritted his teeth. "He could have harmed you – gravely so."

"And I could have healed myself!" she continued, eyes blazing. "He is young, and now petrified because of you!"

"My lady —" he begun, but was interrupted.

"I'm not sure how they do things where you come from, but in Elsior, every single person is treated with kindness and respect! You will do well to register it, and the sooner the better."

Sébastien dropped all pretense of calm, his voice tight with fury as he towered over the princess. "All due respect, your father hired me to safeguard you and that is what I intend to do. Even if it's from yourself."

Vivienne was about to retort, but something in the guardian's countenance alerted her to danger. She realized they were close enough to touch, and there was a heat radiating from him, close to magnetizing.

"I—" she tried, but had to moisten her lips with the tip of her tongue at the sudden dryness in her throat.

Sébastien's eyes lowered at the action, and the magnetism fortified, his scorching eyes meeting hers. Vivienne's body burned with a humming intensity in her bones, even as it leaned towards him.

They were staring at each other, lost in the moment, when Lancelot came up. "You up for a rematch?" he dared Sébastien, blissfully unaware of what he had stumbled into.

"Aye," Sébastien muttered, eyes still on Vivienne. "My lady," he bowed, and retreated.

Vivienne was still staring into space, when Alistair appeared by her side, nudging one hand in question. "Is the new guardian giving you trouble?"

"No . . . not really. He is peculiar, that's all."

Alistair glanced up at his mistress, and back to Sébastien, now further away. "I would say protective."

Vivienne bit her lip in deep reflection, unnerved by their connection and the constant dreams she had of Sébastien. It was bad enough he drew her like a moth to a flame whenever they were in the same vicinity, but now sleep eluded her as well – all thanks to one dark-eyed knight.

Alistair's second nudge to her hand was a jolt, startling from her musings. She smiled down guiltily, realizing he must have come for a reason, yet she was busy daydreaming. Putting Sébastien out of her mind for good, Vivienne concentrated on Alistair.

As usual, he interpreted the unspoken query, and opened his large jaws in a doggy grin. "I assumed you would be interested in practicing some unrestrained enchantments."

"Always!" Vivienne beamed, and followed him off the training grounds.

* * *

Vivienne blinked, slowly waking up. Sébastien's heat was at her back, but a noise had shattered the memory – and sleep. For a moment, it remained unidentified, as she hovered between fantasy and reality.

Then her ears caught a muffled groan, followed by a thud. The young woman got up and slowly trudged down the stairs, to the living room. She stopped dead in her tracks, staring at Alistair's unmoving form lying down in the middle of the room.

"Al!" Vivienne ran to him, knelt down and checked him

for injuries. He appeared unharmed, except for the labored and uneven breathing.

"What happened?" Her hands traveled over his body in an effort to find a remedy to the affliction. Since the cause was uncertain, she was hesitant to use magic.

I had a bit of a run-in with our pal, Carleigh. Alistair's voice was fainter than before in her head, which in itself was concerning.

The name alone was enough to give Vivienne pause, as it brought back a hint of the peril they had confronted in the past. "The man responsible for my death?"

The same one.

Her stomach dropped at the confirmation. Would it have been too much to hope she and Sébastien were the only ones reincarnated, and the last bit of bad luck and creepy stalkers was due to some modern peril? *Apparently.*

With a shake of the head, Vivienne focused back on Alistair. "Are you alright? Should I try to heal you?"

No, I will be fine. This body is not accustomed to the necromancer curses Carleigh used offensively.

"Because it's not your demon dog body?"

Alistair's eyes glinted of a satisfied gleam, and Vivienne could perceive it in his voice when he said, *Good, you are remembering more and more. It pleases me. But yes, to respond to your first question. My old body, being demonic, could withstand any attack of nefarious forces. This one is a normal dog body, and thus, it is taking me longer to filter the curse out of my system.*

Vivienne caressed his fur, then followed the motion by gently cradling his head and placing it in her lap. "Don't worry, I'll be here."

They were silent, the only noises being Vivienne's soft breathing and Alistair's more laborious one. In an effort to distract him, the young woman sifted through her recent memories. "Do you ever think back on how we met? Back then, I mean?"

Yes . . . The dog gave a small, rueful shake of his head, and sighed heavily. *You were a handful, even as a child. When your mother passed away, you kept running away from the castle, until the day when you ran into the path of a bear in the forest.*

"You were going to eat him!" Vivienne accused, laughing softly.

I was, Alistair admitted unabashedly, amusement in his voice. *He was my food for the day. At least, until he tried to eat you. Something about you – your light – woke up even this old monster.*

"You were never a monster, Al." Vivienne whispered, rubbing behind the ears where she knew he enjoyed it. "That's why I ignored your efforts to drive me away, and ended up naming you myself."

Defender of men, Alistair snorted, referring to the meaning of his name. *Nice pick indeed, your majesty.*

Vivienne ignored the title, instead whispering, "Are you feeling any better?"

Yes.

She bit her lip, but the heaviness in her chest was too stifling to ignore. "Why do I have this foreboding feeling that something might happen to you? Did it, in the past?"

Alistair hesitated, and thus Vivienne knew he was being

evasive when he replied, *Everything will be alright.*

They were quiet again, until his breathing became steadier. With a groan, the dog stood up.

Carleigh is here for you.

"For me? Whatever for?"

A couple of reasons, not that they all matter. But his goal is to steal your magic and amplify own.

Vivienne frowned at the words. "But how, if I'm supposedly so full of light? You mentioned how evil his sorcery is."

It is. But if he corrupts your spirit, it will not be a problem.

The enchantress shivered, unable to stop it. The cold that had reached her ever since leaving Sébastien's side was now within her, and she felt exhausted.

Noticing the reaction, Alistair shoved his muzzle to his mistress, and she wrapped both arms around his massive neck. *We will not let that happen,* he assured.

Vivienne nodded, but could not help fearing it. The past remained foggy for the most part, and using enchantments was still something she was unaccustomed to. The major part of what she did was on pure instinct, which would only get her so far. Confronted with a powerful sorcerer, whose trade was the black arts, Vivienne knew she would lose.

"What else did he say?" she probed.

Nothing important. I will fill Sébastien in the morning, but you should rest.

The young woman got up slowly, and went back to bed. As she slid under the sheets, Sébastien rumbled, "You're cold. Is everything alright?"

"Yeah, don't mind me. Rest." But as though guessing at her hidden fears, he wrapped his arms around her tightly, and threw a leg over possessively, for good measure.

Within moments, Sébastien's heat warmed her, and Vivienne was able to relax. In his arms, somehow, she found the sweet peace of sleep once more.

* * *

Sébastien was fast asleep, reminiscing of old times, when the ambiance changed, and he faced himself in the mirror. He tensed, prepared to tackle the nightmare once more.

Except this time, the disembodied voice came from right behind.

"You promised."

Sébastien whirled around, and found himself in close proximity with Merlin. The old wizard was dressed in the beige robes of a mage and clutched an elongated staff, as tall as him.

It was white in color, and a single translucent crystal decorated the top, where spells could be centered when it was called for. Merlin's grey beard was longer than before, and the once sparkling blue eyes were weary and disappointed.

His words shook Sébastien to the core, especially once it registered what they implied. The knight's initial guilt was overtaken by indignation.

"This entire time, it was *you!*"

Merlin's features remained an impassable mask under the attack.

"*You* entered my head, put in these nightmares."

Sébastien stepped towards him, barely controlling himself. "You've been messing with my head ever since I found Vivienne again, haven't you?"

"Yes."

Sébastien clenched his fists, sorely tempted to punch the old man.

"Why!? *Why* would you do this? We're on the same side!"

"No, we are not." Merlin's voice, once full of warmth, was now devoid of it as he examined Sébastien like he was an insect.

"You best explain that while I can still control myself," Sébastien growled.

"I am on the side of nature, of good. Though I am grateful to you for bringing Vivienne back, now you must edge out of the way, so she can become the person she is intended to be."

"No, I won't do that," Sébastien gave a resolute shake of the head, gritting his teeth. "I can help her. Shelter her!"

"She can defend herself, young one."

"Don't patronize me, old man, or else I swear –" Sébastien stopped before saying something he would regret.

Merlin pointed to Sébastien's whitened knuckles with one gnarled hand and asked, "Is this so different than what I revealed to you in the mirror?"

"You were messing with my head."

"Yes, I was," Merlin admitted in that same calm tone. "But is it so different? The same violence you observed in there is now reflected in every bone in your body."

With a subtle hand gesture from the mage, a mirror emerged between the two of them.

"See for yourself," Merlin entreated. "This one is no illusion, Sébastien. It is your real reflection."

"I'm done playing mind games with you," the knight bit aggressively. "You cannot force me away from Vivienne!"

"It is no trick. *Look!*"

The command was so overwhelming, Sébastien felt inclined to listen, though he only saw his own reflection. The shirt was clean, and after a quick overview, there was no immediate sign of violence. However, when he peered attentively for a second look, Sébastien observed the rigid shoulders, the clenched fists, and the same stony glint in his eyes.

The fight went out of him, as though he had been dealt a hefty punch. "No . . ."

"Do you see now, what I'm alluding to?"

Sébastien bit his lip to avoid a retort, instead averting his eyes from the mirror. With a wave of the staff, the object disappeared, and it was only them two once more.

"This is beyond your love for Vivienne," Merlin continued in a softer voice. "What you have done, to bring her back, has changed your very core. You are no longer the same man, yet you are still part of the same whole. If she continues to love you, and you stick around, it will taint her. Vivienne's essence will change, as yours did, and not for the better. Thus, you cannot be there as her partner."

"I've been around her for days, and nothing happened!" Sébastien retorted, a pleading in his eyes.

"Not yet, but it will. It is impossible to avoid it. You are soul mates, and your corruption will hurt her light."

"Merlin, I—"

"You promised you would not corrupt her," the mage's tone held a warning this time around. "The price was clearly stated when you made the deal with me."

"I only need a few days with her," Sébastien pleaded. "I've been apart from Vivienne for ages . . . Please let me breathe her in for a few more moments. Do we not deserve this?"

"Not if it will shift the balance again."

When Sébastien averted his eyes again, Merlin persisted. "What if you aim this violence towards her?"

"I would never lay a hand on her! You have to realize that!"

"Do I? You promise this now, much like your long ago promise. Yet it was easy for you to break it."

"This is not the same thing!" Sébastien glared at him.

"Perhaps. Nevertheless, you swore an oath to maintain your distance. It is one you must keep. Otherwise, I will have to intervene across the ages. Avoid Vivienne the hurt, and end it now. You can be her guard, nothing more. It is the *only* way. Do you understand?"

They faced off, midnight against stormy blue eyes, until Sébastien hung his head in defeat. "Yes. I will rectify it."

"I do wish things were different."

Sébastien opened his eyes, wishing so as well, but his next steps to follow were clear as crystal.

* * *

Vivienne was staring out the window when Sébastien's Jag pulled up. He exited the car, and approached the house.

When she had woken up to an empty bed in the morning, Vivienne had figured he had gone to shower and change, and would come back.

Impatiently, she ran to the door, and yanked it open before Sébastien could knock. "Come in!"

Since recollecting her past life, a feeling of completion overtook the young woman. She had not yet processed all the memories, but they were there, in her subconscious, waiting to be called out. Finally, she had control and understanding of the phenomena – and she was not crazy.

Vivienne was so lost in her own happiness, she did not immediately notice there was something wrong with Sébastien. When he stepped inside, Alistair lifted his head off the couch with a weird whine.

"Lady Vivienne, we have to talk." The formality in Sébastien's tone had the effect of a cold bucket of water being thrown over her.

"What are you—" Vivienne inched towards him, but he backed away, not meeting her eyes. Instead, he kept his stare firmly anchored to the wall behind her.

"What's going on, Sébastien?"

She noticed the tightness in his muscles, his blank features, and the taut jaw – in frustration or wrath, maybe both. Using the same unyielding tone, he said, "I've thought it over, and I have come to the conclusion that in order to be a proper guardian to you, I have to distance myself."

"Distance yourself?" Vivienne's brow furrowed in confusion.

"From you. We cannot be together." She watched in shock as Sébastien knelt, head bowed in submission. "Please accept my apologies for the last days. I have lived without you for too long, and I fell back into the fantasy, when the reality is quite different."

"I don't get it . . ." Vivienne stuttered, aghast. "What changed between yesterday and today?"

"My lady, nothing has. I simply believe it would be best this way."

Vivienne dropped to her knees in front of him. *Will we always be doomed to be worlds apart?*

"Sébastien, please . . ."

When he still refused to meet her searching gaze, Vivienne placed a hand to his cheek hesitantly. "I love you. Do you not know that, by now? After all these lifetimes?"

He still refused to meet her gaze. "I do, my lady. And it is due to the depth of not only your sentiments, but mine as well, that I vow not to let love interfere with my job this time. I will keep you alive, at any cost."

"Even your happiness?" she asked, barely above a whisper.

"Yes. Even so."

Sébastien's head raised slightly, the resolution in his eyes unmistakable – determined, and as serious as he had always been.

"Even at the cost of *my* happiness?" Vivienne shot back, attempting to break the wall he put up.

"You will find happiness elsewhere," he declared evenly. "I believe it is due to my past weakness that I have been unable to save you. This time will be different."

"So you'll witness me with another man?"

There was a flicker of anguish in Sébastien's eyes, which

passed so swiftly she was not sure if it had been imagined. "If he can care for you and bring you joy, then yes . . .my lady."

Vivienne stood up before Sébastien could notice her gathering tears. It took all her strength, but she pulled it from memories of the royal bloodline running through her veins.

"That will be all for today, Dubois. Leave me." She was proud when her voice came out strong, and unwavering.

There was a pause, the air shifting behind as Sébastien also stood. "Good day, Vivienne. I will supervise from the outskirts for now. If you require my presence, you've only to call."

When she glanced behind, a few moments later, he was gone. It was only then Vivienne slumped to the ground, letting the sobs wash over. Alistair was by her side in an instant, finally unfrozen from his shock by her misery.

"What happened here? What did you say to him!?" Vivienne beseeched, tears streaming down her cheeks uncontrollably.

Alistair lay down and placed his head on her knees. *I had nothing to do with this, I swear. When I went to Sébastien yesterday, it was to bring him here to help with your memories. The last thing I want is your unhappiness, highness.*

"What's the point of it all?" Vivienne cried out in despair. "Why bring this all back, only to lose it again?"

Alistair peered over her shoulder at the closed door, and rumbled, *Respect his wishes, majesty. For now, at least. There has to be something here we are both missing, but I vow to find out what it is.*

Somehow, Vivienne dragged herself to the bed, where she drifted into a restless sleep. Her heart felt like it had been torn apart, and she did not think recovering would be possible. The sentiment of loss was unbearable, but if Sébastien truly decided this, she would not beg, nor ask for more.

I've been without him for years, and survived. Surely I can keep doing it – magic or no magic.

* * *

Alistair waited until his mistress was dormant, then snuck out and continued to Sébastien's place. He made sure to leave behind a defensive spell, in case anyone came lurking by.

Down the quiet street, he blew a breath of magic towards Sébastien's door, unlocking it with his mind. When he entered, the guardian was sitting on the balcony, forlorn. There was an unsteady aura around him, edged with desperation.

What happened to you? Alistair enquired flat out.

Sébastien turned to him, his gaze so drunk with agony and liquor, it was puzzling at best. "Let me be, Alistair. I'm not in the mood for lectures."

You are mistaken, I am not here to lecture. Vivienne is hurting, and you caused this. The least you could do is be honest and explain why.

"I've already explained." With a heavy groan, Sébastien slid down to the ground, and emptied the remaining of his drink in one shot.

That's bullshit and you know it. Last night, you were in bed with her. This morning, you leave and come back a different man.

At Sébastien's stubborn silence, Alistair put a paw on his

leg, nudging. *Is it Carleigh? Did you run into him too?*

Something shifted in the knight. His head snapped to the dog, with an alert and focused regard, despite his obvious inebriation. "What do you mean? I didn't run into him. At all."

I did, last night, when I tried to speak with Merlin. Had a nice showdown . . . I will spare you the details. Suffice to say, I lost.

"What happened? And how the hell did he manage to come back?"

Alistair hesitated in responding. Sébastien's aura was stretched enough, without the added information of the battle he had fought. However, they both had a job to do, and knowledge was key for both of them.

I got my ass kicked, Alistair answered the first question. *Carleigh formed a deal with darkness to return, so naturally, he is much stronger than before. And in terms of what he aspires to, well, he has definite father issues, and blames Vivienne for Merlin casting him away.*

"That's nothing new," Sébastien muttered, turning away in disinterest.

No, but the way he's going about it, is. Alistair waited until the guardian met his gaze again, before delivering the last bit of information he possessed. *Carleigh is planning to defile Vivienne's white magic, and accumulate it for himself.*

"Damn it all to hell!"

In one burst of bitterness, Sébastien stood up and flung the glass against the wall, then kicked the first thing in his path – which happened to be a heavy table. He did not notice the discomfort on his leg, but rather continued on a rampage, hitting anything in his way, lost in his own dark thoughts.

The result Carleigh hoped to achieve, Sébastien could have handed him on a platter. The realization was unnerving, and even more so was the fact Merlin had been right all along!

From the beginning, the old man must have comprehended the threats they were facing. Now it all made sense, further fueling Sébastien's rage, to the point he turned the entire living room to shambles in mere moments.

After a particularly heavy punch to the wall, Alistair leapt out of the way, narrowly avoiding a bookshelf hitting him. Having had enough, he lunged, throwing his entire weight on Sébastien. They ended up back on the ground, the dog's paws weighing heavily on the man's shoulders.

What is the matter with you!?

"Vivienne will not be exploited," Sébastien snarled, an agonized tone to his voice. "I will make sure of it."

Alistair searched his expression, barely having time to notice the almost desperate determination animating him, before Sébastien's features smoothed in an unreadable mask. Only his eyes showed flickers of the anguish lurking beneath the surface.

"Leave me alone, Alistair. Tonight, at least."

The demon dog hesitated. This man had once been his friend, and partner. Together, they had protected Vivienne in the past. *What has changed? What am I missing?*

With one last shake of the head at the chaos left behind, Alistair gave in and retreated to his mistress' home. He could not understand the sudden change in Sébastien any more than Vivienne could.

CHAPTER 8

Vivienne returned to the castle from the forest, not quite aware of where she was heading. It was no surprise when she slammed straight into something solid, and lost her balance. The fall was stopped as a strong pair of arms reached out and grabbed at her waist.

"My apologies," she mumbled, "I was not paying attention to where—"

The words got stuck in her throat when her green eyes collided with his. "Sébastien," Vivienne whispered, a blush filling her cheeks.

The guardian peered down, with the intense stare that was his trademark, as though assessing her very soul. When the noise of their surroundings got past Sébastien's scrutiny, he blinked as though dazed, and let go of her waist.

"Lady Vivienne," he bowed.

The princess stood there, missing his heat, and having the most peculiar craving to be closer again. She bit her lip, muttered something non-committal, and retreated before the urge to do something foolish took control.

Sébastien was left staring after her, wondering if maybe – just maybe – Vivienne was affected by his presence as well.

* * *

Vivienne woke up from yet another memory. As if to spite her, now that Sébastien was gone, they came more and more.

Alistair was by the bed, watching her worriedly. Two days had passed since the talk with Sébastien, and it had been complete radio silence on both ends.

She wiped away the tears on her cheeks, and picked up her ringing cell phone, which had woken her up.

"Hello?" Vivienne croaked.

"Viv?" Jennifer's voice was tinted with concern.

"Yeah," she rolled her eyes, staring at the ceiling. "What is it, Jen?"

Vivienne was still annoyed at her friend for being nosy, but the current predicament took precedence. She had no stamina to waste on petty fights.

There was a pause, then, "Are you alright?"

Vivienne waited a beat, and repeated, "What do you want?"

"I was checking in, hoping we might meet for coffee."

"I'm not in the mood."

"Listen, Viv," Jennifer started hesitantly, "I get that I've been a nosy bitch, but I care about you. And, well, it sounds like you might need a friend right now."

Alistair let out a low growl, enough for Vivienne to capture, but not enough to be heard through the phone.

"Alright, coffee," she sighed. "I'm bringing Alistair with me, though."

"Great."

Vivienne chuckled a bit at Jennifer's less than enthusiastic tone, and disconnected the call.

I do not agree with this idea, Alistair pointed out shortly after. Following the showdown with Guinevere, it was taking the dog's entire self-control to keep hiding the truth from his mistress.

If he ceased to exist for revealing things which should not yet be revealed, she would be without defense – and that, he could not accept, especially considering Sébastien's changing moods.

"Well, it's not like I have anything better to do today."

Vivienne got out of bed, but Alistair advanced and blocked her path. *You should talk to Sébastien.*

"No." Vivienne tried to maneuver around him, but his rather enormous body was right in her path, not budging.

Then let me talk to him, Alistair insisted.

"Need I remind you that you tried two days ago?" she scowled. "And it didn't end well. Drop it, Al. It's definitive – me and him, we're done. He prefers to be a guardian? Then that's what I'll allow him."

Your pride is getting in the way of your thinking, highness, Alistair rumbled wisely, but it fell on deaf ears.

"Perhaps. But I was not born to beg, and I will not even for the sake of love. Now, are you coming with me to meet Jennifer, or what?"

With lots of grumbling from Alistair, Vivienne got dressed, put on his leash – *Humiliating!* he grouched – and strolled over to the coffee shop a few blocks away.

Jennifer, much like last time, was already there. Next to her radiant beauty and designer-clad body, Vivienne felt like crap, donning sweatpants and a long-sleeved shirt.

"Honey, you look like you haven't been resting properly!" Jennifer greeted, her voice dripping with fake worry.

Alistair snorted, causing her to glare down at him, intent to stare him down. He lunged in a flash, teeth bared, and Vivienne barely held him back in time from snapping her friend's pretty neck.

"Alistair, what the hell!" Vivienne complained, missing Jennifer's less than shocked expression. "Sit."

He listened, though begrudgingly, and rumbled in her head, *She is fake, Vivienne. Cut her loose – the sooner, the better.*

The enchantress ventured a dark look towards him, an eyebrow raised in silent questioning.

I cannot explain it, Alistair continued, then had to stop, already perceiving the tug of the past.

Something similar to the current collar around his neck was suffocating him, reminding him of his duties. The demon dog knew he had to do things different this time around, as his existence depended on it, and so settled for an evasive warning. *There is something about her . . .*

Vivienne sighed – yet another secret. Before she could say anything to him, Jennifer sat down in front of her.

"So, how have you been?"

"Good," Vivienne mumbled, annoyance creeping up at what she guessed would soon turn into the Spanish Inquisition of gossip, as per Jennifer's habit.

Alistair observed his mistress, taking in the whitened knuckles clasping tightly to the leash, and raised his gaze up to her blank countenance. He glanced quickly to the other woman, who was busy talking, and back to Vivienne.

His eyes glowed for a brief moment, even as he inspected past the physical form, to detect the aura beyond it. It was a soft glow surrounding a person, and in Vivienne's case, it currently flared red at certain spots, as though she was angry.

The dog desperately wished to fill her in on the reason for her oddly instinctual reaction to her so-called friend. With a heavy sigh, he settled his head down on the ground.

"Are you still seeing that guy?" Jennifer asked, an edge to her voice.

Wow, she definitely has a knack for going straight to the point, Alistair commented.

Vivienne shrugged, concealing the anguish and keeping with the indifference. "No."

Jennifer's eyes widened, and she was about to add something, but one peek at Alistair dissuaded her. Instead, she followed it by saying, "How about a girls' night out tonight?"

Vivienne shrugged, and waved the server away without order anything. Instead of committing, she asked, "How've you been, anyway?"

"Oh, just peachy."

It was Vivienne's turn to arch an eyebrow at her tone.

"Found out the guy I was dating cheated on me," Jennifer elaborated.

"The one from the bar?"

"Same one."

"Are you actually surprised? He was sleazy."

"Mm. Guess so. Well, not everyone can get the good ones like you." As she said it, Jennifer took a sip of her coffee, with an odd glint in her eyes that Vivienne could not place.

"What the hell are you implying?" she frowned.

"Oh, come on! You've always gotten the nice guys."

Vivienne shrugged, unwilling to get into the matter. "Anyway, so what about this guy?" Her attempt to change the topic did not go unnoticed by Alistair.

"Yeah, well he can go to hell," Jennifer snorted. "Seriously, let's have a girls' night tonight, and we can find guys to make us laugh."

That's not a good idea, Alistair grumbled.

Too bad, Vivienne replied mentally to him, not entirely sure he would capture it. A shake of his head a moment later informed her the message had been well received.

With another shrug, she nodded to Jennifer, then got up and grabbed Alistair's leash. "I'll see you tonight."

* * *

Later that day, Vivienne stared in the mirror at her slinky little black dress and smoky eye makeup. She had never gone heavy on artificial enhancements, but the effect tonight was eye-catching, to say the least.

"Guess I don't look much like my old self either. Right, Alistair?"

The dog contemplated the outfit, and left the room

without a word. Vivienne shrugged off his disappointment and headed out.

* * *

Alistair waited until Vivienne was gone, then left the house. It was imperative he got to Sébastien, in all haste. When he arrived at the house, the lamps were still on, and he entered like last time.

Sébastien walked into the living room at the sound of the door opening. He had a feeling the dog would return at some point or another.

"What's wrong?"

He seemed as worn out as Vivienne, with dark circles under the eyes and the shadow of a beard.

It's Vivienne, Alistair rushed. *She is upset with you, and does not grasp why you did what you did. She's headed to a bar tonight. I fear Carleigh will use this to his advantage.*

"I'm on it."

With rushed movements, Sébastien grabbed a leather jacket and slid a gun in the waistband of his jeans, then dropped his shirt over to hide it. He was halfway out the door when Alistair, dutiful to the end, added, *And, Sébastien? Do not lose focus.*

"What's that supposed to mean?" the knight frowned over his shoulder.

You'll see, was the cryptic response.

* * *

Sébastien drove in the Jag, speeding among the cars, and arrived at the bar in record time. He entered through the back, and immediately scanned the crowd. It did not take him long to find both Vivienne and Guinevere.

They were by the bar, and men were buying them drinks. It also did not take him long to get Alistair's cryptic warning.

If Sébastien previously had issues with restraint around Vivienne – when she was not even trying to be sexy – they all slipped away when his eyes landed on her. In the little black dress Vivienne wore, she was absolutely stunning.

Like a moth to a flame, Sébastien was drawn, and all he longed to do was drag her away and run his hands all over her body. Apparently, some of the men had similar ideas in mind, as one in particular was in Vivienne's personal space.

Sébastien observed her edginess as she examined the crowd. Their eyes met across the distance, and almost as if pulled by an invisible thread, they stepped to each other.

Vivienne could not believe he was there. How Sébastien had even realized where she was, would remain a mystery. Then again, as a guardian, he would have ways. Jennifer approached them, grabbing her hand and breaking their stare-down.

Her friend glanced at Sébastien warily, then smirked at Vivienne – again, that uneasy sensation. It kept happening where Jennifer was concerned, each stronger than the last.

"Are you okay?" Jennifer asked Vivienne, caring as always. At her nod, she went on, "You look great, by the way! Don't know what you're doing differently, but you're glowing, girl."

The compliments fell on deaf ears, as Vivienne responded

with a tight-lipped smile.

"Is your date joining you?" Jennifer asked.

"No," Vivienne replied in a frosty tone, before she could stop herself. Either Jennifer was playing dumb or, in the dimness of the bar, she did not recognize Sébastien was the same man as last time.

Sébastien inched by, his lips near Vivienne's ear. "I'll be around if you need my assistance."

She ignored him, and concentrated instead on Jennifer, who grinned widely.

"Well then, come on! It's time to have fun."

Vivienne let her friend drag her away from Sébastien, welcoming the escape. The way his eyes devoured her created a yearning for things she could not have. Distance was, after all, the guardian's wish.

* * *

How did it feel, Vivienne wondered, for Sébastien to witness another man's arm around her shoulders, his mouth close to her ear, making her laugh?

And yet inside, she was dying, only wanting him around to murmur tender words. How she wished they had been born in different worlds!

When the dance ended, Vivienne turned to leave, but her current dance partner yanked her towards him. "Where are you going, beautiful? I'm not done with you."

"Oh, but I am," Vivienne snapped through gritted teeth, trying to shove him away.

Next thing she knew, a force of nature came between

them both, drawing her away. Vivienne found herself tucked under Sébastien's rather large muscled arm, with his hand firm on her waist, gripping her tightly.

"I suggest you drop it," Sébastien advised the man.

"Oh yeah? And who the hell are you?" he shot back, eyes squinting nastily.

"No one you want to mess around with."

Vivienne could perceive the possessiveness in his grip, the alpha male coming to the surface, even if no one else did.

When the man ignored him and went to clutch her hand regardless, Sébastien seized his neck and hurled him against the nearest wall. He got up and tried to punch, but the guardian evaded it and hit his gut with such energy he slammed him against the stone once more.

The loud thud echoed off, and some people in the vicinity turned to stare despite the loud music. The man dropped to the ground, grunting in pain and clutching his stomach.

"Let's go," Sébastien grumbled, grabbing Vivienne's hand and dragging her away.

They got as far as the car – and only because the young woman let him lead – but the minute he let go to open the door, she exploded.

"What the *hell* do you think you're doing!?"

"Shielding you." Sébastien's features were a stormy mask in the dimness, his nostrils flaring in anger.

He went to grab her waist to maneuver Vivienne in the car, but she shoved him back.

"Don't you dare get near me!"

Sébastien closed his eyes for a mere second, almost as if annoyed, and snatched her regardless. Vivienne assumed he was about to push her in the car, and aimed all her energy towards deflecting that. Thus, she was completely unprepared for what he actually did.

Which was, he kissed her.

Then Sébastien took advantage of Vivienne's surprise and pushed her in the car anyway.

Bastard.

* * *

Neither of them spoke on the way to the house. As Sébastien accompanied Vivienne to the door, she could not help from biting out, "I was under the impression you being my bodyguard implies you don't get to be personal."

Sébastien stiffened, muscles freezing into place. The action was echoed in the vibrations coming off him. Vivienne was conscious of his every breath, without even looking at him.

Hesitantly, the guardian conceded, "I was out of line, I admit. But the situation needed defusing."

"Next time, keep your hands and lips off me."

Vivienne moved inside and closed the door behind, ignoring Sébastien's stricken look as her words echoed in the air.

* * *

Long after she was out of the car, Sébastien stayed behind, keeping an eye out. The lamps turned on in the house, and shadows drifted. He waited until Vivienne's bedroom light went out, and only then headed home.

Her words had been piercing arrows to his chest. Sébastien had not intended to act that way, not after the heartfelt speech from days earlier, but had simply been unable to control himself.

When his phone beeped, he examined it as one would a snake. A gloom settled on his shoulders when he saw the caller ID. Sébastien swerved into an alleyway, and headed in a different direction than the house – it was time for work.

* * *

Hours later, the guardian got out of the shower stall and entered his dim living room, heading straight to the bottle of scotch. After the night's events, sleep would not be easy.

I have kept my distance, but now I am running out of patience.

At Alistair's words, the guardian whirled around to notice the dog lounging on a sofa, eyes glaring back. *I will not stand around to have you two dance around each other over and over again like in the past. There is simply no time for this. What is it you hide, that eats at you so?*

Sébastien stared at Alistair for a beat, then wordlessly walked to the laundry bin and yanked out the shirt he had thrown in half an hour earlier. The bloody rag landed on the carpet in front of the dog.

He squinted down, then back up at Sébastien questioningly. *What is this?*

"My life now. I'm not the good knight of the past, Alistair. I'm as reprobate as they come." He followed the

| 197

statement by downing half his glass.

Alistair got off the couch, and cautiously approached the garment. He sniffed it, then raised his incredulous gaze to Sébastien. *You kill people?*

Another gulp of alcohol, then Sébastien said, "I get results."

Alistair paused, trying to find his words. This was a development he had not foreseen. *Where is this coming from?*

Sébastien exhaled heavily, then grabbed the entire decanter of scotch and sat down on the sofa next to the huge dog. "It's a long story, but I'll start with when you died. After Merlin got his wish, and Vivienne became Lady of the Lake, they did not speak. As a result, when Carleigh attacked for the last time, we were not prepared. He got to me first, in order to weaken Vivienne."

He refilled his glass and continued, "I'm not sure what happened, but when I woke up, Vivienne was on the ground, and Merlin was there. Together, the two of us managed to stop Carleigh, but by the time we did, it was too late to save Vivienne. Right before she died, Carleigh cursed her. He aimed the words to destroy our soul mate bond, as well as her future potential."

What was the curse? Alistair asked.

"That Vivienne would not be reborn until my soul became dark. When she died, I begged Merlin to let me die of my injuries, that way I would be reborn and do my best to bring her back. We both knew she would be the salvation of the new world if Carleigh ever emerged again. So, in the last two lifetimes, I've done exactly that. And I've acquitted myself of the task admirably, I suppose."

He snickered sardonically. "So much so, Merlin himself thought it imperative to mess with my dreams and warn me I cannot be with Vivienne anymore, because I can tarnish her."

When Sébastien was done recounting the full story, the demon dog's eyes were filled with pity. *You had a choice in the matter, and you chose right in bringing Vivienne back. But you have to find a way to forgive yourself. As for what Merlin mentioned, I do not believe your love could, in any way, taint Vivienne.*

"It doesn't matter anymore," Sébastien shrugged. "When she finds out, Vivienne will abhor me, guardian or not."

I have told you this once before – you underestimate her feelings for you.

Shortly after, once Sébastien had gone to sleep, Alistair rose and left. He had his answer, miserable as it was. *Time to find a solution.*

* * *

It was night when Vivienne took a midnight stroll, Alistair by her side. She was not aware that a few feet away, under cover of trees and bushes, Sébastien matched her pace, keeping an eye out for danger.

"Lady Vivienne!"

The shout had come from far behind. As she whirled, the princess noticed Lancelot running towards her. Alistair barked, once, and advanced in front of his mistress, intimidating in his posture with his teeth bared.

"Yes, Lancelot?" Vivienne enquired when he was near.

The younger knight hesitated, evidently afraid of Alistair.

"You should not be strolling the grounds alone."

"I dare say I have managed quite well so far." For some reason, that particular night, Vivienne could not stand the knight's sickening sweet demeanor, which previously she might have found charming. Her thoughts were occupied with another man altogether.

"My lady –" Lancelot commenced.

Vivienne's eyes narrowed, and her voice came out frosty. *"I am not* your *lady, Lancelot, and it is a lack of respect to be using that term. You will address me as Lady Vivienne."*

The confusion in the guard's eyes was not faked. At the exact moment, Alistair telepathically pointed out to her, *"Yet you let your new guard call you so."*

Vivienne ignored them both, despite having the distinct impression Alistair was laughing at her.

Lancelot glowered at the dog, mumbled an *"As you wish,"* and left. Vivienne resumed her walk with Alistair.

In the shadows, Sébastien smirked, before Alistair's voice came to him. *"Lancelot is irritating. There is something odd I sense around him. You have to keep him away from Vivienne."*

Masking his shock, the guardian became pensive. *"It would be hard, considering her sentiments for him."* He did not realize the words thought could be heard, until the dog's reply.

"You humans truly amaze me, always missing the obvious," Alistair snorted in response, then went silent as Sébastien pondered his words in confusion.

Sébastien continued his watch over Vivienne from the shadows as she strode around. When she approached the lake and called on her magic, he could not help but stare at her *beauty and grace under the full moon.*

The princess had bewitched him without even trying to, and it seemed the entire realm of Elsior was in the same situation.

The moon flashed brighter, and a headache hit Sébastien unawares. Images came to his head – fragments of holding her hand, embraces under the moonlight. His body tightened with the memories, even as he was filled with a desperate longing that nearly crippled him.

At the tumult he felt coming from Sébastien, Alistair stopped his observation of Vivienne and glanced to the shadows. He expanded his mind in an invisible mist, until it attained the knight's thoughts. Hesitantly at first, then more boldly, he probed deeper for the notions, capturing them at the surface, and the aura surrounding him.

In this particular case, when their intellects came into contact, the demon dog's entire body tensed in dismay at the images he found there. It could not be . . . Was there truly more going on with the two lovebirds than they could all discern?

"Come be a good doggie for once, Alistair," Vivienne implored under the moon, and he turned back to her. With a playful growl, the demon dog splashed in the water at her request.

At the sound of laughter, Sébastien was able to catch his breath. The memories faded away, but the longing within his mind and body remained. He willed himself to stay in the shadows, and focus on protecting Vivienne.

Despite his best efforts, the pounding headache remained. The silence he forced upon himself tired him further, but the guardian survived through it for the next hours. When Vivienne retreated to her room safely, he dragged himself to his quarters and promptly passed out.

Alistair waited until Vivienne was dormant, then returned to the lake and the full moon. He gazed at the midnight sky, opening his mind and soul, and reached deep within where his old deity abilities rested. Finally, he was prepared to voice a query.

The dog's entire being was surrounded by a midnight glow, and he waited until the earth shifted under his feet, nature settling to listen. When the only noise was his breath, Alistair dared to enquire, "What are they to each other?"

The lake, previously calm, swirled for a few moments, as a vortex would. Once it settled, the reflection of the moon had changed. Alistair watched, transfixed, as the future played out – Sébastien and Vivienne's fates intertwined, and the incoming trouble.

When he peered back up at the moon, the wind whispered, "Salvation or destruction, that is their fate, as it has been for centuries in their past lives."

With a low whine, Alistair went back to his mistress, pondering the newfound knowledge and what to do with it.

* * *

Vivienne woke up from the memory, drenched in sweat. *Will it never end?* she wondered, with the sinking realization that it would not. She and Sébastien had a shared history, and despite maintaining a distance romantically, they had to figure out a way to work together.

The young woman still had to learn to use incantations as she had in the past, and a guard was required whilst so doing. Furthermore, Sébastien knew everything that had happened, and his information and intuition would be useful while fighting Carleigh.

He had been a great bodyguard in the past, and Vivienne still trusted him with her safety. *Perhaps it would be possible to keep a professional relationship, despite the complications.*

With a sigh, Vivienne picked up her cell and dialed Sébastien's number, before better judgment kicked in.

"Hello?"

Vivienne ignored the way the sound of his voice, rough from sleep, caused her stomach to tighten in a knot of desire and longing.

"We have to talk," she said instead.

There was a pause, then Sébastien replied, "I'll be there in ten."

* * *

Vivienne's call had come as a welcome surprise, though for a moment Sébastien dreaded Alistair had revealed his secret. That was before he remembered what the dog had mentioned about being unable to interfere directly, only at the most with a nudge, due to his fallen from grace status.

Sébastien realized it was simply Vivienne's need to comprehend that had prompted the call. Although he could not be as honest as with Alistair, perhaps he could explain enough to stop the recklessness that seemed to power his beloved. Last night's events were still ingrained in his imagination, not likely to disappear anytime soon.

When he arrived at the house and knocked, there was no response, but the door swung open of its own accord. Sébastien entered, carrying coffee and bagels.

He was sipping out of the cup when Vivienne walked out of the kitchen, wearing a red satin nightgown. The sight of her – dressed like *that* – caused him to ungraciously spit the coffee out.

Vivienne's eyes widened when she noticed him standing in the middle of her living room. "You could have called when you were close!" she yelled in accusation.

"Umm . . ." was Sébastien's less than intelligent retort, as the nightgown covering her body left little to the imagination. Her angry glare changed to confused, before realization dawned.

Blushing crimson, Vivienne ran out of the kitchen, up the stairs to the bedroom, and Sébastien was left staring at the spot where she had been, fighting his own body's desires. *A cold shower would have been a good idea before coming.*

Vivienne returned after a few minutes, this time wearing a pair of sweatpants and a t-shirt. Avoiding her eyes, Sébastien tried for another gulp of coffee, extending the untouched cup towards her.

She refused it, surveying him warily now, the blush long gone. Sébastien noticed the pallor of her skin, and the circles under her eyes. He had to bite back the words of concern trying to escape – in her current state, the enchantress would not appreciate it.

Instead, he moved to place the coffee and bagels on the table.

"What do you think you're doing?" Vivienne asked,

suspicion tinting her voice.

Unburdened with the edible gifts, Sébastien faced her once more. "For starters, my lady, I'd like to feed you. And perhaps to explain myself."

Wrong words, Alistair mumbled from the couch.

"Shut it, Alistair," Vivienne's eyes narrowed his way. "I assume you let him in?"

The dog bowed his head in the opposite direction, ears bent backwards in remorse.

Sébastien frowned at Vivienne's icy tone of voice, so unlike her. At least she was not the same as at the bar, though the image of her in the black dress, with the devil-may-care attitude, would be forever ingrained in his recollections.

"I understand you might not want to listen," Sébastien tried again, "but you've been piecing together the past. Before . . ."

He trailed off as Vivienne crossed her arms defensively, afraid it was already a lost cause. Considering she was not running away – yet – he forced a deep breath, and restarted. "Before we became lovers in the past, and I let the attraction between us fail me at my job, I was a defender, and a friend. Please, let me be that again."

Sébastien met Vivienne's stare steadily, letting her assess his honesty. After a few moments, her gaze drifted to the coffee and bagels.

"Alright, Sébastien," she agreed tiredly. "We'll try it your way. It was, I have to admit, the reason I called you here. Working professionally is my hope for us, as well."

"Glad to hear it, my lady." He tried to ignore the dullness spreading in his chest at Vivienne's quick assent. Instead, he forced a cheerful tone. "So, what's on the agenda today?"

Sébastien watched Vivienne as she snatched the coffee, but left behind the bagel.

"Well, I wanted to practice magic, use some defensive techniques and work on anything rusty. The lake we went to together would be perfect, away from tourists, and the water should help me concentrate. At least, that's my guess based on what I've been remembering."

The knight glanced to Alistair, who pretended he was not listening. With no sign from him of the contrary, he said, "Alright. It might be a bit too far, but there's a spot by the river Rhône that's also quiet. How about it?" At her curt nod, Sébastien tried for a grin. "I'll drive you. But first, please eat something."

Rolling her eyes, Vivienne grabbed half of the bagel, and munched on it. It was a start, and one Sébastien was grateful for.

* * *

The drive to the Rhône was hushed, and even Alistair remained silent on the back seat. Sébastien had informed them the secluded spot was not far from the park where they had been attacked, and Vivienne could practice there, away from preying eyes, so they let him lead.

The entire time, Vivienne was uncomfortably aware of the precarious position they – her and Sébastien – were both in, due to the past.

She had been honest – or so she kept telling herself. But then the burning look in his eyes that morning, and her quickening heartbeat around him, said otherwise.

Vivienne was distracted from her musings at Alistair's panicked command. *Turn around!*

"What?" She twisted in the seat to frown at him, but the dog's opaque eyes were focused on something ahead. His nose had picked the scent first, and now his extended senses perceived the black arts.

Turn around, Alistair repeated. *We are not alone, and they have prepared an ambush. Druids, lots of them. I sense them waiting for us up ahead.*

Vivienne's eyes widened, and she glanced at Sébastien, but the guardian was already shifting gears. In one swift move, he did a U-turn, and pressed on the accelerator as they retreated the opposite way.

"You okay?" Sébastien asked her, jaw tight with tension.

"Quite, yeah," Vivienne reassured him. "We avoided trouble, but now I'll have to find somewhere else to practice."

Perhaps at home, for now, Alistair suggested warily.

Vivienne groaned – she had wanted to avoid neighbors potentially witnessing her magic. But seeing as there was no other option, it was a risk they would have to take.

She leaned back in the seat, and looked out the window for the rest of the drive.

* * *

Guinevere lounged on the sofa, sipping wine in a nightgown, when Braydon strode out of the darkness of a particular corner. She jumped, startled, and some of the wine spilled on the brand new leather couch.

"You could have called ahead," she grumbled, schooling her features in a blank mask. She was hoping against all odds that her trembling hands went unnoticed.

Braydon was not fooled – fear was in every bone of Guinevere's being since their last encounter. He searched deep within himself for an ounce of remorse, but none stirred. Yet he approached his accomplice gently, as one would a frightened doe, since he still needed her cooperation.

"Darling, I have a task for you."

Guinevere arched an eyebrow, still trying to appear disinterested. Nonetheless, a glint of interest appeared in her calculatingly cold eyes. "Do tell."

"You have to cause some chaos. The two lovebirds are too lovey dovey, and my master's main necessity is time. They have to be close enough so they will be destroyed when Carleigh finally breaks them apart, but not *too* close – they cannot get back together."

"Neither of us wants that," Guinevere scowled.

"Indeed." Braydon neared her, raising a hand to caress her cheek. When she flinched away, he grabbed her chin, forcing her to meet his icy stare. "You will do a superb job of interfering, won't you?"

In a complete turn of personality, Guinevere stretched against him, her supple body pliant and eager. "And my reward?"

"It shall be grand indeed," Braydon smiled thinly, before dropping his mouth to hers in a bruising kiss.

CHAPTER 9

A few hours later, Sébastien was restlessly pacing in the living room of Vivienne's house, when his pack pocket buzzed. He pulled out the cell, eyes narrowing at the text message with the unfamiliar address.

With a sigh, he went out in the backyard. Vivienne was sitting cross-legged on the ground, twirling her index finger in the air. The motion would have seemed ridiculous, if not for the water answering her call, and the pool itself following the movement of its mistress.

As Sébastien watched for a few moments, the enchantress paused the action, and instead spread an entire palm, raising it up in the air. The liquid lifted with it, in the shape of a thin wall, and formed a defensive barrier.

Sébastien shook his head in an effort to break the entrancement he had fallen into. "I have to leave," he announced, his tone a tad too brisk.

Vivienne's gaze flew to his, and the wall she had created splashed in the pool. Alistair elevated his head off the lounge chair. *Where are you going?*

"I have to handle some stuff," Sébastien responded warily, as Vivienne's eyes flashed with annoyance and hurt. "I'll call you later," he added. To Alistair, he said, "Take care of her."

He left before the situation escalated, ignoring Alistair's watchful glint. His old pal evidently knew where he was headed, but kept silent.

Later, once Sébastien got home after finishing a job for Tony, it had neared evening. He checked his cell, but Vivienne had not called. Though he longed to hear her voice, his eyelids were growing heavy.

He grunted upon hitting the bed, unable to muster the initiative to budge. The new bruises on his body were wretched, and a rest was most needed before heading out again.

Overwhelmed by fatigue, Sébastien did what any normal man would do, and allowed his mind to go blank, drifting off within moments. It was not long before a memory swam to the surface, invading his dreams . . .

* * *

"You look like crap."

Sébastien blew out an angry breath, wiping the cold water off his face. He forced himself to count to ten, before raising his gaze and meeting Lancelot's sneer.

"Not in the mood, Lance," the knight grunted.

"So I notice. Late night?" the younger man leered with a knowing expression.

"I suppose." Or more to the point, an agonizingly short night. After watching over Vivienne all evening and part into the night, he had barely managed to sleep for a few hours before the morning sun rose.

"Who's the lucky wench?"

Sébastien whirled around to retort, but the words died on his lips when he noticed they were not alone. Vivienne was frozen in her tracks behind Lancelot, looking refreshed – if a little pale. There was an odd glint of betrayal in the princess' eyes, bewildering to him.

"My lady," he bowed, "anything I can help you with?"

Vivienne tried to ignore the tug at her heart, but could not forget Lancelot's words. Sébastien had been with a woman, of course he had. He was young, gorgeously irresistible and free. He spent all day with her, which implied the nights were his to enjoy alone – and he obviously had.

Vivienne rapidly scanned the bloodshot eyes and dark circles of her guardian, and came to the same conclusion Lancelot had. She willed her expression to remain neutral, even as she answered in an even voice, "No, I am quite fine, Dubois."

Sébastien arched an eyebrow in question. Vivienne only used his last name when mad at him. Yet for all intents and purposes, her tone was neutral – or so he thought.

"And please refrain from calling me your lady," she added as an afterthought. "Lady Vivienne will do just fine."

The knight's expression became a full-blown glower at

her words. Out of the corner of his eyes, Sébastien noted Lancelot's victorious grin, and gritted his teeth. On edge now more than before, he bowed respectfully to Vivienne. "I apologize."

She ignored the gesture, and instead turned to Lancelot. "Someone has to accompany me to Merlin's, for some supplies."

"At your service, Lady Vivienne."

Before Sébastien could intervene, they were gone, leaving him angry enough to punch a wall. He marched down to the blacksmith's forge instead, to sharpen his sword and work off the frustration.

The knight was unaware of how much time had passed, when a voice rumbled in his head. "When I urged you to keep Lancelot away from Vivienne, I was not referring to a permanent solution. Temporary and with no blood shed will do just fine."

Sébastien whirled to see Alistair sitting down, eyes glowing in amusement.

"You sure about that?" he muttered, then went back to work, his strokes heavier than before.

"Quite."

"I cannot understand it. It was fine calling her 'my lady' and now I cannot. And she accepted Lancelot's presence around her. The idea of them together—"

At the sudden growl coming from the demon dog, Sébastien stopped, astonished. Alistair had bared his teeth, red flames shooting from his eyes menacingly.

"You had best not be insinuating Vivienne would allow his touch, otherwise I fear my support of you as her champion *has attained its limit."*

"No!" Sébastien put both hands up as a gesture of peace. "That is not what I implied! I meant . . ." He ran a frustrated hand through his hair. "Lancelot is a player and he annoys me, and I do not like him around the princess. I can comprehend Vivienne's affection for him, but he is not worthy."

"If you dislike it so much, why not figure out how you wronged her, and fix it!"

"Because I don't know how!"

Sébastien could have sworn the dog rolled his eyes, then stared pointedly before declaring, "You look like crap."

"Not the first time I heard that today," the knight scowled.

"No . . ." Alistair stared at him for a beat, then repeated himself, this time enunciating each word. "You. Look. Like. Crap."

"Saying it as though I'm an idiot is not making this any better, demon dog."

"Goddess of all—" Alistair stopped midway, and tried a different approach. "To an outsider, it would seem like you spent all night enjoying extracurricular activities."

"What?" Sébastien frowned at the notion. "That is absurd, I was following Vivienne. You know it, you felt my presence in the woods!"

"Yes. But Vivienne does not."

"So she concluded I'm neglecting my duties? Is that why she is upset?"

This time, Alistair did roll his eyes. "My mistress is not so selfish as to not permit you free time. I believe the reason of her being upset with you is more due to what those activities might have been . . . Or with whom."

Alistair peered in amusement at the guardian as reason dawned.

"But why would she care if I'm with someone?" Sébastien wondered aloud.

"Perhaps your perception of her feelings is not quite so on the spot as you believe." At the man's blank stare, Alistair gave up and walked away, grumbling, "This is why I do not get involved in human drama."

* * *

Later that same night, Sébastien cornered Vivienne in the gardens on an evening stroll.

"Lady Vivienne," he called out formally, stepping out of the shadows.

She whirled, eyes widening when they fell upon him. Sébastien took advantage of the surprise and was by her side in two long strides. Before Vivienne had a chance to protest, he bent down on one knee. "I apologize for this morning. I did not neglect my duties last night. I—"

"Dubois, there is no need for details. It does not concern me." Vivienne's tone effectively aimed to end the conversation, but Sébastien was not about to give up.

"But it does. I was out shadowing you."

Her lips parted at the admission. "You . . .what?"

"Your father commanded me to accompany you at all times. So have Alistair and Merlin. And I have done just that, wherever you have been the last days – and nights."

Sébastien straightened his back, eyes never once wavering from hers. His burning gaze dared her to scan for the truth.

"You were up all night following me?" Vivienne wondered, gesturing for the knight to stand up, which he did.

"Yes," Sébastien admitted simply.

"Why did you not come forward?"

"Last time I did, my presence distracted you," he shrugged. "You were enjoying yourself with Alistair, and did not need another companion. I was content being a shadow."

Vivienne blinked in utter shock at the confession, and had the grace to appear contrite. "In that case, I do apologize for my behavior. I was incensed for no reason, and lashed out at you. Thank you for clearing it up."

Sébastien acquiesced, but did not leave.

"Was there anything else?" the princess asked.

"As a matter of fact, yes. Two things, really. First, I would like you to approve of me alone accompanying you when you exit the palace grounds."

A glimmer of laughter filled her eyes, but her expression remained neutral. "I can do that," Vivienne complied good-naturedly. "And the second?"

Sébastien inched closer, effectively breaking the rules, and clasped her hand in his. He did his best to ignore the heat generated where their skins grazed. "I do not call you 'my lady' out of presumptuousness or arrogance," he confessed, voice rough with emotion. "I say it with respect, because you are my charge and I intend it as a threat for anyone who would harm you, to make it known you are protected by me."

Searching her gaze, Sébastien took a deep breath, before

admitting the last bit, "*I have never in my life given an oath as powerful as the one I gave to you when we first met, believe me. If you wish me to refrain from using those two words, I will. But I preferred to explain myself.*"

Vivienne was too stunned by the champion's words to speak at first, able only to search his earnest look. The way her body reacted at his every caress was distracting, reminiscent of the strange dreams she had been having. With a supreme effort, she breathed in deeply.

"*It is fine, Sébastien,*" *she allowed, voice slightly unsteady.* "*I did not mean what I said this morning. Let us forget it and move past.*"

A shadow of a smile played on the guardian's lips when he conceded, "*As you wish, my lady.*" *He bent over her hand, lingering a few seconds longer than necessary, inhaling the skin's fragrance.*

When their fingers disentangled, he regretfully departed.

* * *

Sébastien woke up with the memory still present in his mind. He gritted his teeth at the anguish within, damning Carleigh and Merlin to all hells and beyond. Vivienne was in his head, in his heart, in his *soul*, and there was no denying the torture.

The yearning of being with her was a fire in the veins, and the need to protect her from Guinevere's presence was even stronger. Without a second thought, he took out his phone, and called Vivienne.

Though it was night time, she picked up on the third ring.

"Vivienne, are you alright?"

"Quite, yes. What do you want?"

Sébastien cringed at her abrupt tone, trying hard to steady his heart against it. He knew the enchantress was mad at his disappearance act, and for keeping a distance, but it was still hard to hear it in her voice. This time, there was no Lancelot to blame for making idiot comments.

He sighed instead, pinching the bridge of his nose with his free hand. "Are you going out tonight?"

"Yes, with Jennifer. Same bar as last time."

"I'll be there."

There was a small pause, before Vivienne said, "Fine. Anything else?"

When Sébastien did not respond, she hung up, leaving him to fall back onto the pillows with a grunt of frustration.

* * *

Later that night, Sébastien accompanied Vivienne to the bar. They had barely entered, when his cell vibrated with an unfamiliar text, ordering him to go at the back of the building. Despite previous claims he would drop the current employment, the practice of quitting was beyond complicated.

Considering a major part of Tony's operations was within the area, Sébastien was aware the stakes had exponentially increased.

He grazed Vivienne's hand to get her attention, but she withdrew as if he was a virus. Sébastien did his best to keep his features blank, mumbling a simple, "Be right back."

* * *

Vivienne had noticed the hurt in Sébastien's eyes, but his touch was more than she could handle at the moment. Being close by was complex enough, especially considering all the latest memories floating in her mind were of heated, intimate scenes from the past.

Someone tugged on her arm, and she spun to Jennifer. "Is that the same guy you were with a few weeks ago?"

Vivienne frowned at the panic in her friend's features. Or rather, the supposed concern in her voice. "Yeah, it's the same guy. So what?"

"Viv!" Jennifer clasped her arm, this time with more emphasis. "He's with the *Mafia*! That's Sébastien Dubois, it's why I rushed here!"

"What—" Vivienne stuttered, unable to comprehend and refusing to believe it. Yet at the same moment, Sébastien's words, the urgent messages and the last couple of days played in her head on a loop. It all made sense – the late phone calls, overwrought nerves, evasiveness . . .

Vivienne's keen gaze landed on Jennifer. "What have you learned about him, Jen? *How* did you learn of him?"

As if on cue, Jennifer broke eye contact, refusing to meet her gaze. Vivienne narrowed her stare, suspecting something else did not align with the narrative.

Should I tell her? Jennifer's lips did not budge, but like before at the café, the words were unmistakably hers. Alistair's warning from back then resonated in Vivienne's mind quite clearly. *Cut her loose.*

"Tell me what you know!" she commanded, eyes flashing as she yanked her arm out of Jennifer's grip.

"Only that Sébastien Dubois is a liability, and a man you

shouldn't be seen with," Jennifer started haltingly. "He works for Tony Lombardia, one of the biggest crime bosses around. The old man has underground Avignon and most of France in his pocket, one way or another. There have been rumors he's grooming people to lead his empire. Your guy is bad news, Viv, and he's *real* bad from what they mention – dangerously so. Stay away from him, please."

Her eyes were not lying, but the nagging sensation persisted. Vivienne was unsure of what to do, as her heart suggested one thing, but her head another. To gain time, she nodded.

It was then she felt it – an instinct within, a sixth sense attuned to her old guardian's vibe, blaring loudly in her mind. *Sébastien is coming.* Vivienne looked around, noticing his rapidly advancing form. She hesitated for a beat of a second, then whispered to Jennifer, "Leave us."

When he arrived by her aside a few moments later, Sébastien's eyes were on her friend's retreating back, frowning. "What did she want?"

"Never mind that, we have to talk. Now. Let's go outside."

Vivienne rushed out of the crowd, knowing he would follow. They both exited through the back, letting the door close behind, and ended up in an alley behind the bar. It was deserted, exactly as the enchantress had hoped it would be.

Taking a deep breath, Vivienne turned to Sébastien. He stood facing her, head slightly tilted, trying to figure out her odd behavior. They were almost close enough to touch, and his expression was guarded, wary. He was not her midnight visitor anymore, but rather a stranger.

Emptiness filled Vivienne, and a desperate longing for it to stop. The last couple of visions flashed in her head, and she knew there was only one way to learn for sure if Sébastien was still the same knight from the past.

Listening to her instincts, Vivienne did the only thing she could think of – threw herself in his arms and kissed him.

Sébastien's body froze, a testimony to his bewilderment. For a moment, they stood frozen, then his muscles relaxed and he wrapped both arms around his beloved's waist. He slanted his head to have better access, needing to take control of the kiss, devouring her.

Vaguely, Vivienne was aware the embrace was similar to the déjà-vus. In a way, it was even better as there was no restraint, no need to behave in a certain way. Their mouths moved in unison, their bodies fitting tightly together.

As another vision danced at the edges of Vivienne's sanity, Sébastien drew back. He held her close, whispering above her hair, "I'm so sorry, for all of this."

There was palpable regret in his tone, but reality was what hit Vivienne more as her gaze widened, focused on one thing only. When Sébastien's hand caressed first her hair, then her cheek, she noted his split knuckles and the ugly red bruises there. *Bruises gotten from punching someone.*

"It's true, isn't it?" Vivienne looked up at him with a horrified stare.

"What?" Sébastien's brow furrowed at the accusing tone.

Vivienne backed out of his embrace, instead using both arms to hug herself. Betrayal seeped through her like warm lava, followed by an icy feeling.

"Jennifer was right. You really are with the Mafia."

Sébastien did not respond, instead glancing away. *And so it starts* . . . His shoulders dropped as though he carried a huge weight.

"Answer me!" Vivienne demanded in a voice unlike her own, filled with desperation and the regal tone of her past self.

"You know why," he said. "It was necessary in order to be close to you, to shield you."

Vivienne waited a bit, but Sébastien said nothing more, still as a statue. It was with a heavy heart she asked her second question. "So this was all pretend?"

"Yes," Sébastien admitted in the same dead tone. His eyes drifted close for a mere moment, before he opened them again, and declared, "I'm here to serve and protect you, Vivienne Du Lac. At any cost."

Vivienne reached out for Sébastien, not yet knowing whether to embrace or slap him. When their hands made contact, the déjà-vu hit her without warning this time.

* * *

It was the feast the same night and Guinevere had been invited at the last minute. Her alliance to Arthur was well known, and King Adrien thought it only fair to celebrate, considering he knew both families.

Vivienne nibbled on food the entire night, and Sébastien observed every moment of it, his chest tightening with each passing moment. He glimpsed her furtive glances to Lancelot, whose eyes were glued to Guinevere, over and over.

Like a moth to a flame, the young man was already deep within the siren's clutches, and Sébastien had a hunch it would not be long before their attraction spiraled out of control.

Halfway through the feast, the princess stood up, whispered something to her father and retreated. The old man's eyes scoured the room, finding Sébastien's. With a curt nod, he excused him.

Sébastien inclined his head in agreement, and subtly left the hall. He knew King Adrien was concerned about threats lately, as was Alistair. Keeping to the shadows, he trailed behind Vivienne at a safe distance – close enough to intervene if it was necessary, yet far enough off that she would not notice.

Unaware she was being followed, Vivienne headed to her quarters, her thoughts fixated on Lancelot. She knew come the morning, Merlin had to be warned – yet again – of what she had witnessed. Arthur, according to the old wizard, was to be a great leader, but Guinevere would only ruin him.

Sliding in bed with a deep groan, Vivienne wearily concluded the entire night had only served to confirm her suspicions. Her peers were treacherous creatures, indeed.

In the hallway shadows, Sébastien waited until the door closed, and the flickering light streaming out was extinguished. He could not guess where Alistair was, but since the princess was out of harm's way, it was time for him to retreat.

The guardian's own heart, on the other hand, was in turmoil at the idea Vivienne would be dreaming of Lancelot. Shaking his head ruefully, he walked around a corner, only to run straight into said devil.

"Watch your blasted step, Dubois," Lancelot grumbled.

Sébastien said nothing, attempting to detour around. From the way the other knight stumbled about, he was beyond drunk.

Despite his best efforts, Lancelot still seized his arm. "Are you ignoring me?"

"It is not a good idea to start something right now," Sébastien warned.

"Really?" Lancelot drawled. "If I recall correctly, I drew blood at practice."

Sébastien tightened his fists with barely suppressed rage. Vivienne's countenance at the dinner flitted through his mind. "And I kicked your ass. You are quite drunk. Go sleep it off."

"What? You imagine because Lady Viv pays you some special attention, you're better than us? Hell, you're probably her chosen romp of the month—"

He did not get a chance to finish as Sébastien's fist cut him off, connecting with his jaw forcefully.

The door to Vivienne's room swung open, and she was astonished to notice Lancelot on the ground, unconscious. Sébastien towered over him, breathing heavily, his fist clenched tightly.

"What is the meaning of this?"

Sébastien peered at her, and the heat of the battle in his eyes gave way to something else – something scorching. His ardent gaze travelled up and down her body, and his nostrils flared.

When the burning ardor met her own confused stare, Vivienne realized the nightgown, with the newly lit candlelight behind her, must be transparent.

With a wave of a hand, she got a cape and covered

herself. Sébastien's eyes did not waver as Vivienne's approached him.

"I apologize, my lady," his voice sounded anything but. "The noise must have disturbed you. Lancelot had too much to drink and his words were offensive."

"To whom?"

"It does not matter."

Vivienne might have let it slide, were it not for the crackling fury, almost tangible, emanating from him. "Sébastien, I command you tell me."

"Offensive to you," he mumbled, avoiding her eyes.

"I see."

Vivienne glanced at the younger man on the floor thoughtfully. Then, with a motion of her hand, Lancelot was gone, disappeared into nothingness. Sébastien gaped at his mistress incredulously.

"Merlin has been teaching me to dematerialize things – and people," she explained with a shrug. "I sent him back to his room. He should not be privy to this conversation if his drunken intellect does, by chance, recall it tomorrow morning."

Vivienne stepped to the knight slowly.

"May I check your hand?" she asked softly, coaxingly.

Entranced, Sébastien extended his bruised fist to the enchantress. Vivienne caressed the bloodied knuckle, running a glowing palm over it, before letting the enchantment work. "How is it I keep healing your wounds?"

Sébastien's words were out before they could be stopped, in a rushed intensity. "If only I could do to the same to you, my lady."

"Heal me?" Vivienne looked up from the wound, frowning. "From what?"

The intensity was back again in Sébastien's gaze, and this time Vivienne fell prey to the sentiments urging them both on. With a groan, the knight bent his head and grazed his lips to hers. What should have been a gentle kiss turned into more when she inched near, her body melting against his.

Vivienne moaned in contentment at the soft plundering, her innocence and closeness snapping Sébastien's restraint. In one swift move, he had Vivienne pinned between the wall and himself, as the embrace brought them both deeper down a spiral of pleasure.

When his hand drifted under her cape, stroking the bare skin of her leg through the thin chemise, Vivienne gasped at the sensations. The small noise broke past Sébastien's red haze of desire, and he froze.

Realizing what he was doing, the guardian let her go at once, as though scalded. "I am so sorry, my lady. I had no right. Please forgive me."

Head dizzy from his skillful lips, Vivienne took a moment to register Sébastien was now kneeling at her feet instead of kissing her. As though it was not confusing enough, the fast-drumming pulse in her veins was untamable.

"I – it is fine, Sébastien," she managed to stutter, stepping back to her chambers and leaving the still kneeling guardian behind.

"I am a fool," the knight declared to the shadows, bowing his head.

* * *

Vivienne came to in Sébastien's arms, his worried voice

surrounding her. "Are you alright?"

She got up slowly, but steadily, and met his gaze. It was almost impossible – and too puzzling – to separate the present man from the past one, but Vivienne knew it was important to do so.

Sébastien had changed, that much was true. She could still taste the kiss from the vision, and it was apparent even in that one example the champion of the past was gone. Though Vivienne longed to trust and have faith in him, without full honesty and the details of his transformation, there was no other choice but to cut ties.

"You have your wish, Sébastien," she declared coldly. "You can stay out of my life."

"Vivienne, I—"

"No," the young woman cut him off with a determined expression. "You lied to me about your allegiances ... You lied to me about many things. I was willing to withstand the pain of maintaining a simply professional relationship with you, despite our feelings. But with this, I cannot trust you. I'd rather be surrounded by no one at all than by liars."

Sébastien sighed, running a hand through his hair in frustration, but did not contest the decision. Deep within Vivienne, his hasty surrender hurt more than all the lies, but she hid it well.

Considering the conversation finished, Vivienne was about to depart, but his next words stopped her. "In that case, you might want to re-evaluate your friendship with Jennifer."

"What are you implying?"

Sébastien shifted from one foot to the other, then haltingly admitted, "I wasn't going to mention anything, not to hide it from you, but to shelter you. She's Guinevere. I can't fathom how she reincarnated, but she did. There's no way in hell she has your best interests at heart."

On some level, Vivienne's instinct had warned there was something more to Jennifer, thus the truth Sébastien spoke made sense. "Thank you for telling me."

She approached the bar door but before opening it, spoke over her shoulder one last time. "Take care, Sébastien."

* * *

The guardian watched, unmoving, as Vivienne's disappeared within. He had already decided his next course of action was retreating to being a shadow in her entourage.

Though she did not want him around, protecting her was still his priority – an impossible one to disregard. Sébastien had promised her father long ago, as well as Merlin and Alistair. Despite everything, it was the one oath he could still keep.

Once the door closed behind his beloved, engulfing her in the dimness of the bar, Sébastien wallowed in the agony. The possibility Vivienne would abhor him once the truth was out had always been present, but he only now realized how empty his life would be without her.

The last few days with Vivienne, the romance they had lived, had been what they deserved – a peaceful life, to enjoy their love. Unfortunately, it was not what fate had dealt them.

With no other choice, Sébastien willed the pain away and slipped into the role of guardian, as he had done many times before.

* * *

Vivienne found Jennifer easily. The fake friend scanned her stormy features and got up from the group she was with. In complete silence, she led them into a private booth, where it was quieter.

"When were you going to tell me?" Vivienne demanded right away.

"About Sébastien?" the young woman frowned. "Darling, I tried, but—"

"Cut it out. I'm referring to you, *Guinevere*."

There was a brief astonishment, then her mask slipped for good, instead turning into a satisfied smirk. "Oh well, I guess the cat's out of the bag!"

"What game are you playing?" Vivienne's eyes narrowed.

Her eyes glittered with malice. "The payback one. It's quite fun, I assure you."

"Guinevere."

There was ice in Vivienne's tone, but it did not faze her old rival.

"It was fun," Guinevere sipped on a drink, "watching you blubber about, not remembering where you're coming from." She paused, then sneered, "Of course, that stupid knight of yours had to come back and ruin it all by giving you back your memories. Guess my fun's done now, hmm?"

As she drank some more, pretending nonchalance, Vivienne's anger rose like a tidal wave. With each passing moment, the enchantress was having a distressing time keeping a leash on it.

"Gosh, of course Sébastien's not the same as he was back

then, but damn, talk about being corrupt! Mafia job, couldn't go more unethical than that. I guess it means your happily ever after is off the books. Which is fine, considering you ruined mine with Lancelot!"

"You were promised to Arthur!" Vivienne exclaimed. "Do you honestly not care you broke his faith?"

Guinevere pretended to ponder it for the briefest of moments, before shrugging. "Nope, not at all. I did, however, care I couldn't get my hands on Lancelot as much as I wanted to, what with you running interference. And then, all that drama—"

The slap resounded in the tiny booth, and Guinevere clasped her reddened cheek, glaring at Vivienne hatefully.

"How *dare* you!?"

"You could have been a great queen, had you not been so busy whoring around," Vivienne retorted. "And you best realize, I not only have my memories back, but my powers too."

The wrath she had been keeping a lid on unleashed, filling her. The little wisp of spirit which arose when healing Alistair now became a full blown flood, permeating Vivienne's entire being. She gasped as it gathered right under the surface of her palms, almost burning in its heat.

There was a crack of electricity, and the bar's lights extinguished with a whoosh. The music died off at the same time, and everyone's groans echoed in discontent.

The little candle on the table between the two women was the only source of light. Whatever Guinevere observed in her rival's countenance chilled her to no end, as she got up and ran out of the bar.

Vivienne waited for a few moments, taking in deep breaths for discipline. Once calm, she stood up and left the place, in no haste to be back to a house without Sébastien.

As she stepped through the door, Alistair took one look at his mistress and got up off the couch.

What happened? he pressed, stepping closer warily. He could not tell if her expression was one of sorrow, fear, or something else entirely.

Shaking her head, Vivienne crumbled to the ground and recounted the whole story, hot tears running down her cheeks. It all came out in between sobs: the betrayal of the one she had presumed friend for years, and the break from the love of her life – past and present.

CHAPTER 10

In the stables, Sébastien was busy brushing Illyria and packing provisions. It had been over a week since their kiss, and the guardian was tired of revisiting it over and over – and over again. Vivienne had not spoken one word directly to him, other than ask for companionship wherever it was she had to go.

The knight did not understand her reaction, nor whether she was hurt or simply offended. All he was aware of was the deep longing to do it again . . . And again.

Inside the castle, Vivienne watched from the balcony as a contingent of men prepared to deploy outside the castle grounds. The door to her room opened, and King Adrien stepped in.

"Father, what is all this?"

"All the guards are heading to the border," the old man

disclosed. "There has been a skirmish, and it worries me that it might escalate."

"All of them?" Vivienne frowned, fearing the worst.

"Yes. Can you put a barrier in place to defend the castle in their absence?"

"Of course." She kissed his cheek in passing, then ran out of the room to the gates below

Ensuring there was no one around to get hurt, Vivienne positioned herself close to the castle's gates. Two large, ornate metal doors stood as the official entrance to the palace, and from each started a wall of stone, which circled the grounds. In height, it added up to ten men's, and its width was the same. The rock itself – bricks of a pale grey – had been put together by ancestors of the past. Each area was unbreakable.

Vivienne took a moment to glance up at the wall, then pressed her palms to the stone. She closed her eyes, searching for the incantation within, and forcing it out into the wall itself. At the hotness underneath her palms, she blinked, to glimpse a green glow escaping them and entering the rocks.

The stone vibrated as the spell travelled within it and upwards. It finally escaped past the top, where the sentries were normally posted, and formed a dome.

As the blazing barrier embraced the grounds with its protection, Vivienne looked around the area, searching for her guardian – in vain.

She went to the stables, where Sébastien was adding some items to his baggage, next to Illyria. Both man and horse glanced up at her arrival.

"My lady, you heard?"

Vivienne nodded, stepping closer. "I do not like the idea

of you in a fight."

Sébastien was pleasantly surprised by the admission, and followed it with one of his own. "And I, my lady, hate to leave you here unprotected."

"I will be fine . . . But please come back unharmed." Vivienne placed a hand to Sébastien's cheek in a wordless gesture.

The knight searched her gaze, before turning his head and pressing his lips to her palm. "I vow so, my lady."

The promise vibrated within Vivienne, and they stared at each other for a few moments. She yearned for nothing more than a touch of his mouth, but his reaction to their last encounter was confusing.

The princess' eyes went to Sébastien's weapon, and of its own accord, her hand extended to its hilt. With a basic wish, a spell flew in it and Vivienne smiled in satisfaction as another green glow entered the metal.

At Sébastien's raised eyebrows, she explained, "It will protect you, and allow me a glimpse of how the battle is going, in case . . ." Vivienne trailed off, unable to finish.

The anguish in her eyes unsettled the knight, but he did not dare a single motion, even as Vivienne wordlessly dropped her hand and left.

By the time Sébastien exited the stalls, he noticed Vivienne next to Lancelot's horse. The younger man had bent his head lower, and Vivienne was whispering in his ear. Under the guardian's dismayed gaze, Lancelot clasped the princess' hand in his, and kissed it softly.

Sébastien's heart weighed heavy with what he had glimpsed. It was apparent Vivienne's concern for him was out of duty, but for Lancelot, it was real caring.

He had no idea that in truth, Vivienne was tasking Lancelot with watching after Sébastien. She was also pleading with the rash youth to let Alistair protect them, without intervening, as soldiers frequently did on the field of battle.

Once she was done, the enchantress met Sébastien's burning gaze across the distance, waved a goodbye, and went up to her chambers. Alistair was there, pacing impatiently.

"You are leaving as well, I take it?"

"Yes," he replied simply.

"Be careful," Vivienne begged, now worried for two loved ones.

The demon dog nuzzled her hand in farewell, then departed swiftly.

When night came, Vivienne tossed and turned in bed, unable to rest. She gave in and went to a basin of water, dipped an index in it. When the liquid rippled, she whispered, "Show me Sébastien."

Influenced by the enchantment, the water swirled for a moment before smoothing into a mirror, where she could see the battle itself.

Sébastien valiantly fought for hours against assailants, and Vivienne even caught glimpses of Alistair. But then something struck the guardian, and he went down. There was nothing to see afterwards, as though the connection had been broken. Worried beyond words, the princess kept pacing.

Within the hour, Vivienne tried again, impatiently tapping her fingers against the basin. This time, she witnessed a moving sky, as if Sébastien was being dragged. She restlessly waited until the group of knights returned to the castle, unsure of how long it would take them.

It turned out to be two more days and nights, then a knock woke Vivienne up in the middle of the night. She ran and yanked the door open before the third knock came again.

"Sébastien!" Without thought of anything but relief, she jumped in his arms, burying her head in his chest. "I was afraid you were harmed."

The knight's answering moan of discomfort alerted her that he was, indeed, hurt. Vivienne backed away, and Sébastien saw for the first time the tears in her eyes.

"My lady, why are you crying?"

She wiped at her cheeks, embarrassed. "Of relief. I was afraid . . .." Vivienne trailed off before she could admit to more. "Come in. You are harmed, and I can heal you." She reached for Sébastien's hand, but he would not budge.

"I appreciate the offer, but I only came to ensure you were alright. It is not a wise idea for me to come in."

Vivienne ignored the strained note in Sébastien's voice, and dragged him in regardless. "Do not fight me over this. I care not if anyone notices you, when I can mend you better than any healer around here."

Sébastien gave up and allowed himself to be pulled in and settled in an armchair. The princess drifted around, lighting lamps, while he tried to manage his breathing and reaction to her. It was a lost cause, as his eyes never wavered off her enticing silhouette.

"Can you remove your armor?" Vivienne asked once there was light, critically inspecting what she could see of the wounds.

Sébastien tried to draw the protective shield up, but the

anguish shooting up his arm had him groaning. Vivienne was by his side in an instant, her hand gently restraining.

"Stop, I can do it."

Vivienne used air to help get the armor off the knight, leaving him in a shirt stained with the battle's grit. She could not help a gasp at the amount of blood.

"It looks worse than it is," Sébastien tried to smile, but it came out as a grimace.

Rolling her eyes, Vivienne grabbed the bottom of the shirt and gently peeled it off him, then over his head. She conjured up a bowl of cold water from the lake and a cloth, and got to work wiping off his chest and back, all to better observe the wounds.

Sébastien's shoulder had an awkward angle and developing bruise, and one side of his body had a few deep gashes, which could become infected rapidly if left untreated.

When the clean-up was done, Vivienne said, "I will use magic again, unless you have any objections?"

Sébastien inclined his head in assent, gritting his teeth when the princess' glowing hands progressed across his body. While Vivienne's powers healed the wounds, the knight's entire world narrowed on the healing angel.

Hair cascading down her shoulders, biting her bottom lip, green eyes filled with worry, the princess was completely unaware of the effect she had on him.

"Does it hurt badly?" Vivienne asked after a moment, noticing his tension and expression of torment.

"No," Sébastien gave out a strangled groan. The injuries were not the problem – Vivienne's closeness was.

As soon as she was done, he tried to get up, but the room

spun around him in warning. Without another option, Sébastien had to settle back down on the armchair.

"Where are you trying to go?" Vivienne asked, already reaching to restrain him, both hands resting on his chest.

"To my chambers."

"You are still weak from the loss of blood."

"I have to go," Sébastien gritted out, clenching his jaw against the unreasonable desire heating his blood. A few more moments, and he would utterly lose control.

"No, you do not," Vivienne frowned, not understanding his odd behavior. This was not the cool-headed guardian she was used to. "Let me bring you something to drink, and you can rest. You could even sleep here until mo—"

Sébastien gripped her wrist, a warning to his seriousness. Vivienne peered down at him, noting his rigidity. It was impossible not to also observe the rippling of his muscles, lighted by the fire, and something inside her badly craved to touch the guardian – and not as a healer.

"Please don't," Sébastien pleaded as Vivienne's emerald eyes darkened.

A smoldering rapture resonated within her – similar to the one in his own blood. She met his gaze and clearly noticed in there the barely contained passion, unaware hers were the same.

"Do not look at me that way, Vivienne, or I will lose control."

The enchantress could not fathom which of Sébastien using her name, how it sounded from his lips, or the actual admission unsettled her more and fuelled fascination.

Her lips parted in bewilderment, both at the crackling

excitement and a memory from months back. She had once eavesdropped on guards speak about the thrill of battle and how afterwards all they longed for was to come home to their ladies and bury the newfound ardor in lovemaking.

The yearning for Sébastien's hands on her body was enough to make her dizzy. Throat dry, Vivienne moistened her lips and watched as the knight's last shred of restraint snapped.

In one swift motion, Sébastien tugged on her wrist, and Vivienne ended on his lap. His heat surrounded her like a scorching furnace, seeping through the thin chemise and warming her entire body.

His hands cupped her cheeks, even as he begged, "Please send me away. In the state I am in, this is not something I can control."

"But I can," Vivienne assured him, then closed the distance between them, pressing her lips against his. She had been dying to do it again – and Sébastien did not disappoint.

One hand went to her waist to gather her closer, whilst the other angled her head so he could better plunder her mouth. The fierceness of the kiss continued, and Vivienne could sense Sébastien's last bit of restraint as he tried to rein it in. She was not sure stopping was an option any longer, with the way her own body was close to combusting.

Vivienne pressed closer, and Sébastien deepened the embrace, mercilessly taking over. Both hands slid to her hips, pulling her down on him, pressing against his manhood. The growl that escaped him was more animal than man.

His lips drifted with intent down her jaw, then her throat, and back up again with an eagerness Vivienne registered from faraway. She had one instant of clarity, that if things progressed too far – no matter how much she wished them to – Sébastien would feel guilty in the morning.

With a repressed moan, the enchantress let both her hands roam across his back. Much as she enjoyed the feel of steely muscles, Vivienne pushed past her own desires and sent small jolts of warmth to relax them. It is what he needs, she reasoned against her body's cravings.

Before long, Sébastien's lips gentled, and the pace changed from feverish to more tender, until the princess slowly withdrew away. He rested his head on her shoulder, drawing in deep breaths as if he had run a long distance.

"I had no right," he muttered shamefully. "But I appear to be making a habit of it."

Vivienne grabbed his chin, forcing him to meet her gaze. "I initiated it, Sébastien. And I did not object to it – nor did I the last time." His disbelieving frown threw her off. "You doubt my words?"

"No, but . . . Are your affections not taken by someone else?"

Vivienne raised an eyebrow, disconcerted at the question. "Of course not."

Sébastien sighed – he was too tired for love games. "Please let us finish this conversation at a later time, my lady. I should retire to my chambers now."

"Rest," Vivienne murmured, taking pity on his fatigued state of mind. "I will ensure you sleep in your bed tonight."

With a single hand gesture, the enchantress dematerialized him, as she had Lancelot not long before.

"I do thank you for the concern," a grumble came from the shadows.

Vivienne whirled around to Alistair, and ran to hug her protector. "Of course I was concerned! How are you? What happened in the battle?"

"The usual – blood, human against human, and sorcery involved."

Vivienne frowned at the description, but Alistair jumped on her bed and laid his head down, putting an end to the conversation. She would talk to him tomorrow about taking a bath, as he seemed ready to doze off.

She got into bed, careful not to shake it, presuming the demon dog was asleep. It was only after she was settled that Alistair conveyed his particular brand of wisdom once more.

"Much as the battle was exhausting, observing you two dance around each other is even more so. Please settle Sébastien's heart before it ends up out of his chest, Vivienne. The man loves you."

Vivienne gaped in shock at the darkness for a long moment, Alistair's gentle snore the only background noise. With an inhuman effort, she forced herself to sleep. Despite her best attempts not to, she dreamt of onyx eyes, stony muscles and soft lips on hers.

* * *

Vivienne woke up from the flashback, surprisingly not crying, but rather tingling all over. Her sanity was at stake this time, and not even keeping a distance was helping.

Sébastien had been silent since the night at the bar, and it was going on the third day now.

The young woman got out of bed and stepped to the

window. The moon was bright tonight, and it reminded her once more of all that was lost. Vivienne had an inexplicable urge to comprehend why Sébastien became this way, and what incited him to it. Unfortunately, it was apparent the answers she sought could not be obtained gently.

The enchantress stepped back to the bed, and nudged Alistair awake. Whatever he had been up to these days, it was tiring him out.

"Alistair, wake up."

Your majesty, the dog grunted, eyes still closed, *do you ever sleep? You humans are insatiable.*

She ignored the comment, insisting, "I need your help."

At that, Alistair's eyes snapped open, and he got up warily. *Another memory?*

"Yeah . . ."

Which one?

Vivienne blushed in the dimness, not willing to discuss erotic dreams with her dog. But then it registered he had been there – partly – so she charged past the embarrassment. "When Sébastien came back from battle, and I healed him. You were there too."

And to think you have not even delved into the good stuff yet, Alistair yawned loudly.

"Erm, what?" Vivienne blinked incredulously at the comment.

Alistair shook his head, and his mental voice definitely sounded like he was laughing.

"Well then! Are you going to help me or not?"

The dog sobered up immediately. *That depends on what requires help.*

"Aren't you my guard dog, supposed to do as I command?" Vivienne scowled at him.

My, my, aren't we demanding tonight? he complained instead of responding.

When her scowl remained, Alistair stretched his massive body and yawned again. *Alright, alright. What exactly am I helping you with?*

"Can you track Sébastien?"

Alistair stopped in another mid-yawn. *Why?*

"I would like to talk to him."

What about?

"Why are you so nosy?"

I have a good reason. Namely, you have been cruel to the knight these last days and he does not deserve it. Plus, I happen to have learned—

"Yes? Learned what?"

Alistair was silent.

"I can't believe this!" Vivienne's eyes narrowed at the perceived betrayal. "You're taking his side and keeping secrets!"

Majesty—

"No, Alistair, forget it!" her temper snapped. "I fancied finding out why he's the way he is, but you're obviously not going to help. I'll find him myself."

She grabbed a jacket and was out the door before the dog could do anything.

* * *

Alistair shook his head as Vivienne left. *Humans!*

Then he got up and followed his mistress, staying in the shadows. He used a portion of his abilities to keep himself hidden.

On one hand, the dog could understand why Vivienne searched for answers. His predicament prevented giving them to her. Leading the enchantress to the truth, though, was not forbidden.

Alistair followed as Vivienne angrily marched out the backdoor, crossed the street, and jogged towards Sébastien's place. In the middle of the night, Avignon was hushed, its paths softly lit.

He nearly laughed when Vivienne broke into Sébastien's place the same way he had, and looked around. The knight was not present, but the Jag was, which the dog found interesting.

Concern seeped into Alistair as he realized Vivienne found something. Whatever it was, it led to her picking up Sébastien's car keys and Jaguar, and driving off like a dog on a hunt. The dog followed effortlessly, paws hitting the ground as he kept the pace.

Alistair got worried as they left the safety of the city and headed outside the ancient stone walls. Sooner than he would have liked, they somehow ended up in a secluded industrial spot.

He hit panic mode when, probing in Vivienne's mind, he found out she was heading for a Mafia meeting. Before he could make up his mind on how to act, the enchantress parked around a corner, got out of the car, and headed towards a building at the end of the street.

Even from a distance, Alistair could see a dilapidated bar,

with a big *Ouvert* neon sign – meaning it was open. Luxury cars were parked everywhere around it.

He was about to stop Vivienne and knock some sense into her, when shadows lined the street unnaturally.

Dammit, majesty! Alistair mumbled, picking up speed.

* * *

As it turned out, Sébastien was not very good at hiding his extracurricular activities. There was a note with a date and meeting place in full view of the kitchen. Granted, Vivienne was a bit late, but she figured it would not be hard to crash a party.

All thoughts of fun went out of the young woman's head as the hairs on the back of her neck prickled a warning. She stopped running, and whirled around.

"Wonderful!" Vivienne gritted out.

There were four, nope, five evil-looking druids striding out from the shadows – and she had no backup. *This is not going to end well.*

Within that same moment, the royal sensed a presence rushing towards her at high speed. She glanced over her shoulder, in time to notice Alistair lunging – and kicking to the ground – the sixth druid that had been approaching her from behind.

"Alistair!" Vivienne breathed out in relief.

Do not be so happy to see me, he muttered mentally. *You were mad before, remember?*

Vivienne shrugged, turning her attention to Carleigh's acolytes. Remembering the latest in a long line of déjà-vus, and the strong connection to Alistair, she telepathically shot back, *This makes up for it. Were you following me?*

Of course. As an afterthought, Alistair added, *I am glad you can still tap into our connection. It will be easier to coordinate, communicating this way.*

Vivienne nodded tightly while inspecting their adversaries – trying to find a way out. *Alistair, we're seriously in trouble.*

No, we are not. Concentrate and use your abilities, like we practiced.

Vivienne tried to do as Alistair bid. Busy searching for the blaze in the pit of the stomach, it was a total surprise when a gust of solid air hit her head-on. The enchantress flew in the air and landed on the ground harshly.

There was a growl, and teeth snapping, whilst Alistair ripped apart the sixth druid he had been standing over. The other four faced in her direction, eyes blank in a trance, unmoving as though waiting for a command. The fifth one was advancing towards the dog slowly.

Vivienne, this is not the time for a nap, Alistair said, keeping an eye on the approaching warlock.

She groaned, maneuvering off the ground. An irritating lump was forming at the back of her head, and both her palms and left shoulder hurt, having gotten scraped on the ground.

Gritting her teeth, Vivienne pushed past the discomfort to access the power within. Once her magic was grazed and called to the surface, its warmth filled her, hovering for a command.

Alistair stared from a distance, a pile of ash on one side of him from the first prey, and the fifth druid now a pitiful cloaked figure at his feet, yet not quite disintegrated. The young woman could see the lightning that stirred inside her reflected in the demon dog's irises.

The enchantress elevated one palm up, and recalling how she had defended the castle, decided to first throw a protective barrier over herself and Alistair. She envisioned a bubble coating them individually, able to stop attacks, but at the same time flexible to let their respective enchanted magic escape and hit the targets.

Vivienne could not figure out if it had worked, until there was a vibration – almost a tap. She glanced around and noticed the four druids facing her now lowering their hands, as though they had tried to throw something.

Did they just attack? she asked Alistair, throwing a flabbergasted look his way.

His trademark laugh responded in her head. *Yes, highness. And good job on the barrier. Now let us see some offensive skills, please! It is you who requires practice, not me.*

Rolling her eyes, Vivienne moved her hand and formed air into the shape of a sword, with a glinting wet tip. She aimed it in the direction of Alistair's prey. With a thrust of her palm, she sent the gush of air, reinforced with evening dew, to the man at Alistair's feet. He shattered to dust, much like the intruder in the alleyway.

The four remaining conjurers snapped out of their trance, and advanced as one towards Vivienne. She threw hexes at them, and with each thrust stepped closer to Alistair, until they were side by side. Two of the warlocks hit by her air weapon immediately burst into grey ashes, hastily swept away by the wind.

The remaining two left were now flanking them, one on each side.

Alistair lunged, and Vivienne timed her attack to match his. One druid crumbled in the dog's jaws, the other joining him once the enchantress' sphere struck him.

"Well. That was easy," she mumbled out loud, oddly put off.

Expecting more of a challenge? Alistair coughed, spitting out dust and ashes.

"Sort of, yeah."

He howled in amusement, already prodding Vivienne with his muzzle. *Let us leave here and find Sébastien.*

They edged away fairly quickly, and headed into the direction of the bar.

I cannot believe you plan to crash a closed Mafia party, Alistair said when they got closer.

"I have to understand what's going on with him, Alistair. I was willing to accept him as a guardian, and still am. But I need to figure out if his allegiance is with me. Jenni – Guinevere's isn't. I gather yours is, despite the fact you like him. But Sébastien ... I can't figure out his intentions anymore. Which means I have to get him to talk to me. What he experienced is still alien to me, but it's only by understanding it that I can ultimately decide."

When they arrived at the last building before the bar, Alistair stopped and locked gazes with her, bowing his head in assent. *Alright. Stay here, I will go get him.*

"Won't they find it weird, a dog with no leash? What if they shoot at you?"

He snorted. I would like to see them try. Before Vivienne could add anything else, he was gone.

* * *

Inside the bar, seated among men in suits, Sébastien rubbed his forehead tiredly. The meeting was turning stressful with each minute, and the more he stayed, the more he longed to get away.

Merlin's nightmare kept playing in his head, and one conclusion the guardian had come to was that he would never be good enough for Vivienne, not in this life or the next. At least not if he stayed under Tony's thumb.

Unfortunately, the boss had taken a liking to him due to his violent nature and ability to get results. That was not something easily thrown away.

"Sébastien," said the devil himself, "what's your opinion on this?"

Sébastien snapped out of his thoughts, and tried to pinpoint the purpose of the question, without revealing he had not been paying attention.

"He's got a girl on his mind," Nico, one of Tony's men, leered.

There was no lost love between him and Sébastien. The guardian had had to collect from Nico numerous times, the most recent one being only a few weeks ago.

When Nico refused pay up front what he owed Tony, Sébastien had been forced to get a bit creative. Apparently, kicking his ass had been enough to bring him back in the fold. Not enough, however, to get some respect.

The issue at hand was coming back to him, now. Tony had lost some territory to new immigrant biker gangs, who were slowly trying to take over. Some brought drugs into the area, others different vices. Tony wanted to decide whether to create a deal or eliminate them, as he did not like losing money.

Sébastien commanded his features in a blank mask, conscious of his boss' surveillance. He ignored Nico's jib, instead scrutinizing the Italian man. "My guess is, if you back off and negotiate with the bikers for turf, they'll turn against you. I suggest projecting a strong force, and they'll fear you instead."

Tony broke into a huge smirk. "Rule by fear, not love . . . I like it. That's my boy! Exactly what I've been saying all along."

Sébastien backed away from the table, having now delivered his piece. He was about to call Vivienne, when an instinct stirred within, some deeper warning of a presence nearby.

The guardian glanced around the corner in time to see Alistair poke his head around the door. Though they were now in modern times, their time in the past had been enough to forge a bond between them, enough so they could sense each other's presence, and apparently the leftovers of that still remained.

Vivienne's outside, the dog rumbled warningly. *Come with me before she does anything stupid.*

Frowning, Sébastien followed him out, where his beloved waited nearby – much too close to the Mafia meeting place. Fury bubbled inside him at the sight of Vivienne so close to trouble.

"What the hell are you doing here?" he snapped. "How did you even find me?"

"Well, it's not like you're that good at hiding secrets," Vivienne folded her arms defensively. "At least on paper."

Sébastien's ire deflated, replaced by a now familiar twinge in his chest at the wariness and distrust apparent in her eyes.

"Alright, my lady," he conceded with a slight bow of the head. "What can I do for you?"

It was only after the words were out, that he got a closer look at Vivienne – the scraped hands, the blood around her shoulder and the dust on her clothes. "And why are you covered in—were you in a *fight*!?"

"We were attacked," she rolled her eyes, apparently not impressed by his reaction. "Again. I'm fine. But I've come for a simple answer, and I won't leave until I get it."

When he said nothing, Vivienne finished, "I have to know why you're this way, why *this*," she gestured between them, "is happening, and who your allegiance belongs to."

"It's always been you, Vivienne."

At the resigned, hurt tone of his voice, the enchantress almost backed down, but managed to steel herself against it in time. "Please be honest. *Why* are you this way? What changed from the past?"

Sébastien hesitated, to the point Alistair rumbled to him only, *She will not let it go without a reason, Sébastien. This is her faith in you on the line.*

I cannot, the guardian retorted back mentally. *Anything I explain could bring back the memory of her father, and once she gets the extent of my information, she will expect more. Much as I wish otherwise, I cannot give Vivienne what she seeks. My orders are clear – I'm to protect her, nothing else.*

Alistair stayed quiet as Sébastien faced Vivienne and admitted truthfully, "I can't. After you've recalled everything, I might. But not yet. There's no guessing the harm I'd be putting you in if I do."

When her expression closed, he edged nearer, about to emphasize the point, but a door opened in the distance.

"Dubois, we're ready."

Sébastien froze. So did Vivienne.

He peeked over his shoulder, doing his best to shield– and hide – her with his body. It was a lost cause, as Tony looked past Sébastien and noticed Vivienne anyway.

"I said we're moving," the boss reiterated coldly. "Now. Finish up."

Sébastien turned back to Vivienne, but her expression was clear to him – the fight was lost. She had seen Tony, his entourage, and his own subservience to the man.

Vivienne frowned at him, confused. *Why would he side with the Mafia?*

As if hearing her, Sébastien grasped her arm and rapidly moved away from Tony's Lincoln that was pulling up.

"There's more here than you can grasp, Vivienne."

"Really, Sébastien?" She did not bother to keep the scorn out of her voice. "I doubt that. It appears your allegiance is not to me after all."

The shock registered in Sébastien's features for a swift second, before he masked it all away. The hold on Vivienne's arm tightened. "Believe what you will. My duty is to protect you, and that's exactly what I'm doing."

Vivienne glared as Sébastien towered over, effectively pinning her to the car behind. She tried not to react, but her body's treacherous response was hard to ignore. Her knees weakened, her torso already leaning towards him. She did not want to fight – not with him.

"Sébastien!"

His boss' voice effectively distracted Vivienne out of her thoughts. Sébastien's entire body froze and the grip on her tightened for a tiny second, before he let go.

"Trust me," he murmured, so low she almost did not capture it, but the sentiment was echoed in his eyes. And then he was gone, following his employer.

* * *

Sébastien got in the car under Tony's perusing eye.

"Who is she?"

"No one." It killed him to say it, but if he wanted to protect Vivienne, it was paramount he downplayed her importance to him.

"Really?" Tony dragged it out, in a way Sébastien knew he was fishing and needed a bone.

"She's an old friend. Out of my league, so don't worry. I'm not pursuing, and she definitely isn't."

"Didn't look that way to me."

"Have I ever let you down?"

"No," Tony pondered, "no, you haven't. Make sure it stays that way."

Sébastien acquiesced briskly, and the conversation switched to other topics.

* * *

The forest was quiet, only the sound of wind in the leaves breaking it every once in a while. Vivienne felt she had come home, finally at peace and one with nature.

She had rented a car out of the city after the fiasco with Sébastien, and left his Jaguar at the bar. Driving for hours, she had found the most secluded spot and camped there to practice some enchantments away from prying eyes.

While Alistair lay by her side, Vivienne sat by the stream and let her thoughts flow, unrestrained. The incantation enveloped her, and she let it work with water and air, trying to see how far it was possible to force the elements to work together as shields and weapons alike.

It had been barely been an hour, when Alistair rumbled, *Time to test those defensive skills now.*

The enchantress inclined her head in assent and stood. With a hand motion, the air ahead rippled, becoming her new screen. With help from magic to keep it compact, Vivienne imagined the barrier bouncing any curse aimed at her back to the attacker.

Alistair turned his attention to her, and pawed at the ground as a bull would. From his enormous jaws an orb of energy flew. It hovered in mid-air, undecided and waiting for its master's command. Though it was not quite malevolent, as he did not have his full abilities of the past, the spell was strong enough to counteract his mistress'. Without a warning, he let it loose, blowing it her way.

Vivienne's shield vibrated as the sphere hit it, and bounced the power back with such force it evaporated into thin air, and pulverized into a million little diamonds.

Twigs snapped behind them. The young woman turned

around with a sinking feeling, though not scared considering Alistair's silence.

Sébastien stood there, facing her.

Vivienne glared at Alistair, who was looking away, ears flattened on his head. "Traitor," she scowled, realizing the dog must have given Sébastien their location mentally. "Next time, I'm coming alone."

She turned to face Sébastien, her heart tightening at his blank features. Whereas before there was a connection, the guardian seemed fully intent to destroy it, for whatever foolish reason he thought would eventually protect her.

"What do you want?" Vivienne demanded flatly.

"To make sure you're alright."

"Are you serious?" she gaped at him incredulously. "Don't pretend, when you know full well how I feel! Or you would if you were half the man I fell in love with."

Sébastien's jaw tightened in response, and Vivienne forced herself not to react further.

"You can go. I'll be fine."

The guardian glanced at Alistair, then back at her. "I'd rather stay."

"Suit yourself," she shrugged, turning her back on him and focusing back on magic.

Hours later, Vivienne's frustration had attained its peak, as tumultuous sentiments blocked most access to her abilities. She got up for a stroll in an effort to clear her head – or find something to hit.

It was not long before she became acutely conscious of Sébastien following. Vivienne stopped dead in her tracks, whirling around.

"Stay the hell away, Sébastien. I'm not in the mood."

At his obviously dismayed expression, all the frustration over the last couple of days bubbled to the surface.

"Yeah, I'm pissed. Why would you bring back all these memories to torture me with thoughts of what I can't have? A past that's lost, and a future that will never be!"

"I—"

"No. I'm not done!" Vivienne held up a palm to accentuate the sentiment. "You refuse to talk to me, but still pretend you care for me, despite handling some side business with the Mafia. The damn *Mafia*! You, my most trusted knight, a man of high morals and ethics!" She shook her head, unable to comprehend. "In the name of what we had, Sébastien, you better tell me something, *anything* that can explain your behavior, or else I'm walking out of here and you're not going to see me again."

His responding anguish was astounding, even as she waited, staring at him expectantly.

"Please don't," Sébastien pleaded in the charged silence. "Don't leave."

"Give me *one* good reason."

Sébastien broke eye contact, and she persisted, "I'm not fooling around. You have to realize by now that I'll be true to my promise. If I walk away from you, I won't look back."

He stared at Vivienne for a beat, but still did not voice anything.

"Have faith in me, Sébastien," the enchantress softened her tone. "Before you throw this away, give us a chance. Trust in me as you did before."

"I do," he pleaded. "I always have."

"Then what is it? I have to understand what I'm missing, so that I can help you!"

"I'm . . . I've lived two lifetimes, since before," Sébastien mumbled, rubbing the back of his neck. "Things changed. I did."

"How?"

"Not for the better. My very essence has changed, and because of it, I can't be with you. This is all I can say. I'm sorry I lied about the Mafia. I'm sorry I hid things from you. And most of all, I'm sorry I gave you an illusion to hope for."

Vivienne could see the honesty in his eyes, and her heart constricted painfully. "You're an idiot, Sébastien. You need me, and I need you. We're good together, we always have been, but you're clinging to an excuse to keep away. We could have attempted this, really tried to have at least a friendship."

The young woman paused, hoping against it all that Sébastien would jump in and say something to make it all better. For a moment, she could almost read the emotion in his eyes, and his wretchedness at her words and the distance between them. *Maybe, just maybe . . .*

And then the silence stretched, and Vivienne realized Sébastien would not fight, nor add anything more to what was already said.

"I shouldn't have to tell you this," she continued, biting back tears, "but you must have realized I'm in a vulnerable position, trying to remember anything. Having you by my side would have been extremely helpful. *If* I could trust where your loyalty is. But I can't. You cannot shelter *me* if you're busy running errands for *them*. So stay away from me. I'll handle Carleigh on my own."

Without another word, Vivienne departed.

Alistair lingered for a moment behind, and Sébastien had the time to capture his voice. *I presume you give credence to Merlin's words. On the off chance that he is right, you have to get the full picture – there is redemption for what you've done. But you're going about it all wrong.*

With that, he followed Vivienne to the rental car, and they drove away.

* * *

In the middle of the night, Sébastien woke up. He tried to drift off again, but after much tossing and turning came to the realization it would not happen. Every fiber of his body was demanding he go be with Vivienne, but Merlin's words were too fresh. He did not wish to be the reason Carleigh won.

With a grunt, he got up and headed to the living room. He sat on the couch and poured himself a glass of cognac. He was none too surprised to sense a presence in the room, and even less so when Alistair emerged from the hallway and lay by his feet.

"This redemption you spoke of," Sébastien began, but could not finish – could not hope.

It starts with hope, the dog rumbled, oddly echoing his thoughts. *And with all the emotions contrary to darkness, the ones you have not let yourself feel – strength, courage, and love.*

Sébastien was shaking his head in denial before the dog was even done. "All those involve a connection with Vivienne, and I don't want to –"

Taint her, I know. Which is the whole reason I did not mention this before, though it is quite evident. But you are soul mates and this time apart has been too long, enough to tear you both inside out.

Alistair paused, for the full effect of the words to register, then continued, *I do not believe Merlin's assumption. On the contrary, I think your bond can help you, strengthen you both. But I am also of the opinion you have work to do, and it starts with forgiving yourself.* Another pause. *Consider it, at least.*

Sébastien hesitated, but agreed eventually. After his old pal left, he managed to doze off, only to be assailed by weird dreams in which Vivienne's disappointed face showed up repeatedly.

CHAPTER 11

On the way to Merlin's lessons, Vivienne had to make a conscious effort to ignore Sébastien's presence behind her. Following the night he had so thoroughly kissed her, she had not been able to look at him without yearning to do it again. Which, it was obvious he was not interested in, as per the hasty apology.

Nevertheless, she was slowly losing her sanity by being around him as he sparred shirtless, as he escorted her around... Vivienne fantasized day and night of the knight's eyes, hands, body, and it was fast becoming tedious.

"My lady," the devil himself said from behind, interrupting her musings.

The enchantress schooled her features in an impassable mas, before facing him.

"Lancelot is running this way – with news."

Vivienne peered to where the guardian pointed, noticing the young man rapidly advancing towards them. She acknowledged him with a welcoming nod, and missed Sébastien's scowl.

"What news, Lancelot?"

"Your father declared there's to be a hunting party in an hour, and he requires all his men in on it. I was sent to confirm whether Sébastien will be joining."

"I will be fine without you," Vivienne glanced at Sébastien, "once you drop me off. Merlin can accompany me back, if anything."

He held her eyes for a moment longer, before nodding in agreement Lancelot. "You can inform the king I will take part."

As Lancelot left with the news, Sébastien offered the princess his arm. "I will at least drop you straight with the mage, before I leave. Would you object?"

"Not at all," Vivienne replied, her fingers tingling as she grasped his extended forearm. A slight dizziness hit her, and she had to hold on tightly as though her life depended on it.

The rest of the trip to Merlin's was pure torture. Thighs brushed as they strolled, hips occasionally bumped each other . . . A myriad of movements made Vivienne all the more mindful of his presence. And throughout it all, Sébastien seemed unbothered.

Except when they arrived, as she peered up at him, the flame was back in his onyx eyes. The look he levelled on her before departing warmed her from tip to toes.

* * *

Much later, bustling around the castle finally got on Vivienne's nerves, and she stopped a panicked servant. "What is going on?"

"The men were attacked by a boar. Sir Lancelot was almost impaled alive, but one of the new guardians saved him."

The princess' heart dropped at the news. "The new guardian. What is his name?"

"I do not know my lady, my apologies. I believe he might one of your daily guards."

"Sébastien!"

Vivienne did not stop to consider how it might appear. She picked up her skirts and ran for the great hall where they must have arrived, bursting past the doors. The group of men gathered around all gaped at her, but she only had eyes for one.

In their midst, laid down on one of the benches, was Sébastien. He was ashen, with a shirt full of blood, his stomach cut open by the animal. The king was at his head, Lancelot by his side.

"Get out of my way," Vivienne uttered in such a glacial voice that the men in her way edged away without a single word.

Her father looked up at the sound of her voice. "Darling daughter, can you save him?"

"Yes," was all she responded, kneeling next to Sébastien's unmoving form.

Vivienne lifted the bloody rag which covered the gut wound, and gasped at its severity. She had never attempted healing on such a scale, especially on a human. But if there was a chance to save him, the enchantress would give it her all.

"My lord, it's not good for the lady–"

Disregarding Lancelot's words, Vivienne announced in a deadly tone, "If you attempt to remove me from Sébastien's side, I will petrify you to hell."

She did not have to look up to confirm the men's shocked expressions, as the dead silence surrounding her spoke volumes. Vivienne was not one for threats – at least she had not recently been. She had absolutely no idea where the words had even come from, aware only of her longing to save Sébastien.

"There is so much blood," Vivienne uttered to herself in quite a different voice. With a muttered incantation – one of Merlin's own – some clean linen and fresh water materialized by her side. She got to work cleaning the wound, until only fresh blood seeped.

Once that was done, the enchantress placed both hands above the wound and reached deep inside for the healing capacity, much as Merlin had taught her. She could experience the enchantment at work, but Sébastien's breathing only became more laboured. Healing the wound would only be part of the problem. He would have to handle the rest himself, fighting for his life.

In an effort to block away the astounded and frightened faces – not everyone at the castle was accepting of their mistress' magic – Vivienne closed her eyes. The spell escaped her palms in pale golden wisps, entering Sébastien's wounds, healing the torn flesh and piecing it back together. His features remained of marble during the entire operation, breathing still as weak.

When it was done, Vivienne examined him for any other wounds, but none were apparent. She stood up, and the men in the immediate vicinity backed away a few feet – all except the king. The princess could not tell whether they did so in awe or fear, but she was too numb to bother caring either way.

"He will require transport to a room where he can rest and get about easily. Or be overseen by a servant. Father?"

King Adrien noticed the pleading glint in Vivienne's eyes, and announced loudly to everyone, "Sébastien displayed great courage today. I will have him placed in one of the guest bedrooms in the east wing. He will have everything."

Vivienne kept her counsel, silently content as the east wing was on her side of the castle. As she moved away from Sébastien, a few of the men dared to inch closer. They gently grabbed the guardian for transport, and stepped away.

They carried Sébastien to his new chambers, then left him alone. Vivienne had trailed behind him, sensing her strength waning with each step. By the time she reached her room, she fell on the bed, exhausted and in tears. One thing was clear now to her more than ever – if Sébastien had died, she would have been devastated.

* * *

Later in the day, Vivienne went to check on the knight. She was informed he had a fever, and it was worrisome. As the princess stayed by Sébastien's side, using cold compresses to cool him down, he shifted restlessly whilst sleeping.

"Vivienne."

Startled, Vivienne peered up from the book she was reading, but Sébastien was still dormant – with her on his mind, apparently.

"Lancelot, he is alive," the knight mumbled again.

She frowned in confusion. What is he on about?

"I would rather you be happy with him than sad without, my love."

With a gasp, understanding dawned on Vivienne. Sébastien's words from before, of healing her pain, and having feelings for another – he presumed she liked Lancelot! And the reason he saved him . . .

"Oh Sébastien . . . You did it for me, putting yourself in the path of the boar . . ." Vivienne whispered, incredulously staring at the knight. He had almost died, all for her own happiness.

Uncaring who saw her, Vivienne gripped Sébastien's hand, and his restless motions stopped. "I do not like Lancelot," she declared, voice raspy with emotion. "It is you my heart yearns for. Please get better soon."

Though he did not answer, the hand she clasped gave a gentle squeeze. The enchantress remained by his side until the fever dropped, and only then retreated to her own chambers.

* * *

Vivienne woke up, and to avoid the pity in Alistair's eyes, got dressed quickly. "I'm going for a coffee," she muttered and left before he could do anything.

The walk from the house to one of the closest cafés was brief, but instead of going there, the young woman aimlessly wandered the stone alleyways and cobblestone paths. Unconsciously, she ended up back at the same small place where she had seen Sébastien for the first time.

Stopping there was more a whim than anything else, as Vivienne did not think she would run into him. After all, the guardian had stayed away ever since the meadow scene, and that had been two days earlier.

Vivienne still could not believe how big of a fool she had been. To ignore it from the beginning – the obscurity emanating from Sébastien – was beneath her otherworldly skills. She still could not comprehend why he had changed for the worst, and the lack of honesty nagged at her day and night. She needed closure, and he had all the answers.

And yet, their time together was over. Vivienne had to keep a distance whilst processing everything, hoping that once all the information of the past sank in, the rest would fall into place.

She exited the café and flung the empty coffee cup in the trashcan. It was getting close to the time for Alistair's walk. Before she could leave, her senses caught wind of Sébastien before he even called out to her.

"Vivienne!"

She whirled around, and the breath caught in her throat. Sébastien was leaning against a wall, on the other side of the small street. He was dangerously gorgeous in black shirt and jeans, and vulnerable with a pleading glint in his eyes. In a few instants, he crossed the street and his familiar scent engulfed her.

"Please listen to me," he begged, but Vivienne put a hand up to stop him.

"Stay away, Sébastien. I've said everything back in the meadow. If you wish for more than this distance, you have some explaining to do."

"I can't," he froze, again with that trapped expression. "I wish I could. You have no idea how badly I wish I could . . ."

"Won't you at least explain how you changed so much?"

"Time, my love," Sébastien sounded wistful.

Her eyes flashed. "Don't call me that! A better man than you are did, and I don't like defiling the memory of what we had together."

Vivienne saw the hurt in his eyes, as Sébastien did not attempt to hide it. Instead, he stepped forward and seized her wrist. "Please listen to me. Let me at least be your shadow, like in the past. You need protecting while you piece it all together."

"I remember enough," she said, amazed her voice did not shake from his touch.

As the guardian's eyes fixated on her hands, Vivienne glanced down. She was shocked to notice the magic that had gathered in her glowing palms.

Vivienne raised a gaze to Sébastien's appraising one. "You would use it against me?" he whispered.

"Like I mentioned before – you're not the man I fell in love with. He would have fought evil with all his strength."

The air around them changed at her words, crackling dangerously. Sébastien's eyes flickered to a cold onyx as the outrage seeped in. It was evident in the way he held Vivienne, in the energy brushing against her, and in the way his features tightened.

"What makes you think I didn't fight it?" he hissed. "You

have *no* idea of the hell I went through!"

"And whose fault is that?" Vivienne shot back. When his grip tightened in response, the enchantress enunciated carefully, "Sébastien . . . Let. Me. Go." There was a moment's hesitation, but then he did as she asked.

Vivienne ran off, refusing to look behind even as he called her name. In her haste to get away from what had taken place, she missed the shadow skulking about, who had seen everything.

* * *

Carleigh was pacing impatiently in the church when Braydon entered. Before the newcomer had even spoken, the sorcerer's face contorted in exhilaration.

"Well?"

Braydon paused to catch his breath, then declared, "Vivienne almost used her abilities on Sébastien. They had an altercation and apparently it was threatening enough to nearly attack him."

Carleigh was silent, then a rictus stretched his thin lips. "Excellent! We're almost there."

He walked away from Braydon to the center of the church, where the pool of darkness bubbled. The necromancer could sense the acolytes on the other end, caught between life and death, in between the worlds and at his mercy forever.

Linking them to him, binding them even in death by means of sorcery had been the best idea from his past life. The price of necromancy – as all else – never did come cheap, though he could not complain of the result.

Carleigh's chest shook with a cruel snicker, and he lifted a hand above the pool. "Almost there, my sweet." The mass writhed, as though responding to the cajoling. "Once I am immortal, I will unleash you to feed on this world, as we agreed."

* * *

Vivienne retreated home as fast as possible, rushing past the front door and slamming it behind.

What the hell happened? Alistair ran down the stairs, grumbling. *Your aura is all over the place.*

He found his mistress on the couch, staring in a daze.

"I almost used magic on Sébastien!" Vivienne revealed in a whisper.

The dog's ears flattened against his head in shock, even as the enchantress looked away, breaking eye contact. *How? Why? And what do you mean 'almost'?*

"He waited for me outside the café, to talk – calling me his love. I said something, and it angered him . . . He grabbed my hand, and my magic reacted."

Reacted how? Alistair wondered, sniffing her palms. All his senses expanded to capture what Vivienne was not divulging.

"It glowed in my palm, I felt it there. Had I released it, I could have hurt him!"

Your highness—

"No, Alistair, you don't get it! I didn't even call it to me!"

Vivienne. The dog's calm voice broke past the chaos in her head. *Your magic is your life. It defends you even when you do not call it. It sounds to me as though you perceived a threat and subconsciously prepared for a fight.*

"I did that before . . ." she gaped at him, letting the words sink in. "The night the intruder broke into my home and attacked me. I was falling into a vision, and a bolt of light escaped me . . ." Vivienne trailed off, biting her lip in concentration, before asking, "Is it even possible? Was I able to do this in the past?"

That, and much more, majesty. It will all come back eventually.

Vivienne thought back to the scene, and Sébastien's darkening expression . . ."He never directed it at me," she realized.

What?

"Sébastien's fury. That's what I saw as danger. In the past, though he got annoyed and frustrated, he never directed his discontent at me. But today . . . I could feel it clearly, and when he touched me, I –"

Were you afraid he would hurt you? Alistair's bared teeth interrupted.

Was I really afraid? Vivienne urged herself to give an honest response, analyzing the incident. She had remarked the anger in Sébastien's eyes, but there was also hurt. He had reacted the same way she would have, if the exact same words had been hurled at her.

Despite his wayward emotions, Sébastien never would have harmed her. It was a certainty the young woman experienced in her bones. Though angry, his intent in grabbing Vivienne had been to get her to stay and listen to his words, not to hurt her.

And now, removed from the situation, the enchantress could clearly see it.

"No," she acknowledged to Alistair in a strong voice. "I was dismayed, that's all."

Are you absolutely sure? You have to be.

"Yes, I am. I've accused Sébastien of many things, even of being disloyal, but I don't get the impression he would ever hurt me. No matter whom his loyalties are with, Sébastien will always keep me safe."

At her honest declaration, Alistair relaxed and sat on his hind again, pensive. Then again, so was Vivienne.

"I never would have expected my life to turn out this way, Alistair." She was back to whispering now. "All these memories, these new abilities, and not being able to share them with Sébastien. Magic existing is enough to blow my mind – let's not even bring up the fact I can wield it! My entire life something was missing, and when Sébastien came into my life, that sensation was gone. And now, it's there again. It's tearing me apart being away from him."

I get it, highness. But there is nothing you can do at this point.

"I believe there's more going on, much more than I am aware of."

Alistair broke eye contact with her, and she frowned. "Do you know something?"

Not enough.

"What new information have you gathered?" Vivienne insisted.

I will go talk to him, the dog got up and headed towards the door, still evasive.

"Alistair—"

Majesty. His voice was a growl so harsh, the enchantress cringed. *Let me handle this.*

"Alright," Vivienne backed off, softening to a pleading tone. "But before you go, please . . . Give me something I can hold on to, some kind of hope."

Alistair shook his massive head, and for a moment, she presumed he would not respond. But in the end, he exhaled and revealed, *Sébastien has experienced certain things after you passed away. I did not witness it all. But I can think of one person, aside from him, who can give us more information.*

"Who?"

Merlin.

"What? But—"

I can get to him. A powerful wizard such as him can transcend time, and I presume I can still speak with him. Whether he will tell me the truth or not, I cannot fathom.

Alistair was already up and moving away, when Vivienne's puzzled tone stopped him. "Why wouldn't he?"

Merlin likes games, and I have a hunch he has been playing us all. But first, I need to speak with Sébastien, as well.

"Do you have an idea of where he is? After today . . . He looked bad, Alistair."

I will find him.

With one last meaningful look to his mistress, Alistair was gone, leaving Vivienne to her worries.

* * *

After the fiasco at the café, Sébastien retreated to the only place he belonged anymore. It was the same bar Vivienne had come to, where the Mafia meeting had taken place.

It was fairly deserted in the afternoon, but not even two straight up whiskeys were enough to stop the dark thoughts running through his head. Vivienne had almost used an enchantment on him – that notion alone was still haunting.

"Give me another one," Sébastien ordered the bartender, Francis.

The beefy old man poured the shot, peering at him dubiously. "You alright, Dubois? You look like crap."

"I've heard that before," Sébastien gave a bitter chuckle at the words.

He drank the alcohol in one shot, welcoming the burn down his throat and in the pit of his stomach. And then it was back to reflecting on Vivienne's words, when she had instructed him not to call her "my love," and the anguish and fury that had followed back to back.

Sébastien had not even realized the resentment had filled him, not until he had noticed the wariness in her eyes. It seemed Merlin was right, after all. Eventually, without intending to, he could hurt her.

I'm bad news, period. And Sébastien definitely did not have as much discipline over himself as he had previously believed – he could not trust himself around Vivienne.

So basically, the further I stay, the better. That's nothing new. It was bad enough Vivienne's safety was compromised at Carleigh's hands, he could not have it be so at his own.

"Another one," Sébastien motioned to Francis. When the bartender hesitated, he scowled, "Not now, man. Just pour."

The old man shrugged and served him another drink.

* * *

Far to the side of the bar, Nico, one of Tony's men, supervised the entire exchange. He was not overly fond of Sébastien, as the man had supplanted him with Tony. Furthermore, he was obviously hiding something.

Nico had spent the last few days trailing Sébastien, and it seemed he had a girl on the side. Tony would not be happy, as he expected all his men to be focused on the job and not allow themselves distractions.

Still, before revealing the information, Nico had to find out more – whatever would dig Sébastien's grave properly.

As his rival started on a fourth drink, he got up and approached the bar.

* * *

A hand tapped his shoulder, and Sébastien turned to see none other than Nico. He was still beat up from their last interaction, and the guardian got a distinct hunch of trouble. *Maybe those drinks in public weren't such a good idea, after all.*

"Yo, Nico," Sébastien greeted neutrally.

"Dubois," the man pointed to the drink. "Care if I join you?"

Sébastien shrugged, meanwhile making an effort to filter the booze from his system, and be more alert.

"So, what've you been up to?" Nico asked.

"Same old. Collecting."

Nico nodded slowly, as the bartender poured him a shot of vodka. "Yeah, I bet."

"Listen, man," Sébastien retorted, "I'm sorry about last time. It's my job, you weren't cooperating, and you know how Tony is."

"Forget about it. Water under the bridge and all." Nico sipped his drink, attempting nonchalance, but his eyes were suggesting a different story.

"Cool," Sébastien forced past his lips.

They continued drinking in silence, and Nico got up after finishing. He spun towards the guardian after a moment's hesitation, as though forgetting something.

"By the way, who's that piece you've been banging? She's smoking hot."

Sébastien froze, forcing himself not to react, but the anger was already bubbling under the surface. *Stay focused, there's a lot at stake here.*

"I don't know what you're talking about."

"Sure you do!" Nico clapped him on the back like an old friend would. "She's hot man! I really can't blame you for going after her. Hell, I wouldn't mind me—"

He did not get to finish, on account of Sébastien's fist connecting with his jaw, then his stomach. Nico doubled over and fell to his knees, spitting out blood.

"Bring this outside, guys," Francis grumbled. "I don't want a fight on my hands."

Sébastien glared at the bartender for the interruption, but seized Nico by the scruff of his shirt and dragged him outside in the alleyway. He slung him into the nearest wall, but still the Mafia man got up, sneering. Blood seeped from a split lip.

"I wonder what Tony would think of you being distracted by such a sweet piece of ass."

The last of his control snapped, and Sébastien advanced towards Nico to finish the job. The man clenched both fists, preparing for a fight, but his eyes widened in horror at something behind Sébastien. "What the *hell*!?"

Sébastien sensed it a moment later. He peered over a shoulder to see a cloud of billowing smoke, the color of ash, materialize. It trailed over the ground in a thick form, passed around him, and climbed all over Nico like a viscous mass. It washed over the man, and before he could even cry out in horror, his lifeless eyes were staring at Sébastien, his dead corpse on the ground.

The guardian gagged reflexively, his gut churning. He had killed before, but this was something else. A foul odor emanated from Nico's corpse and it had nothing to do with the dead body, but rather with the murkiness that had killed him.

"So. You're the champion."

The voice had come from behind, and Sébastien whirled to confront it. The adrenaline drumming in his blood did quick work of evaporating the booze from his system, and he was able to properly size up his adversary.

The newcomer was about the same height as him, but lankier. Now that the smoke was gone, Sébastien could see him clearly. Cold grey eyes stared from a hawkish face, lips curled in disdain. He wore the druids' mantle – a dark hood covering his head – but unlike the men he had previously run into, this one was not obscuring any features.

It was not one of the men Sébastien and Vivienne had

already had the luck of meeting, the guardian concluded in an instant. On top of the physical difference, there was a darkness emanating from him that was more potent than what he had confronted before.

"Who the hell are you?"

"I'm called Braydon," the druid introduced himself, also sizing up the knight. "No need to look so wary, I come bearing gifts – a message from Carleigh."

Sébastien glowered at the man's bullshit line. "Oh yeah? I got a message for him, too."

"Shut up and listen, fool!" Braydon snapped. "Carleigh will spare your life if you give him Vivienne."

"Is that all?" Sébastien snickered cynically.

The warlock ignored his tone, instead examining the guardian with a leveled expression.

Wow. He's actually serious, Sébastien mused. Out loud, he announced, "You can advise your master I'm not interested in bargaining with the devil."

To drive his point home, Sébastien stepped closer, itching to get a punch in. Instead of succeeding, he encountered only smoke when Braydon disappeared without another word.

Sébastien circled around, ensuring he was truly gone, and his eyes fell on Nico's body.

"Shit."

The man was well and truly dead, and Sébastien had no way to explain it. He took out his cell and punched in some numbers. "Yeah, it's me. I need a cleanup. Location is Francis' bar, the alleyway behind it."

* * *

Vivienne sat by the balcony, studying the setting sun. Alistair had been out most of the day, until a few hours earlier when he had returned, shaking his head, *No luck. Something is blocking Merlin, and Sébastien is . . .indisposed.*

She had nodded, and turned to the outside. They had been this way, sitting silently, for the last few hours, when a weird noise outside the door startled them both – a thud, followed by a scraping sound.

The young woman got up and called magic in her hands as a pre-emptive measure, waiting until a soft glow filled them before stepping towards the door. Alistair, having inhaled a good whiff and recognized the scent, shook his head. *You will want to open this, trust me.*

As she did exactly that, Vivienne's eyes fell on Sébastien. He was sitting on the ground, a knee oddly drawn up to his chest, his head leaning on a bent forearm.

"Sébastien," she admonished, "I thought I was clear enough last time we spoke."

The guardian started, before his oddly glazed look met hers. There was a pause, then he said, "We have to talk."

Vivienne threw a look over her shoulder to Alistair. *Is it just me, or does he sound odd?*

The dog simply shook his head. *I am as clueless as you are, majesty.*

Vivienne turned back to Sébastien, giving him a wary once-over as he got up slowly. The guardian looked as though he had not slept in days, nor shaved. He was a mess, with dark circles under his eyes, and as he tilted precariously towards her, she distinctly smelled alcohol coming from him.

"You're drunk."

"Yeah," he muttered, rubbing the back of his neck. "It's the only way I'm ever going to have this conversation with you."

"What conversation?" Vivienne frowned, even as Sébastien inhaled deeply to plunge in.

"You're wrong. About what you said. I want to be the same man you fell in love with. But I did things, Viv, in the past two lifetimes, and in this one—"

"Like joining the Mafia?"

"Yeah . . . Like that. There's a reason to all the craziness, believe me."

"So what is it?"

"It was a means to an end." At Vivienne's confused stare, Sébastien added, "You'll find out when you recall everything. I cannot say more, if there's a risk it will tip the balance. I'm afraid of what else it would bring back. In the end, I'm simply following orders not to intervene with your trip down memory lane."

"Orders? From whom?"

"Merlin." A glance over her shoulder to the watchful dog, then, "And Alistair, in terms of protecting you."

"I don't understand how keeping secrets is useful," Vivienne rolled her eyes. "But whatever, it's like navigating a labyrinth of secrets with you guys. So, why exactly did you have to get drunk to tell me all this?"

Despite her nonchalant tone, Vivienne did not expect the honesty in Sébastien's answer.

"To numb the pain. You have to understand, I *didn't* betray you. This, what I am, it has to do with you, but not in the way you're imagining." On some subconscious level,

Sébastien realized he had reached the point where he was supposed to shut up. Now that the words were coming out, though, he found it hard to do exactly that.

"I had to choose, and it was not easy," Sébastien continued, his intense gaze focused on Vivienne's. "I didn't forget about you. As a matter of fact, I did everything I could to keep you alive in my mind, in my heart, until it hurt too much. I never could forget, Viv, that's the entire problem."

"What are you . . .?" Vivienne trailed off, the rest of the unspoken question dying on her lips. In his eyes, she could see the trapped emotion, and was left unable to shake the feeling of missing the entire picture.

Sébastien bowed clumsily, done with his speech, and clasped her hand in his. "If you ever decide otherwise and see me worthy enough to be your guardian again, I am yours, my lady. I always was, always will be, at your service. In the meantime, I'll be a shadow." He left, swaying on his feet.

* * *

Vivienne's despair was nothing compared to the confusion. When Sébastien had admitted his actions were somehow related to her, the full weight of his meaning came crashing down. The fact they had a past, that she had influenced him and somehow contributed to this path, was worrisome enough.

What was even more puzzling, in the end, was the vital information missing that could have explained Sébastien's change. The young woman could not fathom how the white knight of the past had become so corrupted, and yet the latest tidbit of information forced her to conclude she was the cause.

Alistair, having observed Vivienne since Sébastien's departure, was the first to sense a shift in her aura. He moved closer, nudging her insistently with his muzzle. *Highness, what is it? Your energy is all over the place again.*

"It's my fault," the enchantress declared dazedly.

What?

"I'm the reason Sébastien is the way he is," Vivienne explained, focusing on him.

You cannot blame yourself for this!

"But I do . . . You heard him. Whatever the full reason is, it began with me."

Vivienne held onto the wall in an effort to remain standing. She was drowning in a swirl of emotions, somewhere between a need to cry and scream in frustration. Alistair's presence, like in the past, was the only thing effectively grounding her.

You are taking Sébastien's words and twisting them, Vivienne. He is drunk, and has had a shit day. On top of it all, he is utterly lost.

"Perhaps. But at least one thing is clear."

What is? Alistair probed warily, already dreading the answer.

"Before, I decided to keep him at bay to protect myself. But it's well apparent the opposite has to happen – Sébastien needs to defend himself. Whatever life has in store for him, at the very least I can ensure my presence has no bearing on it. He's given too much to guard me in the past, and it's about time he's free to live for himself."

Alistair said nothing, deep in his own reflections. It was evident he had to understand more if he wanted to help

Vivienne snap out of the mood she was in, and to ease her worries. With each moment she concentrated on Sébastien's words, the atmosphere surrounding her escalated into a tornado of despair and guilt, and nothing seemed to distract her from it.

The dog guarded over his mistress as she curled up on the couch, and stared unseeing at the fireplace, in her own mental hell of torment. The minute she fell asleep, Alistair cast a barrier over the house and ran to find Sébastien.

* * *

Sébastien did not enjoy his current predicament. Mere hours after the chat with Vivienne, all he longed for was another drink to forget the world existed. He also craved to be next to her, shielding her, but a direct order from Tony could not be ignored.

The guardian had not yet begun to leave the Mafia, and so was still bound. This was especially true after having used Tony's clean-up crew behind his back to hide a body, killed by means of sorcery, no less.

What a freaking mess.

Sébastien got out of the Jaguar and advanced behind the dry cleaner, in the alleyway where he knew his current target spent most evenings. There was a group of young men by one of the lamps, passing joints, beers, and overall amusing themselves. One man in the middle was the person he was hunting.

Tony's trip to Avignon was partly designed to remind the people he did business with who the boss was and the allegiance owed to him. Men like the young punk Sébastien was about to engage with had forgotten the significance of the very word.

Sébastien approached the group, stepping closer as casually as possible.

"Yo, Lucien," he nodded in greeting.

The dark-haired man faced Sébastien, noticing he was alone. "Seb, what's up?"

"You owe Tony money. I come here to collect."

"You and what army?" he snickered, finishing his can of beer and tossing it aside.

"Come on, man, let's not do this. Just give me the money."

Lucien winked at the group of thugs behind him, then faced Sébastien, smirking. "Make me."

Sébastien shrugged off his jacket, tiredly rolling his shoulders. This was going to be bad – and another couple of vile marks on his soul. First they surrounded him in a circle, glints of metal in a few of their hands.

Then, the assailants came at him one by one. The small alleyway restricted their actions, but left Sébastien free to use full force. Each time he deflected them effortlessly, ducking blows, and handing out punches right and left. He knew nothing but the thrill of the fight, nothing except the crunch of bones under his fists.

When the knife jammed itself in his ribs, he did not even flinch. "What the hell!?" Lucien swore, but Sébastien kept going until the man dropped abruptly.

Sébastien stopped punching, panting heavily. His fists were bloodied, the knuckles cracked. There was an ache in his body, and Vivienne's image flashed vividly in his mind in warning. Angrily, the knight shook his head in an effort to clear it – the time for having a conscience was long gone.

I did not believe you, at first, a voice rumbled.

Sébastien peered over a shoulder to notice Alistair standing not far away, staring at him. "And now?"

Yes.

The guardian looked down at Lucien's unconscious body, then turned back to Alistair. "Did you do this?"

If you're referring to coercing them for a catnap before you killed them . . . Then yes.

"I can't decide whether to thank you or yell at you."

Just get what you have to from him. We need to talk. The dog retreated, stopping at the entrance of the alley.

Sébastien crouched next to Lucien's body and checked both pockets. He snatched two large wads of cash from him, hoping they would appease Tony enough for the moment.

With one last look at the chaos – and unconscious bodies – left behind, the knight then picked up his leather jacket, and joined the dog. He let Alistair climb in the Jag for the short drive home.

Silent until they entered the house, Alistair then took advantage of Sébastien's unprotected back and jumped him from behind. His canine weight was heavy and the guardian was weak enough from the fight and his open wound that he dropped to the floor.

Sébastien rolled over to get some leverage but Alistair clamped his massive jaws around his throat in a matter of seconds. The sharp edge of his teeth dug into the skin, and the once powerful soldier closed his eyes, ready to welcome death's embrace.

Do you wish to die so much? the demon dog snarled.

Sébastien blinked in confusion. He could not talk with the jaws on his throat, but there was one other solution – seeing as the demon dog did not seem intent to move. With no other choice, the guardian sorted out his chaotic thoughts in a vain attempt to communicate with Alistair, hoping it would work like in the past.

No, I don't.

Could have fooled me.

The jaws relaxed from his throat, and Alistair sat on his chest instead. The breath Sébastien had been holding in left him with a whoosh, and he was unable to breathe any better. If Alistair was trying to suffocate him to death, it was definitely working.

The way you fight, knight, it's as if you want to die. Something more than the curse and the last two lifetimes led you here, to this moment, to who you are . . . And I want the full version, so that I can figure out how to fix you.

"Why?" Sébastien wheezed out.

I once had a vision about you and Vivienne. Alistair glowered down at him, eyes glowing in the dimness. *You are meant to be either her salvation or her doom, if you accept darkness. That is what I told Merlin long ago, but now I understand better. Nothing can keep you two apart, and if you reject what fate is trying to give you back, there will be consequences.*

Having said his piece, Alistair got off Sébastien to let him breathe. As the knight slowly righted himself, the dog had the chance to observe the blood on him, seeping from the knife wound.

Soul mates are bound forever, no matter how many

lifetimes are lived. You and Vivienne are both broken due to not being together, and I will not let you ruin your chance at happiness, just because you are convinced of your damaged soul.

When Sébastien remained quiet, the dog went on, *You have two choices, as you did when Vivienne died. Unlike Merlin, I will disclose all the details. Number one, I let you die of your wound, and you pass onto your next existence with a poisoned and heavy heart. Number two, I heal you so that you can fight. Let me be clear – this means you take what little purity is still inside you and use it against the evil attacking Vivienne. The choice is yours, knight. What will it be?*

"What light are you talking about?" the guardian wondered, a stricken look on his face.

There is still something inside you striving to come to the surface. That is why you feel remorse over what you have done. If you had truly become a villain, you would not be full of all the regret and empathy I see in you when you are around Vivienne.

"It doesn't mean anything," Sébastien counteracted, well aware of said emotions.

Yes, it does.

"How was Vivienne reborn then, if I didn't change?"

One simple reason – the curse was not specific enough. At Sébastien's stunned gaze, Alistair elaborated, Carleigh is no master of the arts. You presumed you had met the prophecy, acted as such, and thus it was enough to trick the fates.

"You're implying I still have a chance? Despite what Merlin has been clamoring all along?" It was unbelievable to his ears, yet Alistair was actually giving him hope.

I am saying you could, if you are brave enough. So, I ask again – what will it be, knight?

Despite the dizziness from the loss of blood, Sébastien maneuvered himself into a bent knee position in front of Alistair and solemnly placed his right hand over his heart. "I have no sword to pledge an oath with, but I swear to you here that if what you say is true, and there is still something untainted in me, I will do everything I can to get back the rest. I want nothing more than to be the man I once was, and be with Vivienne. In the meantime, I will not let anything or any*one* get to her."

Good, Alistair replied, satisfied at the turn of events.

As the knight's pallor got worse, the demon dog drifted closer and grazed his muzzle to Sébastien's hand. Currents vibrated all over the guardian's body in red wisps, sharper than Vivienne's soft healing touch. The heat warmed – almost scorching him – but with an audible zap, the sharp agony in his ribs was completely gone.

When Sébastien checked under the shirt, his wound was healed. "Thank you."

Do not thank me yet. You still have a long way to go, knight. Also, do not get used to me healing you, as it is beneath me and not part of my daily duties.

Sébastien had to laugh at Alistair's words, feeling lighter than he had in ages.

* * *

Braydon stopped dead in his tracks, taking in the scene before him. Once more, Carleigh was in a yogi pose by the portal of obscurity. The pool itself had risen in the air, as though it blanketed something – or someone.

When he reached it, muffled cries echoed from within. The tendrils shifted in their eagerness to fully encompass the shape, and a head was distinguishable. It was human, with a beard, old wrinkled skin, and wide eyes filled with terror.

"What is this?" Braydon turned a gleaming gaze to Carleigh. "You started all the fun without me?"

"Hardly," the sorcerer sneered, stopping his mediation. "The darkness was hungry, and I fed it a homeless man. Though . . ." He glanced at it again, cackling, "I do believe there will be demand for more."

The blood-curling screams ended, and Carleigh stood up. The obscurity dropped at his approach, showcasing only a skeleton left, clean of blood or meat. With one wave of his hand, it became ash and dissolved within the pool.

Carleigh then concentrated on Braydon, noticing him shifting from foot to foot, as though impatient. "What now?"

The druid hesitated, before confessing, "Sébastien refused to hand Vivienne over."

"Of course he did," Carleigh sniggered evilly.

"You're not mad?"

"Why would I be? This way, it will be much more fun!"

Braydon's frown clearly implied he disagreed. Rolling his eyes, Carleigh explained, "Now we break Sébastien, so he cannot protect her."

"And how shall we do that?"

"By demonstrating to him just how far he has fallen."

* * *

After the chat with Sébastien, Alistair returned to the Place des Corps Saints fountain. It was a full moon, which suggested contact across the ages would be easier. Especially if Merlin was already reaching out, as he suspected from Sébastien's words.

The dog paused in front of the fountain and dipped his head over its marbled edge as if he would take a drink. Instead, he inhaled deeply, then exhaled.

A wisp of white smoke escaped him and crawled across the surface of the fountain. The water vibrated, and ripples edged out. As they quieted, it was limpid for a few moments, then a fog developed slowly within its reflection.

Once it cleared, Merlin's features emerged. The wrinkles were deeper, but his blue eyes were still as sharp.

Old friend, Alistair rumbled.

"Alistair, you've assumed a great risk contacting me this way, in the open."

It could not be helped.

"Is something wrong?"

Sébastien has brought Vivienne back after two lifetimes apart.

The dog observed the mage for a few moments, noticing his lack of surprise. *But then again, this is no news to you, Merlin. Is it?*

"I cannot say it is, you are correct."

So you have been following what Sébastien has been doing all along. And you never once aided us?

"I did not, you are right, once again. If you know about the curse, you will understand."

I'm not sure I do, Merlin. The dog's voice was tight with

barely repressed anger. *Do explain it.*

"I cannot intervene in their affairs."

Bullshit, Merlin. You love intervening and manipulating people like chess pieces.

"Perhaps. But in this new age you live, it is complex. It requires advantages I do not have. You are in a different time, it is easier to speak for you."

Really? And where exactly are you? I'm truly interested, considering the energy I used to contact you is barely anything.

Merlin scowled for a moment, but conceded, "When Arthur died, I sheltered myself from the world. I now live in between times, waiting for the moment when he will be reborn, so that I may join him in the future and mentor him, as before."

So, what, you're stranded in time?

"Without going into details, no. I have chosen this prison, and it lets me view everything – the past, present and future. I have been able to peek at Vivienne's life. And Sébastien's past two lifetimes. That is how I concluded he is unworthy."

Is this why you've been showing up in Sébastien's nightmares, tormenting him, denying the happiness he has earned?

The old wizard's face became blurry.

Do not dare leave, Merlin! We are nowhere close to finished! To illustrate his point, Alistair sent a tiny bit of enchantment into the water, effectively locking the mage in until they were done.

Merlin's face became less blurred – though more annoyed – and back into focus. "I see you have not changed, still as demanding as ever, old god. But yes, I intervened because they are both playing with fire. The longer Sébastien stays around Vivienne, the more his maliciousness can affect her."

You do not give her enough credit. Vivienne can help turn him around!

"She cannot! His soul is tainted by wrongful deeds."

Merlin, those actions were done to save Vivienne, and the world. At your request! You know as well as I do that through their soul mate bond, they are each other's equals. In the past, Vivienne was passive to Sébastien's aggressive, soft to his hard. And now, his force adds to her healing powers, whilst her light balances his dark.

The mage's face darkened, unwilling to admit the facts laid out in front of him. "The balance will be broken as a consequence of his reprobate soul. The knight is not as uncorrupted as he was in the past, when it was no issue for them to be together."

Stop being a stubborn fool! You must have discerned as well as I have that perhaps the only chance to clean Sébastien's soul is Vivienne healing him, and joining her soul to his, as they did in the past.

"They cannot be together again!" The wizard's eyes flashed with displeasure. "Vivienne will never achieve her full potential with him!"

Is that what this is all about? Alistair's snarl echoed in the night. *You are playing them again until Vivienne attains her potential, to serve your needs and clean up your mess with Carleigh?*

Merlin was silent, and the dog growled his displeasure once more. *You have not changed, old man. But Vivienne will prove you wrong, and achieve her potential. I will ensure it, and you* will *regret your words.*

He released the incantation and connection, ready to depart, though Merlin tried to stop him. "You are meddling, Alistair. The penalty costs more for you, in the end. Are you willing to bet your demon status on it?"

The dog inclined his head towards the fountain, meeting the mage's eyes for a brief moment. *If I lose it for the sake of their happiness, it is a price I am willing to pay.*

"Alistair!" Merlin lost his countenance, the impassable mask finally breaking as he panicked. "Vivienne will be ruined!"

You truly have lost your marbles, old man, Alistair stated, not glancing at the wizard. *I cannot believe you, of all people, have forgotten how powerful love is.*

"I have not. It is you who has forgotten its faithless side. We have both seen it destroy."

Love will save Vivienne. She is not Arthur, and she does not have your weakness.

With the fated words, Alistair did leave, and Merlin's stricken expression evaporated from the fountain.

* * *

Vivienne woke up in tears, cold and shivering. She turned a lamp on, but whatever nightmare had assailed her, she could not recall. Only the memory of the sentiments it evoked remained – the despair, the guilt, the utter hopelessness and gloom everywhere.

The young woman hugged the covers to her and glanced

out the window, where a blood moon stared back. Shivers ran deeper down her spine, and she subconsciously looked around for Alistair.

The dog was nowhere to be seen, and after a few more moments of searching, Vivienne somehow managed to fall back into a troubled sleep.

CHAPTER 12

Sébastien's phone buzzed in his back pocket. A glance confirmed it was Tony's number, and he hit decline. Though not the best course of action, it was the only idea he had for the moment, until he found a better way to make his exit.

He looked out the window of his Jaguar in the direction of Vivienne's house. It seemed she was heading for sleep, which meant he would soon be off duty, and able to hit the sack, too. It had been yet another day when he had not interacted with her and kept his distance, as she wished.

He had, however, spent it considering Alistair's words, and resolved that as soon as Vivienne would be open to it, he would confess the entire truth. Then, she could decide for herself if he had a chance at redemption or not.

Sébastien was about to depart, but a shadow by the thick bushes behind the house stopped him. His eyes darted to

Vivienne's window, confirming she was inside.

In the next breath, he was out of the car, shutting the door behind him quietly. He followed the direction of the shadow, passing through Vivienne's backyard, past the fence – the area was empty.

Though there was no one visible around, Sébastien still captured a menace out of the corner of his eye. He ducked under a breach in the wall next, ending up behind the home, into a dim alleyway.

A white Lincoln was parked there, facing the street. As he observed it, the headlights turned on, and the engine revved, right before it took off at top speed towards him.

Sébastien's body hit the car with an impact, rolling over it and landing heavily on the pavement. He groaned in discomfort, having a strong suspicion a few ribs had gotten bruised.

He pushed off the ground, making an effort to get up. The metallic taste of blood hit his mouth, even as he noticed the car had stopped. The door opened and feet came into his field of vision, and the bottom of a cloak – it was the necromancer.

"Carleigh!" Sébastien spit out, and managed to get back up to a standing position. The ground was not stable under his feet, and a throbbing echoed around his head from hitting it on the fall. Despite it, in that instant, the only thing he was concerned with was facing off the sorcerer without displaying any sign of weakness.

"You're still alive," Carleigh clapped, sneering. "You have no idea how long I've waited for you to finally be alone, without help from your dear princess and her stupid dog. I hoped this would have gotten you out of the way, but I do not suppose it is ever that easy. With you heroic knights, it never is."

With a wave of his hand, dark magic gathered around Sébastien in a thick, grey smoke.

"Fight me like a man if you will, you little shit," the guardian growled. "I'm tired of your games."

Carleigh ignored him, and instead extended his palm abruptly. A gust of air hit Sébastien and he flew in the air, hitting the stone wall behind. Another rib cracked from the impact, knocking the breath out of him.

The sorcerer inched closer, lifting Sébastien in the air with another dismissive wave of the hand. His cruel eyes appraised the knight, even as the air escaped him.

"Are you tired, now? I wonder—" Taking in Sébastien's hateful expression, Carleigh stopped and smirked wider. "My, my. You really *would* kill me if you had the chance."

"Don't you doubt it!" Sébastien gritted out, gasping as the effort of speaking hurt more than staying quiet.

Carleigh sniggered, then proceeded to release Sébastien, before retreating back to the car.

The knight fell to the ground, panting and dizzy from the lack of oxygen. "Come back here!" he wheezed.

"No, I don't suppose I will. I might just let you finish off my work for me."

"What the hell are you implying?" Sébastien managed to shift his head vaguely in the direction of the voice.

Before entering the car, Carleigh sneered back at him. "It means, champion of good, that your dark aura will soon affect Vivienne. My curse did its work, after all! Thus, there is no reason for me to rush and kill you, if waiting the game out will get me the same result."

With his last jab flawlessly delivered, Carleigh left. An odd sense of contentment filled him at the knowledge his words would be more poisonous to the guardian than any voodoo tricks he might have pulled.

It took Sébastien a few moments to digest the new information. Dismayed at yet another turn of events for the worse, he dragged himself past Vivienne's backyard to the back door, to ensure she was alright.

* * *

Carleigh got into the car to find Braydon's scowling expression.

"Why can't we use our abilities rather than ride in this contraption?" the young warlock complained.

"I would rather not attract human gawking," the sorcerer explained, rolling his eyes. "So far, we have managed to stay away from prying tourists and locals alike, and I intend to continue so. Do not give me that look, I am not afraid of these humans. But I have learned the best way to manipulate people is to be out of their sight. They will all ignore my existence, that way when I take over the world, their fates will be at my command entirely."

Braydon pondered the words, then distractedly peered behind at Sébastien's faraway form. "Why not kill him? I assumed that's what we came here to do."

"Much too easy," Carleigh declared smugly. "You ever witness a good man fall, Braydon? I have in the past. And I can assure you, it is quite an entertaining show."

"Be careful not to underestimate them."

The air inside the car changed as Carleigh turned to his second in command. "You dare dispute me?"

Braydon's eyes widened – dying today was not in his books. "No, never," he gulped.

"Good." As swiftly as he had been incensed, Carleigh broke eye contact, snorting in amusement at how quickly he had cowered.

* * *

Unaware of the drama happening a few feet away, Vivienne was sipping on a glass of wine when there was a knock at the back door from the kitchen.

Alistair squinted towards it, then her. *You better get that. It's Sébastien.*

"I don't want to talk to him."

The dog's eyes flashed in warning. *Vivienne!*

Sighing, the enchantress discarded her glass and dragged herself over to open the door. Sébastien stared back at her, all beaten up as though he had been in a fight. He was barely standing, heavily leaning against the door frame.

"What happened to you?" Vivienne gasped.

Alistair was already at his feet, sniffing furiously. *Carleigh's stench is all over you. Did he attack you?*

"Yeah," Sébastien tensed his jaw. "He did. Had a nice little showdown in the alleyway behind here." He looked Vivienne over, almost as if reassuring himself she was in one piece, before telling Alistair, "You were wrong, by the way. Carleigh confirmed it."

"Wrong about what?" Vivienne asked, noticing their crestfallen expressions.

Sébastien broke eye contact, but she snatched his hand before he could turn away. "Give me this *one* answer."

He stared at her hand over his, then sighed heavily before admitting, "Your demon dog was wrong about there being any redemption for me."

What did Carleigh twist your mind with? Alistair interrupted.

"He mentioned Vivienne is as good as poisoned if I stick around. So your plan won't work, and mine is the only one left."

Alistair wished he could say something to dispute it, but even he could tell the knight's mind was closed to all reason, as his aura was.

When Vivienne looked to him for advice, he shook his head. *I tried, highness. He will not listen.*

Panic seized the enchantress at the idea of Sébastien being gone from her life. Before he could add anything, the words tumbled past her lips, "Let me heal you."

Sébastien tried to decline, but could barely stand up as it was.

"Please," Vivienne begged, tugging on his hand.

A wave of piled up fatigue swept over Sébastien. With no will to fight her, he complied and stepped inside, almost toppling over on the couch. Vivienne helped him remove his shirt, and immediately began the healing enchantment.

Having used it a couple of times, it was becoming easier to access. Within moments, her hands glowed and the healing wisps travelled over Sébastien in spirals.

The déjà-vu came unbidden, as it always did, tugging at the edge of her mind until the room swayed. This time, Vivienne did not lose consciousness as it hit, rather falling into a trance.

* * *

It had been two days following the hunt, and Vivienne was worried for Sébastien. She had been told he had awoken, but was still weak. That night, she finished dinner early – barely eating anything as it was – and left the great hall.

As the princess wandered the hallways, she sensed a presence behind and whirled around.

"Sébastien!"

"I did not intend to frighten you, my lady. I was attempting to ensure you got to your quarters safely."

"What are you doing awake?" Vivienne moved towards him, and stopped before reaching the handsome knight. "You should be resting."

"I have had all the rest I could without being able to see you."

Vivienne's lips parted in surprise, and she glanced hopefully into Sébastien's rapt expression. His eyes were devouring her, taking his fill as if she had not been within his sight in ages.

"I–" The princess stopped, unsure of how to go on. The intensity in the guard's gaze was even a bit worrisome, and she backed away instead.

"I had a strange dream while I rested," Sébastien divulged, his stare never once wavering off hers. He

advanced, one step at a time, even as Vivienne kept inching backwards. "I dreamt you healed me, and revealed that it was not Lancelot your heart pined for."

"That is a nice dream, indeed," *Vivienne whispered, having a hard time to get the words past her dry throat. She was afraid of what would happen when they came into contact, knowing her body had no discipline whatsoever around him – truly a chilling notion.*

"It was," *Sébastien agreed, getting even closer.* "I dreamt of your healing touch and kept convincing myself I had to wake up, and tell you in person . . ."

He was now in front of her, barely a hair's breath away. Vivienne had run out of room to back away, and they found themselves in a deserted part of the hallway, behind a pillar. Cold stone was at her back and Sébastien's warmth at her front.

The enchantress tilted her head back to meet his gaze, unaware of how inviting her parted lips were.

"Tell me what?" *Vivienne whispered, an almost daring inflection in her voice.*

Sébastien placed both hands on the wall on either side of her, effectively caging her in. His body moved, closing the last gap between them as he confessed, "I love you. Not as a knight to his lady, but I have fallen for you as a man for a woman. I cannot stay away from you. The only reason I lasted this long is because I presumed your affections belonged to another. If I am overstepping, now would be a good time to shut me down."

Vivienne stared into onyx fire, unable to speak, only shake her head in denial. The small victorious gleam she noticed spoke volumes, before Sébastien gathered her close and his mouth descended on hers. As before, it commenced slow and tender, but soon escalated into more.

The only thing that mattered, in both their minds, was getting closer after the days spent apart. As he embraced his beloved, Sébastien captured her moans, and her lips opened at his gentle prodding. With a barely suppressed growl, he deepened the kiss, grabbing her waist and lifting her up in his arms.

He nearly dropped to his knees when Vivienne wrapped both legs around his hips, pulling him closer. And still the knight's mouth plundered hers, tasting sweetness and innocence.

It was only Sébastien's keen listening skills and years of training that alerted him to the guard patrolling the hallway.

Immediately, he froze. If Vivienne was caught, her reputation would be ruined. Blissfully ignorant of it, she still kissed him, and he did not want it to stop – damnation and all.

With a huge effort, Sébastien drew back from the princess' eager lips. "Open your eyes, love."

He smiled at her glazed, satisfied expression, planning to continue as soon as the threat was eliminated.

"A guard is here," Sébastien murmured, his voice barely above a whisper.

Vivienne's eyes widened at the implied message, but Sébastien placed an index on her mouth for silence. "Shh."

He slowly let her feet get back to the ground and angled his body to hide hers, just in case. They waited with bated breath, but the guard's footsteps drifted further away rather than closer.

"Well. That was ..." Sébastien peered down at the

grinning royal, chuckling softly at her sheepish expression. "I truly apologize, Vivienne. I should have known better than to let it progress this far in public."

"How about in private?" she whispered, and his heart beat faster at the invitation in her eyes. Before he could stop her, Vivienne grasped his hand and dragged him to her room.

Once inside, she locked the door and waved a hand for a sound proof barrier, ensuring they would have complete privacy.

When she circled back to him, however, Sébastien was already retreating, palms held up – to keep her away, or him from getting closer, he could not say. "Vivienne, I cannot in all good conscience take your virtue."

The enchantress could not help a small smile, as his loyalty and principles made him that much more endearing. "Then spend the night with me, and keep me company. I cannot bear to be parted from you now."

His expression softened, and he nodded. "That, I can do."

As the princess stepped away to change, Sébastien removed his boots and left only his breeches and an undershirt on. He hesitated for a moment, glancing at the large bed, but was saved from making a decision by Vivienne's soft curse.

Sébastien raised his eyebrows when she stepped out of her private room, and turned her back to him with an annoyed sigh.

"Would you object to unlacing my corset? My handmaiden usually does it, but for obvious reasons, I would prefer not to call her . . ."

Her timid tone was his downfall.

Sébastien shifted behind Vivienne and slowly unlaced the

corset with expert fingers. Each time his fingertips grazed the bare skin of her back, little electric jolts tingled them both. When he was done, the knight had an impossible time recalling why it was he could not bring the situation to its inevitable conclusion.

And then, Vivienne spun in the circle of his arms, her green eyes wide and innocent, and he remembered. He bent down for a light goodnight kiss, but kept a tight leash on the passion still stirring underneath the surface.

Sensing it, Vivienne retreated once more to the private room to change, before joining him in bed. It was the first night in a long time that Sébastien slept soundly.

* * *

Why did you stop? Alistair asked in both their heads.

Vivienne blinked, coming out of the memory to find Sébastien staring. His wounds were now all healed – though it was the furthest thing from her mind. There was an alertness behind the guardian's gaze, as if he was aware of the past between them as well.

"You had another déjà-vu?" he whispered.

Vivienne acquiesced, and got lost in internal musings once more. It was so distressing, in light of the recent recollection, to remember why they could not pick up from where they had left off. Her entire body tingled from sensations of the past, yet her brain screamed to keep a distance due to Sébastien's obvious inability to be fully honest with her.

I'll be giving you two some space now, Alistair grumbled,

noticing their auras, and retreated to the backyard.

It was enough for Vivienne to snap out of it, at least momentarily. But even as she dropped her eyes to Sébastien's chest, the images still flashed in her mind – his hands on her waist, the way they had kissed, her own reckless abandon. They were fated together, no matter what.

"Sébastien, I—" She met his intent stare, noticing it had not wavered.

He did not let her finish, but instead tugged on her wrist. Vivienne fell astraddle him, and Sébastien pulled her closer still. He cupped her cheek, whispering to himself, "Just one more taste before I go to hell."

He drew Vivienne's lips down to his, and she let him. It was a dance they were good at. Mouths moved against each other, getting reacquainted, tongues battling for dominance, hands on her waist grinding down, until they were touching oh-so-intimately.

Before long, Vivienne was begging for more. Sébastien's lips drifted to her neck, leaving butterfly kisses up until he found a sensitive spot and gently bit on it. She gasped, and he returned to her mouth, drinking her moans. They continued until surrender was within touching distance.

Sébastien disengaged abruptly, bringing himself in check. His eyes were searing, and his hand shook as he caressed Vivienne's cheek. Then the emotion disappeared off his face, replaced with a blank expression. Gently, he moved her off him, and stood up.

"Goodbye, my lady."

Sébastien left, willing himself not to look back, yet torn apart by the knowledge he could never again be close to her.

At least not while his body had any breath left. There was only role left for him – to guard Vivienne with his life.

Alistair entered the room shortly after Sébastien's departure. *I cannot stand by anymore without doing something.*

In a slight daze from the make out session, Vivienne focused on him and frowned at the words. "What do you mean?"

Sébastien needs your help, princess. Carleigh's words got to him, and you partly give credence to them, too. What you both ignore is that there is a way out of this. The first part is Sébastien's to work out, to forgive himself for the past and move forward with good intentions. The second part, however, is all up to you.

Alistair stepped to her, and Vivienne knelt down to be at his level.

You have to become the Lady of the Lake again, in order to use your waters and cleanse him. Before that, however, you have to remember how it happened in the first place, and summon back your strength together, as one – without the noise and chaos I perceive in you right now.

Astonished at his lecture, Vivienne could only gape. Within moments, a dizzying warmth spread within her, forcing her eyes closed. She gave in to the black out, even as she dimly realized it was Alistair who had induced the dormant state.

* * *

Sébastien had come close to giving in to his baser impulses, but the idea that the day before he had been responsible for a man's death, someone who had a family, a wife and kid . . . He could not do it. His self-loathing was definitely attaining new heights.

Lost as he was in his dark thoughts, Sébastien registered too late he was being followed. Tires screeched, and a white Cadillac with tainted windows parked next to him.

Shit.

Two men came out, and he barely had time to punch one. Then a taser came his way, causing him to go down like a rock.

Only moments could have passed when Sébastien woke up, but he was in another car – a limousine, this time. Tony sat across him, pouring himself a glass of wine.

Sébastien got to a sitting position on the seat, rubbing the back of his neck.

"You want one?" Tony enquired, nodding to the glass.

"No, I'm alright."

Tony took a knowing sip from the glass, swished it in his mouth, then swallowed. "Nico's dead." The announcement was devoid of emotion, but his piercing gaze was leveled on Sébastien.

The knight braced himself.

"You called in a cleaning," Tony continued. "Why?"

Sébastien examined his chances, and decided to go with the truth – at least partly. "Nico was falling off the wagon. Last time I went to collect, he aimed a gun on me, and I had to beat him up. He came after me again, and I defended myself."

Tony squinted in deep concentration, searching his collector's expression for a lie. "This wouldn't have anything to do with the girl I saw you with?"

"No. I told you she's nothing."

"Sure she is," Tony leered.

Sébastien chose not to respond – the situation was not going his way, and a tantrum from him would only worsen it.

"My boy, next time you do a cleaning, you run it past me, alright?"

He nodded, pretending submission.

"I run the show here," Tony continued.

"I never argued otherwise, boss."

"And you don't ignore my calls. When I call, you pick up. After taking you in young, it's the least gratitude you can demonstrate for making you who you are. Understood?"

"I get you."

"Good."

Tony sipped some more wine. Sébastien waited a couple of beats before asking, "So, are we good?"

"Yeah. Get out of here."

He tapped the screen separating them from the chauffeur, and the car came to a stop. Sébastien exited without a backwards glance.

* * *

As soon as Sébastien was out of the car, Tony took out a burner cellphone and punched in some numbers.

"Follow him. Get me some proof of what he's been up to. And the girl . . ."

"Should we capture her?" the voice at the other end enquired.

"No, not yet. Wait for my word. Let's see how this plays out."

"You got it, boss."

He hung up, eyes locked on Sébastien's retreating back. The collector had been one of his best men for a while, but even the best fall. *And they fall grievously.*

"Shame," Tony mused aloud. "I might have to kill him, after all."

* * *

Sébastien returned to his home, vaguely aware of being followed, and figured it was probably one of Tony's men. He would have to inform Alistair to keep a distance and double the watch over Vivienne.

The problems keep on coming, apparently.

Once he got inside the house, the guardian removed his jacket and went to shower, sensing the muscles in his body loosening. He figured it would evade him, but sleep came the minute his head hit the pillow.

* * *

Vivienne floated, in a lake or a pond, simply floated and watched the sky above her. There was no past, present or future – only her. She reflected on things learnt and seen, the past blocked in her mind and, most of all, Sébastien.

Eyelids fluttering closed, the enchantress thought of their last time together, and could glimpse the heat in her man's eyes, feel the agitation in his touch, and his despair upon leaving. These were not characteristics of a stranger, but of the champion she knew.

The more Vivienne played the last scene in her head, now without the clutter of reality, she noticed Sébastien's actions, his eyes, and experienced the swirling emotions.

Whatever Alistair and the guardian were keeping hidden, Vivienne realized it was in order to give her time to piece it all together properly. Her original attempt to remember everything at once having failed, there was no choice now but to assess each recollection as they came. And Sébastien, much like always, was sheltering her.

He yearned to be close, that much was apparent. His resolve to stay away was not intended to hurt, but rather because he no longer felt worthy enough of Vivienne. The guardian had craved intimacy back in the past, and still did now. Their few days together at the beginning, when the young woman was still unaware of being a reincarnation, were proof of that.

Yet there was something he hid, something which had happened in the past, and it gave him a reason to constantly withdraw. Vivienne went back to their previous encounters, and recognized she did not help in the matter, either. It was almost as if Sébastien was afraid of being a bad influence, of *tainting* her.

The realization opened her eyes.

Bring me back, she let her thoughts drift to Alistair. *I have to see Sébastien.*

* * *

Sébastien jumped up, not quite sure what had awoken him. He was still wearing the boxers he had dozed off in, when there was a knock on the door.

He squinted at his alarm clock, blinking away the last remnants of dreams.

3am.

Who the hell would be at my door this late?

The guardian snatched a gun off the bedside table, pulled on a pair of jeans, and shuffled to the door quietly. Through the peephole, he saw Vivienne.

Frowning, Sébastien opened the door, and the impact of what she wore hit his body. His beloved stood dressed not in the jeans and shirt of a few hours ago, but in a red dress that hugged her curves, leaving little to the imagination.

He bit back a curse – as if more distractions were needed, when his concentration was already hard enough to find! His dreams had been off these days, with memories of their past intimacy. To wake up to the stiff reality he could never stroke her again was messing with more than just his mind.

Sébastien's eyes stopped travelling up and down her body, only to level on her gorgeous face. "What are you doing here, Vivienne? Late night?'

She grinned, and the understated beauty of that action clenched his gut excruciatingly. "Of sorts, yeah. Can I come in?"

Sébastien hesitated, and Vivienne noticed the gun for the first time. "Expecting somebody else?"

At the mention of the weapon, he snapped out of it and yanked Vivienne inside before any of Tony's men noticed her.

"Did anyone see you come in?" Sébastien muttered as he locked the door, then went by the window to check the outside – nothing odd caught his eye.

"What?"

"Did anyone *see* you?" he repeated impatiently.

"No, no one. It's empty everywhere. What's going on with you?"

"Nothing," Sébastien said, pacing across to the other window – same result.

"Obviously, it's *something*."

"Leave it alone."

"Jeez, you sure know how to make a girl feel welcome."

Sébastien stopped moving, glowering at her instead. "What *are* you doing here? I made myself clear earlier. And where's Alistair?"

"I left him at home," Vivienne shrugged. "And I don't care what you said, I'm here to talk and fix this."

The look in the enchantress' eyes was so earnest that Sébastien melted, almost giving in. Then the meeting with Tony, and the previous day's incident with Nico, came to his head. He willed a closed up expression, resolutely looking anywhere but at Vivienne.

"You need to leave."

"Sébastien—"

"*Now!*"

The cold tinge in Sébastien's voice struck Vivienne, and she could not help the tears that gathered in her eyes. Despite them, she straightened her back and got up off the couch slowly. Head held high, she walked around him to head out.

When she passed by, her lovely citrus perfume floated to Sébastien. His resolve weakened, and he clenched his fists in an effort to stop from reaching out to her.

Vivienne stopped right next to him, in agonizing proximity.

"Look at me," she demanded.

Sébastien locked his tortured gaze on hers.

"Can you truly say this means nothing?"

Her lips pressed to his, a feathery touch that was fuel to his loins. Before he even knew what he was doing, Sébastien grabbed her waist to pull her closer. He faltered at Vivienne's small gasp, then slanted his head, deepening the kiss.

All she could do was hold on, dizzyingly swaying in the circle of his arms, as the embrace brought her closer to heaven with every passing second. Sébastien drew back after a few moments, barely leaving an inch between their lips.

"Stop me." The words escaped with no real conviction as he searched her expression.

"No," Vivienne implored, and pressed eager lips to his again.

In response, Sébastien dragged his beloved even closer, and she moaned as their bodies pressed together, mouths battling for dominance. He hunched over and picked her up, never once interrupting the kiss, and took her to the bedroom.

Near the bed, the guardian laid Vivienne down and peeled off her red dress. Hands trembling, he got to work on his jeans, but she took over impatiently.

Within moments, Sébastien was on top of her, semi-naked against semi-naked skin, and whispered, "I've waited a long time for this."

"I know," Vivienne breathed smugly in his ear.

Sébastien froze.

Abruptly, he jumped off Vivienne as though burned, immediately pulling the jeans back up. The muscles of his back were taut with anger as he panted heavily.

"What—" her shocked expression met his furious one.

"Get the *hell* out of here!"

"How dare you!" Vivienne yelled back.

"Stop the act, *Guinevere*," Sébastien spit her name. "I know it's you."

She smirked, and it was completely wrong on Vivienne's features. The illusion broke, and her face blurred for a moment as though he stared through stained glass. Then, instead of Vivienne on the bed, it was Guinevere's blonde locks on his pillow.

"You're in league with Carleigh now, too?" Sébastien went on, getting more aggravated with each passing second.

The enticing siren shrugged, stretching languorously on the bed sheets. "He made me an offer I simply couldn't refuse."

"Get out!" Sébastien repeated through gritted teeth, barely keeping a leash on his rancor.

Guinevere still did not budge, instead smiling at him and adopting a seductive pose.

"What's he trying to do anyway, forcing me to screw you?" Sébastien grumbled, not impressed in the least.

"Oh darling, I wouldn't call it *forcing*," Guinevere snickered with a mock pout. "You were enjoying it a few minutes ago, and you would have if we finished what we started."

"Answer me!"

Guinevere shrugged, loyal to no one in the end.

"Carleigh realized you're keeping your distance from Vivienne to avoid tainting her. But your soul mate bond is still a thorn in his side, something she could get strength from. If you betray her by being with me, it'll break the bond."

"How?" Sébastien enquired, crossing to the bed despite his better judgment.

"It would enhance the darkness already inside you, and you'd be less likely to get in Carleigh's path. Plus, once you lose Vivienne for good, you'll be distraught and unable to fight him."

Sébastien let out a few well-placed curse words as he angrily marched away. Much as it was tempting to break something – preferably Guinevere's neck – he ended up returning towards the bed once more.

"You were willing to do this only to get back at Vivienne?"

"And why not? She ruined me." Guinevere stood up, realizing she had no chance, and began putting on the dress.

"You ruined yourself." Sébastien forced himself to breathe calmly, stabbing a finger her way. "Now get out of here before I strangle you."

With a last long stare at his stormy expression, Guinevere rushed out.

Sébastien sat back down on the bed, attempting to get his body and mind on a leash. To have fallen for it, held her in his arms, and thought she was Vivienne . . . Hell, he had almost made love to the treacherous siren!

In one movement, the guardian got up and headed for the bottle of scotch. It was as he poured a drink that his cell rang, Vivienne's number blaring across it.

Sébastien closed his eyes at the despair threatening to overwhelm, and hit decline. This would be one more secret to keep from her.

He recalled what Alistair had told him, about soul mates and how they could be torn apart. It definitely felt like it – the ache within his chest, the knot in his throat and stomach, and the urge to cry.

For so many years, Sébastien had worked on bringing Vivienne back, intending to stay away once he succeeded, but at the same time figuring it would be doable. Now, so close to her, the delusion was apparent. It was not enough to defend her from afar. He craved to have Vivienne in his arms, same as before.

And the realization he could not have that, and would have to let someone else take his place, was slowly killing him.

Sébastien downed the shot, and followed it up with another one.

Carleigh will pay for this, he swore.

* * *

The sorcerer stepped to the pool of darkness, waving a hand over it. Within moments, it became opaque and shifted into a mirror.

"Show me Vivienne."

The mirror revealed the enchantress, alone and dormant with the mutt by her side. Carleigh momentarily analyzed the shape of her features, the curve of her waist, the raven black hair.

"My, my, you really are quite beautiful," he muttered, not having truly gazed at his nemesis since the whole journey had begun.

His mouth twisted in a rictus, eyes squinting in hate.

Carleigh spoke with his back to Braydon.

"You can go test her now, but do not kill or harm her. Let Vivienne attack, and make sure she does so with magic. I need to see exactly how powerful she is and how much she recalls."

Carleigh waved a hand over the darkness and two drops of liquid, the size of pebbles, flew in the air. Under his insistent glare, they formed into bullets. With another wave, a gun emerged out of the pool next.

"Use this," he instructed, giving both to Braydon. "The more information you can gather, the better I can deal with it."

"And Sébastien?"

"Vivienne will call him after, I presume. Make sure she's away . . ."

"And then?"

"He's all yours."

"To kill?"

Carleigh merely sneered cruelly. "What do you think?"

* * *

Vivienne blinked, immediately noticing Alistair lying next to her.

I was getting scared, highness, he mumbled.

"Why? I was barely under for half an hour."

You've been under for hours, the dog divulged with a rueful shake of the head.

"Wow, must have been quite a sleeping hex," the enchantress joked.

I am simply content you have returned safely, Alistair sighed heavily.

"Yes. And I have to talk to Sébastien."

The dog pushed the phone off the table towards her, and Vivienne dialed the guardian's number. It rang, but he did not pick up. She tried again, and it went straight to voicemail.

"I'm going to see him."

It is early morning, majesty, and he might still be resting. Wait, and he will come to you.

"Alistair, you don't quite grasp this. I've been so stuck on the image of him in the past, I haven't sympathized with the man he is now."

But you want to?

"Yes. I liked him when I met him without these complications, and I wish to understand this new version of him. I still want him, Al. But I have to get him to be honest with me again. He is still, deep down, a good guy. He simply isn't willing to admit it to himself."

Sébastien is convinced he is damaged. Consequently, he is afraid to get close to you.

"I understand that part now. He thinks he's not worthy, and that his baggage can somehow damage me."

I am glad you figured it out, highness. It is one of the major parts of the puzzle. The dog managed to keep the relief out of his voice – just barely. He was well aware it had been his direct actions that had led his mistress to the truth. *Consequences be damned.*

"Yes. And I also get why you could not admit it, bound by your confidence for Sébastien. I have to do my share, if I want us back together, but there's more at the bottom of this. Our first step forward will be for us to trust each other again."

In that case, go see him, but I will accompany you. It is not a good idea for you to be out by yourself.

"Fine."

They were about to exit, but froze at the sound of the door handle jiggling – someone was breaking in.

Alistair crouched low, ready to pounce.

* * *

Sébastien woke up to the sound of his cell ringing. He picked it up, running a tired hand over his eyes at the pounding headache that greeted him awake.

"This better be good."

"Tony expects you to fix a problem."

"Can't someone else do it?"

"You're the fixer, Dubois."

He clenched his jaw, training his darkening gaze on the ceiling. "Fine. What is it?"

"New recruit family drama. I'm texting you the address now."

"Fine," Sébastien repeated.

"And, Dubois? It's a priority."

"I got it," he gritted out.

Disconnecting the call, Sébastien noticed two other missed calls from Vivienne. He debated on calling her back, but recalled the events of the previous day, and the idea went out the window.

His cell buzzed with the address, which he instantly recognized as an out of town one. "What the hell?"

With muttered curses, Sébastien showered and left his home in a rush.

Less than an hour later, he sat parked in front of a small

house with a garden, wondering what about the place, or the family living inside, could warrant Tony's attention.

When the door opened, Sébastien braced himself. He knew the petite blonde woman, having seen her once before at a get together in Rome. She was Nico's wife.

"What the *fuck*!?"

The phone vibrated again, this time with a picture – his mark to kill. Sébastien squinted at it, and felt his blood run cold.

He dialed back the number.

"Problem, Dubois?"

"Damn right, I got a problem. What the hell is this, some kind of sick test?"

"Not sure what you're alluding to. It's your job."

"You sent me a picture of Nico's *son*."

"Yeah, he's the new recruit."

Sébastien watched as the sixteen-year-old exited the house and hopped on a bike, probably on his way to school. "You've got to be shitting me."

He inhaled deeply, and pushed the question past clenched teeth. "What's the job, exactly?"

"The mom."

Sébastien felt the directive like a gut punch to his stomach. "The mom?"

"Yeah, Dubois. What's the matter with you, going deaf or something?"

"You expect me to kill Nico's wife, the kid's mother, because she's causing drama for her son joining the Mafia?"

"What's the big deal? You had no problem killing Nico."

Sébastien refused to dignify the statement with the

response it deserved. He had never pushed this boundary before, having a hand in a kid becoming orphan, and he was not about to. The decision was made in a snap moment.

"She's off limits."

"What the hell—"

He hung up on the annoying voice, and got out of the car.

The petite woman was about to close the door to the house, but noticed him and her eyes widened.

"You have to get out of town," Sébastien announced, without bothering to introduce himself – recognition was evident in her expression. "I knew your husband and what he was involved in. Your son is going into it too. Leave town while you still can; both your lives are in peril."

"How do you know this?" she wondered shakily.

"Because they sent me here to kill you."

Fear hit her eyes, and she backed away. Sébastien brought both hands up in a gesture of peace, to reveal there was no gun. She stopped moving, and instead eyed him warily, but less afraid.

"I will not hurt you. But you should leave within the next hours."

The guardian departed the same way he had arrived.

* * *

The lock snapped, and the door swung open. With only the light from the outside, as it was still early morning, it was tough to see anything.

The intruder, however, could observe Vivienne. "Finally, highness. We have not yet been introduced."

He stepped into the room, his voice as unfamiliar as his features, once Vivienne had a good look.

The enchantress could sense no supernatural abilities from him, and he was dressed in normal jeans, not a black billowing cape. Yet Vivienne had the impression something was missing, a piece of the full picture.

It was only as the intruder advanced that she registered a darkened aura around him, suggesting he was an accomplice of Carleigh. He was definitely not the Mafia type with the lanky build and hawkish features – much too refined for that trade.

Alistair advanced into the shadows towards the man. He lunged before Vivienne could stop him, and landed on the stranger flat out. The young woman prepared a hex just in case, but the dog had it handled, jaws clamped around his throat in seconds.

When Alistair froze, Vivienne followed suit.

What's wrong? she questioned mentally.

He has a gun, was the chilling reply.

The enchantress used an incantation to illuminate the room, and noticed the tell-tale sign of the weapon shoved under Alistair's ribs.

Let him go! she ordered the demon dog. *Let him go and get out of the way, before you get hurt.*

No. I would much rather kill him and rid us of a problem. Whoever he is, I am no fan.

"Alistair, if you kill him, I won't get any information out of him. I can use him." This time, the words were spoken out loud in an effort to get through to her stubborn protector.

"Then you better get your dog off me," the intruder

croaked, "before my bullets filled with dark magic hit him."

"Carleigh's present, I presume?" Vivienne enquired coldly.

The man tried to snicker, but it came out as a wheeze. "I came prepared," was all he said.

Could this hurt you? Vivienne asked Alistair mentally.

Yes. Not permanently, but this body is not very strong.

Vivienne recalled how long it had taken him to heal, after the fight with Carleigh. Unwilling to take the risk again, she shook her head.

"Let him go," the enchantress ordered out loud again, more afraid for the dog than the situation they were in.

At her command, Alistair edged his canines away from the man's neck, and retreated. He approached Vivienne, but multiple gunshots rang out only seconds later.

"No!" she screamed, watching in horror as Alistair crumpled at her feet.

Vivienne knelt next to him and immediately searched within herself for the healing enchantment to remove the bullet out. She was in the midst of extracting it, and the golden wisps were suturing the skin, when the man shifted behind and snatched her hand.

"You're coming with me. Carleigh asked for you."

The enchantress yanked her arm out of his grip, and turned back towards Alistair. The man tried to mishandle her again, but the minute he reached out, she whirled around angrily.

The air crackled around them, little bolts zapping it, lights flickering in the house wildly. "What kind of a coward are you, shooting someone in the back!?"

Fueled by her anger, a gust of Vivienne's power extrapolated and hit the intruder like a wall of bricks, pinning him against the wall. Her wrath grew, and the man paled at the ice in her eyes.

"If I wasn't supposed to be using my magic for good, I would turn it against you in a second, you pitiful thing," she declared coldly. "As it is, advise your damn master to stop hiding and come confront me himself, if he desires to so badly. And don't you ever, *ever* get near me or mine again."

For a second – a split moment – Vivienne yearned to drive the point home. The air around her foe became a ring she could squeeze, until no breath was left. At Alistair's groan, however, she deflated.

"Get the hell out of here," she muttered, turning her back to the intruder as he hurried to get out.

"This isn't over!" the man yelled before disappearing.

Vivienne worriedly knelt next to Alistair, but he was alright. She continued to get the bullet out, then proceeded to heal him.

I will be fine, the dog rumbled reassuringly as he noticed her tears. *After a nap. The darkness did no harm, other than exhausting me. This body cannot receive too much of it, and what was inhaled will be filtered out by my own blood. My soul can withstand it, and the magic still within me will help.*

Placing his head in Vivienne's lap, Alistair's breathing slowed down.

"Al," the royal pleaded before he dozed off, "please don't tell Sébastien."

Why ever not?

"He hasn't returned any of my calls. And, well, I guess

I'd rather give him some space."

As you wish, highness, the dog agreed sleepily, drifting off.

For once, Vivienne was the one watching over him.

* * *

Whilst dreaming, Alistair was dragged in a vision. He searched his surroundings, but could not notice anything beside the whiteness of the mansion – white walls, white furniture, white everything.

He growled low, but a voice interrupted.

"No need to get your panties in a twist. I've brought you here to remind you of one important fact you appear to be forgetting."

Alistair tilted his head at the slightly familiar voice from so long ago. He opened his jaws to speak, but found it impossible to do.

"Yes. You are here to *listen,* not talk. You seem to be forgetting you were already demoted from demon lord status to your current predicament." There was a laugh like tinkling bells, before the voice continued. "Our warnings were not in vain. If you continue down this path, and interfere in human affairs by helping your charge out when you should not, there *will* be consequences."

Alistair snarled in response, but before anything could be added, a mist surrounded him. Within moments, he found himself in a meadow to continue his normal dream. When he woke up, the encounter itself was already gone from his mind.

CHAPTER 13

"My lady," a different voice than the one in her dreams woke the princess up. "Your father wishes to speak with you. Someone is here to see you."

Vivienne groaned, but got up nonetheless.

King Adrien waited in the throne room, smiling reassuringly as she entered. Vivienne managed to return it, despite the sour mood she was in already.

"Dear daughter, I am aware of our understanding that you will focus on magic, and not marriage, but the son of one of my oldest friends has dropped by to visit. As a favor, could you please show him around? And be pleasant."

"Of course, father," Vivienne rolled her eyes. "Might I get an escort, though?"

"Yes, yes. Bring Sébastien. He is protective of you."

Vivienne dipped into a curtsy, lowering her lashes to hide her joy. Showing a stranger around would be bearable, as long as Sébastien was there for backup.

The man himself was scrawny and awkward, about her height, but respectful and polite. Vivienne could not put her finger on it, but something in his countenance – a glint in the eyes, the way he smirked – was disturbing.

"We have to get my guard," she announced and headed towards the training grounds, the suitor following far behind.

As they neared, Vivienne noticed Sébastien disappearing around a corner. For a moment, she could have sworn glimpsing a flash of blonde hair right ahead.

With a bad presentiment in the pit of the stomach, the princess gestured for the suitor to wait. She went towards the stables, following the voices. One was Sébastien's deep tone, and another was more melodious. Vivienne did not have to see its owner to identify Guinevere.

She rounded the corner just in time to see the young woman step into Sébastien's embrace, and his arms go around her waist, much as they had with her. The cold bite of betrayal was harsh on the enchantress' heart.

Vivienne was about to retreat to nurse her wounds, but was held back by something. The hesitation was enough to notice Sébastien was not gripping Guinevere lovingly, but rather trying to push her away. When he finally did so successfully and backed away, he gave the young woman a wide berth.

"What is the matter with you!?" Even Vivienne cringed at the tone of Sébastien's voice, the disgust and scorn more than apparent. "You are promised to Arthur! Does it mean nothing to you?"

"It is precisely why I have to enjoy my freedom while I still can."

"*Well, go enjoy it with someone else. I am not interested.*"

Guinevere's expression contorted in an ugly pout, but she caught sight of Vivienne and sneered. "*Oops! We have a witness. Lady Vivienne,*" she curtsied in a mocking bow.

Sébastien whirled around, and the princess noted in his eyes the realization she must have witnessed everything. "*My lady, I–*"

Vivienne waved a hand dismissively, cutting the guardian off, and instead marched straight to Guinevere. She had not intended it, but her words came out as glacial as with the men of the hunting party. "*Lady Guinevere – and I do use your title only out of politeness, as no lady behaves this way – you will do me the honor of staying the hell away from my guards, unless you wish your fate to not be so pretty after all.*"

Guinevere paled in front of her anger, but Vivienne was not done. "*Sébastien is off limits. As is every man on these grounds – and all of Elsior. You belong to Arthur and it is to him you shall swear fealty and loyalty. Are. We. Understood!?*"

The dreadfully calm voice, with the ice underneath, gave Guinevere goose bumps, and she dropped in a curtsy so low, her knees almost grazed the ground. This time, there was no mockery as she acquiesced, "*Yes, my lady.*"

"*And, Guinevere?*" Vivienne let an enchantment imbue the words, enthralling. "*Lancelot is not for you. You will stay away from him, as well.*"

Guinevere nodded blankly, and retreated.

"*Vivienne?*" Sébastien's voice came questioning, as if he was unsure it was truly her. The princess turned to him, *ignoring the bewilderment in his eyes.*

All the knight could glimpse was the reined in lightning of her magic reflected in her green gaze. He knelt in front of her, in awe of her powers, and in shame of what had taken place. "Please forgive me. I had no idea she would –"

Vivienne stopped him with a raised hand. "I need you to escort me. There is a suitor here to speak with me, and I have been tasked to parade him around the castle."

Sébastien nodded, though he yearned to add so much more. Vivienne's words only truly sank in as he followed her. The fact that his beloved had a suitor already courting, this only the day after they had spent the night together, was disturbing, to say the least. And so it was with a heavy heart that he did his duty.

Neither of them distinguished the shadow of the visitor in a corner, having witnessed everything. Now he knew Arthur's weakness, and all he had to do was ensure Guinevere did betray him, as he had foreseen. The little charm Vivienne had set, imbued with his shard of the occult, would be enough to unravel Camelot and its king.

* * *

Vivienne spent two days and two nights reflecting, pondering, assessing, and wondering. She picked up the phone more times than she could count, longing to call Sébastien, but giving up. It was now the end of the third day, and still no contact.

Pride was one of the reasons – she wanted to avoid being the one always reaching out. But more than that, it was the uncertainty of what he was thinking. The torment in Sébastien's eyes from their last interaction kept her awake in the middle of the night.

And every day more memories returned, leading Vivienne to wake up from dreams of the past each morning. It only caused her longing to increase, missing his companionship and presence most of all.

Alistair, noticing her restlessness, drifted off the bed and walked over. His soft paws barely made any noise on the floor, but Vivienne faced him anyway.

Dressed in sweatpants and a shirt, the enchantress had been startled from sleep by yet another memory – and always, the waiting tugged at her.

You should not be this exposed, the dog mumbled, having taken longer than anticipated to recover from the attack. *What if the creep is out there?*

"I don't think he is. When I tried scanning for his aura, I wasn't able to pick up much."

Alistair was quiet, and she saw a doggy smile out of the corner of her eye. "What?"

I am proud your abilities are becoming stronger every day. From what I observed of Carleigh, it is essential we have the upper hand.

"I wish Merlin was still around," Vivienne whispered. "He would probably be able to speed this up for me."

When Alistair said nothing, she glanced down at him. "What's wrong? Is your wound still hurting?"

No.

"Then what is it?"

I do not believe Merlin's coaching is required in this

instance. You have done quite well so far on your own.

Vivienne frowned at the words – Alistair acted as if he did not wish to speak of the warlock. "Is there something I'm missing? About Merlin?"

Majesty, it is neither the time nor the place. I will be happy to enlighten you once this matter with you and Sébastien is resolved.

"*If* it ever is," Vivienne murmured to the moon, the mention of her guardian's name tugging at her heart.

It will be.

Alistair sounded more confident than the enchantress felt at the moment. The fear of losing Sébastien forever was nagging, a trap unwilling to let go.

The sound of the phone ringing startled both of them. Vivienne fished it out of her back pocket, thinking it was Sébastien.

"Hello?"

"Don't think you've won yet, highness." The enchantress froze at the intruder's voice.

Alistair barked low, and she fixated a gaze on him.

Let me listen in, the dog ordered, and Vivienne complied, hitting the speaker button.

"Carleigh wants what he wants, and I intend to get it for him."

"You don't scare me!" Vivienne was proud her voice did not shake. "And if he wants me so bad, you should suggest he come get me himself. You're obviously incapable of accomplishing that small task."

"Laugh all you want. I gather your demon dog still defends you, but he won't be there all the time."

Alistair's growl came from deep within at the threat, and Vivienne knew the man had hit a nerve.

"What the hell are you talking about?"

"Ask your protector," the intruder laughed, before continuing in a threatening voice that raised the hairs on the back of her neck. "But I *will* finish what I began. Watch your back. I'll be seeing you much sooner than you anticipate. And maybe we might have some fun before I bring you to Carleigh."

The line disconnected.

A shiver ran down Vivienne's back, even as she asked Alistair, "What was he talking about?"

Majesty—

"Be honest with me."

The dog pawed the ground in frustration, before settling on his hind with his head bowed. *In the past, Carleigh managed to get the upper hand. One of the ways he did so was by hurting me, thus removing me as your protector.*

"Hurting you? How bad?"

Alistair tried to avoid answering, instead saying, *You have to call Sébastien and inform him of this.*

"Stop evading my questions! How bad?"

Bad enough that I was not able to defend you, and you were without a guardian.

"You died, didn't you?" Vivienne pressed, sensing the truth of the words as she spoke them.

It is impossible for me to die, highness, Alistair admitted in a resigned tone. *But yes, I was extinguished from existence at that particular time in space, and my body was eliminated.*

The enchantress tried to process this, but Alistair prodded

a muzzle against her hand insistently. *We need to leave, and you have to call Sébastien. Now.*

Vivienne sighed, grabbed a jacket, and exited out the door with Alistair on a leash, all the while punching in Sébastien's number. He answered after the first ring.

"Sébastien," she greeted.

There was a pause at the other end of the phone, before the guardian whispered, "Vivienne." The longing in his voice stirred the young woman.

"I'm in trouble," she rushed ahead, afraid of getting lost in *ifs* and *buts*, before she had even gotten to the meat of the problem.

This time there was no silence as Sébastien picked up on her urgency. "What's going on?"

"A few days ago, while I was on my way to you, a man broke into my house. He was sent by Carleigh to capture me. I fought him off, but now he called and he's threatening to finish what he started tonight."

Vivienne heard muffled swear words, almost as if Sébastien put the phone away. Then he was back, his voice vibrating with emotion. "Why didn't you come to me that night?"

"I . . . it was too complicated. And I figured you still needed space."

Sébastien was silent for a moment, before asking, "Where are you now?"

"I was home with Alistair when the call came . . . I'm on my way out. Alistair demanded to get out of here and to call you."

"Good, at least one of you has sense. Go to the Palace of

the Popes and stay there." His voice left no room for questioning, yet she tried.

"Sébastien–"

In the background, she could hear noises – the buckling of a belt, the locking of a door. "Vivienne, please listen to me. I get that I screwed up and I can't be your official guardian anymore. But let me handle this. I'll be an hour, then go by your house and end this once and for all."

"Once and for all?"

"It's not the first time it happened," Sébastien sighed, as though the weight of the world was on his shoulders. "Please, Vivienne. I wasn't able to help you in the past, but I can now. Let me do this."

Despite disliking the plan, the pleading in his voice undid Vivienne's resolutions. She consented with a simple, "Alright."

"Thank you. Go where I said, and text me when you get there. I'll meet you when I'm done."

"Okay." The line was already dead.

* * *

Sébastien arrived at Vivienne's place as fast as possible, attempting to ignore the hope in his chest. She had seemed as eager to see him as he did her. Staying away had been torture, something he was unable to continue doing, even if she could.

As the knight parked next to the home, he noticed the front door slightly open – the intruder must have intended to catch her off guard. At the idea of Vivienne harmed, fury boiled underneath his skin.

When Sébastien got to the front door, he slowed down, making no noise. His keen senses informed him someone was on the other side. He yanked the gun out of the waistband of his jeans and shoved the door open with a swift kick, but no one was around.

He entered cautiously, senses triggered at the sound of breathing. The guardian whirled in time to find Braydon there, leering.

"What the hell! You again?"

"Yes, me. I gather her highness sent you here, as predicted after my call to her?"

There had never been a time when Sébastien was more aware of being outmatched, not by physical force, but rather by the dark arts.

Then the shady druid's words sank in. "Predicted?"

Braydon sneered, and spread both hands in a gesture of peace.

"My master is good at what he does, Sébastien. He had me corner Vivienne to test her skills – an easy enough feat. Though I escaped our last encounter slightly bruised. Ah well."

Braydon surveyed Sébastien's gun, turning cold eyes to the guardian. "Planning to use that anytime soon?"

"Not before I get some answers," Sébastien declared, leveling the weapon towards the sorcerer and pointing it straight at his chest.

"Very well." Braydon walked over to the couch and sat down. "Go ahead."

What the hell kind of a game is he playing, pretending to toy around? Sébastien wondered. Regardless, he knew it was the only chance he would get.

"Why do you want me here?"

"To kill you."

"I can't say that's much of a revelation."

"Now that we've grasped what Vivienne can do," Braydon's smugness pointed to the fact he had the upper hand, "and that she remembers, we have to get you out of the way. That is, before you two figure out a way to get past your little hiccup and get back together."

"Why, pray tell?" Sébastien frowned, unable to keep the sarcasm out of his voice.

"Once Carleigh removes her magic for himself, he's promised Vivienne to me. If she's still alive, that is."

Every muscle in the champion's body froze. His teeth clenched so tight that his jaw throbbed painfully. "*What* did you just say?"

"Oh, come now, Sébastien. You know full well that with your wicked soul, you cannot have Vivienne. Someone will have to be there to console her once you're gone. And that someone will be me."

"Vivienne will never fall for it!"

"Ah, but would she be the same woman you know now?" At his furrowed brow, Braydon sniggered. "Do you honestly not realize her powers are as much a part of the little minx as her own soul? It's what makes her so pure and innocent. Without it, Vivienne will cease to be Vivienne, and she'll be . . . Well. If you've ever had a peek at her reckless side, she'll be ten times worse."

At the mention of a reckless Vivienne, Sébastien recalled the night, not too long ago, when she had gone out in search of trouble in the little black dress. If he was to give credence to Braydon's words, the end result would be . . . At the thought of the woman he knew being gone, he snapped.

"I've had enough of your crap!" Sébastien snarled, and took the safety off the gun, aimed, and pulled the trigger. Despite his finger's pressure, the bullet never exited. He squinted at Braydon's permanent smirk.

"Fight fair at least, you bastard," Sébastien growled, realizing sorcery was used to block the gun.

"Now, what would be the fun in that?"

With a wave of Braydon's hand, a gust of wind flung Sébastien into the nearest wall. He struck it with a grunt, before falling to the floor.

"Reconsider, knight. Carleigh's first offer was fair – join him, and maybe he'll give Vivienne to you when he's done." The sorcerer sounded perfectly reasonable, at least to his own ears, but all Sébastien heard was crazy talk.

"No, thanks!" The guardian spit out some blood, and stood up to face him.

"You really would die for her, wouldn't you?"

"What the hell would you know about it?"

"Hmm. Nothing, I suppose."

As he moved for another magical attack, Sébastien saw the wrist action, and this time prepared for the gust. When he landed, it was actually on his feet.

"My, my," Braydon attempted to sound regretful. "What a shame to kill you, rather than put you to use for us. Ah well. Such is life."

He got up from the couch, and this time Sébastien could not evade the attack. He found himself pinned to the wall, with the air around him thinning, his lungs feeling as though they seized on fire.

Pieces of things flashed in his head. Vivienne's image emerged more than once, and he fought against it, but his brain was shutting down. Already, he was slipping into the shadows, his eyes closing.

Sébastien, the dagger! A voice rang with surprising clarity, though he could not place it past the fog. *Get it! The metal is filled with untainted magic, he will be vulnerable after!*

The guardian's eyes snapped open in a last futile effort, even as Braydon departed with finality, believing him dead.

Out of the corner of his eye, Sébastien saw a small dagger out of its leather sheath, on display on the table next to him. He extended a hand towards it, and whether wishful thinking or outside help, it gravitated to him.

Sébastien gripped it by the blade, and threw it with all his might towards the warlock. Braydon fell on the ground, panting. It was a few moments before the champion realized air was filling his deprived lungs once more.

He maneuvered off the ground and approached the sorcerer. Braydon was now lying face down on the floor, the knife wedged between his shoulder blades. Sébastien yanked it out, and flipped him over on the back.

"Shame," he repeated the warlock's earlier words. "If only you weren't so cocky, and had bothered to check I was dead."

"What . . .did . . .you . . .do . . .to . . .me?" Braydon croaked agonizingly. A thin line of blood seeped from the corner of his mouth.

Sébastien clutched the dagger tighter. "Light magic."

"You're . . .no . . .wizard."

"Nope. But I am Vivienne's guardian, and I will do anything to defend her. So thanks for the information, Braydon, but you're done intimidating my lady."

He placed the metal tip next to Braydon's neck and watched unflinchingly as the druid tried to gasp in air, but the magic slowly incinerated his skin. The warlock disintegrated, leaving nothing but dust behind.

* * *

Carleigh was recharging with malevolent energy, breathing it in, when there was a tug in his conscience, like a string being cut.

His eyes flew open, glowing with onyx fire. "Show me!" he commanded to the smoke surrounding him.

It twisted in a circle, before forming a fog mirror. Its surface revealed Braydon on the ground, with Sébastien hovering over and transforming him into ash.

The necromancer jumped to his feet, screaming in rage. The darkness surrounding him writhed, attuned to his emotions, feasting on them and egging him on. It was not loyalty which initiated the rage, but rather frustration at having lost a good lieutenant into the hands of a champion of good.

* * *

A few hours after their chat, Vivienne got a reply text from Sébastien. *"Your home is clean. You can go back."*

"I thought you were coming to meet me here," she texted back.

"I can be there soon . . .if still you want me to."

"I do."

* * *

Vivienne was impatiently waiting under one of the arches by the Palace of the Pope, Alistair by her feet, when Sébastien strolled across the plaza. He wore jeans and a leather coat, as dangerous as they came.

When he noticed Vivienne, the guardian paused for a second, and their eyes met.

Vivienne was not sure what hers revealed, but the way Sébastien's gaze hungrily travelled all over her face and body made it apparent he had missed her.

I will be nearby, Alistair rumbled, before retreating to give them a private minute.

Sébastien advanced swiftly, jogging to Vivienne, and came to a stop right in front of her. Onyx eyes searched hers, before he extended an arm, wrapping it around her shoulders and gathering her in a fierce hug. She returned it with all the strength she could muster, having missed the guardian – and the man out of her reach – immensely.

Too soon, he shifted, and his free hand came up to lift her chin. Sébastien's scorching eyes raked over Vivienne, then his lips crushed hers with no warning. The kiss was overwhelming, demanding, a craving to reassure themselves the other was safe.

When they disengaged, the conflict was apparent in

Sébastien's gaze. Vivienne was about to mention something, but was engulfed in his arms again, before being informed, "Your house is clean, and you won't find the guy again. I added in an extra lock for protection. I know you have your magic, but a little extra security never hurt anyone."

"Thank you," Vivienne replied softly, and his tight squeeze reassured her.

After days apart, Sébastien thought he would be unable to stop the torrent of words on the tip of his tongue from escaping. Instead, he found himself unable to stop hugging the enchantress, and breathing in her scent. They became lost in their own little bubble.

Far away, a group of tourists guffawed, and the noise distracted the lovebirds out of their moment. Sébastien's arms loosened up, as if about to release her.

"No!" the enchantress denied fiercely, tightening her own grip. "Please don't go."

"Vivienne, I . . . I'm not fit to defend you anymore. I've broken my code by hurting lives instead of helping them. You've surely grasped what that means."

"Screw your code!" She peered up at him, attempting to communicate the fear of him leaving. "Don't you get it? It doesn't matter to me. It was still you I called when I was in trouble. It'll always be you, Sébastien."

The guardian frowned down at her, in deep reflection, never once breaking eye contact. When he spoke, it came out conflicted.

"That may be so, but without that code, I'm unable to feel whole, Viv."

"So let me help you!"

He shook his head, a sad smile on his lips. "This isn't something your magic can heal."

"Perhaps . . .but my lake could."

Again, Sébastien frowned, so Vivienne took her chance and said, "It was in it Excalibur was born and returned to at the end. It can also heal and give back what was lost . . . You've lost faith in yourself as a consequence of breaking your code. But you did so to shelter me. It can be forgiven, Sébastien, if only you'd forgive yourself first."

"So you're suggesting I, what, go take a dip in the waters in England?"

"Not necessarily," Vivienne grimaced sheepishly. "In theory, you could . . . But if it hurts you to be away from me as much as it pains me, I could always bless a body of water nearby. Alistair told me I could use it to cleanse you."

There was still skepticism on his face.

"Please, Sébastien, let me help you as you have helped me. I cannot win this fight without you by my side." Vivienne cupped his cheek, much as he had done. "*Please*," she pleaded again.

The guardian's eyes softened and he inclined his head in agreement. Despite himself, Sébastien leaned in and kissed her again, this time even more demanding than the last.

When they broke apart and Vivienne could breathe again, she said, "I suggest we bring this back to my place, seeing as people are gawking. I'd rather not get banned from here."

"Wouldn't that be a shame?" Sébastien joked, his body shaking with laughter. In one smooth move, he shifted Vivienne out of his arms and clasped her hand in his, holding her near. "Let me accompany you home, my lady."

CHAPTER 14

The walk to Vivienne's place was silent, with Alistair following closely behind and keeping an eye out. He entered the home first when they arrived and rapidly inspected it, before declaring, *It is safe to enter.*

Once Vivienne was inside, Sébastien remained at the door. She faced him, a hand extended in invitation. "Please stay with me tonight."

"It's not a good idea, my lady."

Her relaxed expression fell, and she frowned. "We're back to formalities, now?"

"I cannot refuse you, Vivienne," Sébastien groaned, ruffling his hair with one hand. "You know that, but back there, we cannot–" He broke eye contact, trailing off.

Tell her you almost died, Alistair rumbled warningly.

No.

Sébastien, I will if you do not.

He clenched his jaw stubbornly, but finally stated, "When I came to your place, Braydon was here."

"Braydon?" Vivienne narrowed her eyes. "Who's Braydon?"

"The intruder."

"You know him?"

"Yeah. Had a run in with him . . .. Ah hell. Alright, I'll come in. If only until I bring you up to speed. You have to learn everything you're facing, supernatural and otherwise."

Finally, Alistair snorted and moved to the living room.

Vivienne shifted to the side and Sébastien entered, stopping when he came to the dagger that was still in the middle of the living room.

"Must have been quite a fight," the enchantress murmured, inspecting the chaos.

Sébastien acquiesced and picked up the blade, balancing it in one hand for a few moments, then placed it back on the table. "This small knife saved my life tonight. Braydon was a sorcerer, much like Carleigh."

"What?" Vivienne exclaimed incredulously. "But I fought him, and he was normal!"

"He was toying with you – and me, for that matter. To test your abilities, and figure out how much you remembered. He planned to kill me tonight, and serve you to Carleigh for him to take your powers, after which Braydon would keep you."

"Keep me for wh—" Vivienne stopped at Sébastien's dark look. "Oh."

"Yeah," he muttered, with that one word voicing all the hell he would have rained down on Braydon, had he gotten close to succeeding.

There was a pause as Vivienne considered how best to phrase her next query. "You said he *was* supernatural . . . Why the past tense?"

"He's dead."

Her eyes widened in shock, darting to the dagger. "How did you . . .?"

Sébastien shrugged. "Braydon was suffocating me with some occult trick. I was about to pass out, when a voice suggested – in my head – to reach for it."

Vivienne tilted her head to Alistair. "That's why you were acting so weird and unfocused back at the Palace?"

Yes, the dog responded. *But I knew I could not get here fast enough, and defend you at the same time.*

"Thank you," Vivienne replied and knelt to hug him gratefully. From her vantage point, she then looked at Sébastien, tears filling her eyes. "You almost died."

Without warning, she hurled herself in the guardian's arms. He oomphed in surprise, before wrapping both arms around her reassuringly. "I'm alright."

"You could have *died*," Vivienne repeated.

"It's my job to protect you."

She froze at the statement, drawing back from the embrace. "Earlier, what you mentioned about what we cannot do . . . What did you mean?"

"I let my emotions get the best of me," Sébastien admitted softly as he caressed her cheek. "It does not change what I've already said, that we cannot be together. But I will reflect on your offer of healing."

Vivienne's eyes flashed and he braced for an argument,

unprepared for what actually followed.

"Friends, at least?" The three simple words were uttered with an oddly vulnerable glint in her eyes, hitting Sébastien straight in the gut.

"Yeah," he replied, swallowing past the lump in his throat. "If you trust me enough to have me by your side, then I will be here, as your friend. Always."

Vivienne was about to contradict him, but changed her mind at the last moment – it was not the right time. Instead, she switched the subject. "You mentioned you knew Braydon?"

"Yeah," Sébastien answered distractedly, as something else occurred to him – something fairly important to mention. "And there's another thing. We have some Mafia issues, too."

"*We?*" Vivienne frowned.

"My boss saw us together. I tried to convince him you're not a risk, but he's not buying it. He has me followed, and they might attempt an attack on you. Alistair is on high alert."

Realizing it was yet another thing they had kept hidden, Vivienne sighed heavily. "Let's clarify something right now," she declared, voice tight with annoyance. "Since I'm the one with royal blood here, and you're supposedly my subjects, listen to me as I command you this. No. More. Secrets."

"Yes, highness," Sébastien agreed, fighting back a grin.

Vivienne rolled her eyes, moved away from him. "Good. Now, why would your Mafia care about me?"

"They're not mine," Sébastien responded automatically, fists tightening reflexively. At the disbelief in his beloved's expression, he sighed.

You are a distraction, Alistair answered for him.

"Wonderful," Vivienne muttered. "So I have Carleigh and his band of wackos, now your boss and his band of assassins, and probably Guinevere plotting something nasty."

At the mention of the old queen, Sébastien's body tensed. Alistair immediately focused his midnight stare on the guardian, alarm bells ringing.

Vivienne, blissfully unaware, continued, "So what's with this Braydon again?"

"Right," Sébastien snapped out of his thoughts. "I have to first finish with this story, so that you can understand the connection. When the Mafia learned about you, that's where Nico comes in. He's an . . . associate. Was, anyway. Before he tried to blackmail me by warning to reveal our secret to Tony. I kicked his ass, and Braydon came out of nowhere and killed him."

Did us a favor, Alistair pointed out.

"True. But that's where it became a liability and I had to call in a cleaning crew." At Vivienne's confusion, Sébastien added, "They're the people that come and clean the bodies, making sure no trace is left. Anyway, Tony found out and figured it was somehow linked to you. He's suspicious of my weird behavior lately, and set his goons on me and you both."

"Why do you matter so much to Tony?"

"I don't," Sébastien admitted, running a hand through his hair in frustration. "But when I was younger, Tony took me in, and I suppose you could say he's cared for me."

More like used you, Alistair interjected.

Sébastien threw him a look. "Either way, he's under the impression I owe him. And he doesn't accept people abandoning him or contesting his authority, which are both things I've been doing since you came back into my life."

"Even more reason for you to stay with me tonight," Vivienne declared. She held her breath, waiting with bated breath to see if another victory could be counted, on top of Sébastien agreeing to be friends.

The guardian was about to refuse, but at the pleading in her eyes, he conceded defeat with a single nod. "I'll sleep on the couch."

Vivienne turned her head away to hide an amused expression, but Alistair had no such qualms, responding with a doggy grin. *It's on, highness. The fight for his redemption has begun.*

* * *

Later in the night, once Vivienne had dozed off upstairs, Alistair trotted to Sébastien and placed his head on the knight's knees. *What happened with Guinevere?*

Any semblance of relaxation evaporated from Sébastien's body as he tensed. "What makes you think—"

One mention of her name by Vivienne's lips, and you seemed ready to throw up. I ask again, what happened?

Sébastien's face contorted in pain, before he revealed, "She showed up at my place, concealed as Vivienne."

Carleigh's doing?

"Yeah. She accepted his offer, acted vulnerable, and I fell for it."

Alistair waited for the full confession he knew would follow.

"It got much further along than it should have," Sébastien

divulged, his head bowed in shame and avoiding his gaze. "I didn't sleep with her. But it was close."

Alistair was quiet for a beat, then said, Vivienne has to be aware of this.

"She won't trust me after this, Alistair."

She will, specifically because you were honest with her. If she finds out instead from Guinevere, it will be more distressing.

"Alistair–"

Listen to me! the dog insisted, his paw heavy on Sébastien's knee. *Vivienne has begun to believe in this new version of you. Do not ruin it with your silence. If there is one thing watching humans for eons has taught me, it's that honesty is your best weapon in the complicated affairs of love.*

His words were enough to draw Sébastien's attention, and he met the dog's insistent expression. "I was under the impression you don't get involved in human affairs."

And I do not. Ordinarily.

"Does Merlin—"

Merlin is of no concern to us. He plays by a set of different rules.

Sébastien's gaze was filled with confusion. "But you said yourself he was right with regards to me and the curse."

Alistair sighed, removing his paw. Yes, and I am regretting that. I stand by my last advice to you – redemption. The sooner you are truthful to Vivienne about your past, the less it will weigh on you.

With the final statement, Alistair got up and retreated to a corner.

Sébastien pondered the words in his head. Honesty was

the best weapon, but the thought of Vivienne with scorn in her eyes . . . He could not handle it. Tonight, for the first time, he had been a champion again, able to shelter her.

What would the old him have done?

It was following that line of thinking that the guardian recalled the incident in the past with Guinevere, and how Vivienne had reacted. And Sébastien knew he had to try, because honesty was truly his best bet.

He got off the couch and headed to the bedroom upstairs, closing the door behind him. With the moonlight filtering via the open window, Vivienne seemed peaceful, and his heart squeezed. He would have to report the truth formally – and hope she understood.

Sébastien inhaled deeply, then sat on the bed.

* * *

Vivienne was not mad after the incident with Guinevere – not really, and definitely not at Sébastien. She was, however, extremely confused at her reaction towards him. The princess had not expected the all-encompassing hurt when she had witnessed him with Guinevere.

Still with the visitor, she was conscious of Sébastien's presence behind them – and of his taciturn emotions swirling about. Vivienne yearned to speak with the knight, but knew it would be a conversation better suited for the evening, when they were alone.

As they approached one of the armories, the suitor surprised her with a request. "Lady Vivienne, I rather hoped we might have a word, in private?"

She nodded, and ordered Sébastien, "You can wait here."

At the panic in the guardian's eyes, Vivienne tried to reassure him, but could only send a whisper to his mind, "Listen to my call. I will be fine."

Sébastien assumed he was losing all sanity when Vivienne's voice echoed mentally, without the words being spoken out loud. It then dawned on him that Alistair must have shared his skills with his mistress.

As Vivienne stepped away and the door closed behind them, he forcefully relaxed his fists. He tried to wipe off the bad taste the suitor left in his mouth – and it was not jealousy speaking.

It was as he paced back and forth, moments later, that Vivienne screamed in his head. "Sébastien, I need you now!"

The knight rushed in the armory, and his eyes fell on the princess pinned to the wall, the visitor's hands all over her body. With a roar, Sébastien launched himself on the man, aiming only to inflict pain. The thought of his hands on Vivienne was enraging, fuelling him as one fist, then another pummeled the man into the ground.

Lost in the need to deliver justice, Sébastien did not notice Vivienne leave momentarily, then return with three guards.

Moments later, Vivienne's gentle tap on his shoulder and her calm voice managed to break past the red haze. "I am fine, Sébastien. He did not have a chance to hurt me. Let him go."

Glowering, the champion noted the man had a bloodied nose and lip, and his hands were wrapped around the ashen throat to choke him. With a snarl, he released the suitor, whirling to Vivienne instead. His ardent gaze raked over her form, examining for any injuries.

Sébastien craved to wrap his arms around her, to comfort her, but observed instead the royal's countenance was calm – much too calm considering what had transpired.

Vivienne saw the frown, and her explanation tumbled out. "He is magical," she pointed to the man. "Quite probably an impostor, too. Merlin taught me how to interpret auras, and since I met him, I realized there was something odd about him. I knew once we were alone, he would show his hand. And now I have learned what he wishes."

"You know nothing!" the man spat from the ground.

"I have gathered enough," Vivienne retorted, before flicking a wrist to imprison him. One of the pending ropes came and wrapped itself around his wrists. She added an extra spell for strength, so her attacker could not remove it. "As for this Carleigh you speak of, he will realize soon enough you failed in your attempts to hurt me."

With finality, she nodded to the guards and they grabbed the man, dragging him to the prison tower.

Vivienne waited until they were gone, then faced Sébastien, her eyes softening. "The guards will handle him now. Please, come with me to speak to my father." They strolled in silence to the throne room, though Vivienne was conscious they were both bursting with words unspoken.

As expected, when they filled the king in on the events, he was outraged. "How dare he lay his hands on my daughter! Sébastien, if you had not been there, I shudder to guess what could have happened. How can I repay you?"

Sébastien knelt at Adrien's feet, and bowed his head. "All I wish is to defend your daughter with all my might."

The king peered at the knight, and his daughter. Something passed between them, something he knew would be impossible to refuse Vivienne.

"Very well," nodding slowly to himself, Adrien spoke out loud. "You will have quarters next to Vivienne to defend her from this new peril. It appears she is not as guarded as we assumed, even in this castle."

Vivienne managed, only barely, to hide her astonishment at her father's gratitude. To let Sébastien have quarters nearby was a measure of the trust the king put in him. In such a brief time, it was quite an accomplishment.

After Sébastien exited the room, Vivienne approached the king.

"Sweet daughter, are you truly alright?" His kind eyes were full of concern as he clasped her hand in his.

"I was never in any peril, father," the princess reassured him. "I knew the stranger was magical and I lured him away to find out his true purpose. Sébastien was there when I needed him to, for witnessing. Now the man can have a trial, with a knight to give testimony that he was seen trying to assault me."

"Yes, so I gathered. What about this Carleigh? Is he a real portent of evil?"

Vivienne hesitated, preferring not to cause worry, but also not wanting to lie to her father. "I will go speak to Merlin about him, perhaps he has more information. For myself, I have no idea who he is, only that he sent this man here to hurt me. To what purpose, I cannot fathom."

King Adrien was silent for a moment, before leveling an imposing stare towards his daughter. "Do you have feelings for Sébastien?"

"I–" Astounded, Vivienne could not formulate a response.

"I know you promised yourself to the learning of magic," Adrien continued in a voice made wise by age, "and you allow yourself no distractions . . . But not even Merlin can deny you true happiness. While you might not have a conventional marriage, please have faith I will support whichever man you choose."

"Thank you." Vivienne managed to smile past her tears, choked at her father's kindness, and hugged him close. "I do care for him."

"Good, considering I presume he returns the feelings for you." At her bewildered gaze, the old king added, "I have been observing Sébastien for a while and not once does he let you stray from his sight. I am happy you are surrounded by the same love me and your mother had, Vivienne, as it will truly shield you."

"That is what scares me, father. Where my future is headed, there will be plenty of dangers no normal man can chase away . . . I have so little to offer him, since I will not have a family of my own to speak of."

"My dear daughter," the old king took both her hands in his, "you are everything to him, and that is more than enough. Give Sébastien a chance to prove it."

Vivienne assented and, pecking him one last time on the cheek, went to her chambers.

* * *

As she bathed and changed for bed, Vivienne was acutely conscious of Sébastien's chambers being only on the other side. *Excitement tumbled in her stomach, to the point she could not wait any longer and headed for the secret passage that connected both rooms.*

She entered the barely lit room, and for a moment feared to have chosen wrong. Then she noticed Sébastien in front of the fire. He was sitting, naked except for a cloth hung low on his hips. The champion must have just finished washing, as droplets of water still glinted in his hair.

However, the tortured demeanor emanating from him was confusing. He had his head in both hands, seemingly deep in reflection.

Vivienne knew it was bad to spy on Sébastien, but rarely did she have a chance to truly observe him. She took her fill of the only thing visible – his broad shoulders, stretched with whatever burden he carried around, flexing almost in anger.

As the princess stared, a warm feeling spread through her, and her throat became dry, her body aflame.

"This is ridiculous, I have to explain!"

Vivienne jumped when Sébastien spoke, but before she had a chance to make her presence known, he whirled around and saw her. They stood apart, staring at each other, each afraid to start first, until both spoke.

"I did not mean –"

"It was not your fault –"

They both stopped talking. Vivienne offered a tiny smile, and inched closer. Sébastien was frozen, hands clenched as though to stop from reaching out. His gaze burned brighter with each step she took.

Within instants, Vivienne was only a small distance away.

"I know Guinevere threw herself at you. I did not intend

to keep you at a distance today, but I was confused." At his small frown, the princess continued, "I experience too many feelings around you, and I am not used to it. The incident today affected me, and I was trying to understand the emotions it caused."

Vivienne paused, before admitting, "I long to be with you, Sébastien, but I cannot offer you much. My path does not lie in being a wife or mother. There is but one journey that awaits me, and it is dedicated to guarding my realm. To ask you to share that burden with me . . .the price does not seem fair."

The guardian still did not voice anything aloud, and she chewed on her bottom lip nervously. *"Please say something,"* **Vivienne pleaded in a small voice.**

That snapped Sébastien out of his reflections. In one fluid movement, he wrapped an arm around his beloved's waist, pulling her close, lips descending on hers in a new kind of embrace. This one was not restrained, rather possessive and hungry, and the young woman gave in gladly.

Vivienne wrapped an arm around his neck, and placed the other on his chest, close to his fast-beating heart. With a groan, Sébastien deepened the kiss until her knees wobbled. Only then did he slowly draw back, never breaking the intimacy of the hold nor adding space between them.

"Never say please to me again, Vivienne," **he implored hoarsely.** *"I am the one person you never have to ask for anything. As for this price you mention, I gladly pay it for even one more moment in your company, one more taste of your lips. But I cannot compromise your virtue –"*

"My father gave us our blessing," **she interrupted, chuckling softly at the shock in Sébastien's eyes.** *"I was as*

amazed as you. It appears his wisdom is beyond compare."

"When you say he gave his blessing . . ."

"He instructed me to take whatever makes me happy, and if that is you, he stands behind me."

One of Sébastien's hands rose to cup her cheek, and she nuzzled it. "We are free to do as we wish," Vivienne resumed.

"And what is it you wish, my lady?" The blaze in his eyes was now a full-blown fire.

"You."

"In that case . . . Your wish is my command."

Then his lips caught hers again, this time gentler, slower. Sébastien planned to tease her with the kiss, but when Vivienne insisted for more, he matched her pace. They could not get close enough, and so he picked the princess up, and carried her to the bed. There, he worshipped her like the goddess she was for the entire night, until they both fell asleep.

* * *

A hand was shaking her, and Vivienne blinked sleepily, the memory she had been in very much present in her head. Her eyes fell on Sébastien, and her entire body warmed up in response to his closeness.

It was a moment before the young woman noticed the guardian's misery, but once she did, her stomach plummeted in response. "What's wrong?"

"I have a confession to make, then you can pass your judgment, my lady."

The knot in Vivienne's stomach solidified at Sébastien's

formal tone. "Go on," she encouraged him, trying to clear her head of the intimacy of the memory, so different from the reality she was in.

"After I ran into Carleigh, and you healed me, I left because I could not handle being around you. Later that day, I went home, finished getting drunk and went to sleep."

Sébastien hesitated, and Vivienne kept quiet. "There was a knock on my door in the middle of the night. It was you."

"How is that even possible?" Vivienne's eyes widened. "I tried calling you that night, and you didn't pick up."

"Carleigh," Sébastien mumbled, avoiding her gaze.

Vivienne sat up in bed, now fully awake. "What happened then?"

"The version of you that came to me was dressed in party clothes. You came to make peace. I tried to drive you away and you—she—reacted exactly as you would have. I lost control, and gave in to emotions. We made out, and it progressed further."

The knot in the enchantress' stomach tightened at what she feared Sébastien was about to reveal. She yearned to stop him, but knew the importance of honesty and the value they both placed on it.

"Go on," Vivienne ordered.

"We didn't sleep together. It got close, but she mentioned something, and I realized it wasn't you."

"Who was it?"

The enchantress knew the answer even before Sébastien mumbled the name, sounding like he was under torture. "Guinevere."

Vivienne pondered the information, trying to wrestle her

emotions into submission, and not make their situation that much worse.

After agonizing moments had gone by with no word, Sébastien pleaded, "Please say something."

She scrutinized the guardian, noticing the anguish in his expression quite clearly, unaware of how much he could see of hers.

"What did she say?" Vivienne whispered.

Sébastien frowned at the question. "What?"

"For you to discover it wasn't me?"

"I don't think it's a good idea—"

"Tell me, Sébastien."

His stance stiffened, but at the determined expression in Vivienne's eyes, he muttered, "I told her I had been waiting so long for it, to have you in my arms. She responded that she knew."

"How did . . .?" Vivienne trailed off, leaving the question in suspense.

Sébastien scratched the back of his neck in frustration, then said, "You wouldn't know the hell I've been through . . . She would, considering she's been playing you, and hiding your identity. And her voice was smug."

"And what happened after?" Vivienne asked, trying to avoid envisioning the scene – though it was already much too vivid in her mind.

"I kicked her out," Sébastien was saying, "I swear to you."

Despite his words, and the truth in his eyes, Vivienne could not stop her reaction. "Why is it you barely touch me," the young woman murmured, dodging his gaze, "but *her*, you have no problem nearly sleeping with?"

"Vivienne, I thought she was you!"

"But you never even *try!*" She hated the pain in her voice, but simply could not keep it in any longer. "All this time, you won't even attempt to have more with me, for whatever reasons you tell yourself. Yet it all ends in the same thing – wasted opportunities."

The fact Guinevere had – once again – thrown herself at Sébastien, she could live with. And yet Vivienne could not ignore the agony at the idea of the old queen being the recipient of the kisses and caresses she craved.

"I have to fight with myself every second I'm around you, to stop myself from touching you!" The desperation in Sébastien's voice was not lost on her.

They stared at each other for a beat, then Vivienne, under the magnetism of their chemistry, mistakenly lowered her gaze to h Sébastien's lips. The air around them was electric, thick with sexual tension. He dragged in a breath, like a man drowning.

Next thing Vivienne knew, Sébastien pulled her body on his lap, kissing her like the world was ending. His fingers dug in her hip, and she relished the slight pain – because it proved the moment was real, not another memory.

She wrapped her arms around his neck, pressing closer and taking everything Sébastien was giving – and craving so much more he was unwilling to relinquish.

In the heat of the moment, the knight yearned to comfort Vivienne, to show he did want her. But even past the haze of his lust, of her impassioned moans, he knew restraint was his only option.

Despite the desperate desire stirring underneath, Sébastien did not escalate the embrace. Their excitement settled into a calmer flame, and they broke apart.

"I know I can help you heal," Vivienne panted, resting her forehead against his. "Let me. We can be as we were, with these new versions of ourselves. We deserve happiness together, Sébastien. At least consider it."

"I promised you I would," he bowed his head, contrite. "And, Vivienne . . . I am sorry. For Guinevere."

Vivienne sighed and got off him. She ran a hand through her hair, trying to calm her hormones, then settled her gaze on his lowered head. "You wanted a judgment after your confession." Her pause was enough to draw Sébastien's attention to her expression. "Mine is forgiveness, and let that be the end of it."

There was gratitude in his eyes, and something else. But Vivienne was not done. For the first time – the only time – she did something she never had. She knelt in front of him, grasping her hands in his. "I swear to you, we'll get through this – somehow."

After a beat that seemed longer than it was, Vivienne crawled back in bed and pulled the covers to her chin. "I get you can't give me more now, but please remember it's as hard for me as it is for you, with all these memories coming back."

Sébastien nodded and stood, ready to leave. Vivienne's voice stopped him again. "Before you leave, let us clarify something. Where, exactly, do we go from here?"

He met her gaze then, and for the first time in a long time it was less tortured. "I am still afraid of disgracing you," Sébastien admitted hesitantly, "but I would like it if we could work on trusting each other as we once did."

Vivienne eyed him carefully, before replying, "I like the sound of that."

Relief was apparent in the knight's gaze, and he bowed his head in thanks, before staring back at his beloved. "It means more than I can say . . . And I shall leave it at that. I'll let you get back to sleep."

Vivienne waited until Sébastien left the bedroom, then dropped back onto her pillows. Her body still tingled from the déjà-vu, now topped with the reality. She drifted off to sleep, thinking of ways to heal him.

CHAPTER 15

Vivienne woke up the next morning to noises of Sébastien arguing with someone. From the lack of vocal response, she guessed it was with Alistair.

In no rush to join them, she took her time showering, attempting to wash away the memories of the previous night and her body's needs. After dressing in jeans and a tank top, Vivienne headed out to the living room.

By the time she did, Sébastien was on one side of the couch, Alistair on the other, and they were glaring at each other. They both stopped the staring contest to survey her entrance.

"What are you two arguing about?"

"Not arguing," Sébastien retorted.

Difference of opinion, Alistair rumbled mentally.

Vivienne's eyebrows rose, not fooled in the least. "About?"

Sébastien scowled at Alistair, and shifted his gloominess to her. "Your dog has a crazy idea."

His intense onyx eyes reminded Vivienne of the previous night, and the way his lips melted against hers. Her imagination drifted away to happier pastures, thinking of what could be if only his annoying restraint snapped.

"Vivienne?" Sébastien's concerned tone broke past the haze, bringing her back to reality.

The young woman felt a blush spread across her cheeks. Sébastien's brow furrowed for a moment, before his features smoothed as realization dawned. Only his eyes spoke to the tumultuous emotions within, scorching in response to Vivienne's own.

If we can cut past the sexual tension, perhaps I can explain what I was referring to, Alistair mumbled.

Vivienne grinned sheepishly at the dog, now avoiding Sébastien.

"Alright, Al. Hit me. What's your idea?"

Carleigh is in contact with Guinevere, and he is probably doing it in a spot where she is easy to catch. What is the one place you can guarantee she will be at, every night?

"The bar," Vivienne replied immediately.

Exactly! Alistair agreed. *I was proposing we – as in all of us – stake it out, and see what we can find out.*

"Okay, that's a good idea," Vivienne agreed slowly, not understanding what the argument could have been all about.

From the corner of her eye, she observed Sébastien's tense jaw, and glanced between her two protectors. "Am I missing something? What's the problem?"

Sébastien prefers not to put you in danger, Alistair

explained with a roll of his eyes to the man in question.

"But I would have both of you there to keep me safe," Vivienne pointed out.

Exactly.

"Yes," Sébastien agreed, and his voice was strained. "But we're talking about Carleigh and a potential Mafia threat."

Vivienne pondered his words, and the risks associated. It was true the threat was real, but the possibility of even a basic lead, a way to end it all, was alluring enough to risk it.

"I want to do it," she interjected.

"Vivienne–"

"I trust you two to have my back," she glanced at him firmly. "Alistair can stay on the outside, and you on the inside, close to me."

Sébastien's eyes glowed again, hardly able to stop taking her every other word as a sexual innuendo. His sleep after last night's events had been minimal, and rapt with dreams. Whenever his eyes fell on Vivienne, all he craved to do was carry her away in a secluded place, far from all the craziness, and make love forever.

The knight dragged in a deep breath, and broke eye contact. He would have to build up on his discipline, if he truly wanted to defend her.

Released from his burning stare, Vivienne continued as though nothing had happened, "I'll be fine."

"I don't like it," Sébastien grumbled. "It's akin to using you as bait."

"Yes, but I'm agreeing. Plus, we might get lucky."

"And if we do?" Sébastien countered, trying to reason with her. "If we run into Carleigh, will you be able to handle him, in a crowd full of people?"

Vivienne shrugged. "I'll bring him outside where you can both help me neutralize him."

"Alright," Sébastien sighed, realizing it was a lost cause and his best bet was giving in. "But I have to be able to have eyes on you at all times. And if anything goes wrong, we leave on my count."

"Agreed."

* * *

Sébastien was still uncomfortable with the entire plan, but had no chance to detract Vivienne once it was in place. So there the guardian was, dressed in black to blend in with the shadows, keeping an eye on the enchantress at the bar.

Vivienne was gorgeous in a silver mini dress, hiked a little too high on her long legs – more than visible as she stood on a stool by the bar, sipping a drink. If Carleigh was there searching for her, he would be unable to miss the glaring target she made. But the attire also had the advantage Sébastien could keep a close watch.

His gaze remained firmly glued to her, until a group of young men butted in his area. Their unplanned arrival forced him to gravitate around them, but still within earshot.

They were also looking at the bar, and Sébastien tensed the minute they noticed Vivienne.

"Let's flip a coin on who goes first," one of them leered at the others.

"She seems lonely. Bet I can change that," snickered another.

Sébastien scowled, clenching his fists and stepping in

their space. "Watch your language!"

"Hey, back off man," one of the younger men scoffed his way.

The next moment, Sébastien was in his face, grabbing the man by the scruff of his shirt. Blinded by wrath, he dragged him out past the back exit. All he wanted was to get the kid to swallow his words, one way or another.

The others followed behind, but Sébastien did not care. The minute they were out, he let the punk go, shrugged off his jacket, and moved his hands in a come-hither motion.

"Come get me."

And the young man jumped on the occasion – as did his friends. Sébastien was conscious only of the targets to punch, which he did. Restraint snapped, and the red haze of anger took over, to the point he did not feel it when one of their badly aimed hits actually made contact.

He simply kept going, fighting throughout, and bullying his body across human limits of endurance.

* * *

The man sat down next to Vivienne without her assent. She ignored him, focused on an agitated Sébastien a few feet away, almost boiling over.

Her attention was completely overrun when a brawl commenced. Vivienne was so concentrated on it, she did not notice when the man slipped one hand past her drink and dropped some powder in it.

The young woman picked up the glass and sipped it distractedly. Then Sébastien dragged someone outside, and out of her field of vision. Soon, he was followed by a few other shapes. Vivienne immediately got up to go after them.

Alistair, she advised mentally, *there's something up with Sébastien.* When there was no reply, the enchantress tried again. *Alistair?*

Vivienne was well on her way to the exit door, away from the crowd, when the exit sign became blurry. She paused in her steps, confused at the current dizziness hitting her. As she went over the last few moments in her mind, it dawned on her that she had been drugged.

As the realization struck, her senses extended beyond her worry for Sébastien, and she became aware of the footsteps behind. Whirling around, Vivienne noticed a young man following her, a predatory glint in his eyes.

"Bad idea," she warned him. The drug within her body was dispersing, but Vivienne managed to clear her head. When he went to make contact, her instincts – and the fighting Sébastien had taught her long before – took over.

The enchantress angled her body out of the way, then had clear access to the man's wrist. With an iron grip, she seized and twisted it, at the same time dropping to the ground and flinging the man over her head. He slammed into the stone wall, then dropped to the ground, unconscious. The predator would not be hunting anyone tonight.

Vivienne let an enchantment surface, imagining a cleansing wave washing over her and filtering the drug out. Unfortunately, she could only remove the drowsiness, as the rest had been absorbed into her bloodstream. Slightly wobbly on her heels, she continued for the exit door – and gasped. Her eyes struggled to understand what she was seeing, even as she tumbled out into the chilly evening.

Sébastien was in a full brawl with a group of younger men. The way he moved, with such reckless abandon, was enough to give her pause. He was animated by an almost invisible force.

Vivienne soon discovered Sébastien was hurting his opponents more than they were hurting him, and the fury fueling him emanated from the worst recesses of his soul. The guardian's entire being vibrated with it, crossing boundaries it never should have.

This was definitely not the aura of the man she had fallen in love with. There was pure negativity coming off him in waves, evident in the way Sébastien pummeled his opponents into submission. It was a far cry from the feral grace and restraint the champion had once exhibited, even when battling Lancelot.

Nevertheless, it was still Sébastien, and she still loved the man, thus she owed him to intervene before something regretful occurred.

Focusing on that, Vivienne elevated her hand, insisting past the haze of the drug, to command the bodies of the assailants to slumber. A soft pink mist rose from the ground, enveloping the attackers. Within moments, the young men dropped down like rag dolls with their strings cut, fast asleep.

Sébastien faced her with features stony as marble, only his eyes showing the turmoil within. When he finally spoke, the pain in his tone could have filled an ocean. "I warned you I was no good anymore."

"Don't say that!" Vivienne pleaded, and tried to step towards him. Unable to keep a proper balance, she almost fell flat down.

Sébastien was there in an instant, wrapping his arms around her waist for equilibrium. "What's wrong? What happened?" His voice was full of concern, more like the normal man she knew.

"Some guy slipped something in my drink," Vivienne mumbled, placing both hands on his chest to remain standing and steady. "I'm alright."

At the lack of response from the guardian, she looked up to see his features filled with more regret. "Sébastien?"

"I have failed you in every possible way, now." His eyes darkened, and Vivienne could physically feel his walls go up, separating them like the thickest ice.

"That's not true! If you had, I would not trust you, and yet I still do. Can you explain that to me?"

"Vivienne–" Sébastien disregarded her earnest expression, and tried to back away.

"Shhh," she placed a finger on his lips, keeping him close. "The first step in maintaining this trust is to be honest with me. Let me see what's so horrible. Let *me* decide if and how you failed me. Respect me enough to allow me to choose."

Their eyes met and held for a few moments, and the knight recalled his intent a few days earlier to let Vivienne witness everything, and decide for herself. *This is it, then. No more hiding.*

Vivienne saw the conflict in his expression, but also the resignation when he gave up. Sébastien tugged on her hand and brought her over to one of the stone benches, where she sat down. He knelt, bowed his head and lifted both palms face up, offering the enchantress free access to his memories and soul.

"Forgive me," he pleaded.

Sébastien's hands in hers were rough, a testimony to the lifestyle he led. Vivienne gripped them hard and followed the link within, to him. She pictured it, an almost silver string tying them together – their soul mate bond.

The link led the young woman to an obscure cave in her mind. She hesitated for a moment, then entered and was engulfed by Sébastien's memories – the girls, the fighting, the killing, the despair, the anguish. Two lifetimes of pleasures of the flesh and crime, to the point nothing else mattered. There was no love, sympathy, or light, only bad choices and darkness. When the flashes were done, Vivienne slowly blinked, as though awakening from a nightmare.

Sébastien had been watching her the entire time. With no time to school her features, the guardian had front row seats to the horror filling her. She had enough time to catch the anguish in his eyes, before he let go of her hands and stood.

"Now you know."

"Sébastien, wait. Why?"

He stopped in his tracks, but faced away from Vivienne, unwilling to turn around. His entire body was frozen with unbidden tension, and when he spoke, it was with finality. "It was the only way it would ever end, and you could come back."

Sébastien refused to divulge anything else after, but accompanied Vivienne to his car, and brought her home. He waited until Alistair arrived from the bar, annoyed at having been left behind.

Care to explain why you two left? The dog growled at both of them, despite the fact Vivienne was upstairs in the bedroom, and Sébastien, downstairs in the living room.

The guardian studied Alistair from his cup of coffee with a grim look. "I got into a brawl, and failed in my duty to guard Vivienne. Since you're here, I can take my leave."

Without another word, Sébastien got up and drove away. Shaking his head, Alistair climbed the stairs to his mistress' bedroom. He found her in a daze, staring out the window – presumably at the Jag disappearing in the distance.

"He showed me," Vivienne whispered, unprompted. "His past two lifetimes, and why he is convinced of being unworthy."

Why did you not call out to me?

"I got drugged, and my telepathic abilities didn't work, while everything else was weakened." At his nudge on her hand, Vivienne shrugged. "It's okay, I'm alright now. The drug evaporated from my body."

Alistair sat down, tilting his head. *Why did Sébastien run off?*

"He believes, beyond a doubt, that he's a lost cause. Now that he has shown me the full truth, he's convinced I'm of the same opinion."

And are you?

"No. But his past lifetimes did help me realize there's an important piece missing. And I intend to contact Merlin to find out what it is."

Vivienne –

"Don't attempt to dissuade me. Weren't you able to speak to him, in the end?"

I did, because he is in between time dimensions, however –

Vivienne's glare stopped him. "You had your chance to explain your issues with Merlin, and said it wasn't important.

Now I have to speak with him, and clarify a few things."

It is a complex spell, majesty.

"So I gather," Vivienne replied, surveying the moon. "But it's a perfect time to do it, and I still recall how."

Under Alistair's helpless watch, the enchantress sat down on the floor, conjured a bowl of water, fired up a candle, and closed her eyes. She fixated her attention on the bright yellow moon and Merlin's presence, and the bowl wavered.

Bringing magic forth was easier than Vivienne imagined. It stirred like an overeager puppy, filling her within moments. This time, rather than extrapolate it, she concentrated on Merlin's image. She pictured him sitting across from her, separated by a faint wall of glass.

A soft glow enveloped the young woman, then transferred to the bowl. It was barely a halo, as though the moon had focused on it.

Alistair whined, and the hairs on the back of her neck prickled. Vivienne knew it was dabbling in the forbidden, as her old master never would have permitted her to part the curtains of time. Still, answers were required, and only he could provide them.

In the water, Merlin's face emerged. It was blurry at first, but within instants became clearer.

Vivienne opened her eyes, smiling when their gazes met. "It's good to see you again, master. And none too soon, because I need your help." She bent over the bowl to be closer, conscious of the short time they had.

"You should not be doing this," were Merlin's first words, followed by a frown at his pupil across the ages.

"I understand, but I'm desperate. Sébastien believes he is

tainted and unworthy, and I cannot fathom how to help him realize otherwise."

The mage was silent for a beat, and Alistair was nonplussed when he responded, "You're missing some information that would clarify the rest."

The dog would have thought after their last conversation, the old man would have made an effort to dissuade Vivienne from finding out more. Apparently, he had figured wrong.

"What do you mean?" Vivienne asked the wizard.

"First, remember Carleigh's curse," Merlin suggested.

Alistair clued in to the strategy too late. He had the strong impression the mage was aware of the implications, and acting on purpose. Merlin's eyes glowed with the spirit he used.

An eerie breeze entered Vivienne's bedroom, and with it Carleigh's whispered words: *"You will only be reborn when his heart turns to darkness. There will be nothing you can do and you will know despair and lose your light."*

Vivienne snapped out of the trance, accusing eyes narrowing on Merlin. "You knew!"

The wizard did not attempt to hide it, steadily staring back. "It happened after you were gone. I had a chance to save Sébastien's life by healing his wounds, but he begged me to let him die. He promised he would wait for you and guard you from afar."

Vivienne reined in her temper, deflating as realization dawned. "He did it all for me, and now he believes he is unworthy."

Merlin was silent for a beat, but urged, "Stay away from him, Vivienne."

"How can you say that?" Vivienne frowned, forlorn.

"He's done everything – *everything!* – to get me back no matter what the cost. And he refuses to love me so he does not taint me."

"And he is right!" the old mage stated.

"No, he's *not*! I will not let Carleigh break us and decide my future. I will do all within my power to bring Sébastien back and help him appreciate his worth, as he did for me."

Alarm displayed in Merlin's eyes. "The only reason I gave you this missing piece is so you can conclude what I have, and accept it – there is no future for you two. You have to move on."

"I will not toss him aside." Vivienne's narrowed eyes focused on the wizard. "The stakes are clear now, thanks to you, and I won't lose myself, Merlin, I promise."

"And how is it you intend to do this? You do not fully perceive the forces you're meddling with!"

"I honestly can't even begin to guess. But I'll find a way."

Might I suggest something? Alistair butted in, ignoring the resentment in Merlin's eyes. *Sébastien loves you. He has done all this for love, the purest sentiment. Perhaps loving him, in return, would heal him. You have so much spirit, highness, if anyone can banish the shadows in him, it would you.*

"I disagree," Merlin interrupted. "It is much too dangerous, and you have enough to worry about with Carleigh."

Vivienne ignored him, focusing on Alistair instead. "How do I begin?"

Forgive him, was the dog's response. *Go to him and explain your reaction to what he showed you.*

"Vivienne, don't!"

The enchantress focused on Merlin, her gaze speculative. When she spoke, determination made her voice stronger. "This is one matter I will not listen to you in, master. Thank you for your enlightenment."

With a wave of her hand over the bowl, she ended the spell. The glow immediately evaporated, as though someone had pulled the curtains closed and shadowed the moon, and Merlin was gone.

Disregarding Alistair, Vivienne grabbed a jacket and her house keys. She headed out to Sébastien's place, determined the night would not end before she spoke with him.

* * *

"Sébastien, open up!" She scowled at the door, getting more annoyed by the minute. "I'm not leaving until you do."

Vivienne raised her hand to knock again, but the door unlocked. Sébastien stood there in sweatpants and a tank, unreadable eyes glinting.

"We have to talk."

"No, we don't. Your expression said it all, my lady."

"*No*, it didn't," Vivienne scowled at his tone.

She maneuvered past the knight and entered his home, whirling around as he closed the door and leaned against it. A glass with clear liquid shone in his hand – somehow, she doubted it was water.

"You can't read my mind," Vivienne's chin raised to square off with him. "So I'm going to explain it to you. Yes, I was shocked at what I saw. When Merlin explained the curse to me—"

"You spoke with Merlin?" Sébastien's voice was scathing now, the sarcasm apparent. "How unsurprising."

Vivienne lifted an eyebrow. "Why?"

"No reason," he muttered, sipping from the glass.

"Both you and Alistair act weird about him. What is it you're hiding?"

Sébastien exhaled heavily, gulped the last of the drink and poured himself a new one. "Ask Merlin next time you talk to him. All I can say is that he's been messing with my head long enough."

"Sébastien—"

"Fine." Another sip. "You want to know? He's the one who gave me the nightmare you witnessed – with the mirror. That's the truth."

"What? Why?"

He tossed her an incredulous glower, but with a rueful shake of the head realized it was an innocent query. "To remind me of how unfit for you I am now. Guess he was right."

"Sébastien—" Vivienne tried advancing, but he stepped back.

"No. Leave me alone. Please."

"I won't. I still trust you."

"No, you *don't*!" Sébastien yelled, throwing the glass against the wall in rage. Vivienne watched in stunned silence as it shattered to pieces.

"I don't even trust myself, much less when I'm around you!" Sébastien continued angrily, clenching his fists. "I cannot with this destructiveness within me, it's overwhelming. It *cannot* be allowed around you."

"Let me be the judge of that!"

The chaos in his stricken expression spoke more than words. "I can't!"

"Then you're no better than Merlin," Vivienne said softly. "Whatever he did to you, you're now doing to me by robbing me of my choice."

"Vivienne—"

The enchantress approached again, this time placing a hand on his chest, above the heart. "I choose to trust you. And I still yearn for you in my life, still need you, Sébastien. Our soul mate bond is there, lingering between us."

The guardian met her gaze with a groan, and Vivienne sensed the conflict warring within him. "You told me once I never have to say please, that you would be the one person to always be there for me, in whatever way I require you to."

"And so it is," he conceded, bowing his head, fists unclenching at Vivienne's soft voice and soothing touch.

"Then do not make me beg, Sébastien. Shelter me. Let me heal you."

His voice was barely above a whisper. "And if you can't?"

Vivienne yearned more than anything to soothe the anguish in his eyes, but had to give him what he expected – a chance to hope, with no strings attached. "If I cannot, you can do as you wish and I will release you from your oath."

The idea of being away from her was pure agony, but Sébastien forced an agreeing nod.

"We have a deal?" Vivienne confirmed.

"Yes, my lady."

She hesitated, pondering whether to voice out loud the

remaining of her sentiments. At the wariness in the guardian's eyes, she spoke despite the threatening doubts.

"Sébastien, no matter what you might believe, what you revealed to me today does not make me think any less of you. On the contrary, it proves you are the one intended for me, after all you did to bring me back. I wanted you to know this, if nothing else."

Vivienne stood up on her tiptoes, ignoring the way his eyes smoldered, for a light peck on the cheek.

She drew back, intending to exit, but the front door burst open and five beefy men barged in.

* * *

The only thing Sébastien could focus on was, *I have to get her somewhere safe.*

He snapped out of his stupor and captured Vivienne's waist, ignoring her stricken look and hissed, "Sébastien!"

Instead, the guardian yanked her to the side, at the same time advancing forward to shield her with his own body. "What the hell is this?"

He recognized the men as Tony's own, and their leader took charge. "What's it seem like to you, Dubois?"

Like a damn double-crossing execution, Sébastien thought, but said nothing out loud.

They advanced in a semi-circle, blocking all the exits, cornering them towards the living room where there was no escape.

"I'm off limits!" Sébastien growled to them.

"Not anymore."

Sébastien assessed his adversaries, and concluded he could easily battle them. But taking them on and protecting Vivienne was another thing. After the last time she had seen him lose it, he did not intend to showcase his fully unleashed force – despite her reassuring words.

Vivienne saw his hesitation, and wondered why he did not instigate anything. After what she had observed earlier, it was apparent this would be a breeze for him.

A flash of instinct made her realize the reason behind Sébastien's subdued demeanor – he was not lashing out for her. The only way out of the situation was to somehow reassure him there would be no judgment for his actions.

Vivienne reflected back to the past and their telepathic communications, hoping she could do it again. Bowing her head to the floor, she blocked out their surroundings and searched for their bond.

It was there, a tiny link between them, a silver connection in both their hearts. Though thinner than in the past, almost obscured by fog, the enchantress traced it back to Sébastien – and the link snapped into place as they connected.

Sébastien, Vivienne called out softly, *Don't hold back. I can handle it.*

His back muscles tightened in response. The slight tilt of his head to the side was confirmation he had heard – not quite facing her, but listening nonetheless.

Give it your all, Vivienne repeated again for good measure. *I meant every word.*

This time, Sébastien's rage redirected to the five men. After one brief moment of hesitation, he advanced towards them and struck the first one. The other four edged forward as well.

Before Vivienne could even summon an enchantment to help out, Sébastien acted again, striking the man to the right, and shoving him into the wall. The second man to the left, he seized by the neck and head butted, then kicked in the gut.

"Watch out!" Vivienne yelled in warning.

Sébastien twisted around to the man behind, and hit him under the chin in a swift but effective motion. The adversary fell down, hands clutched onto his choking throat.

The last man standing sprung both hands up in a gesture of surrender, but Sébastien's fist connected with his nose regardless – the bone crunched mercilessly.

The champion whirled to confront his next opponent, but there was no one. They were all on the ground, in different levels of pain.

Sébastien faced Vivienne, breathing heavily, and extended a hand. "Come on!"

She ran and grasped it, and they were off. They exited out the front door, but had barely gotten out when bullets from silencer guns whizzed by, and more men progressed inwards.

Sébastien dragged Vivienne back into the house, and this time went out the back exit. They managed to get out into an alleyway, running towards one of the public plazas. He drew his gun out with his free hand, keeping it ready but tucked out of sight against his sweatpants, in case they ran into bystanders.

They made it all the way to the end of the alleyway, when a navy SUV came from behind. Sébastien maneuvered Vivienne out of the way and aimed the gun, shooting at the vehicle. The deafening sound of the gunshots rang all around them, as it rained bullets past their heads.

Fueled by her small telepathic victory, Vivienne acted instinctively. She crouched down close to the ground, and put both palms down on the cold cement. Imbued with an enchantment, they vibrated for a brief moment. Then, a thin barrier visible only to her eyes lifted up from the ground and surrounded them both.

Sébastien stopped shooting when he noted the Mafia men's bullets were not making contact with them. He searched around for Vivienne and saw her getting up, beaming like the proverbial Cheshire cat.

With a shake of his head towards his beloved, the guardian could taste the spell she had used. It imbued the air with a soft fragrance, like Vivienne's skin, so similar to the past.

"Get out of here!" Sébastien pleaded.

She shook her head and smiled. "I'm not leaving you."

"Vivienne!" he roared.

"No!"

Sébastien gave up, and instead motioned for Vivienne to join him. Once she was by his side, he could afford to breathe.

"Let's go to my Jag and get out of here, then."

They detoured right, planning to backtrack towards the home where the Jaguar was parked, but noticed another car moving their way. Sébastien aimed to shoot the tires out, but only the click of an empty chamber echoed instead of a gunshot. "Shit!"

Vivienne noticed the approaching car, and froze. Sébastien tried to tug her out of the way, but was unable to.

Instead, one graciously slender wrist rose slowly in the air. Air was intangible, the enchantress had been taught in this modern world. However, Merlin had once informed her everything could be influenced by magic.

Focusing intently on it, the air around the vehicle became a physical force to Vivienne. Her palm clenched in a fist, using the air as a barrier. In a single movement, it slammed into the car.

With a flick of her wrist, the car was shoved to the side, flipping into the stone wall, and the sound of metal crushing passed them. It came to a stop, hitting one of the lamp posts.

Vivienne gaped at the damage, and met Sébastien's half-frowning, half-proud expression.

"What?" she asked.

He simply shook his head. "It's pretty damn amazing what you've recalled in a few days only."

"Oh." Vivienne shrugged. "What's the point in having supernatural abilities if I can't use them, right?"

Sébastien glanced at the crash, then back at the enchantress. "So long as you only use them for good."

"It was to keep us safe, Sébastien," Vivienne reassured him softly, realizing where the worry came from.

"I know."

An unspoken communication went between them, then Vivienne shrugged. "I cannot manage its strength sometimes."

Sébastien moved closer, pulling her in a half hug. "It's alright, you're almost there. Control comes with piecing it all together. Plus, I'll be here to stop you if you go overboard."

Vivienne froze, not quite believing her ears. Their gazes met, hers disbelieving, and attempting to see if he was serious. The determination in Sébastien's eyes could be measured clearly.

Before she could reply, he let her go and grabbed her

hand instead. "Time to move."

As they jogged back to the house, tensions were high – both were expecting more goons to show up. None appeared though, and they got to the Jag without further issues.

"Where to?" Vivienne wondered, snapping the seatbelt into place.

"Your place. Alistair and I can take turns keeping watch, seeing as Tony won't let this go so easily."

"Has he figured out where I live?"

"Chances are, no. So long as I can stay out of sight for the next day or so, I can find us a getaway spot."

"And Carleigh?" Vivienne wondered, reminding him of their most pressing issue – as if he needed a reminder.

Sébastien shifted gears and hit the gas, taking off the parking lot. "I have a hunch he might use this as a chance to get to you. So, for the time being, you get your wish. You're in my sights day and night, whether you like it or not."

Vivienne turned her head to the side to hide the smile threatening to escape. "Whatever you want."

* * *

Hours later, Vivienne got out of bed and went into the living room. She had only rested for a few hours, but Sébastien was still asleep on the couch, a gun on his chest.

Probably loaded, the enchantress mused ruefully.

The young woman tiptoed and placed the gun on the table, still within reach but not endangering his life. After, she walked past Alistair who was snoring by the door.

They were both taking their protective duties more

seriously than before, seeing as peril was overwhelming from multiple sides. Vivienne mulled over the return home, and the first stressful moments between Alistair and Sébastien.

Her protector had peered at them, then growled to Sébastien, *What the hell happened?*

"Secondary effects is what happened," Sébastien had glowered in return.

What do you mean?

"Tony must have seen us at the bar. He sent Mafia goons after both of us. We fought them off and fast tracked it out of there."

Alistair had been quiet, scanning Vivienne. *Are you alright? You feel weak to my senses.*

"I used some incantations to defend us," she had admitted.

Were the humans that bad? I would rather you keep your offensive magic for Carleigh.

"There were a lot of them, Al."

You should get some rest, the dog had advised, scrutinizing her.

Vivienne had been wary to leave the two alone, considering they seemed ready to come to blows. "Will you two be alright?"

They had shared one long stare, and the tension had gone out of the room as they both nodded in agreement.

Vivienne had gone to shower, and figured rest would probably not come. But the minute her head hit the pillow, she had passed out. The murmur of Sébastien's voice, talking to Alistair about securing the place, had lulled her to dreamland.

Now, close to early morning, the young woman went out

on the patio to watch the sunrise. She was alone for only moments, when tiptoes were heard behind.

"Morning, Alistair," Vivienne greeted casually. With her senses back, her ability to recognize a presence by their energy was more defined, especially for someone she cared about.

Majesty, the dog grumbled, stretching his huge body. *Is everything alright?*

"Hmm . . . Yeah," she murmured pensively. "Odd dream, is all."

Dream?

"Mhmm." Alistair waited until she turned to him. "Did Sébastien have a sword? In the past?"

Yes, every knight did.

"But not now."

No.

"Where is it?"

You would have to ask him, as I honestly have no idea. He still had it when I last saw him in the past. I have not seen him with it here.

Vivienne tapped her chin. "Where do you suppose it is?"

Alistair mulled it over, cocking his head to the side. *You sure are full of questions, highness . . .*

Vivienne shrugged, pointing out, "It's not like Sébastien will confess . . . I preferred to see if you knew anything before potentially bringing it up with him."

If I was to guess, the dog conceded, *I would say he probably lost it ages ago.*

"Why do you suppose that?"

Alistair hesitated, then declared, *A knight's weapon is symbolism, as well as protection. If he does not have it, it is as though he is missing part of himself.*

"Could it be contributing to his current feelings? The ones that he doesn't belong, that he's less worthy than before?"

Part of it, maybe.

Vivienne's eyes unsharpened as she realized that maybe, just maybe, another piece of the puzzle had just emerged. "So it could help him summon back what he lost," she murmured, almost to herself.

Perhaps.

"I will get it back for him," the enchantress decided, peering back at the disappearing moon.

It might not be as easy as you imagine, Alistair warned, not quite keen to see his mistress launch onto another quest, when they already had enough on their plate. He knew Vivienne well, and once she got an idea, it would be hard to change her mind.

"It will come when he needs it, I presume," Vivienne declared. "Excalibur did for Arthur, didn't it? In the legends."

Alistair bowed his large head in assent, surmising the real story behind the myth was quite different. He kept silent, not eager for Vivienne to focus on that part of her memories yet, and instead watched the sunrise with her.

CHAPTER 16

"Carleigh?" Merlin's features betrayed shock, staring first at Vivienne, then Sébastien, who had accompanied her.

"Do you know him, Merlin?" the princess asked.

"Yes."

The old wizard snapped out of his daze, and sat down on one of the boulders, clasping his staff as was his custom. Vivienne took a seat on another rock in front of him, and Sébastien, after a rapid going over of the landscape to ensure they were alone, joined her.

"You both have to hear this," Merlin commenced in a weary voice. "Carleigh was an apprentice of mine – an incredibly cunning and competent young man, but also obscure. He dabbled in the black arts and I refused to teach him further. On the other hand, you, Vivienne, I kept as an apprentice. I believe him targeting you is due to his belief you usurped him."

"Be that as it is," Sébastien interrupted, "we have to stop him before these attempts escalate."

"I am afraid it is much too late for that," Merlin admitted. "I have captured his damnable aura lately, but now I am most sure he is past salvation. He will keep trying to attack." Merlin met Vivienne's worried expression and said, "You have to be careful. Do not underestimate him. However, let him underestimate you."

She shared a glance with Sébastien, before probing, "What are you implying?"

The old wizard got up, and motioned for the youngsters to do the same. "From your mother, you have inherited great powers. But now you have grown into a young woman, and they have multiplied. Let me show you."

Merlin clasped one of Vivienne's soft hands in his withered one. "Focus on your magic, and your feelings for Sébastien. I want to show you what the force of love can do."

Vivienne did as the wizard bid, closing her eyes to better concentrate. A blinding blaze escaped past her eyelids, and she blinked in astonishment, gasping. Her entire being radiated from within, and from her palms emanated a pure, golden glow.

Despite the blinding radiance, the princess studied Merlin and his sparkling blue eyes. "This power is tangible. You can transform it into a healing light, or into a harmful one. You can have rays to scorch anyone who opposes you, or soft glows to heal the deepest of wounds. I will teach you how to sharpen and use it wisely. But now, you must let it retreat back to the earth. Gently."

Vivienne had to focus on the enchantment again, reining

it in as one would an overeager puppy, until the exuberance was gone. The glow retreated from her being, flowing into the ground beneath her feet, imbuing the earth with ancient power.

When the enchantress opened her eyes again, her skin was back to its normal tone. She met Sébastien's awed gaze, her heart singing with joy.

* * *

Sébastien woke up from the memory, and stared at the ceiling for a few moments, confused. *Is this how Vivienne feels each time, as though she belongs in the dream and not the reality?*

He got up from the couch and checked his beloved's bedroom, finding the bed empty. Hearing the shower on, he realized she must have woken much before him. It was an opportunity he could not ignore, and he decided to handle some urgent matters.

Closing the bedroom door carefully, Sébastien headed out to the backyard. Alistair, peacefully guarding the front door, ignored him.

The business with the Mafia was a headache they did not require, and as it was his problem, Sébastien knew he had to deal with it sooner rather than later.

He flipped the cellphone open and dialed Tony's number. It rang, but his voicemail picked up. Sébastien muttered under his breath, redialing. "Come on, pick up, dammit!"

Voicemail again.

He threw the phone on the little table, running both hands through his hair in frustration.

"Is something wrong?"

Sébastien glanced over his shoulder to Vivienne standing in the doorway. In the morning sun, with the light reflected in her inky locks, she was beyond gorgeous, and his heart lurched excruciatingly.

"No." He sighed, biting down the lie he had been about to voice, and instead opted for the truth. "I was trying to eliminate a problem for us."

"The Mafia?" Vivienne questioned, raising an eyebrow.

"Yeah."

Sébastien turned towards the pool and the fenced bushes surrounding the property. "I want to keep you safe, and this is a problem of my own doing."

He smelled the citrus perfume of her skin as she approached, and steeled himself against it, despite yearning for nothing more than to hold and shelter her. Vivienne bit her lip and grasped his shoulder, hesitantly at first, then more firmly.

"Sébastien, you *are* doing it, keeping me safe. Don't you see it, in my eyes?"

He moved around at her persistent nudge, his breath catching in his throat. The enchantress was watching him openly, all guards down, and despite his worst fears, she was unharmed. He raised one hand to caress her cheek, permitting himself this one, small touch.

"If you say so, I must have faith," Sébastien agreed.

Vivienne hesitated, then ran her fingers through his hair. "I wish we were far away from here."

The vibration of his phone broke the moment, and Sébastien recognized Tony's number. By the time his gaze fell on Vivienne again, she was walking away to the corner of the patio, allowing him some privacy.

With a muttered curse, Sébastien picked up the cell and hit the answer button. "Tony."

"Dubois." A pause, then, "You called?"

"Yeah." Sébastien schooled his voice in the menacing tone which worked so well in that environment. "Why the hell did you send your goons after me?"

"You needed to be taught a lesson," the man retorted coldly, unimpressed.

"With a *squadron*? Isn't that overdoing things a tad?"

There was another pause, and Sébastien recognized he might have pushed his luck.

"Are you lecturing me on how to make decisions, boy?" This time, Tony's tone was less than friendly.

Sébastien gritted his teeth and kept quiet. The call was intended to de-escalate the situation, not worsen it.

"Dubois, now's the time to get back in line," Tony continued. "Else that squadron won't be the last one. Am I making myself clear?"

Sébastien opened his mouth to agree, but the words escaping surprised even him. "I'm out, Tony."

"What did you just say?"

Sébastien heard a gasp from behind, and turned to Vivienne's shocked expression "I'm out," he repeated, eyes locked onto hers. "Done. No more jobs."

Her green eyes softened, and the acceptance read in their depths was enough for the guardian's heart to expand in size. It took him a moment to focus back on Tony's words, now a mere inconvenience.

"You do realize it's not quite so simple. After all these years, you owe me," his old boss was interjecting.

"I don't care. I'm out."

"No one leaves without my permission."

"I just did, Tony."

"You're making a big mistake!" The boss' voice vacillated, as if barely keeping his temper in check.

"I doubt it."

Tony was silent for a beat, before informing him, "I know about your girl."

Sébastien's eyes narrowed as he bit out, "You go near her, and you're dead. It's not an empty threat."

"We'll see!" the Mafia boss sniggered, then disconnected.

Sébastien stared at the phone in his hand, taking a beat to register he was now free.

Diplomacy is evidently not your strong suit, Alistair rumbled.

Sébastien sighed, tempted to agree. He had not intended the conversation to end quite that way.

All worries were driven to the back burner when Alistair froze, nose in the air. His entire body arched forward, hair rising on the back, claws digging in the ground.

They all tensed, barely breathing.

"What is it?" Vivienne whispered.

Go back inside, Alistair ordered. *We are not alone.* His glare fixated on the fenced bushes, trying to discern what – or whom – used them as cover.

It was a few moments before he realized the threat was not close, but further away. Yet the energy emanating from it – almost an invisible cloud – was aimed at his mistress' house.

Sébastien, having caught on to the dog's alarmed stance, maneuvered Vivienne back inside the home. They had barely entered, when a breeze hit them from behind. When it passed by Vivienne, she swayed, oddly weakened, and shivered.

More of these nefarious acolytes of Carleigh's, Alistair grunted, following them inside for a moment. *Stay here and wait for me. I will return shortly.* Before either of them could say anything, the dog ran out past the back door, across the backyard, and via one of the holes in the fence.

Alistair exited into the cobblestone alleyway and lifted his head, sniffing. Once he caught a whiff of evil, he began running towards it, pounding the pavement, desperate for a lead that could end Carleigh's menace once and for all.

He lost track of the time spent running, making sure to use back alleyways to avoid people, until his muscles irritated him. When soreness spread, he peered up in the sky, becoming conscious of the fact it had been hours since the pursuit was initiated, and now the sun was close to setting.

For a moment, Alistair feared having lost the trail. He was now at the exact opposite end of the city, and just as he wavered, he caught a stronger scent. With renewed enthusiasm, he headed towards it once more.

This time, the dog ended up at the Pont Saint Bénézet, overlooking the river Rhône. The location was a remainder of the only bridge connecting the French and German kingdoms eons earlier.

Now abandoned, the stone structure's past majesty was still apparent in the four surviving arches. At first, it had been a wooden skeleton supported on stone piers, but when the bridge was rebuilt after a siege, it was done so entirely in rock.

Nature had been cruel over the decades, mercilessly eating at the stone and causing major collapses. Alistair found himself moved by the remnants, perhaps due to his own fall from a great pantheon of deities. He took a moment to glance at the structure, and the little chapel of Saint Nicholas sitting on the second pier. If faith had ever been his to choose, perhaps he would have felt inclined to say a prayer.

With a shake of the head, Alistair snapped out of his thoughts, and moved once more. Though he did not have his powers of the past, the dog was still able to ensure invisibility as he passed the few bystanders – with a nudge of the mind, and a translucent coat covering him like a blanket. It created an optical effect for the humans and they only saw what they wished to.

He kept the invisibility until arriving at the end of the bridge. The scent, however, continued on the other side. With a growl, Alistair jumped in the river, and swam with the current until he reached the shore.

Shaking the water out of his fur, the dog headed towards what was an abandoned building. There were no signs of warlocks or Carleigh, but he slowed down nonetheless, scouring left and right for a trap.

Instead of being jumped, Alistair perceived a shift in the activity around the house, as though it vibrated. Ears perked, he focused on the voices coming from within.

He approached it, eyeing a pile of boxes and containers under a window. Extremely cautious, he hopped on top, and poked his head above the frame.

Alistair captured the chanting before setting eyes on them – thirteen warlocks, grouped in a circle. They were all wearing hooded mantles the color of murky earth, and clasping hands. At the center of their circle, they had gathered precious stones, and earth.

Once upon a time, they had been druids, worshipping nature and its purity. Now, they were mere shadows at the mercy of an evil man, using darkness to their own ends.

Dammit. They're attempting to recharge their depraved sorcery, probably for an attack, the dog mused. It was a ritual he knew well, having participated and encouraged quite a few in his time as demon lord.

As Alistair supervised them, a ray of black energy came out of the circle of stones. A murky snake, it floated for a moment, then headed towards one of the cloaked figures and hit him in the chest. The man inhaled deeply, and opened his eyes – all dark. Another bolt exploded, and hit the vile druid next to him. On and on it went, each individual ray highlighting a man.

When their stares were all the color of the night, reflecting the newfound powers, they broke the circle – but not before one last snake escaped the stones. With no corrupt druid to hit, it hovered in midair, forgotten. Then, sensing Alistair, it made its way towards him, as the warlocks headed towards a corner of the warehouse to plan their attack.

Alistair widened his jaws, hoping his present body could withstand at least this much malevolent energy. It was a risk, as he could well die from it, rather than inherit extra strength. With one last thought for Vivienne, he closed his eyes.

The bolt entered the dog and filled him whole. For a moment, his entire body vibrated, on the verge of exploding. Then Alistair inhaled, wrestling the energy to his own needs, and the tremors eased away. The buzz of newfound abilities rang in his ears, and his eyes glinted dangerously. With one last glance to the warlocks, he strode away and back to Vivienne's place.

* * *

"He should be back here already!"

"Vivienne, would you please calm down? Your pacing isn't helping."

"We should have been his backup!"

The door opened and Alistair entered mid-argument. They both turned to him, Vivienne stepping closer. With one tilt of Alistair's head, however, she stopped dead in her tracks.

"What–" Sébastien came around her. He dropped his gaze to Alistair, and froze as well.

The dog's eyes had a glint in them the guardian recalled all too well – full midnight, as if staring in a pool of obscurity.

"Alistair?" Vivienne asked softly.

The demon dog shook his massive mane, and rumbled, *Of course it's me!*

Sébastien captured Vivienne's relief as she sagged against him.

"I was afraid something happened," she murmured to the protector. "You were gone for hours, and you look . . .."

Like a demon dog?

"Pretty much," she admitted, eyeing him questioningly.

Alistair sat down, looking as smug as a dog could. *I tracked Carleigh's minions to an abandoned house, across the river Rhône. They were accessing a raw, evil power, recharging to come after us.*

"Was that what we all felt?"

Yes, highness. Their darkness in this world and age is upsetting the balance of all which is right. They were never supposed to live here, let alone have access to the occult.

Sébastien crossed his arms over his chest, frowning. "So what happened?"

When the evil hit all of them, it must have perceived my presence nearby, and was drawn to my essence. I absorbed it.

"But your body—" Vivienne's eyes widened, recalling the last instances when malevolent energy had touched the dog, and the consequences that had followed.

Apparently, it can withstand it, Alistair reassured. *Or perhaps my body is learning to endure more.*

"Whatever it is," Sébastien interrupted as an idea struck, "you have some of your old abilities now, don't you?"

For a brief time, yes.

"Then let's go get those bastards!"

Alistair stood and wagged his tail. *I was about to suggest the same.*

Sébastien went to pick up his gun from the table, and the dagger he had used on Braydon. When he turned, Vivienne had her arms folded over her chest, watching both of them.

"What?" he asked.

"I'm coming with you two."

"Like hell you are!" Sébastien exclaimed, resolutely shaking his head. "Absolutely not. Do I have to remind you how last time ended?"

"Last time, there were other factors," Vivienne retorted with a furrowed brow, lips pressed together. "This time, we can work together."

Sébastien went to argue, then glowered at Alistair for help. "Tell her it's too risky."

It is, the dog rumbled, *but she would also have an advantage with her particular brand of magic.*

"Great! So it's settled," Vivienne jumped on the occasion.

Sébastien was about to disagree some more, but Alistair rumbled in his head, *Let her come. We can defend her better together, and it sure beats leaving her here to cook up some crazy idea without either of us to say no.*

Rolling his eyes, Sébastien packed his gun, and they headed for the Jaguar. As they got in, he examined the area. No sign of Tony's men – yet. He could only hope it would stay that way until they dealt with Carleigh, and could get out of the city.

* * *

Alistair led them all the way to the opposite shore, at the Pont Saint Bénézet, instructing them to get out of the car once they arrived.

Vivienne was the first one out, evaluating the distance between the two shores. "How exactly did you get across?"

I swam, Alistair answered.

Her shocked expression met his calm one. "That's a huge distance!" As Alistair rolled his eyes, Vivienne added, "Even for a dog with supernatural capabilities and high endurance."

"I think the better question," Sébastien interrupted, "is how *we* are going to get across?"

Get down on your knees and put your hands together, Alistair rumbled to both of them. Once they did as he bid, the dog advanced and grazed his muzzle to their joined hands.

A clear bubble escaped the protector's breath, and expanded in size until it surrounded all three of them in a shielding screen of sorts. When it stopped forming around them, the bubble elevated off the ground, with the three companions in, and headed towards the water.

Sébastien peered at the few human shadows he could distinguish on the bridge –tourists.

They cannot see us, Alistair explained, having guessed his query. *The circle ensures it. I would have materialized us there, but it takes a bit more strength to do so, and I preferred to keep the best for the so-called warlocks.*

Chuckling at his doggy grin, both humans settled in for the ride, which was shorter than they imagined. In a matter of moments, they found themselves on the opposite edge, where a bedraggled house faced them.

Alistair sniffed the air, and tilted his head to the barn behind it. *In there.*

With him leading the charge, the three headed towards it, keeping all noise to a minimum. The front door was open, and it was larger inside than on the outside. The walls were littered with pieces of broken things, but a long hallway winded on a few feet.

The barn was unlit, so Vivienne called an incantation, and held a hand pointed to the ceiling. A ball of light emerged, illuminating the place.

"Where the hell are they?" Sébastien grumbled.

Alistair froze, nose in the air, then looked behind in time to glimpse the door they had passed, seal itself.

Here. Hidden.

"Reveal yourselves!" Sébastien bellowed, taking his gun out.

The walls shimmered, and the cloudiness dissipated as the druids dropped their camouflage. Vivienne backed into the guardian, with Alistair by their side.

Get your shield up! Alistair had time to yell, before a cursed bolt headed for them. In the next breath, he emitted a loud, thunderous bark. The voice vibrations, part of his old powers, formed into a blockade, which slammed straight into the supernatural disc heading their way.

The force was so great, the attack was returned and slammed back into the two conjurers who had thrown it, exploding them into nothingness.

Alistair focused on the others surrounding them, while Sébastien fired his gun. One warlock was hit, but he still brought his hands up, mumbling until they glowed with a hex.

Since a gun was useless, Sébastien grabbed the dagger from his back pocket and launched it at the warlock, hitting him in the chest. The opponent went down, disintegrating as well.

The knight ran to him, retrieved the knife, and headed for close contact with the others. He used the gun to distract his enemies, and in the blink of an eye, would get close to them, blade at the throat or in the heart.

Vivienne, on the other hand, had drawn up protective barrier. She used it to keep her two companions guarded, while materializing small spheres of pure spirit to divert the dark ones. Between the three of them, they wiped the floor with the foes.

In the moments that followed, Alistair was distracted

grappling with a particularly stubborn druid, when the last one standing confronted Vivienne and Sébastien.

He was oddly calm, in contrast to the couple, who were trying to control their panting chests. The man smirked, then lifted a hand with a knife glinting in it.

"What the hell?" Sébastien frowned.

The druid pointed the tip to his own throat, lips moving in a chant.

STOP HIM! Alistair roared as his own prey dissolved, but it was too late.

They watched helplessly as the corrupt warlock cut his own throat from ear to ear, and collapsed to the floor. They shared an incredulous look, but could do nothing when the spell took hold. His body melted, then from its remains a shady pool was formed, almost a mirror. Within moments, a smoke rose out of the mirror and, with it, shapes.

"What's happening?" Vivienne gasped.

More foul druids! Alistair turned to them, panicked eyes locking with Sébastien. *This is how they are constantly being replaced. Carleigh has given them enough juice to bring forth their counterparts. With one sacrifice, a portal of darkness opens, and their dead souls pass through, manipulated by his damned will.*

The dog cased their surroundings, noticing the expanding number. *Their corruption is overwhelming and Vivienne cannot stay here. I have witnessed what happens when a pure of heart is surrounded by their evil stench, and it is not pretty. Get her out of here,* now*!*

Sébastien hesitated for all of one second, then snatched Vivienne's hand, and yanked her away.

"No!" She tried to disengage from his grip, but his insistent gaze fixated on hers.

"He can handle them with his old abilities. Alistair says the evil in here is stifling, and it'll eat at your soul. We have to go!"

Vivienne hesitated, peeking behind, and Sébastien took advantage of the split moment of inattention to yank her after him, towards the door. He stopped abruptly, and she slammed in his back.

Five warlocks were now blocking their path. To top it off, more emerged behind them from the shadows, despite Alistair attacking them one by one as they exited the shadowy pool. Those escaping his ferocious teeth headed straight for the two humans, as though listening to a command only they could hear.

The sorcerers contented themselves with surrounding the two companions, blank regards facing them. They were puppets at their master's command, instructed only to attack, basic vessels for Carleigh's plans – and replaceable ones, at that.

Vivienne and Sébastien soon recognized they were trapped. The warehouse had only one exit, which was now blocked by more than a dozen sorcerers, rapidly expanding. They clasped hands, and a chant vibrated in the air, though their lips barely budged.

Sébastien advanced in front of Vivienne, evidently planning to use his body to shield her from harm. He longed to have his sword and rip them apart as in the past, presuming the blessed blade would be enough to attack hundreds of them at once.

"Where's your old weapon?" Vivienne asked, echoing his thoughts.

"I don't have it," the guardian retorted with his back to her, eyes busy still exploring the surrounding area and trying to find an exit. Though he could not understand the sorcerers' chanting, it was clear their time was limited, at best.

"I see that. *Where* is it?"

Sébastien glanced at Vivienne, tormented. "I lost it long ago."

"No, you couldn't have," the enchantress denied, with a slow shake of the head. "You can still get to it."

"Not likely," Sébastien retorted, still surveying the druids. "Besides, we have bigger fish to fry right now."

Vivienne did not reply, instead silently raising a palm up. Ignoring the warlocks and their incessant incantations – and ensuring the defensive barrier was still doing its job – she recalled a previous conversation with Alistair, and focused her thoughts on one thing. *Sébastien has need of his sword to protect me.*

She conjured the image of him as a champion in the past. Letting the enchantment do the work, Vivienne simply added in a wish and hope for the knight to be restored. A glow elevated from her palm, and a simple ring of fire floated in mid-air, suspended a few inches above Vivienne's hand.

Sébastien whirled around at the sudden radiance, eyes widening. "What are you doing?"

Vivienne did not respond, intent on the incantation. She pictured reaching through the past, making contact with the metal, and wishing it in her hand.

The blaze vacillated, up until the weapon called out and materialized. It was heavy, and the young woman's hand sagged under its weight. Sébastien's shocked gaze met hers.

"Here," she pointed the ruby-covered hilt towards him.

The knight backed away, as though afraid.

"Sébastien, we don't have time for this."

She glanced at the chanting warlocks behind him. The shadows surrounding them had thickened, and coated the walls like a blanket, heading in their direction.

Alistair's warning was clear now. If the blanket of darkness was to touch Vivienne, it would affect her clean spirit, sucking it dry. Only the shield kept them safe momentarily, and not for much longer if her energy wavered.

"Please," Vivienne begged, pushing the hilt towards Sébastien. "With this, you can fight them, too. The blessing I bestowed upon it in the past has always kept you out of harm's way. Fight off whatever fear you have. You have enough strength to wield it. It's always been your companion."

Sébastien hesitated, before reaching out and gripping the hilt. It was as though a missing piece of the puzzle had been put back. The haunted glint in his eyes settled to a determined one, and he faced the fight.

The blade belonged to him, was a part of him, and the champion used it as such, with Vivienne's incantations sheltering them from sorcery. In a few moments only, Sébastien cut a path amongst the warlocks, then grabbed Vivienne's hand and rushed out.

He dragged his beloved into the woods behind the house, looking for a safe spot to wait for Alistair. The knight maneuvered them behind a large tree trunk, his own body coming around to hide Vivienne's in case they had been followed.

* * *

Alistair peeked behind, no longer sensing his mistress' aura or the knight's. The confirmation they were no longer there was all he required before letting loose.

Come and get me!

His roar shook the ground, in complete defiance of the warlocks. With one shake of his head, Alistair supernaturally enhanced his body to twice its original size. His muscles distended, mass added on, until he was the size of a grizzly bear.

The euphoria filled him along with the long lost power. Incited by adrenaline, the demon dog went on a rampage. He bit everything in his path, blew gusts of cursed shards towards the sorcerers, snapped at them with his huge claws – enhanced with a poisoning dosage of the correct rotten energy which would be disastrous to them.

Eons ago, Alistair had been a fierce warrior as well as deity, thus he was well versed in transforming his body into a weapon. Under his skilled strikes, it was only mere moments until the profaned druids were in tatters, pieces only left.

The demon dog then advanced towards the black mirror, and shattered it with a sturdy hit of his paw. Satisfied at the carnage, he reduced his body back to its regular size.

Only then did he exit the warehouse, locking it behind him with magic in an effort to ensure no mistakes were made, and no one would follow them. Sniffing the ground imbued with traces of Vivienne's aura, he tracked his charges.

* * *

When a twig snapped behind them, Vivienne jumped. Alistair's head showed between the bushes, and Sébastien exhaled in relief.

Time to get out of here, the dog growled. *Do as before.*

Both Vivienne and Sébastien knelt and were engulfed in the bubble again. They had barely made it to the other shore and into the Jag, when Alistair collapsed, exhausted.

Sébastien drove them back to Vivienne's place, taking a few detours to ensure they were not being followed. Once there, the guardian picked Alistair up in his arms and carried him to the couch.

"Guess the fight exhausted him," the champion murmured.

Vivienne simply breathed a sigh of relief, and put a pillow under the dog's head. She glanced at Sébastien, noticing his peculiar look. "What's wrong?"

He had kept silent the entire ride home, but now struck her as almost dazed. Sébastien shook himself out of whichever rumination, muttering, "We keep asking each other that, too many times."

Realization dawned on the young woman, and she shrugged in response. "One of these days, we won't."

Noticing he still clasped the blade, Vivienne suggested, "We should get you a sheath for it."

Sébastien surveyed the sword still glued to his hand. The cross guard was plain, as he had chosen long ago. A rough leather strip wrapped around the grip of it, ensuring the hilt fit and stayed properly in the palm. The pommel was decorated by a single ruby, and the Damascus steel from which it had been forged shone brightly.

He ran a hand across the metal, his expression filled with wonder. "I never imagined I would hold it again."

Vivienne observed the guardian for a moment, amazed at the change in him. He looked . . .like *her* Sébastien. There was a burden still hanging around him, but the way he maneuvered the weapon, and the new glint in his eyes at that moment, full of hope, was so unlike the anguished one she had viewed for days on end.

"How did you get it?" the young woman whispered, hoping to converse freely, with no restraints, as they had before.

Sébastien chuckled, though his eyes never moved from the blade. "My father put me in training with a hard-core mentor at the ripe age of twelve. Most trainees that age had a smaller metal weapon, but he only let me carry around a wooden one. He told me the day I knew how to master it like a man, and give it the respect it deserves, I would get a real one."

Vivienne bit her lip, preferring not to distract Sébastien out of his trance as he caressed the metal blade.

"By the time I was seventeen, I was young and cocky. I got in plenty of fights – always with my wooden sword. I used it as a weapon, nothing more. But over time, it became a part of me. During this one fight, it got cut into two. I was so mad, I finished the fight bare-handed, disarming the guy. I then collected the splintered pieces, and carried them back to my mentor. He asked me what happened."

Sébastien paused with a nostalgic smile, and Vivienne dug her nails in both hands, forcing herself not to reach out to him.

"When I recounted the story for him, he pointed me to a

knife and a piece of wood, and told me I could carve a new one. I refused, adamant to fix my wooden one, because it was my companion. I'll never forget his pride. That same night, he brought me in a forge, where the blacksmith made this one for me only – I helped. When it was done, I named it Éimhín. It means *swift* in Gaelic."

"It's beautiful," Vivienne murmured, fascinated by the rapture on his face.

Sébastien's onyx eyes locked on hers again, and he inched forward, just out of her grasp. "Thank you, Vivienne. You have no idea how much this means to me."

She gulped, stirred by the sincerity vibrating in his voice.

The champion lifted his closed fist over his heart, and bowed his head. "I am forever in your debt."

Vivienne closed the remaining distance, and seized his hand in her smaller one. "You owe me nothing, Sébastien." She paused, uncertain on how to continue, but barreled past her doubts. "But I would like to know, how did you lose Éimhín?"

Sébastien braced as though for a fight, then his shoulders hunched. The suffering in his expression was apparent when their gazes met again.

"You can be honest with me, I won't judge," Vivienne encouraged him.

Sébastien sat on the free couch, next to the one Alistair occupied. He placed the weapon on the table, and dropped his head in his hands.

"When I lost you, and was reborn, I found Éimhín in my first lifetime. I was able to fight the corruption, despite everything I did, as it kept me sane. But you were still not reborn, and I realized if I wanted to truly bring you back, I had to let the shadows inside me."

He paused, then admitted, "So I let go of everything that was me, including the sword."

"Oh, Sébastien," Vivienne murmured, tears burning as she sat next to him. "I'm so sorry."

He lifted his head up, love shining in the expression. "You're worth everything, Vivienne. I would do it all over again if I had to."

They stared at each other, and he gently caressed her cheek. "If all I can have for the rest of this life are small touches like this, it will be enough."

"But it's *not* enough. I want—"

"It will have to be enough," Sébastien placed a finger to her lips. "I won't run the risk of losing you again."

Vivienne searched his expression, then wordlessly got up to retreat to her bedroom before the guardian could glimpse the tears running down her cheeks. She had hoped, against all odds, that with Éimhín back, he would give them both a chance, trust himself more around her.

The only thing the enchantress had managed to reiterate was a sense of duty and protection. Though their love was great, Sébastien was, first and foremost, always and forever, a knight. It was ironic he was the only one blind to the truth.

* * *

"So he thinks a sword a knight makes?" Carleigh muttered, dragging an unconscious man to the pool for sacrifice.

It writhed in response to his perceived anger as he tossed

the man in – he was immediately swallowed by the darkness.

"We will see about that."

Carleigh let the corrupt energy wash over him, recharging and feeding off him. He had a plan to stick to. "Time to see for myself what Vivienne's new powers are worth."

* * *

Merlin captured the presence long before the dog approached him, and exited the cave to meet him. "Old friend, what brings you here?"

Alistair paused and sat on his hind with a peculiar glint. "Vivienne and her champion – they are being pulled together and it is not normal."

"You suspect witchcraft?" Merlin enquired politely.

"No. But there are outside forces involved. I am of the impression they are soul mates." Ignoring the dismay in the old wizard's eyes, he carried on. "From the strength of their bond, more than a few lifetimes before this one."

Merlin's only response was a furrowed brow.

"There is a way to find out for sure," Alistair continued. "We should bring them here and have them perform a ritual."

"Why is this important?" Merlin wondered. "If they do not yet perceive it, maybe we should stay out of it. Would this not harm, more than help them? What if they prefer to ignore the past?"

"I know you keep your secrets, old mage, and there are things in the future you have foreseen. But this is one you have not, unlike myself. I had a vision – Sébastien can be Vivienne's salvation or her doom, if he turns to darkness."

"Then it cannot be ignored," Merlin agreed, brows narrowed in concentration. *"Bring them here at the earliest opportunity."*

* * *

Blinking sleepily, Alistair stirred from slumber. The memory had assaulted his subconscious for a reason, but he was too tired to understand why.

You better not be playing games with me too, old friend, he said mentally to Merlin, before dozing off again.

CHAPTER 17

The next morning, Vivienne walked in on Alistair and Sébastien having breakfast. One was on the floor, and the other at the kitchen table.

"I want to go grocery shopping," she said in a neutral tone, heading straight for the coffee machine.

Silence answered the announcement. Vivienne shifted away from the pot of coffee, noticing the two exchanging glances.

What did you do now? Alistair asked Sébastien.

For his part, the guardian was surveying Vivienne. He steadily met the dog's scrutiny, confessing mentally, *I had to push her away last night.*

Alistair refrained from rolling his eyes – barely.

Majesty . . . His mental rumble was meant for both humans, but his head faced Vivienne alone. *It is not a good idea, what with Carleigh and the Mafia out there.*

"I'm tired of being cooped in my own place. Plus, we need food." The young woman fixed a stubborn gaze on Sébastien, daring him to contradict her. "If you won't come with me, I'll just sneak out."

He put down his fork, and raised his expression to the ceiling. With a half-amused, half-frustrated shake of the head, Sébastien got up from the table. "Alright, you win. We'll go, but at the tiniest sign of trouble, we leave."

"Fine. Whatever."

Vivienne sipped some coffee, and left the kitchen to get dressed in record time. They drove to the store in the Jaguar for added safety, though it was only a brief walk away. The minute they got in, she picked a cart and started down the aisles.

"Do you have a list?" Sébastien wondered innocently.

"Nope."

"Do you have any items in mind?"

"Nope."

"Vivienne –"

"I'll know it when I see it."

Sébastien clamped his mouth shut at her icy tone, and resumed following in silence. Her anger bubbled under the surface, directed at him – a fact he was well aware of.

If he had given in to Vivienne's desires – and his – it would have either tainted the enchantress, or distracted him from performing his job properly. Yet if he did not, she was left hurting, and him longing. *There really is no way out of this,* Sébastien had to admit with a heavy sigh.

Down a couple of aisles, Vivienne tried to reach

something on the top shelf. She struggled with the height, and he stepped closer to help.

"I got it," she mumbled, still stretching towards it.

Sébastien ignored her and captured the item before she could. Vivienne whirled around to yell at him, only to realize they were standing close, barely an inch between them.

Head spinning at the nearness, the déjà-vu came on strong. "Not here, damn it," Vivienne pleaded, then seized Sébastien's arm before her knees gave way.

* * *

Vivienne jumped awake at the insistent knock on the door. She wrapped a cape around herself quickly, and approached it on tip toes. Sébastien was there, his entire body coiled with tension.

"We have to go."

She glanced behind him, then moved so he could enter her room. "What is happening?"

"Your father was hurt. Carleigh ambushed us on our way back from the hunt. Alistair came in time to deflect the worst of it, and the king is unharmed for now. I am to bring you to Merlin, as per Alistair's orders."

With a swift nod, Vivienne rushed to put on a thicker cloak, and followed Sébastien out the chambers, and down the empty hallways to the entrance doors of the castle. Once there, she paused, tugging on his hand.

"Wait. Let me conceal us with an enchantment to avoid detection."

Sébastien acquiesced briskly, and Vivienne placed both

hands on his. A soft glow enveloped them both, sank into their skin, and disappeared. They were now invisible to anyone's eyes but each other's.

The lovers kept their hands joined as they rushed across the gardens, past Vivienne's usual spot with Merlin, and the large prairie separating them from the forest where the wizard's lair resided.

When they passed the barrier to Merlin's grounds, Sébastien looked around, then murmured to Vivienne, "You can uncover us now. I do not wish for the magic to tire you."

Vivienne was about to disagree, but at the glint in his eyes, shrugged and removed the cloaking spell. They moved again, rushing to get to Merlin's as rapidly as possible. Sébastien kept his body shielding Vivienne, alert and scanning the surroundings, even whilst never slowing his strides.

Moments later, they had exited into a meadow Vivienne knew to be close to Merlin's, when a hiss echoed in the air. She whirled around, and noticed the arrow coming her way. One raised palm stopped the weapon in time with a barrier, and it plummeted to the ground, inert.

The princess peered over one shoulder to Sébastien to alert him, but it was too late. He let go of her hand, stumbling backwards into a tree – an arrow protruding from his shoulder.

The knight closed his eyes for a brief second, then clenched his jaw and unsheathed his sword. A deep breath later, he moved in front of Vivienne, just as two men appeared from the shadows.

"Stay behind me!" Sébastien ordered. He advanced to the two druids in cloaks, whose lips were moving in wordless

incantations aimed at the two lovers.

From behind Vivienne, leaves rustled, and she confronted her two opponents with a barrier of protection. Thankful more than ever for Merlin's insistence to learn both defensive and offensive techniques, the enchantress conjured small balls of magic, and concentrated their assailing strength towards the druids.

As Sébastien cut one of the adversaries in two, there was an odd crackling in the pit of his stomach. The world around him evaporated, nothing except the rage of the fight left behind.

By means of their bond, Vivienne also perceived the rippling energy, and tasted the bitterness of evil. She looked over her shoulder, distracted from her own fight, to witness Sébastien swiftly disposing of his assailants – at the expense of his own strength.

"We have to get the arrow out!" Vivienne yelled to her lover.

The champion did not react, instead moving towards the next challenger.

"Sébastien," Vivienne linked to his mind, warning telepathically, "you have been poisoned by the arrow. I can sense it obscuring your aura and sapping your strength."

With an annoyed cry to her opponents, she blasted orbs towards them and they disappeared into nothingness. Now free, the princess went to Sébastien. As if sensing her close, the knight whirled around with the blade held high, almost cutting through her.

Alistair materialized out of nowhere between Sébastien and Vivienne. The metal hit the barrier he had erected between them, inches away from his mistress' head.

"Alistair!" Vivienne's cry did not deter the demon dog from his defensive stance.

"Stay away!" he commanded, tilting his head a little to the side, but not letting Sébastien out of his sight. "Carleigh did a number on him. The arrow had a rage-inducing spell, and he could gravely hurt you, if you get close. I can tolerate the darkness, and remove it from him."

"No," Vivienne pleaded. "You have done enough for my father, and you have your limits. I can get him to listen."

"Vivienne—" The demon concentrated fully on the princess, and noted her determination. With a sigh, he bowed his head. "Not here, and not now."

He dug his paws in the ground, and a translucent panel covered them. It shimmered and, in a blink, they found themselves in front of Merlin's cave. Alistair ran in to get the wizard, while the young woman headed to Sébastien.

The guardian was on his knees, breathing heavily, when Vivienne inched closer. He stood up and gripped her hand, hard enough to bruise. Though she winced at the discomfort, the princess did not draw away. Instead, she stared into his eyes and begged softly, "Come back to me."

With her other hand, Vivienne yanked the arrow out of his shoulder, following the action by pressing a glowing palm to heal. The tension of the fight left Sébastien, until the knight sagged in her embrace.

Sébastien blinked, eyes no longer glazed, but fixated on Vivienne. At the pain etched on her features, he glanced down and released his tight grip. The bruise forming on her wrist was visible to his horrified look. "I am so sorry."

"No harm done," Vivienne smiled reassuringly, clasping his hands in hers. "You are unharmed, and it is all that matters."

The knight did not appear it, though – pale and covered in dirt, eyes haunted by the guilt of what could have happened. By means of their connection, Vivienne captured his shock, and a remnant of the darkness that had entered him.

Alistair's arrival interrupted her words, and this time he had Merlin in tow. The wizard's magical staff was raised and glowing, believing the princess was still in danger. But it was Alistair who realized Sébastien was no longer under the curse's dominance, judging by the clear aura surrounding him.

He tilted a satisfied grin to the wizard, and declared for all to hear, "I told you I was right."

"Not now," Merlin hissed.

"Now is a good a time as any," Alistair rumbled.

Vivienne surveyed them both, as did Sébastien. "What are you two going on about?"

With a scowl to his canine friend, Merlin explained Alistair's theory of them being soul mates. When he was done, Vivienne peered at Sébastien and read his shock, mirrored only by hers.

"How do we learn for sure?" the guardian enquired.

"It is a simple thing of unlocking your past memories, and reconnecting you with your old lives." Merlin paused, searching both their expressions. "Are you quite sure you would like to witness this?"

Vivienne hesitated, but Sébastien gripped her hand in his, and squeezed it reassuringly. His gaze was still not quite right, haunted by what had transpired, but he murmured, "We want to know."

The princess' eyes landed on Alistair and Merlin, nodding for both of them. "Yes. We want to see it – all of it."

"Hold hands," Merlin recommended.

They did as they were bid, and the wizard approached the staff over their joined hands. The crystal on top of it shone brightly as a sun for a moment, before it extinguished. Merlin then touched the air surrounding their hands, and under the lovers' stunned gazes, ripped a transparent piece out, as though from a book. It would be the gate which would let them see into the past.

The cloth, if it could be called such, took the color of whatever it was cast over. When the mage set it over their joined hands, it became tan, blending in. Alistair came closer and breathed on it, a faint white fog that surrounded their clasped hands, hovering and immovable. This would be the essence grounding them, so they would not lose track of the reality awaiting them.

Merlin stared at their handiwork, then lifted his gaze to Vivienne, followed by Sébastien. When they made no move to stop him, he spoke. "Let it be remembered, all that was forgotten."

The cloth shone softly as a glow enveloped their joined hands, and a blinding radiance escaped. Recollections hit them both – a life in the desert, one in the mountains, and another in the glaciers.

It was as though the couple was surrounded by a bubble of light, with the memories swarming, assailing them. All the lifetimes, the love and agony, losing each other because of calamities and enemies – everything was there for their perusal.

Each lifetime followed the same pattern. They met, fell in love, and lost one another due to a hidden, nefarious energy which followed them across time and space, forever haunting and stealing away their happy ending.

Among the flashbacks, Vivienne saw herself in a vibrant garden, and witnessed Sébastien dying in her arms. Another memory was of when he came to warn of danger in the chambers. On and on it went, until they had both born witness to their entire past together.

When it was over, the glow evaporated, and Vivienne turned to Merlin, her cheeks bathed in tears. "Are we to be always doomed?"

Alistair advanced before the wizard could respond, having glimpsed it all through their minds. The potent vitality of love had imbued the couple, to the point the demon dog had been dragged in the memories despite his better judgment.

"No," he answered truthfully. "Whatever happened in the past does not have to repeat itself. Whoever hunted you, threatened you, can be thwarted. It means nothing. We can rewrite your fate, highness."

Merlin did not join in the conversation, lost in his own reflections. Not even visions had prepared him for the strength of their love, let alone the extent of their shared past. He could not help the thought that if only Arthur had fallen in love with Vivienne, she could have been his and Camelot's salvation.

At the growl by his side, the wizard noticed Alistair's black look.

"Do not listen to my thoughts if you do not like hearing

them," Merlin advised mentally, and the dog broke his stare.

Overwhelmed by emotions, Vivienne went to Sébastien's arms for safety and comfort. The guardian leveled a discouraged gaze to the dog and wizard, comprehending now what the flashes in his head had been all about.

"We will find a way," Alistair reassured, meeting his gaze steadily.

* * *

Vivienne came to, blinking – the whole thing had lasted less than two minutes. She was holding onto Sébastien's strong frame, and to any outsider they would have appeared to be embracing in the middle of the aisle.

Shaking her head to clear it, she stepped away and lifted a pained gaze to his worried expression. The neon lights in the background caused her to squint, too strong for her sensitive eyes.

"Are you alright?" Sébastien whispered.

Vivienne tried to come up with a reason to be mad at him, but the way he looked at her, and the suddenly charged atmosphere, left her at a loss of words.

"It was a memory," she murmured, breaking eye contact.

Sébastien was about to enquire further, but backed away at the tension radiating off his beloved. Vivienne held back a sigh of relief, watching instead as the guardian dropped the item from the shelf in the cart.

"I'm sorry about last night."

The young woman's eyes snapped up to Sébastien's, noticing the sincerity in there. Her body reacted in response, almost yearning to admit he was forgiven. Almost.

Instead, she grabbed the cart, and edged away. "I'd prefer not to talk about it."

"Vivienne—"

"I said drop it."

Sébastien groaned as she continued on, pretending to be engrossed in the pursuit of every item, on every shelf, looking everywhere – all to avoid the dark-haired knight.

It was a few moments before Vivienne realized he was not following. She glanced over a shoulder to notice him staring at a woman who had entered the aisle – around forty, petite and blonde.

"Sébastien?"

The guardian snapped out of his daze at Vivienne's voice and immediately turned to follow, leaving the lady gawking behind. The young woman played it to one of those weird coincidences, and continued shopping.

Sébastien put one foot in front of the other, without paying any attention to what they were doing. He knew who the woman was only too well, and his imagination was busy wondering why the hell she was still in town – at a grocery store, to boot.

They got to the lineup after another few minutes of shopping. As they waited, Vivienne asked, "Do you know her?"

"Who?"

"*Her.*"

Sébastien craned his neck to where she pointed, to see Nico's wife staring back. This time, as their eyes locked, she did not glance away.

He was the one to break eye contact, piling stuff on the cash register. In record time, Sébastien bagged and paid for the groceries, and they were exiting when Vivienne persisted, "You didn't answer me."

"Keep moving," he commanded through gritted teeth.

"Wait!" a voice came from behind.

Sébastien quickened his pace, but it was to no use, as Vivienne stopped.

"Dammit!" he growled, followed by a few choice curse words under his breath. *Of all the times she has to be stubborn . . .*

The woman's voice interrupted his thoughts. She had reached them, eyes wide and glued to him. "It *is* you!"

Vivienne stared between the two.

"I'm sorry to bother you," the petite woman continued in a soft voice, "but please help me."

"You have the wrong person," Sébastien lied through his teeth.

"No, I don't," she frowned. "I'm Sofia, and you're the man who came to warn me to get out of town, because of what Nico did."

Sébastien clenched his jaw, but out of the corner of his eye he could see Vivienne registering the name. *Shit.*

"I went against my orders that day, yes," he finally admitted. "And you're still in town. Why?" He tried to manage the anger in his voice, but was barely successful, as per the woman's paling face.

"I couldn't leave!" Sofia's eyes filled with tears. "It's Antonio, my boy. He's so much like his father and—"

"I'm sorry," Sébastien interrupted, in a completely

unapologetic tone. "But this has nothing to do with me."

"But it does! They're initiating him, tomorrow night! I can't do this again, and I don't think he understands what he's getting into."

The guardian had a hard time believing his ears. "And just what the hell do you expect me to do?"

"Please talk to him," Sofia pleaded. "Warn him against it. Perhaps if it comes from a man such as you, it would mean more."

Sébastien was shaking his head before she was even done talking. "I can't get involved."

"Please, I'm begging you. I would have left when you advised me, but he threatened to run away at the first opportunity. I couldn't take the chance."

Sébastien gave up making an effort to be even remotely nice. "As I mentioned before, I can't get involved. You'll have to find someone else."

He spun around, but Sofia rushed over and grabbed his arm. He scowled, towering over the tiny woman. At the warning in his eyes, she let go, but still pleaded, "He's only sixteen, my only boy."

"Call the police," were Sébastien's parting words before he left, cursing the fates for throwing more problems in his path.

Tears streamed down Sofia's cheeks, and she clasped a hand over her mouth to stifle the sobs threatening to take over.

Vivienne, who had not intervened, stepped up at that moment and patted her free hand gently. "I'll try to change his mind. I'm sorry." Then she pursued the guardian, heading to the Jaguar.

Sébastien was putting groceries in the trunk when the

fiery brunette rounded the corner, folding her arms over her chest. "Is that Nico's wife?"

"Get in the car," Sébastien ordered, his stormy gaze clashing with hers. "You're exposed out here."

"Answer me, and I will."

"Yes, she is. Now can you go in?"

Vivienne huffed, but listened, and Sébastien waited until the slamming of the car door confirmed she was within its safe confines. He finished putting the groceries in the trunk, and then joined her in the car.

"Why is her son being initiated?" Vivienne accosted him the minute he was in.

"Simple – Nico's death left a vacant spot to be filled."

Sébastien drove off the parking lot, waiting for the next string of interrogations.

"Okay, but why the kid? I doubt he understands anything."

"If he doesn't, he'll learn soon enough. Tony's play is to go for family blood. Keeps everyone closely tied together."

"But you're not blood."

Sébastien clenched his jaw. "I was an exception."

"Why?"

"Tony guessed at what I could do, and had a use for my talent."

Vivienne hushed, pondering the response. Of course, joining the Mafia was the perfect opportunity for someone to become corrupt. But for a young boy, barely out of his teenage years . . . She pictured a younger Sébastien, dealing with the choice. "How old?"

The knight frowned, thrown off by her softer tone. "What?"

"How old were you when Tony got to you?"

"Young," was all he responded, knuckles whitening on the steering wheel.

"Sébastien, we have to do something!"

"No, *we* don't have to do anything. It's their problem."

Vivienne's eyes were burning on him. "How can you say that?"

"Because it's the truth."

"I refuse to let a young boy get into this life without trying to stop it!"

Sébastien pulled over on the side of the road and faced Vivienne, invading her personal space, his chin jutting out. "I'm going to explain this once, so listen well. Some guy under Tony ordered me to kill this kid's mom, probably to make the decision easier on him, and to eliminate any future problems. I refused. Instead, I went in and warned her, clearly instructing her to get out of town. She didn't. End of story."

Vivienne was about to protest, but he beat her to it. "I've figured, since then, the order came directly from Tony in order to teach me a lesson. So far, he's stayed out of my way and I intend to stay out of his. To defend you, I *will* do whatever I have to."

Sébastien scanned Vivienne's expression, noted she pondered his words, and shifted back into the driver's seat. Without a word, he started the engine and took off again.

Vivienne was in deep reflection the rest of the ride home. It made sense, as a defender, that Sébastien would prefer to shelter her. And yet to stand by and let the initiation happen was not a decision she agreed with. Their past selves would never have let someone pay the price for their safety.

This is wrong.

They arrived in front of her home, and silently brought the food inside. Alistair observed them – and the change in their auras – carefully, but chose to stay out of it.

Once they put away the groceries, Sébastien leaned against the counter and pinched the bridge of his nose. "Are you going to give me the silent treatment for a while?"

"No," Vivienne confessed truthfully. "But I don't agree with this."

Sébastien exhaled loudly, looking away.

"Hear me out, please," Vivienne continued. "I get you're doing this to protect me, but it's at the expense of someone else's life. I won't – *can't* – let this happen."

"This isn't just a matter of defending you. If I get in Tony's way, it's him after us forever after this."

"So what? We can beat him together."

His conflicted expression did not appear to believe her. "It's suicide, Vivienne!"

"It's the coward's way out!" she yelled in frustration.

Sébastien's body stiffened, and she froze. They stared at each other in silence, Vivienne desperately wishing to snatch the words back, now unable to read his expression.

"It's the truth," she whispered in the end. "It's not who we are."

"No," Sébastien corrected, his voice roughened by fury. "It's not who *you* are, my lady. I, on the other hand, am a guardian who'll do anything for your survival."

Vivienne advanced towards him, but his abrupt shake of the head stopped her dead in her tracks.

"Be a champion again, Sébastien," she pleaded.

"Not in the cards for me, my lady." At the wariness in his eyes, Vivienne knew she had lost the fight. "I apologize if it disappoints you, but that's the reality we live in." To Alistair, he said, "I'll be patrolling from the outside tonight."

He left without another word.

"Damn it!" Vivienne yelled in frustration, kicking the table. Then her eyes landed on its bare surface, and she froze – Éimhín was gone, too.

* * *

Sébastien threw Éimhín on the passenger seat of the Jag, and settled in. Frustration still boiled underneath the surface, both at Vivienne's words and his predicament.

As he analyzed her words, the guardian came to the conclusion the enchantress had been right. The decision would have been a no brainer in a past life. *I'll be damned if I let another kid be dragged under Tony's influence, as I was.*

"Damn it all to hell, Vivienne!" Sébastien cursed aloud, slamming his hands on the steering wheel, before starting the engine.

You're on your own for a few hours, Alistair, he advised the dog telepathically.

Driving away, he broke every speed limit, until he was back in the suburban neighborhood where Nico's house was. There was a car in the driveway, and he parked behind it.

Sébastien got out of the Jag, leaving Éimhín behind. He knocked twice, and waited tensely. The petite lady, Sofia, opened the door with bloodshot eyes, as if she had been crying for the last few hours.

"Where is he?" Sébastien examined the empty house behind her.

She blinked in confusion. "Who?"

"Antonio, your son."

At her blank face, the guardian shifted on his feet, rubbing the back of his neck. "I'll help you out, so long as you leave soon after. Tony's retribution will be swift."

"He's gone," Sofia whispered, fresh tears streaming down her pale cheeks.

"What do you mean, *gone*?"

"Antonio said he had to do it tonight, to make up for his father's sins."

"I'll find him," Sébastien assured her firmly. "And I'll bring him to you. Pack, get your car ready, and wait for me at the grocery store from earlier. It's right next to the main getaway highway. Get far away from here, promise me."

Sofia assented, pulling herself together, and wiped at her cheeks. "You're a better man than most."

"No, I'm not," Sébastien denied. "Only someone looking for redemption."

At his anguished look, Sofia added timidly, "In that case, I hope you find what you seek."

Sébastien nodded, then departed without another word.

"May God bless you," Sofia whispered to his back, hoping he could bring back her boy, unharmed.

* * *

Sébastien drove through three different locations Tony owned in the city, but there was no sign of any initiation going. Then he recalled one place, on the outskirts, that was used for more unofficial meetings, and headed there.

Now, stationed in front of the old barn, he knew it was the right spot by the number of expensive cars parked nearby.

He got out of the Jaguar, with Éimhín this time, and Vivienne's words echoing in his ears. *Be a champion again.*

Maybe I still can be.

Sébastien got to the front door and kicked it open. In the middle of the room were seven of Tony's men, plus a young kid, and a blindfolded man on his knees, hands tied at the back.

The kid – Antonio – had a gun in one hand and was facing the blindfolded man.

Sébastien gritted his teeth at the sight, even as images of a similar scene from years ago flew in his mind. They were going to coerce Antonio to commit his first murder, much as he had, long before.

"Dubois, you're persona non grata here," one of the men declared. "Fair warning – this is none of your business."

"Thanks, but I'm here for the kid."

Antonio peered at him, ashen under the tanned skin, his eyes wide and full of fear. Vivienne had been right, he was definitely not meant for the world of crime.

"Come on," Sébastien held out his hand to the teenager, maintaining eye contact. "Let me drive you to your mom."

The boy began to lower the gun, but the other seven men moved in, closing him off from Sébastien.

"Don't think so," replied the one who had spoken before.

Sébastien sighed, and gripped Éimhín with both hands, raising it. "Hard way it is."

He took advantage of their incredulous stares – how many times had a Mafia operative used a sword instead of a gun? – and advanced to the closest adversary, butting him in the head with the hilt. The six others snapped out of their stupor and charged, guns and pipes in hand.

Sébastien struck one man's crow bar out of his hand, then kicked him in the gut and thigh – he went down. Another man attacked from behind, choking him with an arm around the neck. The knight contorted and stabbed him in the leg with the blade.

Two others came at the guardian, weapons drawn to kill – then gunshots rang out. He used Éimhín to duck the bullets, recalling Vivienne had long ago blessed the sword to always defend him.

Nonetheless, Sébastien perceived the fatal intent of the bullets as they hit the metal and ricocheted off, and Éimhín vibrated in anger.

He ducked another shot, and rolled towards his opponents, coming up within striking distance of one and knocking the other in the head – both dropped down.

Sébastien walked to the kid, who cowered in a corner, and had two more men left to fight off. At his determined stride, one ran off, but the last one took aim and shot a few times.

The knight avoided two of the bullets, but sensed the impact of the other two. He bent over in two, the pain slicing through him. With a huge effort of will, Sébastien gritted his teeth against it, and stood up.

In one smooth action, he moved to the last man and struck the sword's hilt on the side of his head. He fell to the ground, joining the others in unconsciousness.

Holding onto his side, Sébastien marched to Antonio. On the way over, he stopped to free the blindfolded man, who ran off gratefully. Reaching the kid, the champion held out his free hand.

The teenager grasped it, shaking like a leaf. Not wasting any time, Sébastien trudged to the car, with Antonio dragging his footsteps behind.

When Sébastien held the car door open for him, the teenager noticed the blood staining his shirt. "You're hit!"

The knight glanced down at his soaked clothes, then hugged his jacket closer to his body. "I'll be fine."

He drove as rapidly as possible, delivering Antonio to Sofia at the meeting spot within mere moments. Her gratitude was heart-warming, but Sébastien extricated himself out of her embrace.

Urgency filled his every fiber – to see the one he loved. One-handed, Sébastien drove back to Vivienne's place, his vision getting blurry with each passing second as he lost more blood.

I have to see her one last time before I die.

CHAPTER 18

There was a knock on Vivienne's door. Alistair lifted his head off the bed, but did not budge or otherwise show a sign of being worried.

When she opened the door, Sébastien was there. The young woman glared at him, still mad about earlier and his storming off.

"What the hell are you doing–" The words died on her lips at the pleading in his eyes.

Vivienne swallowed her rage, and moved aside to let him enter the house. When Sébastien passed by, she vaguely noticed his arm was clasped to his stomach at a weird angle.

Before she could ask him about it, Sébastien turned to her and dropped to his knees, his head bowed in contrition.

"I'm sorry, my lady. I've done the unthinkable." Then he dropped like a log, a pool of blood spreading underneath him.

Vivienne lifted her hand to her mouth, frozen in shock. She could clearly see through the shirt two gunshots to his stomach. She tried not to freak out, to no avail. There was the love of her life, the one guy she had already lost many times over the centuries, and he was bleeding to death on her floor – with bullet wounds, of all things!

Part of her brain dimly wondered what Sébastien had meant, but she disregarded it, more pressed to heal him.

Vivienne! Alistair's insistent roar seemed to come from far away.

The enchantress peered at him, and could hear an echo of his words, but not quite make them out. The warning in his eyes went by unnoticed as well, until the whirl of sensations hit.

"No!"

She tried to fight it off, in a real panic for the first time in her life. Sébastien was badly hurt and she could not – would not – let him die. But the déjà-vu was too strong, and it overwhelmed her anyway.

* * *

Vivienne strolled in the castle's garden, the moon high in the sky, waiting for someone – Sébastien, her heart conveyed.

There were footsteps behind, and she whirled around eagerly, but her smile died at the apparition.

"Carleigh," the princess greeted, her voice firm and unshaken.

How he had passed the guards, was a mystery. Though Vivienne's first instinct was to engage him in a supernatural duel, the shadows surrounding him were enough to give her pause.

"What are you doing here?" she asked instead.

The sorcerer ignored the question, instead glancing at the flowers. "Not quite who you expected, princess?" She cringed at his voice, so raspy to her ears.

"Not sure what you are alluding to."

"Your lover, Sébastien." Cold grey eyes narrowed on her, well aware of the risk taken. He had come alone, but he was apparently unconcerned by an impending capture. "That is who you were expecting, is it not?"

The royal training took over, and Vivienne's voice was icy as she met the sorcerer's disturbing stare. "That is none of your business, nor do you have the right to defy your princess."

"Oh, but you will not be so for long. Enjoy your reign, highness," he sneered malevolently, "while you still can."

Vivienne watched as Carleigh skulked out of the gardens, blending with the obscurity, until his presence was gone.

Sébastien entered a few minutes later, but his grin faltered at her worried frown. "What's wrong?"

"Nothing."

The guardian's gaze, though he tried to mask it, displayed his hurt. Contrite, Vivienne bit on her bottom lip, before whispering, "I did not intend it that way. It was a poor attempt not to worry you . . . Carleigh was here."

The fury in Sébastien's expression was unmistakable.

* * *

Vivienne woke to Alistair's whine and insistent paw on top of her stomach. She jumped up, slightly dizzy, but needing reassurance that Sébastien was still alive.

Leaning against a wall for support, the young woman looked to her left, but there was no one – only a pool of blood on the carpet. Panic seized her.

Her wide eyes turned to Alistair. He was getting up as well, shaking his massive head as though in agony.

"What happened? Where is he?"

A growl tore the nightly silence. *Carleigh! He came out of nowhere and knocked me out.*

"*Where*, Alistair?" Vivienne pressed, her voice tinged with desperation. They were running out of time.

Follow me. I can find his scent.

* * *

Alistair led Vivienne off to an abandoned building not far from the house. Apparently, Carleigh had a liking for those kinds of shelters.

The darkness surrounding it hit the enchantress strongly, even from afar. She extended her senses, to find Sébastien in there. By means of their bond, she was aware of his weakness – from the continuous loss of blood – and longed to have him out of harm's way.

"Carleigh!" Vivienne yelled, blasting the door open. "I know it's you, you bastard, get out here and fight me!"

Nothing happened.

Vivienne looked around, but could hardly distinguish anything past the shadows cloaking the place. A faint light came from the dusty windows, barely there. The entire place was way past abandoned – dilapidated and barely standing, paint falling off the walls, and what used to be neon lights now completely extinguished.

Giving up all pretense of safety, Vivienne ran to Sébastien's unmoving form in the middle of the room – but never got there. Instead, she slammed into a transparent barrier, flying backwards in the air and hitting a wall on the way down. The landing was brutal on her backside.

Alistair, having stayed behind, immediately ran to ensure she was alright. Then his eyes narrowed on Sébastien. Unfocusing his gaze past the reality in front of him, he finally saw what he had missed at first – an invisible barrier, almost like a dome, that surrounded the champion.

He sniffed the air and the sudden darkness suspiciously, before growling in warning, *Carleigh is here.*

As the words were spoken, a shadow edged away from the wall, and Carleigh slunk over. "The mighty Lady of the Lake," the sorcerer sneered from only a few feet away.

Vivienne stifled a grunt as she got up, unwilling to give him the satisfaction of seeing her weak. She glanced at Sébastien again, and his increasingly pale skin.

"I kept him alive enough for you to show up. Wouldn't it be horrible to watch him die before your eyes?" Carleigh continued, his voice coated with mocking sympathy. "Ah, but the sad truth? He's already been there. Too bad you missed the spectacle of your own death in the last life."

Vivienne tried to block the words out, but he kept on going. "Merlin's protégée . . . I never understood what was so special about you. Other than your royal blood and snotty attitude, you're not even that powerful."

Alistair snarled and stepped between the two of them, not liking the man's nearness.

"Out of my way, mutt," Carleigh smirked.

When the demon dog kept his stance, the necromancer elevated one palm towards him, with a malevolent energy forming in it. Vivienne reached deep within herself for an incantation, urging it to create a defensive shield around Alistair.

Feeling it snap into place with a tug on her senses, the enchantress lowered her gaze to Alistair's back. Past his furry self, she forced herself to examine his aura – and held back a relieved sigh when she noticed the thin transparent line of the barrier protecting him.

Satisfied, Vivienne commanded, "Step back, Al." He peered behind, uncertain. *Do as I tell you,* she continued telepathically. *Go to Sébastien and try to break past the barrier.*

Be careful, majesty, he urged. *I hope you realize what you are doing.*

Step by step, he moved away. Carleigh glared after him, then faced his old nemesis once more. They now stood facing each other, the royal and the pauper.

Carleigh jerked his palm, and a murky orb flew towards Vivienne, only to hit her own protective barrier and bounce off. "Learned some tricks, have you?" he sneered.

Undeterred, the warlock waved his arm in a circle, high up, calling air. Vivienne could only frown, trying to guess what he was up to – unaware of her own weakness.

The necromancer was well aware that Vivienne's shield

could block all attacks of darkness. The elements, however, were trickier and harder to block – a side effect of being taught by the same mentor.

Since he could not use fire as it was too purifying for his taste, nor water – it being Vivienne's element – the necromancer was left with earth and air. Earth had stopped acknowledging Carleigh's call long ago, considering it was closely linked to white magic, so, really, all he had left was air.

Satisfied with the gathering in his palm, Carleigh snapped out of his thoughts and sent a blast of air towards Vivienne. It hit her barrier but rather than bounce off, it vibrated through it. The enchantress dropped down, groaning out loud this time at the pressure in her head.

Rather than let go of the hex, Carleigh whirled it around the enchantress in circles, effectively blocking her from Alistair – and creating a wicked migraine by means of the air. It was enough to block her abilities.

"See? All I need to drop you is the tiniest of incantations."

Vivienne glared at him from her viewpoint. Out of the corner of her eye, she noticed Alistair attack the barrier around Sébastien repeatedly. He even tried lunging at it with his claws and teeth – to no avail.

The anger and fear of losing Sébastien fueled her, and energy vibrated in her being. At the sudden change in her demeanor, astonishment glinted in Carleigh's eyes.

Listening to old instincts, Vivienne slammed both her palms on the ground. A thick flow of green spirit entered it, ran through the earth, and surfaced in front of Carleigh with all the bulldozing grace of a tsunami.

When the blast hit Carleigh full force, he flew in the air and slammed into the nearest wall. Vivienne watched in satisfaction as he dropped to the floor, grunting in pain. Once he lay unmoving, she ran towards Sébastien.

At the same time, there was a popping sound, and Alistair tilted his head in the direction of his mistress, *The barrier is gone.* Noticing Carleigh on the ground, he added, *Good job making him lose concentration. He could not have kept maintaining it.*

Ignoring the praise, Vivienne knelt next to the guardian. "Sébastien," she whispered, trying to shake him awake. Her shoulders sagged in relief when his eyes flickered open, though his gaze was lost and unfocused. Slowly, he came to, recognition flickering.

"Vivienne?" he rasped out. "What are you doing here? Carleigh, he's—"

Alistair glanced behind them, but the sorcerer was gone. *Coward,* he grumbled. To his mistress, he added, *Well done, highness. You truly held your own.*

Vivienne vaguely nodded, her attention on Sébastien. "Carleigh's done for today," she said, positioning one hand above his stomach. The healing flash escaped her effortlessly, but by the time the wounds closed up, her strength waned.

That is enough, Vivienne, Alistair recommended, prodding her away from Sébastien with his muzzle. She shook her head to clear it, but saw only blurry fur. *You have done enough for today.*

Alert now that the loss of blood was stopped, Sébastien stood up, not even dizzy. Alistair had trouble keeping Vivienne standing, thus he picked the young woman in his arms, resting her head on his shoulder.

"You've used too much," Sébastien scolded, but the enchantress had long since passed out. His gaze shifted to Alistair. "Did she really defy Carleigh on her own?"

Oh yeah, the demon dog rumbled. *And she kicked his ass.*

* * *

Vivienne woke up in the middle of the night in an empty bed. She got up, and joined Alistair by the window of the chambers. He was standing guard, ears pricked forward, fixated on something. Glancing outside, she noticed Sébastien by the lake shore, pacing restlessly.

"How long has this been going on?" the princess wondered.

The demon dog squinted up at her, and admitted, "A few nights. He feels guilty for hurting you, and succumbing to Carleigh's influence. I tried to explain to him that he did not fail in his duties, but . . ."

Vivienne petted him gently, and grabbed a shawl. When Alistair went to follow, she shook her head. "I have to do this myself."

Going by the servants' tunnels, the royal was soon outside in the crisp air. She approached her lover, speaking only when she was by his side. "Sébastien?"

The guardian whirled around, eyes haunted. The minute he recognized Vivienne, his body froze.

"You should not be here alone," Sébastien advised, then turned away from her.

"With you, you mean?" Vivienne finished for him. "Yes, I

should. I can help."

"I do not anticipate you can, my lady. I failed you in this, and hurt you."

"You did not fail me. On the contrary, you used your body as a shield, and without you, I could have been the one hurt." The enchantress moved around him, and caressed his cheek gently. "Please let me help you."

"I can refuse you nothing," Sébastien murmured, inclining his head in assent.

Vivienne beamed, letting the shawl fall off her shoulders, and entered the lake. It was not cold, warming with her basic wish. Sébastien stared after her, mesmerized, until the water was up her waist.

"Come join me," she invited, extending a hand towards him.

Sébastien hesitated for a moment, before removing his boots and following in, until he was by her side. He was pleasantly surprised at the warmth of the liquid, until he realized the princess was dominating it.

"Do you trust me?" Vivienne asked him.

"Always."

She immersed her hands in the water, always maintaining eye contact. It bubbled at her touch, until two jets of clear liquid splashed up like a fountain. They rose in height on either side of the guardian, then joined on top of Sébastien's head. Through it all, he held her gaze.

Vivienne's green eyes flamed with power as her soft, melodious voice, imbued with an enchantment, recited a spell from deep within. "With this water, I cleanse you. Let the remnant shadows be expelled, your spirit be purified, and your soul lightened. You are, and will be, untouched once more. I, keeper of this realm, so cleanse you."

As the liquid poured over him, Sébastien closed his eyes, allowing it to sink into his clothes, under his skin, and into his very soul. A warm, gentle wave flowed within him like a torrent, taking away the remnants of the darkness and weight on his soul.

When he blinked, Vivienne smiled at him, eyes an emerald green once more. He bent his mouth to hers and pulled her into a soft kiss, thanking the fates for his luck.

Up in Vivienne's room, Alistair surveyed the moon, recalling the prophecy he had foreseen. "They really are soul mates," he muttered, and knew it was time for Merlin to keep his end of the bargain.

* * *

Vivienne woke up from the déjà-vu with a pounding headache. The sun filtered past the blinds, and each sun's ray drilled a hole in her head.

She stretched towards the nightstand, and found a glass with two painkillers next to it. Gulping them down, she rested her head on the pillow once more. The previous night's events flitted in her head – Sébastien injured, under Carleigh's control, and her small victory over the sorcerer.

It was not done by far, that much she knew. The hatred Vivienne had seen in Carleigh's eyes was profound, going deeper than even Merlin rejecting him. There was a piece of the puzzle eluding them all.

Exhausted, the young woman was about to go back to

dreamland. As her breathing slowed down, falling in a semi-conscious state, Sébastien's features entered her mind. Once more, she could hear the anguish in his voice as he said, "I've done the unthinkable."

Vivienne's eyes snapped open with newfound determination. She had to find out what the guardian had meant – and pray it was not another black mark on his soul. She slid out of bed, her head pounding with each movement.

After a shower, she still had a hard time moving about with the constant pounding. "Time to take more pills," she groaned, having disliked medicine since her stint with the psychiatrists.

Vivienne wandered out of the room, only to run into Alistair.

You're awake!

"Keep it down, Al," she winced as his loud voice echoed in her head. "Yeah, I'm awake. And I need another pill."

She went to the kitchen cabinet and plopped another one in her mouth, gulping some orange juice to wash it down with. Alistair lay down on the floor, observing her strangely.

"It hurts so bad," Vivienne groaned, massaging both sides of her temples in a useless effort to extinguish the migraine.

You were using an extra burst of energy, something you have not in a long while, and it exhausted you. The pain is a secondary effect from the entire ordeal.

Vivienne headed to the kitchen table, but her knees wobbled. She grabbed the counter in time to avoid falling.

Perhaps you should relax today.

The enchantress shook her head at the alarm he projected. "No. I've seen firsthand how powerful Carleigh is now compared to the past. He even used air to put me down! I only won because he underestimated how much I remembered. I'd say it's pretty much essential I match him for our next encounter."

I would not worry about him bending elements to his will, highness. In his current malicious state, he could barely summon one of them, and the others will not stir. Fire is too purifying, and water and earth navigate more towards your type of magic.

"Then how the hell was he able to use air?"

Alistair rolled his eyes, muttering, *Air is the most fickle of the elements. Either way, it is not worrisome. However, in your current state, if you use spells, you will tire yourself easily, and that in itself is more perilous.*

"I have to master elemental incantations for our next face-off." When Alistair looked like he was about to argue, Vivienne added, "Whether you like to admit it or not, even *you* were scared when I confronted Carleigh."

Alistair sighed, out of options to change her mind.

"Where's Sébastien?" Vivienne wondered, recalling the reason for getting out of bed in the first place.

He went to check on something.

"Where?"

No idea.

"I have to talk to him," she scowled at the dog, feeling silly.

Alistair displayed his canines in a flawless imitation of a doggy smile. *You will have to wait, majesty.*

Slowly, Vivienne drifted away from the kitchen counter, and got all the way to the table before dropping into a chair heavily. Alistair followed and sat at her feet.

"Did he explain what he meant last night? About having done the unthinkable?"

No, and I did not ask.

Vivienne hesitated, and voiced her doubts out loud. "Alistair, I'm afraid of what it might be. What if it's another mark on his soul?"

The dog's eyes shone with sympathy, and he licked her hand in a comforting gesture. *Trust him, highness. It really is all you can do.*

"I do trust him."

Alistair placed his head on her lap. *You could call him.*

"I already did. Got voicemail both times."

As soon as Vivienne mentioned it, her cell phone rang. She picked it up, once more disregarding the caller ID. "Sébastien?"

"No, darling." She did not recognize the voice at the other end, but he sounded pissed. "But if you run into him, advise him he signed his death warrant last night."

"What?"

"Tony doesn't take lightly to his fish being skimmed from under him."

"I'll pass it on," Vivienne replied in a frosty tone, then disconnected.

Her thoughts were churning, but she could draw only one conclusion. *Sébastien must have intervened in Antonio's initiation, drawing attention upon himself.*

Vivienne was struck by the realization the guardian had made this choice for himself, something selfless for the side of good. And in so doing, he had also stepped closer to a joint future with her. The young woman's heart warmed at the idea, and the need to be with Sébastien became almost unbearable.

Majesty?

Vivienne peered down at Alistair, grinning from ear to ear.

Good news? he probed, tilting his head.

"Nope, not at all," she chuckled. "It was a Mafia guy, calling to threaten Sébastien that he signed his death warrant last night."

Alistair waited for more, but once Vivienne beamed wider, he ventured, *Am I missing something? Why are you so content about that?*

"I'm not happy. I'm *ecstatic* at what it means," she laughed. "Don't you see? To have done this, Sébastien must have gotten involved and saved Antonio!"

Realization dawned on Alistair, and he rumbled, *Which begs the conclusion that he is now permanently out of the Mafia.*

"Yes!"

I advised Sébastien a while ago he can still seek redemption, and he is now well on his way. I am happy for you both.

The young woman grinned, her headache less agonizing now. Hearing the growl of her stomach, she got up and made breakfast, sticking with some crêpes to avoid exhaustion before the day had truly started.

Vivienne had finished the last round of crêpes when she heard the front door opened. She stepped into the living room, anticipation in the pit of her stomach, until Sébastien entered.

Unrestrained, Vivienne jumped to hug him, and was

pleasantly surprised when Sébastien returned it, holding her tight. Having nearly died last night, he had a new appreciation for how right she felt in his arms.

"You're unharmed!" Vivienne whispered in his chest.

"Thanks to you, yes," Sébastien murmured, pressing his lips to the top of her head.

The enchantress drew back, her eyes shining with joy, content to have him alive.

* * *

Vivienne cursed for the fifth time as the flames of the candles extinguished. She had been playing with enchantments for the last three hours, concentrating on the elements, and the spells were simply not working.

Merlin had taught her long ago there was one strong source of raw power inside her, which was amplified when near water – her preferred element. On top of that, other elements she could bend to her will existed – fire, earth and air. Though air had been easy enough, the rest were proving uncooperative.

Vivienne, you should rest, Alistair suggested, not for the first time.

"I can go on a bit longer," the royal mumbled, and aimed her hand at the candles again.

Vivienne had ten facing her, of different sizes, laid down on the grass. The exercise consisted in trying to set them ablaze simultaneously, then remove their fire and use it as a weapon. It was a good thing they were outside, by the pool, considering a few patches of grass had accidentally been incinerated so far.

Under her hand, a flame emerged. Vivienne focused her intent on making it climb higher and higher, feeding on itself.

After growing for a bit, a portion of the flame split from the rest, and jumped to the other candles, hopping onto each wick until they were all fired up. The small flickers combusted in tandem and the candles grew together for a few moments. Just as the young woman was about to collect them into a blazing sphere, they extinguished.

Sébastien got up from his spot on the grass, and sat beside to Vivienne.

I'll get her to rest, he promised mentally to Alistair. *Give us a moment.*

The dog retreated to the far corner of the backyard, extending his senses to scan for trouble. There had been no sign of the druids since the warehouse fight, and none of Carleigh, either. It was worrisome, to say the least.

Alistair yearned to contact Merlin for advice, but could not count on his duplicity. Thus, he kept watch.

Sébastien, meanwhile, grazed Vivienne's arm to get her attention. She glanced at him, giving up on the newest candle.

"Time for a breather."

She rolled her eyes, then sighed. "You won't let it drop, will you?"

"No."

"Alright. What would you like me to do?"

Sébastien stood and tugged on Vivienne's arm, dragging her to her feet. She wobbled, having been sitting for too long. A true gentleman, Sébastien picked her up and carried her bridal style into the house.

Vivienne was quiet in his arms, enjoying the closeness

and drawing comfort from Sébastien. She was on the edge of a precipice, attempting to read his body language to figure out if the near-death experience had changed anything – such as removing his determination to stay away.

Sébastien brought them into the living room and on the couch, placing Vivienne in between his legs, with her back to his chest. She fidgeted, unable to sense what he planned.

"Relax," he instructed softly, pressing his hands to her shoulder blades and massaging gently, taking his time.

As Sébastien's fingers dug into her back, the knots of stress from the past few days tightened. Under his expertise, as he went over each and every one of them, they loosened until Vivienne was floating in a state of utter peace.

From his position, Sébastien could smell Vivienne's sweet perfume, and it reminded him of countless mornings spent by her side in previous lifetimes. By the time he worked out the last kinks in her neck, she was leaning into him, her breathing slow and relaxed.

Sébastien stopped, believing she had fallen asleep. He would allow himself this one moment of peace, of intimacy. The feel of her body against his made him crave more, but he was content with the certainty Vivienne was safe, alive, and well.

The guardian had not expected to survive the bullet bounds. The fact he had, suggested his life was still worth living. It was a surprise – an eye-opening experience to say the least – that there was still something in him to save.

Much as Sébastien knew he could not be a husband to Vivienne, he could allow himself to be a friend. As such, their love would not be tainted, and the white magic inhabiting the enchantress would remain clean.

It would not be easy to stick around and watch Vivienne live her life with another man, when the time came, but he could do it – had to.

Sébastien exhaled heavily.

"Why the sigh?' Vivienne murmured, and he tucked a strand of hair behind her ear.

"Just thoughts . . ." Sébastien paused, then added, "I thought you were asleep."

"No . . . I was enjoying the closeness. You've been so adamant to keep me at bay that I didn't want to risk spoiling this unexpected show of affection."

Sébastien caught the pain in Vivienne's voice and wrapped his arms around his beloved, bringing her nearer. "I'm sorry for hurting you."

"I know you have your reasons – noble as they may be."

He hesitated, not eager to elaborate. Despite himself, after a few moments, the words tumbled past his lips: "How are you feeling now?"

"A bit more relaxed . . .but I still have to practice. After seeing Carleigh's strength, I know I have to match it."

"Rome was not built in a day, beloved."

"You're right," Vivienne smiled against his arm. She bit her lip, struggling with the words, but finally chose to be honest. "I found out about Antonio."

Sébastien froze only slightly, before relaxing, "What about him?"

"Someone from the Mafia called today . . . Said to tell you you're done for, as far as Tony is concerned."

"I expected as much," Sébastien chuckled without humor.

After a beat, he asked, "What's your take on it?"

"I'm extremely grateful . . . Thank you for choosing to save him."

"It was the only right decision," he admitted after another brief pause. "Your words were true."

The crackling of the fire got to Vivienne, and his encompassing heat and heartbeat lulled her to sleep. Sébastien convinced himself that in a few minutes, he would get up and bring her to bed. But he drifted off, holding the enchantress tightly in an embrace.

* * *

Guinevere cowered in fear at the lunatic.

"This is your last chance," Carleigh hissed, getting in close proximity, his putrid breath washing over her. "Sébastien must screw you. Seduce Vivienne's guardian, or else it will be the last attempt you ever make."

As soon as Guinevere was gone, the sorcerer walked to the darkness, and the mirror became cloudy. "Now let me see these dreams of yours." When Sébastien appeared, he snarled. "You still imagine you've got a chance to survive, to be redeemed? I shall prove you otherwise."

Carleigh inhaled deeply, braced himself, then knelt and sunk both hands in the pool. "First, for her highness . . ." The obscurity agitated underneath his touch, sensing the intent behind the words.

The warlock could see Vivienne lying dormant in the guardian's arms. From the mirror, a drop of darkness detached, and fell across her reflection, where it was absorbed.

Almost immediately, Vivienne twisted around in her sleep, moaning as though in pain.

Carleigh smirked in victory. "And now, Sébastien. If Guinevere does not tempt you, I shall ensure you fail."

The shadows concentrated on the knight's features, almost zooming in, and a drop entered him as well, sinking into the skin. His aura flared dark for a moment, before it was gone.

Carleigh withdrew from the mirror, his hands dripping with stained liquid. He cackled maniacally as the creatures of darkness scurried at his feet, forever around.

* * *

Vivienne was on the edge of a lake. A beautiful palace was upon it, but in a brilliant blaze, it went under. She stepped closer, shuddering at the sight before her. Dead bodies and gaping faces floated in the limpid pool, with blood oozing from them and tainting it.

Vivienne put a hand out to use magic, but noticed the blood on her skin for the first time. A wordless scream escaped her lips, and she fell to the ground.

* * *

Sébastien woke up to find Vivienne twitching in his arms. It was nightfall outside, and with a start he realized they had slept for a few hours.

The young woman moaned as if in anguish, and shifted once more. He tightened his arms around her, whispering,

"It's only a dream. You're okay." Despite his reassuring words, Vivienne kept trashing, and Sébastien felt tears on her cheeks.

It is not just a dream! Alistair's voice came from behind, and the guardian craned his neck to see the dog rushing around the corner of the couch. His opaque eyes glowed with an uneasy light.

Alistair approached and sniffed Vivienne curiously. No sooner had he inched closer, that he backed off with a confused snarl.

Wake her up, now!

Something in Alistair's voice spurred Sébastien on. He sat up, bringing Vivienne with him, and tried to shake her awake.

"Vivienne!"

A blood-curling scream escaped past her lips, raising goose bumps on his arms.

Touch her head! Alistair instructed, at the same time sending a nudge of his own supernatural energy to coat the knight's hand.

When Sébastien's fingertips touched Vivienne's forehead, a zap of electricity passed amongst them, and her eyes finally snapped open.

"It's okay. It was just a dream," Sébastien murmured in a soothing voice, attempting to calm her down.

"Oh, it was horrible!" Vivienne cried, pressing into his chest and bursting into tears. Sébastien gathered her closer, futilely hoping by the gesture alone he could remove the nightmare from her mind.

He glanced at Alistair over the top of her head, and the dog read the doubt in his eyes.

Whether you like to admit it or not, the soul mate bond is still there. You are fooling no one by imagining you can stay away from Vivienne, knight. It was you who brought her back.

Sébastien could not fathom what to respond. Despite the truth in Alistair's words, the belief – nay, the certainty – that he had enough darkness in him to be a valid risk to Vivienne kept him away. He loved her enough to set her free, as long as it meant safety and a happy life for her.

In between sobs, Vivienne recounted something about a lake, a city under the water, and deaths. She did not detect Sébastien's alarm, soon reflected in Alistair's eyes.

"The worst was the blood on my hands," Vivienne revealed, having calmed down. "I couldn't . . ."

"Shh," Sébastien whispered, tightening his grip on her. "You're alright."

"Doesn't feel that way, though. It wasn't one of my normal flashes, but it wasn't a simple nightmare either."

The guardian could only hold her close, until Vivienne drifted off again.

"Alistair," he called aloud, seeing as the dog had left the room to scan the backyard and surroundings for traces of a threat.

His claws on the floor clamored his return. *I am here.*

"Could it be the memory of her father?"

No. I am of the opinion it is an altered version Vivienne saw, conveyed as a dream.

"Who would be toying with her like this?" Sébastien scowled.

I can think of two who would, Alistair stated, meeting his worried stare with a furious one.

"But Merlin wouldn't –" Sébastien stopped mid-sentence, recalling how the wizard had manipulated his own dreams.

Vivienne only truly became Lady of the Lake after her father's passing, and my own. If that is what Merlin wants her to be again, he would coerce her into remembering.

Sébastien peered down at the enchantress' relaxed form in his arms. "I wish I could spare her the past."

You and me both. But it is a ticking bomb, waiting to burst. No matter what either of us does, it will explode eventually.

Sébastien pressed his lips to Vivienne's forehead, breathing in her unique citrusy perfume. She shifted, cuddling closer, unknowingly losing herself in another memory.

* * *

"Absolutely not!" Alistair bellowed.

"You cannot stop me if I am attempting to put an end to this feud!" Vivienne yelled back.

"Like hell I can't, majesty. I will go to your father and he will have you locked up in an ivory tower before you can act on this madness!"

"Alistair—"

"No!" he shook his massive head, eyes flashing. "It is much too perilous!"

"What the hell is going on here?" All the yelling had attracted Sébastien. He took in their defensive postures, subconsciously already angling his body to defend Vivienne.

"Rest easy, knight, I am not the danger here. If you want to protect Vivienne, protect her against herself!"

Sébastien focused on the princess, frowning. "What is he referring to?"

Vivienne avoided his look.

"You will not even tell him?" the dog growled, and advanced to Sébastien. "Vivienne received a message from Carleigh, to meet for a so-called parlay. That lying bastard pretends it is in order to call a truce and work out terms."

Vivienne saw Sébastien tense out of the corner of her eye, and glowered at Alistair. "Now you've done it."

"He is absolutely right," the champion agreed. "It is much too dangerous to meet him. And I assume, on top of that, he expects you to go on your own?"

"Of course he does!" Alistair snarled. "This has gone on long enough, and Carleigh is toying with us. I will involve Merlin, perhaps he will be able to talk some sense into her."

"No!" Vivienne protested. "He has enough on his plate with Arthur and Guinevere. Please let me do this. If I can avoid more attacks, it is worth an attempt. Alistair, you always say I have untapped potential . . . Let me try."

The dog walked towards Sébastien, rolling his eyes. "I give up. Your turn."

The knight faced Vivienne, cupping her cheek in his palm. "Love, if you go and get hurt, I will never forgive myself. But I also cannot restrain you. What I propose is you let me come with you."

"No!"

"Then you will not go," Sébastien clenched his jaw at the refusal. "I agree with Alistair. We can go to your father and Merlin."

Vivienne's eyes darted from him to her massive demon

dog. Neither one showed the tiniest sign of relenting. In the end, she scowled at her lover. "Fine, you can come."

"I as well, then," the dog jumped in.

"Alistair—"

"No negotiating, princess."

"Alright!" She glared at both of them, annoyed at having lost her ground. "But we depart now."

They saddled only one horse, Vivienne's Shadow. Sébastien rode behind her, one arm wrapped around her waist the entire ride. It was a reassurance for the enchantress, giving her strength for a task she was not quite sure she could accomplish, despite all the bravado portrayed. Alistair followed them on foot, more than able to keep up with the horse.

They had no sooner left the castle grounds – and Vivienne's safeguard – when a grey sphere materialized in front of their eyes. It hovered in mid-air, before heading down a path into the forest.

"Fascinating. Now we follow a glowing orb. This is a great idea, majesty," Alistair muttered in their heads, and pursued the sphere with an annoyed snarl.

After a few hours' ride, they arrived at a clearing, and the orb evaporated. They were long past Elsior's grounds now, having delved deep into unfamiliar territory.

"You brought guests, despite my warnings?" Carleigh walked out of the shadows abruptly.

Vivienne dismounted, with Sébastien doing the same. He placed himself next to her, prepared to step in at the slightest provocation to remove the princess out of harm's way.

"Sébastien is my most trusted knight," Vivienne declared.

"My father would have been suspicious and dispatched an army if I had left without him. I can enchant him to sleep if it would put you at ease."

Annoyance flashed over Carleigh's face at her defiant tone, and the implication he was fearful of one mortal man.

"Your lover can stay awake," he snickered, not fooled in the least. His spies had informed him about the monarch's tryst with the knight. "To witness and report back to his king."

Alistair bared his teeth, stepping in front of Vivienne, and Carleigh levelled a dismissive stare to him. "Nice dog."

The demon's body shook with coiled tension as a thunderous bark escaped him.

Carleigh lifted his palms and made a come hither motion to the woods behind him. Seven corrupt druids strode out, dressed in mantles the color of midnight.

"You promised this was a meeting for a truce!" Vivienne gasped.

"I lied." The sorcerer smirked. "Or are you so naïve to believe everything you hear? You truly have led a sheltered life, Vivienne. But that is about to change."

"I highly doubt that," she hissed, and Sébastien was proud of the strength in her voice.

Vivienne backed away, one palm glowing for a mere moment, before an invisible barrier escaped her and surrounded Shadow. It was done subtly, and neither the druids nor Carleigh noticed the new protection the horse had acquired.

Then, she elevated both hands in front of her. In full view of the warlocks, a spell formed between her glowing palms, and she hurled it towards Carleigh without further ado.

Sébastien unsheathed his sword, and went back to back with the princess, facing the conjurers surging behind them, as well.

In the midst of the battle, they got separated, but Alistair's bark could be heard above all noises as he jumped from one warlock to another.

It was only a few moments later, as they each faced different opponents, that Sébastien heard him warn, "Vivienne, no!"

He whirled around to notice the young woman facing Carleigh. The sorcerer gathered dark magic in his palms, in the shape of a coated ball, and flung it towards Vivienne. Just as it would have hit her, Alistair lunged with his jaws wide open and absorbed it all.

Carleigh's stupefaction would have been worth a laugh, had Sébastien not caught the slight wobble in the dog's paws when he landed. Focusing on him, he saw Alistair bend a paw to the ground as if unable to stand following the heroic action.

"I see it is not a dog after all you have there. A demon, Vivienne? How intriguing." Carleigh cackled, then continued, "If only my magic was not overpowering him with the new poison I have created."

"Alistair!" Vivienne knelt by the dog's side, checking for injuries, and leaving herself completely exposed. By means of their unbroken bond, she realized the damage came from the spell Alistair had inhaled, and its poisonous tendrils that paralyzed both his powers and body.

"Get out of here," Alistair's voice came in her head, weaker than before. Yet he still got up and defied Carleigh.

"No, I will not leave you here!" Vivienne tried to reach

for him, but he moved out of her way.

"Get out, princess! For once, listen to me. This is no game."

Vivienne froze at the authority in Alistair's tone, and turned her gaze to Sébastien. Across the distance, he read the indecision in her mind as clearly as if he had been by her side.

"Get her away!" Alistair yelled in the guardian's head, whilst remaining focused on the sorcerer. "I cannot afford the distraction."

Sébastien whistled to Shadow, who galloped towards him. He latched onto the saddle and jumped on the horse, racing to Vivienne. The exigency in Alistair's tone was not feint. He bent down, captured the princess by the waist and yanked her on the horse as well.

With a nudge, the knight rode Shadow in the direction they had come from, leaving the dust and chaos of the battle behind. He glanced behind only once, and was met with Alistair's gratefulness.

"Keep her safe."

Then, the massive demon dog turned away, confronting Carleigh and the remaining conjurers alone.

"Why did you take me away!?" Vivienne twisted in the saddle to Sébastien and lashed out, smashing her closed fists against his chest. "We should have stayed and fought by his side!"

"I was only listening to Alistair's orders, beloved."

Sébastien's soft voice got past her outrage, and Vivienne collapsed against him, sobbing her heart out.

* * *

The young woman stirred in the champion's arms, and Alistair edged away again. *Rest is useless to her while she is afraid,* were his parting words.

Vivienne blinked sleepily up at Sébastien, shadows of the past shimmering in her gaze. Probing her mood, he noticed she was no longer traumatized, but rather pensive.

Sébastien squeezed her close again, waiting until she spoke. It must have been the dim light, or the full moon – or denial at having nearly died . . . But when Vivienne's green eyes met his again, his entire body felt awake.

The air crackled with their energy, and Sébastien was even more sensitive to the enchantress' soft body cradled against his muscle, their uneven breathing, her eyes smoldering with desire. He glanced down to her lips, mesmerized despite his better judgment. Vivienne parted them slightly – an open invitation – and his control snapped.

When Sébastien lowered his mouth to hers, it was intended as a comforting embrace, with the conviction she needed it at the moment. Yet the minute their lips grazed, everything else ceased to matter.

The guardian rolled over, pressing Vivienne against the couch with a muted groan. His leg slid between hers, even as she wrapped her free arm around his waist to pull him closer.

Sébastien groaned against the kiss, fire fueling his blood, and still Vivienne was asking for more. His mouth drifted to her neck, nibbling on the sensitive skin, and she gasped at the sensations.

He froze in his movements, only to hear her plead, "Don't. Please don't stop."

With a supreme effort, Sébastien pulled back, ignoring his

body's roar of torture. "It's not right I take advantage of you when you're vulnerable."

Vivienne's eyes rose to his, half-reproachful. "Why do you still pull away, now that you've decided to be better?"

"I'm still the guy with a corrupted soul, love," Sébastien murmured self-deprecatingly. "The way I see it, if I'm around guarding you, comforting you, being a friend, I'm not fulfilling the soul mate bond. The minute we get involved romantically, as deeply as before, it will go wrong."

"No, it won't!" Vivienne denied fiercely.

"I will not run the risk and lose you."

"And I won't risk losing you either," Vivienne admitted as she bit her lip, caressing his chin. "I can be happy with this little, at least for a while. One day, I will crave more."

"Not with me, Vivienne," Sébastien shook his head for emphasis, not wishing to give her false hope. "It will have to be with another."

"I only want *you!*" she argued, eyes flashing at the statement. "No one else but my soul mate will do."

Though his expression softened, there was only regret in his eyes. "For me as well, my love. But to have our hearts beat as one, and have mine engulf yours with darkness, is not an option I can live with."

Vivienne battled with herself to stop the torrent of words she wanted to unleash on him. What she would have said might have appealed to Sébastien's rational side, but it could also make things worse.

With a sigh, she chose pleading instead. "After all this is done with Carleigh, promise me that you will consider my words."

"I swear it. You should rest," Sébastien suggested, rolling

to his back and tugging her on top, back to their previous position.

Vivienne relaxed against his chest, the memory of the nightmare still vivid in her mind. A shiver ran down her spine, and Sébastien rubbed her back.

"I'm afraid to dream again," she admitted, her voice slightly tinged with panic and an unspoken wish for reassurance.

"I'll be here with you," Sébastien said, tightening the circle of his arms. "Hold on to me and you'll be safe, even in your dreams."

Vivienne snuggled deeper and drifted off into a restless sleep, soon followed by Sébastien.

CHAPTER 19

Asleep in the cottage where Sébastien had stopped for the night, Vivienne dreamt of her last meeting with Merlin and Alistair – the dear protector, whom she might not see again.

"I must leave the kingdom before it gets worse," Vivienne declared, standing before them. "My father has been hurt once, and I fear my staying here will only further incite Carleigh to keep attacking."

"I disagree," Merlin said, ignoring Alistair's dark look. "You are a lady of light. You should stay and fight."

"You trust that I am strong enough?" Vivienne demanded.

"Yes, I do."

The princess peered at Alistair for confirmation, but he remained silent.

"Alistair?" she prompted.

"I cannot intervene further than I have. The decision is your own. For what it is worth, you do have pure magic, highness, and that in itself is a gift."

Vivienne woke up from the recollection at the sound of a door closing. She stood up in bed as Sébastien headed towards her.

"Where have you been?" the enchantress whispered drowsily.

She knew something was wrong when he knelt by the cot. In the dim light, Vivienne could see Sébastien's shoulders were hunched, his head bowed as he grasped her hand in his.

"I rode ahead to scan the surroundings and ensure there were no traps. And I got all the way up to the riverbank, from where we could see the castle. Vivienne—" Sébastien choked on the words, unsure of how to announce the news.

With a hand movement, Vivienne lighted the candles around them, illuminating his pain-ravaged face. "What happened?"

"Carleigh took his revenge," the knight revealed, maintaining her gaze.

Vivienne swallowed the despair threatening to overcome, and instead got out of bed. "Show me."

With a heavy heart, Sébastien helped her mount Shadow and led her to the destruction site.

* * *

Vivienne was dragged away from the memory into a dream. She found herself in front of a lake again. This one was larger, with the moon's shape and radiance reflected in it. She dreaded what its depth would reveal, but a feeling within invited her to look.

When she did, there were no dead bodies, only her own reflection staring back. Vivienne dipped one hand in the water and observed as it rippled on and on, until she lost sight of it.

Enthralled, she did not hear the footsteps behind, until someone spoke. "Beautiful and entrancing, is it not?"

Vivienne whirled around at the sound of his voice. "Merlin!"

Clad in the usual pale ivory garment, wooden staff in hand, her mentor appeared the same way she recalled. His blue eyes crinkled at the corners, and he chuckled softly at her surprise.

"How is this even possible?" Vivienne went on.

"Much the way you contacted me between the ages, child."

"Yes, but that . . . It was mostly instinct. I didn't imagine it would be possible to actually see you face to face."

Merlin shrugged, motioning for the enchantress to walk with him around the lake. "Depending on the person, it is, much like now. I project myself through time, from where I now exist. Between dimensions, it is not impossible. Of course, it is easier and less taxing on this old body if there is someone reaching out at the other end."

"And was I?" Vivienne's eyes widened. "Reaching out, I mean."

Merlin rested both hands on the staff, pausing in the walk, and leveled a piercing gaze to hers.

"That is for you to discover, my dear. I captured your call over the last few days and decided to answer. So what ails you?"

"I—" Vivienne paused in the lie, aware of the sharpness still animating the old man. "I used a spell last night, the kind I have in the past, and it exhausted me."

Merlin pondered the words for a moment, then questioned, "Why did you use it?"

"To fight Carleigh. He captured Sébastien and I freed him, but it took a lot out of me."

The mage's lips pressed tightly at the guardian's name. "Vivienne, you will not want to hear this, but you have to cut him loose."

"Who, Carleigh?"

"Sébastien."

"Why would you say that?" the young woman asked, brow furrowing.

"If you keep putting your life in danger to save him, it will kill you."

"Sébastien is my soul mate!"

"Not anymore," the old wizard shook his head. "He is no longer the same man."

"He still is, Merlin. See for yourself. Do you not notice the bond linking us?"

The wizard continued to watch her, silent.

Vivienne marched to him, pointing at her heart insistently. "*Look!*"

Merlin's hands did not budge, nor did his lips, but his eyes flashed briefly with a spell. As he examined beyond her physical form to Vivienne's soul inside, he saw the distinct golden gleam of half a soul.

"This should not be possible," Merlin snapped out of the trance, narrowing his eyes. "What Sébastien has done in order to bring you back should have broken the bond. It cannot still connect you."

"But it does. Do you see it now?"

"I do . . . Yet it changes nothing, Vivienne, rather complicates things. The more you stand by Sébastien, the more you will lose."

"That's a lie!" she yelled, and retreated away, but Merlin's next words stopped her dead in the tracks.

"You will not get to your potential as Lady of the Lake on this path!"

Vivienne slowly shifted to her mentor, not even bothering to hide how much his words hurt. "Is that all you care about, Merlin?"

"You know it's not true!"

"Are you sure about that?" Alistair and Sébastien's cryptic warnings and demeanors now made more sense, whenever the subject of her old mentor came up.

Merlin noted the lightening appear in Vivienne's eyes, and tried to use logic. "You require all your strength to fight Carleigh. Sébastien is sapping it away, with all you are doing and will do to help him regain his purpose. He cannot help you in this, and will drag you down. He is only human, Vivienne."

"Is that the future you foresee?"

"The future is not clear."

Vivienne's anger dimmed immediately, a headache beginning in its stead. She clutched a hand to her head, massaging the side in an effort to stop the throbbing.

"What is it?"

Merlin tried to approach, but Vivienne held her palm up to stop him.

"My head, it's—" She gritted her teeth to stop from screaming out loud. The agony hit each nerve, and her head felt as though it was splitting open.

"Vivienne!"

She tried to look up at Merlin's alarmed tone, but fell to her knees instead. The world narrowed to only the pain – and something trying to make its way out of the shadowed corners of her mind.

"No!" Merlin yelled. "It's not supposed to happen this way. You should not be summoning all of this back at once!"

The discomfort hit stronger at the words, dragging the enchantress into a tornado of chaos. Vivienne was conscious of the cool lap of the water behind, and Merlin's incantation at work in front of her.

"Let me help you."

"No!" Vivienne gritted out. "You were never after my well-being."

She placed her free hand to the side, submerging it under the water and calling the element forward. It washed over her in a wave, and she woke up, gasping.

* * *

Vivienne got out of bed and stumbled into the living room, her head still hurting as the last of the memories pushed forth insistently. "Alistair!"

The demon dog came running from the kitchen at her yell. He stopped dead in his tracks at his mistress' odd behavior, examining her aura. *What is it?*

"*This* is what you've been hiding!" Her accusation was

stony, outweighed only by the pain in her expression.

Vivienne, what happened? You make no sense.

"I remember!" she continued yelling. "The rest of it! My father dead, my entire realm. It was *my* foolishness that killed them!"

No, that isn't true, highness! The dog's ears bent backwards. *You did everything you could to stop it!*

"Stop lying!"

Alistair looked around, alarmed as the house shook from its foundations. Whatever had spurred Vivienne's memories was also amplifying the force of her resentment, and thus her abilities.

The enchantress had always been influential, but had been able to dominate it. Now, the demon dog was afraid she was losing control.

Princess, Alistair tried to keep a firm and rational voice, inching closer. *Explain to me what happened.*

The young woman clutched the side of her head, flinching in anguish. "I was dreaming something, and Merlin showed up. He warned me to stay away from Sébastien when—" She stopped, holding on to her temples tightly. "Make it *stop!*"

Alistair watched helplessly as his mistress slumped to the floor, anguish pulsating around her. He cautiously stepped closer and placed his muzzle to her forehead, in an attempt to cool her down. Instead, the dog was dragged in Vivienne's mind, and the chaos within.

* * *

Sébastien watched, helpless, as Vivienne faced the ruins of her castle, her silhouette ramrod straight, the fragile girl in her crumbling. The entire place was in flames, with no sign of any survivors – least of all her father.

"This is not your fault," the guardian declared.

He could feel the princess' – now queen – heart breaking into a million pieces by means of their bond, and his own clenched in pain.

"It is," Vivienne's voice answered, but there was only hollowness in her tone. "I called this despair upon my realm. Carleigh wanted me, and when he could not attain his goal, he sought an easier way to destroy me."

"We will ensure he pays."

The young woman only shook her head, tears streaming down her cheeks. "They deserve a proper burial, more so than vengeance."

Pushing past her despair, Vivienne waved her hand towards the mass of rocks. From the earth, a blaze was born. It was not the usual orange, but rather a cold, icy color, and it grew in height, washing over the castle. In mere moments, the entire structure, and its grounds, glowed faintly with the incantation.

With a stifled scream, Vivienne clenched her fist. In front of her eyes, the once majestic towers wavered, before the foundation shattered in tiny pieces. The towers were next, crumbling to the ground, and the rest of the structure followed in a domino effect.

When it was all only a mass of ruins, the enchantress attacked the grounds. The earth itself vibrated, groaned, then split into two with a sigh. With her free hand, Vivienne called forth the lake, swirling a palm to raise a wave high up, before dropping it onto the ruins.

The leftovers of her kingdom were submerged underneath, buried and obsolete. Under their gloomy gazes, the chaos was smoothed out, the lake now larger than before – a tomb worthy of the realm.

Vivienne fell to her knees, barely holding herself together. Her back was rigid with the strength it took her to avoid crumbling, when all she wanted was to let go and fall apart. Sébastien helped his beloved up, attempting to comfort her to the best of his ability.

It was not long before someone appeared behind them. The guardian whirled around, and his eyes fell on Merlin, surveying the lake's depths.

"I gather it is not what you hope to hear," the old wizard revealed, "but fate cannot be changed. In the end, all of this furthers you becoming the Lady of the Lake, as you were intended to be."

Vivienne backed out of Sébastien's embrace, her beautiful features distressed with anguish. "Answer me truthfully. Were you aware of what would happen?"

"I foresaw it, yes."

"So when I came to you, wanting to leave, and you advised me otherwise, you knew this would happen."

Merlin did not respond. Vivienne clenched her fists in anger, his betrayal cutting deep. "You lied to me!" she accused. "You knew what would happen, even foresaw that Carleigh would go as far as this!"

"The future is not clear," Merlin admitted. "What it predicted, to my eyes, was a tragedy. I realized it could not be stopped, but that it would drive you to new challenges." He

glanced at the ruins underneath the water. *"This never should have happened."*

"So what did I do wrong?" Vivienne's voice broke.

Sébastien advanced to her, glaring at the wizard. Could he not see the guilt he was adding to with his rash words?

"Nothing, my dear," the old mage retorted. *"It was Carleigh's sorcery that over tipped the balance, and my fool mistake that cost you, in the end."*

"You had no right! No right *to hide this from me!"*

"You are correct," the wizard agreed. It was the first *Sébastien saw of his remorse, but Vivienne had already turned away from him.*

"Leave. Please leave me alone. I do not wish to set eyes upon you again."

"Listen to me, just this once," Merlin pleaded. *"Do not give in to revenge, otherwise this will have been for nothing."*

Vivienne tilted her head to him and met his eyes blankly. "I have no strength for revenge. I will build Aisling Caisleán here, my own 'castle of dreams', in memory of the shattered innocence you helped cause."

When she gazed back to the lake, Sébastien shook his head to Merlin and with a dark look invited him to leave. Once he was gone, he gathered Vivienne back in his arms, taking her sobs as they came. In the queen's mind, the dam was breaking, and she fell to pieces as the entirety of her loss dawned on her.

* * *

The sound of crying stirred Alistair awake. He got up, noticing

Vivienne still in a kneeling position, her head buried in her hands as sobs racked her entire body.

Vivienne . . . I am so sorry you had to recall it like this.

"You should have told me," she whispered, breathing in deeply. She withdrew her hands and stood, her eyes flashing despite the tears. "Why did you hide this from me!?"

Sébastien chose that moment to enter the house from his morning patrol. He stopped in his tracks, noticing the standoff between the two.

"What's going on?"

She remembered everything, Alistair answered, his eyes never wavering away from the enchantress. *About her father, the kingdom . . . The lake.*

"And the curse!" Vivienne exclaimed, fixing her accusing stare on Alistair. "Why didn't you say anything!?"

It was yours to find out.

"Bullshit! You were afraid I would seek revenge."

I was not!

"But Merlin was."

Highness—

"No, Alistair. You knew Merlin manipulated me in the past, you have to have known it."

I did not. I grasped he hid something, but I never found out what. The full story about your father, I never knew!

"You both lied to me!"

Vivienne–

"I can't believe I was the cause of my father's death!" Overtaken by grief, she ran out of the home to the backyard.

Go after her, Alistair glowered at Sébastien. *Now! This is Carleigh's doing, the coincidence is too grand.*

The guardian found Vivienne not far off, in a corner of the backyard. Her head was bent over her knees, and she was rocking back and forth. There was chaos in her, and pain, much as in the past. Sébastien knelt by her side, gripping her shoulder firmly.

The torture in Vivienne's eyes faded away to shadows as he whispered, "You can't blame yourself for this."

"Yeah, you told me that in the past, too," she croaked. "We both know it's not true. And Merlin, all along, he knew. It's like having it happen a second time. I know it's not quite the reality, but the agony is so real."

Sébastien sat next to the young woman on the grass and wrapped an arm around her shoulders. Vivienne moved into his chest with a quiet sniffle, then the sobs overwhelmed her. He could only tighten his grip, letting her cry it out, damning Carleigh to all hells for the pain he caused.

Moments later, as he rubbed her back, Vivienne hushed. The sound of the lapping water of the pool was the only noise as they breathed in unison. After a deep breath, she finally drew away, recalling the events before the memory had taken over.

"Merlin instructed me to cast you away," she informed him.

Sébastien's body stiffened in response. "What?"

"He visited me in my dream. He had nothing to do with me remembering all of this, at least I don't think he did . . . I believe it happened despite him. But he was there to warn me off you, saying I would never attain my true potential with you at my side."

"Because of my corrupt soul." His words were not even a question.

"Yes."

The champion sighed, debating with himself. Though Sébastien realized it was not the right time, he wanted to keep being honest with his beloved. "He's probably right, Vivienne."

"I disagree," she held his guarded eyes. "And I have my proof. He looked to see if our soul mate bond is still there."

The knight held his breath in anticipation.

"It still is, Sébastien. I belong to you, and you still belong to me. For better or worse."

"I want to trust that, believe I'm not bringing darkness to your light. But looking at the last few incidents, how you were harmed, saving me instead of the other way around . . ." Sébastien trailed off when tears filled her eyes.

Vivienne blinked them away furiously. "I can't handle this without you by my side. There are too many emotions for me to sort through by myself, don't you see?"

"I'm here, Vivienne," Sébastien grasped her hand reassuringly, squeezing it for emphasis. "And you have a right to be hurting. You have a right to feel whatever you wish."

"Even towards you?"

At Sébastien's silence, Vivienne searched his expression and noticed the raw anguish he could not hide from her.

"I can't—"

"I don't need you as a champion or defender, Sébastien, but as my man."

The knight let go of her hand, resting his forehead against hers instead. They breathed in sync for a few moments, before he pulled away. It was tearing Sébastien apart, the longing to be with Vivienne, to eliminate both their agony. But he couldn't.

"I can't."

"Why not?" she pleaded.

"For the same reasons as before."

"The darkness?" Vivienne enquired tonelessly.

"Yes. I will not be the cause of your doom."

Sébastien silently pleaded for her to understand, but it was to no avail. Vivienne turned away from his penetrating gaze, hiding her expression and the despair spreading through her.

"I'd like to go back inside now."

Sébastien grabbed her cold hand in his, and accompanied the quiet enchantress back into the house. Alistair's eyes worriedly followed them when they entered, then headed upstairs.

Vivienne was unmoving, almost like marble in his arms when the guardian helped her to bed. She got under the blankets without fighting him, then turned away and buried her head in the pillow.

Sébastien hesitated, before getting up to exit the room.

"Close the blinds," Vivienne rasped past her dry throat.

He did as she commanded, then whispered, "I'll be outside. Call me for anything."

When the young woman did not respond, Sébastien exited the room, not realizing he was walking out of her heart.

* * *

Over the next few days, Vivienne was conscious only of the darkness, of the days going in and out, and all she yearned for was to sleep forever. Full days were spent in bed, reflecting on the past and her father's death. She would wake up in the middle of the night crying, only to doze off again.

One night, Sébastien captured her muffled crying and entered the room. His heart lurched at the sight of Vivienne's pain. Heart-wrenching sobs shook her body, and in an effort to hide it, she ended up gasping for air as though suffocating.

He sat on the bed and wordlessly gathered her in the circle of his arms. She began to fight, hands flailing with closed fists, punching him and mumbling incomprehensible words.

"Vivienne, quit it," Sébastien murmured softly, gently grasping her hands in his. "I'm trying to help."

She managed to yank her wrists out of his grip, and curled back under the blankets.

"You have to talk about this," he persisted.

"No, I don't. Leave me alone."

The enchantress did not notice the guardian's worried frown, but felt his presence in the room even as she dozed off. When she woke up, much later, Sébastien was gone.

Vivienne did not care anymore that Carleigh was out to get her. She wished he would come already, to finish what he had started. The guilt at the past, to have left Elsior defenseless while attempting to strike a truce with him – what a fool she had been! – was overwhelming.

In and out of nightmares, the enchantress went. Reality blurred with fiction, to the point she was no longer sure of her identity. Was she the monarch from the past, or the impostor of the future?

Alistair entered the room at some point. *I am sorry for keeping it from you.*

Vivienne was unresponsive for the longest time, then

croaked past a dry throat, "It's my sin to bear."

Highness, please, talk to us, Alistair begged.

The young woman kept her back to him, and her eyes firmly shut.

At the silence behind, she figured Alistair had left, and drifted away – until there was an unfamiliar probe in her mind, as though someone poked her with a needle.

Calling on the remaining strength she had, Vivienne called forth magic and effectively blocked the demon dog. With a small whine, he left the room.

* * *

Alistair retreated out of the bedroom and down the stairs, to the living room where Sébastien paced relentlessly. At the dog's appearance, the guardian stopped, and a flare of hope shone in his eyes.

For all response, Alistair shook his head dejectedly.

Sébastien headed to the couch, taking a seat and aggressively running both hands through his hair. He had tried talking to Vivienne, but she would not let him in.

Reflecting on their last conversation over and over, the champion had understood his mistake. Vivienne had been in an extremely vulnerable place. In an effort to shield her, he had caused more hurt with his rejection and stubborn will to keep a distance romantically. *If only –*

Alistair advanced in front of him, interrupting his musings. *This cannot go on.*

"I agree," Sébastien replied, lifting his head up.

If I could wring Merlin's neck right now, I would, the dog grumbled.

"Vivienne is sure he didn't mean for the memories to come back."

He might not have. But Merlin, more than anyone else, should have been conscious of how much mess his involvement could cause.

"You intervened with us," Sébastien pointed out.

And it was not right.

"I've managed to not damage her, thanks to his advice."

Sébastien, he played you! He played us all. To this day, I have the impression there is more to this Carleigh feud, and it involves Merlin, one way or another. That vile sorcerer is fixated on Vivienne with too much hatred in him, it cannot be all over the loss of a mentor.

The guardian pushed off the couch and resumed pacing, his body tense and white-knuckled. In his fury, he could imagine having Carleigh in front of him, and wringing his neck with his bare hands to avenge Vivienne.

Sébastien . . . Alistair rumbled a warning at the knight's rising indignation.

He stopped, inclined his head to the demon dog and inhaled deeply. "He's powerful, Alistair. When I fought Carleigh by myself, he had me pinned to the wall without even blinking."

Perhaps, the dog conceded, *but each villain has a breaking point. We must find his and push him past it.*

Sébastien exhaled heavily, peering in the direction of Vivienne's bedroom. He could sense her within, heart breaking over and over, and he was helpless – again.

"She's in bad shape, Alistair."

Worse than before?

Sébastien looked down in surprise, then realized the dog had not seen Vivienne in the past. Alistair had already been out of the picture when the princess had been mourning the loss of her realm, and all she held dear.

"Yeah," he answered honestly. "When she lost you, and her father, it brought Vivienne to her knees."

What raised her up?

"See for yourself."

Alistair observed, expectant, as the former champion knelt in front of him and bowed his head. With one movement, the dog placed a paw over his shoulder, and pressed his muzzle to his forehead.

As he had done multiple times before, Alistair expanded his mind to encompass Sébastien's, picturing a smaller bubble being swallowed by a bigger one. He knew it worked when the knight's breathing slowed down, falling into a trance. Only then did he immerse himself in the memory awaiting.

* * *

Sébastien entered the solarium, where Vivienne was seated on a chair facing outside. Following the destruction of Elsior, she had used an enchantment to build a smaller version of the castle on the lake, envisioning and creating it from nothing. She had hidden it to mortals' eyes, baptizing it Aisling Caisleán – Castle of Dreams.

Only the queen and Sébastien lived there, along with a few servants found in adjoining villages. For the most part, they were outcasts and work at the new castle provided them with a purpose.

Anyone who required an audience with Vivienne could get it, and would be shown a way to Aisling Caisleán if their intent was pure. More often than not these days, the lady kept her sorrowful eyes away from peers, and Sébastien was running out of options to help her.

Thus, it was with a heavy heart the guardian observed Merlin arrive, and headed to announce it to his beloved. He gravitated past the entrance of the sun room and approached the queen, resting a hand on her shoulder.

It took her a few moments, but Vivienne eventually looked up at him, her eyes bloodshot and with dark circles underneath. She was still gorgeous to his eyes, but he felt helpless at her devastated expression.

"Love," Sébastien whispered in a soft voice, "Merlin is here."

"I do not wish to set eyes on him." Vivienne's voice was devoid of emotion, her eyes blank as she twisted away.

"Please. It is for Arthur," Sébastien said.

The enchantress wearily shifted to him, as if each movement took all her energy. Tiredly, she ended up nodding. She appeared frail, so unlike the strong and exuberant royal he had first met.

The mention of Camelot's king moved Vivienne, only due to the fact she felt all realms representing the golden age should be defended as Elsior had not been.

Sébastien glanced over his shoulder and motioned to the valet who kept to the shadows. Merlin was let in within the minute. As the mage observed Vivienne, the knight noted the sadness in his eyes.

Always the cunning wizard, Merlin masked his emotions

and instead declared, *"You were right about Guinevere and Arthur. He is losing faith, and her affair with Lancelot has progressed...gotten worse. I would not ask if it was not absolutely necessary, but only a weapon will restore him when the time is right."*

"Why come to me?" Vivienne enquired blankly. "I am no blacksmith."

"You are pure of heart. A weapon forged by you would trump all others, Lady of the Lake. Please."

A flash of anger hit Vivienne's eyes at the wizard's manipulations. It was soon gone, replaced by a vacant look. "Do not call me that. I have listened to your query, and have no response to give. Now get off my grounds."

The old wizard looked to Sébastien for help, but the champion only shook his head. Merlin's back hunched over and he departed, unfulfilled, wondering if he had mistakenly meddled this time.

* * *

Alistair stumbled into Vivienne's solarium that same evening, bursting the large doors open with a push of his magic.

The queen, lost in ruminations, jumped up to her feet immediately. "You're alive!" she exclaimed in surprise, unable to believe her eyes.

The demon dog met her shocked gaze for a beat, before collapsing on the marble floors with an audible thud.

"Sébastien!" Vivienne yelled and ran to Alistair's side, kneeling down and running her glowing palms over to heal him.

The champion rushed in, alerted by the noise. He joined the queen on her knees, immediately noticing Alistair's weakness and labored breathing.

"I do not have much time left," his voice rumbled in both their heads, his eyes still closed. "I escaped Carleigh's clutches, but could not yet come back to you. While hunting him, the damn sorcerer's trail led me to Arthur. He is still out there, Vivienne, planning to do the same to Camelot as he did to your realm. Do not let him."

"How can I help Arthur when I failed my own people?" the enchantress cried.

"Trust in yourself, Lady of the Lake," Alistair nuzzled her hand. "Own your title and your spirit, open yourself up to the old and the new. Listen to the song of my mourning tonight, under the full moon by your element, and you shall understand. It will come to you."

The dog blinked, focusing on Sébastien one final time. "Defend her. At all costs."

Then his eyes closed, the massive body exhaled its last breath, and he became still. Vivienne dug her hands into his fur, sobbing quietly. She was startled when the fur became dust, raising her head in horror. Under her distressed stare, Alistair's body crumbled apart, until there was nothing left.

She picked up a handful of the ashes, and clutched them to her heart as the sobs shook her. Sébastien picked the queen in his arms, holding her close, unable to hold back the tears streaming down his cheeks at the loss of his friend.

A gentle breeze picked up, sweeping away the remaining ashes until it was as though Alistair had never existed – except for the memories in their subconscious.

Later that night, when Vivienne was done crying, she stepped out by the lake with Sébastien trailing behind. The guardian kept a small distance, watching as she let her head fall back, surveying the moon.

When it was at its apex, nature stirred in unity, and the wind picked up a beautiful song of mourning and loss, as the leaves joined in. The rustling was the tempo, the howling a crescendo. Water sloshed back and forth, forth and back, and the moonlight shone stronger, illuminating Vivienne's radiant features.

Sébastien registered as he never had before just how much their lives were intertwined. After having shared such a major loss with his beloved, he was more attuned to their own mortality than he had ever been. Having lost each other multiple times before, the knight dreaded their own fate, at times. The song stirred him deep, with an irresistible longing to have Vivienne in his arms and never let go.

The guardian was distracted from staring by the glow coming from the lake. Vivienne walked in, and it seemed to part, allowing her passage. And there, in the middle, something glistened.

The enchantress crossed her arms and bowed her head, and when she blinked, her eyes shone with the force of the magic she weaved. Sébastien could detect its pale glow filling each fiber of her body. Through their bond, he could experience its vibrant murmur.

The light in the middle grew stronger. Vivienne extended her hand and the water parted. From its midst, a sword floated forward, the metal shining strongly under the moon.

As the creation approached, the monarch was breathless

at its beauty. An exquisite dragon design shaped the hilt, of both gold and silver nuances depending on how the radiance touched it. The sharp edge of the blade effortlessly cut through the surface of the liquid, barely creating a single ripple in its journey.

When it got to her, the blade hovered in mid-air, pointing its hilt towards the enchantress. The grip was adorned by highly refined leather, wrapped around the strong neck of the beast. The pommel was where it stood – an impeccably designed head, scowling viciously at all those unworthy to wield it, its ruby eyes shining menacingly. Glorious wings substituted the cross guards, superbly constructed for strength and speed without sacrificing the grace of the mythical legend.

The sword seemed filled with a life of its own, as though it would viciously tear apart armies of evil with or without a mighty warrior to wield it. When Vivienne gripped the weapon by the hilt, the beam shone blindingly, and Sébastien had to shield his eyes with one hand.

The young woman, attuned to the sword already, heard the name whispered clearly in her subconscious, and voiced it out loud. "Excalibur. So shall you be named."

When she walked out the lake, the queen was renewed. Vivienne's every step was confident and determined, wafting past on sure footing. Her shoulders, long having slumped and turned inwards for protection, now straightened into a regal posture. Her chin was raised up, eyes shining brightly with newfound magic and an iridescent gleam within.

After a moment, Sébastien was able to look at her directly, once the radiance behind and around her softened. He was immediately enthralled by the sudden changes in his beloved.

Vivienne's face was no longer the deathly pale he had grown used to, but glowing instead, her joy fully visible. Her entire body, approaching him, did not simply radiate power; it was as if the royal had become the sun itself, banishing evil and returning hope to anyone in her vicinity.

She was no longer the fragile person of the last few months. Rather, an enchantress, sure of her abilities and realm – indomitable, unstoppable.

Before reaching him, the queen stopped and studied the treasure in her hand. "Go find Arthur," she softly commanded, "wherever he is. His quest should be hard, but not too much. He needs you at his side."

Excalibur shimmered, then evaporated altogether, to reappear much further away, embedded in the stone from which Arthur alone could withdraw it.

Back in Elsior, the couple embraced under the moonlight. And for the first time in what seemed like forever, Sébastien sensed Vivienne's passion in her caresses. She ran a finger across his jaw, smiling wickedly as the muscle jumped under her fingertips.

"You have been patient, my love," she whispered, her voice husky with forbidden temptation.

Sébastien gulped, attempting to rein in the stirrings of his desire – and failing. He let his forehead drop against Vivienne's, inhaling her sweet fragrance.

"I have missed you," he murmured back.

Vivienne threw her head back, lips invitingly parting for his. With a groan, Sébastien dropped his mouth to hers, unprepared for the response of their bodies – clutching, gripping, melting beyond closeness.

Aflame with desire, neither noticed the glow slowly surrounding them as the union of their spirits sanctified their soul mate bond. When their garments came off, the only thing that mattered was the scorching flame driving them both, rising always higher, until they found heaven together.

* * *

Alistair removed his paw, stepping away from Sébastien, who stood back up. The demon dog pondered what he had witnessed.

Vivienne, despite the depression she was in, would still want the knight to be healed. Thus, if he could convince her that a trip was needed with that sole purpose, she would get out of bed for it.

That just might work, Alistair mused, a plan slowly forming in his mind.

Both protectors froze as the door to her bedroom opened, and Vivienne came down the stairs. Disregarding them, she went into the kitchen, picked up a glass and drifted around the sink to get something to drink.

Sébastien hesitated, but when Alistair motioned for him to join her, he followed into the kitchen.

Vivienne was above the sink, washing a glass, when he grasped her shoulder. She jumped, dropping the item, and it smashed into the metal sink and broke into pieces.

"Crap, I'm sorry," Sébastien muttered, snatching both her hands away from the shattered glass – too late. An errant shard had already cut her, and trickles of blood spread across the countertop, in stark contrast with its whiteness. "Let me clean it."

Instead of moving, Vivienne stared, transfixed, at the blood running over her hand, spilling into the other palm. Sébastien probed their link and captured her horror, before he realized what she was thinking – and the depth of her guilt over the loss of Elsior.

"No!" he growled fiercely, squeezing her hands in his. "This is not their blood on your hands, Vivienne. Stop it!"

When she still stood frozen, Sébastien shook her by the shoulders. The young woman blinked furiously, but could not stop the tears gathering in her eyes and overflowing onto her cheeks.

It was only upon seeing her distress so fully, that the guardian was struck by how deep the enchantress had fallen in the pit of despair. *Just how much did we miss over the last few days?*

"Don't you see?" Vivienne whispered. "You were so worried of not being good enough for me, but it's always been the other way around. *I* am not worthy of *you*."

Sébastien's eyes widened, shocked at the words. Something took over him, as much frustration at her words and their situation, as being deprived of what he craved most of all. The new feeling spread through him like hot lava, and he reacted.

At the sudden shift in the guardian, Vivienne's body responded, leaning towards his as though physically touching. Electricity crackled again, and for a moment, time stood still and they both tethered on the verge of a precipice, trying desperately not to fall in.

It was Sébastien who consciously decided to let go of all principles, and in free fall, dropped his mouth to hers in an angry kiss.

At first, Vivienne did not respond and remained still, like a doll in his arms. But as he pressed closer, her lips parted, and it was as if he was the water and she had been in a scorching desert.

The enchantress dragged him closer by his shirt, demanding more contact, sliding both palms under the fabric. Sébastien flinched as her cold fingertips touched skin, but did not stop, aware only of the relief at having gotten through to her despite the barrier of despair. In the end, he got swept away by the raging desire invading his bloodstream.

Vivienne's hands drifted up, to his back, her body craving his – longing to feel more of being alive. Sébastien had only intended the embrace to shake her up and illicit some type of response. In his wildest dreams, he would not have foreseen losing sight of his goal so rapidly, as though control was a word he had never learned.

He gathered Vivienne up in his arms, groaning as she wrapped her legs around his hips, pulling Sébastien even closer as he settled her on the counter. It became a battle of who could get under whose skin, and who would end up winning.

What the hell!?

Like cold water being poured over him, Alistair's roar penetrated Sébastien's mind.

The defender drew back from Vivienne's tantalizing lips instantly, in a daze himself. She blinked, her glazed eyes fluttering as if waking up, her lips swollen by the kiss.

There was a glint in Sébastien's eyes that warmed the young woman's bones to the point of melting, something she had sorely missed in the last few days. It brought her out of the cold, dreary world that had become her reality.

"Why did you stop?" Vivienne raised her eyes to the champion, her voice normal now.

Sébastien was about to answer, but made the mistake of glancing down at her lips. Subconsciously, he started to lean towards her again.

Cut it out! Alistair growled again, and this time the ground shook under their feet when he pawed it in anger.

Vivienne pulled away, and peered past Sébastien's shoulder to Alistair. Having heard – and ignored – him both times, she glanced back at the guardian. "When will you do what *I* want?" she accused.

Ignoring his pained expression, she slid off the counter and retreated. Within moments, the bedroom door slammed shut upstairs.

Sébastien focused his blazing glare to Alistair. "Why the *hell* did you intervene? I was getting through to her!"

You should not go there. Not in her current emotional state – or yours. You know it too, deep down. I am only reminding you of what you chose to ignore in your haze of passion.

Gritting his teeth, Sébastien had to admit the dog was right. Though he was relieved at having breached Vivienne's walls, he never should have let it get so far. Yet the feel of her in his arms was a euphoria he could not wait to repeat.

"When will this torment finally end?" he exclaimed, angrily slamming a fist on the counter.

Soon, Alistair responded, though he was not so sure himself, for once.

"Alright, demon dog," Sébastien conceded with an incline

of his head, rubbing his fist absentmindedly. "You've made your point."

No, I have not. If you want Vivienne so badly, you have to do a heck of a lot more than you have been doing. Redemption will not serve itself on a silver platter.

Sébastien clenched his jaw harder. "Do I look —"

You look lost, the dog interrupted. *You have to figure out how to go about it and do it.*

"Fine. I got it," Sébastien clipped.

Good. Now on to better things.

"Such as?"

Ignoring the guardian's stormy expression, Alistair continued, *Carleigh can strike at any moment. We need to get Vivienne out of this depression, and back to strengthening her magic.*

"And how do you propose we do that? She won't talk to either of us."

Then we make her.

Sébastien frowned. "How?"

One thing Merlin was right about is that Vivienne must accept her Lady of the Lake status.

"He also warned I'm standing in the way of that," Sébastien reminded him.

That is where he was wrong. There is a way to bring Vivienne back to us, but it will require your full trust in me.

"You have it," Sébastien did not hesitate in responding. He glanced at his beloved's closed bedroom door and whispered , "You already know I'd do anything for her."

Yes, I do. And make no mistake. This time, I will hold you to that promise.

"What do you expect me to do?"

Meet us at the Pont Saint Bénézet tomorrow morning before sunset. There is a pathway there that leads to a more secluded spot of the river.

Sébastien acquiesced briskly, indicating he knew which spot Alistair alluded to. "How will you get Vivienne out of bed?"

I have my ways, knight, the dog retorted.

"You know I'm no longer that," Sébastien pointed out darkly.

You still do not see yourself clearly. Being a champion can never leave you. It is part of you. But I shall not wasting time explaining this right now. Stand watch tonight, will you? For what I must do tomorrow, rest is essential.

Sébastien observed the dog as he camped in front of the door, dimly wondering what the hell he had agreed to.

CHAPTER 20

"Where are you taking me?" Vivienne grunted at Alistair's mysteries. As if she needed them at the moment, when all her body craved was rest and to wallow in misery.

You will see, was the dog's cryptic response.

Alistair felt slightly guilty at having used a tiny spell to ensure the enchantress was more amenable. It was not coercion, per se, but she never would have listened to an innocent suggestion of a stroll otherwise. The supernatural nudge had helped enough to get her out of the house.

Afterwards, he led Vivienne in an alleyway by the shore of the river Rhône, where she was confused to find Sébastien. He inclined his head in greeting to Alistair, not even glancing her way.

Vivienne scowled, studying both of them. "What is this?" Her annoyance was made worse by the fact it was so early, with the sun barely rising over the horizon.

Carleigh is strong, as you have undoubtedly noted, Alistair started, facing her. *You must tip the balance. The only way you can do so is by getting your full abilities back. This means learning to draw strength from the water, not just use it, and access all your elemental sources.*

"What?" Vivienne's scowl faded, and her brow furrowed instead. "I lost those with my realm. I have my magic now, why isn't it enough?"

Carleigh has much more. And at the risk of correcting you, highness, those powers are not lost. They are trapped within you, waiting to be unleashed.

"Alistair—"

You have more magic than you can currently perceive, highness.

"No! Stop trying to make me to jump through hoops like Merlin did." Vivienne knew the minute the words were out of her mouth that they were the wrong ones. In Alistair's eyes, she could see some of the old demon nature as they glowered.

That is not nearly what I want to do, the protector warned, *but since you will not listen to reason . . .*

The dog focused on Sébastien, who nodded in assent to something. Next thing Vivienne knew, the guardian was elevated in the air by an invisible energy, and dropped above the river. He sank, and did not resurface.

Free him of the water's dominance, Alistair demanded, meeting the young woman's horrified look.

"What are you talking about it? Let him go!" Vivienne scanned the lake with her faint senses, and could tell Sébastien was imprisoned in its depths. *He's not bluffing . . .*

I am not, indeed, the dog confirmed, having followed her thoughts. *Now free him, or else he dies.*

"Alistair, don't you *dare* take away from me another person!"

Then free *him.*

"I can't!"

Sense the element. It will listen to you.

Vivienne was too busy freaking out to feel anything other than her own panic. "Alistair, please!" she begged again. "I can't do this."

Then I suppose Sébastien is as good as dead, Lady of the Lake.

The use of her old title sparked something, causing Vivienne to look at the water differently. She then turned to Alistair, appraising him. His eyes were not full of malice, rather, he seemed just as edgy. He was not testing her, rather pacing back and forth as she hesitated between acting and . . .

There is no other option. I have to get Sébastien out.

Vivienne concentrated on her love for the knight, calling to mind the memories of the past she had tried to block off.

As they came, so did a hum of energy deep within her, attempting to burst to the surface. The enchantress had been mindful of it before, but now it was stronger – yet still unattainable. Vivienne closed her eyes, blocking everything else out, and extended a hand towards the water in the vicinity.

Unfortunately, the flashes behind her closed lids were not those she was looking for. All she saw was her kingdom destroyed, the agony overwhelming, the memories deep within, and creating Aisling Caisleán – the new realm of the Lady of the Lake.

Vivienne focused on that last bit, on the sensation of the water being at her command as the old castle was submerged, and building the new one. The element became one with her, fluid, graceful and bending to her will.

Her eyes snapped open. "I feel it."

This time, Vivienne's hand was not just within reach of it. It *was* the water, cold and fresh, slipping between her fingers. She shifted her hand over, and noticed the previously calm liquid move with it. When turning it the other way, it stirred again. The hum was everywhere in her body now.

She inhaled deeply and fixed her entire attention on Sébastien – his heartbeat, his aura, deep within the river. Vivienne breathed out, then in once more, clenching and unclenching her hand with each breath.

On her second try, the water parted at the same time her fingers stretched out. In its middle, Sébastien was surrounded by a scintillating glow, completely unharmed, yet the burn in his gaze scorched even from far away.

You did it, Alistair praised from behind.

The globe inched nearer, and Vivienne beamed and repeated, "I did it." Her grief over the past was somehow settled by the victory. It felt good to have her unleashed abilities back.

The pain at losing her father was still fresh, but it was something the enchantress knew she could turn into strength – a fuel to the fire, a reason to the fighting.

"You were amazing," Sébastien's voice came close by.

Vivienne whirled around, finding him closer than expected. Her grin slipped off as the scorching look he gave her struck deep. "I wouldn't have been able to, without my feelings for you."

Sébastien knelt at Vivienne's feet, and her joy faded away when he said, "I am happy to be of service, my lady." The guardian formally kissed the back of her hand, lingering one second too many, then got up and moved past her.

Alistair stepped in his way, rumbling, *What is it?*

Her light shines brighter today than ever before. I will not taint it.

Seeing Alistair was at a loss for words, Sébastien retreated. He stopped once the woods hid him from their sight, and exhaled the tension within him. Then, he stepped to the nearest tree and punched it. His arm vibrated from the impact, yet the heavy weight in his soul was not gone. The champion watched from the shadows, doomed to be away from the enchantress that had his heart.

Vivienne's gaze got lost in the river. The chaos in her head was overwhelming, as was the yearning to go for a swim, hoping the exercise would submerge it all.

Having assured his mistress' safety with a shield, Alistair ensured it also kept her away from prying eyes. Letting Vivienne frolic in the lake, the dog headed to sort out yet another problem.

He entered the forest where Sébastien had disappeared, to find the knight lying down on the ground, his back to a tree. Both his fists lay white-knuckled on the ground by his side, bruised and sore. His eyes were shut tightly, in an apparent losing battle to find some peace.

I know you are not sleeping. The guardian did not budge at the dog's words, a true statue of silence. *Your wrath is pretty hard to miss, knight.*

Sébastien opened his eyes, and Alistair paused in his

perusal. The anger emanating from him was not the only thing he perceived. There was now control within the knight, and a restrained love eating him up.

Alistair stepped closer, tilting his head to the side. *Why did you leave? You say Vivienne's radiance shines bright, but you could let it shine on you, allow it to heal you. She can do that now.*

Sébastien did not answer, only shook his head abruptly in denial.

Yesterday you were ready to move to the next level. What changed?

"Today's experience. The way ... her light ... Alistair, I'm damaged goods. Merlin is right. I'll only be a burden to her."

You have been defending Vivienne this entire time. Without you, she would not even be reincarnated, here to save this world. Now you have a chance for her to help heal you. Why the hell would you say that?

Sébastien's shoulders sagged – he had to come clean. "Come and see for yourself," he invited.

As he unclenched and clenched both fists, fresh blood oozed out of the wounds around his knuckles. Alistair stared, uncomprehending, until black liquid seeped out, instead of the normal red of blood.

What the hell? His confused gaze fell on Sébastien's tortured expression.

"I noticed it when I punched the tree. Whatever it is, it's proof of the corruption within me – the one I allowed in. Not even Vivienne can heal this."

Alistair shook his mane. *I refuse to believe that.*

"Why?"

Because are Vivienne's soul mate. You cannot be apart, unless my prophecy comes true – which would suggest you are here to destroy her. Instead, you are lifting her up, helping her achieve more than she could on her own.

Nothing changed in Sébastien's countenance, as though the words fell on deaf ears.

How are you missing this? the dog persisted. *It is the test of true soul mates, and you are passing with flying colors.*

The guardian shook his head, pointing to one fist. "Then explain this to me!"

Alistair hesitated, before advancing cautiously. He whiffed once and smelled the destructive power.

"You can sense it, can't you?" Sébastien's enquired bleakly, but Alistair captured the anguish vibrating in his voice, just underneath the surface. "Don't lie to me! You were a demon lord once, in the midst of darkness itself. You have to feel it."

Alistair dreaded to confirm it, but the truth was undeniable. If there was one thing he could recognize after all the years, it was the foul stench of darkness.

He peered into Sébastien's eyes, unable to avoid it. *I do sense it there, my friend. I will not lie to you.*

The knight closed his eyes as if the words had been a sentence of death.

Wait, Alistair urged, even as he reflected back to the battles they had been in. *When you bled before, this was not the result. I would have felt it.*

Sébastien blinked, and a small flicker of hope appeared in his eyes.

So what changed? Alistair wondered.

Sébastien mulled over the last few days, then informed him, "My anger has been getting worse. And I've been having these nightmares. Like with Merlin, but worse. This morning, I woke up after I plummeted in a black hole."

This is unnatural, Alistair growled. *I smell Carleigh's hand in this.*

"Carleigh? Could he actually do this?"

Influential sorcerers can wield all kinds of tricks, Sébastien. I was able to spin the thickest of nightmares, once upon a time. He examined the wound one last time, before licking it closed. *Come. I will contact Merlin. This has gone on long enough, and he has to reveal what makes Carleigh so powerful.*

The guardian got up slowly, veins throbbing on the side of his neck with the effort it took to keep himself calm.

Wait.

Sébastien glanced down, noticing Alistair was gazing intently at his fists. *Though this may be temporary, do not give evil an excuse to stick to you. Otherwise, you will not be able to shake it off, no matter what we do to try to heal you.*

That's probably what Carleigh is counting on, Sébastien ruminated morosely.

* * *

After dropping Vivienne and Alistair back to her place in the late afternoon, Sébastien offered to go pick up food. The young woman hesitated to ask him to stay, but eventually let him go, unable to understand his mood.

The guardian avoided meeting her gaze, and instead drove off in the Jag. He ended up at the same grocery store he had run into Antonio's mom. Sébastien got out of the car and went in, picking up things in record time, lost in brooding over the events of the last few hours.

When he was done paying for the items and got outside, it was nightfall, the sun setting earlier nowadays.

Sébastien observed a group of four men close to his car. It did not take him long to recognize them – and even less for them to stare back expectantly, as though they had been waiting for him.

"Yo, Dubois!" yelled his old buddy Lucien. "Where've you been, man?"

"Away." Sébastien put the groceries away in the trunk, keeping his responses curt. They either had not learnt about his problems with Tony, or knew and were there because of it. Either way, it was best he left as soon as possible.

"Oh yeah? We hear Tony's got a price for your head."

There goes that idea, Sébastien thought moodily.

"Yeah," another added. "Rumor on the street is he'd pay good bucks."

Sébastien clenched his teeth, and maneuvered to the side car door. He intended to drive away, but found his way blocked.

"What do you say?" Lucien faced him eagerly. "For old time's sake."

Sébastien threw him a dark look, then shook his head. "As I recall, old times was me kicking your ass. You'd still like to attempt it?"

"Hell yeah! Whenever you're ready, old man."

The other young men gravitated behind in a circle, smelling a fight. Sébastien tried to keep himself in check, replying, "Get out of my way."

Lucien smirked, "Afraid of a fight now that you're getting fu—" He did not finish as in one fluid movement, Sébastien brutally bashed his head against the car.

The man grunted and fell to the ground. Sébastien then faced the other three, his fists clenched. The first attacker, he tossed a few meters away, and the crack of his bone snapping was music to his ears. The second, he ducked a punch, sent one of his own to the man's stomach, and head barreled into the assailant until he flew and landed a distance behind.

The third opponent managed to land a blow with a crowbar to the guardian's head, and Sébastien literally saw red. He seized the kid by the neck and slammed him into the hood of his car, watching unflinchingly as he dropped to the ground, his forehead bleeding.

Sébastien then picked up the crowbar, heading to where the kid was slowly getting up. He raised the metal tool, intending to strike, but Vivienne's image popped in his head, making him pause.

What the hell am I doing?

The red haze lifted, and Sébastien dropped the crowbar – noticing, in passing, the kid's relief. Without a word, he got in the Jag and drove back to Vivienne's place.

As he picked up the groceries to bring them inside, the knight noticed the thin line of inky blood oozing from his knuckles. He wiped it on his jeans, then entered the house.

When he cleared past the door, Alistair approached him.

"Where's Vivienne?" Sébastien enquired, scanning the

living room for his beloved.

Resting. What happened to you?

"Nothing."

There is blood on your forehead. Mixed, murky *blood.*

Sébastien glanced down at the dog. "I got attacked outside the grocery store. Four guys."

Alistair paused, then followed him in the kitchen. He perused Sébastien's rigid muscles, the way the knight avoided meeting his gaze, and the overall darker aura surrounding him. *Are they still alive?*

Sébastien faced him, narrowing his eyes. "Of course! I kept your advice in mind."

Alistair was not fooled. *How close?*

"Not close enough," Sébastien shrugged nonchalantly – he knew the dog was referring to how close he had come to losing control. "I almost bashed one kid's head in with a crowbar. *After* he gave me this." He pointed to his bleeding temple for emphasis.

The air in the room changed with Alistair's rising alarm, a fact Sébastien quickly caught on to.

"I'm going to sleep," he scowled. "Maybe then I can get away from this crap." He followed the final statement by plopping down on the couch, and throwing an arm over his head.

Alistair observed Sébastien, his anxiety evermore rising. If the resulting darkness was a play by Carleigh to mess with the knight's head, it was doing an admirable job. In one day, it had destroyed all hope and increased his rage, effectively putting Sébastien on the path to ruining himself.

The dog stepped closer to ensure he was asleep. Gently,

he sent a wave of supernatural energy to clean and heal his wounds, before they developed into a concussion.

Knowing the guardian would have Vivienne's back, he retreated to the fountain in the Place des Corps Saints. It was now pitch black and the night was hushed, as usual.

Once more, Alistair put his muzzle close to the fountain, parting the curtains between the ages. Merlin's face cleared from the foggy liquid.

"Old friend," the mage greeted shortly.

You sound tired, Merlin.

"I grow weary of the voyages of time." The wizard paused, concern showing in his eyes. "How is Vivienne?"

Alistair scanned his features closely. It seemed Merlin had put on ten years since they had last spoken.

She is fine, Alistair mumbled. *Mourning her father, but pushing past it with the strength of character we both know she possesses. That was quite a trick, making her recall everything.*

"You must believe me, I did not intend her harm."

But you did intend for her to remember, Alistair insisted.

Merlin avoided the dog's attentive gaze. "What is it you want, demon dog?"

More explanations. About Carleigh.

"I fail to see how I can be of help. I knew the young boy, not the monster he has become."

True. But you can brief me on why he is so intent on destroying Vivienne. It is not —

Alistair stopped and glanced behind him, in the direction of Vivienne's house. He captured an almost imperceptible menace, but could not locate it. Intrigued and vaguely worried, he extended his mind, scanning the house from top to bottom.

"What is it?" Merlin enquired urgently, noticing the dog's distraction.

Alistair ignored him, focused on finding the source of the threat. He inspected Vivienne's bedroom, but found her still resting – the danger was not there.

"Is it Vivienne?" Merlin tried again.

Alistair extended his senses to Sébastien's form, and perceived the tentacles of darkness.

No. It's Sébastien!

Without wasting time on further explanations, the protector ran towards the house. He pushed his body as fast as it would go, paws pounding the pavement.

He burst through the door, then headed to the living room where Vivienne had joined Sébastien. Whatever obscurity plagued him had woken up the enchantress, and she was attempting to shake the guardian out of his trance.

Feeling Alistair nearby, Vivienne turned to him, panicked, "He won't wake up!"

Use your abilities, Alistair nudged her out of the way, and pressed his muzzle slightly in her hand to center her chaotic energy. *Shield him with your light magic.*

The enchantress placed her free palm to Sébastien's chest, the other one channeling Alistair's calm, and breathed in deeply.

Picture him safe, the dog murmured. *It works the same as the normal barriers, but stronger, as it feeds on your soul mate bond.*

Vivienne imagined a luminous glow protecting Sébastien, wrapping him and keeping any negative influences away. The spell left her fingertips and she blinked in time to notice a golden glow surrounding the champion in a cocoon.

She turned to Alistair. "What's going on?"

The dog only shook his head. *After, I will explain.*

Vivienne nodded vaguely and focused back on Sébastien, silent tears falling on her cheeks. "Please come back to me," she pleaded.

* * *

Sébastien was in agony. The cavern surrounding him was cold and damp, with a foul smell about. It was unlit and he could hear the lap of water.

He was unaware of how he had arrived there, but rapidly realized he was stuck. At first, the knight had attempted to move, but his hands and feet were bound by chains. When he tried to get free, they had only tightened.

Then the shadows parted, and a hooded figure advanced. "Funny place you got yourself in."

Sébastien groaned and the cuffs squeezed even more around his wrists. "Who the hell are you?"

"You don't recognize me? Here, let me shed some light." The figure shone a beam into Sébastien's face, hurting his eyes.

"Carleigh, damn you!" the champion snarled.

"You damned yourself, so called defender. Look at your bindings."

Sébastien glanced down, noticing the chain links were formed of his own inky blood. He pushed down the panic threatening to gain, instead glaring at the sorcerer. "Let me go, you bastard!"

"You're in a prison of your own making," Carleigh sneered. "I barely had to do anything."

A different light emerged out of nowhere, brighter than the fake one the sorcerer had conjured.

"Release him immediately!" a familiar voice ordered.

"Merlin?" Sébastien's eyes widened in surprise. The wizard was the last person he would have expected to come to his aid.

Carleigh disappeared without asking for his due, and Merlin emerged from the shadows, stepping towards the knight.

"Wake up," the mage ordered, his blue eyes narrowed on Sébastien. "*Now!*"

Merlin aimed his staff at Sébastien, and the brightness that escaped from it hit the guardian fully in the chest like a bolt of lightning. He inhaled, then blinked rapidly at the sudden fire burning in his veins, purifying whatever darkness Carleigh had set on him.

The chains loosened around him and with a single yank, Sébastien's wrists broke free. He squinted at Merlin to thank him, but instead found himself staring into a blindingly white sun. The following instant, the knight was engulfed in a big hug, Vivienne's soft perfume now in the air around him.

"You're back!" she whispered against his neck, tightening the embrace.

* * *

Alistair waited for a few moments, observing them both. Once assured Sébastien seemed fine – he did, the obscurity now diminished in his aura – he swiftly returned to the fountain.

This time, Merlin appeared after a delay, as though there was a bad connection. The wizard's eyes were weary. "You were right, my friend."

What about?

"There is something I have been hiding about Carleigh. Having meddled in the past, I am afraid this time he might win if I do so again."

I am not asking you to intervene directly, only to share what you have learned. I can handle it from there.

Merlin hesitated, going into a brief trance as he scoured the future to foresee the consequences. When he focused back on the dog, it was with a firm head shake. "No. If I do, you will lose your life like before, and Vivienne will be left without protection."

Merlin! Alistair bellowed.

"No, my friend."

Alistair was about to insist further, when the liquid rippled. *What's the matter?*

"The fight with Carleigh was exhausting."

What fight? Alistair tilted his head to the side in confusion.

"In the realm of the dreams. There was so much evil generated, not even you can imagine."

The image faltered, but Alistair jumped forward. *Wait!*

After a few turbulent moments, Merlin's face solidified again. "I cannot hold on much longer," the mage warned in a whispery voice.

You went in Sébastien's dreams?

"Yes."

Alistair pondered the confession. Merlin being a wizard of good, he had to keep replenishing his strength in nature. If he had used his magic while in a shadow domain, the corruption within must have hit him hard, by the looks of it.

Why?

"He needed saving."

From Carleigh?

"And from himself." Merlin's eyes sharpened on Alistair. "You should have informed me the darkness has materialized in him physically."

It is only recent.

"If I had listened to you earlier, we might have prevented it," Merlin admitted.

Then you are agreeing with me that Sébastien is salvageable?

"He *was*."

Alistair took a step closer to the fountain. *Do not allow this, Merlin. Do not back down because we are faced with a tougher fight.*

"My friend, this one is lost. Sébastien, with or without your help, will give in to his darker side. It will not be long until he turns against you both. When that time comes, you must be ready to do what is right."

I will not kill him!

"Then you might as well let Carleigh win."

With the final statement, the old mage was gone.

Alistair stayed behind a while longer, contemplating the moon and refusing to give credence to Merlin's words. *Sébastien would never turn against us!* After the night's events, the obscurity within the knight was lessened, though its shadow was still very much apparent.

Yet despite all reassurances, the dog could not help wondering . . . If it came to pass, would he be able to defend Vivienne at all costs, even by killing his friend – her soul mate?

CHAPTER 21

Vivienne was out by the pool, practicing enchantments in the safety of her own backyard while Sébastien rested. After the previous night's events, he had slept most of the day away, recharging.

Alistair, in an effort to distract his mistress, was teaching her to dematerialize and rematerialize small objects, despite her obvious lack of attention. After a few failed attempts, he noticed her unfocused expression and suggested, *Break time.*

"Why?" the young woman frowned his way.

Your head is not in it. Alistair hesitated for a moment, unwilling to bring back painful memories, then tried, *Is it your father?*

Vivienne bit her lip, looking past the water as if searching for answers. "No . . . I made peace with my father's death in the past, and again last night. It was extremely distressing to relieve everything again, but … I will survive, as I did before." She inhaled deeply, voicing what was truly bothering her: "What happened yesterday?"

What do you mean?

"With Sébastien. He was so … subdued."

Alistair thought hard on what he was allowed to reveal. After his last conversation with Merlin, he had found sleep hard to come by. Instead, he had spent the night observing Sébastien's dormant form, attempting to see him as a menace – and failing.

The dog made up his mind and peered into Vivienne's worried green eyes. *Sit down and I will tell you what I know.*

As she sat cross-legged on the grass, he bluntly divulged, *There is something wrong with Sébastien. His blood is the color of coal.*

Vivienne's brow furrowed. "What are you implying?"

The obscurity he feared has manifested itself physically. It is not a natural phenomenon, and I got my confirmation that Carleigh is involved with it, as of last night.

Realization dawned on the enchantress. "You mean the nightmare I couldn't wake him from."

The same one, Alistair conceded.

"Sébastien wouldn't talk about it after, only held me until we both dozed off."

What I am aware of, is that Merlin went into the dream and saved him.

"For his own designs, no doubt." Vivienne was still distressed by her mentor's manipulation and possibly purposeful actions to recall her father's loss.

Alistair did not respond, only gazing at her as though he

wanted to reveal more.

"How bad is it?" Vivienne asked.

Sébastien's corruption? At her nod, he continued, *It would only be temporary, until we figure out how to get rid of it. Except . . .*

"What is it? Alistair, you promised you'd be fully honest with me."

Everything he does that is remotely violent, or acted on with bad intentions, causes the shadows to stick more to him.

"But Sébastien hasn't . . ." Vivienne had been about to deny he was violent, but at the glint in the dog's eyes, trailed off. "Has he?" she wondered aloud instead.

He almost killed a young man yesterday. The assailant cornered Sébastien with three of his buddies, and he defended himself. The corruption within him caught on to the violence and spiraled out of control. He barely stopped himself from killing one of the attackers.

Vivienne sighed. "What can I do? I want to help, but he won't allow me."

If you were together, the issue would be fixed. Seeing as you are not, it is still growing.

"It's not for lack of trying on my part," Vivienne muttered.

You have to understand, with the way Sébastien is now, he craves nothing more than to be with you. The manifestation of evil is the only thing keeping him away.

"I know his soul is pure," the enchantress declared, surveying the water again. "No matter what his opinion of it is."

Perhaps once he refuses the darkness, he will believe he

can control himself again. Only then will you be able to truly aid him.

Vivienne pondered his words, dissatisfied at the lack of an imminent solution. There had to be something she could do, before Sébastien was lost forever to the forces that had brought her back.

* * *

By the time their little lesson finished, it was close to nightfall. Vivienne and Alistair retreated back inside the home, only to find it empty. They searched everywhere, to no avail. Eímhín was still there, but Sébastien was gone.

"Where is he?" she asked Alistair.

The dog closed his eyes, breathing in the scent in the air. *It was not Carleigh – or anyone else, for that matter. Sébastien left of his own accord.*

Vivienne went to the bedroom and tried calling him, but it went to voicemail. On her second attempt, she got the same result. Not liking the new predicament one bit, she started looking for her house keys, wanting to head out to find him. The ring of her cell stopped her.

"Sébastien?"

"Oh no darling," Guinevere's voice came giggling, "but I do plan to take a bite out of him, and soon."

"Where are you?" Vivienne tried to keep a calm voice, and barely succeeded.

"Where else?" her old friend snickered, then hung up.

"Bitch!" Vivienne hissed under her breath, then ran out of the bedroom to Alistair. "He's at the bar. Guinevere just called me."

Why would she do that?

"Don't know, don't care, but I'm going." Vivienne went to get the house keys, but Alistair beat her to it, grabbing them in his jaws and passing them over.

It could be a trap, highness. She is probably still working for Carleigh.

"I'm going anyway."

Let me come with you.

Vivienne hesitated, then conceded. "Fine, but stick to the outside. Let me know if you sniff out Carleigh or one of his wackos."

They jogged to the bar and got there within the half-hour. As Alistair went through the back alley, the enchantress headed inside. Loud music immediately hit her, and she tried to scan the sea of people, hoping to locate Sébastien.

She thought having glimpsed him at one point, but it was someone else. Frustrated, Vivienne tried looking instead for Guinevere, when Alistair's voice came in her head.

I found him. And you should get here fast.

The enchantress moved past the bodies immediately. *Where?*

Back alley, by the exit door.

Vivienne shoved against a few more people, then finally exited. She explored the shadows, not noticing her dog or her guardian. She was about to give up when there was a thud, followed by the sound of something – or some*one* – hitting metal. She headed that way.

When detouring the corner, the enchantress noticed Sébastien fighting with two men. She gasped at the sheer brutality of their punches, and his defensive ones.

Took you long enough, Alistair reproached her, stepping out of the shadows behind a bin.

From their point of view, Vivienne and the demon dog could not be seen, but could observe the altercation perfectly.

"Inside was a mess," Vivienne whispered, "and I had a tough time finding you here until –" She stopped, cringing as a body hit metal again. "The noise gave it away."

Shouldn't we intervene? She asked mentally, biting her lip in worry.

Wait, Alistair instructed and grabbed her hand gently in his large canines, holding Vivienne back.

The young woman did as he bid, stifling the urge to interfere as Sébastien continued to fight defensively. It was due to their bond – and how attuned she was to his reactions – that Vivienne became aware before Alistair when the intention behind his punches changed, becoming darker, hitting to injure.

When Sébastien hurled one of the adversaries towards the stone wall as if his life meant nothing, Vivienne knew it was time to step in.

* * *

Unaware of his audience, Sébastien knew only the thrill of the fight. He had come to the bar in search of something – though what, he knew not. Despite making a huge effort to avoid it, the guardian had still ended up in a brawl.

At first, it was all defensive, but now he was in too deep to stop. It was a rhythm, almost a beat in his head. Hit, punch, evade, hit again. And again.

Nothing mattered except the pound of flesh. Vivienne's image flashed in his head for a moment, making Sébastien pause. Had Alistair not stressed the importance of maintaining control?

Then an assailant punched him in the jaw, and the image disappeared. He wiped the blood off his lip, noticing the darkness stain his skin.

Sébastien's jaw clenched at the realization the battle for his soul was already lost. There was no option left – Vivienne would have to be advised he could no longer be a guardian.

The hopelessness and isolation struck him deeply again, along with the certitude he would have to leave Vivienne's side for good, if he truly wanted to ensure her happiness and survival this time around. His chest constricted painfully, but another punch to the gut threw him down.

Breathing quickening, Sébastien got up again and clenched his fists. His opponents had gotten up as well, facing him – unfamiliar names in the shadows.

The champion held a hand up in a come hither motion. "Come at me," he growled.

They studied each other, sharing an incredulous look, but his defiant nature made them want to break him – so they lunged.

Sébastien ducked one attacker, then tackled him with his shoulder. The man rolled off his back, hitting the ground with a grunt. The knight then captured the other assailant's wrist and heard the satisfying crunch of the bone. The man's scream of agony did not even register as he fell down.

Sébastien got up to confront his next challenger, except there was no one around. Panting, he winced at the very real anguish in his chest, even as his sanity returned.

"What—" He scanned his surroundings in shock, but before he could grasp what had happened, a door opened nearby.

Sébastien whirled to the incoming person, fearing it was Vivienne. Luckily – or unluckily – it was only Guinevere. She sashayed towards him, studying the two unconscious bodies on the ground.

"My, my, you've created quite a mess."

"What the hell are you doing here, Guinevere?" Sébastien's brow furrowed.

She stepped closer, now within touching distance. Tilting her head to the side, the vixen smiled in a cold way that never attained her eyes. "You know how I like bad boys, don't you?"

"I recall you break hearts," he cut coldly.

"Can't be helped," she shrugged.

Sébastien was about to suggest she back off, but the siren pressed her hands to his chest, licking her lips suggestively.

"Your tricks don't work on me, Guinevere."

"Perhaps," she smirked. "But you are still a man with male needs, and that, you cannot resist."

Ignoring the tension radiating off the champion, Guinevere wrapped an arm around his neck and dragged his mouth down for a kiss. Sébastien stood frozen for a millisecond, stunned at her audacity, before placing his hands on her waist to push her away.

The minute he touched Guinevere, however, the need to get her off him was gone, and Sébastien only craved to draw her closer. Blood pounded in his head, nothing but lust stirring underneath, as the longing from the make out session with Vivienne on the kitchen counter filled him.

It was the difference in the kisses that helped Sébastien realize some type of spell was augmenting his lust, probably courtesy of Carleigh. The haze filling him lifted, and he shoved Guinevere away. There was dismay on her face, before the siren saw something behind him that made her smile.

Sébastien glanced over his shoulder, noticing Vivienne headed their way. *Shit.*

* * *

Vivienne had been shocked when Guinevere came out of nowhere. From her vantage point, she could not hear anything, only read their body image.

The young woman watched as Sébastien froze at whatever the old queen was saying, right before Guinevere threw herself at him. Vivienne frowned as the guardian reached for her waist, and the scene played like the one from memories long past.

She shook her head to clear it, and once again peered at Sébastien – only to witness him push Guinevere away. Having seen enough, Vivienne began approaching them.

Guinevere noticed her first and sneered victoriously, just like in the past. "Darling, doesn't history just repeat itself?"

Sébastien moved, meeting his beloved's expression. His eyes flashed for a second with unspoken regret, before he turned away.

Vivienne clenched her fist, itching to slap the smirk off Guinevere's face. Instead, she retorted, "Yeah and like before, you're wasting your time. He's not interested."

"Really? Shall we try again?" Guinevere purred, and inched forward.

Vivienne moved in front of Sébastien, blocking her way. "Stay the *hell* away from him!"

"You can't have her anymore," Guinevere sniggered, looking past Vivienne to Sébastien. "The only way to forget her, is to replace her. You should reflect on *that*, pretty boy."

There was a slight pause, then the guardian's hand was on Vivienne's shoulder. In a pained voice, he said, "You should leave."

The enchantress glanced at him, shaken by his tone. The expression in Sébastien's eyes was proof enough that if she left, something bad would happen and cause yet another rift between them.

"No." Vivienne willed herself to speak calmly, hiding the hurt at his words. "I refuse to let you soil our memory. Come with me."

Sébastien was shaking his head before she was even done, mumbling, "Guinevere has a point."

"Like hell she does!" Vivienne muttered low, seizing his wrist. "I'm not taking no for an answer!"

The exercise Alistair taught her flitted strongly through her mind. Fueled by anger and desperation, the spell began on its own with little input from her.

A mist surrounded and hid them, and as Vivienne wished it, their bodies dematerialized. They became blurry at first, then completely translucent, until they were gone.

As they evaporated, Vivienne clearly heard Guinevere's cry of frustration.

* * *

Guinevere screamed as they disappeared, in rage as much as in fear. Her petite body trembled, even as she hugged herself, taking in deep breaths to calm down. Twice now, she had failed Carleigh's orders, even with his supernatural help. This time, there would be no forgiveness.

She retreated to the car, deciding to get out of the city while the drama calmed down – and Carleigh was, hopefully, defeated.

Parking her car in front of her townhouse, Guinevere rushed into the house. Still shaken, her hand shook and the key would not open the door, until finally it did. She ran up the stairs, finding a suitcase and throwing it on the bed, already piling clothes inside.

Moments later, she had finished packing some accessories and was about to close it, when a voice behind startled her. "Going somewhere?"

Guinevere whirled around, hand rising to her heart to stop it from beating out of her chest. Carleigh was in the doorway, a cruel smirk playing on his lips.

"You scared me half to death!" she cried reproachfully, ignoring the sorcerer's query.

He did not reply, instead observing her like a cat playing with a mouse. The glint in his eyes was distinctly predatory.

Guinevere focused on the suitcase, zipping it closed. Behind her, Carleigh stepped into the room.

"Nice place you have here."

At the silence following, her hands' trembling increased, despite holding on to the handle of the suitcase in an effort to hide it.

"How did it go with Sébastien?"

Guinevere inhaled deeply, then faced the necromancer. "It didn't. I didn't get a chance to act," she lied through her teeth, hoping to buy some time.

"That's not what I saw," Carleigh murmured, moving closer. He raised a hand to her cheek, caressing it slowly. Guinevere tried to draw back, but was frozen by fear.

"Sébastien did not desire you. Again."

"There's something wrong with him, Carleigh," tears filled Guinevere's eyes. "I tried. He's just not biting."

Something flashed in the sorcerer's display, before he coldly declared, "My dear, I'm afraid you've outlived your usefulness."

He let go of her cheek abruptly, as though about to depart. Guinevere fell to the floor, her legs unable to keep her standing.

Carleigh whirled to her, hand raised for the deadly blow, magic gathering within, and—

"Jennifer? You in there? Chérie, let's talk, I miss you . . ." There was a pause, then, "Why's your door open?"

Guinevere's eyes widened, recognizing her ex-boyfriend Jacques' voice. "What the hell is he doing here?" she whispered, horror dawning.

Carleigh tilted his head to the side in amusement at her predicament. In a voice perfectly imitating Guinevere's, he simpered, "I'm up here, darling. Come join me."

There was a pause, then Jacques climbed up the stairs, his heavy footsteps too loud in the silent house. Guinevere tried to scream a warning to stay away, but the warlock's evil magic prevented any such actions. Dread filled her, as she knew without a doubt Carleigh planned to kill Jacques out of pure cruelty.

The minute Jacques came up the stairs, and saw Guinevere on her knees, he shifted to Carleigh with clenched fists. "What the hell, man?"

The necromancer lifted his hand, levitating the Frenchman without breaking a sweat. Suspended in mid-air now, Jacques desperately attempted to get some oxygen in his lungs caught on fire, to no avail.

"Stop it!" Guinevere begged.

Carleigh cackled, then directed the potent magic in his hand to Jacques. The man's lifeless body fell to the ground, paler than a ghost, a putrid scent awash him. The sorcerer focused back on Guinevere, and she closed her eyes. With one wave of his hand, her neck snapped.

* * *

Meanwhile, Vivienne and Sébastien materialized back at the house, their bodies regaining color and form.

We're home, the enchantress informed Alistair.

Leaving me behind again, I see. In retrospect, I suppose I should be content you have learned to use that portion of your abilities, the dog shot back. *I will join you soon.*

Vivienne tuned him out, already feeling Sébastien's mood rising. Sure enough, the guardian whirled around, eyes flashing, and dug his hands into her arms.

"What the hell do you think you're doing?" he roared.

"Saving you," Vivienne retorted calmly. "You try to stay away from me, but I will not let you allow more darkness into yourself than you already have."

Sébastien let go as if scalded, shock written all over his expression. "You know?"

Her voice softened and she nodded. "Yeah, I do."

"Since when?"

"Since I recalled everything back periodically. I've sensed your somber aura – so at odds with what I knew of the past – and the chaos in your head. I knew there was something wrong, but I couldn't figure out what. When Alistair explained it to me, the pieces fell into place."

Sébastien ran a hand through his hair in frustration. Vivienne inched closer, reaching for his shoulder, but he withdrew with a brusque shake of the head. "Don't."

"Sébastien–" Vivienne kept her expression blank, but the hurt still tinged her voice.

He jerked away, and a flash of anguish crossed his beautiful, martyred face. "I don't like doing this . . . Hurting you."

"Then don't!"

"I'm unable to promise you that, Vivienne. You know everything now, you should un—"

"Don't tell me to understand, I *refuse*! You've previously told me we cannot be together like before, now you say you cannot be in my life, at all." At the surprise in his eyes, Vivienne laughed humorlessly. "Oh yes, I can read you. And I know you're planning to leave for good."

The young woman moved forward, and this time Sébastien did not back away, only flinching when she extended her hand.

"Stop acting like you're a bomb about to explode!"

Vivienne yelled angrily, losing her cool.

"But I *am*!" His eyes flashed dangerously. "Why can't you see that!?"

"What I see is that twice now you've let Guinevere get nearer than you allow me. What I'm convinced of is that you still love me, as you've demonstrated on numerous occasions. If you'd just get on with it, we could fight this together, not apart!"

Sébastien cringed at her tight-lipped expression. "If only you knew how much I want to do that, be by your side as a partner should. But I *cannot*. I will never be good enough for that in this lifetime, and we're only deluding ourselves in believing otherwise."

Vivienne threw her hands up in frustration, screaming in anger at the skies. As she stomped into the kitchen, the guardian concluded she had accepted the reality, and walked to the door. The moment his hand wrapped around the knob, he was blasted back by an invisible force.

Sébastien landed on his feet, shaking off the enchantment, and whirled to the enchantress facing him. She folded her arms across her chest, a defiant lightning shining in her eyes.

"You promised you would let me go when the time came. You cannot hold me here, Vivienne," he tried to reason, fighting his own frustration.

"Watch me!" she bit out.

"Don't do this," he pleaded, inhaling deeply in an effort to calm down. "Don't push me past my limits and cause me to hurt you!"

"You won't."

"Vivienne—" Sébastien growled.

"You *won't*! Hell, why can't you see that? The worse you've done is give me an angry kiss. Or two. When you're around me, your negative side shies away."

"Really?" he snickered sarcastically. "And when I *do* lose control, and hurt you, will you find some other excuse? That you fell down the stairs? Knocked your head, perhaps?"

Vivienne's eyes narrowed at the tirade, before it finally struck her that Sébastien truly gave credence to his own words. "You really believe this tainted crap, don't you? You don't trust that you can form your own choices, but rather that once they are formed for you, they cannot be changed."

Sébastien did not reply, his silence an assent.

"Do you even have faith in yourself?" Vivienne continued.

"I lost that long ago."

It was her turn to be silent, though it did not take long for her to make a split decision. "Fine. Let's test your damn theory, and Merlin's while we're at it."

Vivienne marched up to Sébastien and grabbed his hand. He tried to yank it out of her grip, but the enchantress immobilized him. With a spell, she ensured his muscles would listen to no command until otherwise suggested by herself.

If there had been one beneficial development following the incident at the river Rhône, it was that she had a much better mastery of her powers. So it was without breaking a sweat that Vivienne was able to keep the guardian frozen, yet at the same time extend her free hand and call a knife from the kitchen to her.

Sébastien's eyes widened as they fell on the blade floating straight to her extended palm. "What the hell are you doing?"

The young woman peeked up at him, her features set in determination. "You believe despite your soul, our love, and despite regaining Éimhín, that your past can still contaminate me. Merlin keeps going on and on about how you being around me will taint me – my magic *and* blood. I'm testing that."

Without further explanation, Vivienne cut a thin line across Sébastien's palm. He clenched his jaw as the black blood poured out. Vivienne then let go of him, raised her hand and cut a similar line. She let the blood drops fall in the knight's palm, then clenched her hand in a fist to stop the flow.

"Now watch," she ordered, unfreezing Sébastien.

They both observed intently the spot where the two types of blood united. They remained separate for long moments, neither staining the other. When they did converge, a soft glow emanated for a moment. Once it was gone, the blood left behind was of a pure red color, the lighter having cleansed the tainted.

Vivienne peeked up at Sébastien expectantly, finding him still staring at the blood. She pressed her cut hand over his, healing them both with one touch. "Don't you understand? Our soul mate bond, Sébastien, means I can heal you. You only have to let me."

The champion could only stare at her in response, as though seeing her for the first time. After long moments, he slowly shook his head. "I'm not sure what to reply to that."

"Then stay here and defend me. I need you here."

"I'm not good at that anymore." Sébastien's tortured tone hit her all the way to the core. "You recall what happened last time I was protecting you in public – you were drugged under my very nose!"

"I disagree. You *are* still good at it," Vivienne contradicted him, ignoring his last remark. "And this is a request, not a suggestion. I am still your lady and responsibility."

Sébastien grunted in defeat, then inclined his head in assent – as Vivienne had hoped he would. "Good. You can have the couch."

She left him there and headed to her room. Before going in, the princess whirled around one last time. Sébastien was sitting on the sofa, hunched over, his head buried in his hands as though the weight of the world rested on his shoulders.

Vivienne longed for nothing more than to comfort him, but instead forcefully closed the door. It was time to push the guardian out of his pity party – much like Alistair had done with her.

Just before dozing off, the young woman had one clear thought. If Sébastien could once more see himself worthy enough of her forgiveness and protection, he could then let go of the darkness surrounding him.

* * *

After Vivienne went to sleep, Sébastien stayed on the couch, eventually lying down. He was startled by footsteps mere moments later, but it was only Alistair returning.

The dog stopped in his tracks and tilted his head, peering curiously. *Why do I smell blood?*

"Vivienne's idea of an experiment," Sébastien muttered,

studying his newly healed hand.

Really? Too bad I missed it.

Sébastien chuckled despite himself, not noticing Alistair's stare fixed on him, and his aura.

As the guardian was about to doze off, he persisted, *Did it serve its purpose?*

Sébastien hesitated, still wondering about it. Observing proof that Vivienne's blood could indeed clean his had been both confusing and elating. He was still afraid of an extended effect his presence would have on her. Yet somehow, the fates were shining on them and there seemed to be a way to stop the shadows from taking over him, after all – and potentially be together as well.

"I'm not sure," he confessed to Alistair. "But it has given me room to reflect."

Finally, the dog rumbled, and headed to his mistress' room. Sébastien ended up asleep within minutes.

* * *

Vivienne was dreaming, another recollection from before losing her father. Buried within all others, it came to her mind, unbidden.

* * *

The princess was out riding Shadow across the castle grounds, when Sébastien caught up with her at sunset at one of their favorite spots. He unsaddled Illyria, then stepped by Shadow, smiling.

"My lady," the knight extended a hand in invitation. Vivienne slid off the horse, against his body, and straight into his arms.

"Where have you been all day?" She beamed at Sébastien, dizzy from her tumultuous sentiments, yet aware of the shivers running up and down her body.

"Your father had me running errands."

Vivienne laughed, then wound her arms around his neck, pressing closer. Sébastien's mouth descended in a sweet and tantalizing kiss. It was a slow dance of yearning, a promise of what was to come later.

When the champion drew away, she smiled. "Are you all done now?"

"All yours, yes."

Sébastien captured her hand in his and walked to the shore. They had no sooner reached it, that in a fit of silliness, he pretended to fall to the ground and dragged the princess with him. They tumbled on the soft grass, nearly landing in the lake, but the knight stopped them at the last minute.

Hovering over Vivienne, Sébastien dropped his enamored gaze to hers. She lifted her hand, caressing his chin and stubble, confessing, "I love how secure I feel in your arms, like nothing can get to me."

Sébastien's expression softened, and he buried his head in her neck, inhaling her citrus perfume until he could not get enough. "You always will be. I will always keep you safe, at any cost. It is what makes me worthy of you."

When he lifted his head again, Vivienne was beaming, gorgeous in the sunset's light. Unable to hold back any longer, Sébastien bent his mouth to hers, needing a taste like he needed his next breath.

* * *

Vivienne woke up, the dream hovering around her like an annoying fly. Slowly, an idea was beginning to form in her mind.

Alistair lifted his head off the bed. *You are much too awake, majesty. What is it?*

"I think I've come up with a way to get Sébastien to give in."

Highness . . .. There was a warning in the dog's tone, which Vivienne ignored as her eyes lighted with excitement.

"In the past, Sébastien revealed that keeping me unharmed is what makes him worthy of me. He seems to now be of the opinion that he isn't worthy because he failed. All I have to do is demonstrate to him he can still keep me safe!"

Alistair got up, now facing her. *And how exactly will you do that?*

The young woman was about to reveal exactly how, but decided against it at the last moment. If she informed Alistair of her plan, he would believe she was crazy, and stop her from acting it out.

Vivienne! he insisted again.

"Never mind," she muttered, snuggling back under the blankets.

Unhindered, Alistair yanked them off with his teeth, and Vivienne scowled.

You are planning something. With Carleigh desperate, it is not a good idea to go solo and play the heroine.

"I know what I'm doing."

Let me come with you.

"No, Alistair. I have to do this for Sébastien."

The dog pawed the blankets in exasperation, before dejectedly instructing, *Promise me you will call upon me if anything happens.*

Vivienne nodded, then buried her head in the pillow, blocking her thoughts. If Alistair knew what she was truly thinking of, he would not be so accepting. *In fact, he'd probably bite my head off before letting me do what I came up with.*

The plan forming was beyond hazardous, but it was the best chance Vivienne had of saving her soul mate.

CHAPTER 22

Tied to a chair, Vivienne reflected this might not have been her best idea yet. At the very least, she should have brought backup. The young woman racked her brain to figure out where it had gone wrong, but could only blame it on her badly timed déjà-vus.

* * *

A few hours before . . .

Early in the morning, Vivienne snuck past the slumbering knight and guard dog. She borrowed Sébastien's Jag and drove to the bar she had seen him last with the Mafia.

She was unsure of how the plan would work, but hoped Sébastien would tap into their soul mate bond and come to her rescue – preferably, before it was too late.

In the meantime, she waited outside the bar until a well-dressed man entered with an entourage. From afar, it looked like Tony.

Vivienne waited a few seconds, then entered the bar. It took her only a few moments to realize she had crashed a meeting, and another to come to the conclusion she had to get the hell out of there.

All the men had their eyes trained on her – and Tony's flashed in recognition. *Oops.*

Her original plan had involved only him, but as usual, it was misfortune that smiled her way. *I really bit off more than I can chew this time.*

"I'll be on my way," Vivienne chuckled nervously. "Got the wrong address."

She tried to retreat swiftly, but barely managed to clear the door when scraps of chairs on the floor board could be heard. *Shit, they're coming after me!*

Vivienne knew a spell was out of the question. First, there was a strong chance she would end up hurting them, considering she could not fully control her magic yet. Second, the idea alone of using her supernatural abilities in front of regular people made her nauseous – too much could go wrong if she was captured.

Shaking her head to clear it, the enchantress ran for Sébastien's Jag. She reached for the driver's door, but bullets whizzed past her and shot out the tires.

"Damn!" Vivienne bit her lip and whirled around. Tony was fast approaching, two other men trailing behind him.

She put her hands up in a gesture of peace. "No need to get all testy, fellas, I didn't see anything."

"I don't believe that," Tony sneered. "You seem like a smart girl."

If I was smart, I would have come up with a plan B, Vivienne brooded. She dropped her hands and, in a stroke of creativity, lunged in a kick at the closest man. It was only the good training of the past that permitted her to throw him off and – with a tiny spell – seize his gun.

Vivienne aimed it at Tony, trying to find a better way to get out of the situation than taking a life – even if it was in self-defense. It did not help her nerves that the Mafia boss was watching her, apparently not impressed at having a gun pointed at him.

"You won't shoot me."

"Shut up."

He was right, of course. Vivienne had never shot anyone, let alone held a gun. But she had to do something.

It was at that very unfortunate moment her throat closed up, and she felt the ground coming closer. Vivienne shook her head in an effort to clear it, to no avail.

This can't be happening again. It was a déjà-vu pushing past, even while she attempted to keep the goons away.

Alistair! Vivienne screamed mentally.

His response was swift. *Where are you?*

Umm. The Mafia bar. I'm in trouble.

Damn right you are, majesty. She cringed at the anger vibrating in her head.

No, you don't get it. Tony's here and I'm about to fall into another memory.

A pause, then his exasperated voice muttered, *I will be there soon.*

No! Send Sébastien.

Vivienne! Alistair's impatience was evident.

This is for him, she pleaded. *Please.*

Alistair went quiet, and Vivienne could only hope begging would be enough. She tried to concentrate on Tony, but a stab in her neck area distracted her.

Less than a few seconds later, her vision blurred and the gun dropped out of her hand. Tony's man dropped the syringe he had shot Vivienne with and picked the young woman up in his arms. She noticed the limo they entered, and then everything turned dark as the déjà-vu dragged her away, aided by the drug.

* * *

Vivienne was strolling in the gardens when Sébastien came to get her.

"Arthur is here."

It had been months since the queen had forged Excalibur. She had never expected the king of Camelot himself to come, but then again . . .

"Let him in," she commanded, following Sébastien back to the throne room.

The enchantress had barely sat down when the large doors opened, and the young leader entered. Vivienne noted the strength of the knight's shoulders, but his weary eyes stirred her soul.

"Arthur, welcome."

"Lady of the Lake," the monarch bowed in her direction, and nodded to Sébastien. "I come to seek your counsel."

"I am flattered, and hope the journey was not for naught. How can I help?"

Arthur's request was swift, though bewildering. "Do you believe in soul mates?"

Vivienne glanced to her own love for confirmation. "Yes," she said.

"And is there . . . Do you suppose it is possible that soul mates are incompatible in a second life?"

"I am afraid not." Though Vivienne softened her voice, she could tell her words had dealt Arthur a blow. "I can only speak from my own personal experience, but soul mates always meet up, and live another life. The true significance of the term is that they complete each other, live in harmony with one another."

Arthur sighed heavily, having realized as much.

"If I may be blunt . . . What ails you?"

"My wife, Guinevere, and Lancelot, my best man . . . I believe they are betraying me, breaking their vows."

Damn you, Merlin, and your meddling. With all your powers, and you could not save Arthur the hurt? *Vivienne pushed away the distracting thoughts, then got off her throne.*

She approached Arthur, then raised a hand to his cheek, imbued with a tiny spell to boost his spirit. "Soul mates do not hurt each other. She is not yours, only borrowed. Guinevere follows her own path, as do the ones who follow her. You, dear king, have a kingdom to rule. Do not let this destroy you. What you require is something to bring back your faith, both in yourself and in the world."

Smiling, Vivienne then placed her glowing palm on his chest. "Follow your heart on a quest. Rediscover your strength, and forge ahead, Arthur. With or without her."

* * *

Head still woozy from the drug, Vivienne watched warily as Tony Lombardia stepped closer.

"What a pretty face you have, *cara*," he caressed her cheek. She twisted out of his grasp, but he grabbed onto her chin menacingly. "Since you came into town, my best collector has gone off the books. I don't like surprises. And you, my dear, are a constant one."

You have no idea, Vivienne mused silently, yearning to show him just how *surprising* she could be. Annoyance filled her that the drug – whatever they had injected her with – had not seeped out of her system yet, and her magic would be useless for another few minutes.

"I didn't come into town," Vivienne hissed, well aware a fight was the worst idea to gain time – yet unable to stop herself. "I was already here, you moron. And Sébastien isn't *your* collector, he's *my* protector."

Tony let her go and burst out laughing, his goons following suit. "The only thing that boy does is fight and kill. And he's damn good at it."

Vivienne glared in response. If only she could will a spell out . . . Though the young woman would not use it to escape, at least it would permit her to dominate the situation. Despite her agitation, it remained inaccessible.

Tony focused on Vivienne again, this time with a different glint in his eyes. "It's a shame to put such a pretty face to waste. Maybe we can have some fun while waiting."

He snagged a handful of her hair and yanked on it, forcing her head backwards. Vivienne refused to give him satisfaction and yell at the discomfort, so instead bit the inside of the cheek to stop her cries. Just as Tony pressed nearer, and her panic rose, Sébastien's voice echoed across the walls – except, it did not sound like him.

"Let. Her. Go."

Tony dropped her as though seared, and tensely shifted around. Upon recognizing Sébastien, he snickered.

The guardian, unamused, kept advancing. Vivienne was mesmerized by the change in him. No longer the gentle knight, his entire body was a hard wired muscle machine intent on killing – something Tony either did not notice, or ignored, flapping his mouth.

"Don't be selfish, Sébastien, we can share the little–"

He did not get to finish as the champion's fist slammed into his gut, followed by an upper hook to the jaw – and he kept going. Tony's boys jumped in the brawl, but Sébastien was not in a mood to be stopped. He delivered blows with chilling precision, to the point Vivienne could only watch, fascinated.

Unbidden, Merlin's words came to her mind. She had not believed it, but the proof was in front of her eyes of the darkness consuming Sébastien. The defender's being vibrated with unleashed fury, his punches delivering deadly strikes, breaking bones and damaging internal organs. And the more it went on, the further he ended from her.

I have to do something! Vivienne realized. Her plan was backfiring, and her previous panic was nothing compared to the alarm bells going off in her head. If Sébastien committed more murders, it would only enable his darker side to take over.

"Sébastien!" The knight did not even flinch at her desperate cry. Tony's goons were on the ground, and he was battling with the boss himself now

Please stop! Vivienne projected her thoughts in his head, as loudly as possible.

Sébastien paused, and for a moment she almost cried in relief – but it was short lived, and he went back to fighting Tony.

Vivienne closed her eyes to concentrate better, almost sensing it – their time in the past, the memories of their love. Powers flowing within her veins once more, the enchantress rapidly dispelled the remnants of the drug from within, and loosened her binds. She faced Sébastien, and gaped.

The guardian had Tony on his knees, a gun pointed to his head. His face a stony mask, Sébastien took off the safety and was about to pull the trigger.

Don't do it, Vivienne implored mentally, afraid of what speaking out loud would do. *Don't give in.*

For you, I have to, he answered back, avoiding looking at her. *To protect you.*

No. I'm here. You have me here, *Sébastien. Walk away. Don't let it drag you further away from me.* Nothing changed in the knight's stance.

Tony, angry at being defeated, taunted him. "Go ahead and do it then!"

Sébastien pressed the gun closer to his head. Within him rose an unreasonable need to kill Tony, as though that action alone would protect his beloved.

Remember us! Vivienne tried again.

Out of options, she racked her brain and projected the memory of their first night together, hoping it would be enough to cause a distraction.

Sébastien's hand shook as the memory of their love, the way she had looked at him, was imprinted in his mind. He recalled clearly everything he had been for her in the past, and everything he silently wished for now. The red haze of his rage deflated, the murderous feeling evaporated, and he focused on Vivienne.

You are master of your own fate, she smiled reassuringly, waiting with baited breath as he battled with himself. Finally, he lowered the gun.

"I knew you didn't have it in you," Tony sneered.

Sébastien glowered at the man, his expression scary in its calmness. "You don't know anything about me. I choose to spare you, Tony. In return, I cut my ties with you. You will not pursue me or those close to me. Otherwise, I'm feeding your entire operation to the police. And we can both know I have enough proof and don't care if I go down with you. Are we understood?"

Tony paused, reading the determination in his eyes. In the end, he acquiesced, fully aware that after years under his tutelage, the young man had more than enough ammunition to carry out his threat – and he was not bluffing. Respect tinged his voice when he muttered, "You did alright, kid. And you got yourself a deal."

Sébastien turned away and approached Vivienne, grabbing her hand to bring her to safety.

"Let's get out of here."

* * *

"You did *what*!?"

Vivienne cringed at the rage in Sébastien's voice. They had barely been back at the house for an hour, having had to taxi. On their way, the knight had called a mechanic acquaintance of his, who promised to get his Jag new tires by morning.

Once back safely inside the house, Vivienne had shared her crazy plan with Sébastien. To show him he was still worthy, she had thought to get herself in trouble, thus leading to him saving her.

Luckily, Alistair was not around – though the young woman knew a lecture would follow from him shortly after.

"It wasn't a big deal—" She stopped when Sébastien held up his hand.

"Not a big deal?" he enquired in a flat voice.

The knight closed his eyes, and Vivienne noticed his tension as he struggled to keep calm.

Calm? Sébastien was attempting not to throttle his beloved. The image of Tony's body leaning over her was enough to rile him up again. He had never been so furious at Vivienne's irresponsibility – or so relieved she was safe.

"Sébastien." Soft hands touched his chest.

His eyes fluttered open, and Vivienne noted the muted fury in there, as well as the relief. She faintly wondered if he was, once more, trying to figure out how to keep a distance.

Merlin's warning was the furthest thing from Sébastien's mind, as his entire being centered on the fact Vivienne was in his arms, unscathed, and safe – and it was all due to him.

Saving her despite all the odds stacked against them was something he did not believe was possible anymore.

In that instant, peering into her eyes, Sébastien also realized another thing – Vivienne had been right all along. He had found her using the soul mate bond. He had been able to save her aided by the depth of their love. Lastly, he had been able to let go of the urge to kill, to keep her safe – and found the strength to do so in their love.

The previous reasons for staying away from Vivienne – tainting her, hurting her – flew out of his mind, and only the love and desire remained. A craving burned within his veins, one only she could put out.

"I'm fine," Vivienne whispered, searching his expression, desperately wanting to believe they had attained the point of no return – yet afraid to do so.

With a strangled groan, Sébastien drew her close and crushed his mouth against hers. She responded instantly, more than ready for it. He placed one hand on her waist and yanked the enchantress to him, his head slanting and covering her lips with his.

The kiss was rough, exigent, a hungry possession as their tongues battled for dominance. Sébastien's hands drifted to Vivienne's hips, navigating around the room to the couch, where he tugged her down to straddle him. His lips moved to her neck, nibbling on the sensitive spot he knew so well, watching through half-closed eyes as she flushed in pleasure.

He shifted his mouth to her shoulder, past the strap of her tank top, alternating between butterfly pecks and grazing his teeth against her tingling skin. Sébastien then made his way languorously to her mouth, but stopped at her pulse point, and it fluttered wildly against his lips.

"Sébastien," she gasped out loud when his fingers dug in her hips, grinding her down on him, and shivers of pleasure shot up her body. Their breathing quickened in response to the sensations flaring everywhere they touched.

"Vivienne," Sébastien practically growled out, and the enchantress managed to draw away from the kiss enough to see his eyes. The torment and fear of having come close to losing her were evident within, yet the walls usually visible in there were now gone.

The knight lifted a hand to her cheek, caressing it gently, an unlikely pause in the midst of the fire consuming them both. For a moment, an achingly despairing second, Vivienne feared he would withdraw – as it always happened when they got too close.

Sébastien read the flicker of hesitation in her eyes and smiled – as if he could ever stop, now that they had reached the point of no return. He let his hand drop slowly to her front, trailing over her chest, to her hips, then his fingers dug in hungrily.

Vivienne's heart gave way and she pressed closer, deepening the embrace. Sébastien's shoulders relaxed, the tension leaving them, as he returned her kiss. Engrossed in each other, their excitement only stroked higher and higher.

When his hands slid under her shirt, Vivienne did not stop him. She arched her back to give him better access, moaning when his hardened fingers stroked a particularly sensitive spot.

Sébastien got up with Vivienne in his arms, and walked over to the bedroom, laying her down on the bed. With extreme slowness, he peeled off their clothes, until she was naked on the bed, aching for him, her body flushed under his gaze.

"You are truly gorgeous," Sébastien reveled in caressing her skin softly, gently, as if he did not trust she was real.

Vivienne gripped his wrist and tugged on it, dragging him atop her. She removed the last bit of clothing, enjoying the hardness of his muscles as the champion hovered above her, his arms strained with tension.

Sébastien bent down to kiss her again, this time trailing his lips down her neck, and she shivered at the delicious sensation. Her body stretched against his, begging for more.

"I've missed you," Vivienne confessed, her voice hoarse with emotion.

Sébastien paused in his actions and pulled back a bit. His eyes softened, the intensity still there, but more muted as he whispered, "And I, you."

When his mouth found hers again, the kiss was gentler. He continued the slow, tortuous pace as he slowly worshipped her body. His expert fingers found her deepest desires, bringing forth pleasure until she saw stars.

Vivienne stirred under him impatiently, panting, begging for more. She was desperate to have him within, as it should have always been. Sébastien's eyes met hers, smoldering onyx to glazed emerald, and he read her impatience. Only then did he enter her.

They gasped in unison – it was as if two pieces came together, completing each other. Nothing had ever felt this right, for either of them. They both froze in movement, the sound of their panting breaths alone in the room.

Sébastien then kissed her earlobe, gently biting on it,

regaining some control. When he could breathe past the suffocating ache in his chest, he lifted his head enough to observe Vivienne's beautiful face.

"Do you feel it?" he wondered hoarsely.

"Yes," Vivienne breathed, nails digging in his back, silently begging for more. When he remained frozen, she met his scorching gaze and bit her bottom lip. "Please, Sébastien. Now."

His jaw tensed, even as he tried restraint – he did not want to hurt her. But when she wrapped her legs around him, pulling him in deeper, it was a lost cause. With a sigh of defeat, the knight let go, sliding deep within her, his groans of pleasure echoed by her moans of delight.

Sébastien lasted until Vivienne came apart under him, then joined her, dropping his head to her chest in a final surrender.

They were silent for a few moments as their pulses went back to normal. Vivienne gently ran a hand through his hair, enjoying the feel of his weight on top of her.

When Sébastien peered into her eyes, it was the first time Vivienne had ever glimpsed his expression so open, vulnerable and trusting. He stared silently, before placing a hand to her cheek. "How did I ever get so lucky?"

Vivienne turned to his palm, kissing it softly. "I'm the lucky one." At his soft chuckle of disbelief, she added, "To have met you again. And had another chance at this."

Sébastien's eyes flashed with a glint of something – possession, satisfaction perhaps – before he murmured, "Trust me, love, luck is on my side. You never gave up on us."

He rolled to his back, taking her with him until Vivienne

was spread over his chest. Then he hiked one of her legs over his own, running a hand in circles over the sensitive skin on the underside of her knees.

"If you don't stop, it's going to lead places," Vivienne murmured drowsily, cuddling into him.

Sébastien laughed, his chest vibrating with each chuckle. He wrapped an arm tightly around her, happy and relieved beyond doubt. "I was lost without you, and you brought me back," he declared.

Vivienne grinned against his chest. "I only helped. You regained your own freedom."

She dozed off, content to have her champion back. There were still shadows in Sébastien, but he was able to walk away from them, and that control was all that mattered.

* * *

Sébastien's heat against her back, Vivienne slept peacefully, when she was dragged in a dream not of her own volition.

The enchantress was back at the lake from her memories. She scanned her surroundings, guarding her mind and half-expecting Carleigh to show up. Yet it was her old mentor who strode out of the trees.

The wizard walked slowly, heavily relying on his staff.

"Merlin," Vivienne greeted, inclining her head ever so barely.

"I come in peace," he stated with tired eyes. "You can put your magic away."

At his words, she noticed her own fists were white-knuckled, glowing and ready to attack. Inhaling a calming breath, the enchantress let the energy flow back to the earth.

When Vivienne studied Merlin, pride shone in his expression, despite his obvious fatigue. "You have grown into your abilities, my dear. I always knew you would."

His kind words did not get past the defensive walls she had already put up.

"Let us not fight, Vivienne, and make peace instead."

"Why?"

"I care about you, and I would like to help you in your fight with Carleigh."

"We have it covered."

Merlin was silent, searching her eyes. Vivienne squirmed uncomfortably under his gaze, recalling their last encounter. "These powers you detect so strong, it's my love for Sébastien that helped unlock them."

"I had a feeling," Merlin admitted.

"You were wrong," Vivienne went on, her chin raised in a defiant gesture. "I tested his blood and mine, and it did not sully me. Our soul mate bond cleansed the darkness in his."

The old wizard frowned. "How is that possible?"

"You still don't get it, do you?" Vivienne shook her head wryly. "We're soul mates and we belong together, it's as simple as that. I can heal him because of everything that exists between us. You forgot love is stronger than anything else."

Vivienne paused, her expression unflinching. "Sébastien is finally beginning to have faith in me." There was an edge to her voice, bordering on icy.

"I only wish your happiness," was all Merlin replied, attempting to placate her.

She scoffed, crossing her arms over her chest. "I find that

statement hard to trust."

"Vivienne –"

"Twice now you've stood by while evil invaded my life, and let it destroy my happiness. How does that show you care?"

Merlin took a step closer, but stopped at her icy look. "You say you don't believe it, and I get that. But please, see it from my point of view. I had the mistaken belief I was protecting you."

"Were you doing that when my father was killed and you stood by?"

Anguish flashed across Merlin's features. "I respected king Adrien and did not wish him harm. My gift is a blessing and a curse, Vivienne. I could not guess it would happen as it did. Please, let us reconcile."

"No. What you did warrants no forgiveness." Merlin could only stare, bereft, in her cold green eyes as she warned, "And don't enter my dreams again."

The enchantress turned her back to him and willed herself to wake up.

* * *

The sun filtered past the curtains, right on Vivienne's resting form. Her sleepy eyes fluttered open, blinking against the rays. With a wave of her hand, air listened and swung the curtains shut, blocking out most of the shine. The young woman buried her head back in the pillows, only to hear a chuckle nearby.

Vivienne froze, then became conscious of another's warm body next to her, and an arm thrown across her waist. As she analyzed this, the events of the previous night came back, and she lifted her head off the pillows, turning around.

In the dimness, Sébastien was watching her. His arm was curved under his head, and an amused smile tilted his lips sexily.

"You're here!" she blurted.

The guardian's eyebrows rose in mock concern. "Am I not supposed to be?"

"I thought I imagined it," Vivienne blushed, hoping the dimness would hide it, but his widening grin informed her otherwise.

The glint in his eyes softened, and Sébastien inched closer. His body pressing against hers, he maneuvered Vivienne on her back and hovered over.

"So did I," he confessed, lowering his mouth to hers.

The embrace began slowly, but soon their hands joined in, roaming all over each other's bodies. Sébastien could not get enough of it, this moment he had fantasized of for ages. All the mornings he had woken up in an empty bed, aching for his beloved, were a faint echo of the past.

When she arched underneath him, her body silently begging, Sébastien gave in to the raw, primal need exhibited, and slid back inside her.

Vivienne's eyes fluttered open with a glazed, bottomless expression within. It ensnared his, even as she bit her lip, imploring, "More."

With a sexy grin, he pressed closer, giving in to what they both desired. But this time, Sébastien watched Vivienne's every expression, keeping his strokes slow and deep, until her nails dug into his back, begging for the ultimate pleasure.

Only then did he let go of his restraint, and they found heaven together.

Later, Vivienne was spread on his chest, smiling happily, his hand drawing lazy circles across her back.

An idea occurred to her, and she peered up, alarmed. "Alistair!"

Sébastien's body shook with laughter. "He's fine. In the living room."

"How do you know?"

"I heard him come in, and he stopped at the door when he noticed us both here."

"Mm . . . I bet he did."

"We should probably get up," Sébastien suggested. "I'm sure he'll rip you a new one after your little stunt."

Vivienne buried her head back in his chest, hoping to avoid the lecture.

Sébastien waited a few moments, then chuckled and urged, "Come on, love. Up we go!"

Vivienne reluctantly followed him into the shower. She had no sooner entered, that an idea occurred to her and she froze.

Sébastien, reacting to her sudden mood change, whipped his head around. "What is it?" His body had predictably tensed, ready to protect.

Momentarily, Vivienne got distracted by the hardened muscle, so tempted to give in to her body's new longings. Then the more urgent matter came back to her mind, causing another blush, "Umm . . ."

Sébastien's body relaxed, though his brow furrowed in concentration, trying to figure out her odd behavior. "Okay . . .

Now I'm getting concerned."

Vivienne bit her lip, and mumbled, "We forgot to use protection."

"We what?" Sébastien gently lifted her chin up with his index, searching her features. "You'll have to repeat that, love."

With a sigh – and even deeper blush – she muttered, "We forgot to use protection last night. *And* this morning."

Sébastien tried to hold it back, but the laughter escaped him anyway. At her scowl, he forced a serious expression. "You're right, that's unacceptable. I'll handle it, starting now. I'll head over to the convenience store, won't be longer than a few minutes."

He was halfway out the bathroom door when Vivienne tugged on his hand, and he turned back to meet her mischievous regard. "I have a better idea. I can use magic for it."

His eyebrows rose, but as Vivienne tugged insistently, Sébastien gave in and retreated to the shower stall. She beamed at him, whispering, "Close your eyes." He hesitated for a moment, and finally did as he was bid.

Vivienne took his hands in hers, imitating him. Memories once more at the forefront of her mind, she sifted among them for the one she wanted. Long ago, the enchantress had raided her father's library – and Merlin's – for any and all mentions of incantations.

There had been one spell she had used, once her and Sébastien had become lovers, to avoid pregnancy – unless she chose otherwise, which would never have been the case.

As the incantation came unbidden to her mind, she

reached within, letting it envelop her. It glittered across her skin, then latched onto Sébastien's. The magic pushing it forth caught onto its mistress' wish, and transformed it into reality.

When the radiance evaporated in diamond droplets, Vivienne opened her eyes, and saw Sébastien staring lazily. With a grin, he closed the distance between them, his mouth moving to her ear.

"We good now?" She nodded, and Sébastien closed the door to the stall, pulling her in his arms under the hot water.

It took them longer than normal, as they lost track multiple times while washing each other. After long moments, they got dried off and dressed, and exited the bedroom hand in hand, to the kitchen.

Sébastien had barely put stuff together for coffee, when Alistair headed towards them from the backyard. He sat down, studying both humans.

So. Finally stopped dancing around each other, have you?

Vivienne smiled tentatively, "Yup!"

If in your next life you go through the same dance, I will be taking a vacation and coming back after it is all done.

"Fair warning," Sébastien chuckled.

Vivienne tossed a glare his way, but before she could say anything, Alistair coughed to get her attention. The enchantress focused back on him, pouting in advance at what she knew would follow.

Now. About your little stunt yesterday—

"I know it was stupid," Vivienne interrupted, putting up her hands in mock surrender. "I figured it as soon as I got there. But I thought I'd be able to handle it." She stopped, sighing. "They injected me with some tranquilizer drug, and I wasn't able to use any magic."

Sébastien fidgeted next to her, and Vivienne squeezed his hand. Though he said nothing as he made coffee, his taut jaw was an indication of the turbulent emotions within. The memory of the risk she had taken was still raw in his mind, enough to set his teeth on edge.

Vivienne grasped his shoulder – a basic, lingering touch – and the Sébastien met her reassuring gaze. "I'm okay . . . You got me back here safe."

The tension eased off him, and Sébastien gave her one of the mugs to sip.

Alistair smacked his paw on the floor, reclaiming their attention. *This better be your last bright idea, highness!*

"It is!" Vivienne agreed fervently, as the guardian next to her choked on his coffee, laughing.

Ignoring him, Alistair announced, *We have to talk about Carleigh.*

* * *

In the abandoned church, Carleigh effortlessly hurled a table against a wall in rage.

"They were not supposed to be back together!" he lashed out at the audience behind.

The sorcerer glowered at his pitiful acolytes, cowering in a corner at his unleashed anger. "Go get them. Attack and kill Sébastien. Do not fail me!"

They scrammed to do his bidding, scurrying about like rats attempting to avoid a fire. They had no sooner run out the door that Carleigh flung a blazing sphere to one of the wooden benches, screaming his wrath to the empty building.

"No matter," he gritted his teeth, studying the cross in front of him. "I will simply have to advance my plan."

After the druids were gone, Carleigh turned his wrath on the pool of darkness. He coerced it to fixate around a bar area, and within its reflections found a convincing thug.

As before, when inducing Vivienne and Sébastien's dreams, the necromancer forced one of the drops of the liquid towards him, and the man froze. Evil spread within his pitiful human mind, his expression going blank as he became just another puppet, his will no longer his own.

"Attack Sébastien," Carleigh ordered. "Make him kill you."

CHAPTER 23

Vivienne tried to remove the blindfold covering her eyes, but a pair of familiar hands stopped her.

"We're almost there, hang on a little longer."

The young woman could not help the flutter in her stomach at whatever it was Sébastien had planned.

Vaguely, her mind recalled how Sébastien had tensed when Alistair had brought up Carleigh. His reaction had been enough to then suggest a day off was needed to recharge their batteries.

Alistair had studied them both, and given a little snort, saying, *Right. Okay, lovebirds, be careful and stick near a lake if you can. Vivienne's magic will be stronger in its vicinity.*

Sébastien had nodded and, before the enchantress knew it, he had packed a bag for them and they were headed down the highway, her blindfolded.

Vivienne was brought back to the present when the car came to a stop, and Sébastien got out. He opened the door and helped her out, steadying her with a hand on the waist when she swung precariously.

"Easy," the guardian murmured next to her ear, and shivers of delight ran up and down her spine. Vivienne stretched against Sébastien, grinning at his sudden intake of breath.

"You little minx," he chastised, then pushed her away, leading to where she presumed the surprise waited.

Vivienne inhaled deeply, sensing water nearby – the element radiated her being with its power. The smell of pine cones and grass also assaulted her senses.

Sébastien came behind, interrupting her perusing, and removed the blindfold.

Vivienne had been around bodies of water before, but this one was beyond gorgeous. It was larger than the one they had been to last time – and quite further away from Avignon, if she was to guess by the time they had spent in the car.

Something about its brilliance, the way the sun shined on it, and the sky reflected, perhaps even the flutter of the leaves around, reminded her of Elsior. Vivienne's heart constricted painfully for a moment, before she grinned widely.

Turning to Sébastien, she noticed he had been gazing at her with a soft look in his eyes. His lips twitched in amusement at her expression. "Like it?"

"Yes!" she beamed. "This is gorgeous, Sébastien, thank you!"

"Anything for you," he murmured, moving closer, and his mouth descended on hers.

Sébastien kept himself in check, the kiss soft and sweet. Much as he wanted to, the time for lovemaking would come later. When Vivienne tried to insist for more, he drew back.

"Let's eat!" he ordered, laughing at the enchantress' disappointed expression.

For the next few hours, they were in bliss. Eating, talking about the past and the present, staying away from anything too heavy by unspoken agreement, and focusing instead on the subject of *them*.

As the night neared, Vivienne used a spell to throw orbs of light above the lake, where they kept the fish and mosquitoes entertained.

Sébastien was content to watch his beloved, until she became restless and stood. With a wicked grin, she removed her top and shorts, and jumped in the lake.

The guardian burst out laughing, and with a small shake of the head at Vivienne's antics, happily joined her in. It was nice not to worry, to be carefree and enjoy each other – though they were still mindful of the menace waiting at bay.

As he swam to Vivienne, Sébastien extended his arm and pulled her close. She gasped at the sensations running through her body, naked skin upon naked skin, and the water between them. With a sigh of surrender, she wrapped her arms around him and drifted closer.

This time, his kiss was anything but restrained. He unleashed the full extent of his fervor, hands roaming across her body, groaning, even as Vivienne melted into him.

"I can't wait much longer," Sébastien whispered after long moments of making out, his voice hoarse with restrained passion.

"Neither can I," Vivienne breathed.

And there, under the moonlight, in the eclipsed lake, they made love slowly, languorously, lulled by the waves.

Later, once they had crashed back from the stars, Sébastien picked Vivienne up in his arms and brought her to shore. He snatched two blankets from the car, one to lie down on the ground, the other to cover them. Though the air was warm, night tended to get cooler.

He laid Vivienne over his chest, keeping her close, and dragged a blanket over their tired bodies. As slumber overtook him, the guardian had one last thought for a certain wizard.

You were wrong, Merlin. Vivienne does accept me as I am.

* * *

Vivienne was dying, and Sébastien was helpless to stop it. He had taken his eyes off her and the dueling sorcerer for a mere moment, to kill off his final opponent, and turned back to see an orb of darkness hit his beloved full front.

She flew into the air and landed closer to him, but this time, she did not get up. He ran to her side, pulling her into his arms, but Vivienne was unresponsive.

"Merlin!" the guardian roared in need, holding her close. "Help me! Do not let her die!"

"She is too far gone," a voice snickered behind mockingly.

Sébastien kissed Vivienne's forehead, then lunged for his sword and stood up to confront Carleigh. "You will pay for this!"

"I highly doubt that," the malicious sorcerer smirked.

He flung a sphere of dark magic at Sébastien, which the

knight deflected with his weapon.

The duel went on, and he held his ground. He managed to injure Carleigh, but could tell by means of their bond that Vivienne was slowly slipping away.

Noticing he could not win by pure blade skill alone, the sorcerer sent a wave of witchcraft to attack Sébastien from behind, causing him to drop to the ground. Deep, bloody gashes spread across his back, even as he screamed in agony.

Carleigh strode towards Vivienne, his midnight robes – and the shadows at his feet – trailing him like a second skin.

"Get away from her!" Sébastien roared.

Helpless, he saw the warlock approach Vivienne and whisper in her ear. He could not hear what was expressed, but the enchantress' eyes fluttered open and he perceived a sudden burst of hate through their bond.

"I said," Sébastien croaked, "get away from her!"

There was a blinding flash, and Merlin appeared. Sébastien let the wizard handle the fight with Carleigh, far more concerned for his beloved than the fate of the world. He crawled to Vivienne, desperately searching for a pulse.

Her hand was cold, almost translucently pale. "Please stay with me, my love," Sébastien pleaded.

Vivienne opened her eyes and smiled weakly, tears streaming down her cheeks.

"I will always love you, remember that," she whispered.

When shouts clamored from behind Sébastien, he could not help but glance, torn between a need to help Merlin, and a longing to save Vivienne. It was the idea of Carleigh running free, after all the damage he had inflicted, that helped the knight decide.

"Please wait for me, beloved, do not give in just yet," Sébastien implored, squeezing Vivienne's hand.

He waited for her weak nod, and only then got up one last time to help Merlin, despite the loss of blood he had already suffered.

With Sébastien blocking the attacks with his sword, Merlin was able to use the staff's concentrated power to fatally wound Carleigh. They managed to get the warlock down, pinning him to the earth, where the old wizard's power captured him.

His evil no match for Merlin's acute abilities, the sorcerer gargled blood, choking on his own viciousness. Before perishing, Carleigh smirked at Merlin. "You are too late. Your precious is already cursed."

Sébastien grabbed him by the throat, snarling in his face, "What did you do?"

"Keep your strength, pretty boy, or else you shall join her in the grave."

"Speak!" Merlin commanded.

"I cursed her. She will not be reborn until her dear champion's heart turns to darkness."

With a furious shout, Sébastien picked up the blade to end him. Yet it was Merlin who gave the final blow, sending a wave of spirit so strong into Carleigh, it caused the execrable sorcerer to turn to ash.

The mage then helped Sébastien get to where Vivienne lay dying. "Please save her," he begged. "I will give my life in exchange if I have to."

"I cannot. You have no idea how much I wish it, but it is too late."

At the words, Vivienne gasped, as though running out of breath. Sébastien gripped her hand, sobbing hot tears of shame and regret, having been unable to save her life.

"Please don't leave," he cried.

The enchantress' beautiful green eyes opened one last time, and her gaze locked onto Sébastien's, love shining through. Then they fluttered closed, and Vivienne exhaled her final breath.

Merlin's sorrowful eyes turned to Sébastien, barely keeping his own emotions in check. "Listen to me well. Did you hear Carleigh's curse?"

Focused on Vivienne's last few breaths, Sébastien pleaded, "Let me die of my wounds, so I may join her in the next life. You explained soul mates find each other."

"Yes, they do. But you heard what Carleigh said – only when you turn evil, will she be reborn. If you let it enter you, the darkness of the curse will affect Vivienne, as well."

At the words, the guardian peered up at Merlin, realizing their meaning. "You mean to say if she is reborn, I cannot be with her, as it would taint her?"

Compassion shone in the old man's eyes, but he did not disagree. Sébastien knew his fate was sealed. He contemplated Vivienne, her beautiful features frozen forever in death.

"The world cannot be denied her radiance. Let me die of my wounds, Merlin, and I will wait for her, and defend her from afar when she is reborn. I give you my oath. I would die a million deaths if it helped her."

Merlin acquiesced, and pressed both hands to Sébastien's forehead. "Then be at peace, good knight."

The flame was blinding, entering his forehead, and

Sébastien felt himself slipping away. "See you soon, beloved,"
he murmured, tightening his grip on Vivienne's hand one last
time, before letting go.

* * *

Sébastien woke up later in the night from the recollection, not understanding what had shaken him awake. The stars were still shining bright, the night was hushed, and Vivienne was tucked into his side, safe and sound.

Yet something had bothered the guardian, a nagging impression of danger. He pulled on a pair of shorts and walked away, tucking the blanket around Vivienne to keep her warm in his absence.

Eyes on the lake, Sébastien's reflections focused inward. He recalled Vivienne's death in their last life together, the loss present in his mind, all over again. Now that they were together romantically, he was worried she would get hurt again – not by him.

Carleigh definitely had an agenda, and no matter how they avoided him, its dark intent was heading towards them.

* * *

Vivienne had been warm and slumbering peacefully, when the warmth evaporated. She tossed and turned for the next hour, eventually giving up and blinking awake.

She understood her restlessness almost immediately. Sébastien was no longer lying next to her, but rather sitting by the shore, throwing pebbles. Putting on some clothes, she tiptoed towards the knight.

"Hey," Vivienne greeted softly.

He looked up at her approach, then turned back at the lake. The few seconds were enough for the young woman to notice the anguish in his eyes.

"Sébastien, talk to me."

There was a long silence, then the guardian whispered softly, "You should get some sleep."

"If only I could . . . I can sense your torment even while resting." Vivienne pressed on his shoulder, forcing him to meet her gaze. "I'm right here, Sébastien. *Talk* to me."

The uneasy glint as he met her gaze was enough, even before he expressed anything out loud.

"You feel guilty . . .About last night." Even as Vivienne spoke the words, her heart stiffened wretchedly at the fear he would withdraw away again.

As if on cue, Sébastien looked away, biting on his lip. The enchantress frowned, at a loss on what to say. Through their bond, she could experience his mood, but it was a tangle of tumultuous emotions.

Realizing she had to tune in subconsciously, Vivienne closed her eyes for a brief moment, concentrating solely on their link. Its strength now renewed with their growing relationship, she could read Sébastien's emotions better – among which, the chaos that threatened to overwhelm the joy underneath. Amongst it, there was one idea alone which kept going on a loop in his mind.

Vivienne's eyes flew open, flashing warningly. "It wasn't a mistake!"

"I didn't say that."

"You didn't *not* say it, either."

His shoulders sagged in defeat. "I knew the stakes and still—"

Vivienne placed her index on his lips to get him to stop. "I refuse to hear this. Not after what we shared last night. I love you, Sébastien, that has never changed. Let me help you. I see the good in you, and I accept the bad. Let me heal you, and learn to forgive yourself as I have, so we can move past this."

The champion glanced up, wanting to believe it was possible, as much as she did. As if reading his thoughts, Vivienne extended a hand to him. When he hesitantly grasped it, she tugged him towards the lake, her determined steps getting closer.

"Vivienne—"

"No," she gave a resolute shake of the head. "I get now where this is coming from. You're as happy as I am at our newfound intimacy, yet the shadows that haunt you want to remove even that away. And I will not let them."

Sébastien sighed, knowing deep down she was right – always had been, when it came to the matters of the heart.

"You told me you'd consider it – letting me heal you. Well, now we have a moment of peace, and it's high time you let me return to you a little of what you lost in your efforts to bring me back."

At her enticing grin, Sébastien gave in. He walked fully into the lake, joining his beloved in the middle. As she had done in the past, Vivienne immersed her palms in the water, and ordered it above the champion's head.

"Water of my realm," the enchantress instructed in a

voice imbued with ancient magic, "this man gave more for me than anyone ever has for a loved one. Please ease some of the burden on his soul, and help cleanse him from evil and pain, so that he may see the brightness and hope of the future once more."

With one command from its mistress, water poured over Sébastien. As in the memories, it infiltrated, cleansing him. What he had done in the past could not be undone, it was an undisputable fact.

However, when Vivienne's pure enchantment entered Sébastien's skin, through the element, all the apprehension, anger and negative sentiments he had carried around with him were swept away on a tidal wave. In mere moments, the weight lifted off his shoulders, as the torrent running over him washed away the sins, and restored the knight to hope.

When Sébastien opened his eyes, Vivienne was peering at him with tears in her eyes and trembling lips. "Did it work?" she asked, already knowing the answer. Even blind, the strength of their bond would have told her that it had succeeded beyond her greatest expectations.

"Yes," Sébastien whispered and reached for the young woman, gathering her close to him. "But you have to know, my love, the things I did in the past are ingrained in me—" He stopped again, choking on the words, the fear of disappointing her a reality he still had to tackle.

The images from his past two lifetimes came to Vivienne's mind. "You did it for me," she stated firmly. "But you don't have to anymore. You can be my champion again, here in this modern world – my partner, my lover. What you did in the past can remain there."

"What if I can't stop?"

"Give yourself more credit. I do."

And without giving him time to answer, Vivienne dragged Sébastien's mouth down to hers, kissing him softly. Her unwavering belief removed his last doubts, and he allowed the healing nature of their lovemaking to wipe everything else away, under the shining stars.

* * *

The ride back to the city the next afternoon was quiet, but there was a closeness and connection between the two lovers which had not been there before. Hands laced together, their communication was subconscious, no spoken words needed.

When Sébastien pulled in front of Vivienne's home, she smiled his way. "Thank you for yesterday."

"Thank you for last night," he replied.

Purely out of a need to touch her, the guardian placed his hand to her cheek and Vivienne nuzzled it. The glint in Sébastien's eyes changed, from soft to smoldering, and he lifted her chin up, bringing his mouth to hers. She leaned in happily for the graze of his lips.

At her breathy moan, Sébastien deepened the kiss, and within a few moments he had Vivienne out of the passenger seat and on his lap, hands roaming under her shirt.

They jumped apart guiltily at a sudden tap on the window. Peeking out, they saw an amused senior passerby, gesturing to roll down the window.

Sébastien did as the elder bid. Vivienne tried to shift off him, but his hand on her waist was an iron grip.

"You might want to do that somewhere more private," the older man suggested, biting back a laugh. "Lots of tourists here around this time of day."

"Right away, sir," Sébastien nodded, while Vivienne stifled her giggles in his neck.

The passerby left, and Sébastien gave his love another swift kiss, before opening the door. They both headed inside the house, still chuckling.

Alistair greeted them at the door, and Vivienne bent down to hug him.

You seem happy, the dog rumbled in her head.

The young woman disengaged, unable to hide the joy filling her. "I am," she acknowledged, and noted the satisfaction in his canine gaze.

Good. You both deserve it.

Alistair concentrated on Sébastien, and bowed his head in greeting. He immediately detected the easier way the guardian carried himself, as though a huge load had been taken off. The demon dog bit back his satisfaction, and waited for them to settle in, before bringing them up to speed.

Since we do not have to worry about the Mafia any longer, we can now focus on the druids. Carleigh is off into hiding. I have picked his conjurers' trail in more than one spot in Avignon, but his has been rather more complex to find. He may be camouflaging it, or perhaps he is simply so gone to the evil side there is no human scent left.

"Maybe if we attack his minions, it might force him to show his hand," Vivienne suggested.

Not a bad idea, Alistair agreed. *Carleigh might not care for their lives, but I bet he requires them alive – or his definition of alive – to help him attain his goals. He will not be happy at the inconvenience.*

"I agree, it's a great idea. Minus the fact it's risky, for Vivienne especially," Sébastien cut in.

Right.

The buzz of a phone interrupted them. Vivienne glanced at Sébastien, as it came from him. "Shouldn't you answer it?"

"Don't know who it is, don't care." He shrugged, throwing an arm around the enchantress' shoulders to drag her closer. "How can we minimize the danger?" The question was directed at Alistair.

Vivienne smiled at the knowledge he was stating a claim, guarding her, and appreciated the effort more than she could say. The notion entered her mind that it was surprising how normal their transition had been. Their relationship's survival had never been the focus in the past, as there had been too much going on. Yet she was immensely enjoying the newfound closeness.

"Vivienne?"

Having lost track of the conversation, she blinked dazedly, and found Sébastien grinning at her.

"Where did you go just now?"

"Oh, places . . ." With a sheepish smile to Alistair, she added, "Sorry, what were you guys saying?"

Alistair gave a shake of the head in amusement, and repeated, *I suggest we ambush the druids, making sure the fight is on our terms and fully predictable.*

"Seems reasonable to me," Vivienne agreed.

The buzzing began again. She studied Sébastien, then his pocket. "Maybe you should get it."

He resolutely shook his head. "Whatever it is, it'll remove me away from this, and today my priority is to make headway to get to Carleigh and secure our future."

Vivienne grinned at the words, and the response in his eyes, before Sébastien turned to Alistair. "So where did you pick up their trail?"

Once at the warehouse we fought the druids, then again behind an ice cream parlor. Another was by the lake where they almost ambushed us a couple days ago, and there were a few other spots.

They fell quiet, attempting to figure out what the best spot to attack would be. Sébastien was about to speak, but the buzz of his cell interrupted him.

"For fuck's sake!" he swore, and withdrew the arm away from Vivienne's shoulders to get the annoying contraption out of his back pocket.

Although Vivienne did not hear who was on the line, Sébastien stiffened the minute he picked up. At the sound on the other line, his brow furrowed. "And why would I—"

He listened for a brief moment, then nodded, "Fine. Be there in ten." He was up the instant after disconnecting the call. "I might have a lead on Carleigh. I'll be back within the hour."

It could be dangerous to go alone. Why not let us come with? Alistair suggested.

"It's a potential sighting, might not even be much," Sébastien sighed. "I'm going to check if the information is worth it, and if it is, I'll come get you."

He was about to exit, when Vivienne grasped his hand and tugged him down for a quick peck. "Be safe. And bring Éimhín."

Sébastien complied and headed out the door. She squinted after him for another few moments, then shrugged off the odd behavior and turned to Alistair. "How about we go get some ice cream?"

Alistair snorted her way, not fooled in the least at her innocent question. *Funny. Not until Sébastien comes back. He would skin me alive.*

"Fine," Vivienne laughed. "So help me with some spells. Let's test those fireballs again."

That, I can do, the demon dog did his doggy grin, eyes starting to glow.

* * *

Sébastien pulled up in front of the bar. It had been Guinevere on the other end of the call, begging him to meet her and promising to reveal Carleigh's location.

Now, arriving in the middle of the day, the knight had doubts. For one, her sudden desire to help them out was disputable at best. On top of that, her car was not by the bar.

Sébastien parked in the alleyway behind the building, where Guinevere had pleaded to meet up. Already convinced it was a trap, but willing to see it to the end, he grabbed Éimhín and stepped out.

He had barely turned a corner, when rushed footsteps came up from behind. Sébastien whirled to face whoever it was, and something hard hit him on the side of the head – he saw stars.

* * *

Vivienne sensed a hit on the side of her head around the same time. She dropped the conjured orb, luckily extinguishing it before it hit the floor.

Her confused gaze landed on Alistair. "Did you do something to me?"

What do you mean?

"Some type of telepathic attack to see if I could multitask?"

No . . . Why?

"There was a tug just now, as if I'd gotten hit . . . It's tough to explain."

Dammit! Alistair rumbled, getting off the couch. *It comes from Sébastien, not you. You probably felt it due to the strength of your bond, now that you two are romantically involved again. Follow the link between you. It should give you an idea of where to find him.*

Vivienne closed her eyes tightly, forcefully searching and expanding her senses. She got flashes of a fight, an alleyway, and the name of the bar.

"I know where he is!" she declared, opening her eyes, lightning flaming deep within.

Then let's go!

* * *

Vivienne got to the bar in time to witness Sébastien throw the man into a stone wall. The guardian's words of the night before came back to her, about how he doubted using violence could be unlearnt.

It was not long before she discovered the champion's

punches, though he was attacking, indicated restraint. Apparently at the end of his wits, Sébastien put his opponent in a chokehold, and he collapsed to the ground.

He then waited a beat to make sure the man was not getting back up. Satisfied, Sébastien scanned his surroundings and noticed Vivienne a few feet away. "What are you doing here?"

"I felt the fight."

"You *what*?" He frowned, glancing to Alistair for clarification.

"Apparently," Vivienne expanded on her statement, "one of the perks of soul mates is heightened sensitivity to each other. Except in this case, I was able to find you due to the bond."

Sébastien blinked in surprise, then shook his head. He glanced down at the unconscious man, muttering, "He attacked first."

"And you showed restraint," Vivienne pointed out, approaching and clasping his hand in hers.

"Yeah," Sébastien's eyes flashed with bewilderment, then pride. "I guess I did."

"I knew you could."

Sébastien opened his arms, and Vivienne walked into his embrace. The guardian held her tightly, inhaling her sweet perfume. "I wouldn't be able to do this without you."

"I believe you could," Vivienne asserted against his neck.

How did you end up here, anyway? Alistair questioned. *I thought you had a lead on Carleigh.*

Vivienne pulled back, her eyes narrowing thoughtfully. Sébastien cringed under her scrutiny. "I did. Guinevere called, promising she would tell me his hiding spot. I came here, got attacked by this non-magical person, and never actually got to blondie."

"And you *believed* her?" Vivienne scowled. "She's been so adamant to show me how low you've fallen, it doesn't even amaze me she staged this!"

Sébastien did not have to read minds to realize Vivienne was annoyed, evidenced by her lips pressed tightly together and folded arms.

"Honestly, I'm surprised she was even alive after failing twice," he grumbled defensively.

She is not. They both glanced down at Alistair's words. *Carleigh killed Guinevere the same night you two reconnected. I followed her home and saw the body after.*

Vivienne closed her eyes for a few moments, and reopened them wearily. "Guinevere was not the nicest person, but her alter ego Jennifer had been my friend for years. I would not have wished this on her."

The sentiment is appreciated, majesty. I should have informed you earlier, but I preferred you both to have some time away without this on your mind.

"Thank you," Sébastien said simply. "But the question remains, if Guinevere didn't call me, then who did?"

I would guess Carleigh, using an impersonation spell.

"To what ends, though?" Vivienne wondered out loud. "He could not have actually assumed this guy could win against you."

Sébastien shrugged in response, but Alistair had more to say. *Maybe that is what he hoped. Not so much for you, Vivienne, to witness Sébastien fighting. But rather for him to kill the man, for the evil to expand. He is probably aware by now that you two are back together, and it has become a thorn in his side.*

"Makes sense," the guardian agreed. "But back to our conversation before I had to leave . . . I definitely agree this is an appropriate time as any to strike."

Right. Vivienne was in the mood for ice cream earlier.

"Of course she was," Sébastien rolled his eyes. "The ice cream place will be our first target, then."

And I will scan the grounds, see what else I can track down, Alistair offered, then took off.

The lovers, meanwhile, got into the Jag to drive the brief way to the location Alistair had given them. They arrived within moments, and took a seat on one of the benches behind the building. Luckily, since it was closed, no one else was around.

"So, how exactly do we attract the druids?" Vivienne wondered.

Sébastien placed Éimhín out of sight, but within easy reach, and shrugged in response. "Maybe you could try some spell? It should be enough to peak their interest."

Vivienne grinned, and with one hand gathered an orb of brightness, making it explode into tiny fireworks. She had no sooner sent the energy away, when the breeze shifted.

Sébastien immediately stood up, moving with his body to shield her. He grabbed the blade, holding it by his side. The clouds in the sky grew more ominous, then shapes approached from behind the ice cream place.

"Here they come," Sébastien muttered.

There were four in all. He gripped the sword tighter, and

Vivienne cast a protective shield over them. The four warlocks surrounded them in a semi-circle, hands gathering dark magic in flashing onyx orbs.

They threw it at Vivienne, but Sébastien advanced with Éimhín and slashed through the energy. The knight then stepped to the side, attracting two of the druids, as the other two went for Vivienne.

Sébastien got close enough to one and with a single stroke of the sword, he became sooty dust. The other was harder to get rid of. When the knight tried to hit him, it was as if Éimhín struck an immobile wall.

He took another swing when the druid was busy throwing a spell, and this time drew blood. It was enough for Sébastien to realize the warlock's shield was down whenever he struck. Once that was figured out, he dispatched him at the next attack, and turned to Vivienne.

The enchantress had one conjurer imprisoned in a glowing orb, and the other on the ground, though still alive. Sébastien stepped to him and with a swift slash of Éimhín, he was gone.

"Where's Carleigh?" Vivienne questioned her prisoner.

The man did not answer, and the young woman concluded she would not get any information out of him. With a cry of frustration, she tightened the ring surrounding him until he, too, was transformed into dust.

With a disgusted shake of her head, Vivienne turned to Sébastien and grinned, "We make a pretty good team."

For all response, he drew her tightly in an embrace, glad she was safe.

* * *

Later that evening, after the grit of the battle was washed off and they had eaten, Sébastien went to get some shuteye. Vivienne stayed up, waiting for Alistair.

The dog trotted in around two in the morning, in good shape and unharmed. He stopped in the living room, surprised. *Still awake, highness?*

"I wanted to make sure you got here unharmed."

Alistair moved closer, placing his massive head on Vivienne's lap. *Yes, no trouble on my end. Only dead ends everywhere.*

She petted him, scratching behind the ears where he liked it – though never would admit out loud. "We'll find Carleigh. You mentioned yourself he's fixated on me. It's only a matter of time before he does something stupid."

How did it go at the ice cream place?

"We won."

How many?

"Only four."

How the hell he keeps getting them here is beyond me, Alistair growled. *Sacrifices like the one we witnessed are not a long term solution, there must be something stronger leading it.*

"Because they're the same ones as from the past?"

Yes. That is why when they meet Sébastien's sword, they become dust. I realized it clearly following our last battle with them. They are strong in the black arts, but it is also the reason why blades of light or of the past cut the strings of the invisible evil that keeps them alive, and kill them.

"Perhaps I should forge another sword, then."

Vivienne was only half-joking, and Alistair did not respond, but the words reminded her of the flashback she had when kidnapped by Tony.

"Alistair . . ." the young woman started, a query in the voice.

Hmm?

"The weapon I forged, in the past. Excalibur."

Yes?

"Do you suppose I could get ahold of it?"

The dog mulled it over, before tentatively answer, *I don't see why not. It would still have a connection to you, as its maker. In the legends they mention here, after Arthur died, Excalibur was returned to the lake. I cannot be certain, considering I was no longer in that time when it happened, but . . . You could attempt to, it is the only way to learn the truth.*

They were silent together for a few moments, Vivienne pondering his words, Alistair wondering.

Why do you ask?

"When I was kidnapped, I recalled something of Arthur and Excalibur. I figured, from what I advised the king in the past, that it could vanquish Sébastien's last doubts, and give him peace of mind."

Be careful that in your wish to help him, you do not harm him.

"What are you alluding to? I'm too tired for riddles."

Excalibur is a particular blade, from what I observed and heard. If it was to reject him, Sébastien could see it the wrong way.

"You're right," Vivienne agreed.

You would have to piece together the exact words you used when you created it, as they determine whom it accepts and rejects.

Vivienne bit her lip in concentration. "I guess I can try."

Good. Alistair was silent again, then asked, *What about your waters? They have healing abilities.*

"Took care of that on our little day off," Vivienne admitted. "It cleansed and purified Sébastien, but of course, could not remove the darkness he willingly let in."

At least he is on the right path, Alistair pointed out.

Vivienne nodded, and got up to go join Sébastien.

Majesty? The dog stopped her at the top of the stairs.

"Yeah?"

Sébastien has his demons. But he is fighting them by being with you and controlling himself.

"I know. To be honest, I don't care if he keeps darkness within him, so long as we can be together. But it bothers him."

You being with him will eventually remove the last of it.

Vivienne smiled. "Thanks, Al." Then she opened the door and walked into her bedroom.

Sébastien was asleep in the moonlight, but when Vivienne slid in the bed, he wrapped an arm around her, dragging her close.

"Are you awake?" she chuckled softly, placing her fingertips to his chest.

"Mm, maybe," Sébastien mumbled sluggishly.

Vivienne laughed, and kissed him lightly on the lips, "I love you."

"I love you too," he grinned, arms tightening around her.

As she snuggled next to him, Vivienne dozed off within

minutes in the comfort of his arms.

Sébastien waited until Vivienne's breathing relaxed, enjoying the hushed peacefulness. In his wildest dreams, he never would have believed it possible to hold her again. Now that he did, nothing would keep them apart ever again.

* * *

The druids entered the church, each carrying a homeless man, woman or child. They were innocents, victims of a cruel fate. But they would not be missed, thus perfect for Carleigh's scheming, their blood a feast.

The sorcerer directed the druids to the pool, where they coerced the people to kneel. Darkness stirred, slithering like a snake.

The humans' eyes widened, and some tried to scurry away, only to find out their bodies would not budge. Immobile and helpless, they waited as the darkness rose in the shape of a large worm. It squirmed closer to them and swallowed each person, one by one, in its slimy body.

Their silent cries of horror disappeared, as did the bodies, underneath the large worm. Once it was bloated and returned to the normal flat pool shape, Carleigh moved closer.

"Now forge me a sword powerful and poisonous enough to cut anything."

The mass bubbled, and out hissed a weapon. It flew in the air, implanting itself at Carleigh's feet. "Time to test it out," he grinned.

CHAPTER 24

Vivienne was dreaming again, this time in front of her lake.

"Merlin, this better not be you again," she grumbled against the fog.

"Tis not the warlock, young royal."

The mist dissipated, and there was a glow above the lake, floating. As Vivienne stepped closer, she discerned within it Excalibur, whom she had forged and sent to find Arthur. The voice was coming from it.

"You have been calling to me, princess."

Vivienne's eyebrows rose in amazement. She had been informed, in the past, that some supernatural objects could possess a soul of their own and approach their creator, but to experience it was another deal altogether.

"I was not aware I did so, Excalibur," the enchantress spoke respectfully. "I did not even think it possible."

"When you forged me, some of your supernatural spirit and essence was placed into me. Despite the gap in time, I still feel your call."

Vivienne was speechless. This was one hell of a secondary effect neither Merlin nor Alistair had warned her about.

"You should not fear the bond."

"I suppose nothing should astonish me anymore," Vivienne sighed.

She paused, and advanced further to the element lapping at her feet. The beacon inched closer as well.

"Why was I calling to you, do you know?"

"I do. You do as well."

It struck the young woman in a flash – her last conversation with Alistair, wondering if Excalibur could help heal Sébastien, and the dog's own warning against the liability. And now, here she was, faced with the choice.

"For Sébastien," Vivienne voiced her musings out loud.

"Yes."

Excalibur shone brighter. "Is it possible? Would Sébastien be able to wield you?" Vivienne pushed past the lump in her throat.

"I can go to whomever you command me to, princess. I will stay in the knight's handling until his death, be he pure of heart only."

"You cannot be handled by a corrupt soul?"

"My abilities are vast, and due to being forged by you – a being of light – I should only be used by a good soul. If I was to fall in the hands of evil, wielding the occult or tainted by it, the conflict in energies would destroy me."

Vivienne pondered the sword's words for a moment. Excalibur had been a sign of hope, a symbol whilst in Arthur's hands. She recalled a modern legend prophesizing of the king's return, and how the blade would be one amongst many puzzle pieces he would have to put together, to accomplish his destiny.

If the enchantress was to command Excalibur to Sébastien, and it was destroyed, Arthur would be one weapon short – *if* he ever reincarnated.

"Sébastien needs you," Vivienne stated, biting her lip in concentration. "If he could wield you, it would put him at ease as he would recognize redemption truly has resulted in good. Excalibur, you once helped Arthur regain his faith."

"I did. Arthur was a powerful and just leader. If your champion is much the same, I can be of aid to him."

"And if he has corruption in him?"

"I cannot foresee until we make contact."

Vivienne's brow furrowed with the certainty this was not a choice she should be making. It was not hers to mess with. Perhaps Alistair was right at the end of the day. "Thank you for responding to my call."

The sword wavered, sensing its mistress' inability to decide. "If you change your mind, majesty, search but to water, and call me to your side. I will answer you – always."

"Thank you."

The fog picked up again, and Vivienne stirred to the sun's rays entering the bedroom.

* * *

Vivienne awoke to voices outside the bedroom. She dressed swiftly and joined Sébastien and Alistair in the living room.

"Alistair found another lead during the night," the knight said as he kissed her. "There's a place by the church in this neighborhood with traces of Carleigh."

"The one next to the cemetery?"

Same one.

"I'm coming with you two," Vivienne announced.

Sébastien peered to Alistair, who shook his head in defeat. "Alright," he repressed a groan, "but you keep close to me, Vivienne. I mean it. No heroine business."

"Of course."

The short drive was filled with tension, especially considering it was still twilight hours and the place would be deserted.

Sébastien parked behind the cemetery, and pointed to the church. "We'll go from behind, and hopefully with some concealment, we can stay undetected."

Vivienne nodded in understanding. "I might be able to hide us better than normal." A faint grin graced her lips as an idea formed, spurred by her dream.

The enchantress got out of the car and closed her eyes. Her first order of business was to search deep inside, for a particular shard of power which allowed her to mess with reality. She used it to mask herself, and the two companions now shadowing her.

Vivienne followed it by lifting both hands out in front of her, palms down and facing the earth. The mist, evaporated with the sun's first rays, was now conjured by means of an enchantment. It rose in the air and settled the cemetery under a gentle blanket, not thick enough to be suspicious, but good enough for extra coverage.

Great job, princess, was Alistair's praise, and Vivienne grinned.

Sébastien wrapped her hand in his larger one, and gave it a squeeze. "No matter what, we cannot get separated," he reiterated.

Vivienne acquiesced, and they advanced. The eerie silence of the cemetery, coupled with the early morning, was enough to raise the hairs on the back of her neck. It did not help that waves of sorcery were coming off the ground, impregnated as it was with the evil warlocks' presence.

I feel their malevolent essence, Alistair grumbled from in front of them.

Vivienne inclined her head in assent, whispering, "Me too. It's oppressive."

The closer we get, the more there is a chance of them sensing you, highness. Keep your magic handy, ready to defend yourself.

"Got it."

They kept advancing in silence, until Alistair abruptly stopped.

"What—" Vivienne started, only to be thrown to the ground by Sébastien, his body shielding hers.

She raised her head to witness an orb of witchcraft about the size of a watermelon – but the color of night – shatter against a headstone not far off. Sébastien jumped back to his feet, extending his hand to help her get up.

The enchantress got to her feet, hastily gathering an enchantment in the palms of her hands, preparing for the next attack. Sébastien swung Éimhín around, attentively scouring their surroundings for threats, his body taut and coiled to strike.

The next destructive sphere came from the right, and he whirled to strike it with Éimhín, even as Vivienne noticed another one headed for Alistair.

"Al, watch out!" she yelled.

She backed away, intending to help him, and let go of Sébastien's hand to throw an orb of brightness into the dark one. They exploded together, shattering into tiny fragments.

Alistair got enveloped by the fog, now stronger than before, and disappeared out of sight. Vivienne searched for Sébastien, but he was gone as well. He called out to her, from not far off to the side.

"Dammit," the enchantress muttered realizing they had managed too easily to get separated. To top it off, someone else dominated the fog now, using their idea against them.

Vivienne ducked another round, and this time sat down on the ground, enveloped in a barrier. She placed both hands directly to the earth, but yelped as they were zapped, removing them – a telltale sign her instinct was right, and someone else was behind it now.

Highness, a little help with this damn fog would be nice! Alistair complained in her head.

Give me a few moments.

The young woman placed her hands on the ground again, ignoring the zap this time. *Water is* my *element, and I alone control it.*

She followed the connection and tugged on it, forcing the fog back into the ground. As the mist cleared, Vivienne got up and examined her surroundings. Sébastien was caught between druids, and Alistair was nowhere to be seen.

Another presence entered her field of perception. Though she could not see him, Carleigh's aura was too wearying to ignore, pulsating violence as it was. It triggered faint memories of the past, when she had dueled with him.

Vivienne could sense the sorcerer somewhere in the distance and was afraid of history repeating itself, and her dog being harmed.

Alistair, where are you!? Vivienne screamed mentally. At the same time, she caught sight of a group of conjurers heading towards her.

I am off to the side of the church, not far off. Carleigh is here, his stench is everywhere.

Don't go after him alone! Vivienne panicked.

I will not. Heading back to you as soon as I finish with these damn cloaked pricks.

There was a fountain not far off, liquid spurting in jets from it. Vivienne extended her magic and called the element to her, forcing the spell to cool as she had practiced. By the time it surrounded her, the enchantress had transformed it into sharp ice picks, glinting dangerously in the morning's rays.

The warlocks were still advancing. She flung a beam of radiance first, expecting them to deflect it, then threw in the wall of ice picks. It hit two of the conjurers. One went down for good, but the other got back up, his fists clenched and teeth bared.

Damn.

* * *

Not far off, Sébastien swung Éimhín in time to cut through another nefarious sphere of dark magic. His arm was scraped from hitting the headstone earlier, after being separated from Vivienne.

At least now he could see his beloved, and she was holding her own in the fight.

Sébastien, Alistair's voice alerted, *Watch out. Carleigh is close. If I do not get to you in time, get Vivienne out of here.*

The dog disappeared as soon as he had emerged in his head. Sébastien swung the weapon high above his head, and let it loose. It hit his enemy in the chest, and he shattered.

The knight stepped over and picked Éimhín from the ashes, shaking his head to clear it. A hiss in the air was his only warning. Sébastien whirled around, swinging the sword up in time to par another.

"Carleigh," he muttered. *Found him.*

The sorcerer smirked at his bewildered look, clashing his blade against Éimhín. His new toy was strong, Sébastien's own sword bending under its weight. The champion shoved him off, disengaging with a grunt, and then they were circling each other like boxers in a ring.

* * *

Vivienne saw Carleigh next to Sébastien, alerted by his potent sorcery. With a compelling blast, she dispatched her last opponent.

Alistair, to me! Carleigh is here.

Get to the church and block him, came the instructions. *We are here to deplete his forces, not tackle Carleigh. But if we have to, we are better off cornering him, and attacking all at once. Create a barrier like you did in the past.*

Understood, Vivienne replied mentally, already running to the church. She sent one last blast of magic behind her, watching as it hit Carleigh, destabilizing him. Sébastien locked eyes across the distance and read her intentions.

As he headed closer, Vivienne created a spell to surround herself in a semi-circle, blocking off the evil attacks. This way, she would have the church behind her, and Carleigh and his evil druids facing her. If there were any conjurers in the church, they would be easier to dispatch than Carleigh.

Vivienne snapped out of her thoughts at the loud clash of metal, noticing her lover embroiled in another match with Carleigh. He struggled under whatever incantation the sorcerer was using.

The enchantress turned away from them to focus, forcing the enchantment to work more rapidly, building the shield as she had once for Elsior.

She peered over a shoulder again at the sound of a crash behind, to see Sébastien sprawled on the ground, Éimhín shattered in front of him.

"Sébastien!"

Carleigh moved towards him, but a growl tore through the air and then Alistair was there, facing them. Thankful for his well-timed intervention, Vivienne put out a hand and extended the barrier to include Sébastien.

She was about to run to him, when a hand grabbed her. Angrily blasting a druid away with a gust of air, the young woman ran to her lover. The shield would protect them for a while, but they were cutting it much too close.

Sébastien struggled to get up as if a weight pinned him down, the muscles in his arms straining.

"What's wrong?" Vivienne asked, trying to help him up – to no avail.

"Some spell," Sébastien grunted.

She drew back, this time inspecting the knight with her other senses, and understood his meaning. An air incantation was pressing down on him. Vivienne dissipated it with a push of her own magic, leaving Sébastien gasping in relief.

With a resolute shake of the head, he got up and met her gaze. "I have no sword again."

Vivienne smiled, longing to wash the vulnerability off him. "I can help with that." *After all, everything happens for a reason.*

The enchantress confronted her opponents, this time inciting the shield towards them. Within a few moments, they discovered they could not advance further, and the couple was now untouchable underneath the dome of the barrier.

Vivienne glanced one last time behind, letting her senses penetrate the church to ensure it was empty. Satisfied, she then focused on Sébastien.

"What are you doing?" he wondered.

The young woman dipped again into the fountain for energy, her fist clenching as she urged it to do her bidding and open a way to the past. "Finding you a sword," she whispered for Sébastien's ears only.

Once the link clicked in place with the element, Vivienne ordered, *I need you, Excalibur.*

There was a faint resistance as the water, pliable normally, responded to the force of good. Vivienne's request was unknowingly asking for a parting of the gates of time, since Excalibur existed in the past.

With one final push, the element gave in, bending the rules of time, and creating a tear to get the weapon to her, effectively opening a pathway between the past and the present. In that precise moment, the fighting around the couple ceased, and everything froze.

Vivienne opened her eyes in shock, having perceived the change in her surroundings. She glanced around, but everything – the acolytes, the environment, even Alistair and Carleigh – was immobile except for her and Sébastien, still under the barrier.

Noticing her shocked gaze, the knight looked around as well, and blew out an exasperated breath. "What did you do?"

Vivienne shrugged in response and closed her eyes again. She could see, in her mind, a shining beacon making its way to them. When her eyelids fluttered open, she beamed in victory.

"What—" Sébastien began, and peered over a shoulder to see what she was studying intently. The shining beacon was very much real, as Excalibur emerged from the fountain before both of them, suspended in mid-air.

"You can't be serious!" Sébastien exclaimed, shock displayed as he whirled to her. He remembered only too well the dragon hilt of the sword, and its previous owner.

"I am."

"This is Arthur's!"

"It was returned to my lake upon his death, and has waited for my command ever since."

"Command?"

Vivienne glanced behind at the druids, ensuring they were still frozen, then hastily explained, "As Lady of the Lake, I forged this blade in mourning of Alistair and all that had been lost, to give hope for the future. Its strength comes from me, and the faith of its wielder. Excalibur will go to whomever I command it to, but it will only truly belong to a strong, true heart of light and fairness."

"I can't—"

"Try, Sébastien! Just *try!*" Vivienne implored, staring straight into his eyes. "You have nothing to lose."

Sébastien read her features, saw her unfailing belief in him, and acquiesced tightly. "Alright, my lady. Bless me," he murmured, kneeling at her feet.

Vivienne held Excalibur flat on her palms, facing upwards. *Please accept him,* she begged silently. *He has done right by me.*

Out loud, she declared, "Sébastien Dubois, with the power vested in me as Lady of the Lake, I hereby offer you Excalibur to be your companion in battle, as defender and ally. Do you accept?"

"I do, my lady."

Sébastien looked up in her eyes, and so many vibes passed between them in that one moment. The past was more present than ever, as they both recalled the first time they met, and the first oath he had pledged.

His gaze then fell to the blade, and he hesitantly reached for it. When his hand grasped it, nothing happened. Sébastien wrapped it firmly around the hilt, and unsheathed the sword in one smooth movement.

Two things happened. First, everything and everyone was

in motion again. Second, a whoosh of air escaped from the weapon, passing the two lovers, and lacerating the warlocks like a whip. Their eyes met in mirrored shock – the druids were now on the ground, pulverized.

Sébastien stood, weighing Excalibur in his grip, afraid he could not wield it. But when he swung it around, it weighed no more than a feather, as though it had been created for him alone.

"How is this possible?" he murmured.

Vivienne touched his arm, and the knight peered in her beautiful green eyes. "Having a heart of light and fairness implies sometimes doing things no one else likes, to serve the side of good. You have brought me back at a huge cost to yourself, and Excalibur grasps this. Ultimately, this proves you have cleansed yourself, Sébastien. Now, light can truly be served when we fight Carleigh."

The champion swung the blade again, relishing as it sang in his hands. He then looked to where Alistair, now unfrozen, was circling Carleigh. A group of eager conjurers approached, but the lovers were still under the security of the shield.

Sébastien turned to Vivienne, eyes blazing with determination and a fierce hunger to get involved. "Are you ready to jump back in?"

She inclined her head in assent, and stirred a hand in a wave to remove the barrier. The minute she did, dark magic began flying at them from all corners, courtesy of the warlocks.

Vivienne moved in a section near Alistair, while Sébastien went to the other side, ready to jump in and get rid of the necromancer once and for all. The demon dog, meanwhile, was busy focusing on Carleigh and his new weapon, dismayed at the evil coming from it.

What the hell have you done?

"Oh, this?" Carleigh smirked, swinging it in the air to better show off. "A little gift to myself. It was not easy, of course, to conjure this much black magic. But in the end, I was able to find some lost souls to sacrifice."

So that is the source of the blood I smell, Alistair growled. It made sense Carleigh had found some innocents to sacrifice, all the better to create a weapon of destruction. The metal itself reeked of an obscurity he had only felt in the underworld. He know, without a doubt, it could poison whomever with a single blow.

"Come at me, demon dog," Carleigh cackled. "Or are you afraid?"

Alistair hesitated, eyeing the sword.

It had a full metal hilt, and caught the sun's blazing rays, turning them into darkness. The blade itself was made out of Damascus steel, with a red velvet strap wrapping. The pommel had a silver snake coiled around it, and as Carleigh slashed it, its onyx eyes glinted maliciously.

The dog clenched his jaw, attempting to figure out the best way to remove it out of the sorcerer's hands. The only solution he could think of would lead to him being harmed, and out of commission.

So be it.

Alistair glanced to the side, where Vivienne defended herself against the attackers with bright beams of fire. He then threw a look to his other side, and did a double take. Sébastien was wielding a sword, and it was –

Is that what I think it is?

Sébastien met his gaze for a moment, grinning, before focusing back on his opponents.

Alistair did his doggy laugh, then lunged at a bewildered Carleigh, slamming into the sorcerer hard enough to throw him off balance and to the ground. The demon dog then went for his throat, but the blade cut into him, seeping darkness and paralyzing most of his canine body.

Carleigh pushed Alistair's limp form off him and got up, dusting his robes. The druids were keeping Sébastien occupied, and he was about to head for Vivienne.

Except, the glint of the metal in Sébastien's hands caught his eye, and he froze. The damn knight now swung Excalibur!

Disregarding his replaceable men, Carleigh evaporated. This was not a battle he was willing to fight – yet.

* * *

At the sudden lack of malevolent energy behind her, Vivienne glanced away from her disintegrating enemies. Carleigh was gone, but a furry mass was left sprawled on the ground.

"Sébastien! Alistair's hurt!"

The enchantress ran to him, throwing the protective barrier around them both. With a trembling hand, she touched his bleeding wounds, gasping at the amount of blood already lost.

"Alistair," Vivienne sobbed, her bottom lip quivering.

He groaned and opened his eyes – they were pitch black, cold and unfeeling, with none of the usual warmth Vivienne was used to. Noticing her, Alistair snarled viciously, foam dripping at the corner of his jaws. She realized that whatever was in the blade had affected him, much like the arrows with Sébastien in the past.

The enchantress placed one hand up in a supplicating gesture, and with the other she put the dog under a sleeping spell. Due to his massive form and magic wielded, it would not contain Alistair for long, but it would be enough to complete his healing.

"Sébastien!"

At Vivienne's cry, the champion redoubled his efforts, swinging Excalibur swiftly and slicing through the remaining conjurers. Once they dissipated, he approached Vivienne and the barrier.

"Carleigh cut Alistair with his poisoned blade," she explained, lowering the shield to allow him entrance. "It's done something to him, but I can reverse it if I bring him to the same lake where we went, to heal and purify him. Meet us there, please, I don't think I can dematerialize all of us at once."

Sébastien nodded, pulled her in for a rapid, arduous kiss that left her breathless, then jogged to the Jag.

Vivienne emptied her mind and grasped Alistair's fur. She bent over the dog, eyes shut tight, and pictured the lake clearly in her mind. She opened them and looked around only when the smell of the battle was replaced with that of grass, and the nearness of the lake strengthened her.

Despite the sun up in the sky now, no one was around the secluded spot. The enchantress dragged Alistair in the lake, placing an incantation to keep him afloat and sheltered. Afterwards, she directed the element to surround the dog in a cocoon, where the droplets would pour on him, be reabsorbed as poisonous and purified, until he was fully cleansed.

She sat on the side bank, watching the tendrils of darkness seep out of him. Less than an hour later, Sébastien entered the forest, a hand clasped oddly behind his back.

Vivienne got up and ran into his arms, enjoying the secure feeling she got when he wrapped his arm around her waist to pull her closer. Pressing her lips against his neck, she whispered, "Thank the fates you're unhurt!"

She drew back for a moment, searching Sébastien's features. He seemed like himself, but the nagging doubt could not be pushed away. "Where's your sword?"

Sébastien's brow furrowed for a split second, before smoothing. He lifted Excalibur for her perusal, having held it hidden all along.

"I was afraid Carleigh might have gotten to you," Vivienne whispered, relaxing against his hard muscle.

"I'm fine," Sébastien replied, and dropped Excalibur to the ground.

Peering down at Vivienne, the glint in his eyes changed from soft to predatory. The young woman's body responded, melting against his. She tilted her head up, begging for his lips.

Sébastien's hand fisted in her long, dark locks, placing her head just so, before his mouth descended with a vengeance. The kiss was arduous and urgent, full of unrestrained fervor, much as in her heated memories.

Vivienne moaned against his mouth and Sébastien picked her up in his arms, walking to the nearest tree. Her back against it, Sébastien at the front, he quickly got their clothes out of the way, and slid inside her within minutes.

Vivienne gasped against his mouth at the sheer pleasure of it, groaning when he paused. She wrapped her legs around him, dragging him closer, pressing her mouth to his ear. "Don't stop," she pleaded.

With a groan, Sébastien buried his head against her neck and lost the last remnants of his self-control.

* * *

Much later, fully clothed to protect against the chillier evening, Vivienne was lying against Sébastien, by a tree.

"This is what you were avoiding that one time, in the past," she murmured, finally working it out.

"Yes." Sébastien grinned sexily, remembering the time he had come back from battle, and the princess had healed him.

"I'm glad you didn't hold back this time," Vivienne admitted, stretching her pleasured body against his.

Something stirred above the lake, and she got up hastily. Sébastien followed her to the edge of the lake, and they watched in silence as their companion awoke.

Alistair, unaware yet of their presence, slowly got up in the cocoon. Glancing at his surroundings, he growled low, then started barking furiously.

"Alistair?" Vivienne whispered.

He stopped mid-snarl and contemplated them for a few breath-stopping moments, before finally rumbling, *Are you going to explain to me why I am being washed in a flying ball of water?*

Vivienne laughed in relief, and moved her wrist, allowing

the magic to release him. The bubble surrounding the dog popped like a balloon and he swam to shore, shaking his fur once on dry land.

"Carleigh's sword cut you and–"

Poisoned me, Alistair finished for Vivienne. He surveyed the lake, then his mistress. *Thank you for bringing me back, highness.*

"It was the least I could do."

Alistair concentrated on Sébastien. *If you can wield Excalibur, it is safe to admit your road to redemption is all but finished.*

"What do you mean?" the knight frowned, glancing at Vivienne. For all response, she chewed her lip guiltily, avoiding his eyes.

If you had not been pure enough of heart, your touch – and swinging, and handling – would have destroyed Excalibur, Alistair divulged.

Sébastien's jaw dropped, gaping at his beloved. "You *knew* this?"

Vivienne's sheepish smile was an answer on its own.

"And if Arthur ever came back?"

Vivienne stared at Sébastien for a moment, before recalling his other two lifetimes – of course he would be aware of the old king's return. She shrugged in response to the query. "I would have forged him another sword."

The champion's midnight eyes bore into hers for a moment, and she tried to decode any annoyance. In the end, Sébastien only grinned, and pulled her to him.

"Thank you," he whispered in her ear. "I will never, in this entire lifetime or the next, be able to express to you how grateful I am."

Eyes shining, Vivienne murmured, "You can keep trying – for lifetimes on end, my love."

At the risk of interrupting this sappy moment, they both turned to Alistair at the half reproachful tone, *there is the other matter of how Vivienne got you the sword. While I fought Carleigh, I sensed a shift in the time momentum.*

"The *what?*" Sébastien chuckled, throwing an amused glance to the enchantress.

Time itself, Alistair explained with a roll of the eyes. *It is an old term I used as a deity, in a long ago past. It describes time itself, as well as the different dimensions and reactions.*

Vivienne shrugged, mumbling, "How was I supposed to guess time would stop with one tiny incantation?"

She was relieved when Alistair chortled, *Majesty, you will never cease to amaze me.*

They decided to spend the rest of the day in the wilderness, to recover from the morning's events.

CHAPTER 25

Vivienne let the last of the water drop in the pool, and retreated inside the house. She noticed Sébastien's eyes on her from the living room, and knew Alistair must be back.

Three days had come and gone since their last battle, and they had spent it sparring, both physically and magically, to prepare for the next one. Meanwhile, Alistair was desperately making an effort to pick up Carleigh's scent on independent excursions throughout the city. He had become hell-bent on making the sorcerer pay, and it worried her.

Vivienne took her time heading back in, and felt her lover's presence before she got to the back door where he was waiting. Her heartbeat quickened as Sébastien scanned her up and down, his eyes scorching. Without a word, he bent his mouth to hers, lips an inch away, body deliciously close, a reminder of their morning activities.

As she peered up at him, Sébastien's mouth tilted in a sexy grin. It only took one lick of her lips, and he took control, taking her on a teasing journey.

When they came up for air later, Vivienne was left clutching his shoulders, her body melting closer. Sébastien rested his forehead against hers, and the young woman placed a hand to his cheek.

They remained like that, breathing each other in for a few minutes, before the knight drew away, and the smile died off his lips.

"Alistair is back," Sébastien mentioned with a slight hesitation.

"How is he?"

"You'll see for yourself." He took her hand and pulled her inside.

Alistair was on the couch, staring intently at something on the table. Vivienne headed nearer, locking gazes when he lifted his head at her approach. Sébastien hovered by the entrance, giving them some privacy.

Highness, I may have found something.

"Before you show me," Vivienne placed a hand on his mane and tugged on his ear for attention, "we have to talk."

It is a good lead—

"Alistair, I insist."

The dog bowed his head in submission.

"You've been fixated on finding Carleigh. Though I admire your perseverance, we cannot afford to go on our own vendettas. He might get to us because of our blindness."

Alistair stared back, fighting an internal battle. Vivienne understood his quest was as much about wounded pride, as to ensure the sorcerer would never hurt anyone again. However, the risks he was taking sank in, and the dog placed one paw in her lap with an enormous sigh.

You are right, majesty. I have let my fury cloud my judgment. My first duty is to protect you, like your champion does.

Vivienne took the huge paw in her own hands. "We *will* get him, Al. And he'll pay for what he did to all of us. But I don't want to lose you, not ever again."

Alistair nodded in understanding, ears bent low on his head in contrition. He then turned back to the table, and Vivienne followed his gaze.

There was a poster the size of a normal page, which Guinevere – back when she was still Jennifer – had left there a while back. It had a picture of a man and a woman dressed in medieval costumes, and her friend had mentioned it was a masquerade event she wanted to attend.

"Knights in shining armor and damsels in distress," Vivienne mumbled out loud, recalling Guinevere's words.

"What?" Sébastien frowned, focusing on to the table as well.

"Guinevere left this here," Vivienne said without taking her eyes from the poster. "She said I had to go, and was quite insistent on it. She told me with knights and damsels in distress, what's there not to love?"

That is where he will be, Alistair declared surely.

"Carleigh? But why?"

He intends to cause chaos. And after losing so many druids, it is where he plans to bring more over. His strength comes from evil and death, and a room full of innocent bystanders is the perfect sacrifice for those vile souls.

"Why not a mall, or anywhere else where it's easier to get an invitation than some posh party for snobs?" Sébastien enquired. At his beloved's mockingly outraged look, he cringed, recalling she was, as a matter of fact, one of them by birth – both in the past and present. "Sorry, love. You get what I mean."

Carleigh has a flair for the dramatic, Alistair said instead. His mistress' life was not something he would risk – no matter the consequences for his own soul.

What I gathered from Guinevere's mind as she died, is that he was planning to lure Vivienne somewhere to create a false reality, imprisoning her within her own mind. Considering that is no longer an option, as you have regained your memories, I am of the opinion he intends it to confuse you.

"To what end?" Vivienne's brow furrowed. "I'm still not following."

Sébastien's hand touched her shoulder, and she glanced up at him. "I think I get where Alistair is going with this. Carleigh's hate for royalty reincarnated with him. The people attending this party will be among the city's richest – and most perfidious. It's a debauchery in the making, not some classy affair."

The knight met Alistair's unflinching gaze, and backed away, pacing as the words tumbled in a frenzy. "Think about it. All the greed, lust, madness, despair, envy . . . These are all emotions that contribute to darkness. Since we last beat him, Carleigh needs a conduct to open the portal. It's the most negative energy he can get in one place – way better than any market, mall or otherwise public place, where innocents foster."

Vivienne stood up, clenching her fists. "We have to go and stop him. It's no longer just a matter of our lives in danger; we have to defend these people!"

She could hear the wheels rolling at the back of Sébastien's mind, before he inclined his head in assent. "Alright, but we have to be careful. You and I have to be in constant contact."

"It shouldn't be too hard, considering we've been working on our bond," Vivienne grinned, standing up. "Go check out the place, get a layout if you want. The location is a villa on the border of the city. Alistair and I have to go and find us both costumes."

With a quick kiss, she headed out the door, closely followed by the dog.

* * *

The masquerade party was ongoing. Vivienne's dress, of an emerald green the color of her eyes, had a corset tightening her waist, and flowed fully and sensually down her legs, all the way to her ankles.

It was slightly puffy, like a princess gown, though the satin and lace it was made out of gave it a more whimsical flow. The only embroidery was around the heart shaped corset of the bust, but the off the shoulder straps gave it a romantic air.

Vivienne had chosen to let her hair loose and wavy, the long inky locks shiny in the candlelight, and wear a simple emerald necklace, with tear-drop earrings of the same color. The silver half-mask she wore hid the top part of her features, but her gaze shone bright with the silver eye shadow used.

The villa itself had a great ballroom, where over two hundred guests were twirling to the sound of music. All had various costumes, some from the seventeenth century, and others even earlier on. Most attendees wore masquerade masks of all colors – full, half masks, death masks, Venetian masks.

Sébastien, having chosen a spot on the balcony above, had a perfect view of the dance floor, as well as the entrance. His idea of a knight costume, to blend in with the décor, had been a more medieval version of Prince Charming – a thin white chemise, and black everything: pants, boots, and a vest. Excalibur was at his hip, now in a proper leather sheath.

The knight could understand why Carleigh had chosen this particular place to bring Vivienne – it oddly made their situation even more unrealistic. He had no choice but to watch as his beloved danced with various partners, never alone for too long.

I don't like this. Sébastien muttered telepathically. Their connection had been growing stronger each day, and now he was able to communicate without straining himself.

Is Carleigh here? Vivienne shot back, while attempting to concentrate on the dance steps with her current partner.

No. A pause. *But that guy's about to lose his hands if he doesn't watch himself.*

Vivienne bit back a laugh, liking that Sébastien was fully focused on protection, and not fighting. Issuing warnings first was much better than impulsively attacking.

If I'm to bait Carleigh, I have to put on a good show, she shot back.

Sébastien's reply was swift, and Vivienne had confirmation he was still watching. *I get it.* Another pause. *I still don't like it.*

It is our less risky plan, knight, Alistair chimed in. *Now all we have to do is wait until Carleigh makes an appearance.*

* * *

An hour later, Vivienne was getting aggravated. She backed out of her new partner's arms, excusing herself to go freshen up, and left as if the hounds of hell were on her heels.

The short stroll to the bathroom was more demanding on her feet than she had imagined. Luckily, the inside was empty, and the young woman was able to breathe quietly for a few moments. Too many innuendos and flirting had contributed to a nasty headache, and still nothing to show for it – no druids, and especially no Carleigh.

Vivienne finished freshening up and placed the mask back on, heading outside. She had barely entered the hallway when someone grabbed her from behind, and she twirled into a familiar embrace.

The enchantress peered up into Sébastien's face. He was positively pissed, and she could not blame him, considering the amount of flirtations he must have observed throughout the evening.

The knight maneuvered Vivienne into the closest alcove, where they were shielded only by dimness and wall, and his body blocked hers from anyone's view. Half out of breath, she raised her gaze to his features, but Sébastien proceeded to kiss her as though they had been apart for ages.

Vivienne gave in, body relaxing against his, pressing closer still. Minutes later, they parted for air and she gasped, "Not that I'm complaining, but what the hell, Sébastien?"

"I couldn't stay away anymore," the knight admitted, voice strained as though barely controlling himself. "It was killing me. I had to get close to you."

Vivienne was about to say something, but with one hand Sébastien grasped her hips, pulled her closer, and with the other removed the half-mask. It fluttered to the floor like a forgotten dream, and the enchantress wrapped her arms around his neck, melting as they embraced again. This time, there was no stopping.

When she teasingly bit his lip, Sébastien groaned into the kiss, and got carried away, reassuring himself she was well and unscathed. All he yearned for was to take Vivienne out of there, away from harm. Yet all his body craved was closeness and contact.

* * *

Vivienne twirled with the latest partner, and came back to a different set of arms, eyes widening when they fell upon Sébastien. "What are you—?"

He drew her close and without another word, shut her up with his lips. She was about to give in, as always, but something weird stirred her instincts. The gleam in Sébastien's gaze as he pulled her in had not been burning in intensity, but cold.

Realizing the trickery, Vivienne opened her mouth under his, but only to better bite down on the unfamiliar lips. The man disengaged immediately, cursing, and the illusion faltered. With a push of the enchantress' own magic, his true features were revealed.

"Carleigh!" Vivienne hissed, keeping her voice low. "You should know better."

Thankfully, despite the unfolding drama, the guests around them were none the wiser, happily involved in their own dances underneath the candlelight.

Hate glittered in the sorcerer's eyes as he wiped the blood from his lips. "Should I? You think too highly of yourself, princess."

"Let's do this outside," Vivienne pleaded with a hasty glance around, ignoring the jib. "Please. I don't wish the death of innocents."

Carleigh only sneered cruelly, and his gathering, darkening aura indicated he was preparing to attack.

Alistair, Sébastien, Carleigh is here!

Disregarding her, the necromancer closed his eyes and brought his palms together as though in prayer.

There was no reply from Vivienne's lover, but the demon dog was quick to respond. *The humans are in danger. I believe Carleigh is gathering enough strength to obliterate them. You have to save them!*

How? Vivienne panicked.

With a protective spell of sorts. Merlin did it once with Arthur's army, or so he told me. Try envisioning the magic at your command, and ask it to contain your duel.

The enchantress cut the contact, instead concentrating on the enchantment. Much too close to the occult magic at work, she was aware of Carleigh's tenebrous energy, filtering from the shadows surrounding. Closing her eyes, Vivienne pictured a wall circling them both, and wished the incoming events would not harm her fellow humans, but rather contain their duel within, away from their blissfully ignorant selves.

When she blinked, the royal noted a faint barrier all around her and Carleigh. They were, indeed, now stuck in a ring of transparency. She also observed the people around them had stopped moving, frozen as if time itself had stood still.

Vivienne! Alistair's voice was alarmed.

I'm fine.

What happened? It is as if time itself stopped, he echoed her thoughts.

I'm not sure. We can figure it out later. Carleigh's about to attack and I need to focus.

Highness, wait! We cannot come to your help now. The barrier around you is too powerful.

Then find Sébastien, Vivienne pleaded. *And let me know if he's harmed.*

A few moments later, Alistair answered, *Found him. He is only knocked out, but fine otherwise. We are heading coming down.*

Vivienne snapped back to the more pressing matter, just as Carleigh opened his eyes. He noticed the circle, and the immobilized people on the outside, and his smugness slid off. "How the *hell* did you do that?"

The enchantress ignored him, instead defending herself with a thin barrier, and egging him on. "Don't you keep clamoring you're better than me? Let's see it, then. Now's your chance, considering we're as alone as we'll ever be."

Carleigh's scowl was the first indication, right before he shot an orb of witchcraft towards her. It shattered on the barrier, not even harming the young woman.

Vivienne turned her palm upside down, gathering in it some air. When a sphere formed, she flung it towards Carleigh – this time, it shattered on *his* shield.

They circled each other, each trying to find a weakness to pounce on.

* * *

On the outside of the barrier, Alistair arrived with Sébastien at his side. They watched, helpless, as Carleigh and Vivienne faced off, throwing rounds of light and dark magic. On both sides, the energies ended up destroyed, without ever attaining their targets.

Sébastien looked around in amazement at the frozen people, recalling the same situation happening when Excalibur was gifted to him. "Did Vivienne do this?"

Yes, the demon dog retorted, barely sparing a glance towards them, concentrated only on the fight. *Time momentum shifted again. The first time, with Excalibur, was a mistake. This is intentional – of her magic, at least. I'm unsure the princess realized what she was doing.*

When he spared the knight a glance and noticed his focused attention still on the humans, Alistair growled. *Forget them! I am more concerned about the sheer amount of power Vivienne is using now. We have to get in there and help her.*

Sébastien turned his focus towards Carleigh, attempting to guess his tactics and search for a weakness. He was beginning to despair, when a pattern emerged: whenever the necromancer would pause to gather and throw another curse, there was a delay of a few seconds.

"Alistair," the guardian voiced his concern out loud, "I think neither of them can attack without dropping their barrier. But Vivienne is using the raw energy within her. Carleigh isn't. There's a delay whenever he throws his dark magic, almost as if he has to search elsewhere to get it."

Pondering his words, Alistair examined the sorcerer and noticed the same thing. *You are correct. It must be a price of the darkness he is in bed with. Or . . .* The dog trailed off, then peered closer. *Could it be he is converting Vivienne's?*

At Sébastien's confusion, he added, *Each time Vivienne uses her pure energy, it has a negative counterpart. Normally, it would flow back into the earth and disperse, but if Carleigh figured out how to use it, he will end up exhausting her before long.*

"How can we stop him?"

We cannot. I can see nothing with my senses past Vivienne's barrier, so I cannot confirm this. But she could.

With the cryptic answer, the dog turned his thoughts to the mistress. *Highness, you have a problem.*

* * *

Once Alistair shared their theory with her, Vivienne created a small orb of light in the palm of her hand. It was a trick Merlin had once taught her, to use a shard of pure magic to see past anyone's treacherous intentions.

With the other hand, she projected a larger orb towards

Carleigh, as a distraction. As soon as his attention was diverted, Vivienne raised the small orb of clarity in front of her eyes, and looked through it as with a looking glass.

As the larger orb travelled from the enchantress to her enemy, she saw the few sparks of obscurity that escaped it, and followed their progress. They ended up absorbed by Carleigh's own aura.

Damn him to hell, but you guys are right! Vivienne communicated to both protectors, getting rid of the small orb as Carleigh destroyed the larger one, not noticing the subterfuge. *How do I stop it?*

You cannot, Alistair explained. *Every spell you use has a counterpart, so there is no filtering yours to avoid this. The only thing you could do is rather than use your raw magic, attempt to use one of the elements. They only have one energy, whereas your spiritual magic has both positive and negative. Begin with something powerful.*

Sensing nothing nearby to drag to her, Vivienne decided to use her second best element. She had not used it since her previous life, and the failed attempts back home were not encouraging, but an effort had to be made.

Though her abilities were not yet at their best when using elemental enchantments, the enchantress had to trust in fire. Due to its purifying nature, fire only had one solid balance, suggesting the sorcerer would not have anything to counter it.

With that in mind, Vivienne focused on the candlelight around the ballroom and drew it to her. Soon, she was surrounded by multiple spheres, each no larger than a fist, flaming wildly. Carleigh stopped his incessant attack to frown, aware of the shift in the atmosphere.

Vivienne launched the fireballs towards him, one after the other. The first scattered on his shield, but the second went past and hit the sorcerer in the shoulder, incinerating the cloak material. As he tried to put it out, another one struck his opposite shoulder, also inflaming it.

"Damn you!" Carleigh yelled and dematerialized from the circle, realizing the fight was lost.

The minute he disappeared, Vivienne dropped the barrier and turned to her companions. "I won't be able to keep them here for much longer," she pointed to the frozen humans. "I'm going to guess that since he left, Carleigh has given up on this particular sacrifice. Get out and I'll meet you at the back."

Sébastien hesitated, but Alistair was already edging away, *She is right, no point in the humans seeing us.*

The knight stepped to exit, but kissed Vivienne quickly, and thoroughly. "Be safe," he urged against her lips, his voice rough with affection. Having his beloved in harm's way, and out of sight, was slowly giving him an ulcer.

Vivienne nodded and waited until they were gone. She replaced the candlelight she had stolen, thanking fire for its help. Then, she moved away from the center of the dance floor behind one of the pillars, preferably wanting to avoid anyone witness her magic.

Once hidden from their eyes, the enchantress elevated her palms. She caught hold of the barrier of time and nudged it in its rightful pace. In a half moment, the music was back, the dancing continued, and no one paid any notice to the lonely woman in the shadows.

Vivienne was about to depart, making her way to the back exit. She had barely gotten up a few stairs when her vision blurred. Holding onto the wall for support became a necessity, as was stopping to catch her breath.

When the walls stopped spinning, the young woman advanced some more. The minute she stepped away, the ground seemed to get closer. A strong pair of arms caught Vivienne right before she hit the floor.

"I got you," Sébastien murmured and picked her up bridal style, carrying her to the Jag where Alistair waited impatiently in the backseat.

What happened? The dog sniffed his mistress' unconscious body, scanning her with his abilities.

Sébastien placed Vivienne in the passenger seat, put the seatbelt on, and got in the driver's seat. "She must have used a lot of power."

Alistair was silent as they took off, watching his mistress' peaceful form.

I have only ever met one human who could agitate the barriers of time as she has done twice now, he revealed to Sébastien.

"Who?"

Merlin.

Sébastien glanced up in the rear-view mirror to the dog. "Are you saying her supernatural skills are to par with Merlin's?"

No. At his confused frown, Alistair added, *I am saying Vivienne is* more *powerful. Once she sharpens the edges and truly masters her powers, my mistress will be a force to be reckoned with.*

The knight was silent, letting the words sink in. He had always known Vivienne was strong and influential, but now he was confronted with the reality of their destiny. They would never have a normal life, a family. She would be in danger from whoever would seek to challenge or use her – and he would always be guarding her.

Sébastien glanced at his beloved's dormant form, then set his eyes on the road. *Any life with Vivienne is better than one without her,* he mused resolutely.

Alistair, who had been following his thoughts, spoke, *Are you sure about that? This will be a decision you cannot change halfway through without consequences.*

"I loved Vivienne in the past when she was a royal," Sébastien answered out loud. "I fell in love with her again as a normal girl. And my heart still beats as one for her now, no matter how strong she becomes. I will stand by and defend her, as I always have."

Then you truly deserve her, knight. Vivienne has given you the one gift she has to give unconditionally – her heart.

Their gazes locked in the mirror.

"I will guard it forever," Sébastien vowed.

Be it so. The menace was left unspoken in Alistair's words.

The Jag pulled into a country road and after a few detours, ended up in front of a cabin by the river Rhône. Alistair was the first one out, checking the grounds for intruders and setting a protective shield around the perimeter.

"No one is aware we're here," Sébastien informed him. "We'll be safe."

He carried Vivienne inside, placing her on the bed. He undid the corset, and left on the chemise she had under the dress, covering her with a blanket.

The enchantress' eyes fluttered open, glazed with the drowsiness of dreams. "Another surprise?"

Sébastien got lost in her beautiful green stare, his body responding to the unspoken invitation within. However, he settled for kissing her forehead. "Rest, my love, and recharge."

"Stay with me."

"I'm here," he reassured her and climbed into bed, holding Vivienne until she fell asleep once more.

* * *

Sébastien woke up with a start half an hour later, only to discover the noise he had heard was Alistair entering the cabin. His fist unclenched from Excalibur's hilt – placed by the bed for easy access – and he dropped it back to the ground. Alistair went and settled by the fireplace, where he could have the best view of the entrance.

Vivienne shifted in her lover's arms, drowsy, "What's wrong?"

"Nothing, Alistair woke me up. Go back to sleep."

She stretched, her delicious curves pressing closer. Sébastien gulped at the stirring of his blood, but with a huge force of effort ignored his body's insistent demands. Instead, he focused on the enchantress' solid heartbeat.

"Where are we?" Vivienne wondered, blinking tiredly.

"One of my safe houses." At her confusion, he added, "From my time with Tony. They're off the radar. We can loosen up while we recharge to better attack."

Vivienne's only response was to cuddle further into him. Sébastien held her in silence for a few moments, but the uneasy question slipped past his lips.

"Love, I've been meaning to ask . . ."

"Hmm?"

"Maybe you should talk to Merlin."

Vivienne's entire body tensed and she tried to draw away from him, but Sébastien tightened his hold on her. "Hang on, hear me out."

"No. He's done enough harm."

"Vivienne–"

"I said no."

Even in the dimness of the cabin, Sébastien saw the flash of her eyes. He waited apprehensively.

If I were you, I would drop it, Alistair suggested.

"Alright," Sébastien sighed, realizing the dog was right. "I'm sorry I brought it up."

Vivienne relaxed, and dozed off again. Listening to her breathing slow back into a relaxed slumber, Sébastien felt awake, but his lids grew unnaturally heavy just the same.

* * *

It was not a normal nightmare he fell into, rather in a semi-radiant cave.

"I'm happy to see you, Sébastien."

The guardian was not even surprised to hear the wizard's voice. "What is it with you and caves, old man?"

"I like the solitude," Merlin's eyes twinkled, for once not reproachful.

"No kidding."

They were silent, eyeing each other. The old man's

countenance changed as he noticed the blade for the first time. Sébastien peered down to notice Excalibur on his hip, even whilst asleep.

"You wield Excalibur?"

Sébastien frowned at Merlin's shocked tone. "No need to sound so amazed."

"Let me see."

With a roll of his eyes, Sébastien unsheathed Excalibur and lifted it up, swinging it a couple of times and slicing the empty air, as though blocking blows. He stopped shortly, feeling silly and on display. "I'd rather keep my strength for the real battle, if it's all the same to you."

When only silence answered, the knight faced Merlin once more. The old man was flabbergasted, tears running down his cheeks. Sébastien was sure the confusion was now mirrored on his face.

"Merlin, what–"

To his utter astonishment, the wizard moved closer. When they were but a few feet apart, the mage bowed low to Sébastien. "I would kneel, but these old bones won't stand the pain."

"Merlin, it's not necessary—"

"I was wrong, Sébastien, I can admit that now. Not only have you helped Vivienne, but you fought your own darkness to become the kind of leader Arthur wanted to leave behind – a just and loyal man."

Sébastien was stunned as the words sank in. "You still serve him, after all these years?"

"I do."

The knight assessed the wizard's expression, trying to see

if it was another trick. When he only detected sincerity in his blue eyes, he extended his hand. Merlin shook it, and Sébastien pulled him in a half-hug.

"You are forgiven, Merlin. At least by me. But we both know it's not my forgiveness you need."

His blue eyes shone with unshed tears. "I have tried, but Vivienne refuses to meet me, and has blocked me from her mind."

"Let me make an effort. I know, before long, she will need your guidance to prepare for the final fight with Carleigh."

"Why do you say this?" the wizard frowned. "She is strong in her own right."

"Yes, and able to win against Carleigh, which happened for the second time today. However, the bastard was using her own spells against her."

"The opposite energies created," Merlin muttered, frowning. "How did he learn to do that?"

"As he learned all things," Sébastien shrugged. "Sorcery, the druids, who can fathom? The important thing is that Vivienne has all the weapons at her disposal to beat him. I will not lose her again."

"I understand," Merlin nodded. "And I agree. Has she used elemental magic?"

"Yes, but that's where you come in. A large portion of her enchantments come as instinct, and Vivienne is marvelous at using them. But she will need more tactics than what she currently is capable of."

The old mage exhaled, deeply regretting having lost his former pupil's trust. "I will do my best when the time comes.

Alistair can get in contact with me, as he usually does."

With one last shake of hands, the dream dissipated, and Sébastien woke up.

In the shadows, Alistair lifted his head, peering closely at him. He sniffed the air, growling low when he recognized the scent. *Merlin's aura surrounds you, knight.*

"We had words in the realm of dreams," Sébastien whispered, trying not to wake Vivienne. "And I've forgiven him for his unnecessary meddling."

You have proven more lenient than the old mage deserves, the dog disclosed wonderingly. *It is quite a change from a few days ago.*

Sébastien chuckled, albeit a bit grimly. With a glance at his beloved, he murmured, "Perhaps. But Vivienne needs Merlin's guidance, you know it as well as I do."

Alistair's silence was his agreement.

CHAPTER 26

Vivienne woke up to an empty bed, Sébastien gone. She got up and dressed in jeans and a t-shirt she found in the closet – thankfully, the safe house seemed to be packed with necessities.

She stepped out into the morning air, breathing in deeply. Getting out of the city had been a good idea, both to draw Carleigh out, but also to come up with a plan he would not foresee coming.

There were noises farther off, and she advanced in their direction, beaming when her eyes fell on a certain knight. Under the rising sun, Sébastien was wielding Excalibur and training his body. He was evidently less tormented, his movements as fluid and feral now as they had been in the past.

Good job, princess.

Vivienne was so lost in her thoughts, that Alistair's words

made her jump.

You did it.

"I only played a part," she whispered timidly. "Sébastien and Excalibur did the rest."

Well then . . . Alistair stood up, as though leaving.

"Where are you going?"

To see what your champion's fighting skills are like after all these years.

Before she could add anything, he lunged, his massive paws pounding the ground. Alistair swiftly crossed the distance down, approaching Sébastien from behind, silent as a wolf. Vivienne was about to cry a warning, but she figured Alistair would never hurt her lover . . .

Would he?

* * *

Sébastien had felt Vivienne nearby, but willed himself to keep training. Allowing distraction would mean getting back in bed, making up for lost time, and it was essential he be ready for Carleigh.

It was moments later, as he concentrated on training, that a different presence came his way. Excalibur hummed warningly in Sébastien's hands and he gripped it harder, whirling around while slashing the air vertically. Alistair jumped out of the way, but a patch of his long fur still floated to the ground from where the sword had sliced it.

They stared at each other for a beat, then Alistair opened his big mouth in a doggie grin. *Let's see what you are capable of, knight.*

He lunged again, and Sébastien blocked. The dog's teeth, fortified by his demon force, hit the blade. He tried to remove it out of Sébastien's hands, but the knight yanked it away in time.

On and on they went at it. Alistair offered brutal force with spells here and there, while Sébastien blocked them with Excalibur, avoiding multiple attacks at once. Vivienne sat on a rock, enjoying their sparring. The perils of the outside world faded away, and all that mattered was the moment of peace they existed in.

Eventually, Alistair grew tired of losing patches of fur. He bowed his head to Sébastien, then addressed Vivienne. *He is definitely ready.*

The enchantress grinned at Sébastien, well aware of his ever-burning stare. She sensed the magnetism of the not-so-distant past, but willed herself to snap back to reality as she approached them.

Sébastien tugged her to him, and what Vivienne imagined would be a gentle peck was in fact a deep kiss, a promise of more. They withdrew away at Alistair's annoyed bark and sheepishly peered down.

Happy as I am for you two, highness, there is still something you must do before you battle with Carleigh.

"What are you referring to?"

Contacting Merlin.

She frowned, not intent to be baited into it. "I couldn't even if I was interested. I cannot reach him."

That is not true. You were able to speak to him when you needed help.

"You did?" Sébastien questioned.

"Yes," Vivienne admitted, "for you." Addressing Alistair, she scowled, "I have not forgiven him."

But you have to, majesty, for this. Unless you prefer Carleigh to be truly killed.

"Why shouldn't he be?" Sébastien growled. "After all he's done, I'll be happy to behead him myself."

Vivienne noted Alistair's warning look, and shook her head in defeat. "I will not have that the consequences of such an act fall on you. The right thing to do is to neutralize and imprison Carleigh, which is something only Merlin has the power and means for. Alright," she sighed, "you win, Alistair. What do I do?"

As she suspected, the spell was fairly easy, but the mental burden on her, not so much. Nonetheless, the enchantress inclined her head in agreement. "Give me some time to come to terms with it, and I will eventually do it."

Much as I hate to say it, do not take too long, Alistair warned, then took off and left her and Sébastien alone.

Since he still had her in his arms, Vivienne was none the wiser when the champion gathered her closer, and let himself fall down on the grass. The young woman fell on top of him with a surprised squeak, and met his devilish regard.

Sébastien ran a hand through her hair, then cupped her cheek and brought her lips to his for a soft kiss. Once Vivienne responded, he deepened the embrace, plundering her mouth, hands roaming up and down her body.

Though she enjoyed the make out session, Vivienne soon realized what he was doing, and pulled away.

"You're trying to distract me!" she accused him.

"Is it working?" Sébastien enquired, amused.

Vivienne was about to argue, but he kissed her again. Unable to resist further, she gave in happily.

* * *

Carleigh entered the church and the druids moved away to let him pass. In his hand shone a brass chalice he had finished digging from around the old building's sheds.

The sorcerer went straight to the dark pool and cupped some of the liquid within the cup. He lifted a palm, and circled it over the object once. An orb the color of coal emerged above the chalice. Within it was imprisoned a small speck of good magic, stolen from Vivienne when she had not been paying attention during their duel.

"It's a shame the dog and knight had to ruin my fun," Carleigh muttered aloud to himself, nonplussed at what they deemed a loss. "No matter. I have one last surprise ready."

The necromancer let the orb fall into the chalice, where it was absorbed with a hissing sound by the tenebrous liquid, fizzing and bubbling for long moments.

Carleigh waited until the liquid stopped bubbling, and with his free hand pulled out a ring found in the old priest's chambers, with a ruby stone. He threw the circle of gold in, and the obscurity seeped into it, gathering in the stone, ready to be unleashed again.

When the darkness was fully absorbed in the ring, Carleigh took it out and placed it on his right ring finger. "Merlin can help all he likes, but not even *he* will be able to undo this."

The chalice clattered to the floor and he turned to the pool of darkness. "And now for the final touch."

With a muttered incantation, he breathed a nightmare over it, inciting it to find Vivienne when she was next in the realm of dreams.

* * *

After spending the entire day concocting attack plans and discarding them, Vivienne welcomed the bed with open arms. She anticipated a dreamless rest, but instead found herself dragged into a nightmare.

The young woman was in the middle of a field, a small hill not too far away. The sun was setting, tinting the sky with the color of blood.

Sounds of agony escaped from the top of the hill, the drawling moans of a beast – or person – dying an atrocious death. Vivienne climbed up slowly, but at the sight of a metal gleam, rushed forward.

From her standpoint, she could observe a field littered with bodies of soldiers. The grass had become red-stained with their blood.

"Vivienne . . ."

The groan came again, and this time she noticed Sébastien on the ground, among all the corpses. He was ashen, wearing a knight's armor, and blood flowed from a wound on his side.

"Sébastien!" Vivienne ran over, removing the armor with magic to better examine the wound. It was similar to the one from the boar hunt in the past, when she had healed him.

The knight captured her hand in his, squeezing it, and Vivienne could no longer ignore his dulling eyes. Death was within arm's reach.

"No!"

Vivienne put up her hands above the wound, but no healing enchantment came out. She tried again.

"Carleigh took your magic," Sébastien croaked. "You cannot help me, my love."

"No, I refuse to believe that!" The enchantress shook her head fiercely, tears streaming down her cheeks. She attempted again, searching within for a spark, but nothing responded.

"It's alright, my love," the champion whispered in a resigned tone. "It's time."

"No. I cannot lose you. It's not enough time!"

"We will meet again in the next life . . ."

"Sébastien!"

Vivienne clasped both his hands, and he squeezed back, weakly. Her tears were replaced by trembling, a coldness filling her entire body, anguish at the thought of losing the man she loved.

"Please don't leave me," she sobbed, clutching onto Sébastien.

"I cannot help it."

"Where's Alistair?" Vivienne lifted her head off the knight's chest, but the demon dog was nowhere around. "Alistair!" she yelled, but nothing responded back.

Sébastien gasped in agony. "Alistair . . ." He stopped, gritting teeth against the suffering. "He was hurt by Carleigh's weapon. He's gone, Vivienne . . ."

Fresh tears joined the ones on her cheeks, even as her lips quivered in dismay. "No . . . We cannot have lost."

"My love, I'm sorry. I cannot hold on much longer. I will

see you again, soon." With one last squeeze of her hand, he let go, and closed his eyes.

"Sébastien!"

He did not respond. Vivienne searched within for their connection, the soul mate bond, but only emptiness existed where there had been warmth. A searing pain shot through her, leaving her gasping as though part of her had been cut off, to never be replaced again.

Sébastien was truly gone.

She laid her head down on his chest, heart-wrenching sobs shaking her body.

You can avoid this, a voice came in Vivienne's head, and she froze. *With a truce.*

Wiping at her cheeks, the enchantress threw her head back and screamed in rage at the bloody sky. "Carleigh, you *bastard!*"

* * *

Vivienne woke up, feeling her wet cheeks. Anger overwhelmed the desperation in her nightmare, and she got up from Sébastien's embrace, moving off the bed and outside.

There was no moon out this time, but the myriad of stars were just as calming. Within a few moments, her breathing calmed down and she was able to analyze her options with a clear head.

So Carleigh had managed to get in her sleep, showcasing the worst fear in her soul. That she had lost not only the battle, but Sébastien and Alistair as well. The sorcerer no doubt imagined she would go and ask for a truce, as she had long before.

Vivienne was no naïve young woman, having already fallen for it in the past. Last time, she had lost Alistair – a mistake she was not about to repeat.

Yet upon further reflection, she realized Carleigh's biggest error of judgment was underestimating her, which he had done in previous battles. If she could get close to him, pretend to play his game, it would be possible to use magic and bring him down. Elements had been used once against him, and the enchantress could do it again.

The only problem to the emerging plan was her two companions. Sébastien and Alistair would never agree to such a risk. The best recourse, Vivienne realized, was to do it alone while Carleigh was under the impression his plan had succeeded. It was risky, but if it worked, she could neutralize him and they would all be safe.

The door behind opened and Alistair came out, sniffing the air. *I can faintly smell Carleigh's odor. What happened?*

Vivienne glanced behind, then broke eye contact, "He got in my dream, and tried to scare me. I snapped out of it."

The demon dog watched her closely, sensing she was hiding something.

"I had to clear my head." A pause. "You can go back inside, I'll be there soon."

Alistair did the exact opposite, parking his butt on the porch instead. *I think I would rather wait here for you, majesty, if that is all the same to you.*

Vivienne bit her lip, turning away. There was no way she could depart, not with Alistair standing watch. At the slightest weird action, he would probably wake Sébastien to enlist his help.

There was only one way to go about it, though the young

woman was not proud about it. She hated the option, but if it would save both their lives, it was a necessity.

"I need to meditate," Vivienne mumbled to her protector and knelt down, digging a hand into the ground. To Alistair, it appeared she was almost in a prayer position.

The demon dog had a hunch his mistress was up to something. He tried to breach her mind, and got a hint of her intentions even as the first wave of the sleeping enchantment hit. It was a white mist rising from the ground, which he inhaled before he could stop himself.

Vivienne, you can't! Alistair warned, already wavering on his paws.

"I have to," she insisted in a pleading tone, even as she watched him lie on the ground, the sleeping spell fully taking effect.

It is beyond foolish!

"I can do it, Alistair. Please trust in me."

Once his eyes closed, the enchantress extended the incantation to Sébastien, putting them both under. They would be dozing off for the next few hours, by which time she would be back.

Probably.

With a sigh, Vivienne held her palm up and the car keys flew to her. She got in the Jag and took off, willing herself not to look back.

It would not be hard to find Carleigh if she put herself out there. As she drove, Vivienne deliberately sent a bolt of her light energy ahead as a ball of light, heading for the city.

She had barely crossed the Avignon city line when obscurity pulled towards her, almost like a magnet. In the distance, near the area of the cemetery where they had last fought, a darkened bolt shot up in response, and she headed there.

The area was much creepier in the middle of the night, especially as she was alone. Everything was quiet, not even a cricket nearby, the tombstones glowing eerily in the darkness.

And once more, Carleigh was cocky enough to believe he could handle her himself. Vivienne discovered with a rapid sweep of the grounds that none of his minions were around.

She smirked, got out of the car and approached the abandoned old church. Leaves crumpled under her determined steps, echoing loudly. Vivienne opened the door to the building and stepped in, looking around. The sorcerer stood in front of where the altar would have been, his back to her.

There was something beyond evil witnessing him surrounded by effigies of saints and blessed statues.

"Carleigh," the enchantress greeted coldly.

He whirled around, a cruel grin on his lips. "Welcome, Lady of the Lake."

CHAPTER 27

"You came," the heinous sorcerer smirked, moving closer to Vivienne.

"That was a cheap trick, Carleigh, getting in my dreams."

"Perhaps," he shrugged. "But you're here now. And alone, too, I gather."

"I was not willing to let the people I care about get hurt," Vivienne retorted, ignoring his satisfied expression.

"People?" he snorted. "That demon dog hardly counts as one."

"I guess you wouldn't understand," Vivienne kept a leveled stare, watching him closely. "Now, what is this about a truce? Last time you offered that, it was a trap."

"Water under the bridge, *princess*," Carleigh mocked, and she frowned at the disdain in his voice.

"Hardly. But what is your proposal?"

Carleigh surveyed Vivienne calmly, then with a flick of his wrist ensured the doors behind her were locked. "Surrender your powers to me, and I will let you and your entourage live."

"Not likely."

"Not *likely*?" His eyes narrowed. "Do you not realize how outnumbered you all are?"

"I don't recall that being a problem in the last few fights," Vivienne replied, raising her chin in defiance. "We managed your acolytes just fine."

Displeasure flashed on the necromancer's face, but he rapidly regained control. "It will not last, majesty. Get out while you can."

"Umm . . . how about no?" Vivienne countered. "My turn now. How about *you* give up, and I'll make sure you end in a proper institution?"

"Give up? Me?" Carleigh's laughs were effectively giving her goose bumps. "You obviously do not understand what's at stake here."

"No, I don't quite get a lot of things you do, like killing Guinevere. But then again," Vivienne shrugged, "I don't have your evil mind. All I see is your futile attempts at . . .whatever it is you want to do."

"That's where you're wrong," Carleigh warned, his voice lowering with menace. "I've managed to upset the balance once, and I can do it again."

"Your curse didn't work," Vivienne pointed out frankly, ensuring her features did not give away any emotion – especially fear. "Sébastien and I are together now, and stronger than ever."

"I didn't care about you two," he sneered. "That curse was designed to get me what I needed – time to build on my powers."

Vivienne's eyes narrowed, and her powers reacted at the words. "Let me get this straight. You're admitting the suffering we endured was simply for your own gain?"

"Of course. And it was pleasurable seeing you lost, unaware of where you came from. Guinevere was not my agent from the beginning, but it was easy to get her on board. She was useful . . .for a time."

Vivienne gathered the enchantment in her palms, fueled by her rising agitation. She was aware of the tidal wave within her, taking a life of its own to shelter her.

Carleigh glanced down at the enchantress' hands, unperturbed – as if she would kill him!

"Once this is over," Vivienne gritted out, confirming his suspicions, "I will make it my mission to ensure you are never again free."

"And you will fail," he smirked. "I managed to come back to life despite everything stacked against me. Do you even know how? It's because I knew what the occult could offer me, and I took advantage of it. I even managed to bring back the druids that served me in another age."

"Those men were always bound to you as a consequence of your sorcery," Vivienne spit out. "I grasped that much. They're not back by loyalty."

"Perhaps not, but they do serve my purpose quite well."

"What I don't get, is why you want my magic of all things."

Carleigh tilted his head, peering at Vivienne as though she

were an experiment. The instinct to squirm under the lengthy observation was there, but she willed herself to avoid it.

"To become immortal, both sides of dark and light are required. Surely Merlin showed you."

Vivienne frowned, but kept silent.

"Ah, I see," Carleigh smirked maliciously. "Of course he didn't. He must have regretted everything he taught me. Either way, I do not wish to die anymore, and your powers are the key. Once that is done, I can do whatever I please in this world, including get to my old mentor and serve him some of my vengeance."

"You won't get your way," Vivienne said, "so you might as well go search elsewhere."

He cackled at her words, shaking his head as if he couldn't believe it. "You still haven't realized it, have you?"

"What?" Vivienne's brow furrowed in confusion.

Carleigh's cackle became a snigger at his own private joke. "Oh my. And you believe you're so pure."

"Answer me!" The enchantress ordered, raising her palms, already glowing with the energy forming.

The sorcerer smirked and waited for a beat, building up the tension, before sweetly asking, "Would you hurt your own brother, sister dear?"

Vivienne's eyes widened and she dropped her hand, extinguishing the enchantment in shock. "*What* did you just say!?"

* * *

Sébastien was resting – not quite dreaming – when the

ambiance changed. Much like last time, he got dragged in a meadow where Merlin was waiting, as was Alistair.

"What's going on?" the champion asked.

Alistair jumped to his feet. *Vivienne put us under a sleeping spell.*

"What?" Sébastien glanced from the dog to the wizard, brow furrowed.

She had a nightmare, induced by Carleigh. It affected her, and she got this crazy plan—forget the details, we have to go now!

Sébastien tensed. "Are you saying she somehow charmed us to stay asleep?"

"She did, Sébastien," Merlin intervened. "To save your lives, Vivienne believes she can fight Carleigh on her own, as he underestimates her."

"Merlin, that's crazy!"

"Not so much. I know my pupil well. She is strong, and probably right in this matter. But Carleigh is a master manipulator, and he has a few tricks up his sleeves."

"So wake us up," Sébastien demanded. "Get us back into the real world."

He tried, Alistair growled. *Vivienne put on a strong sleeping enchantment, and we had to be in the same place for him to attempt again.*

Sébastien was about to ask how his beloved's magic was stronger than Merlin's, but recalled his last conversation with Alistair on the subject, and instead said, "Tell me what to do."

"Wait!" Merlin lifted a hand, eyes focused on something in the distance – a future only he could foresee. It lasted for a few moments, before his entire body was overtaken by trembling, and naked fear showed on his face.

"He told her!" the mage uttered in a horrified tone, just loud enough for the knight to hear.

"Told her what?" Both Alistair and Sébastien advanced, but the wizard snapped out of the trance without responding.

"I have no choice. Get out before it's too late. *Now.* Stand back!"

Merlin held up his hands towards the sky, pointing his staff upwards as well. The clouds gathered above, then lightning struck the ground close to him.

Sébastien and Alistair jumped out of the way, startled by nature's anger. The second time it struck, the fire bolt gathered in the staff, where it illuminated the crystal with a roaring blaze.

Merlin studied the tree trunk behind them briefly, then extended his free hand and the staff towards it. The bolt exited the crystal and struck the tree, but instead of combusting, it was transformed into a transparent portal.

Sébastien gaped, having never seen one before – even when Vivienne had teleported them, she had used a different type of enchantment. Portals were used to transport people from one end to another, but only extremely capable and experienced mages could create them. Now, he understood why.

A large hole was where the trunk had been. The color of the sky, it rippled like water. Merlin moved his hand, maneuvering and expanding it to his liking. If he was to let go at the wrong moment, it could explode and send them all to hell.

"Go! Now!" the wizard ordered.

Sébastien glanced to Alistair for guidance.

We have to enter it, the dog instructed. *Concentrate on Vivienne and your bond when you do.*

The knight nodded, and they both headed towards it. Alistair went in first, evaporating within seconds. Sébastien followed him in, focusing on the link between him and Vivienne.

His entire body aflame, he willed his thoughts into a coherent string. Next thing the guardian knew, he was no longer at the cabin nor in the illusion created by Merlin, but in the middle of the cemetery where they had fought the druids.

Excalibur was on the ground by his feet. He picked it up, scanning their new surroundings. Alistair got off the ground, shaking his head.

"What the hell are we doing here?" Sébastien muttered in confusion, before he noticed his empty Jag.

Merlin's idea of expediting the process. Vivienne is in the church with Carleigh, I can feel them both.

"Then let's move!" Tightening his hold on Excalibur, the knight broke into a run towards the church.

* * *

"So let's put it this way," Carleigh persisted through Vivienne's bewilderment. "It's due to our blood bond that no magic but yours will do, sister."

"That's not true," she murmured, referring to their being related.

"Oh, but it is," Carleigh smirked, pacing. "Imagine my dismay when *I* found out. This was after our encounter in

Elsior. Once you died, Merlin and your damn champion managed to overpower me. When I died, things from the past I had not recalled came back to me. Memories that cunning old wizard deliberately blocked so I would not remember everything."

"You are *not* my brother!" Vivienne declared with disgust.

"Well, half-brother, really. But who cares about semantics?"

"It's not true! You're a liar, you always have been!" The young woman fought off her shock, but the glow in her palms dimmed due to her swirling emotions.

Carleigh's expression only showed satisfaction at her despair. "Oh, it's true. I didn't want it to be either, but it couldn't be helped. Maybe had our father, as a youth, learned to keep it in his pants, we wouldn't find ourselves in such a precarious situation."

"Our father?" Vivienne whispered, still unable to wrap her head around the revelation.

"Yes, dear sister, *our* father," Carleigh mercilessly continued. "He had a one night stand with a kitchen maid when he was a teen. When she became pregnant, king Mihail, his father, sent her away. And then our father met your mother, had you, and forgot all about me."

Vivienne attempted to process the history, but there was only one horrific thought looping in her mind. *This psycho is my brother, blood of my blood.*

"Of course," Carleigh continued, "I tried to have my revenge in a few different ways. All I knew at the time was that I wanted those of royal blood to pay. I didn't quite grasp why I hated them. After Merlin figured out I learned the dark arts to take over the kingdom and eradicate the monarchy, he cast me away."

He glowered at Vivienne with hateful eyes. "I tried to curse our father, not realizing who he was, but your damn demon dog kept absorbing the hex, keeping him alive. Then I tried attacking you, and after you got together with that cursed guardian of yours, it was almost impossible to get to you."

"We cannot be related," Vivienne voiced aloud, mainly to herself.

"But we are," Carleigh chortled with the same smugness.

Bile rose in Vivienne's throat at her next thought, and she raised troubled eyes to his cold ones. "You're saying . . . When you killed . . . You're the one who . . . ."

"Killed our dear father and destroyed his realm?" The sorcerer pretended to mull it over, then beamed. "Yes, princess, it was all me."

Vivienne clasped a hand over her mouth, forcing herself not to throw up.

"And now, I can end his lineage altogether. Then I can absorb your powers and coerce Merlin out of his hiding place to have my revenge on him. Once he's out of the way, I will transform this damaged world into my idea of utopia."

Snickering, Carleigh gathered black energy in one hand, flicking his wrist towards her. Vivienne was elevated off the ground and thrown against the wall. Air suffocated her and she could not fight against it, the chaos in her head preventing her from accessing her powers.

I screwed up. I should never have come, Vivienne thought. She closed her eyes, fearing she would never again see her lover. *I love you, Sébastien. Forgive me.*

* * *

I love you, Sébastien. Forgive me.

The guardian heard the words as they arrived by the church, and sensed his beloved's anguish.

"Vivienne!" he screamed out loud, trying to yank the door open, but it would not budge. "Open the damn door, Alistair!"

Sébastien felt Vivienne inside, as well as her shock and distress. "She's in trouble!"

The demon dog threw the entirety of his magic at the door, but it only bounced off it and disintegrated. *I sense it as well. She is not using an enchantment to defend herself, but this damn door will not budge!*

Sébastien lifted Excalibur, gripping the hilt with both hands. "Step back!" He threw all his weight behind the sword, slamming the door with it. The magic holding it frozen released, and the wooden panels burst open with a bang.

They entered in time to catch Carleigh pinning Vivienne to the wall, moving in for the killing strike. Without hesitation, Sébastien flung Excalibur to the sorcerer as he would a dagger, grasping it by the metal blade and throwing it with all his might.

The necromancer turned to them, saw the blade headed his way, and his eyes widened. With a muttered curse, Carleigh waved his hand and called the shadows to him, disappearing within their depths and becoming one with the occult.

Excalibur implanted itself in the wooden wall, and

Vivienne slumped to the ground. Sébastien and Alistair rushed to the young woman. She clutched her throat, coughing and breathing heavily, tears running down her cheeks.

"Vivienne!" Sébastien gathered her in his arms, tightening his grip when he felt her trembling. "What happened, beloved?" Chaos suffused their bond, and he was unable to pinpoint the source of her distress.

To top it off, Vivienne would not elaborate, only shaking her head against his chest. Sébastien stood up, picked the enchantress in his arms, and retreated out of the church.

His face was a stormy mask, hate for Carleigh filling his veins. Alistair followed close behind, snarling furiously. At the pallor of his mistress' face, he whined pitifully.

What did he say? Alistair enquired, eyeing her. *Your aura . . . I have never seen it so scattered.*

Vivienne drew away from Sébastien's embrace and whispered one word. "Brother." When the déjà-vu came, she welcomed the blackout.

* * *

Vivienne was ten years old when her grandfather, the old king Mihail, was on his dying bed. King Adrien brought his daughter up to the man's room to speak to him one last time.

Thus, she was there when Mihail pulled Adrien close, whispering with his last breath, "You have another heir – a male, son from the kitchen maid."

Shocked beyond words, Adrien called Merlin and ordered him to find this son he had not been aware of. After weeks of searching, the mage returned with empty hands, deploring he could not find anything, and the boy must have been lost.

Neither Vivienne nor Adrien knew the truth. The moment Merlin found Carleigh and his lineage, he used magic to blind him and his mother to their past. He also paid them a good sum of money to leave Elsior and never come back.

Merlin had plans for the young royal Vivienne, and nothing should disturb those. Least of all a bastard child whose soul was already corrupted with envy and jealousy.

* * *

Back at the church, shadows detached themselves from the wall and Carleigh stepped from within their midst. He had never truly left, only using darkness as a distraction to camouflage his physical body.

The sorcerer moved to the pool of darkness, hidden under a blanketing cloak, to ensure the curse he had placed upon it had held, and it had not been discovered.

To his utter satisfaction, it was still untouched. Smirking, Carleigh stepped over to where he had captured Vivienne, and the last ingredient lying on the ground – a lock of her raven hair.

He carefully picked it up and placed it above the ruby ring on his finger. The stone glistened menacingly in the dim light, and Carleigh hastened to add the hair to it. A satisfied grin escaped him when it was absorbed with a hiss.

* * *

Back at the cabin, Vivienne stirred in bed. Sébastien stepped away from the window – where he had been standing guard – and rushed to the bedside.

"If I wasn't so happy you're unharmed, I would gladly throttle you." Though his words were half-joking, the enchantress did not answer, instead turning away.

"Vivienne?" Sébastien probed softly, but the young woman kept silent.

She is still in shock.

"Alistair, she's slept for hours." He sat on the bed and nudged her again. "Love? Talk to me."

When all Vivienne did was stubbornly avoid them, Alistair let out a low whine. Sébastien glanced at the dog, trying to find a way to bring her back.

"Give us a minute," he pleaded in the end.

Once Alistair left, the champion lifted his beloved on his lap, forcing her to meet his gaze. "I get you're scared and avoiding this is easier than tackling it head on, but you have to come back to me, love."

Gently, Sébastien pressed his lips to hers. At first, Vivienne remained frozen, much as when she had found out the truth about her father. But the guardian was patient, kissing her softly, lips coaxing, cajoling, and attempting to communicate heat to her cold body.

He was rewarded when Vivienne finally stirred. Her hands went up to his hair, tugging him closer, and she eagerly returned the embrace.

Sébastien drew away, breathing rapidly, smiling as some color returned to her face. "You're back."

Vivienne stared for a beat, then nodded.

"Alistair, come back in," Sébastien announced louder.

The demon dog was quick to re-enter, eyeing them both. *What happened?* he asked Vivienne.

She cleared her throat and moved off Sébastien's lap, but stayed within the circle of his arms. "Carleigh is my half-brother," she announced matter-of-factly, the flashback having convinced her of the truth.

There was a stunned silence as the two protectors shared a shocked look.

Sébastien opened his mouth to deny it, but Vivienne interrupted, "It's true. I had a recollection of my grandfather confessing to my father on his death bed. He sent Merlin to get the child, but the wizard came back empty handed."

Of course he did.

"Carleigh killed my father," Vivienne divulged, tears coming to her eyes again. "I knew it before, but . . . It was his father too! And he murdered him out of vengeance."

So he knew?

"No. He mentioned he had an inexplicable urge to get revenge against royalty. Merlin apparently blocked his memories as a child."

That is why he went after your realm, Elsior, and Camelot.

"Yes."

Alistair had to will himself to be calm, despite the fact the wizard's manipulations were close to sending him in a blind rage. *So this is what he was hiding from us, when we tried to find out more,* he said to Sébastien alone.

When the knight only nodded morosely, the dog addressed them both. *How did Carleigh realize the truth about his lineage?*

"When Sébastien and Merlin killed him, his death broke the chains in his mind."

"So he was reborn with a new vengeance," Sébastien mused.

"Yes," Vivienne confirmed. "He intends to get my powers not just because of the light magic, but more so for our blood bond."

All the pieces of the puzzle finally fell into place, and Alistair grasped the rest in a flash. *To gain immortality,* he finished when the enchantress could not bring herself to say the words.

Vivienne nodded, then whispered, "And to kill Merlin, then change the world to his idea of utopia."

Alistair and Sébastien communicated wordlessly, then the dog acquiesced to an unspoken query. The guardian groaned in response, but shifted Vivienne around to him. "Love, it's time."

"For what?"

"We need Merlin."

Vivienne did not stiffen as before, but the wariness in her eyes pained him.

"You should know," Sébastien rapidly added, "that Merlin showed up in my dreams and apologized for what he put me – us – through. I forgave him. He's also the one who woke us up from your enchantment."

"Alright," she agreed, facing Alistair. "We do it as you explained, then?"

Yes. It is a powerful incantation. Merlin can open a portal on his end, but you have to, as well. We must go to the lake, where your magic is at its top strength.

Vivienne's only response was to stand up.

"Can you handle this?" Sébastien tugged on her hand, concern etched on his face.

Vivienne could only shrug in response, before answering, "Just stick close by, please. Remember when you said you'd help keep my powers under control?" At his brusque nod, she added, "I'll need it today."

"I'll be right here, love."

Sébastien stood up and they strolled hand in hand to the lake. As they walked, the knight took a chance and tried to aim his thoughts towards Alistair alone. *This immortality Carleigh seeks, why does he need Vivienne's powers? Aside from the blood bond, what motivates him? Why not someone else's?*

Without pausing or otherwise reacting, the dog responded, *Her magic is not an ingredient he needs, but a price to pay. The forces he deals with require only the best.*

Sébastien frowned, not reassured in the least. *How can I protect her then?*

Do not let her out of your sight, and I will do the same.

They reached the lake in silence, and Alistair was the first one to speak. *Concentrate on Merlin's energy. You will feel it on the other side, and you have to pull him through, parting the gates of time as you did when you brought forth Excalibur.*

Vivienne entered the water up to her knees, and held both hands parallel to the clear liquid. She searched for the raw energy and it rose to meet her hands steadily. Halfway there, the young woman lost focus, and the magic dropped back into the lake.

"Give it another shot," Sébastien urged softly from behind.

Vivienne shook her head, swallowing past the lump in her throat. "I can't."

Sébastien's heat was suddenly close behind, and he placed both hands on her shoulders, whispering, "Yes, you can. I have faith in you."

It was the right words, at the perfect time. Vivienne inhaled deeply and closed her eyes, lifting her palms again. When the element rose to meet them, she drove against it, pushing until it created a flat oval mirror on top of the lake. It spun with a wave of her hand, creating a vortex.

Once established, it looked like a large mirror had been dropped in the middle of the body of water. Its translucence was in odd contrast with the blue of the sky reflected in the rest of the lake, and the ripples resembled more sea creatures than they did water.

Vivienne pushed past the portal, sensing Merlin on the other side, and held onto it. When it snapped into place, like the last piece of a puzzle, she sagged against Sébastien.

"Now, it's Merlin's turn."

She had barely finished the words, when lightning escaped from the vortex and Merlin appeared in the midst of it.

CHAPTER 28

The wizard stepped out of the lake, parting it with a movement of his staff and ensuring it did not wet him. In mere moments, he joined Vivienne, Sébastien and Alistair on the shore.

He bowed his head to the knight as in the dream, nodded in recognition to Alistair, then glanced at Vivienne. The young woman was watching him warily, tucked against Sébastien's side.

"Vivienne," he greeted.

"Merlin."

They scrutinized each other, evaluating moods and weaknesses.

You really screwed up, old man, Alistair intervened, willing himself to remain calm as he addressed him alone. At the mage's flashing gaze, he continued, *Not only did you hide Carleigh's true parentage from me, but you taught him how to become immortal?*

The wizard clenched his jaw, responding simply, *I made a mistake, yes. Is that why you brought me here, for punishment?*

Peering at Vivienne and Sébastien's expectant expressions, Alistair continued, *No. We will finish this later.* To all three, he declared, *Vivienne must harness her powers, and we were hoping you could help remove the last piece that is blocking her.*

The wizard masked his annoyance. Instead, he nodded in agreement, inspecting their surroundings. "We have limited time. Now is a good a time as any to commence . . . If you are ready."

Vivienne edged away from Sébastien's side, whispering to him, "You should back away."

The enchantress waded back in the lake, intending to gain strength from it. Long ago, when Merlin had been her mentor, they had dueled in a friendly manner, but this was different. The anger for everything he had kept hidden mounted to the surface, obscuring her intentions.

Without lifting a finger, Vivienne elevated a wall of water and transformed it into ice picks, launching them towards the wizard.

Merlin held his staff up, easily deflecting them. "You have to reach deeper," he advised. "Carleigh will get to your light with his malevolent force, but you can use your elemental skills against him."

The enchantress gritted her teeth, rejecting the advice, and formed the same attack again.

"Vivienne!" When he realized she was ignoring him, the old mage frowned, keeping a protective barrier up. "You have to listen to me!"

She extended a hand to the water to obtain more energy. Merlin noticed the aggravation in her eyes, even so far away, and her rising wrath.

"You used me!" Vivienne accused.

"I did not. My fault was not mentioning to you all I knew."

"Like the fact Carleigh is my half-brother!" she yelled, hurling energy towards him.

Merlin blocked the attack a second too late, and it threw him off his feet. The staff dropped out of his hand a few meters away.

The wizard was astonished at the power Vivienne had learned to dominate in such a short time. However, he knew fury was amplifying it, thankfully not in nefariousness, only in sharpness. *If only I could find a way to get her to use it productively,* he mused.

As Vivienne inched closer, he fixed a placating gaze on her. "I did not tell you because he was uncontrollable."

"Is that why you hid it from my father, too?"

Merlin's eyes widened. "You unlocked the memory for that as well?"

Vivienne disregarded the question, and aimed another burst of energy at him. Thankfully, this time he was prepared, and held out a hand for his staff. It flew into his grip in time, deflecting the attack back onto the enchantress.

Unprepared, Vivienne went flying into the nearest tree. Sébastien moved forward to help, feeling her emotions spiraling out of control, and remembering her earlier words.

Wait, Alistair ordered. To the mage, he added, *You might want to play the vulnerable old man card, Merlin, before she gets* really *mad.*

The man's blue eyes threw an annoyed look to Alistair, but he offered a brusque nod. He focused back on Vivienne, who was now marching towards him again.

"Perhaps if you had bothered to reveal it," she was saying, "I would have figured out the reason he's so good at taking bits of my spells away is because we're related!"

The old mage sighed and placed the staff down, extinguishing the flame within it. "Yes, perhaps it would have helped. And perhaps you, being a good person, would have tried to connect with him, not realizing how much of a snake he is."

Vivienne did not reply, instead staring at him with mistrust. Nevertheless, the aura around her person was calmer, less combustible.

"You do not trust me," Merlin continued, "and I understand that. But please let me help you." Once the flashing in her eyes calmed, he was certain she was open to suggestion. "Water is your truest element, but in your last battle you used another."

"You saw?" Vivienne arched an eyebrow. *Then again, I shouldn't be surprised.* Out loud, the young woman admitted, "Yes, I used fire, due to its purifying properties."

"And it was a great idea, as it burns through dark magic. I am of the opinion that if you use both water and fire as your main element, you will have a better chance. You also have to learn to imbue your attacks with raw magic, drawing onto both to fuel each other, thus purifying the last of the obscurity."

Vivienne frowned, understanding the idea, but not entirely sure she could manage it.

You can do it, Sébastien's voice came in her head, having felt her doubt.

With a deep breath, Vivienne brought both palms together in a prayer gesture. She closed her eyes, concentrating on the raw power within, bringing it to the surface. In so doing, she created a glowing orb easily.

"Good," Merlin praised her. "Now add the fire."

Brow furrowed in concentration, Vivienne managed to add a second blazing sphere on top, which engulfed the first one. She narrowed her eyes as the sheer amount of force used weighed on her.

"Why do I feel so strained?" The question escaped her through gritted teeth, and she darted a side glance to Merlin.

"For one, your last confrontation with Carleigh sapped your energy. Also, this is something you have to use your vital energy for. When incantations act of their own accord, or you use them instinctively, the path between nature and you is not clouded by human emotions."

Merlin paused for a moment, hesitant to continue, but gauging her reaction. When Vivienne imperiously arched an eyebrow in his direction to continue, he shrugged, "When you use it as you do now, you become the conductor of the energies. It is not something our human bodies are used to, which is why battles such as the one you will have with the necromancer are rare – and usually avoided."

"Not that I have much of a choice," Vivienne muttered, then shifted her stance, inhaling deeply and focusing on the unyielding force at her command.

"Steady," the old wizard counseled, inching closer. "Now, use your favorite element to forge a path, and this as your main weapon."

Holding the blazing circle in one hand, Vivienne placed

the other to the river and created an ice pick wall. Much as she had done with the ball of light, she imbued the ice picks with the raw energy of her magic. Merlin held his staff up, opposing a barrier to it in the middle of the lake.

Gasping, Vivienne let the ice picks go, and they formed enough of a breach in the shield, that she was then able to launch the fireball. It passed through, and exploded further down the river.

"You did it."

Vivienne was breathing heavily when she turned to her old mentor.

"You might not forgive me," Merlin murmured, "but you are ready to confront Carleigh, with this as your main weapon. If you listen to me in nothing else, then at least hear this: guard your thoughts. Carleigh will do anything to get in your head, considering he cannot beat your light fairly. He also knows you will not kill him, and will prey on mercy."

Vivienne sighed, the fight going out of her. Sébastien came over and gathered her in his arms, offering wordless support and rewarding her with a thorough kiss.

"I'm proud of you," he whispered when they disengaged, and she grinned weakly.

They glanced to Merlin, but he was back in the lake, his staff already parting the waters to clear a way for him.

"Alistair, be the eyes at the back of their heads," Merlin instructed the demon dog.

The mage then evaporated, sinking into the lake. The portal disappeared with Merlin, and the water was calm once more. Vivienne blinked to stop the tears escaping her. She had not forgiven him, nor expressed any of the peace words she had in her head.

"I have a hunch we'll be meeting him again before all this is over," she whispered.

Perhaps. But in the meantime, let us rest, Alistair suggested, joining them. *You have done remarkably well, highness.*

She inclined her head in agreement, and they all headed back to the cabin.

* * *

Later in the evening, as the three companions slept, Sébastien jumped awake. The night was quiet – too much so.

Alistair lifted his head up, sniffing the air, then pawed the ground impatiently. *They are here.*

Sébastien got up and shook Vivienne awake, whispering, "It's time."

Luckily, they had both slept in their clothes, half-expecting a blitz attack – thus, they were swift to react. The knight grasped Excalibur and lined the walls before he got to the door, Vivienne and Alistair close behind.

Sébastien opened the door and they all stepped out, instincts on high alert – only to be greeted by utter darkness, and no one there.

"Reveal yourselves!" Vivienne ordered, getting goose bumps from the darkness filling the air.

There was movement in the trees, and the warlocks were the first to stride into the moonlight. Sébastien lifted his blade up.

"Little sister, last chance," Carleigh's disembodied voice

came, but he was not among the thirty or so shapes advancing.

"Show up and fight me, Carleigh!" the enchantress commanded.

The reply echoed all around them, taunting. "Find me, and I might!"

Vivienne advanced, but Sébastien seized her hand, pleading, "Don't. It's a trap."

The knight noticed in her eyes the need to defeat the sorcerer once and for all, but she held back, nodding softly, "Alright."

Without aloud communication, they fanned out. Vivienne hit the druids closest to her with a white sphere, while Alistair and Sébastien used their teeth and sword – respectively – to fight the others.

Vivienne was quick to realize that for each druid evaporated, two more would materialize from the shadows.

"Carleigh!" she screamed, whirling around to locate his malevolent essence.

"No need to yell, sister," the voice came from up close.

"Stop calling me that!"

"Suit yourself. I'm here now."

Vivienne's eyes narrowed at the shift of air behind, and she whirled to see a smug Carleigh standing there. He was wearing dark clothes, as well as his permanent black cloak, a ruby ring, and a sword on his hip.

Locking eyes with hers, the necromancer raised his palms up and the patch of earth they were on cut off from the rest. Separated, it floated away onto the river, where they could not be inconvenienced.

"Vivienne!" Sébastien yelled, having witnessed what happened.

She faced Carleigh, but mentally pleaded with her lover, *Be safe. Come to me after you eliminate the wackos.*

Sébastien snarled in response, angry at being separated, and whirled to the adjoining conjurers.

Carleigh must have a portal opened here, Alistair rumbled, disintegrating a warlock trying to strike the knight from behind. *They will not stop emerging while it is functioning. I will go find it, and destroy it.*

Sébastien waved him off, and the dog ran away on a hunt. A few moments later, deeper in the forest, he found himself in front of a hole in the ground. No larger than a small pond in diameter, its depths were unknown and pitch black.

The demon dog strode to it and snatched the next druid emerging from it. He clamped his teeth into the warlock, throwing in a burst of magic to keep him frozen. The man became immobile, and Alistair dragged him back to the hole. Before throwing him in, the dog blew a sphere of magic on top of him, designed to put a stop to it.

The portal wavered, engulfing the conjurer, right before the orb exploded. Light shone within its dark depths for a half-moment, before disappearing. As if on cue, there was a vibration, then the hole seemed to widen, patches of earth detaching from the walls to fall in.

This is not supposed to happen! Alistair snarled, jaws open in shock. He realized Carleigh must have put a curse in effect, in case they tried to tamper with his baby.

What's going on? Sébastien enquired, having caught the astonishment in the dog's voice.

When Alistair did not respond, the knight dispatched his remaining opponent and ran towards the forest the dog had disappeared through. He tripped over a branch, and got up in time to block a malevolent orb aimed at him.

He wheeled towards the warlock who had followed him and slashed his gut, effectively ending him.

WATCH OUT!

At Alistair's roar, Sébastien looked behind and noticed he had been about to fall into nothingness. There was a gaping crater separating the two companions from each other, and it was rapidly expanding, the earth on a landslide.

The champion glanced in the deep pit, but could not discern an ending. His eyes met Alistair's across the distance. *What the hell?*

Carleigh must have realized we would find it, and set a trap. We cannot allow this to expand, it will end up swallowing whole cities!

Sébastien scanned the obscurity for more conjurers, amazed to find none. *Why is it so quiet?*

Following his lead, the dog, across the distance, sniffed the air. With a nudge of his inner self, he created a bubble as he had at the lake, and let himself be transported across the pit, to the guardian. It was better to float and see where he was going, rather than dematerialize onto a nonexistent patch of ground.

Alistair was halfway across when a tentacle whipped from underneath him, popped the bubble, and wrapped itself around his lower half. With a howl of agony, the dog tried to dig his teeth into the membrane, to no avail.

"Alistair!" Sébastien screamed, watching helplessly as the tentacle tried to drag the dog down. Another one slithered out, aiming for the knight. With a swing of Excalibur, he managed to cut through it, and a potent smoke came out, making him cough.

"How do we get rid of this thing!?"

When there was no response, Sébastien glanced to notice Alistair limp in the tentacle's grip, being pulled lower still. Gritting his teeth, the knight gripped Excalibur by the hilt. There was only one way to save his canine friend – he jumped into the pit.

The fall had him suspended in midair for a few moments, before he finally hit the hard ground. He landed on his shoulder blade, rolling into a kneeling position, lifting Excalibur up to block any incoming attacks.

In the surrounding obscurity, something agitated. Excalibur hissed a warning, and Sébastien swung it in time to cut into another tentacle aiming for him. He followed the dead membrane to the monster hidden deep within, one of Carleigh's other necromancy tricks.

The octopus-like creature was the size of a small elephant, with beady red eyes and a body full of scales. A stench of sewer came off it, overwhelming in the small space. Its multiple tentacles slithered on the ground, constantly searching for prey.

When Excalibur hissed, Sébastien swung it again, cutting another one. Before the creature could detect him approaching, the champion moved up to it, and sunk his blade in the monster's body. There was a loud howl, and the creature melted like ice cream in the warm sun, soon absorbed within the earth.

Alistair was left on the ground, panting. *You saved my ass, knight.*

"You're welcome," Sébastien grinned.

There was a rumble and they peered to the sky above. The sinkhole was reversing, like curtains being drawn.

Alistair advanced in front of him, and lifted a paw. *Grab onto me.*

Once Sébastien followed suit, they were both surrounded by the transparent bubble, and elevated into the air, escaping the closing earth just in time. Back on normal ground, they gaped in amazement at where the crater had been. Instead of a dark hole, there was now a normal meadow, with grass and flowers to boot.

"I don't believe this!" Sébastien snarled. "The son of a bitch was distracting us!"

Alistair's deep growl answered him. *Time to finish this off.*

Sébastien nodded tightly, swung Excalibur above his head, and took off with renewed strength. They rapidly disposed of the rest of the faithless druids lying in wait in the forest.

* * *

On the lake, Vivienne ducked Carleigh's attack, and counterattacked with one of her own. She imbued each elemental strike with another incantation, rendering them stronger. Though the sorcerer pushed back, there was bewilderment in his eyes at the force behind her magic.

"I will not let you win," Vivienne predicted. "I have too much to fight for."

"Really?" he smirked. "A champion, a dog . . . And your father and realm are lost."

Vivienne did not answer, except to throw him an annoyed

glare. As with Merlin, she conjured an orb of light, added the fire within, and flung it towards him at the same time as a wave of liquid formed in the shape of a blade.

It broke past Carleigh's shield, and he landed on his back, the fireball having entered him. It was as though he was aflame, unable to breathe. He grabbed the earth on his side, digging his fingers – and the ring – in an effort to ground himself.

Vivienne marched to the sorcerer, and he noticed for the first time the burning in her gaze – justice about to be handed out to him.

"I will not kill you," the enchantress muttered. "You've gathered as much already. But Merlin will imprison you."

"I don't believe that, sister. You should have disposed of me when you had the chance."

Vivienne did not understand the words until she felt a pinch on her ankle. Glancing down, she noticed a snake the shade of midnight retreating. Half of its body was still underground, controlled by Carleigh's sorcery which had seeped into the earth.

She gasped as the tiny bite started burning within, then cooled to the temperature of ice, causing her entire body to tremble. Carleigh's victorious features became blurry, even as she was left gasping.

The poison filled Vivienne, affecting her supernatural forces. It felt as though the magic was exiting her in little droplets, the same effect as air being let out of a tire – though nothing could be further from the truth.

Flashes of the past hit her – different than before. They were not happy recollections, but the worst the enchantress had. She screamed, falling to the ground in pain. The shield she had used before disappeared, leaving her vulnerable.

Once she was captive to the turbulent emotions, Carleigh inched closer. With his dark sword, the sorcerer cut Vivienne's wrist and watched as her blood poured in his cupped palm.

Extending his senses across the ground, he went all the way back to the church where the darkness lay in wait. With a call from the necromancer, it evaporated, only to reappear in front of him – a viscous mass.

"I promised you the blood of the purest champion of good," Carleigh stated to the darkness. "You asked for a few drops. She is yours."

The mass stayed still for a few long moments, then turned to Vivienne and the blood pooling in Carleigh's hand. It inched closer, until it was right underneath the wrist. Drops of the enchantress' blood fell and were absorbed with a hiss.

Greedy, darkness tried to inch closer to engulf the royal completely. The second it attempted it, a lightning bolt shot from the sky and a shield rose from the ground, covering Vivienne completely and healing her wrist in the same process. Her magic, having sensed the evil nearby and its mistress' inability to defend herself, had reacted protectively.

The tumultuous entity vibrated, then pulled away, hissing, and turned to the sorcerer.

"You've had your price. Now give me what you promised," Carleigh snarled.

Under the necromancer's waiting gaze, the mass dissolved. It its place remained a chalice, white on the outside, black on the inside. The warlock picked it up, feeling the spell of immortality vibrating off it.

"The drink of eternity," Carleigh laughed. He closed his eyes in satisfaction and drank the entirety of its contents. He then discarded the goblet, and it evaporated into the nothingness it had come from, as the coldness of immortality entered him

Carleigh shivered at the sensation, like a lover's caress, running through him. Immortality was all he had ever wanted – the power to be anyone and anything, and control all within his path. Now, it was singing in his veins, a gift of the occult he had served for so long.

Black, unfeeling eyes opened, and he turned to his sister in captivity. Vivienne was comatose, staring unseeing at a point in the horizon, the barrier still protecting her.

"And now, I wait."

In the distance, the guardian and dog swam towards him. Carleigh waited patiently, a faint smile on his thin lips. It was time to test his newfound powers in a way that showed Vivienne's companions just how pitiful their lives were. Vengeance for the past would be his, once and for all.

CHAPTER 29

With the acolytes all gone, Sébastien looked to the river, as there was a keen tug in his mind. "Something's wrong. We have to get Vivienne, now."

Hold on to me, Alistair instructed, then entered into the lake.

The guardian followed him in, wrapped an arm around the dog's massive neck, and they sank in the water. An invisible energy propelled them forward, much quicker than if they had actually swam.

They arrived at the small patch of earth and could glimpse Vivienne in the distance. She was on her knees, bent over, with a semi-translucent barrier surrounding her.

The companions got out of the water and Sébastien immediately inched towards his beloved, while Alistair kept an eye on Carleigh. The necromancer was standing with a satisfied smirk, simply observing his half-sister.

Try as he may, the demon dog could not understand the behavior. He could sense something had happened. Darkness's footprints were all over the unseen world his senses could capture, but he could grasp nothing concrete from its trail.

As he approached Vivienne, Sébastien observed the protective shield around her, and the energy crackling on its surface – like little zaps of electricity.

"Vivienne!" he yelled above the noise of the vibration.

The enchantress did not respond, keeping her head bent and hands joined as if in prayer.

"Vivienne!" Sébastien yelled again, desperation tinting his tone.

He moved Excalibur and struck the shield with it, only to be shoved back by an invisible force. The brightness and sparks glinting off the metal attracted Vivienne's attention, and she peered up at her lover.

Sébastien willed himself not to react, but the young woman's blank look shook him to the core. It was no longer the warm emerald shining with joy, rather cold and empty, as if she no longer experienced anything. There was no focus within, no shine of recognition – only a bleak, glazed stare and blank countenance.

The knight noticed Alistair out of the corner of his eye, but dared not blink away from Vivienne for fear of losing her completely. "Love, it's me, Sébastien."

Her lips moved and, with a sinking presentiment, he realized she was casting an enchantment, and remained unattainable to him.

Sébastien turned to Carleigh, pointing Excalibur at him.

"What did you *do*!?"

"I did nothing," he chortled. "I simply reminded her of past mistakes."

She is putting up a defensive shield, Sébastien, Alistair rumbled. He sounded unsure, and the knot in the guardian's stomach got heavier. *Something odd took place here, but I cannot get a good read on it. Keep Carleigh occupied while I get closer.*

No problem, Sébastien promised.

He advanced to the necromancer with Excalibur humming in his hand. "You and me, it's time we end this unfinished business."

"You can always try!"

Carleigh used dark magic, while Sébastien relied on Excalibur to block attacks. Promptly realizing he was at a disadvantage, the sorcerer pulled his own weapon out of the cloak, and they went metal to metal. When the swords clashed, sparks shot out.

His blade is the opposite of yours, Alistair warned. *Darkness in its raw state. Do not let it cut you, as death will not be merciful.*

Got it, Sébastien assured him. *But what's wrong with Vivienne?*

I cannot figure out what he did to her, but she has externalized her spirit. All she has left are emotions.

How is that possible when I sense none coming from her?

Alistair hesitated, then informed him, *I can feel Carleigh's particular brand of magic within Vivienne, almost as if somehow it infected her. There is a bite on her ankle that I isolated as the origin, probably one of Carleigh's tricks. The problem is, in Vivienne's case, the darkness has no ambitions to feast on, so instead it is crushing her hope. Despair and remorse are taking over and she is poisoning herself, with nothing to pull her out of it. We must stop this before it is too late.*

Blocking the necromancer's blow, Sébastien growled, *Will killing him fix it?*

No.

Alistair, don't lie to me!

It is the truth! If your murder Carleigh, Vivienne will still be lost. You have to somehow reach her heart and remind her she has something to fight for.

Sébastien got distracted with Alistair's words – wondering how to get to his beloved. He blocked the blow a second too late and Carleigh's blade grazed his shoulder. A whoosh of something struck him and he gasped, Excalibur growing heavy in his hand.

"There, that wasn't so complicated," Carleigh smirked triumphantly. "Now, to finish off my lovely sister." He stepped to Vivienne. "Your champion is dying. Do you want more remorse?"

In a flash of desperation and fury, Sébastien used his remaining strength to creep on the sorcerer and bash him in the head with Excalibur. Carleigh dropped to the ground, unconscious.

"Keep an eye on him," he grumbled to Alistair, then stumbled to Vivienne's bubble.

* * *

The shadows in Vivienne's heart overwhelmed and grew until there was nothing but the worst of sentiments left. The curse was oppressing, crushing her, taking away her ability to breathe, yet not killing her – not yet. It was as though it yearned for her to give up, to taste the bitterness of defeat, before she would be put out of her misery.

Love, Carleigh, the world no longer existed, buried far away in an unattainable abyss where nothing could get to the memories. There was no salvation to cling to, no fire to light a way out.

Vivienne observed everything via a haze, unaware of the battle happening on the outside. Until *he* was in her head.

Love, I need you!

Sébastien's mental cry for help got to her. In the most obscure corner of her heart, something flickered, and Vivienne blinked at the surrounding reality. She noticed the knight outside her shield, bleeding, tendrils of obscurity flowing out of him.

In front of her eyes, Sébastien slumped to his knees, breathing heavily. She crawled to him, blocked in by her own barrier.

"Carleigh cut me with a poisoned sword," Sébastien said, his gaze trying to lock onto Vivienne's. "I need your help."

The enchantress bit her lip, wanting nothing more than to come to his aid. When she tried to search deep within, there was no tangible magic, only a wave of negativity.

"I don't have it," Vivienne confessed shamefully, attempting to bring down the shield – to no avail. "I can't even get out of here, Sébastien." Tears streamed down her cheeks as she noticed, helpless, the life edging out of him.

You must drop the barrier, Alistair informed her.

Vivienne looked in his direction, but gave a small shake of the head – freezing once her gaze landed on Carleigh's unconscious body next to the dog. In that moment, she knew that to save Sébastien, it was time to reach into the unknown, whatever the cost.

The enchantress closed her eyes, searching deep within, for what was left – a pool of obscure emotions and tainted magic. She attained and gathered some of it, keeping the image of Carleigh's unconscious body in view.

A life for a life! Within moments, Vivienne directed the darkness towards the sorcerer, and let the force loose.

Stop it! Stop her! Alistair cried in both their heads.

I can't, Vivienne admitted frankly, pleading with her eyes for understanding. *I will not stop and lose Sébastien. If I can't escape this makeshift prison, he has to live.*

Having heard the words, the champion lifted his heavy eyelids. Though woozy from the loss of blood and darkness eating at him, the knight vaguely recalled Vivienne's shields could only be entered by someone pure.

What's the chance that this whole fight with Carleigh didn't *take away the last shard of light I had left?* he thought, dismayed at failing yet again.

Despite the doubt, Sébastien knew there was no choice now. To be Vivienne's salvation, he had to stop her from making the biggest mistake of her existence.

Please, he implored the fates, *let me get to her.*

Sébastien urged himself to stand up, then passed the barrier, almost crawled through the transparency. There was a ripple as if he was walking under a waterfall, and he fell to his knees in front of Vivienne, mere inches between them.

"It's not necessary, love," he whispered. "Leave the shadows, and come back to me. I'm here, Vivienne. Accept your light magic back in."

Sébastien grasped her cold hand in his, and the pull was immediate. Their soul mate bond re-emerged to the surface, strengthened by the physical connection. Images of the past and present ran in the young enchantress' head, this time not distorted by her own agony.

Vivienne inhaled deeply and willed herself to let go of the darkness. Resistant at first, the tendrils finally released Carleigh.

Instead of calling them back to her, the young woman shunned them. She closed her eyes and breathed in deeply, begging pure spirit to come back to her and cleanse the darkness out.

The protective shield – reinforced by light magic – transformed into liquid, falling like rain showers to the ground, and trickled in tiny diamonds back to Vivienne. It covered the young woman's body in its entirety. In a blinding blaze, it was absorbed into her skin, reintegrating her body – the final missing puzzle piece.

The enchantress could now access her center again, filled with spirit. A burst of warmth went through her, warming her cold extremities and giving her the breath of air she desperately craved.

Vivienne opened her eyes, shifting her focus to heal Sébastien. He was lying down on the ground now, smiling weakly. It only took a scan with her otherworldly senses to realize the evil within him could not be cleansed away.

"It's alright," Sébastien whispered, reading the horror in his beloved's eyes. The fresh tears streaming down her cheeks were more vocal than any verbal warning. He squeezed her hand in his, proud to have kept her safe.

"No," Vivienne cried, "I've seen this before. *No!*"

With a resolute shake of the head, the enchantress placed both hands above his wound, the incantation forming subconsciously. It glowed brighter than any others, due to Vivienne's intensity and the love backing it. Though the wound could not be mended, there was a way to extract the occult from within it – at a cost.

Vivienne, no! Alistair pleaded, reading the intention behind the magic, and inched towards her.

The young woman flicked a wrist to the dog, creating a barrier he could not penetrate. Alistair pawed at it, attempting to cut through with his claws and teeth, all the while continuously begging her to stop.

The shield did not budge, reinforced as it was by the Vivienne's intense emotions. Without a care for her own life, she attracted the shadows to her instead, her magic extracting them out of Sébastien. At first hesitant, the tendrils of darkness crawled over the enchantress eagerly, being absorbed in the skin, feeding off her life energy.

The whole thing took only a few moments. The guardian blinked, conscious of his strength returned. Uneasiness stirred deep within him and he looked to the side, where Vivienne was lying down, close to unconsciousness. Alistair howled in anger, still blocked by the barrier.

Sébastien stood up and crawled nearer, cradling her in his arms. His lips hovered a few inches from Vivienne's, but she could barely move. He clutched her hand, hoping it would be enough to keep her with him.

"What have you done?" he whispered, chest constricting painfully, as though he was being torn in two.

"You saved me once," Vivienne stated, inhaling deeply as her life force seeped out. "Now I can do the same for you. You can have a life with a good woman."

Tears came to Sébastien's eyes, and he willed the words past the lump in his throat. "It's always been you, my love, no one else. In all these lives we spent together. Please don't let go . . . Don't leave me again." He choked on the words. "I've tried to do everything different this time. *Please* stay with me."

Vivienne heard the words and tried to squeeze his hand, but her muscles would not listen. She slipped into a blackout, no longer in control of anything.

* * *

"No!" Sébastien yelled, gathering Vivienne's inert body to his chest. "Not again!" He sobbed against her cheek, hot tears streaming down his face.

Merlin! Alistair roared. *If you care so much about her, come and do something!*

There was no response for a few moments. Then, a rumbling vibrated in the lake next to them. Alistair headed over, lending his own magic out. Though the demon dog did not have the powers Vivienne now did to part the curtains of time, he could add his force to Merlin's, and help him push through – consequences be damned.

With a huge nudge from his side, to contribute for the dog's lack of power, Merlin emerged and ran to Vivienne, having followed the fight from his time. With a wave of his staff, the barrier she had created disappeared, and both he and Alistair could pass through.

The mage moved his staff over the young woman, and it glowed fiercely. "She has absorbed all the evil, and it is potent. I can heal it, but some will remain in her." Merlin scanned Sébastien for his approval and consent.

Why is she unable to heal this herself!? Alistair growled loud enough for anyone within the vicinity to hear.

"Even Merlin knows mages have limits."

The three males whirled around to see Carleigh standing, smirking, not unconscious in the least. A malevolent orb was conjured in his hand, and he was bouncing it up and down as he would a tennis ball.

At their shocked expressions, he flat out snickered manically, while they could only stare at him – and each other – in dismay.

When neither male joined in, Carleigh's laugh slowed to a chuckle, then a snort as he continued, "I knew my dear sister would not be able to heal herself, after having spent so much energy fighting me. And I knew you would come, old fool." The last words were spoken directly to Merlin, his evil glare fixated on the wizard.

Merlin stared back unflinchingly, still kneeling next to Vivienne's motionless body. He glanced at his pupil's body, then to his staff on the ground, and finally back to the necromancer.

"And what is it you wish to accomplish?" his deep voice

thundered. "All this misery, this hate, to get what, exactly?"

"VENGEANCE!" Carleigh roared, his restraint slipping. With a deep breath, he pressed his lips tightly together and continued, "You ruined my life, hiding my real identity. And you cast me away. I expect what is due to me."

Merlin stood up slowly, leaning on the staff as though in pain. "And I suppose none of this has anything to do with the evil forces you struck a deal with?"

"And if it does?" Carleigh was still playing with the sphere, though his eyes flicked briefly to Sébastien and Alistair, who had moved next to Vivienne.

"How can you imagine I will let you destroy this world, letting darkness feed on it?" Merlin questioned.

"I don't care what you intend to do, *master*. I will get what is due to me. Starting with her." He pointed an index to Vivienne, chortling in amusement as the three males closed ranks, effectively blocking her from his sight.

Sébastien advanced in front of Merlin, Excalibur drawn, his body a shield. Alistair faced Vivienne and blew a barrier over her, before joining the wizard's other side.

"Look at you, the three stooges," Carleigh cackled, before throwing the orb towards Sébastien.

The knight lifted Excalibur to cut through it, but at the last minute it did a wide ark and instead hit from behind, blowing him in the air. He landed a few feet further, rolling onto the ground, and got up almost immediately, gritting his teeth. With a meaningful look to the demon dog, Sébastien charged again.

Alistair, reading his intent, went to strike on the other side. They both arrived by the necromancer at the same time.

Sébastien swung Excalibur, slashing him. At the same time, the dog barked thunderously and a large circle exiting his jaws, hitting the sorcerer full force.

There was an explosion as both Excalibur and Alistair's attack hit Carleigh, and the two protectors were blown backwards by the force emanating from it.

Merlin was about to step forward, but glanced over his shoulder as he heard a moan behind. Vivienne's hand was tightly clenched, and the sounds coming from her were of agony and affliction, like a hurt animal that was drawing its last breath.

The wizard glanced back at the thick cloud of smoke now emerging from where Carleigh had been. Sébastien and Alistair were getting up, approaching it cautiously from both sides.

Merlin passed the staff in a circle over Vivienne's form. The crystal blazed with a blue glow first, then red, alerting him to danger. He raised it closer to his left eye and surveyed the enchantress using the crystal.

"No . . ." Coughs from behind unfocused the mage from the disturbing picture he was seeing.

The smoke was so potent both protectors had to back away from the sorcerer. Alistair whined, making an effort to shake the ash out of his eyes, whilst Sébastien furiously wiped away at his face with both hands. He felt a burning sensation as though he had entered a room filled with chemicals. When he finally managed to clear his vision, his jaw dropped to the ground.

What the hell!? Alistair echoed the sentiment.

Carleigh stood smugly where they had left him, not

harmed in the least – not even a speck of dust. "You didn't really figure I had been standing next to your precious princess all this time without doing anything, did you?"

Sébastien glanced at Alistair, then Merlin. Throughout the entire fight, the wizard had stood there, observing, eyes glowing softly while in a trance.

Now, he shook his head, and there was fear in his gaze. "You couldn't have!"

"Become immortal, you mean?" Carleigh smirked wider. "And if I did? What will you do now, old man?"

Sébastien, unfazed, circled around the necromancer and arrived by Alistair's side.

It matters not what his powers are, he stated for good measure to the dog. *All we have to do is capture and imprison him. Then we can figure out a way to neutralize him.*

Alistair gave a tight nod, not once taking his opaque glare off from the sorcerer. *It will not be easy.*

When has it ever been? Sébastien retorted, and gripped Excalibur tighter.

With his newfound immortality, Carleigh's ego had also increased, no longer careful of multiple attacks, as though he could withstand anything.

"No . . ." Merlin murmured, glancing from Carleigh to Vivienne, his shoulders sagging in defeat.

Snap out of it! Alistair threw at him, but the wizard's frame seemed more fragile compared to Carleigh's potent corruption. The shadows around the necromancer were larger, obscuring his feet to the point they resembled tentacles.

Carleigh brought both palms together, as though in prayer. For a few moments, his lips budged in an incantation neither of the defenders could capture, then he slowly disengaged his palms. A ball formed betwixt them, growing with each movement he made, until it was the size of an extremely large volleyball.

The orb was the same color as the previous ones – pitch black – but electricity crackled from it, like it was filled with lightning. From the mass of darkness at his feet, a snake slithered up Carleigh's leg, then over his forearm. Gluing itself to the ball, it was absorbed.

Merlin, be careful! Alistair roared a warning, but it was too late.

The mage used the staff to defend himself, the crystal shining brightly for a moment as a barrier was cast. When Carleigh launched the sphere, it hit the shield, and normally should have been shattered. Instead, it bounced a few feet away, hovered in the air, and went back to attack.

Carleigh cackled, eyes shining in delight as he watched the show. Merlin with both hands gripping onto the staff, maintaining a shield, and the orb incessantly striking. With each hit, the barrier wavered, and the ball gained in mass, expanding as it stole the magic and grew.

Sébastien gripped Excalibur and was about to head towards Merlin to help him. Alistair advanced in front of him with a meaningful stance.

Merlin can take care of himself. If we do not manage to injure Carleigh, or render him unconscious, this world will be lost.

Sébastien glanced at Vivienne, then her mentor, before nodding tightly to Alistair. *What do you propose?*

Alistair glared towards Carleigh, still lost in his own

arrogance. Then he looked to Merlin, who was now on his knees, holding onto the staff as though his life depended on it. Strain showed on the mage's expression as he came close to breaking.

We can only attack him repeatedly, hoping we can distract him long enough for Merlin to attempt a counterattack. You got that, old man?

Merlin gave a tight nod in response across the distance.

Sébastien gripped Excalibur and without further ado, ran towards Carleigh. Alistair matched his pace, jaws open and ready to attack.

The dog lunged first at Carleigh, only to be driven away by a wave of the necromancer's hand. He landed heavily on the ground, whining in pain. Still, he got back up and lunged again. At the same time, Sébastien swung Excalibur to attack the sorcerer's shield.

The singing sword hit the screen, cut past it, and there was a whoosh of air as the barrier collapsed. At the same time, Alistair aimed for Carleigh's throat – he never got to it. The tentacles at the necromancer's feet struck out, wrapping around his paws, and yanked the dog down to their mercy.

Seeing his predicament, Sébastien swung again high at Carleigh's head, with the certitude it would be blocked. He then dropped to a knee, cutting instead through the creatures at his feet. When Excalibur hit the darkness, the metal shone brightly, as though it was bathed in moonlight. The creatures hissed and edged away, releasing Alistair.

"You two are annoying me," Carleigh muttered, moving his gaze away from Merlin.

He raised both palms, one facing each defender, and

released two bolts of malevolent energy. Before they could block it, the spell hit them full force and they flew back, landing to the ground – unconscious.

Carleigh laughed maniacally, then approached Merlin. "What say you, o great mage of the past? Ready to give up and accept your fate?"

Merlin's blue eyes met his, and the defiance remained as he declared, "Never. I will not let you win. I should have arranged for you to be suffocated in your crib, and saved us from all this."

"You *would* say that, wouldn't you?" Carleigh scowled at him. With a head signal from him, the orb of darkness increased the frequency of its attacks, constantly hitting onto the shield.

Merlin grunted, white-knuckled as he gripped onto the staff.

"Know this before you die, consumed by my darkness. I will let it take over this world, feasting onto each living thing. And when and if your king Arthur is reborn, I will ensure he is corrupted, as I did with your precious Vivienne."

"No!" Merlin glanced again at his pupil, lying unconscious, and it was the split move that cost him. There was a crack, and the staff broke in two. The wizard slumped to his knees, palms on the ground, panting heavily.

The sphere hovered in mid-air, waiting for its master's command – there was nothing defending Merlin now. With a nod, the orb hit the wizard full frontal, blowing him in the air until he landed roughly a few meters away, unmoving.

"Finally. My revenge is complete."

Carleigh placed his back to both Merlin and Vivienne,

and elevated both palms to the sky. All that was left was to open a portal, and let the darkness swarm in. As he brought his hands together, a voice stopped him.

"Didn't your father teach you to never turn your back on your enemies?"

The necromancer froze, and the sneer died off his lips as he whirled around. Vivienne stood facing him, head bowed, shoulders straight, hair obscuring her visage. Carleigh's eyes narrowed. Something was different about her, something . . .

"Oh, that's right," the enchantress continued with an evil snigger, her voice cold and devoid of emotion. "You never had one."

When she raised her chin, Carleigh's jaw dropped in shock. Vivienne's eyes were midnight black, her skin the color of cray. There was nothing human left in her features, as though they were now made of marble – all unnatural pallor and sharpened edges.

"You bitch!" Carleigh yelled, throwing a ring of energy at her.

The young woman raised her palm and caught the orb instead of deflecting it, to the necromancer's increasing shock.

"You're thinking, let's see . . ." Vivienne murmured softly, caressing the sphere as one would a puppy, " . . .that there's no way I should be able to hold anything dark. That it should burn me, affect me . . ." She laughed, meeting his gaze. "Surprise!"

The orb ascended in her hand, twirling at its mistress' command.

"You're bluffing," Carleigh muttered. "You cannot handle darkness, this is some trick you're pulling. When I took your light –"

"Yes, yes, you became immortal." Vivienne rolled her eyes, as though it was a story she had heard many times before. "And you left me in agony. They," she waved a hand carelessly towards Sébastien and Alistair's unmoving forms, "tried to get the good back into me. And it worked. Except you cut my poor, poor lover with your evil weapon, and guess who had to come to the rescue?"

"You couldn't have, unless –"

"Unless I let the darkness in me. Which I did. Ta-da!" Vivienne spread her arms, the sphere still bouncing in her palm, and twirled around in a circle.

When she faced Carleigh again, there was black lightning in her eyes, and her hair was flying wildly, animated by an unseen energy.

"Then join me."

She tilted her head, assessing the sorcerer as one would a bug. "Join you?" Vivienne repeated, forming the words as though foreign.

"Yes! Don't you see, sister? This is what we're intended to do, rule the world together. Join me . . .and we can both reap the benefits!"

Vivienne threw her head back and sniggered. "There can only be one master of darkness, brother. Or, in this case, *mistress*."

With that, she threw the orb back at him – but Carleigh had been prepared, a shield drawn up. He conjured another sphere, this one similar to the one used on Merlin, and threw it back to Vivienne.

The enchantress waited until the last moment, when the sphere almost hit her, before lifting a palm and stopping it in midair.

"You forget," she murmured so softly Carleigh could barely hear, "the darkness you put in your sword, which I absorbed from Sébastien, was potent, not diluted, like yours. Immortal or not, you are nothing compared to me. I am your queen, and once and for all, you *will* recognize it." Eyes flashing, Vivienne added, "Time to see some of my own wonders, *brother*."

With that, the young woman raised her other hand, a fire sphere in it. Carleigh could not believe his eyes – the element was still responding to her call!

He stared in shock as Vivienne added the sphere to the orb he had thrown her way, and rerouted it. The darkness flew his way and came to a stop outside the barrier, hovering for a beat, immobile in the air.

Then, it attacked – except once it hit the shield, it multiplied. With each strike, the orb duplicated, until there were hundreds such orbs hitting at once.

With a cry of defeat, Carleigh fell to his knees, and the spheres all fell upon him at the same time. Vivienne watched in satisfaction as he was brought to within an inch of defeat. She strode closer, to better hear his pleas for mercy.

"Why would you do this? To protect them?" Carleigh whispered instead.

"I care nothing for either of them. You ensured that, silly brother," Vivienne admonished softly.

Carleigh dropped to his back, weak from the attack, and gave into the blackout. Though he was immortal, what Vivienne had used with the fire and curse had sapped his strength. It was the perfect time to feed him to the same forces he served.

The enchantress raised her palm, ready to finish the necromancer.

"Vivienne."

She tilted her head to the side, to Merlin. He had crawled over, only a few feet away. Still on his knees, he lifted a hand pleadingly to her. "Please ... You cannot give in to the obscurity. You are the best of us."

Vivienne smirked his way, her black eyes uncaring, "Which is why it's only fit I become your Queen of Darkness."

"This is not you," Merlin whispered, shaking his head. "Please ... I beg of you, think of Sébastien. Your lover, you did so much to help him. Will you shun him, too?"

There was a flicker in the enchantress' eyes and she turned away from the wizard, scanning the grounds for Sébastien's unmoving form. The moment of hesitation was enough, as Merlin's palm shone with a light, which he aimed at the back of her head. Vivienne dropped down, unconscious as the sleeping spell took over.

Merlin crawled next to her body and waved a hand in the direction of the other two defenders, bringing them back to consciousness. When Sébastien and Alistair came to a few moments later, he was still next to the young woman's inert body.

"Vivienne!" Sébastien cried, and staggered to her side, kneeling by Merlin. "Will she be alright?"

Alistair sniffed the air, noticing Carleigh's battered body, Merlin's demeanor, and Vivienne's unconsciousness – yet she been moved from her previous spot. He observed her unnatural pallor, and growled low.

What the hell happened here?

Merlin cased their surroundings, then declared, "Carleigh is defeated."

And you *did this?*

"Yes." The wizard locked gazes with the dog, daring him to defy.

Alistair concentrated his attention to Vivienne. *There is more potent darkness in her than before.*

"I can heal her, as I mentioned before. But there will be a shard of it left."

The mage had addressed the last words to Sébastien, a query in his blue eyes, to which the knight pleaded, "Bring her back."

Merlin put one hand over Vivienne above her chest, and with the other levitated Carleigh's body nearer, placing the other hand on him. He closed his eyes and began withdrawing the obscurity from Vivienne.

The tendrils of evil were slow to exit, unwilling to let go of the power lying dormant within her. As soon as they poked their head in the middle of her body, the wizard unflinchingly yanked them out like weeds, and threw them into Carleigh's body to be reabsorbed.

She is still not breathing! Alistair panicked when Merlin finished the procedure.

Sébastien grazed her lips with his own, tears falling on her cheeks. "Come back to me, my love."

Vivienne's eyes fluttered open at the words, inhaling deep. Her irises were dark, but as she blinked, they cleared to a normal emerald green color.

Sébastien gathered her to him, crying in relief, and she wrapped both arms around him tightly. There was an odd sensation in her stomach, as though there was something she should be aware of, but had forgotten. In her lover's strong embrace, it went away, and Vivienne breathed in the fresh air.

When Merlin went to stand up, the enchantress clasped his withered hand. "Thank you," she murmured, her eyes shining with tears.

The mentor bowed his head and pressed a kiss to her forehead, warm once more. "You are most welcome, my dear."

"Merlin, I . . ." Vivienne gulped past the knot in her stomach, and continued, "I forgive you. For the past. I realize now you had tried to shelter me. My stubbornness to see you as the enemy could have cost me my life. I cannot, and will not, err that far in judgment again." She surveyed Sébastien, then Alistair. "I need all of you by my side if I'm to fight evil here and defend this world. My sentiments, though important to me, should not come first in the fight for good. And Merlin . . . I hope you forgive me, too."

"There is nothing to forgive, Vivienne," he declared, the corners of his eyes creasing as he smiled. He was proud beyond words that she had managed to get past the hurt and perception of betrayal she had carried within for so long.

Merlin beamed at the couple, then inclined his head to Alistair, who was by his side. Undeterred, the dog warned, *You must bring Carleigh back with you and imprison him in such a cage he can never get out of, until we can figure out how to remove his immortality.*

The old mage acquiesced and levitated Carleigh's body back into the waters. As he was about to disappear, Alistair's voice stopped him again. *Something happened here, which you are hiding. I will find out eventually, old friend.*

Merlin squinted back at him, then at Vivienne in

Sébastien's arms, but said nothing. He had faith in his pupil. With one last glance to the couple, the mage evaporated with the sorcerer's still unconscious body by means of the portal.

The transparent mirror wavered once he was gone and, with a nudge of Alistair's power, contracted until it was smaller, then finally disappeared. The water was once more limpid and blue, a true reflection of the sky.

Alistair turned to Sébastien and Vivienne, who were now embracing passionately under the morning sun. He woofed in happiness, and they turned to him, smiling.

I dare say we all deserve a long vacation after this, the demon dog rumbled, and they laughed out loud.

Sébastien peered down at the gorgeous woman in his arms, eyes locked with hers, and whispered, "Anywhere you want, we can go. We have this life and the next to enjoy together."

"We did it, Sébastien," Vivienne grinned, tears of joy streaming down her cheeks. "We rewrote our fate, changed its conclusion. We can truly enjoy our happy ending now."

"As you wish, my lady." The knight bent his mouth to hers, this time in a longer embrace. When he drew away, his heated gaze was the promise of passion to come, and the enchantress' body warmed in response.

As the sun rose behind them, Alistair narrowed his eyes. For a moment, a fraction of a second, he had noticed Vivienne's aura flare dark.

He opened his jaws to mention something, but found he could not. As he tried again, a familiar voice snickered in his head, *You will reveal nothing. You are bound to me from now on, demon lord.*

The dog whined low, but the two lovebirds were too caught in their moment to notice his distress.

The end . . .

. . . for now
Turn the page for a sneak peek
at Book II of The Avalon Chronicles
series:
"Avalon Wishes"

Preview

"Avalon Wishes"

Before he was Alistair, meet Atrox . . .

Ardea knew the three facing them supposedly deserved the punishment. Vulper had shown them the proof of Atrox's disobedience, his rallying of the smaller deities, how the three had planned to overtake the current trinity.

And for what? Ardea's scowl deepened. *All for more power.*

According to Aequus, they would have taken the lesser deities' powers, absorbed them for their own. They would have invariably kicked the current trinity out. They were not the first, nor the last to do so . . . But they certainly were the first who had gotten so close.

The middle one, Atrox, had still not learnt his lesson. Ardea could tell from his proud stance – one she knew well enough by now, to decode.

"Is this your idea of a court of justice?" Atrox spoke, his thunderous voice echoing across the empty surface. His words were followed by a sneer. "Even humans can do better."

"Silence!" The warning came from Aequus, earning him a laugh. "You are not here to speak, lower –"

"Cut through the shite, *brother*," Atrox taunted, enjoying the sudden silence, as though no one dared breathe. "Let's face it, you and my dear sister want me out. You have ever since you let Vulper into our little trio."

He threw a fiery look to the red-haired man, before glancing into Ardea's bi-colored eyes. "You know what I mean."

The tone was accusing, but she refused to let it get to her. Raising her chin in a gesture that truly showed their familiar liens, Ardea stated, "You were never pushed out."

"You let him poison you against me," Atrox rumbled low, his gaze growing more intense, a fire in its pit. "You thought I was too ambitious."

"And you were!" Aequus burst, standing up as though to step towards him. "This is all your fault, and you know it!"

Atrox stood to his feet, though not as quickly. He lifted one knee, then the other, and stretched himself into a standing position. His every movement was feline, full of power and grace, unhurried. Even captive, he outranked them all.

Ardea's hand on Aequus' quieted the god down, and he sat back on his chair. He watched with narrowed eyes as Atrox remained standing.

"Back on your knees," he ordered, pointing a finger to his brother. "Where you shall stay when faced with your superiors."

Atrox stared in silence for a few moments, enjoying his brother's ever more frustrated expression. Then, he smiled. "Yes, we are all quite aware you outrank us," he continued in the same insolently bored tone, refusing to kneel. "Can we get it over with or is our punishment to stay here being forever stared at?"

Ardea met his arrogant gaze, the midnight black eye firing shots of poison, the emerald one steely in its gaze. "Did you really believe there will be no consequences for your actions?"

Atrox simply shrugged, unfazed. "We all know this has nothing to do with dispensing justice, but rather with establishing power. And control over me."

"Enough!" Vulper interrupted. "Atrox has a point. This has taken too long already. Let us bypass the internal squabbles, and put an end to this."

Atrox turned his gaze to the god, letting his hate show. "You *would* want this over with, and me gone, wouldn't you?" he growled low, but knew the god heard him.

Before he was Merlin, meet Emrys . . .

The sun was setting, hours later, and Emrys was still in the meadow. He now had not one, but over fifty of the small light balls floating around, like fireflies. His mind was at peace, as was his body, unaware of the approaching storm.

He was so busy playing with his magic, he did not hear the voice until it was close by.

"Emrys!"

Startled, the young man lost hold of his magic, and it dropped to the ground. The patches of grass the balls fell on immediately caught fire. With a muttered curse, Emrys took off his tunic, and put the fires out before they caught volume.

When he turned around, his mother had her hand to her mouth, frozen in shock. Her eyes were wide, staring at the burnt patches of grass.

Emrys sighed, then pulled his tunic back on, watching out of the corner of his eye as she slowly breathed in, as though to steady herself. His mother had been beautiful, once. Her long, wavy brown hair was now dulled, with white locks through it.

She was thin, and the brown eyes that used to smile with laughter were now dull and unseeing.

His father had transformed her so, blaming her for putting on earth a devil's spawn, as he affectionately called his son. Both son and mother had been victims for far too long.

Straightening himself as best he could, Emrys faced his mother again, sadly noticing that she was keeping a wary distance between them.

"Your father is looking for you." she murmured, barely audible. He was used to her softspoken tones, especially lately, and his attuned ears caught the urgency in her voice. "You have to come!"

Emrys thought back to his last *talk* with his father and winced, massaging his bruised shoulder again. His mother's eyes went to his shoulder, and the look in them told the young man she was thinking of the same incident.

She turned her head to the side, unwilling to hold his gaze. "Please come back home, before he gets upset again."

Emrys stepped closer to her, slowly, as though she was a frightened doe – and in some ways, she was. "Mother, why do you stay with him?" he asked softly, noticing even now how he towered over her.

She looked up at him briefly, before pursing her lips in an attempt to appear mad, "Stop saying such things. It will do neither of us any good to think we have a way to escape, you hear me?" She turned to leave, muttering under breath, "As if we had anywhere else to go!"

Emrys hesitated for a brief moment, taken aback by her outburst. It was not the first – nor would it be the last – time she had gotten mad at him for suggesting a way out. His mother was a non-confrontational person, and his father had beat into submission any remnant of strength she had.

It saddened the young man to no end, and was the main reason why he stayed. If he was not there to protect his mother, who would?

With a sigh, he glanced behind himself at the meadow one more time, then followed in his mother's footsteps. Outside the quietness of the meadow, it was night now, but their decrepit house was near enough that he arrived within only short moments of his mother.

As Emrys stepped through the door, he only had a second of warning, before a fist struck him in the face. The force behind it, as well as the angle, threw him off his back to the ground.

"You been out doing the devil's work again, boy?"

Emrys glanced up from the ground, blue eyes burning in hate. His father towered over, a burly bulk of a man, three times his size. He could smell the alcohol coming off him in waves, if the red nose and glazed eyes had not yet alerted him to the drunken state.

"No," Emrys hissed in answer to the question, before spitting out blood. "I finished all the chores and the field work, and went for a walk."

"As if I'd believe such lies!" the man growled, and kicked his son in the gut.

Emrys curled up in a ball, coughing to catch his breath, before pushing himself back to his knees. He inhaled deeply, trying to gather that same peace that had filled him in the meadow.

He knew it was best to stay quiet and avoid his father's

look, but it was stronger than him. He looked up again, glancing behind the man to see his mom in a corner, cowering in fear. He would get no help from her.

A movement above him made him raise his face to the man, to see he now had a wooden stick in his hand. Thicker than a staff, it seemed heavy enough to inflict damage.

"If I can't get you to listen to me, maybe this will teach you to leave magic alone."

The words alone confirmed what Emrys already feared. He bowed his head to protect his face and tensed his back, even as his father brought the object down with all his strength. The wood hit to the left of his spine and Emrys lost his breath once more, falling back to the ground.

He gritted his teeth, refusing to give him the satisfaction of showing pain. He pushed himself back up, this time raising his gaze to his father.

The man had stepped back to take another gulp of his beer, and noticed his son staring at him.

"How dare you look at me!?"

He slapped the mug down on the wooden table, and lifted the stick again. This time, it came down harder, and Emrys held back another groan of pain – but did not break his stare.

Another blow followed. And another.

It seemed the unflinching stare of his unnaturally blue eyes only angered his father even more, as the blows came stronger every time.

Emrys refused to look away. But in doing so, he noticed his mom turned away, well versed in the art of denial.

It was that instance, more than the beating he was taking, or the soring of his back muscles, that hit the boy the hardest.

The realization that her weakness would never change. That his father would always hate him. And this would be the rest of his life, unless he did something to stop it.

Now.

No sooner had his father raised his hand to strike again, that Emrys moved.

He moved away from his reach, standing up. On wobbly feet, adrenaline pumping through him and holding the pain at bay, he managed to keep straight.

His father was gaping and his mother's eyes widened, begging him not to make any trouble.

"Sorry, mum," Emrys whispered.

He lifted a hand up, and drew a circle in the air. The circle grew in shape, until it enveloped Emrys in a slight silver glow.

His father stepped away in fear, sputtering, "Evil! Devil!"

Emrys turned disdainful eyes to the man he used to call family.

"You are done striking me. I will not apologize for this gift I have."

"Get out of my house! You're the devil's son, not mine!"

Emrys' eyes flashed of lightning, and his father was thrown into a wall. His unconscious body fell to the ground. "You are quite right, I cannot be yours."

More than one love story awaits . . .

"You must be the new advisor."

The soft, melodic voice, penetrated Merlin's haze, and he blinked.

As he caught her presence out of the corner of his eyes, he

turned his head slowly to the side.

Morgana.

She had not introduced herself, but every fiber of his being felt it. Her alabaster skin was almost translucent in the early morning. Long, straight black hair to her waist, cinched by a belt. Her soft blue gown did little to hide the curves of her body, something his eyes lingered on.

"I did not mean to interrupt," she spoke again, and his eyes settled on her rosebud mouth, her lips moving so softly.

Merlin gulped, then looked away. He could not, would not. A promise had been made, one he had to uphold. Something within him was emphasizing that he *really* needed to uphold that promise.

"You did not interrupt," he replied, voice hoarse.

Extinguishing the magic, Merlin reluctantly let go of the earth, and stood. He had no choice, now, but to turn towards her.

As he did, he noticed she had moved a few steps closer, as though pulled to him by the same force he was fighting against.

Their eyes met and held, cerulean blue to silver. Then her gaze roamed over him in a way that did nothing appease his unsettled body.

What is this!? He fumed internally.

Never had he been as weak around a woman – especially not one as young as her. For though Morgana was very much of age at her two decades of life, there was an innocence still within her eyes that drew him in like a moth to a flame.

"I am Merlin," he cleared his throat, bowing in greeting. "The new advisor, you are correct. I presume you are Lady Morgana?"

There was a brief hesitation, as though she wanted to try her hand at lying to him, then she inclined her head in assent. "I am."

Their gazes locked again, and Merlin cursed the fates for putting him on the path of this temptress. Her eyes were not so innocent now, a look within he very well recognized. One, he was sure, was reflected in his own eyes.

Lust, pure and simple.

"I was surprised," she spoke again, drawing his gaze to hers, "to hear my father sought you out. Apparently, tales of your exploits reached him from afar."

Merlin was silent, unsure of how to answer. Morgana held his gaze for a few moments longer, before smiling briefly. "At ease, Merlin. I shall leave you to your secrets."

As she turned to leave, the mage could not help his eyes from roaming her form. He turned away, cursing against his own weakness.

And through it all, witness the rise and fall of Arthur, Mordred and Carleigh . . .

Continue reading!
Visit www.alexawhitewolf.com/books for more

ABOUT THE AUTHOR

Alexa Whitewolf was born in Romania a little after the fall of Communism, 1992 to be exact. Growing up in the Transylvania region surrounded by epic mountains and a never ending stream of legends and stories was bound to create an overactive imagination. From a young age, she started rescuing pets–abandoned dogs in warehouses, kittens about to be drowned–and spent her childhood talking to animals. This devotion to the furry creatures shows up in her writing, as most of her series will have one–or more–pets involved (think Alistair if you read *The Avalon Chronicles*, Tyr in *The Sage's Legacy*).

The move to Canada in her teens was a sometimes rough adjustment, and Alexa overcame it by burying herself in books–both reading and writing. She started her young adult series at that time, and continued with the fantasy of Avalon in university. Nowadays? She's working on a few other upcoming series, among which a werewolf paranormal romance.

Alexa currently lives nearby picturesque Ontario, where Starbucks locations abound. When not at home writing–or awake in the middle of the night trying to put her characters to sleep–Alexa can be found enjoying walks with her husband and two masters of mischief, Zeus and Achilles. Her social media feed is always inundated with animal posts, so if you're looking for some sunshine in your day, you know where to find it: Facebook, Twitter or Goodreads, so don't be shy!

When the mood strikes, Alexa also dabbles in handmade

jewelry and stationery for special occasions, as well as the occasional website creation for friends. And if that's not enough to keep this night owl busy, she's still trying to convince her husband to get another puppy–sadly, a work in progress.

You can read more on her books, enter giveaways and follow her blog on travel, dogs and life in general at **www.alexawhitewolf.com**

Be sure to sign up for Alexa's mailing list for exclusive perks!

ALSO BY THE AUTHOR

The Avalon Chronicles series
Avalon Dreams
Avalon Wishes
Avalon Nightmares

The Sage's Legacy – YA series
The Dragon Medallion
The Dragon Manuscript
Relics of the Underworld

Moonlight Rogues series
First to Fall
Second to Surrender
Third to Tumble
Last to Love

Standalone novels
Blood Ties, Love Binds
Unconditional Love
Blazing in a Storm of Ashes (Coming Soon)
More novels coming soon!

Sign up for my readers' group **at www.alexawhitewolf.com/contact** and receive a copy of *Unconditional Love* for **FREE,** as well as first dibs on cover reveals, discounts, giveaways, prizes **and more!**

www.ingramcontent.com/pod-product-compliance
Lightning Source LLC
Chambersburg PA
CBHW030737030726
47497CB00001B/17